I0760779

This book is a work of fiction. The characters, incidents, and dialogues are products of the author's imagination and are not to be construed as real. Any resemblance to actual events or persons, living or dead, is entirely coincidental.

eBook 978-1-964509-02-0
Paperback 978-1-964509-03-7
Hardback 978-1-964509-04-4

Published by JK Franks Media LLC, 2025
Editor: Debra Riggle

Email the author at author@jkfranks.com
Friend him on Facebook at facebook.com/groups/JKFranks
Visit the author's website at www.jkfranks.com

First Edition

For Kevin

Watching you find your own path and become the person you're meant to be has been one of life's unexpected gifts.

EMERGENCE

COMMAND + CONTROL
BOOK 1

JK FRANKS

JK FRANKS MEDIA, LLC

"Those people have seen something. What it is I do not know and am not curious to know."

ALBERT EINSTEIN.

AUTHOR'S NOTES

The UFO phenomenon has captivated me since childhood. Like many others, I have witnessed unexplainable lights in the sky—some fitting the patterns described throughout this book, others defying easy categorization. While I've never experienced a close encounter, I don't dismiss such accounts universally. The challenge lies not in blind acceptance, but in maintaining the open-minded skepticism necessary to navigate this complex subject.

When people demand evidence for UFO phenomena, it is often claimed there simply isn't any. In reality, we face the opposite problem: there's too much evidence. We have thousands of years of documented sightings, witness testimony from credible sources, photographs, and video footage captured by military personnel, law enforcement officers, commercial pilots, and other trusted members of society. Yet these accounts are routinely dismissed, debunked, or relegated to the realm of hoax and delusion.

There is a serious possibility that we are being visited and have been visited for many years by people from outer space, from other civilizations.
— Lord Admiral Hill-Norton, former Chief of Defense Staff, UK

Physical evidence exists as well, though it tells an incomplete story. Metal fragments, soil samples from alleged landing sites, radiological readings, and gamma ray detections have been documented and analyzed. However, this evidence hasn't revealed new elements or materials that couldn't have been manufactured on Earth—a fact that supports one of this book's central arguments.

Much of what we're witnessing may indeed be of terrestrial origin: advanced human technology developed in secret, decades ahead of public knowledge. Consider the exotic flight systems of the SR-71 Blackbird, the B-1 bomber, and stealth fighter aircraft. These revolutionary designs were developed and tested in complete secrecy for decades before entering mainstream awareness. Today's unexplained aerial phenomena could very well represent the next generation of experimental craft, both military and commercial, undergoing classified testing.

What troubles me most is the apparent pattern of evidence removal. Time and again, when crashes, explosions, or other undeniable events occur, officials seem to quickly remove or obfuscate the facts, sweeping away any physical proof. While some cases may involve the recovery of classified technology to prevent foreign acquisition, many incidents clearly don't fit this straightforward explanation.

This pattern suggests something beyond routine military security. What are they concealing from us?

One possibility is that what's being hidden is absolute proof—evidence so profound it would fundamentally alter our worldview in ways we can barely comprehend. The disclosure of this truth would represent the biggest revelation in human history, and if so, I question whether we're prepared for such a paradigm shift.

The implications could be staggering across multiple domains—scientific, philosophical, and yes, spiritual. Perhaps the revelation that we're not alone in the universe would expand our perspectives rather than shatter them. But are we ready for that expansion? Are we prepared for the truth?

This book approaches these questions through a hard-science lens, exploring fictional "what-if" scenarios that I fear our leaders are not currently considering. What if these phenomena represent advanced technology—whether terrestrial or otherwise—with capabilities that could fundamentally disrupt our military, economic, or social systems?

What if we're facing threats that operate by principles we don't yet understand?

For most of the encounters described in these pages it is accurate to the reports I had access to. I don't claim they are all true and some of the more incredible I decided to omit simply because I knew they would cast doubt on the remaining incidents.

Our military and intelligence agencies assess threats using the traditional framework: **Threat = Capability × Intent**. This model works well for conventional adversaries—foreign militaries, terrorist organizations, cyber attackers—because we understand the basic parameters. But this framework fundamentally breaks down when applied to truly anomalous phenomena. How do you assess capability when you're witnessing technology that appears to violate known physics? How do you determine intent when the intelligence behind it might operate according to logic patterns completely alien to human thinking? How do you plan for threats that fall into the category of "unknown unknowns"—dangers we don't even know exist?

The traditional threat assessment model assumes we can accurately evaluate what we're facing. But what if we're dealing with deliberately concealed capabilities, paradigm-breaking technology, or intelligence that thinks so differently from us that we can't even recognize intent when we see it? Our institutional blindness may not just be about secrecy—it may be about using 20th-century analytical tools to assess potentially 21st-century threats.

The U.S. needs to take a serious, scientific look at this and any potential national security implications. The American people deserve to be informed. — Senator Marco Rubio, former Acting Chairman of the Senate Intelligence Committee

Through speculative analysis grounded in scientific methodology, we can begin to model potential scenarios and their implications. This isn't about proving aliens exist or don't exist—it's about conducting the rigorous threat assessment that should be happening at the highest levels of government and scientific institutions, but apparently isn't.

The pages that follow explore these possibilities not with definitive answers, but as exercises in preparedness. By thinking through scenarios from a position of scientific skepticism combined with strategic foresight, we can better understand what we might be facing and how we might respond.

Whether the truth emerges gradually through disclosure or arrives suddenly through contact, our survival may depend on our willingness to think beyond conventional paradigms. The question isn't whether we believe—it's whether we're prepared for possibilities that could reshape everything we think we know about our place in the universe.

ACKNOWLEDGMENTS

A huge thank you to the many experts, witnesses and unnamed sources who helped this story come together. Also a very special thank you to Retired Navy Captain Todd Creekman for his invaluable insights and assistance.

PROLOGUE

0431 GMT February 27
59°30′N, 27°00′W
North Atlantic

Dr. Ethan Novak gripped the controls of the submersible, his heart and pulse rate steady despite the danger as he descended into the inky depths of the ocean. The titanium hull groaned under the immense pressure, a constant reminder of the hostile environment that surrounded him. At 5,029 meters, the darkness was absolute, broken only by the feeble glow of the sub's exterior lights.

Leaning over, he switched the lights back off. "Save the batteries," he said to the other occupant of the Woods Hole Institute team. They were heading to a smoker, a volcanic vent 1,500 miles south of Iceland. It was a part of the Atlantic where the Eurasian and North American tectonic plates were trying to rip each other to pieces.

"Six thousand seven hundred eighty meters to bottom," the voice in the darkness said.

Novak leaned forward, peering into the abyss, searching for any sign of life in this desolate underwater landscape. Suddenly, a flicker of movement caught his eye. He squinted, trying to make out the shape in the murky water. It was unlike anything he had ever seen before – a sleek, metallic object that seemed to defy the laws of physics as it glided effortlessly through the water.

"What the hell is that?" he muttered, his voice barely audible over the hum of the submersible's motors.

"Pete, full thrust, aft now!" He pulled hard on the joystick. "Stand by on the release."

The grad student running the instrument bank couldn't see anything from his position but the camera feeds, which were all still dark. The submersible lurched back and banked sideways to the sudden thrust.

As if in response, the object suddenly changed course, hurtling toward them with incredible speed. Novak's eyes widened in horror as he realized the thing was heading straight for them.

"Hold on to something solid, kid!" he yelled over his shoulder as a brilliant blue light filled the cockpit.

He then braced himself, gripping the controls tightly as he waited for the impact to send shockwaves through the hull. The tiny sub cost almost seventy million dollars and was the star of the fleet, but it was not going to be any match for this.

Whatever the thing was swept by within inches but, thankfully, did not make contact. Still, the submersible shuddered violently, sparks flying from the control panel as the lights flickered, then died. Novak and Pete were plunged into complete darkness, the only sound being their own ragged breathing and the creaking of the straining metal around them.

"Was that a biologic?" Pete asked in confusion.

"Flip the breakers, release the ballast," Novak ordered. Of course, it was no whale or giant squid or anything else natural to this underwater world.

Novak fumbled for the emergency flashlight, his hands shaking as he clicked it on. The beam of light cut through the gloom, revealing the extent of the damage. The control panel was a mess of fried circuits, the main flat panel display had a crack, and the port frame around the main viewport had a bead of water on the inside. "Oh, shit! Why aren't we rising?" he yelled.

"The release is jammed," the grad student yelled back, panic growing with every word.

Novak's mind raced as he tried to comprehend what had just happened. The object, whatever it was, had vanished as quickly as it had appeared, leaving them alone in the depths with a crippled submersible. He knew he had to act fast if he wanted to survive, but the shock of the encounter had left him momentarily paralyzed.

As the minutes ticked by, Novak forced himself to focus, running through the emergency protocols in his mind. He had to get the power back on, or they would be trapped down here forever, victims of his own scientific curiosity.

Topside, the crew of the Woods Hole ship Discovery II tried frantically to reach Novak and the sub nearly a mile below. They had seen the camera and sensor feeds as well before it all went dark.

"Sonar?" Adrian Anders yelled. "Get us a fix on our boys." The young man at the workstation lifted his eyes to the expedition commander and shook his head. He'd briefly had two objects on the downward-pointing sonar array. Now he was showing none. There had been no sounds of a breakup, but that was no guarantee.

The sonar operator adjusted his settings, fingers flying over the keyboard, eyes narrowing as he expanded the range. He held his breath, waiting for something, anything, to show up on the screen.

"Got it," he whispered to himself, spotting a blip moving away at an incredible speed. It streaked across the display like a shooting star in reverse, heading away from their location.

"Adrian!" The operator's voice broke the tense silence. "I've got something. Moving away fast."

Adrian rushed over, leaning in close to peer at the screen. "What is it?"

"No idea. Definitely not our sub, but it's gone now."

"Where's Novak?" Adrian's eyes darted back and forth across the screen.

The operator fine-tuned the settings again, casting a wider net across the ocean floor. "Hold on," he muttered, squinting at the display. Another blip appeared, faint, but there.

"Got it!" He exhaled sharply. "The submersible—it's sinking."

"How far down?"

"Looks like another 700 meters."

Adrian's face tightened. "Damn it!" He turned to the crew around him. "We need to get them out of there!"

"Bottom here is over two and a half miles, sir."

Adrian didn't need to hear the rest. The expensive little submersible wasn't rated for those depths. Their only hope was if they could separate from the launch platform.

Back in the submersible, Novak fought against rising panic as he worked to bypass the fried circuits and restore some measure of control. Pete watched him with wide eyes, trying to stay calm but failing miserably.

"We're sinking," Pete's voice wavered.

"I know." Novak didn't look up, focused on his task.

"What do we do?"

"Working on it." Novak gritted his teeth, connecting wires and flipping switches. A flicker of power surged through the controls but then died again.

On the surface, Adrian barked orders into his headset. "Prepare the recovery team. Get ROVs ready for deployment."

The sonar operator glanced back at Adrian, worry etched on his face. "We don't have much time."

Adrian nodded grimly. "I'm aware. We need to move faster."

In the submersible, a sudden jolt threw Novak against his seat as another system sparked to life briefly before going dark again.

"We're running out of time," Pete's voice trembled.

Novak shot him a steely glance. "Then we better hurry."

He found the connection he wanted and ripped the wire out, bypassing the control board and touching it directly to the small silver screw holding a thick wire securely inside a plastic holder. "Release! Release! Release!" he yelled as the sounds of the crippled sub became too loud to ignore.

~

Elsewhere, in the bustling heart of Tokyo, screens flickered and failed without warning. People halted mid-stride as if the city itself had taken a sharp inhale. A collective shiver ran down the spine of the metropolis. The brilliant lighting of the gigantic screens going dark immediately struck fears of an earthquake, but the brief outage lasted only seconds. They flickered and resumed their unabashed march toward consumerism.

In a sleepy village in Norway, radios spat static, and dogs howled in unison at an unseen provocation. An old fisherman stared at the sky; he whispered to old Norse gods, fearing the tales of sky spirits. Far out over the ocean, he thought he heard an explosion.

In the rugged hills outside Antofagasta, Chile, Police Chief Ramon Ortega wiped the sweat from his brow. As he surveyed the route, one of his trackers came down the trail, his face ashen. "¿Qué encontraste?" he asked the shaken man.

The tracker ignored the question but stopped and turned slowly, facing back up the trail. He shook his head, his mind visiting some dark thing, Ramon decided, before venturing up the incline himself. The ground rose steadily from here to Atacama. Up there, nothing grew, nothing but scientists with their big domed telescopes pointed toward the sky. The high desert was 150 miles inland, but Ortega had tried working there when he was younger. The air was too thin, the nights too cold, but the view... that was something else.

He smelled it before he saw it. His father would have described it as a killing field. The grim scene before him had no equal in his memory. It was alien, unreal. He had been searching for four missing campers, but what he found was a nightmare beyond comprehension.

Scattered across the rocky terrain lay the remains of not just four, but what must be nearly a hundred bodies. The stench of decay hung heavily in the air, mixing with the coppery tang of blood. Ortega's stomach churned as he took in the gruesome sight.

Most of the bodies appeared to be foreigners; many were young, and most were female, their tattered clothing and pale skin suggesting they had not been here long. But it was the condition of the remains that truly horrified Ortega.

Limbs were contorted at unnatural angles, faces frozen in agonized screams. Some bodies were missing parts, as if they had been torn apart by some savage force. The ground was stained dark with dried blood, and bits of flesh and bone littered the area.

Ortega had seen many terrible things in his years on the force, but nothing could have prepared him for this. His mind reeled as he tried to comprehend the scale of the carnage. Who were these people? What had happened to them?

He felt a chill run down his spine despite the heat of the day. He knew he was looking at the work of something truly evil, something that took pleasure in inflicting pain and terror.

With trembling hands, Ortega reached for his radio to call for backup. He knew this was undoubtedly just the beginning of a long and harrowing investigation, one that would test him to his very limits.

As he waited for the rest of the department's crime scene team to arrive, he couldn't shake the feeling that he had stumbled upon something far more sinister than he could have ever imagined. The secrets buried in these hills would haunt him for the rest of his days.

CHAPTER ONE

1414 GMT Oct 25
White House Press Room
Washington, D.C., USA

The White House press room was in chaos. Reporters shouted questions, their voices tinged with panic and desperation. At the podium stood Jessica Thompson, her usually immaculate appearance now disheveled, her eyes wide with shock.

She had witnessed the unthinkable—an alien creature, flanked by heavily armored human soldiers, had stormed onto the Rose Garden, killing a full protective detail, then into the battered remnants of the Oval Office where a heated exchange with the president took place, and then taken several of the remaining cabinet members away. The country was in ruins, cities burning, and people vanishing without a trace.

Jessica cleared her throat, trying to steady her trembling hands. "Ladies and gentlemen," she began, her voice cracking. "The President of the United States."

A hush fell over the room as the tattered remnants of the White House press corps tried to anticipate what President Martin could possibly say that would help. Jessica glanced down at her notes, also hoping her boss could find the right words to reassure her as well as the terrified nation. She knew it had been a rough few days for the man. Marine One had flown him in from wherever he'd been secreted away, only to be met by that repulsive alien thing.

President Martin took the podium, his face lined with exhaustion, his eyes carrying the weight of a world teetering on the edge of collapse. The room fell silent, the only sound the distant hum of generators struggling to keep the White House lit.

The president scanned the room, the gravity of the moment settling into his bones. He gripped the edges of the podium, knuckles white.

"Aliens are real," he began, the words heavy yet devoid of hesitation. "As if anyone has any doubt anymore."

A murmur rippled through the press corps. Faces that once carried skepticism now wore a mask of grim acceptance.

Martin continued, his voice steady but carrying an undercurrent of regret. "Secrets were kept from you, from the public, for reasons I won't bother getting into. Reasons that seemed justified at the time but now seem... irrelevant."

He paused, letting the weight of his confession hang in the air. The silence in the room was thick, oppressive.

"Disclosure should have meant truth," he said, his tone growing sharper, more accusatory. "Instead, it just meant more politics. More maneuvering, more lies. We told you half-truths, cloaked the reality in shadows. And now, we all must pay the price for your leaders' hubris.

“If humanity survives this, our political system must change. I feel certain you will make sure it does. Currently, the sole mandate for any candidate is to get re-elected; the side job is to raise money and accept donations. You can well see where that has gotten us: leaders who lie, massage the truth into acceptable sound bites, question the facts, and publicize falsehoods that suggest a difference between political parties but drive a dangerous wedge between our citizens and your leadership.”

The reporters scribbled furiously, their pens a desperate attempt to capture the enormity of the moment. Camera lenses zoomed in, capturing every line of fatigue on Martin's face.

"We thought we could control the narrative, manage the information," he continued. "We were wrong. Horribly, disastrously wrong."

A reporter near the front, his face pale, raised his hand. "Mr. President, what does this mean for us? For the world?"

Martin met his gaze, eyes filled with a weary determination. "It means we are at the mercy of forces beyond our understanding. It means we must come together, not just as a nation but as a species, to face this new reality. We can no longer afford to be divided."

He took a deep breath, feeling the weight of his words settle over the room. "This is not the time for fear or blame. It's the time for action, for unity. We must find a way to survive this, to adapt. The very existence of our species depends on it."

The room remained silent, the gravity of the situation sinking in. President Martin stepped back from the podium, his heart heavy with the knowledge that his words, though true, might not be enough.

"As we confront this harrowing reality," he began, each word deliberate and heavy, "I utter words I never thought I would say: the America we believed in... the country we love and have fought for has been dismantled by forces far beyond our capabilities. Forces that I failed to prepare for or protect you from."

A collective gasp rippled through the room. Journalists exchanged glances, some scribbling furiously in their notebooks, others too stunned to move.

"We are," he paused before beginning again, his voice strained. "I am attempting to negotiate for a peaceful end to hostilities. Some attempt at coexistence, but I understand how hollow that sounds. I stand here, facing you, knowing that the assurances I offer are ones I do not believe myself."

A reporter in the front row stood, his face flushed. "Mr. President, how can we trust any negotiations? We've seen cities disappear, our people taken—"

Martin raised a hand, silencing him. "I understand your fear, Cecil. Trust me, I share it. But this is the only path left to us. Our military is outmatched. Our technology, our might—none of it matters against these beings. What we face is our very survival, not just for America but the world, hell, for all humanity."

He paused, looking out over the room, each face a mirror of his own despair. "Our priority now is helping one another. Our world has changed, and we must change with it."

The silence was thick, the weight of his words settling over the room like a death shroud. The press corps, usually so quick to fire off questions, seemed paralyzed, their pens hovering above their notepads.

Jessica, standing off to the side, felt a chill run down her spine. She had known this day would be historic, but not like this. Not with the president admitting defeat, negotiating with an unknown force that had already wrought so much destruction.

A murmur started at the back of the room, growing louder as it spread. The reporters were breaking out of their stupor, questions bubbling up, their voices a cacophony of disbelief and even anger.

"How can we know any peace won't be just another ploy?" another voice demanded. "We don't believe them, and frankly, Mr. President, many will not believe you."

"What about reports that the North Koreans are behind this? They were seen with the alien envoy earlier today, weren't they?"

Martin's shoulders sagged. "We don't have answers. Only the hope that by negotiating, we can find a way to stop the devastation. It's not enough, I know. But it's all we have."

The room erupted into chaos, the president's words offering no comfort, only a stark, bitter truth.

Martin looked to where Emily Carter would normally be standing but saw only emptiness. She'd tried to warn him, but it hadn't mattered. Nothing they had done had made any difference.

President Martin's eyes suddenly blazed with a fire that hadn't been seen in months. He gripped the edges of the podium, his knuckles whitening as he leaned forward, his voice rising above the din.

"But hear me now," he thundered, silencing the room instantly. "We will not bow. We will not surrender. This nation was built on the foundation of liberty, justice, and an unyielding spirit. Our ancestors faced insurmountable odds, and they did not falter. Neither shall we."

He took a deep breath, his voice echoing with the fervor of a leader who refused to concede defeat. "The words of Churchill during the darkest days of World War II ring true today. 'We shall fight on the beaches, we shall fight on the landing grounds, we shall fight in the fields and in the streets, we shall fight in the hills. We shall never surrender.'"

The reporters, once filled with despair, now sat up straighter, their pens poised, capturing every word.

Martin's voice grew stronger, each syllable a beacon of defiance. "This alien force may have technology beyond our comprehension, but they do not understand the human spirit. They do not understand that when faced with annihilation, we rise. We unite. We fight back with every ounce of our being." He paused, letting the weight of his words settle.

"To every American, to every citizen of this planet who hears my voice, I say this: we are not only fighting for survival. We are fighting for the very essence of what it means to be human. To stand together, to resist oppression, to choose freedom over fear."

The room was electric, the tension replaced with a palpable sense of unity. Reporters nodded, some even cheering softly, their despair giving way to a newfound resolve.

"Let history remember this moment," Martin continued, his voice unwavering. "Let them say that when the darkness threatened to consume us, we did not yield. We did not cower. We stood tall, shoulder to shoulder, and faced the unknown with courage and determination."

He straightened, his eyes scanning the room, connecting with each person. "We will fight. In our homes, on our farms, in our streets, in every corner of this Earth. We will resist with everything we have, and if we fall, we will fall knowing we fought for our humanity, our freedom, and our future."

The room erupted in applause, the sound echoing through the halls of the White House. In that moment, defeat seemed a distant concept, replaced by a burning hope, a collective will to fight back, no matter the cost.

Martin's replacement protective detail all took notice of something at once and rushed the president offstage and to safety just before the entire room disappeared in a massive explosion of concrete and dust.

CHAPTER TWO

SIX MONTHS EARLIER
Private Residence
2144 GMT April 05
Oregon Coast, USA

In the chill of a clear Oregon night, Dr. Kaden Trembley peered through his telescope, eyes fixed on the vastness above. Stars twinkled in their ancient light, indifferent to the tiny Earth below. Yet something in the serene sky moved with an urgency that betrayed the calm. Fast-moving lights, like celestial fireflies, danced across the heavens in a pattern that defied any logic he knew.

"Not the best night for stargazing," came a voice from behind Kaden. Sarah Mitchel walked up behind him, embracing the man before planting a kiss on his cheek. She was right; it was too cold, and he was getting too old, but here he was.

He grunted, his focus unbroken. "Those aren't stars, Sarah." His voice still echoed with the British accent that had attracted her to him in the first place.

The lights seemed to merge, then paused as if considering their next move before shooting off at an impossible velocity. Kaden scribbled notes in a worn leather notebook with a trembling hand.

"Satellites?" she asked, looking at the laptop screen displaying what the telescope was focusing on.

"Hmm?" he muttered absently before catching himself. That was probably why he was still single at 56. Work always came first. "No... we call them fast-movers, and if you lot haven't done the math on their speed, you're in for a rude awakening." He turned around and saw her smile. "But you're well aware of that, aren't you?"

"Maybe, you old goat, but come inside. It's too cold out here." She slipped her arms through his, and he pulled her close. They kissed as she closed the telescope's external display screen and pulled him back toward the cottage. The fast-movers raced overhead, unabated and undeterred in whatever their mission was.

Kaden fell into an overstuffed sofa as Sarah handed him a Scotch neat. He took a deep drink and smiled. "Cheers for that."

"For what?"

"Standing by me through all this rubbish," he said.

She smiled and placed a hand on his knee. "You are all I have. I can't let academia run you out of town just because you believe in little green men. Not again, at least."

Dr. Kaden Trembley was an astrophysicist who taught two classes each semester at Colgate in New York. The head of the department had suggested... strongly suggested he take the next semester off after he'd published his most recent paper. Earlier in the week, he'd been told they'd scheduled a video conference that would include him, the dean, and various other department heads. That call would be tomorrow morning. He knew all too well what to expect from that.

Cosmologists and astronomers routinely believed in other intelligent life among the stars. Far fewer of them felt comfortable saying that life was visiting Earth. Trembley knew he was ruffling some feathers when he submitted the article.

"You're onto something," Sarah said, her gaze fixed on his face.

Kaden nodded slowly. "I think so, yes. But the real question is—what if it's onto us?"

Sarah sipped from her wine glass and leaned back. "Then we must decide if we want to be alone in the universe... or not."

Kaden leaned back against her, Sarah's head nestled into his neck.

"You're rather assuming we have a choice in the matter, aren't you?" He felt her stiffen slightly.

Sarah had a brilliant mind in her own right but saw things in a more detached way than he did. She was perfectly happy with the abstract; he preferred the raw discovery.

"You should call Nathan," Sarah said.

"I've tried; he's gone all quiet on me at present."

"Surely he isn't abandoning you over that article, too."

Trembley laughed. "Him? Good heavens, no. I doubt he's even bothered to read it, but he's far more of a believer than I am. No, he's tied up with the Aurius project; it's running dreadfully behind schedule and hideously over budget."

"SOP for a government project," she said.

"You remember Javier, my intern from last semester?" Kaden asked, not looking up from his search.

Sarah nodded. "The kid with the tattoos and piercings? He was brilliant."

"He is indeed," Kaden agreed, pulling out a folder from the pile. "I've got him working on something rather fascinating: a system to track and catalog all UAP and USO sightings and unexplained incidents worldwide." He handed the folder to Sarah, who flipped through it with a raised eyebrow. "This is impressive, Kaden. But what are you hoping to find?"

Kaden leaned against the desk, crossing his arms. "Patterns, Sarah. I believe there's a pattern emerging, but it's not what I expected."

Sarah looked up at him, her eyes searching his face. "What do you mean?"

Kaden sighed, running a hand through his graying hair. "I thought we'd see an increase in sightings, a clear trajectory of extraterrestrial activity. But instead, it's almost like they're retreating. Pulling back."

Sarah frowned. "Why would they do that?"

Kaden shook his head. "I haven't the foggiest. But I fully intend to find out."

He walked over to the window, staring out at the night sky. The fast-movers were long gone, but their presence lingered in his mind.

"I hear what people say about me, Sarah. That I'm obsessed, that I've lost touch with reality. But I know what I've seen. And I won't stop until I can prove it."

Sarah stood up and joined him at the window, placing a gentle hand on his shoulder. "I believe in you, Kaden. And I'll stand by you, no matter what."

Kaden turned to her, his eyes softening. "Thank you, Sarah. I'd be utterly lost without you."

They stood there for a moment, the weight of Kaden's quest hanging in the air between them. Then Sarah smiled, breaking the tension.

"Come on, let's get to bed. You've got a big day tomorrow, Professor Trembley."

Kaden chuckled, allowing her to lead him toward the bedroom. Tomorrow, he knew he would be facing the skeptics and the naysayers once again. But tonight, he had Sarah and the knowledge that he might one day find proof of extraterrestrials visiting Earth.

CHAPTER THREE

0445 GMT May 10
Robert-Bosch-Strasse 5
Darmstadt, Germany

The ESA ground control room buzzed with activity as scientists and engineers huddled around monitors, guiding the remote rover across the Martian landscape. Dr. Elena Schmidt, the lead scientist, leaned forward in her chair, eyes fixed on the live feed.

"How's the terrain looking, Luca?" she asked the rover operator.

Luca Rossi's fingers moved over the controls. "Smooth so far. We're making good progress toward the target site."

The team watched as the rover's camera captured the rust-colored expanse, an alien world waiting to be explored. Suddenly, Luca paused, his brow furrowed.

"Dr. Schmidt, take a look at this." He pointed to the screen. "There are some unusual patterns in the soil."

Elena squinted at the image. The rover's camera had picked up a series of indentations, seemingly too symmetrical to be natural. "Luca, can you zoom in on those markings? They don't look like typical erosion patterns."

"Got it. Enhancing now." Luca's fingers skipped over the keyboard.

As the image sharpened, the team collectively held their breath. Luca elevated the camera as high as possible to gain more perspective.

"They look too..." Luca muttered.

"Precise? Symmetrical?" Elena questioned.

"Wish we had NASA's helicopter to get a larger view."

Elena nodded and then triggered the AI analysis. It was always running in the background of all ESA photo processing. She clicked the buttons to calculate the distance between indentations and the circumference of depressions in the beige rocky soil.

'Anomaly detected,' popped up on a red block on the screen. Luca pushed the zoom and lowered the camera arm currently located over 100 million miles away from the European Space Operations Centre in Darmstadt, Germany.

"Move in closer."

Luca sent the commands, and they waited long minutes as the view slowly shifted. Elena and several others leaned in toward the monitor. Between the two-meter-wide depressions, something was catching the light. Small, polished segments of brown stone came into view. The stone was elongated and rounded on one end and broken off on the other.

"Where's Pierre?" Elena asked loudly.

"He was lying down," one of the assistants said, rushing off to get him.

Elena used the AI to virtually measure the stone. "1.2 centimeters by .85 centimeters," she repeated for everyone as they waited on the astrogeologist.

"What is that? Polished stones on Mars?" Elena leaned closer to the screen.

Julie, the bouncy, brunette member, chimed in, "It looks like a riverstone."

Elena had already considered and dismissed that. The shape was too precise, almost a perfect contour from front to back on each of the visible sides.

An older man with thinning hair wormed into the small group. "Take a look, Pierre," Elena said, stepping to the side. "Does that look like basalt?" She knew that basalt was one of the more common rock types on the red planet, but this one seemed wrong.

The geologist made some random sounds and leaned in even closer. "No, I don't believe it is. You see, Dr. Schmidt, where that straight line of scarring shows the color beneath, it is significantly lighter. Martian rocks aren't exposed to natural weathering like that, and basalt rocks in particular would show much less contrast."

Pierre's hand moved to the camera control, and Luca brushed him away. "I'll do it."

"Yes, yes, sorry. Please pan to the upper right quadrant."

The view shifted and zoomed.

Elena saw what the geologist had noticed. "More, Luca. Move off the target entirely." The polished brown stone disappeared off the screen, and almost as suddenly, another just like it came into view. Members of the team looked at each other with shocked expressions. What set of circumstances could have created two matching stones in the same location?

"Can we use the arm to collect them?" Elena asked.

Pierre shook his head. "No, there's something else I want to see. Can we move that first stone?"

"The articulation is not that precise; this is a really small target, but I can try," Luca offered.

"Don't bury it in the sand, Luca. We might never find it again," Julie said unnecessarily. He'd already marked the exact coordinates into the tracking system. The delicate mechanical arm came into view, looking like a giant metal strut. Using an edge, he slowly moved it toward the stone.

"The lag is going to be a problem," Luca said. "The system isn't designed for this level of detail work."

"You're doing fine, my boy," Pierre said, placing a hand on the pilot's shoulder.

Luca maneuvered the rover slowly closer, its high-resolution camera focusing on the stone. The manipulator arm attempted to roll the stone multiple times but missed. On the next try, he got it, and the stone rolled millimeters; then another side came into view. He used a nozzle to blow a puff of air onto the surface, brushing away the thin layer of dust. "I'm enhancing the image."

"Oh my! Look at this... those... those...," Pierre stammered. "There are engravings on these stones!"

The room fell silent as the team stared at the intricate patterns etched into the surface of the stones. Geometric shapes and lines intertwined, forming a language they had never seen before.

"Incredible," Elena breathed. "These markings appear symbolic, maybe something tribal."

"They aren't natural, for damn sure," Luca said.

The team erupted into a flurry of activity, analyzing the images and comparing them to known Earth symbols. Hypotheses flew across the room as they grappled with the implications of their discovery.

"Get high-resolution images of both of these, Luca. Do not lose the spot. These symbols could suggest a form of communication or artistic expression," Elena mused. "We need to compare this with any known symbols from Earth and other findings. This could be the most important discovery in human history."

Another team member piped up, "This could be evidence of past life or an ancient Martian civilization."

As the team meticulously documented their findings, preparing reports and transmitting data back to Earth, the atmosphere in the control room was electric. They knew they were on the cusp of something monumental.

"We need to compile all this data and share it with the international scientific community," Elena said, her voice trembling with excitement. "I repeat, this could be one of the most significant discoveries of our time."

Luca nodded, his eyes still glued to the screen. "I'll ensure all the images and coordinates are logged. We'll need more time to explore this area."

"Should I add them to the collector?" Luca asked.

That is a good question, Elena thought. If they didn't, a sandstorm could bury them forever. If they did, people might not believe the images were real. She didn't want anyone to suggest they were an AI creation or some natural aberration.

"If we leave them here, NASA will send a mission to take them."

Elena looked at the geologist and gave a nod. "You aren't wrong, but they have the only technology in the solar system that can retrieve a sample from another planet."

"This could be worth a manned mission," Julie blurted out.

The Elysium Rover had cost billions and was nearing the end of its planned mission life, but this could extend it and the team's timeline by years. Elena knew the rover would never move more than a few feet from this location. Somehow, they had to get these rocks back to Earth.

CHAPTER FOUR

1203 MST May 11
State Road 54
Havenbrook, Nevada, USA

The dilapidated postal Jeep banged and rattled with every bump on the country road. Inside, Jack Simpson fumbled to get his next batch of mail ready to go. His mind was elsewhere; the job was monotonous, and the midday Nevada heat was stifling. Jack adjusted the small fan to blow on his face for a while. His USPS shirt was already clinging to his chest and back.

Using his left hand, he arranged the piles for the next four houses. People he rarely saw, leading lives that few would ever notice. Like them, his life was on autopilot, working for the weekend and praying for something better. Pulling up to the Weyland's, he automatically reached for the mailbox. His hand froze in midair. The box was... gone. His eyes focused on the strangeness, then beyond. He stared in disbelief at the empty plot of land where the house had once stood.

Jack rubbed his eyes, thinking perhaps the heat was playing tricks on his mind, but the vacant space remained. A curious whine filled the air, like a distant swarm of bees, making the hairs on the back of his neck stand on end.

With a shaking hand, he reached for his phone to double-check his location. He'd driven this route for over three years—he was sure he was where he was supposed to be. Looking to the other side, he realized with a start that the Murphy's house was missing as well. Cars, yard, grandkids' swing set... everything.

"What in the hell is going on?" he asked.

He dialed his supervisor, but there was no signal this far out. Apparently, no one needed to talk to anyone in Havenbrook, Nevada. Jack's heart raced as he looked around, searching for any sign of life. The desert stretched out before him, vast and unforgiving, with no indication that anyone had ever lived here.

He stepped out of the Jeep, the scorching heat hitting him like a wall. The air shimmered, distorting his vision, and for a moment, he thought he saw a flicker of movement in the distance. Jack squinted, trying to make out the shape, but it vanished as quickly as it had appeared. Heat waves distorted the view ahead, but he knew it didn't look right.

Stepping back into the faded white mail truck, he eased down the road another mile and then another. This community had dozens of homes and a large trailer park full of ramshackle mobile homes that hadn't moved in half a century. That was yesterday; today, there was only an empty expanse of desert.

The whine intensified, now a deafening roar that seemed to come from everywhere and nowhere at once. Jack clutched his ears, the pain almost unbearable. The fan stopped, then the truck rattled, coughed, and died. Jack stumbled out of the Jeep, still clutching the bundle of mail for the Weylands. Something was very, very wrong here. Jack was desperate to escape the noise, but as he turned back to the Jeep, he realized it was also gone. In its place was a pale shimmer of bluish light that was fading by the second.

Jack stood there, alone in the desert, his mind reeling. He looked down at the mail in his hands, the envelopes now meaningless. Abstractly, he knew he should understand what they were, but his mind wasn't making the connection. The world around him seemed to shimmer and warp, like a mirage on the horizon. The letters and sales flyers fell to the ground, and then Jack's world imploded.

In the French Alps, Jean-Pierre Dubois pedaled furiously up the winding mountain road. His legs burned with each rotation, but he pushed on, determined to shave precious seconds off his time. The crisp mountain air filled his lungs as he leaned into a sharp turn, his bike hugging the curve of the road.

Several kilometers back, Coach Luc Moreau and mechanic Antoine Lefevre followed in a support vehicle. Luc's eyes were glued to the tablet on his lap, monitoring Jean-Pierre's progress. The small GPS transponder on the bike relayed speed, position, and other telemetry to the team's training app.

"He's making excellent time," Luc muttered, a hint of pride in his voice. "This could be our year at the Tour."

Antoine nodded, keeping his eyes on the road ahead. The car wound its way through picturesque villages, past bubbling streams and towering peaks. The scenery was breathtaking, but neither man paid it much attention, their focus solely on their star rider.

"We'll be ready for the Danes this year," Antoine said.

"You're doing great, Jean-Pierre," Moreau said. "Keep the cadence up. Push, push, push."

The rider didn't respond, but he was undoubtedly focused on the grueling incline. The late-season high-altitude training had been his idea. The Belgian champion was fighting for a podium finish this year, having missed out the prior year by fourteen seconds and two places.

"His speed looks good, no?" Antoine said, his face breaking into a huge grin.

Moreau checked the numbers against his sheet. "Yes, this circuit will be fast..."

Suddenly, the blinking dot representing Jean-Pierre on the screen vanished.

"What the hell?" Luc tapped the screen frantically. "Antoine, speed up. We've lost his signal. He must have gone off the road."

The car accelerated, tires screeching as they took the switchbacks at dangerous speeds. Both men scanned the roadside, looking for any sign of their rider or his bike. The tracking app gave precise coordinates of the bike's transponder. "It should be up ahead," Moreau said, his voice cracking with nervous anticipation.

"There!" Antoine shouted, pointing to a wide outside turn ahead. But as they pulled up, there was nothing there—no bike, no rider, not even a small skid mark on the road. The drop-off on the other side of the safety rail was steep but not dangerously so. If Jean-Pierre had gone over, they would be able to see him.

For hours, they searched the area, calling Jean-Pierre's name and checking every ditch and crevice. Other team members and eventually emergency services joined the search, but as night fell, they had found no trace of the Belgian cyclist.

Back in the car, exhausted and bewildered, Luc absently retraced his rider's route on the tracking app, hoping for some clue. He replayed the last 30 seconds time and again. Then he decided to zoom out the screen to see more of the area. His eyes widened in disbelief as he took in what he was seeing on the screen.

"Non, non, ce n'est pas possible." Indeed... it was not possible.

CHAPTER FIVE

0903 EST MAY 12
WHITE HOUSE OVAL OFFICE
WASHINGTON, D.C., USA

Emily Carter, the assistant chief of staff, strode through the bustling West Wing, her heels clicking against the polished floors. She nodded curtly to the staff who acknowledged her as she passed, her mind focused on the task at hand.

The president's voice boomed from the room as Emily entered the Oval Office. "Another disclosure briefing? Christ, how many more of those damn things do they have to put on?"

Emily straightened her jacket, stepping forward. "Mr. President, I understand your frustration. But with the recent incidents, the public is demanding answers."

"Did you read the report about the guy in France?"

"The cyclist? Yes, sir. I had our people review the data feed and confirmed what the DST already released."

"So, he did just disappear?"

"Mr. President, the rider was just over a kilometer ahead of his tail car when they lost his signal. Approximately seven seconds later, the transponder showed he was over 700 miles to the northeast, and more advanced tracking indicates that less than ten seconds later he was over 4,700 miles away."

The president sighed heavily, rubbing his temples. "Jesus Christ, Emily. This thing is getting away from us. Some of the other events might be explained away, but this one has witnesses and left a digital trail."

"Yes, sir," she answered noncommittally.

"I take it Raymond's still away?"

"Chief Whittner is... indisposed, sir. Yes... the umm... health issues. And the other things..." Emily kept her tone neutral, though they both knew full well the extent of Whittner's problems.

The president waved his hand dismissively at the screen. "Fine, fine. But we need this crap wrapped up quickly, you hear me? We can't add fuel to the growing rash of conspiracy theory fires."

"Of course, Mr. President." Emily nodded, her expression unreadable. The multiple reports of strange lights days earlier hadn't helped.

The president grunted, reached for the remote, and turned up the sound.

The head of the influential House Defense Oversight Panel, Senator Alex Reynolds, released an enigmatic statement hinting at a "grave national security risk" looming over the nation.

This cryptic announcement from the senator urged President Jacob Martin to reveal details about the mystery, though specifics were scarce.

"What details? Why do they automatically assume we are covering something up?" the president yelled.

The anchor switched to a live shot out on the House Triangle, as they called it. Emily knew she could walk over to a window and see the perfectly crafted attractive woman caught in the glare of the camera lights.

"We inquired about the issue at the White House. National Security Advisor Pete Cavanaugh informed us that he had proposed to personally brief the elite 'Gang of Eight,' which includes leaders from both parties in the House and Senate, along with the top members of the House and Senate Defense Intelligence Committees. Mr. Cavanaugh later added that the Martin administration is 'committed to safeguarding the national security of the United States and its citizens.'"

The president walked to the bar, his frustration with the legislators evident. "Goddamn blowhards, do they not understand this is not a public forum? I know half of them are up for reelection, but painting this office as the problem is ridiculous."

Emily agreed but felt it was best to keep silent.

"Hell, the economy is for shit. That asshole running France is causing all of Europe to move to a war footing, and all these clowns want to discuss is a bunch of weather balloons."

It was more than that. A lot more, in fact. Emily Carter had been plowing through the files for the past week. Something was up... something serious. The president was right, though. The senators weren't interested in finding the truth... they were simply wanting to find out who it was that knew the truth.

"I can run point on this for you, sir, I mean if you want," Emily offered.

President Martin looked at her and grinned. "Yes, I believe you can, Emily. With your background, I feel sure you are the right one to be the point person for this office. Make it happen; you have my full authority."

She nodded, but inside she was overjoyed. This is how one got ahead at this level of power. You seized opportunity, and this was one that fascinated her more than most. Now, if she could keep her other boss from meddling in it, assuming he came back to work anytime soon. Between his high blood pressure and the fact that his wife had been sleeping with the assistant DA back home in Arkansas, she felt sure he would not be a big factor.

Still, it was not Emily's top priority at the moment. Her brother Paul's disappearance years earlier had resurfaced again. A long-missing report from someone on the same ship. Still, one thing you learned in this business was how to compartmentalize, and personal problems were way down the list... hell, they didn't even make the list. If she was ever going to take advantage of her position, this was certainly the time to do so.

"One thing, Emily," President Martin said. "Get a committee together to do the real work. With Raymond gone and Reynolds making a racket, we will have our hands full with the media for a while. I can't have my chief of staff distracted, but I really would like to understand what is going on with all these incidents."

"Should we schedule a meeting with Reynolds?"

The president snorted a laugh. "That blowhard? No, he would have a cadre of friendly reporters stationed on the driveway, so he could blast all of us as soon as he exited this office." Martin took a sip of coffee, then looked pensively. "The man's a snake; if he is looking into something, it's not out of concern for the country. More likely political currency, something he can bargain with later. His 'disclosure' is less about getting to the truth than positioning himself to take advantage of the media spotlight right now. UFOs are this week's shiny object. Let's not give him any added credibility."

Emily was all too familiar with Reynolds and all the other politicians exactly like him. Politics in the nation's capital was all about personal gain, not the good of the nation. An individual's personal feelings mattered little as they positioned their political sails to take advantage of whatever the prevailing wind might be.

"So what will your approach be?" President Martin asked as he picked up the daily security brief folio from his desk.

She wasn't one to jump to conclusions about UFOs or alien life, but the recent events demanded a thorough investigation.

"Mr. President, if I may," she began, her tone measured, "whether these incidents are extraterrestrial in nature or not, they represent a significant unknown. And in our line of work, unknowns are dangerous."

The president raised an eyebrow, intrigued. "Go on."

"We need to approach this pragmatically. If there's even a remote possibility that we're dealing with advanced technology—terrestrial or otherwise—we need to understand it. The national security implications alone are staggering."

Emily paced the room, her words carefully chosen. "Think about it, sir. If these are some kind of experimental aircraft or swarms of drones, we need to find who's behind them. If they're some natural phenomena we don't yet understand, that knowledge could also be invaluable. And if... well, if they are something more, we can't afford to be caught unprepared."

She turned to face the president directly. "I'm not saying we should jump to conclusions about little green men. But we can't dismiss these incidents out of hand either. The truth, whatever it is, could reshape our understanding of the world—and our place in it."

The president nodded slowly, considering her words. "You're right, of course. We need answers, not speculation."

"Exactly, sir. By forming this committee, we're not validating any particular theory. We're simply doing our due diligence. It's about gathering facts, analyzing data, and being prepared for any eventuality."

Emily's pragmatism shone through as she continued, "If it turns out to be nothing, we'll have peace of mind. If it's something more... well, we'll be ahead of the curve. Either way, we're serving the country's best interests."

He nodded as he scanned the main points in the brief. Emily had long ago learned how well the man could multitask.

"I like it," he said, glancing up. "Let's keep it dark for now. Emily, remember you can't unring this bell. Looking for aliens is inviting a spotlight you don't want." He paused to consider his next words. "Use your best judgment on whom to bring in, but I would steer away from anyone who has already appeared before a congressional committee. They will be tainted and likely under observation. I don't need the national security advisor asking me why we are inviting nutjobs to the White House."

"Good advice, sir. I'll meet all the nutjobs off-site."

The president laughed. "Okay, Chief, what other fun and games do you have on tap for me today?"

Elysium Mars Lander Malfunction Attributed to Radiation Glitch — ESA to Reboot Mission Software

"Earlier today, mission control confirmed that the Elysium lander's anomalous signal burst was the result of a rare gamma-ray spike affecting onboard systems. Contrary to social media speculation, no foreign signal was received or transmitted. ESA Director Henri Solvay called the event 'a fascinating glitch, but ultimately a non-issue.'

"We'll be resuming normal telemetry within 48 hours,' Solvay added. 'There is no reason to believe the lander encountered anything unexpected on the Martian surface.'"

—ESA Press Briefing Summary | Source: European Space Agency Communications Office

CHAPTER SIX

Colgate College
Hawthorn Lane
Hamilton, NY, USA

Kaden glanced at the name on his screen before answering. The caller ID still managed to send a jolt to his system despite the years.

"Hello, Elena."

"Kaden, darling," the familiar voice said.

It had been a few years since Trembley had seen his former star student, but he could tell from her tone that something was off.

"What's wrong, Elena? Did something happen with the rover?" He knew the Mars mission had been her obsession for the past decade.

There was a hesitation.

"Kaden, something's happening with the Elysium Mission. The control lab's been shut down, all access revoked."

Dr. Elena Schmidt's voice crackled with urgency over the phone. Kaden gripped the receiver tighter, his mind already racing.

"Good Lord, when did this happen?" He started pacing, his free hand rifling through the scattered papers on his desk, looking for the tattered folder he kept on the Elysium program.

"Just now. I went to check on the overnight data analysis and found the doors sealed, guards posted. They're not letting anyone in."

Kaden froze. The Elysium Mission, aimed at studying geologic and atmospheric anomalies on the red planet, had been his and Elena's shared obsession for years. For the government to abruptly lock it down...

"Did they say why? What about the research, the data feeds?"

"All communications are cut off, Kaden, but yes, I think I get the reason why—we've found something." The words felt heavy.

"Such as...?" Kaden asked.

"It must be the Americans," she continued, ignoring his query. "If their government's involved, if they're classifying our findings..." Elena trailed off, the implications clear.

Kaden's thoughts whirled. Elysium had been an ESA project; NASA, or more accurately, the U.S. government, had no authority...

"I'm going to try to get inside, find out what's really going on."

"Elena, no, it's too risky—"

"I can't just let them bury this, Kaden. You know that. You remember what they did to Kincaid."

He tried hard to ignore her reference. "Tell me what you found up there?"

Silence crackled over the line for a long moment.

“Come now, Elena. You can’t dangle the word ‘discovery’ and then ghost me like a bad date.”

Then a sigh. "I can't...not over the phone. But I have a feeling it is bigger than even we realized. Someone from Washington has also been trying to talk to me...I have no idea what to do."

“Well, that’s not ominous at all,” he said, flipping through a stack of paperwork like it held answers it most certainly did not.

“Be sensible, Elena. Be careful and do what they say."

"Elena? Elena!"

The line had gone dead, an ominous double-click the only answer. Kaden stared at the phone. Had someone been listening?

He shook his head, forcing himself to focus. Elena wasn't prone to overreaction—quite the opposite, in fact. Still, something had her rattled.

Kaden set the phone down, his mind replaying the conversation with Elena. Something about her mention of Kincaid nagged at him. It had seemed too random, too out of place to be mere coincidence.

He rifled through his cluttered desk, searching for the old research notes he'd compiled on Dr. Kincaid's controversial work. The man had been a brilliant astrophysicist, but his claims about discovering evidence of extraterrestrial life on Mars had gotten him ostracized from the scientific community and eventually driven him to a nervous breakdown.

As Kaden looked at the worn pages, he realized something. Elena's mention of Kincaid had been on purpose. She was pointing him in a certain direction. Elena Schmidt was a brilliant woman and a dear friend back in the day. He knew better than to ever underestimate her.

He remembered a conversation he'd had with Kincaid years ago, just before the man disappeared from the public eye. Kincaid had rambled about a secret research facility in the Nevada desert, a place where the government was allegedly hiding proof of alien technology recovered from Mars. It had all seemed like delirium, but Kincaid was not stupid.

At the time, Kaden had dismissed it as the ravings of a man on the brink of madness. But now, with Elena's hidden message, he recalled something else. Area 52, a private server that he and his former assistant had set up mainly to schedule secret rendezvous.

Elena was beautiful, and even though fifteen years his junior, Kaden had found her to be irresistible. Sleeping with a student was less of a problem in college, but he still regretted it. Somehow, they had held on to the friendship, but something about the illicit relationship had stained them both.

He glanced at his computer, fingers itching to start digging into the mystery. But he hesitated. If there really was a cover-up afoot, if powerful forces were trying to bury whatever the Elysium Mission had uncovered...

He had no idea if the Area 52 cloud server would even still be operational. He hadn't looked at it in years. Using his own devices, or even the university's network, suddenly seemed like an unacceptable risk. He needed to be smart about this, cover his tracks. He couldn't afford to tip off the wrong people, not when the stakes were this high.

Kaden's gaze drifted to the lights of the small town a few miles away.

It was not that late. He knew what he had to do. Grabbing his keys and a scrap of paper from an old file, Kaden headed for the door, his heart pounding. He didn't know exactly what he was getting himself into, but Elena needed his help. She wouldn't have called otherwise.

Thirty minutes later, the screen of the computer at the internet café glowed with advertisements for everything from treatments for erectile dysfunction to low-cost burial insurance. He swept them from the screen, then opened up a VPN service. He logged in to the private server network and then entered the old IP address on the scrap of paper.

Surprisingly, the crude Area 52 logo appeared. The low-resolution logo was decades out of date, but apparently, the server was still operational. He tried to recall where the login link was; he knew it was nothing obvious, and after several failed attempts, he recalled the correct process. Click inside one of the letters of the logo, the lower left corner, then the middle of the top line of the bounding box. A small login screen appeared.

Kaden referred to his paper again and entered his ancient credentials, then held his breath. The file system appeared as it always had. Two folders, Alpha and Beta. His was Beta; as expected, it was mostly empty. Old notes, an ancient PowerPoint file, and various calendar entries.

His mind skipped back to those days, making love to the beautiful woman who filled him with unbridled joy. The illicit meetings and bits of subterfuge to keep the relationship private added to the thrill.

Of course, it had ended badly. So badly, he'd had to leave the university system and come to America. That, combined with his rather public spectacle after his claims of alien visitations, caused his blood pressure to climb. Forcefully, he willed that memory out of his mind as he moved the cursor to the Alpha folder. Elena's folder.

Fifteen minutes later, he was hurriedly walking back to his car. The contents of that folder were now duplicated on the flash drive in his pocket. The artifact in the photos he'd seen was etched into his mind.

"What does it mean? The stones had obvious signs of tooling. “Intelligent life on Mars?" He checked himself and his muttering as he crawled behind the wheel of his hybrid Volvo coupe. "Now, I've got to figure out why a few tiny rocks on Mars are causing my dear friend such distress."

CHAPTER SEVEN

COLGATE COLLEGE
HAWTHORN LANE
HAMILTON, NY, USA

Kaden poured over the data from Javier, his eyes darting between the glowing screens. The UFO sightings seemed random at first glance, but as his intern had dug deeper, patterns emerged. Triangular formations, synchronized movements, recurring locations—it couldn't be a coincidence.

He leaned back in his chair, running a hand through his disheveled hair. The implications were compelling. If he was right, if this was evidence of a coordinated extraterrestrial presence...it could change everything. Still, he needed more proof. Most scientists refused to accept his level of support even for hinting at alien visitation.

A knock at the door startled him from his thoughts. Dr. Sarah Mitchell, his friend, occasional lover, and former colleague, stood in the doorway, her expression one of concern. In her hands was a bottle of wine and what looked like two boxes of take-out meals.

"How was your meeting?"

"My what?" he asked absently. "Oh... oh, it was... rather as expected, I suppose." He shrugged. "So, you still have a job?"

"Hmm? Oh, right... well, after another forced sabbatical. Javier is going to take over the mini-semester for me. It'll be fine, I expect."

"Kaden, when was the last time you really slept? Or ate something that didn't come out of a vending machine or the microwave?" Sarah asked, eyeing the empty coffee cups and energy bar wrappers littering his desk.

Kaden waved off her concerns. "I'm perfectly fine, Sarah. You know how I get when I'm onto something. I can feel it in my bones."

Sarah sighed, stepping into the cluttered room and setting the food and wine down. "Kaden, I know how much this means to you. But you're going to burn yourself out. Your obsession with proving the existence of extraterrestrial life... it's consuming you."

Kaden bristled at her words. "It's not an obsession; it's my life's work. You of all people ought to understand that."

Sarah's eyes softened. "I do understand, more than you know. But I also know what happens when you let that drive blind you to everything else. It can destroy you, Kaden. I've seen it happen before."

Kaden turned away, his jaw clenched. He knew she was referring to her own past, the secret government projects she'd left behind. But he couldn't let that deter him. Not when he was so close.

"I appreciate your concern, Sarah. But I can't stop now. Not when the truth is within reach."

Sarah shook her head, a sad smile on her lips. "Just be careful, Kaden. Don't lose yourself in the pursuit. Sit for ten minutes and eat. Have a nice glass of Merlot."

He started to protest, not wanting to lose his train of thought, but she was right. He was becoming obsessive, and he knew all too well how that ended.

"Thanks for the takeaway. It looks rather delicious."

"We call it take-out, Kaden, and after this long, we expect you to know how to speak properly." She laughed as she dug into the curry chicken.

"Properly? I'll leave that unbelievably absurd statement right there, shall I?"

He took a few bites, then poured them both wine. "It's not bad at all. I usually hate the bloody mess you Americans call wine, but you've done quite well, Sarah," he lowered the glass. "Now tell me why you're home early."

Her lips pursed, and she wiped them with a napkin. She knew better than to be less than truthful. Kaden was way too smart for that.

"I got a call today."

One of Kaden's bushy eyebrows raised noticeably.

Sarah went on. "Your protégé, Elena, has people talking."

"Well, she should. Her team stumbled onto something incredible."

Sarah sipped her wine and then shook her head. "Not the good kind of talk." Her eyes glanced furtively around the room before continuing. "Kaden, a serious question. One I feel sure I know the answer to. Do you think there really is a government cover-up regarding alien contact?"

The question momentarily threw him off. He wasn't expecting such a tangential and problematic topic next. "I... don't know that I would ever feel comfortable putting it that way." He, too, glanced at the walls and ceiling. "I do believe there is compelling evidence of visitations and maybe a cover-up. That does not implicate the entire government, though. Why the sudden change of topics?"

She leaned in close. "I know where things went off the rails... you know... before. I see how much this means to you, and I don't want to see you or your reputation harmed."

He could tell there was more. "And...?"

"I've been asked by some high-ranking officials to suggest a short list of names for a possible cabinet-level committee to investigate the veracity of the recent UFO events."

Kaden was shaking his head. "Oh, no, Sarah, not you. Please don't tell me you're signing on to anything like that. You know how Washington operates. No one gives a toss about the truth, especially the Oval Office."

"This is from the assistant chief of staff, and off the record, it seems personal, Kaden. But to answer your question, no. I am not joining. You are. I volunteered you."

Doctor Kaden Trembley was completely gobsmacked and unable to utter a single word. For her part, Sarah continued to empty her wine glass and refill it again, all the while wearing a sick grin.

"You... you can't possibly be serious."

"I am, Doctor, and I believe you will thank me. Us believers—and yes, some days, I do count myself among you—need a voice. We need an advocate because if you are right, and other parts of the government are hiding the evidence, there must be accountability, and more importantly, we need to know why."

They talked for another hour, but Kaden was still very unconvinced he was the right person to take on this role. After Sarah left, he turned back to his screens, the data swirling before his eyes. He thought of his strained relationships with his former colleagues, the funding rejections, the whispers of 'crackpot' and 'conspiracy theorist' that had followed him for years. Did he want to start all that again?

His phone buzzed, and he checked the screen. 'Unknown caller.' He sent the call to voicemail and returned to work. Seconds later, it rang again from the same number. He was about to end the call but decided to see—few people had that number.

"Trembley speaking."

"Trembley? It's Nathan. We need to talk."

CHAPTER EIGHT

Private Residence
Ojai, California, USA

Marcus Smith sat in his sleek, minimalist living room, sipping on a cup of black coffee. The room's clean lines and modern furniture belied the subtle presence of survival gear woven seamlessly into his daily life. A stylish bookshelf housed more than just novels; hidden compartments contained first aid kits and water purifiers. A decorative wooden trunk doubled as a cache for non-perishable food supplies.

He glanced out the window, watching his neighbors go about their mundane routines, unaware of the potential threats that loomed beyond their suburban bubble. Marcus knew better. His years as a successful investor allowed him to afford this lifestyle, but his prepper mentality stemmed from something far deeper.

His mind drifted back to his days as a Navy SEAL. The memory came unbidden, sharp and vivid.

Afghanistan, 2010. The mission had been simple on paper; simple did not equal easy. Extract a high-value target from a heavily fortified compound. Marcus and his team had moved under the cover of darkness, their gear heavy but familiar. They communicated through hand signals, each man knowing his role down to the smallest detail. They had trained, not for weeks but months on this single mission. Sadly, someone had passed them bad intelligence.

As they approached the compound, everything went sideways. An unexpected ambush erupted, bullets flying from all directions. Marcus remembered the adrenaline coursing through his veins as he took cover behind a crumbling wall. His commanding officer barked orders through the comms, trying to regain control.

Marcus peeked out, firing off rounds to suppress the enemy fire. He spotted their target—a terrified informant huddled in a corner, flanked by insurgents. He signaled to his teammate, Jackson, and they moved in tandem, covering each other's backs.

Jackson reached the informant first but took a bullet to the chest in the process. Marcus grabbed Jackson's vest and dragged him behind cover while shouting into his radio for medevac support. The seconds felt like hours as he applied pressure to Jackson's wound, watching his friend's life slip away.

"Hang in there, brother!" Marcus shouted over the din of gunfire.

But Jackson's eyes glazed over; he was gone.

The mission ended in success—they extracted the informant—but at a cost Marcus couldn't forget. That day and several others much like it had changed him profoundly. It wasn't only about surviving the mission; it was about being prepared for anything life threw at him.

The exhaustive training regimen for the team had brought a false sense of invulnerability. "Work the plan!" was one of the CO's favorite lines. Sometimes, though, shit just happened. Plan on it going sideways, and you learn to be smart about how you react to it. When the plan goes out the window, whatever you do next is the most important thing of all.

Back in his suburban home, Marcus set down his coffee cup with a resolute clink on the glass table. His prepping wasn't paranoia; it was prudence born from hard-earned experience. He had a team once more, not of soldiers but of survivors. He'd taken the leadership role when the group's founder had passed away a few years back. Now he called the shots.

They were well-funded, relatively well-trained, and included a mixture of skills and personalities that worked well together. Six years earlier, they had divided themselves into an alpha and a beta group. The thought was that two groups and two bug-out sites were better than one single large one. Marcus was now in charge of Beta, their enclave in the Ozarks.

Marcus often thought back to the day his prepping instincts truly ignited. His military life had given him the skills, but it was a business trip to Southeast Asia years later that forever altered his perspective.

He had been in Jakarta, closing a very lucrative deal for a major investment firm. The city buzzed with energy, skyscrapers piercing the sky amidst a labyrinth of streets and markets. At that point in his new career, Marcus was used to navigating complex financial systems, predicting market shifts, and seizing opportunities before others even noticed them. His ability to read patterns had made him one of the most sought-after investors in the industry.

That morning, he had been sipping coffee at a local café, reviewing charts on his tablet when the ground began to shake. At first, it was subtle—a mere tremor. But within seconds, it escalated into a violent earthquake. Buildings swayed ominously, and the café's windows shattered, sending shards of glass raining down.

People screamed and scrambled for cover. Marcus instinctively dove under a sturdy table, his military training kicking in automatically. He watched as chaos unfolded around him—streets cracked open, cars overturned, and debris fell from above. The earthquake lasted only minutes but felt like an eternity.

When the shaking stopped, Marcus emerged to a scene of total devastation. The city's infrastructure had literally crumbled; emergency services were overwhelmed. For hours, he wandered through the wreckage, helping where he could but feeling an overwhelming sense of helplessness.

That night, huddled with other survivors in a makeshift shelter, Marcus fully realized how fragile modern life truly was. Despite all his wealth and expertise, he had been as vulnerable as anyone else when disaster struck.

Returning to the U.S., Marcus couldn't shake the experience. He saw parallels between market volatility and life's unpredictability. Just as he diversified his investments to mitigate financial risk, he began diversifying his physical life to mitigate existential risks.

His success in investments provided the means to build up his personal survival stocks and eventually develop the plan for a robust prepper enclave. One thing he felt separated him from many preppers was the absolute belief that one man, or one family even on their own, was not enough...not long-term. You needed others, not a lot and not just anyone. You needed people who would work hard, understand the need for leadership, and were focused on more than surviving.

He leveraged his skills to eventually use the group's burgeoning nest eggs to procure land in the Ozarks—remote yet accessible—as well as Northern Florida. His analytical mind plotted out everything from food storage systems to renewable energy sources.

Marcus's business acumen translated seamlessly into organizing and maintaining their community. He used data-driven strategies to allocate resources efficiently and ensured that their operations were sustainable long-term.

"Diversify or die," he often told his team during the virtual meetings. It wasn't just about stock portfolios anymore; it was about life itself. Every active member of the enclaves contributed member fees every year to the communal fund and was assigned to one of the enclaves for site work for a minimum of two weeks each six months. No outside contractors were used, ever.

With each passing year, Marcus felt more secure knowing that he wasn't just prepared for financial downturns but for whatever catastrophe might come next. His enclave thrived under his leadership—a testament to his belief that preparation wasn't paranoia but prudence in an uncertain world.

His gaze drifted towards the corner of the basement where even now supplies were stacked—canned goods, water filtration systems, and tactical gear—all carefully integrated into his daily life. It was an oddity, an outlier in his affluent neighborhood, but for Marcus, each item represented a shield against uncertainty. He wondered briefly what Natalie would say if she saw this load-out.

Two hours later, Marcus adjusted his webcam, ensuring his face was well-lit before logging into the secure video conference. One by one, the members of the prepper enclave appeared on the screen. There was Lynn, an EMT with a penchant for herbal medicine; David, a former engineer who now focused on renewable energy projects; and the Johnson family, a couple with two teenage children who had recently been struggling to meet their annual financial contribution. Others filed into the meeting room over the next few minutes.

"Good evening, everyone," Marcus began, his tone firm but welcoming. "I appreciate you all making time for this meeting. We have a lot to cover."

Lynn chimed in first. "We need to discuss our stockpile rotation. Some of the older food and medical stocks are nearing expiration."

David nodded in agreement. "I've also been working on improving our solar grid, but I need more panels. We should consider reallocating funds."

The conversation flowed easily among the members, each offering updates on their respective projects. It was a testament to their collective dedication and shared beliefs. However, Marcus noticed the Johnsons' discomfort. He knew this moment would come and had prepared for it.

"Alright," Marcus said, directing his attention to Mike Johnson. "We need to address a very sensitive issue."

Mrs. Johnson shifted uneasily in her seat while Mr. Johnson stared at the floor.

"I'm sorry to bring it up like this, Mike, but you know our protocols. We're aware you haven't been able to meet your full annual payment," Marcus continued. "You know this is crucial for maintaining our resources and planning future projects."

"We've had some unexpected medical expenses," Mrs. Johnson said. "Our youngest needed surgery."

A murmur of sympathy rippled through the group, but Marcus knew they couldn't afford leniency... not without a plan.

"I understand," Marcus replied, softening his tone slightly. "But we need to find a solution that ensures everyone contributes fairly."

David leaned forward. "Maybe we can find another way for them to contribute? Extra labor hours or specific projects?"

Lynn added, "I agree. They're valuable members of our community."

Marcus nodded thoughtfully. "That's a good idea. How about this: You commit to additional work at the B-site compound and take on more responsibility for maintenance tasks? Also, the food stocks being rotated out can go to you. This should help partially offset your financial contribution until you're back on your feet."

The Johnsons exchanged glances before Mr. Johnson spoke up, "We can do that," he said, relief evident in his voice.

Marcus nodded; kicking someone out of the group at this point was a last resort. They knew where everything was anyway, and in an emergency, did anyone think they wouldn't simply show up?

"Great," Marcus concluded with a nod of approval. "Let's make sure we're all pulling our weight and supporting each other as we move forward. Make no mistakes, though. No free lunches here. No matter the circumstances, everyone contributes equally or you're out. That's the way it has to be."

With that resolved, the meeting continued smoothly, reinforcing the community bonds and shared commitment that made their enclave strong and resilient in uncertain times.

They went through several more points of order, and Marcus authorized the installation of an updated security monitoring system for the Beta site. It was a large capital expense, but the site was unoccupied for nearly half the year. They needed to protect what was there.

They also had two more cabins to build, one of which was his own. They'd started out on the larger family cabins, leaving the singles for later. Sadly, for him, it was only him and his dog, Retro, now.

The meeting ended right on schedule as usual. The designated leader of the Florida site should be getting ready for his in about an hour. They maintained good discipline and focus. Now that tensions were running high around the world, that seemed even more necessary.

As Marcus thought about his empty cabin waiting back in Arkansas, Natalie Reeves again came to mind—his ex-girlfriend who had once been the love of his life. She was passionate about her work as a MUFON UFO investigator, as he was about prepping. But while she chased the stars for answers, he dug into the earth for security.

Their breakup had been inevitable. While they'd both been in the Navy, Natalie had been through some pretty challenging stuff. She also couldn't understand why he felt the need for such extreme measures for safety; she saw it as paranoia rather than prudence. They argued endlessly about it until the day she had enough and left.

Marcus often wondered if he'd made the right choice—choosing security over love. Yet every time he heard another report of chaos or disaster, he felt vindicated in his relentless pursuit of independence and safety.

He shook off the melancholy thoughts as his phone buzzed with an incoming alert from their private network. The call from the Alpha site was being delayed. That was odd but not that unusual. Isaac generally could handle those without him, but Marcus still liked to sit in. He sent a text in acknowledgment, then snapped a leash on the German Shepherd smiling up at him, and they went out for a walk.

CHAPTER NINE

White House, West Wing
Washington, D.C., USA

"Now that you are the acting chief, I can finally show you this."

Emily took the red folder from the man she'd known most of her life. She unsealed it and laid it on the table.

"This is about Paul?" she said nervously. The man nodded.

"Yes, his final mission. The umm...the unredacted version."

She quickly scanned through the folder, then went back and began digesting each page fully. "UAPs, not mechanical failure?" she said without looking up. "Not pilot error," she said more softly. The rumors of UFOs, or the now more acceptable UAPs, in the carrier fleet's operations area had been around for years, and now she knew.

General William 'Bill' Briggs told her, "Yes," in a tone he'd used with her since she was a young girl. "Paul was a great pilot, Emily. He and his wingman encountered something unexpected, and well, it's all there."

"And the Navy covered it up?"

"Navy... no. Someone did, though. Buried it deep."

Emily read the classified document again, the words blurring together as frustration and worry gnawed at her. Her brother's disappearance, the mysterious circumstances surrounding it, and now this bullshit report—they had to be connected. She couldn't see how, yet.

General Briggs was retired but still very much in the loop. He noted the dark circles under her eyes and the tension in her shoulders.

"Emily, this may seem odd, giving you the information I just did, but I would ask that you step back from this." His voice was gentle but firm. He was well aware that Emily was already digging into the UFO issue at the request of the president himself. Still, she now had a personal stake in it as well, and he'd seen what happened when asking too many questions on this very subject. Now he had thrown gasoline on the fire with the contents of that file.

She shook her head. "I can't, not when Paul is still missing and no one will give me a straight answer."

"I do understand, Em, but know that pursuing this could destroy everything you've worked for—your career, your reputation, not to mention your faith in the system."

Emily met his gaze, her heart filled with conflict. "But if there's a cover-up, if Paul's disappearance is part of something bigger..."

"Then you'll find yourself up against forces you can't begin to imagine." Briggs placed a hand on her shoulder. "I've seen good people broken by less."

She thought of her brother, the distance that had grown between them over the years. The missed calls, the canceled plans, the unspoken resentments. Guilt twisted in her gut.

"This is the right thing to do...I have to do this, not only for Paul. The president and the nation deserve the truth." Her voice wavered, but her resolve held.

Briggs sighed. "Your father was the same way. Stubborn as hell when he believed in something."

Emily managed a small smile. "It's the Carter family curse."

"Let me ask you something that might be uncomfortable." She nodded. "How certain are you that POTUS really doesn't know? I mean, he is the most powerful man on Earth—right? I'm sure he knows all about Groom Lake, Area 51, and Roswell. Hell, even COVID-19," the general said. "If it has a known name, then I am certain he has been fully briefed."

“Bill..." she began, then looked around her office, wondering how recently it had been swept for eavesdropping devices. "You and I know how compartmentalization works in this town. The president, Congress, and the joint chiefs are kept in the dark on anything important. Hell, especially the politicians and appointees. Even if they hold the highest security levels. No one is going to trust them with the real secrets."

The older man nodded and grinned. "Mushrooms," he said. "Keep 'em in the dark and feed them bullshit."

She gave a sad grin before agreeing.

"Just be careful, Emily. Don't let your drive for justice blind you to the dangers."

"I'm the assistant chief of staff, General; I think I'll be okay."

He stood slowly. "Others who worked in these walls felt that way, too...but they were wrong, Emily. You ever hear of a man by the name of Bill Rich?"

She thought for a moment, then shook her head.

"Probably wouldn't. Well before your time." The retired general leaned against the back of his chair, eyes distant as if recalling a ghost from the past. "Bill Rich was a brilliant engineer at Lockheed Skunk Works, the division responsible for developing some of the most advanced aerospace technology: stealth bombers, reconnaissance aircraft —stuff that still seems like science fiction, even today."

She leaned forward, her interest piqued. "Okay?"

"Before his death, he made some extraordinary claims. He stated that extraterrestrial life exists and that the U.S. government has had contact with them. According to him, not only had we recovered alien technology, but we'd also reverse-engineered it."

Emily's eyebrows shot up. "He actually said that?"

"Yes, and more.” Briggs continued, “Rich mentioned that Lockheed had been working on anti-gravity propulsion and other technologies far beyond our current understanding, all based on what they'd learned from these extraterrestrial craft and artifacts. He said, 'We already have the means to travel among the stars, but these technologies are locked up in black projects, and it would take an act of God to ever get them out to benefit humanity.'"

She shook her head in disbelief. "Why would he go public with this? Didn't he fear repercussions?"

"He was dying," Briggs said flatly. "Cancer. When you're staring death in the face, you tend to worry less about the consequences. He felt it was his duty to reveal the truth, to give humanity a glimpse of what could be."

Emily processed the information, her mind racing to catch up. "So, you're saying the technology that could solve our energy crises, our transportation limitations, all of it... is simply sitting out there somewhere, hidden?"

"That's exactly what I'm saying. Rich claimed that these technologies were kept secret to maintain power structures and control. Think about the implications, Emily. Free energy, advanced propulsion—these would revolutionize society, but they'd also dismantle the status quo."

Her fingers tightened around the edges of the folder. "And you believe him?"

Briggs turned to meet her gaze. "I do. I worked in this town long enough to know that the most outlandish rumors often hold a kernel of truth. Bill Rich wasn't a crackpot. He was one of the most respected engineers of his time. If he said these things, there's a good chance he wasn't lying."

Emily's resolve hardened. "Then I need to dig deeper, Bill. If there's even a fraction of truth to this, it changes everything."

"Just remember," Briggs said, "some doors, once opened, can't be closed."

She nodded, eyes blazing with determination. "I know. But I have to try."

After Briggs departed, Emily returned to the papers in the file, more determined than ever. She and Paul came from a family of patriots. Now, it was her turn to serve her country, even if it meant uncovering unpleasant truths about her own government.

CHAPTER TEN

NovaCore Offices
McLean, Virginia, USA

"Talk to me." The voice was all sharp angles and lacked any sign of pleasantry.

"It's just as they claimed, sir. The entire community has been cleansed." Daniel Groves wanted to spit the words out. 'Cleansed' was an operational euphemism for what had gone on in this corner of Nevada.

The other man stared out the windows overlooking K Street. "Make sure there is no trace remaining. No mailboxes, no stuffed animals. You know the drill, Groves. We need to be able to deny that Havenwood, Nevada ever existed at all."

"Of course, Mr. King. I'll take care of it."

King had already disconnected and was waving another man into the spacious office. The other man was younger, better dressed, and clearly enamored with his own place in the universe. He walked over to a wall monitor to ensure the room's privacy settings were all enabled.

"May I?"

Owen King nodded as the younger man moved toward the sofa and helped himself to the contents of the vintage, crystal, scotch decanter on the coffee table.

"Was it them?" the man asked after downing a modest sip.

"Who the hell else would it be, Gibson?" The words came out with more emotion than Owen preferred. He took a few moments to reduce his stress.

"This is more than us cleaning up after them. The Observers are trying to tell us something," Gibson said.

No shit, was what Owen wanted to say to his younger protégé. They hadn't heard a peep out of the aliens in over twenty years. Not even after the USS Nimitz UFO incident in the Pacific in 2004 or the multiple USS Theodore Roosevelt incidents ten years later. Incidents that clearly violated the pseudo-agreement both sides had reached over half a century ago.

"Something is definitely up," Owen said before pouring himself a drink. "Groves can clean up this one, but damn... there's shit going on all over the world, and I don't just mean what's hitting the internet."

Gibson nodded. "The president is authorizing his own committee. Cabinet level this time."

Owen glanced out the massive windows in the direction of the White House and cursed under his breath. "Just to keep the press at bay or something more serious?"

Gibson's face pursed as he considered the question. "I think we need to assume this is serious. It's gotten no press coverage at all and is being headed up by Emily Carter, the assistant CoS."

"Oh, fuck," King said before sitting down heavily in his desk chair. "She's the one..."

The other man nodded. "Yeah, her half-brother was one of the victims in the incident off the Southeast Coast."

"That woman will be like a dog with a bone," King said.

"We can handle her," Gibson said confidently.

"Can you?" King asked, his voice rising sharply. "She's right down the hall from the president of the goddamn country, Gibson. She's the goddaughter of one of the highest-ranking generals to ever serve at the Pentagon. She can't simply come up missing."

The younger man shrugged.

"We are businessmen, not psychopaths," Owen said. "The work we are doing is of vital importance. Jesus, man, look at the technologies we've directly or indirectly brought to market over the years."

It was true, NovaCore Technologies had been at the forefront of high-tech defense weapons systems for years, as had their predecessor Precision Avionics back in the fifties. NovaCore ranked right up there with RTX, Grumman, and Lockheed Martin in the valuation of government contracts. Some of their systems were so far ahead of the competition, it seemed impossible.

Owen King swirled the scotch in his glass, staring into its amber depths as if the answers to all his problems lay within.

"Remember the Valkyrie Drone Program?" he asked Gibson. "Autonomous drones that can identify, track, and neutralize targets without human intervention. We deployed them in Syria two years ago. The Pentagon couldn't believe how quickly we neutralized those high-value targets."

Gibson leaned back, smirking. "Yeah, and the EPDS. Electromagnetic Pulse Defense System? Wiped out an entire enemy communications network without firing a single shot."

Owen smiled. "Our pulse tech didn't only disrupt communications; it fried every electronic device within a ten-mile radius. Effective, clean, and no collateral damage. By the way, they still haven't given us a final order on that."

"And let's not forget about the Neural Interface Systems," Gibson said, his eyes gleaming with excitement. "Direct mind-to-machine control for pilots and operators. Reduced reaction times to nearly zero."

Owen raised an eyebrow. "Our F-35s outfitted with those interfaces outmaneuvered every adversary in war games, even dodging hypersonic missiles. What's bad is we sat on that tech for over twenty years simply so we could slowly roll out more crude versions and maximize our market positions."

"True," Gibson agreed. "NovaCore's innovations are unmatched. That's why we can't let anything jeopardize our work, especially not Emily Carter."

Owen took a long sip of his drink, savoring the burn as it went down.

"Carter is smart," he conceded, "but she may now be driven by personal vendettas and idealism. She wouldn't understand the bigger picture."

Gibson's expression turned serious. "We need to handle her very carefully then."

Owen's eyes narrowed as he stared at Gibson. "You think I don't know that? This isn't some amateur-hour operation we're running here."

Gibson gulped visibly but said nothing more.

"We'll use our resources wisely," Owen continued after a moment. "Track her every move, anticipate her actions, and make sure she never gets close to the truth. Put one of our people on the committee."

The room fell silent as both men contemplated their next steps. The tech they had created was powerful, transformative even, but it also made them a target for those who sought to expose them.

Gibson set down his empty glass.

"Are you going to make contact?" Gibson's eyes looked skyward.

"With them? How? You know damn well that isn't how this works."

"They are changing the rules, Owen. Maybe we should, too."

The city below buzzed with activity, oblivious to the high-stakes game being played above.

"We stay invisible, as always," King said, his position and his words echoing another King, another former leader of the organization.

CHAPTER ELEVEN

Owen King sat in his plush leather chair, his office exuding an aura of power and affluence. Floor-to-ceiling windows overlooked the bustling city, while mahogany shelves held numerous awards and mementos of his success. Yet, the room was not without its secrets. A wall, almost hidden behind a polished oak panel, displayed a myriad of artifacts, blueprints, and schematics—some of them describing items and concepts that were distinctly non-terrestrial.

Alien technology combined with human ingenuity, all carefully drawn out. The room was rich with hidden desires and secrets, most of which Owen had a detached interest in at best.

As he stared at the set of plans open on his desk, Owen's mind drifted back to a dinner long ago. His father's stern face loomed across the table, eyes piercing through Owen's youthful enthusiasm.

"You think success comes without sacrifice?" his father had said, his voice gruff from years of smoking and hard liquor. "Recognition isn't given, it's taken."

Owen had nodded, absorbing every word. The figure beside him back then, Mr. Hargrove, a family friend and a self-made millionaire, had chimed in. "Your father is right, Owen. Ambition requires relentless pursuit. Never let anyone stand in your way."

Those two people had been more secretive in their own ambitions than anyone knew. The memory of that night had partially fueled his drive for decades. It was not only about copying their success; it was about proving himself worthy of his family's name and legacy. A legacy that had, over the years, become as much a burden as a trophy.

Back in the present, Owen felt the weight of those words pressing in on him. He glanced over at the field reports sprawled across one side of his desk—accounts of power outages, mysterious disappearances, and horrific scenes that defied explanation. The chaos wrought by the aliens, as well as those who were trusted with their tech, was far-reaching.

He rubbed his temples, feeling a headache brewing. "Have we gone too far?" he muttered to himself, though he knew there was no one to answer.

He picked up a Groves report detailing the incident in Nevada—homes vanishing without a trace. The precision of the event mirrored some of their own technological advancements, except on a more elevated level, but carried with it an unsettling consequence.

A knot tightened in his stomach as he flipped through more pages. A doctor's underwater encounter in the mid-Atlantic basin and the discovery made by Dr. Elena Schmidt's team on Mars weighed heavily on his overworked brain.

For all his achievements, Owen did grapple with the moral ramifications of their work. The fine line between progress and peril seemed increasingly blurred.

Yet quitting was never an option; that was drilled into him from that pivotal family dinner all those years ago.

The door to his office swung open, and his teenage daughter, Emma, stepped in. Seeing her bright, hopeful eyes was like a balm to his troubled mind.

"Hey, kiddo." His daughter scrunched up her face. She hated when he treated her like a child. Still, he couldn't help it. Even in her loafers and CoExist T-shirt that barely covered her stomach, he still always saw his little girl.

"Dad, can we talk?" she asked, glancing at the chaos spread across his desk.

"Of course, sweetheart. What is it?" Owen put on his mask of confidence, but he knew Emma could see right through it. He was a single parent; her mom had passed seven... no, eight years ago now. She'd had him wrapped around her finger since her tiny hand first grasped his, reaching up from her crib.

"I heard something about the new... what did they call it? The ZPG something project," she hesitated, biting her lip. "People in the plant are saying it might be dangerous. Are you really sure we're doing the right thing?"

Owen's heart sank. "Emma, I—"

"No, I mean it!" She stepped closer, passion igniting her words. "You're obsessed with NovaCore's success, but you have to protect the planet, Dad! How many people will get hurt?"

He felt a sharp pang of guilt. Owen liked having Emma around; she was bright, if not a bit naive... like most teenagers. "Honey, I'm doing this for us, for our future."

"But at what price?" Emma pressed, her eyes shining with tears. "What if it comes at the expense of other futures?" Emma had a social calling and a strong enough moral compass for the entire family; still, she would likely take over the organization at some point just like he had.

But her words struck deep—a painful reminder of the moral ambiguity he had immersed himself in. The weight of responsibility bore down on him, and suddenly the P&L statements and design specs around him felt more like shackles than dreams.

"Sometimes, to protect what you love, you have to make hard choices. There are greater powers at play here, and we don't understand..."

But even as he said it, he sensed the lies. The truth gnawed at him: was he not simply passing the burden of responsibility onward—removing the potential for redemptive action because the stakes felt too high?

From a few offices away, Gibson watched as the young girl left her father's office. Having no children himself, he felt having her around was a mistake... a liability. One that showed how weak his boss truly was. Thankfully, young Emma wasn't allowed around anything truly sensitive, but still, she picked up on things quickly and asked questions that no one else in NovaCore would ever dare.

Gibson knocked lightly on the wooden door before easing it open and walking in. "Problems, sir?" He knew the drill. Hell, everyone knew the drill by now. When the boss's tree-hugging daughter caused distress for Owen King, everyone paid the price.

"Where are we with the Zero Point Energy research?" Owen asked without looking up.

"Just out of the concept phase, sir. I can get the project manager in here if you want the full scope."

"Do it. I need to know who is so open-mouthed about this and what dangers we may be facing."

Ten minutes later, Operations Manager Dr. Evelyn Cross sat across the table from Owen and Gibson. "It's... complicated. The core concept behind tapping into zero-point energy is theoretically sound, but the challenges are, well... significant. We're dealing with physics at a level where even small fluctuations have catastrophic consequences."

"Give me the high-level issues. What's holding us up?" Owen asked.

"Notionally, we understand most of the processes involved. The primary challenge we're facing is one of containment. The energy density at zero-point is off the charts. We're talking about harnessing the quantum vacuum itself—the energy fluctuations that exist even in a 'perfect' vacuum state. The amount of power that could be drawn is theoretically infinite, but safely tapping into that without causing massive quantum, possibly even spacetime distortions, is the tricky part."

"Spacetime distortions?" Gibson asked, shaking his head.

"Yes," Cross answered. "We've detected minor quantum tunneling effects during the few small-scale tests we've run. We're talking localized anomalies—essentially small rips in spacetime—but nothing sustained or stable. And these tests were run at energy levels far below what we'd need for a viable power source. Imagine scaling that up without tearing reality apart."

"So, it's a stability problem. When can we solve it?" King asked.

Evelyn looked increasingly uncomfortable. "We're working on it. But here's the next hurdle—materials. We've run out of viable options with terrestrial materials. The pressures and energy densities at the interface where the ZPE extraction occurs are so extreme that traditional alloys and composites just break down. Even exotic elements like hafnium carbide or rhenium aren't holding up."

"I thought we were past that with those alloys from Project Exile," King said.

"We thought so, too. But even those materials, which are miles ahead of anything publicly available, aren't enough. We need something that operates outside our known material properties—something that can withstand forces on a quantum scale. We're currently trying to synthesize a crystalline lattice based on some of the data recovered from the alien tech."

"Any luck there?"

"Some. The crystalline structure we're attempting mimics the properties of material Zeta-12—one of the alien alloys we've isolated from the, uh, 'retrieved' tech. It appears to have a unique atomic binding energy, but synthesizing it in usable quantities is proving difficult. Our best attempts so far have resulted in only microgram samples. And even those are unstable at room temperature."

"Unstable how?" King asked.

"The atomic bonds decay quickly once removed from vacuum conditions,"Cross explained. "The material starts to lose its properties, and the lattice collapses. We think it might need an electromagnetic field to stabilize it, but we're still running simulations."

"And without that material...?" Owen said, growing increasingly frustrated.

"Without something that can endure those energy densities, even our best reactor designs will fail catastrophically. It's not just about generating energy; it's about sustaining and containing it without vaporizing the entire facility."

"So, what's the next step?"

"We're exploring a few options. One is trying to reverse-engineer the alien containment systems more directly. If we can figure out how their energy fields work at the subatomic level, we might be able to adapt the technology. We've also reached out to external partners with expertise in theoretical quantum mechanics for fresh insights."

"Like who? And who authorized it?" Gibson demanded.

"The... the Israelis and the Argentinians, and Mr. King, umm, you okayed it."

"Hell, I probably did. We've sunk millions into this damn boondoggle. Can't give up if the end is in sight. Time frame?"

"Best-case scenario?"Cross said. "Six to twelve months for stable material synthesis. After that, we're looking at years to develop a functioning ZPE reactor. But if the next few breakthroughs fall into place, we could accelerate that. Of course, if something goes wrong... well, it could set us back decades."

"Decades isn't an option,"King said. "Throw whatever resources you need at it. We need this device operational sooner, not later. However, this can't be a threat to any of us. Build it somewhere safe, or the whole damn thing is off."

"I do understand. But just so we're clear—this isn't like tweaking a conventional reactor design. We're dealing with technology that defies our current understanding of physics. It very well could blow up in our faces. Literally."

"Understood. Just make sure we're on the side of history that figures it out first. Also, Doctor..."

She looked at King worriedly. "Yes?"

"Someone on your team, probably a young male, has a problem keeping his mouth shut. I am betting you already know who that is."

The look on the woman's face let him know he'd been on target with that comment.

"Get rid of him. Today. Off the team, out of the building. You can transfer him somewhere remote or just can his ass. Either way, he will not be a problem for us ever again. You got me?"

She nodded and hurriedly left the room.

"I assume you want me to follow up on that."

"Of course I do, Gibson. Why the hell else are you here? Like you said, you don't know shit about ZPE devices."

CHAPTER TWELVE

0903 EST May 10
White House West Wing
Washington, D.C., USA

Emily Carter sat at her desk, a stack of personnel files spread out before her. As she flipped through the pages, she couldn't help but feel a sense of accomplishment. This was her pet project, the UFO task force, and she needed the right people to make it work.

She knew that this committee would never see the light of public scrutiny, which gave her a certain level of freedom in her choices. Credentials and background were important, but not as crucial as the other qualities she was looking for. Emily wanted people with conviction, individuals whose specialties aligned with the questions that would inevitably arise during their investigations. Most importantly, she needed people she could trust to operate independently—curious decision-makers who could think on their feet.

As she scanned the files, Emily realized that finding this particular combination of skills was proving to be quite a challenge. It wasn't every day that you came across someone with the right mix of scientific expertise, curiosity, and trustworthiness.

A light tap, then the door to Emily's office cracked open, and Agent Trent Rogers stepped inside, a familiar figure in his crisp suit and easy smile. He held a folder tucked under his arm, moving with the confidence of someone who had seen the inner workings of government and military operations alike.

"Hey, Ms. Carter," he greeted, closing the door behind him. "I see you're knee-deep in personnel files."

She looked up, offering a weary smile. "You could say that. I want the best for this task force."

Trent nodded, taking a seat across from her. "May I?"

She nodded and pushed the folder toward him. He spread it open on her desk, revealing potential candidates. "I've got those other names you asked for," he said, still reading. "A lot of them are military—given the nature of your task force, you'll probably want their expertise."

Emily leaned forward, scanning the list he had placed on the desk. "Makes sense. We'll need their tactical experience and protocol knowledge." She trusted Trent implicitly; he had been her first addition to the task force for good reason. His high security clearance allowed him to go places she couldn't, and his disarming personality made him an excellent liaison. She still wasn't totally sure what agency he was with—NSA, Homeland, CIA, Secret Service. Ultimately, she liked and trusted him, and unlike most in the intelligence community, he was very personable and forthcoming. That and the fact that her personal recommendation of him was enough.

"Colonel James Walker," Trent began, pointing to one name on his list. "Tactical expert with experience in asymmetric warfare. He's solid. Has been one of the top military advisors to POTUS for the last fourteen months."

Emily nodded, jotting down notes. "Walker's good. We'll need someone who can handle unconventional threats and unconventional thinking. Not always easy for a military mindset. Think he can handle it?"

"I do. There is some additional background that is relevant in his file. One of which is that he has an advanced degree."

She scanned the file. "In Philosophy of Science."

Trent smiled and nodded. "Could have likely done Theoretical Physicist if not for his military duties. The guy is whip-smart but very low-key; doesn't show his hand."

Trent leaned back, his gaze steady on Emily's face. "We also have Dr. Constance Hughes—Connie—historian and anthropologist. She can give us insights into historical contexts and unexplained artifacts."

Emily scribbled another note, feeling a bit more at ease with each name they discussed. Trent, it seemed, had a knack for finding the right people for the job.

"What about Professor Kaden Trembley?" Emily asked, recalling the astrophysicist whose work had often skirted the edges of controversy. An acquaintance had suggested him.

Trent raised an eyebrow but nodded approvingly. "He's a Brit, but yes, on my list, too. His insights into astronomy and extraterrestrial phenomena could be invaluable, even if he's... a bit intense."

Emily chuckled softly. "That's one way to put it."

Their conversation flowed seamlessly as they continued to review potential candidates, each name adding another piece to the puzzle they were trying to solve.

"Trent, they're going to laugh at us, but we're building something important here," Emily said finally, looking up at the agent with determination in her eyes.

"I know, and hopefully somewhere in here I can find someone to take you out on a date."

"Get out of my office," she said, teasing.

Her love life had been part of a running banter for most of their working relationship. Neither was willing to share a single detail, but to Trent, that simply meant Emily didn't have one. A fact that was sadly true but one she would never admit to.

"Back to the list." Emily tapped her pen against her notebook. "What other disciplines should we include? We don't want it to be too large, or it'll be too unwieldy to get anything done. For now, though, this is just a wish list. Some may decline anyway."

Trent leaned forward, flipping pages in the folder. "Well, you may want to ask them. Like, I would suggest someone who can decode potential alien communications. A cybersecurity and cryptanalysis expert would be ideal, but they may not agree."

Emily nodded. "That's a good idea, and Avery Martinez comes to mind. Former Cyber Command operative, right?"

"Exactly. Avery's cracked some of the toughest codes out there," Trent confirmed, "but I'm not sure you can pry her away from Silicon Valley long enough."

Emily Carter made a note next to Avery's name. "You're right, we can make this list all day long, but who knows who will agree?"

"They will need to relocate here at least for the initial session, right?"

Emily nodded; they had discussed this previously. She had wanted the members to commit to ninety days but later realized that was probably too long for them. They were all going to be people at the top of their profession. No way you could pull them out of their research or jobs for too long.

"Personally, I think we also need someone who can handle the abductee and missing persons reports," Trent continued. "Someone with a knack for finding patterns in chaos."

"I thought that was going to be you, Agent Rogers," Emily said, smiling.

"Not my forte, Boss."

"Detective Rigel Thomas" Emily said, recognizing the name from a recent report she had read. "He's apparently well-known for uncovering unusual patterns in disappearances linked to UFO activity."

"Exactly," Trent agreed, pulling the man's file from the folder and adding it to a pile.

Emily paused, considering their selections so far. "We've got science, military, history, environmental expertise, and investigative skills covered."

"Pretty well-rounded," Trent agreed. "May need more on the scientific side, though. Some of these academics' knowledge is very siloed. They only seem smart in their own discipline."

Emily's pen hovered over the paper as she considered Trent's statement and thought about potential gaps in their team's expertise.

"What about someone who understands our own space missions?" she suggested suddenly. The one that was in the news recently about the

Mars thing. “Dr. Elena Schmidt, the Mars Rover specialist; her experience could possibly offer a broader perspective on planetary sciences.” While Emily had been briefed on the off-the-record findings of that mission, she wasn't ready to share that with Rogers.

Trent nodded approvingly. “Good call. We might find that there’s something more going on in places beyond Earth. Besides, reading here, she was a former student of Trembley.”

Emily added Dr. Schmidt’s name to the growing list. “Trembley seems very tied into several of the top experts in the field. I think we need to get him on board first, next should be Walker, and then let both of them sign off on other members."

He smiled and nodded.

"And no—I am not dating any of them."

Over the last few months, Emily had become well-versed in the history of UFO investigations in the United States. The Robertson Panel, formed by then-Congressman Gerald Ford in 1953, had been a turning point. Dr. H.P. Robertson and his committee had evaluated the evidence, concluding that most sightings could be explained conventionally and posed no national security threat.

But Emily knew better. The panel's debunking strategy had set the tone for decades of skepticism and dismissal. Subsequent government investigations had been influenced by this approach, leaving the truth buried beneath layers of secrecy and denial.

She couldn't let that happen to this task force. This committee had to be different. They needed to operate with discretion, away from the public eye and the forces that had derailed previous task forces. Emily was determined to uncover the truth, no matter how uncomfortable or world-shattering it might be.

As Trent left and she finalized the committee's structure, Emily made a silent vow. Hers would not fall victim to the same pressures and influences that had plagued its predecessors. They would follow the evidence, wherever it led, without fear or bias.

She glanced at the dozen or so names on her list once more. Each brought a unique perspective and expertise to the table. Together, they would form a formidable team, ready to tackle the greatest mystery of their time.

She also needed to reach out to an old family friend for some recommendations. Trent was right; they would have to put a minimum of two military advisors on the team, which could be problematic. No matter how bright a military mind was, they tended to think in a box. Everything is either a threat or an asset. Also, she needed to be able to trust every person on this list. She had no doubt that some would fail the vetting process, both her own and White House security.

With a deep breath, Emily hit send on the email to the office of White House protocol, officially launching SCET, which was what she'd decided to call it. The die was cast, and the journey had begun. Whatever came next, things were going to get interesting around here.

CHAPTER THIRTEEN

Colgate College
Hawthorn Lane
Hamilton, NY, USA

Kaden's computer buzzed as the video call connected, and Dr. Nathan Carlson's lined face filled the screen.

"Carlson, what's this all about? Cryptic phone calls and urgent messages that I must see something," Kaden started, trying to keep his tone neutral.

Nathan's eyes held for a moment, fatigue evident in the man's demeanor. "Kaden, you need to know something about those stones Elena uncovered on Mars."

"Of course," Kaden replied, leaning forward. "But what's so urgent? And why aren't you at your lab?" Kaden could see what looked like a beach in the background.

"Too many eyes at work," he said.

Kaden thought for a moment. "You know someone has frozen out Elena's entire team?"

The other man nodded slowly. "I could have guessed as much. What they found... well, this is big, Kaden."

Trembley decided to just let his old friend speak. He knew Nathan well enough to know that interrupting him with questions might derail the entire conversation.

"I've been examining the image data," Nathan began, "and while Elena's discovery is groundbreaking, there's something I think you, in particular, need to know."

Kaden frowned. "What do you mean?"

"The markings on the stones... they're engravings."

"What? How?" Kaden's voice echoed through his apartment. He struggled to process the information. "How could that even be possible?"

Nathan swapped the view of his face for a bit of video that had the faint ESA watermark in one corner. Kaden leaned in to see the detail better. So far, he'd only seen a single screen grab of the tiny stones. It had been impressive, but the video was astounding.

Nathan leaned closer to his camera, his voice dropping to a conspiratorial whisper. "I shouldn't be showing you this. These stones don't match any known Martian geology, nor could the marks be caused by atmospheric weathering or any other natural conditions."

"Then where are they from?" Kaden's mind was spinning with possibilities.

Nathan took a deep breath. "That's what my team and I have been trying to figure out. Had been trying to figure out, I should say." Nathan showed another clip of video and froze the image. Kaden saw as the raw photo went through filters to lighten, increase exposure, and add contrast.

"That looks rather like..." Kaden stared at the screen, unable to finish his sentence for a moment. His thoughts tumbled over each other as he tried to make sense of this revelation.

Nathan continued, "It's a perfectly drilled hole. I've run every modeling scenario I could think of, cross-referenced with all known databases. The results are consistent—these stones are absolutely not from Mars."

Kaden rubbed his temples, feeling a headache coming on. "What does that mean?"

"Wait, there's more, old friend," Nathan said. "My assistant Natomi —I think you met her at that conference in Brussels last year. She had an idea and used our AI system to extract what we can see of the carvings. They also managed to pull fragments off of the other stone."

Again the video replaced Nathan's face, and Kaden could see the bits of etched lines being extracted and the shapes laid out on a new image. They looked like a more ancient form of picture language.

"That seems almost like Mayan or Hieroglyphics," Kaden said, realizing at once how preposterous that sounded.

"Yes, it does," Nathan agreed before pulling up an image of a necklace made out of stones that looked remarkably similar. "This is in the National Museum of Nairobi. It's an ancient part of a high priest's ritualistic headwear. The language is Nsibidi, which Natomi discovered employs pictograph and ideograph symbols to convey messages.

That is the language of the Ejagham peoples of southeastern Nigeria and southwestern Cameroon in the Cross River region. It is also used by neighboring Ibibio, Efik, and Igbo peoples. The point is, Kaden, these stones found on Mars are actually from Africa."

Trembley nodded slowly, still absorbing the gravity of Nathan's words. There were Earth rocks on Mars and vice versa. Asteroids had blasted countless tons of both planets out into space over the eons. "How old are these?"

"No, no..." Nathan said, shaking his head. "Not that old. I know what you're thinking. That necklace is only about 15,000 years old at most. The original tribes were maybe a few thousand years older than that. It's old, but it is not ancient. I wanted to discuss it with you first. Given your experience and our history... I trust you'll know how best to handle this information."

Kaden took a deep breath and nodded again. This discovery supported his belief that aliens had been visiting Earth for years. It was a breakthrough, but it also brought new challenges. Someone or something had transported ritualistic stones from Africa to Mars in the last 15,000 years.

"I do appreciate your trust," Kaden said. He was totally unsure as to what to do next. "Send me what you have, please, or whatever you can get past your watchdogs."

"Might not be that easy, but I'll do what I can." The call ended, and Kaden stared at his own dark reflection in the screen. Aliens had been visiting Earth for a very long time. That coincided with many of his own theories, but going public again would just see him pushed further out of mainstream science. Neither his career nor his sanity could handle more of that.

Ancient aliens, extraterrestrial visitors, government cover-ups... it was all fringe elements of something much bigger. He'd alluded to it publicly years earlier and subsequently lost his tenured position back in England and now threatened his current one. While this latest find had his mind going into overdrive, he would force himself to be cautious. Follow the clues, be methodical. In other words, be a scientist.

CHAPTER FOURTEEN

1930 CDT June 02
42°08'N, 93°32'W
Central Iowa, USA

Natalie Reeves squinted at the hazy photographs spread across her makeshift desk in the dingy motel room. The fading sunlight filtering through the dusty blinds cast an eerie glow on the grainy images of alleged UFO sightings.

She sighed, rubbing her tired eyes. After her own harrowing encounters with the unexplained phenomena during her time as a Navy pilot, the MUFON organization had become her lifeline—a way to channel her burning need for answers into positive action. But the endless stream of blurry photos and crackpot theories from wannabe investigators was enough to make even her resolve falter at times.

A sharp knock at the door jolted Natalie from her thoughts. She tensed, her hand automatically reaching for the concealed pistol at her hip as she rose to peer through the peephole. Too many days in the field, too many cheap hotels.

"Reeves, open up. It's me." The gruff voice of her fellow investigator eased her nerves.

She unbolted the locks and let him slip inside. "Christ, Larson, a little warning next time?"

He shrugged off her irritation, pulling out a thick manila folder from inside his jacket. "Thought you'd want to see this ASAP. Got some action on those missing hikers in the Ozarks."

Natalie raised an eyebrow. "The Ozarks? That's a bit out of my jurisdiction. Thought Jacobson was on that case."

"He was," he said, holding up the folder. "Until he also upped and went off the grid two days ago. Vanished. Jacobson is our new lead."

That got her attention as she flipped open the folder, scanning the contents. Maps of the wilderness area, more grainy trail camera photos, and hastily scrawled notes littered the pages—but it was the police report on top that made her blood run cold.

"Jacobson's Jeep was found a few hours ago abandoned on a service road. No sign of a struggle, but..." Larson hesitated. "Locals reported strange lights in the sky that night. Lots of rumors flying around about military black ops teams, secret bases..."

Natalie slammed the folder shut; her face went rigid. She knew all too well the lengths the government would go to keep their secrets buried. And now another investigator had been swallowed up by the conspiracy. She checked flight time from the small local airport and made up her mind.

"I'm taking the case." She grabbed her go-bag, already mentally cataloging the gear she'd need for a trek into the backcountry. "You with me?"

Larson frowned. "Look, Reeves, I know you're the best we've got, but you know, this... this feels different. Whatever Jacobson stumbled onto, not sure it's anything we've dealt with before. I've just got a bad feeling..."

Natalie met his gaze, her blue eyes blazing with determination. "Then let's hope we're better at it than he was."

~

Natalie Reeves was 34, from Wilmington—the one in North Carolina, not Delaware. She stepped out of the terminal at the Little Rock airport, and the humidity hit her full force.

"Please, God, tell me the rental car has a working A/C."

MUFON was a self-funded organization and generally considered a bunch of rank amateurs. She'd spent the last few years helping change that perception, bringing scientific rigor and established forensic techniques to every assignment. As such, the number of 'legitimate' incidents the organization claimed was way down. That was good, though, as most of the others stood up well to scientific and public scrutiny.

Natalie slid into the driver's seat of the rental car, cranking the A/C to max as Larson climbed in beside her. Sweat already dampened her shirt in the Arkansas heat. She pulled out onto the highway, heading toward the stretch of mountain road where Dennis Jacobson's rental truck had been found abandoned three nights ago.

As they neared the location marked by their high-end GPS locator, Larson fidgeted with a file folder. "Something's not adding up here, Natalie. Those hikers disappeared a good six or seven miles from here. Why would Jacobson have parked this far out?"

Natalie frowned, considering the possibilities. "Could be he needed a break, or maybe foul play. Let's see what the scene tells us before jumping to conclusions."

Twenty minutes later, she pulled the car onto the shoulder where the pickup still sat, yellow police tape fluttering in the breeze. Natalie and Larson ducked under the tape with their MUFON credentials. The local police didn't give her badge the scrutiny it deserved. Technically, she was not allowed in scenes of active investigations; however, she still had her attitude and a commanding presence from her years in the military. Assume you belong, and usually you do.

She pulled on nitrile gloves as she peered into the cab, taking in the typical detritus of the local investigators' transient lifestyle—fast food wrappers, cigarette butts, dog-eared magazines. A faded picture of a woman and two kids was tucked into the visor.

"Larson, check this out." Natalie pointed to the driver's side door. Scratches marred the paint, and the handle was bent at an odd angle. "I thought you said no signs of a struggle. Looks like it was forced open from the outside."

As Natalie moved around to the side of the truck, something glinted in the gravel, catching her eye. She crouched down, using a pen to carefully lift a silver chain with a rectangular pendant. Initials were engraved on it: 'D.J.'

"Dennis Jacobson." Larson peered over her shoulder. "Looks like it was ripped off his neck."

Natalie stood, surveying the dusty roadside. A flash of color in the scrub brush caught her attention. She moved down the slope about twenty yards and extracted a torn flannel shirt, the pattern distinctive. "This matches the one Jacobson packed, according to his wife." For some reason, the shirt's pattern made her think of her former fiancé. He would have been right at home in these woods.

She examined the shirt, noting the missing buttons and ragged edges. "I'm no alien expert, but this looks more like a plain old human struggle to me. Let me point out a few things to the police. I think Dennis Jacobson was attacked. Maybe he ran across a meth lab or something up here."

Larson nodded. "The hikers, too?"

That was possible, but so far, Natalie knew nothing connecting the two incidents other than general proximity and timing. She demanded correlating facts before she drew conclusions, but her mind was already moving to the next part of their mission.

"Let's move on to the other location," she said.

"But what about Dennis?" Larson said, his voice holding a pleading tone.

Natalie knew the missing man—not well, but he seemed decent enough and competent in his work. She was good at compartmentalizing non-essential things like emotions and obligations. "Sorry, but this is a police matter, Larson. We can do nothing else here. We're UFO hunters, so maybe we can at least do something for those missing hikers."

CHAPTER FIFTEEN

Colgate College
Hawthorn Lane
Hamilton, NY, USA

"You're becoming obsessed again, Kaden."

Sarah Mitchell's voice held a gravity that cut through the static of his cluttered apartment. He reluctantly looked up from his notes, but her presence demanded attention.

His friend's observations weren't requested, but they were not wrong. She'd helped pull him out of the previous fiasco when he'd made such a bloody fool of himself, and she had let it be known then that she wouldn't be doing that again.

"I know, I know. You've said that before," Kaden muttered, eyes still glued to the information from the Mars stones and new UFO sightings from Javier. There was a pattern to all this—coordinates, timestamps, all pointing to something that was beginning to actually scare him.

"And you didn't listen before, either," she countered, stepping closer. "Look at yourself. You haven't slept in days. Your apartment looks like a crime scene of paperwork and old coffee cups."

He sighed and rubbed his temples. "This is rather bigger than sleep, Sarah. We're on the brink of discovering—"

"Discovering what?" she interrupted, a rare edge to her voice. "That aliens are real? That the government is hiding them? What then? Who do you think wants to know that?"

Kaden finally met her eyes, frustration simmering beneath his surface calm. "The truth matters. People deserve to know."

"Do they?" Sarah folded her arms, skepticism etched on her face. "Or is this about you proving you're right? About vindicating your career?"

He clenched his fists. "It's really not about me."

"Isn't it?" She stepped closer, her tone softening but remaining firm. "Kaden, your work has merit. No one's disputing that. But this obsession... it's isolating you. Even before the call with the dean, you had canceled your spring classes, and now you're on a forced sabbatical. You're pushing everyone away."

"I can handle it," Kaden snapped.

She shook her head slowly. "No one can handle the world-shattering truth you're chasing alone. You think uncovering extraterrestrial life won't break you? You think exposing a government cover-up won't leave you shattered?"

"I have to know," he insisted, his voice almost pleading.

"And then what?" She paused, letting the silence sink in before continuing. "What happens when you've burned every bridge? When you're left alone with the truth and no one to share it with? When you're isolated and broken?"

Kaden's jaw tightened, but doubt flickered in his eyes.

"You need balance," Sarah urged. "Stability and purpose beyond your work. If you keep going like this... you'll be consumed."

He looked away, staring at the scattered papers and blinking computer screen.

Kaden took a deep breath, trying to steady his thoughts. "Do you remember me telling you about the Varginha incident in Brazil, which happened in 1996?"

Sarah raised an eyebrow. "The supposed UFO crash and alien sighting? A bunch of teenagers and a whole lot of hearsay?"

"Oh, I have to say, it's rather more than mere hearsay, and it was nearly the entire town," Kaden countered, leaning forward.

"Three young women claimed to have encountered a strange creature while walking through a field. They described it as being around five feet tall, with a large head, large red eyes, and brownish skin that appeared greasy or oily. The creature allegedly made a groaning sound and seemed injured.

"Shortly after the sighting, there were reports that the Brazilian military and police captured one or more creatures and transported them to a local hospital, where they were allegedly treated before being transferred to a military base.

"According to the story, a military officer involved in the operation fell ill and soon after died under mysterious circumstances, which fueled further speculation about the incident.

"Multiple witnesses, including a deputy, reported seeing a creature —again described as short with brown skin and large red eyes. The military was involved; there were reports of strange activity and cover-ups."

"And you believe that?" Sarah's skepticism was palpable.

Kaden nodded. "Yes. And here's why. It's not just about that one incident. Varginha fits into a larger pattern. For centuries, there have been reports, sightings, and evidence that points to extraterrestrial visits."

"Centuries?" Sarah's voice held a mix of disbelief and curiosity.

"Precisely," Kaden said, the intensity in his eyes growing. "Think about it. The Varginha incident wasn't an isolated event. What we're seeing now, these UFO sightings, they're part of a continuum. Look at these images of the stones Elena found on Mars. They apparently closely resemble Nsibidi, an ancient African script. How did those stones get there unless there was some form of contact, possibly transportation, thousands of years ago?"

Sarah's eyes narrowed at the mention of Elena, but she didn't interrupt.

Kaden continued, "What if the Varginha creature was a remnant of a much larger, much older interaction? A piece of a puzzle that's been hidden from us. These sightings, these incidents, they're not random. They're deliberate, part of a long-standing observation or interaction with us. Increasingly, I wonder if we aren't dealing with multiple species of aliens interacting with our planet."

"And the government's just covering it all up?" Sarah asked, crossing her arms.

"I think it's quite likely, yes," Kaden shot back. "The implications of such a truth are staggering. Admitting extraterrestrial contact changes everything—politics, religion, societal structures. They've been keeping this under wraps for years, and now we're just scratching the surface—a surface that many people apparently want left undisturbed."

Sarah's face softened slightly, the weight of his words settling in. "And you think you can uncover this all alone? Reveal the truth?"

Kaden shrugged. "I have to try," he said, his voice firm. "We're at a pivotal moment. The truth is there, and it's our responsibility to bring it to light. Not for personal gain, but because people deserve to know. They deserve the chance to understand our place in the universe."

Sarah sighed, rubbing her temples. "People don't care, Kaden. They either believe it already, or they likely never will."

"Exactly," Kaden replied, determination etched in every line of his face. "And that's why I can't stop. Not now. We must find proof."

"You can stop," she said gently but firmly. "And you should."

Kaden felt shaken but refused to show it. He turned back to his work with renewed determination. "If you think that, why did you recommend me to the presidential committee?"

Sarah sighed deeply, realizing she had done all she could for now.

"You need an outlet. You're brilliant, Kaden, but you struggle when you are in a vacuum. You need other scientists and experts around with the rigor and fundamentals that, well... sometimes you overlook."

"That's not fair," he began, but he knew she was right.

"Don't let this destroy you," she said quietly before leaving him to his obsession once more.

He barely heard the door click shut behind her as he returned to the work that truly did consume his every thought.

Years ago, Kaden had latched onto an incident like a dog with a bone. It was in Exeter, and he had corroborating statements from police and military officials, not just of a craft but a landing. He'd blown half a semester's budget dragging a team of researchers and grad students out to the woods near Exwick.

Looking back now, even he had to admit the story was weak and the proof just as thin, but something about the incident had captured the public's attention, and he found himself in front of the press. Several times, his department heads warned him to step back and let the officials do the detective work, but he hadn't listened.

One of his grad students had been the one who eventually realized the town leaders had organized the entire story to drum up tourism. The councilman had a few too many pints and started bragging about how much money they were bringing in. Kaden's reputation was trashed in the next day's news cycle. He was a laughingstock, a fool. His career trajectory took a dive, his colleagues disappeared, and eventually, he was forced out of the university.

He wasn't stupid enough to ignore Sarah's admonition. Hell, she was likely right, but he also wasn't going to ignore the facts. Believing in alien intelligences and encounters on Earth came with a massive amount of public skepticism.

Why was it so hard for people to accept the possibility of extraterrestrial life? The universe was vast, unfathomably so. He could quote the numbers by heart: over 100 billion stars in our galaxy alone, and there were more galaxies in the observable universe than grains of sand on all the Earth's beaches.

He turned to his whiteboard, covered in equations and star maps. "There are at least 2 trillion galaxies," he muttered to himself, eyeing a line from one scribbled note to another. "Each with billions or even trillions of stars. And around those stars, countless planets."

He paused, picking up a marker and circling a set of numbers. "The Drake Equation," he whispered, almost reverently. "It estimates that there could be anywhere from 1,000 to 100 million civilizations in our galaxy alone."

Kaden's thoughts naturally followed the logic to the age of these potential civilizations. Some stars were billions of years older than our sun. Any intelligent life forms orbiting them could be millions, if not billions, of years ahead of us in technological development.

"Imagine what they could achieve," he muttered to himself, pacing the room. "Technologies beyond our comprehension. Methods of travel that make our fastest spacecraft look like children's toys."

He stopped in front of his computer, tapping the screen to bring up an image of those mysterious polished stones discovered on Mars. "Ancient cultures that could have existed long before humanity even crawled out of the primordial soup," he marveled.

Kaden knew these thoughts made people uncomfortable. It shattered their sense of human exceptionalism—the belief that we are somehow unique and alone in the cosmos.

"But why?" he wondered aloud, frustration creeping into his voice. "Why is it so hard for them to see? To understand?"

He thought back to his lectures, how students would nod politely but remain unconvinced; how colleagues would smile indulgently but dismiss his theories behind closed doors.

"It's fear," he concluded quietly. "Fear of the unknown. Fear of change."

His eyes flicked back to his charts and data points, each one a potential piece of the larger puzzle.

"Or maybe," he added bitterly, "they're just too wrapped up in their own lives to care about what's out there. Our egos just can't accept that we are somehow not special, maybe even inferior."

He slumped into his chair, feeling the weight of isolation pressing down on him again.

"Billions upon billions of stars," he murmured, eyes unfocused as they stared into the depths of space on his screen. "And yet we insist on remaining willfully blind."

CHAPTER SIXTEEN

42°08'N, 93°32' W
CENTRAL IOWA, USA

It wasn't just that Natalie Reeves liked planes; more like she was born to be in the air. She could still see her younger self standing at the edge of the tarmac, her eyes fixed on the planes taking off and landing at the bustling airport. The roar of the engines filled her ears, and the smell of jet fuel permeated the air. Even at the tender age of eight, she knew this was where she belonged.

Her father, a former Naval aviator, stood beside her, his hand resting gently on her shoulder. "You see that, Natalie?" He pointed to a sleek fighter jet as it soared overhead. "That's an F-14 Tomcat. I used to fly one of those back in my Navy days."

Natalie's eyes widened with awe. "Really, Dad? You got to fly that?"

He chuckled, his eyes crinkling at the corners. "Sure did, kiddo. Best years of my life."

"I want to fly one, too, someday," Natalie declared, her voice filled with determination.

Her father knelt down, meeting her gaze. "You know what, Natalie? I have no doubt you will. You've got that spark in you, just like I did at your age. The sky's the limit for you, my love."

Natalie beamed, her heart swelling with pride and excitement. She knew, in that moment, that she would stop at nothing to make her dream a reality.

As they walked back to the car, her father's words echoed in her mind. "Remember, Natalie, being a pilot is a lot of work. It isn't just about the flying. It's about dedication, discipline, and a love for the craft. It's not an easy path, but if you've got the passion, you can make it happen."

Natalie nodded solemnly, absorbing every word. She knew she had a long road ahead of her, but with her father's encouragement and her own determination, she felt ready to take on the challenge.

That night, as she lay in bed, Natalie's mind raced with visions of soaring through the clouds, the controls of a fighter jet at her fingertips. She drifted off to sleep, dreaming of the day when she would finally take to the skies and make her mark on the world.

Little did she know that less than a year later, her father would be gone, killed in what was called at the time a weather-related flight accident. He, his co-pilot, and the safety engineer were on an air freight flight out of Portland. Her mom was convinced Natalie would forget about flying afterward, but it seemed to have had the opposite effect.

Natalie's journey to becoming a Navy aviator was far from smooth sailing. As a woman in a male-dominated field, she faced countless obstacles and skepticism from her peers and superiors alike. But Natalie was no stranger to adversity. She met each challenge head-on, fueled by an unwavering determination to prove herself.

In the cockpit, Natalie was a natural. Her instructors marveled at her instincts and quick thinking, even as they pushed her harder than her male counterparts. She spent long hours studying flight manuals and running drills, honing her skills until they were razor-sharp.

Despite her undeniable talent, Natalie often found herself the target of harassment and discrimination. Male pilots would make snide comments about her appearance or question her abilities, but she refused to let their words get under her skin. Instead, she channeled her frustration into her flying, pushing herself to be faster, stronger, and more precise.

As she slowly climbed the ranks, Natalie's reputation as a skilled and fearless pilot grew. She took on the toughest missions, flying into hostile territory again and again, navigating treacherous weather conditions with ease. Her wingman, Lieutenant Paul Klaussen, became her closest ally and confidant, always watching her back in the air.

But everything changed on that fateful mission. It was supposed to be a routine reconnaissance flight over the Atlantic, but something went terribly wrong. By the time she regained control of her aircraft, it was too late. Paul's jet had vanished into the sea.

The official report cited pilot error as the cause of the incident, but Natalie knew better. She had seen something out there, something she couldn't explain. And the brass seemed all too eager to sweep the whole thing under the rug.

Natalie was haunted by the loss of her friend and the nagging sense that there was more to the story than anyone was letting on. She couldn't shake the feeling that Klaussen's disappearance was connected to something bigger, something that the military was desperate to keep hidden.

Over time, that belief had turned into an obsession, one that eventually drove her from the Navy and pushed her then-fiancée out of her life. Both things came with tremendous regret, but Natalie had the innate ability to compartmentalize things. She put the hard times in a box until she was at a place she could give them the attention they needed. It wasn't all that healthy; she would be the first to admit that, but it allowed her to cope, to function, and, most importantly, to seek the truth.

After her career and then the romantic breakup, she needed to refocus her life's direction. That had proven to be more challenging than she expected. The strong, independent woman who needed no one to get ahead found herself floundering. She had been diagnosed with PTSD, but like everything else, she put that into its own box for now.

When Natalie found herself driving hours and sometimes days to locations of reported UFO encounters, she wasn't sure if it was morbid curiosity or part of something bigger. She did know unraveling the clues had become cathartic. It helped keep her own personal demons at bay. When one of the minor UFO research centers offered her a position, she jumped on it, even though the money was anemic.

Now, that had turned into a full-time senior role with one of the largest UFO hunter networks. People still scoffed when she showed up, but what people thought of her had zero impact on Natalie. She was obsessively focused on the truth, whether that truth pointed toward alien contact or, more often than not, a fake or misidentification of something much more mundane.

As one of her trainers had told her shortly before he retired, "People believe what they want to believe, and no amount of evidence will change their minds."

Natalie had evolved a somewhat different mindset over the years: "People are entitled to their own opinions but not their own facts." She was not sympathetic to people who, in her opinion, were trying to force a false narrative on others. She no longer allowed herself to get pulled into those verbal dogfights; she simply tried to avoid those she viewed as stupid, manipulative, or opportunistic.

Natalie sat at the worn, wooden desk in her motel room, the dim light of a single lamp casting shadows across the stacks of case files. She flipped through another report, her fingers brushing over the smudged ink and hastily scribbled notes. The document in front of her detailed an encounter that had occurred only a month ago—an alien craft sighted over the Nevada desert. Not in her region, but the report was filed as 'Unknown.'

Her eyes scanned the witness's description: a sleek, pale ovoid with no wings and no noise. The hairs on the back of her neck stood up. It was almost identical to what she had seen that night over the Atlantic. The night they said never happened. What was described as an ovoid others described as a Tic Tac shape. To Natalie, though, it had appeared as a gleaming, almost metal-looking cube within a clear oval shield of some kind.

That was not the only time she and Paul had seen it either, but it was the closest. Often, she and many other pilots encountered the strange lights, phantom radar contacts, and even stranger things, but nobody talked. Not so much because of the SF-312 Classified Information Non-Disclosure Agreement they all routinely signed, but because it was a potential career ending admission. Just like it had ultimately been for her. People had bills to pay, mortgages, insurance, and groceries. No one, not even fighter pilots, wanted to be out of a job, especially with the stigma that an OTH or 'Other Than Honorable' discharge could follow you around for years.

She leaned back in her chair, closing her eyes for a moment as memories flooded back. That familiar rush of adrenaline, the jet's sharp turn into the unknown, and Paul's voice crackling through the radio. She had been so sure she could bring them both home safely. But when she opened her eyes again, he was gone.

Natalie shook off the memory, focusing back on the document in front of her. The witness had described feeling an intense pressure, as if gravity itself had shifted. That matched her own experience—an inexplicable force that seemed to pull at her very soul.

She pulled out a map, checking the location against other phenomena. But no matter how many pieces she connected, one question always lingered at the edge of her mind: had she done everything she could to save her wingman?

A knock on the door pulled her from her thoughts. Larson stepped in, a grim expression on his face.

"Find anything new?" he asked.

Natalie gestured to the document on the desk. "Not really," she lied.

Larson frowned as he looked over the report. "We have to head out early. You good for five AM?"

Natalie nodded but felt a pang of doubt gnawing at her resolve. How long could she do this? How long could she keep chasing ghosts?

Natalie met his gaze and forced herself to nod again. "Yeah," she agreed softly. "I'll be waiting out front."

As Larson left, Natalie allowed herself a brief moment of vulnerability. She glanced back at the map and sighed deeply. For all her determination and strength, there was still that small voice inside that whispered doubts and questioned past choices.

She turned off the lamp and settled onto the bed. Tomorrow would be another day of chasing shadows and seeking truth. But tonight—one of her many emotional boxes had crept open, and she needed time to close it again. Eventually, she would find out what really happened to her and Paul—and perhaps find some measure of peace for herself in the process.

CHAPTER SEVENTEEN

0814 EST Sunday, May 10,
New York City, NY, USA

High over New York City, the relative calm of the late summer morning was interrupted by a booming sound so loud it shattered windows over a two-square-mile area. The echoes bounced off buildings down streets that, on most days, would have been packed with people. This was a Sunday, and at 8:14 AM, it felt like the world had come to an end.

The booming sound was accompanied by a blinding flash of light that illuminated the sky, visible for hundreds of miles. Across the globe, almost a dozen similar phenomena were being reported—a coordinated display that couldn't be ignored or easily explained away.

In Times Square, the giant screens flickered and went dark, along with scores of electronic devices in the city. For a ten-block area, cars sputtered to a halt, their engines dead. Phones were rendered useless, leaving people cut off and confused.

Panic began to set in as reports flooded in from around the world. The International Space Station had gone silent, its crew unreachable. Satellites were failing left and right, their orbits decaying rapidly. For the next twenty-four hours, the global positioning system (GPS) was once again down, crippling global navigation and communication.

Amidst the chaos, a video went viral, shot by a terrified teenager in Central Park. It showed a massive, silent craft hovering over the trees, its sleek black surface absorbing all light. The craft emitted a pulse of energy before vanishing in a burst of speed that defied physics.

The video was quickly scrubbed from the internet, but not before millions had seen and shared it. Governments scrambled to contain the situation and control the narrative, but the cat seemed to be out of the bag. The possibility of extraterrestrial life was no longer a fringe theory —it was looking more like a terrifying reality.

In the rented townhome, Kaden watched the news in stunned disbelief. In his mind, years of research and speculation had just been confirmed in the most dramatic way possible. That was not to be the reality shared by all.

In the following days, the online clips were increasingly shown to be false. Eyewitnesses were deemed to be less than credible. A studio in San Jose, California, used AI to create a video that looked almost identical to the large craft in New York City and claimed it was just a cut scene for an upcoming video game—a massive PR stunt. The power and GPS outages were being blamed on unusually powerful solar flares.

An entire metropolis had seen the truth, but within a month, more than half the global population thought it was fake. Within two months, even the people who had seen it were doubting themselves.

"Are we that easily manipulated, Sarah?" Kaden said as they watched the repairman replacing more of the glass cladding outside the small, walk-up flat they'd rented for the weekend trip.

"You know what Sagan said: 'Extraordinary claims require extraordinary proof.'"

"That's not exactly what Carl said, but close enough." He nibbled absently at the sandwich he'd been eating. "I rather liked Sagan—brilliant mind—but that is simply a wrong statement on so many fronts. The basic premise of scientific inquiry is that evidence should be evaluated based on its quality, reliability, and reproducibility, not inflated to match the nature of the claim it supports."

"So, aliens in spaceships just need what?" Sarah asked.

"You're a doctor, too. From an epistemological standpoint, if any piece of evidence meets the criteria for being considered valid and reliable, it should be sufficient regardless of the claim it supports. The nature of the claim should not necessitate a higher threshold of evidence —yes, even aliens. At some point, the scientific community has to take a more reasonable approach to this."

She laughed. "Like an open mind? Scientist?"

"You're quite right," Kaden said. "What was I thinking?"

~

2100 Eastern Ohio, USA

The Ohio woods were quiet, the only sounds the occasional rustle of leaves and the distant call of an owl. The four men, all clad in camouflage, sat around a flickering campfire, their fishing poles propped up against nearby trees. They had just finished cleaning up after supper, their laughter echoing through the trees.

"Good day for fishing," Jake muttered, putting a few logs in the fire and then stretching out his legs.

"Yeah," replied Mike, poking at the fire with a stick. "Still can't believe I got that big one."

As they settled into their chairs, stories and jokes began circulating like mosquitoes. Mike was a civil engineer with the Cleveland Transportation office. He and Tom had been hunting together since their high school days. The other two men were also familiar with the biannual wilderness hunts: Jake Mas and Bill Underhill. Jake had founded a tech startup in Chicago, and Bill was a near legend in the cybersecurity industry. His counter-intrusion team had not only stopped the famed Black Hole virus but also tracked its source back to an office park outside Shenzhen, China. All of them were grateful to get out, enjoy nature, and spend time with friends.

"Your new bride keeping you on a tight leash?" Tom teased Bill.

Bill took a pull from his beer before responding. "She's ready for me to retire. Says she wants to travel and shit."

"Makes sense," Tom answered. "Do it before you have to worry about stuff like prostate issues and ED."

"Too late for that," said one of the others. The laughter abruptly went silent as a sudden light pierced through the trees, illuminating the campsite with an eerie glow. The men looked at each other, eyes wide.

"What the hell is that?" Tom whispered, standing up slowly. A high-pitched sound like a distant siren began softly and steadily grew in volume.

The light grew brighter, soon enveloping them in a blinding radiance. Then, just as suddenly as it appeared, it vanished, leaving them in darkness once more. The silence was deafening.

Bill staggered back from the fire, clutching his head. "What the hell?" He tripped and nearly fell into the fire, which was now merely glowing embers.

"I think they did something to me!" Bill cried out, panic etched across his face.

"Calm down, man," Jake urged, grabbing Bill's arm. "You're just spooked. The thing was there for a second."

"No," Bill insisted, his voice trembling. "I felt it. They did something."

"The thing just shone its light on us. Probably just a National Guard chopper hit us with the high beams," Jake said. "Still, that was weird as shit."

"Yeah," Mike said. "When that wailing sound got really loud, it made me almost feel like I was falling...or flying."

Tom glanced at his watch and frowned. "Wait a second, guys... something's not right."

"What do you mean?" Mike asked.

Tom held up his wristwatch. "It's past midnight. It was just before nine when we first saw the light."

"You're full of shit, Tom," Mike said. "Take some of that money and buy yourself..." his words trailed off as he saw the others looking at their phones.

Mike pulled out his own iPhone and checked the time. His eyes widened in disbelief. "He's right. We lost nearly three hours."

Jake shook his head, trying to make sense of it all. "How's that possible? We were just sitting here."

Bill's breathing grew heavier as he clutched at his chest. "I told you! They did something to us!"

"Calm down," Tom repeated more forcefully this time.

But Bill wouldn't be calmed. He was shaking uncontrollably now, eyes darting around like a trapped animal. "We have to get out of here," he stammered.

Mike nodded slowly. "Yeah, maybe he's right."

They packed up the campsite in record time and doused the fire. As they shouldered their packs in the dark, Tom was the first to realize the obvious: Bill was no longer with them.

~

1500 June 5, Arkansas, US

Chad trudged through the overgrown grass, his backpack weighing him down. He hated being stuck in summer school, but his dyslexia made it hard for him to keep up with the rest of his class. As he walked, the trees seemed to close in around him, their branches creaking in the wind. He shivered, despite the sweltering heat.

Then he heard it—a low, persistent hum that seemed to vibrate through his bones. It grew louder, filling the air around him. Chad's heart pounded as he looked around, searching for the source. The hum intensified, accompanied by a series of bright, pulsating lights that flickered through the trees.

"What the heck?" he muttered, stepping backward. His feet tangled in the underbrush, and he nearly fell. The lights grew closer, casting eerie shadows on the forest floor. Chad's pulse raced, his breath coming in short gasps. He dropped his backpack and bolted, running through the trees as fast as he could.

The hum followed him, relentless and inescapable. He glanced over his shoulder, but the lights were already upon him, illuminating the forest with an unnatural glow. Chad's vision blurred, and his head felt like it was being squeezed in a vice. He stumbled to a halt, clutching his temples.

The forest around him shifted, the trees warping and bending in ways that defied logic. Chad tried to scream, but no sound came out. The lights enveloped him, their brilliance blinding. The hum reached a fever pitch, and Chad felt himself lifted off the ground, his limbs paralyzed.

His mind raced, thoughts colliding in a chaotic whirl. He remembered the stories he'd heard—the rumors of strange encounters, people vanishing without a trace. It all seemed so far-fetched, so impossible. But now, caught in the throes of this bizarre phenomenon, Chad realized those stories might have been true.

As the lights grew brighter, Chad's vision dimmed, the world around him fading into a blinding white. He struggled to move, to break free, but his body remained unresponsive.

Chad knew he wasn't like other kids. People at school called him weird...sometimes they called him worse names. He was mostly okay with that. It didn't hurt as much as it once did. Still, he knew this wasn't right. He might be slow, but he wasn't stupid.

Suddenly, a figure emerged from the trees lining the clearing. Chad's heart skipped a beat as he took in the thing's gray skin, large black eyes, and slender body. It was unlike anything he had ever seen before. The creature didn't move toward him, but Chad felt a strange sense of calm, as if it was somehow communicating with him.

"Who...what are you? Are...are you God?" Chad stuttered, his eyes fixed on the creature.

He didn't hear a response, but somehow, he felt an answer. It was as if the creature was speaking directly to his mind.

"No, I'm not God," Chad mumbled, repeating what he thought he'd heard. "Are you going to hurt me?"

Again, he felt a gentle, reassuring presence in his mind. The creature didn't move but tilted its head curiously. Chad sensed no hostility, only kindness.

"What do you want?" Chad asked, his voice just above a whisper.

The creature tilted its head again, its large eyes fixed on Chad. He felt a wave of images wash over him, like a gentle flood. He saw flashes of cities in ruins, people running in panic, and strange, glowing ships in the sky. But amidst the chaos, he felt a sense of reassurance, as if the creature was trying to tell him something important.

"This isn't a movie? It...it's something bad?" The creature gave a subtle nod.

"It's not you, is it?" Chad asked, his eyes locked on the alien creature. "You're not the one who will be doing this."

The creature's gaze never wavered, but Chad felt a sense of confirmation. This creature was something else, maybe a neutral party, a watcher. Chad knew he was only getting part of this right. Having no control over his body was unnerving, and he was having a hard time concentrating on the alien.

"What's going to happen?" Chad asked, his voice trembling.

The creature's eyes seemed to bore into his soul, and Chad felt a sense of foreboding. He didn't know what was coming, but he knew it wasn't good. The creature's presence began to fade, and Chad felt a pang of loss.

"Wait!" he cried out. The words formed in his brain but did not come from his mouth. "What can we do? What should I do?"

The alien pointed back past Chad's shoulder to the mountains in the east. Then, in a flash of light and sound, the creature was gone. Chad was able to move again and spun around in a circle, looking for any sign of the strange little man-beast.

Then he just stood there, his heart pounding, as he tried to process all that had just happened. He knew no one would believe him, but he didn't care. He had felt the creature's kindness, and he knew that their encounter was special. His foster mother sometimes took him to church, and while he didn't understand the singing or much of what the man in the suit said, Chad decided that he'd just encountered an angel. An angel that was showing him a way to escape the horrors that were coming.

Multiple Explosions Rock Midtown Manhattan — Early Reports Suggest Gas Line or Possible Meteor Strike.

"Chaos unfolded near 5th Avenue this morning as multiple loud concussive events sent pedestrians fleeing. Witnesses described a 'wave of energy' and 'a flicker in the sky' just before the first blast. Emergency services responded within minutes, securing a multi-block perimeter.

"Though the origin of the explosions remains unclear, city officials suggest a possible underground gas rupture triggered by an earthquake or possible meteor impact. NYPD is urging calm and discouraging speculation.

"Mayor Grant called the situation 'under control,' emphasizing that there is no indication of terrorism or foreign activity."

CBS Breaking News | Field Report by Elena Rojas, Midtown Bureau

CHAPTER EIGHTEEN

K Street
Washington, D.C., USA

Laura Bennett strode into her editor's office at the Washington Post, a determined look etched on her face. Her editor, a grizzled veteran named Jack Thompson, looked up from his desk.

"Laura," he said, leaning back in his chair. "Thanks for coming in."

"Well, shit, Jack. Did I have a choice?"

"Don't be like that. You're one of my top reporters. You know we give you free rein to pick your features. I just want to be kept in the loop."

She tossed a folder on his desk. "I'm investigating the recent disclosure briefings. Not just the UFO sightings but the government's potential involvement in a cover-up."

Jack sighed, rubbing his temples. "Laura, we've talked about this. Chasing UFO stories is a surefire way to tank your career."

"This isn't about UFOs, Jack," Laura insisted, her voice firm. "It's about a potential government conspiracy. And that's exactly the kind of story the Post should be covering. Besides, have you seen the videos over the weekend from New York?"

"Yeah, a Hollywood special effects team is taking all the credit. Thought you would know that."

Laura shrugged. "Still a good story. People are primed for it now more than ever."

Jack picked up the folder, flipping through its brief contents. "You have a source?"

She shook her head. "A lead, but it seems to be a good one."

He read more, making some notes on a pad as he did. "You've got a few interesting points here, but I'm not sure it's enough to justify a full investigation. I can okay it as a filler piece."

Laura leaned forward, shaking her head. "Just give me a chance, Jack. I need two weeks. Maybe ten days. If there's a story here, I'll find it."

"Look, Laura, we're hemorrhaging money here. Hell, most of our revenue now comes from our online editions. Hardly anyone goes out and actually buys an actual paper."

She knew this; her own travel budgets had been cut so many times that she often found herself paying her own expenses.

Laura inhaled deeply. "Jack, now more than ever, the free press and good journalism are important. We're one of the last checks on power, the voice of the voiceless. Our job is to shine a light where others won't."

Jack raised an eyebrow, but she continued.

"If we back down just because a topic might be unpopular or not get enough likes or shares, we're failing in our duty. We can't just be chasing clicks. We're pursuing the truth. Journalism matters to people whether they realize it or not."

She leaned closer, her voice steady and clear. "You taught me that, Jack. You taught me that our stories have the power to change lives, to expose corruption, to make this world a better place. If we start censoring ourselves, afraid of controversy or backlash, then we're no better than the people we're supposed to hold accountable."

Jack's expression softened somewhat as he listened.

"I've exposed corporate scandals, government cover-ups, and I've done it all because I believe in what we do. This story? It's no different. It might even be bigger than anything we've ever tackled before. Yes, it's a polarizing topic with a stigma that scares most people from ever having a frank discussion on it, but you know what? A very significant portion of the population is open to the idea of extraterrestrial life and unexplained aerial phenomena. People under thirty are the most open to the prospect. Isn't that the missing demographic for us?"

He tapped his pen against the desk, considering her words. She wasn't wrong. As always, Laura Bennett had done her homework. Jack just didn't want the front page of his paper looking anything like tabloid sensationalism.

"You done with the sermon?" She laughed and nodded. "And you really believe this could be something major?"

"Yes," Laura said without hesitation. "I wouldn't be here if I didn't."

"You run it by your old man?"

Laura tilted her head and gave him the look. Jack smiled and put up his hands apologetically. Laura's dad was a near legend around D.C., a maverick newsman and later editor who had connections to everyone and anyone back in the day.

Jack studied her for a long moment, then nodded slowly. "Alright, Laura. You've got two weeks. But if this turns into a wild goose chase, I'm pulling the plug."

"It won't," Laura promised, a smile tugging at the corners of her mouth. "Trust me, Jack. You're going to love me even more. This story is going to be big."

As she turned to leave, Jack called after her. "Laura, be careful. If you're right about this conspiracy, you could be stirring up a hornet's nest."

Laura paused at the door, looking back over her shoulder. "I know, Jack. But that's what we do, isn't it?"

With that, she left the office, already thinking about what she needed to do next. Her father wouldn't like it, but this story had all the elements of a big exposé. Personally, she really didn't believe or disbelieve in the things. That was not the story. Getting to the truth was.

The following day, Laura began working her contacts. A congressman from Nebraska who was on the subcommittee that began the disclosure hearings suggested she contact one of the witnesses they had brought forward. The problem was, the woman didn't exist. She checked every database she could but found no match. She even used facial recognition to track her down on social media. She found a few matches on Facebook, but they were empty profiles, either bot accounts or fakes.

This didn't disappoint Laura. In fact, it confirmed what her source had suggested. The disclosure hearings had been a sham, just a show orchestrated by someone to make the American public think their elected leaders were doing something about the rash of unexplained activity in our skies. She flipped her notepad open and began crossing off more names, more witnesses and experts called before the House committee. She would track down every last one of them or expose them as actors and frauds.

CHAPTER NINETEEN

Outskirts of Abilene, Texas, USA

Kaden leaned closer to the screen, his eyes narrowing as he scrutinized the footage. The video quality was surprisingly crisp, showing a beautiful tropical beach with palm trees swaying in the breeze. The person filming seemed to be on a boat just off the coast. The camera movement rolled side to side with the waves. Suddenly, a thick cloud formation appeared, unnaturally fast and localized.

"What is that?" Kaden muttered. The leading edge of the cloud began to dissipate as a craft unlike anything he'd ever seen began to emerge. It defied conventional aerodynamics, lacking wings or any visible means of propulsion. The object's surface gleamed with an otherworldly sheen, its geometry so bizarre it made his eyes hurt to look at it directly. It was not a beautiful ship but harsh and, somehow, aggressive looking.

"This can't be real," Kaden said, shaking his head. "The CGI is impressive, but—"

"It's not CGI, Professor," a man's voice interrupted. "This was captured near Exuma, Bahamas, just three weeks ago."

Kaden turned to the older gentleman with salt-and-pepper hair standing behind him. The man's eyes were fixed on the screen, a mixture of fascination and concern etched on his face.

"Maxwell, why isn't it public?" Kaden asked.

Maxwell nodded. "Look at the water below the craft," he said, pointing to the screen.

Kaden's gaze shifted downward, and his breath caught in his throat. The turquoise-blue Caribbean waters were behaving impossibly. Directly beneath the craft, the sea appeared to be bulging upward, defying gravity. Tiny droplets hung suspended in the air, creating a shimmering halo around the object.

"That's... that's not possible," Kaden whispered, his scientific mind reeling.

"And yet, there it is," Jasper Maxwell replied grimly. "We've analyzed this footage extensively. No signs of manipulation or CGI trickery. Whatever this is, it's bending the very laws of physics as we understand them. If it were released, it would likely be debunked just like the Times Square event."

Kaden rewound the video, watching it again and again. Each time, he noticed new, impossible details. The way light seemed to bend around the craft's edges. The eerie silence, despite the churning waters below.

"If this is real," Kaden said slowly, "it changes everything we thought we knew about propulsion, gravity... hell, the nature of reality itself."

Jasper nodded gravely. "That's why I wanted you to see it, Trembley. You are one of my oldest and dearest friends. You know that."

He did know. Jasper Maxwell had been another one of his lone defenders years ago when it seemed Kaden was determined to sabotage his own career. Jasper had not been as public with his support, but that, too, was part of his friend's demeanor.

"Tell me your opinion," the older man said. "No other context, no second-guessing. As one of the leading worldwide experts on extraterrestrial visitations, what do you think was going on?"

Kaden clicked the play arrow once more and watched the forty-two-second clip twice again.

"It's never been described before. It's something or someone new. While the craft is large, it is not 'interstellar' large, meaning it's either something from Earth or... there is a larger craft somewhere that this thing came from."

"What else?"

Kaden knew his friend would have his own ideas, maybe even answers. Still, this was a mental exercise they had used many times to break complex problems down into more manageable bites.

"Pure speculation here, but I believe they're testing some type of weapon, possibly gravitic—something that they could only do near the ground. They likely felt this was a relatively uninhabited place to see how it worked in our biosphere. Since this video has been suppressed, I imagine the U.S. government came to a similar conclusion."

"Yes, Professor, yes on all counts. People are very afraid of this object and the implied threat it represents. The person filming, as well as everyone on the beach that day, are gone—missing. The phone was found by a search crew a day later. It was not a large resort; rather, it was one of the isolated cays. Still, over forty people are now missing without a trace."

"Jasper, I'm an astronomer. Why show this to me? No one would believe anything I said."

"Please, Kaden, we both know that isn't true. You have a brilliant mind. Your classes are always full, and your students love you. More importantly, the people that matter respect you."

Kaden wasn't buying it, not all of it at least. "So, what do you want from me, old friend?"

"Do you trust me?" Maxwell asked.

"Of course," Kaden said without hesitation. "You've been a steadfast friend and advisor for more than half my life."

The older man pursed his lips, and Kaden could see the old mannerisms of when his professor smoked a pipe. Something was on his mind—something important.

"Trembley," he began, then stopped. "Kaden, I'm... not well."

He took a small sip from the water glass. Kaden now sat rigid, waiting for the conversational bombshell to drop.

"It's one of those damn cancers," Maxwell said with a sigh. "Not even one I deserve. I smoked too long and drank too much brandy in my early years. Now they say it's the ultra-processed food that's going to kill me." Dr. Maxwell gave a dry chuckle. "I had to look up what the hell that even was. You know, lunch meats and breads and just normal stuff we all eat every day."

Kaden felt terrible for his friend and could see he was winding up for a rant on the commercial food industry. Maxwell looked at him and winked.

"We don't need aliens killing us. We do a damn fine job doing that all by ourselves. Sorry to drop that on you, but I wanted you to know. That's part of why I wanted to see you."

"Does your daughter know?"

Jasper nodded. "Mostly. Laney and her family are in San Francisco. She knows I'm in treatment, but no, she doesn't know the end is close. I hope to see her and her babies once more, but this—this right here today is more important than anything else. Having closure on my life means nothing if we lose the world."

Kaden had never known the man to be morose or overly dramatic. "I...I don't understand."

"The death of one person is a tragedy; the death of a million is a statistic. Listen—I lived," Mitchell said. "That in itself was enough. I've beheld some marvelous things. Married a wonderful woman who stayed with me until that damn accident took her. Laney was only ten at the time, and you know she and I basically raised each other after that." Mitchell saw the look of compassion and confusion on Kaden's face.

"Forgive me, old friend. At this point, I do think a lot about the past, but you are here because of our future—your future, my daughter's future. You see, I have always known you were right about the UFOs." Kaden started to speak, but Dr. Maxwell put up a hand to stop him. "No, not because I believed in you, which I do, but because I had access to information that you and the public at large never did—information I have never shared with anyone, not even Katherine."

Kaden was on the edge of his seat now. If this was more important than the man's imminent death, a secret he'd kept from his late wife even, he needed to know what it was.

Maxwell set a block of charred meteor on the table. Kaden had seen it on the man's shelf for years.

"Aliens have visited our planet for hundreds of thousands of years."

He proceeded to cite eyewitness accounts, artwork, temples, and passages that had no other commonality than an alien visitation. "In 1561, in Nuremberg, Germany, an aerial battle took place. This was well before man had flown anything. One of the alien craft taking heavy fire was said to resemble a black triangle. This piece of slag was recovered by a small boy in the aftermath."

"I always assumed it was a meteorite," Kaden said.

"Pick it up."

Kaden did so. It was light—way too light to be rock or metal.

"I had it analyzed—a few times, actually. Had to wait years for the diagnostic tools to improve, but it seems to be a long-strand mono-fiber with highly interlocked atoms of carbon—closer to diamond than carbon fiber. This stuff is amazing; there are other exotic elements they still can't identify."

Kaden had heard rumors of more than one battle in ancient Germany but knew most had been clouded with religious events in the years since. Some of what Maxwell said was very familiar, but much was not. Kaden took out a small pad and began taking notes just like he had decades earlier when he was just a grad student looking to pass Dr. Maxwell's courses.

"They call themselves Observers."

"Who, the aliens?" Kaden asked.

Jasper nodded. Kaden could now see how tired and weak his friend truly was.

"The aliens and their appointed humans around the world. The small grayish aliens are the only ones we officially know of. But there are other...maybe many others." He pointed to the screen where the ugly UFO was frozen in flight. "Here's the thing, that is not one of theirs. This is why I am telling you all this now."

A million thoughts ran through Kaden's head. How did Maxwell know this? Was there proof? Can we communicate with them?

"You were one? One of the human Observers?" Kaden asked, coming to an obvious conclusion.

Maxwell nodded weakly. "Just like my father. It is a very small group."

"The, umm...Men in Black?" Kaden asked, wondering if the supposed government cover-up was part of the organization as well.

"There were always cover-ups, but I left after a particularly nasty incident down in the southern U.S. I'm not a cruel man, and I found I had no appetite for the level of harshness the Observer organization would now use when required." He took another sip of water and reached for a nearby pill bottle.

"Officially, I am still part of them, as no one leaves and lives, but my situation was unique. I was a legacy member. As such, I had a few extra privileges, more access than most. You are going to want to know a great deal more about the aliens and the human Observers, but that will have to wait. Some things I can pass along only in death. That is what I must do to keep Laney and her family safe, you see."

"So, what am I to do with this?" Kaden asked. As much as he loved and trusted the old man, he had no additional proof than when he'd walked in the door—possibly just ramblings from a dying man.

"Stupidity is the only universal capital crime. The sentence is death. There is no appeal, and execution is carried out automatically and without pity."

"Heinlein," Kaden said worriedly.

"Yes, my friend. The man was spot on with that one, and let me assure you, we have been incredibly stupid. The aliens have communicated to us with fewer than 400 words in all of recorded history, but the messages were pretty clear: 'What you have is special; don't mess it up.' The other part was for us to keep them secret. It seems we failed at both.

"Mankind is going to be a statistic, Kaden; I see no way around it. You may—no, you will—have a better chance to stop it than I ever did. I've been watched my whole life. I couldn't have breathed a word of this until now. They weren't even happy with my friendship with you.

"I am certain Dr. Mitchell already mentioned it, but someone from the White House will be contacting you. When they do, go with them. I've backed your recommendation for this special commission. They are taking a hard look at alien threats. I have to say, they may be too late, but it appears this group has the right people and the right objective—non-political, which is impossibly rare in that town. You need to be part of it. More than that, you need to take the lead."

CHAPTER TWENTY

1443 EST May 10
Colgate College
Hawthorn Lane
Hamilton, NY, USA

Kaden returned home, his mind a chaotic storm of conflicting thoughts. He tried working through Javier's growing database, but with a growing sense of frustration, he finally gave up. His fingers tapped on the table, a nervous reflection of the turmoil inside his mind. By and large, the scientific community was staying out of the ongoing debate. Those who did make statements generically ridiculed anyone like him who might take the UFO phenomena seriously. His phone buzzed. The caller was not in his contacts, but he braced himself and answered anyway.

"This is Trembley," he answered curtly. He expected it was someone from the media or one of his many critics, but you never knew.

"Trent Rogers," came the gravelly voice on the other end. "I hate to bother you, Professor, but I have something important I'd like to discuss. Would you have time to talk?"

Kaden's eyebrows knitted together. "I'm sorry, who?"

"Agent Trent Rogers."

"You're with the government?" Kaden asked, confused. He wasn't generally on any official radar; he mainly stirred up trouble in the dusty halls of academia.

"Yes, sir. I am a security agent, though that's not something I'm proud to admit these days."

"Yes, well...neither are telemarketers, and they also usually call during dinner." The man's admission had piqued Kaden's curiosity despite himself. "What can I do for you?"

"I've been following your work, Dr. Trembley," Rogers said, his tone carrying a weight of urgency. "I can assure you that you're not wrong about the UFOs, and there's more going on than you realize."

Kaden leaned back in his chair, skepticism creeping in. "Look, Agent Rogers, if this is some kind of prank—"

"It's not," Rogers interrupted. "I have been asked to read you into a special White House task force investigating these incidents, sir."

So, this was what Sarah and Dr. Maxwell had both suggested he look into. Still, he decided to make the young man earn his cooperation. "I've seen the silly congressional hearings supposedly trying to solve the questions of aliens once and for all. Just a bunch of bollocks. A roomful of tossers, if you ask me. No, thank you, good sir."

The man was quiet for a moment. "We do have access to classified information about top-secret projects related to some of these sightings. Our directive is to mainly determine if there's a conspiracy within the government to cover this up, and frankly, sir, we need your help to expose it."

"A government committee to investigate a government cover-up?"

Rogers laughed. "I do know how ridiculous that sounds, but I can assure you, this group will get to the truth."

Kaden hesitated. He'd been ridiculed by his peers, dismissed as a crackpot. His work had cost him nearly everything—relationships, credibility, peace of mind. But this? This could be the validation he needed.

"I don't know," Kaden began slowly. "I'm focused on my research right now—"

"Your research won't mean a damn thing if they continue to bury the truth," Rogers cut in. "You want proof of extraterrestrial life? This might be the best chance in your life to get it."

Kaden stared at his cluttered desk, papers and books scattered like the remnants of a shattered dream. The scientific community had mocked him for too long; this could be his vindication. *This could be the validation I need... or just another bloody footnote in my obituary.*

“Alright,” Kaden said finally. “What do you need me to do?”

"We would like you to come to D.C.," Agent Rogers said. "You have to go through a full background check before you will be allowed into the sessions. Most of that is just routine, but you will need a high security clearance. It will take us a day or two for that. Shouldn't be a problem. We know you are on sabbatical from your teaching but will compensate you more than double what you are currently making."

"How do I know you’re for real, Agent Rogers? I have many people who would love to see me embarrassed by a prank call."

"Sir, there is an Air Force major standing just outside your door with a first-class ticket and some papers for you to sign if we are in agreement."

Kaden pushed the curtain back and saw a young man in uniform standing at attention. He was holding a brown portfolio with what looked like the presidential seal embossed on it.

“Fine,” Kaden agreed, "but I won't be signing any damned NDAs. What I discover, I can publish. Is that understood?"

"The director simply wants the truth, sir, same as you. No NDAs about the work you will be doing."

Kaden hung up the phone with a sense of finality.

He opened the door and signed for the material from the man, who only asked to first see his ID. He sat down in his chair, staring at the ceiling as doubts gnawed at him. Yes, this could just be another wild goose chase or worse—a trap set by those looking to silence him once and for all.

But deep down, he knew he couldn't ignore it. Not now. The truth he was after was elusive, and he badly needed a win.

The next day found Kaden boarding an early flight to Washington, D.C. His palms were sweaty as he perused the information in the program brief. He didn't know anything about this Director Carter, but he did recognize many of the other names on the short list. The group was heavy on scientists. That could be good, he thought optimistically. As the jet touched down a short time later and the terminal came into view, he couldn't shake the feeling that this was only the beginning of something far greater than he'd imagined.

"Professor?"

The young man near baggage claim was no doubt looking at his photo on a tablet. Kaden recognized the voice. "Mister Rogers?"

"Indeed," the young man said. "Welcome to my neighborhood."

The very American reference seemed to be lost on the professor, who simply smiled and nodded. Rogers took the carry-on from Trembley and pointed to a white sedan parked at the curb.

"So, are you part of the... what are they calling it? 'Task force'?"

Rogers smiled. "Sort of. Right now, I am just the... hmm. Not sure what I am. Glorified gopher, maybe. Ms. Carter is running the show, but she is also filling in for the chief of staff at the moment, so she needed some help pulling the group together."

"Chief of staff to the president?" Trembley asked uncertainly.

"Yes, of course. She is the deputy CoS."

"But this task force?" Trembley let the unfinished question hang in the air.

"Seems odd to be a White House committee-level topic?" Agent Rogers asked knowingly.

"I suppose so," Kaden agreed. "Also, your own enthusiasm for the topic on the phone just doesn't fit my assumptions about the executive office."

Rogers nodded. "The government, by and large, Professor, is just people. They are not different from anyone else you might meet. Hard-working, honorable, but POTUS does have a lot on his plate. National security dominates most of his agenda, and, at least in my opinion, the increased incidents of aerial incursions now are a qualified threat to national security."

"The truth is, my boy, we have no idea what is up there in our skies. Never have," Kaden said ominously.

Kaden saw the Capitol building approaching. Rogers turned into an underground garage several blocks away. "We'll get your credentials finalized here," Rogers said. "A few of the others are already being processed."

"Will I meet Ms. Carter today?"

"She is meeting you for dinner. Can't get you into the White House until the Secret Service signs off, probably be tomorrow or Tuesday. The director will get you guys started tonight, and you all will have a meeting room in the hotel to use until then."

Kaden Trembley allowed himself to be led into the labyrinthine corridors of the generic-looking building. What had he gotten himself into? A scientific advisor on a presidential commission. This could redeem his career or sink whatever was left of it if they were looking for scapegoats. It was a chance he felt compelled to take. As Agent Mulder said—the truth was out there.

CHAPTER TWENTY-ONE

1404 CDT
Ozark Mountains
Arkansas, USA

Marcus Smith leaned closer to his computer screen, his brow furrowed as he studied the intricate patterns of UFO sightings scattered across the digital map. The concerned faces of his fellow preppers stared back at him from their respective video windows, clearly not ready to embrace that this was as serious as Marcus believed.

"Look at this cluster here," Marcus said, using his cursor to circle an area. "It's not random. These sightings form a clear pattern."

"Marcus, this could still be coincidence," replied Susan, a former military strategist. "We've seen false alarms before. It's UFOs, Marcus. They aren't even a line item on our threat analysis."

Marcus shook his head. "They should be, and no... we haven't seen interactions like this. The frequency and consistency are unprecedented."

Only a few members of the enclave knew of the man's former fiancée and her work on UFOs. They now had to weigh that emotional connection against the reality being presented. Something was going on. That was clear. Was it a bug-out moment, though?

"What are you suggesting, Marcus?" asked David, his voice tinged with skepticism. "That we bug out to the compounds over some lights in the sky?"

"No, not everyone, not yet," Marcus said. "But we need to be prepared. I'm proposing full readiness checks at both primary locations. Assuming we can even reach the Alpha site, and I want everyone else on high alert. A few others and I will head to Beta just in case."

A chorus of groans and protests erupted from the group.

"Come on, Marcus," Susan interjected. "We're not doomsday nuts. We're professionals who believe in being prepared, not paranoid. This sounds a bit 'tin foil hat,' you know?"

"I'm not being paranoid," Marcus shot back. "I'm being cautious. Look at the data. Something is happening, whether we want to admit it or not."

Marcus had been the de facto leader of the small unnamed group for the last seven years, ever since Pete Simpkins, the founding member, passed away.

"And what if nothing comes of it?" David asked. "We'll have wasted time and resources on another false alarm."

Marcus took a deep breath, steadying himself. "Then we'll be better prepared for the next potential crisis. Isn't that the whole point of what we do? Yes, some of us will have to schedule time off work, take vacation time, and spend money getting our load-out gear up to current requirements. This is why we exist, people."

The group fell silent, considering his words.

"Fine," Susan conceded. "I'll coordinate the checks at the mountain compound. But can we keep this low-key? Members only, no need to spook the families."

David nodded reluctantly. "I'll get with Isaac and help handle the coastal site. But Marcus, if this turns out to be nothing..."

"Then I'll take full responsibility," Marcus finished. "But if I'm right, we'll be glad we took these precautions."

Marcus disconnected the web call and triggered an encrypted SMS text message to the full group. It was a color-coded threat scale similar to what Homeland Security used for terrorist threats. The message raised the threat from condition Yellow to condition Orange, high. That was all that was needed for each of the forty-seven members to begin final preparations to be ready to move to either the Alpha or Beta compounds. Ideally, no one should be more than twenty-four hours away from either site during condition Orange. Many would simply go on to the designated camps.

Staring out over the brown smudge hugging the LA skyline, Marcus knew he had to get moving east. The closest compound to him was deep in the Ozark Mountains between Arkansas and Missouri. Each member did their part in maintaining the compound. Truthfully, no one minded as both were in beautiful but remote parts of the country. They were like working vacations, and having over forty families meant someone was on-site at each location nearly year-round.

He was worried, though. The group was smart, capable, well-funded, and used to hard work. Were they truly ready for what might be coming? He moved his Land Rover Velar to the front and hooked up the enclosed trailer.

Even Marcus admitted this was probably overreacting, but he did have a personal connection to a UFO encounter that he wasn't willing to talk about. It hadn't happened directly to him, but it had cost him someone he loved dearly. The memory gnawed at him like a splinter lodged too deep to remove, and it drove his determination to keep his group safe.

He pulled the trailer door open, revealing an array of meticulously organized supplies. Each item had a designated place, and Marcus checked them off mentally as he loaded the rest of his gear. His movements were efficient, methodical. This wasn't just a drill for him; it was life. His training had left an almost obsessive need to be prepared.

Once everything was secure, Marcus climbed into the driver's seat, signaled for Retro to jump in, and fired up the engine. The familiar purr of the Velar's motor was comforting, a reminder that some things still worked as they should. He navigated the streets of Los Angeles, weaving through traffic with practiced ease.

His phone buzzed with incoming messages from the group, confirming their readiness. He acknowledged each one with a terse audio reply, his focus unwavering. The drive east was long, and he preferred to make it in one go, stopping only for fuel and the occasional stretch for him and the dog.

As he merged onto the interstate, his thoughts drifted back to the encounter that had forever changed his perspective. He clenched the steering wheel, forcing the memories back into the recesses of his mind. Now wasn't the time for distractions. The group's safety depended on his clarity.

The miles ticked away, the landscape shifting from urban sprawl to open desert, and then eventually, to the lush greenery of the Ozarks. Marcus welcomed the change, the sense of isolation that came with it. Here, amidst the towering trees and rolling hills, he felt a semblance of peace.

Just before noon, he turned onto a narrow dirt road that wound its way up nearer to the compound. The secure gate loomed ahead, a symbol of the group's resilience. He punched in the access code and waited as the gate creaked open.

Pulling up to one of the main outbuildings, Marcus stepped out, followed by his dog, and was greeted by the familiar faces of the compound's current caretakers, Dixon and his larger cousin Oneal. They exchanged nods, understanding the gravity of the situation without the need for explanation.

Marcus set to work immediately, coordinating with the two men. He inspected the generator, checked the water supply, and ensured the perimeter defenses were operational. Every detail mattered; every contingency was planned for.

By the time the sun dipped below the horizon, casting long shadows across the compound, Marcus felt a measure of satisfaction. There was much to do, as always. But, given the circumstances, he was comfortable with where they were. He took a moment to breathe, leaning against the sturdy frame of the main building. God, he prayed this was another false alarm, but deep down, something gnawed at his gut. Something that made him think that wouldn't be the case.

CHAPTER TWENTY-TWO

0903 EST May 07
White House West Wing
Washington, D.C., USA

Emily Carter hung up the phone, frustration still etched on her face. General Briggs' recent help had renewed her vigor in the fight for answers. It amazed her that after all these years, there was still no update from the Naval investigation into her brother's disappearance. The new information Briggs had shared had convinced her to push even harder.

Even Paul's mission confidential Navy debrief had yet to reveal any real evidence as to the cause of the accident. A lone radar operator's report of anomalous radar contacts was the only entry she could verify. It had been years now, and even in her senior position in the White House, she was still being stonewalled.

The president had appointed her with all the rights and legal avenues she needed to make it happen. She'd been given a mandate, a blank check to investigate the disappearances, the strange artifacts, the recently rumored alien virus hitting parts of the globe, and any other anomalies that had been plaguing the world. She knew the stakes were high, and she was determined to get answers.

SCET wouldn't be the first, or likely the last, with a very similar mandate of learning the truth about aliens, but she was determined that it wouldn't succumb to the pressures of its predecessors. She really wanted to base it loosely on the COMETA group, which was a group of high-ranking military officers, scientists, and aerospace engineers, many from France's defense and intelligence sectors. The study was coordinated by COMité d'ÉTudes Approfondies, or Committee for In-Depth Studies, operating under the aegis of the Institute of Higher Studies for National Defense (IHEDN), a government-affiliated think tank.

France's views on UFOs were very different from those of the United States. In fact, much of the world seemed more open-minded to the possible reality that we are not alone. After a very thorough examination of the evidence, the report from the COMETA group stated flatly that UFOs were real and very likely extraterrestrial in origin.

The COMETA report was an independent French initiative, partly driven by frustration with the lack of transparency from the U.S., especially after decades of official denial and secrecy. At the time, the U.S. government maintained a policy of disengagement from UFO topics following the closure of Project Blue Book in 1969.

The report implicitly criticized the U.S. for withholding information and not collaborating more openly with allies on the issue. Here in the States, the term UFO was equivalent to saying you believe in aliens. They were not necessarily the same thing. Unidentified objects do appear in our skies; even the U.S. Air Force admits that. In truth, Emily's research indicated that ninety-five percent of reported UFOs could be explained by much more common phenomena. It was that five percent she was interested in. That was where SCET would focus its efforts.

A soft knock at the door broke her from her mental wanderings. Emily stood and welcomed Kaden Trembley, followed by Trent Rogers, into the secure conference room. The room, nestled in a quiet corner of the West Wing, offered both privacy and a sense of urgency. She motioned for them to sit as Colonel James Walker joined them, his presence commanding attention.

Emily made quick introductions without bothering to add any details. The men could do that later if they wanted. Her secretary had prepared briefs for them.

Emily sensed tension already in the air. "We're here because we each bring something vital to the table. Our task force needs a blend of scientific insight and military strategy to tackle the challenges ahead."

She laid out a folder on the table, flipping it open to reveal several documents and charts. "First, thank you for taking this initial step. Once I lay out the group's agenda, my hope is you will be willing to continue. If not, I do understand."

Emily continued, "In developing this group, we first needed a name because... well, this is Washington. Everything you spend tax dollars on has to sound official. I went through a handful of possibilities and then settled on SCET: the Strategic Committee for Extraterrestrial Threats.

"Now, let's outline our strategy. We'll focus on three pillars: resource coordination, intelligence gathering, and then 'what-if' scenarios and tactical response."

Emily's voice was firm but inclusive as she continued, "Resource coordination will ensure we have the right tools and people at our disposal. Intelligence gathering will help us stay ahead of any threats, while our tactical response will prepare us for immediate action."

"Not to be overly crass, Ms. Carter, but can I ask something? Is this group simply for show?" Kaden asked.

She pursed her lips and smiled. "Not on your life, Professor. This country, as well as I personally, have a vested interest in knowing the truth about potential extraterrestrial contact. The president has officially authorized this committee and obtained the necessary official agreements to let us borrow key people as needed, but the administration does not want this group to go public. We are here primarily to advise President Martin."

Trembley nodded. "You mention several key points that certainly intrigue me, Director. However, there is one you have not included: a very human component."

Kaden was not ready to bring up the matter of the Observers. He did want to gauge this group's stance on the topic, though. "A potential cover-up," he continued. "Your famed Men in Black. Let's be honest—

eighty percent of people believe in UFOs, and I would suggest nearly as many believe that your very government is already aware and keeping it a secret."

Out of the corner of her eye, Emily caught Trent smiling smugly. "That will be an aspect we will absolutely address as well, Doctor Trembley, but let's go ahead and clear the air right now. I am one of the highest-ranking members in this administration. Walker is near the highest levels at the Pentagon, and Agent Rogers is obviously well-placed within our intelligence community. Why don't we all share right now what we know or suspect about this potential cover-up?"

Emily leaned forward, hands clasped on the table. "I'll start. To my knowledge, there is no organized government cover-up. To be honest, we mostly have our hands too full with national security and foreign policy to even deal with it. Yes, I've encountered whispers and hints, but nothing concrete. But let me be clear: I do believe UFOs are real, and I strongly suspect there's a group out there working to keep the truth hidden. However, I will stake my career on the fact that if such a group exists, President Martin is unaware of it. He's as committed to transparency as anyone in this room."

Colonel Walker nodded thoughtfully before speaking. "Within the military high command, it's a topic that's simply not discussed. We don't even trust our own intelligence departments on the subject—officially, anyway. However, every field division has had numerous encounters that defy logic and belief—unexplainable events that leave even our most seasoned officers baffled." He paused, looking at each person in the room. "Rumor has it that if there's a cover-up, it would be the intelligence community pulling the strings."

All eyes turned to Trent Rogers. He shrugged, maintaining an air of nonchalance. "I don't have strong opinions one way or the other about a cover-up," he said carefully. "But if one exists, I would agree it's likely that someone in the intelligence community would be aware of it, at least at some level. Keep in mind the intelligence community is not a single entity. It is a multi-headed beast—eighteen different agencies, well over 100,000 people."

Emily noted his evasiveness but chose not to press him further at this moment.

"Thank you all for your candor," she said, leaning back in her chair and opening another folder on the table. "This only reinforces the importance of our mission."

Kaden studied each face around the table before speaking again. "I have concerns and would like to revisit this topic periodically, but thank you. I've spent my entire career chasing the truth about extraterrestrial life, often feeling like Sisyphus pushing that boulder up a hill, only to watch it roll back down and often land right on top of me. But this group," he gestured around the table, "this feels different. It's the first time I've seen a genuine, coordinated effort to uncover the truth, backed by people with the power and resources to make a real difference."

He paused, his voice thick with emotion. "Please, now, this isn't about proving myself right or wrong. It's about uncovering the truth for the sake of humanity. The implications of extraterrestrial contact could reshape our understanding of the universe, our place in it, and our future as a species."

Kaden's gaze locked onto Emily's. "Ms. Carter, I implore you—don't let this group lose its way. We can't afford to get bogged down in political maneuvering or bureaucratic red tape. The stakes are just too high. This isn't about any one person's agenda. It's about the future of our planet and our species. We need to stay focused on our mission, no matter what obstacles we encounter."

His voice grew softer, but no less intense. "I've faced ridicule, setbacks, and countless closed doors. But I've never given up because I truly believe in the importance of uncovering the truth. Now, with this group, we have a real chance to make a difference. Let's not squander it."

Despite her research on the man, Trembley's passion on the subject still surprised her. He seemed consumed, obsessed even, but that could be a good thing. "I'm glad to hear that, Professor, because I have a request." She pointed at Kaden and the Colonel. "I would like you both to be Task Force Leaders of SCET. As such, you will help steer the committee, and each of you is free to bring in additional experts as you feel is necessary."

Walker nodded with no outward show of emotion. Kaden was visibly overwhelmed. This was what his friend had suggested, but clearly, he wasn't expecting it.

Then they got down to business. The brainstorming session became increasingly dynamic as they reviewed the list of potential members for their task force and prioritized immediate actions.

"We'll need experts from a few more disciplines," Kaden suggested, jotting down a few more names on a notepad. "Some will also want off-site work areas. Elena, in particular, is still going over some of the data feeds from Elysium."

Emily glanced at the growing list, then looked up at both men in agreement. "I think we can manage that. This is just the beginning," she said emphatically. "But let's be clear here. Our primary mission is to protect this country and our allies—not little green men or finding the secrets to the universe or even faster-than-light propulsion systems. Is there a threat? Where is it coming from? And how can we prepare and hopefully counter it?"

"FTL drive would be pretty awesome," Trent said almost under his breath.

Kaden started chuckling, then fist-bumped the agent. "He's not wrong."

It's a good mix and a good beginning, Emily thought. No oversized egos and real passion for the truth. What Kaden said did stick with her, though, and it would be just as hard as he suggested to keep this group on track.

"Okay, Trent has more of the members being vetted now, and others are mulling it over. But let's schedule our next official meeting for late next week—say Thursday at 2:15," she said, consulting her personal planning calendar. "In the meantime, you all have each other's numbers and emails. If you need to coordinate without me, feel free. Thank you again."

CHAPTER TWENTY-THREE

Several days later, Emily sat at the main West Wing conference table, scanning the mostly empty room. Normally, anything within these walls would have scores of reporters with boom mics and cameras. Her new committee was almost complete, but a late addition was now being forced upon her. Despite the obvious D.C. games playing out, she had reluctantly agreed to meet with Agent Groves, though she had her reservations. The door buzzed as he entered, his imposing figure cutting through the workspace. He moved with purpose, taking the seat opposite her without a word.

"Emily Carter," he started, his voice low and steady. "I know you probably aren't looking for additional agency involvement, but I do think I can help you. I also have information about your brother's disappearance."

Her heart skipped a beat. "What do you know?"

Groves leaned in, lowering his voice even further. "Your brother's disappearance is linked to a classified military project. It's possibly bigger than even you think," the man lied.

Emily narrowed her eyes. "Why bring this to me and not your bosses at the agency?"

"They know this, and mainly because I think you need to know it, too," Groves replied, his gaze unwavering. "But do be careful whom you trust."

Her skepticism flared. Something about this guy gave her the creeps. "And why should I trust you?"

Groves gave a tight smile. "You shouldn't. You shouldn't trust anyone in this city. Check me out after I leave. If I fail the sniff test, you've wasted fifteen minutes of your day and never have to see me again. I just happen to believe you are on the right track and would like to help in whatever way I can."

Groves' boss had given him the latitude to offer her a few crumbs to get him added to the committee. If that failed, he did have one other option to keep an eye on Emily Carter.

He slid a small envelope across the table. "This might help," he said before standing up and walking away without another word.

Emily watched him leave, then quickly opened the envelope. Inside were a few grainy photos and a cryptic note: Project Sentinel, Warehouse D.

Half an hour later, Emily was staring into the faces of her committee around the conference table in the West Wing of the White House as the investigators recounted a curated list of the strange events of the past few weeks. UFO sightings, disappearances, cryptic messages - it was a lot to take in.

"Confirmed sightings in New York. Three partially verified landings and animal mutilations in Ohio. Bright lights in the sky led local investigators to another mass casualty event in Argentina. ISS transponder and comms were down for over four hours last Friday. Rumor is they had a close encounter, but no one at NASA is confirming. And then there is this," Dr. Kaden Trembley said as he passed over a group of close-up photos. He gave the select group time to come to their own conclusions before telling them what he'd learned about the stones on Mars.

Emily stared around the room, dumbfounded. "Does anyone know why the White House hasn't been informed of this yet?"

The group was mostly apolitical, but they all knew how Washington worked. "No way to verify it, ma'am," Dave Kim, senior analyst with one of the government cybersecurity departments said. "No one in NASA or Space Command wants to put their neck on the line with unverifiable data, especially about UAPs, much less connections to ancient aliens here on Earth."

Emily shook her head, knowing Kim was correct.

"This information is also being very tightly held," Kaden added. "ESA locked down the Rover's lab, and few people at NASA even have a clue."

Emily nodded and moved on down her list.

"Okay...has anyone heard of something called Project Sentinel or Warehouse D?"

The room fell silent, eyes darting between each other. Finally, the stern-faced man in a crisp military uniform spoke up.

"I have," Colonel James Walker said, his voice steady. "But it's highly classified. May I ask where you heard about it?"

Emily hesitated, not wanting to reveal her source. "We all have the highest levels of clearance in this room, Colonel. Besides, I have my ways. What can you tell me about it?"

Walker leaned back in his chair, considering his words carefully. "Project Sentinel was a joint military-intelligence operation. It dealt with...unconventional threats."

"Unconventional how?" Emily pressed.

"The kind that aren't from this world," Walker replied, his gaze intense. "As for Warehouse D, it's where they supposedly stored the evidence."

A murmur rippled through the room. Emily's heart raced - this might be true and bigger than she had imagined.

"Colonel, I need to know everything about this project."

Walker's jaw clenched. He glanced around the room before speaking in a low voice. "I'll tell you what I can, but not here. We would need to move this conversation to a SCIF."

SCIFs are Sensitive Compartmented Information Facilities; they are enclosed areas within highly secure buildings used by defense and security agencies to discuss or process very sensitive or classified information.

"We need to be able to discuss all of that in these meetings. We are two dozen yards away from the president," Emily said.

"I do realize that, but I have my own orders, and while I am here to help, I have to obey the security apparatus that exists in my own organization."

"Colonel, I will work on that. In the meantime, schedule us time in a SCIF. You have my calendar links, so set it up."

She turned to the rest of the committee. "I want every scrap of information on these incidents on my desk by tomorrow morning. I think we can all agree something big is going on, and we need to get to the bottom of it."

She turned to the older man at the other end of the wooden table. "Professor Trembley, could I see you for a few moments after we break?"

As the meeting adjourned, Emily couldn't shake the feeling that she was only seeing part of the picture, and at least initially, she didn't seem to be getting any closer to finding out the truth.

"Ms. Carter, you wanted to talk?" Kaden said, walking up as the others filed out of the meeting space.

She nodded. "First off, thank you for your input. I find your insight into all this to be quite..." she searched for the right word, "unbiased."

He smiled. "I'm a scientist. It's part of the job description."

"Yes, but you are also a believer."

He pursed his lips and nodded. "I am, but many people believe in the encounters, especially now. Proving it is what has always been the tough part."

She pointed to the adjacent chair, and he sat, realizing this might not be the quick chat he'd expected.

"Dr. Trembley."

"Please, just call me Kaden," he said.

She smiled. "Kaden, let me be clear. I don't need to be convinced. I am working under the assumption that they are real. Now what I really need to know is, what do they want?"

Despite her earlier statements, her words still shocked him. No one in the government would ever go on record as being a believer, and this woman was a senior administration official.

"What do they want?" he repeated slowly.

"Yes, Kaden, the events, the incidents, the activity levels are increasing. Taken as a whole, what does that mean?" Emily said.

"Well, there is very little common ground between most of the events, but I was in New York last month when... well, you know."

"Your gut feeling, Doctor. What is going on?"

"I was scared. I felt like they were trying to intimidate us. 'Shock and Awe,' I believe, is what your government used to call the tactic."

"That was a first-strike initiative in a war scenario. Do you think we are at war?"

He shook his head. "Maybe I misspoke. I'm just giving my feelings, my gut. Not war, but they are being more obvious, more overt. If I had to guess, I would say they are testing their plans."

"Plans?"

"Plans to conquer, Director Carter. I think they are probing, testing... practicing for an eventual invasion."

CHAPTER TWENTY-FOUR

38°48'N, 104°31'W
Schriever Space Force Base
Colorado, USA

"We've lost two more, Major."

The airman's eyes were glued to his screen, with his C.O., Major Adams, not far behind. "What is the total percentage of losses?"

"Just over eight percent, ma'am, and climbing. The system predicts a ninety-seven percent loss of all GPS satellites within the next seventy-two hours."

Jesus Christ, Monica Adams thought. *Everything on the planet now relies on GPS. Ships, planes, cars, and it's disappearing on my goddamn watch.*

"Run the PreDawn system once more. I need to know a cause for this before I call the general."

PreDawn was mainly a diagnostic system designed to troubleshoot system failures. It could also handle some simple maneuvering if one of the tiny satellites needed to evade other space debris. They had been using it regularly for the last few weeks.

It had to be a meteor storm. Earth's orbit had undoubtedly passed into a previously unidentified cloud of dust and rocks. Moving at over

7,000 miles an hour, anything they hit would be catastrophic. Her group only had twenty-four satellites up there, and her people were telling her they would essentially all be gone in the next few days.

"Shit, this is going to be a career killer."

"Ma'am, PreDawn isn't finding any evidence of a meteor storm or other space debris," the airman reported, his brow furrowed. "The satellites are just... disappearing, going offline one by one."

Major Adams clenched her jaw. This didn't make sense. Satellites don't just vanish. She turned to her team, a group of the best and brightest in the Air Force. "I want every available resource on this. Pull in whoever you need from other departments. We need answers, and we need them now."

The room burst into activity as people rushed to their stations, fingers flying over keyboards, and voices rising in urgent conversation. Major Adams watched them work, her mind racing. *If it wasn't a meteor storm, what could it be? A foreign attack? Some kind of new weapon? The Chinese supposedly have space-based lasers in testing. Maybe they were having some target practice.*

She picked up the phone and dialed the number for her superiors in Washington, D.C. The call was answered on the first ring.

"Major Adams," a gruff voice said. "What's the situation?"

"Sir, we have a major problem," she said, trying to keep her voice steady. "We're losing GPS satellites at an alarming rate. PreDawn isn't finding any evidence of a natural cause."

There was a long pause on the other end of the line. "We've been having problems for weeks, Major. What's the projected signal loss?"

She hesitated. "Yes, sir, but this is not just signal loss. We project ninety-seven percent of our birds will be dead within the next seventy-two hours, sir." She heard the man swear under his breath.

Another pause. "Understood. Keep working on it, Major. We'll spin up a remote team to assist you."

"Yes, sir. But, sir... do you have any idea what could be causing this?"

The voice on the other end of the line hesitated. "I'm sure command will have some... theories. I'll get back to you. Just focus on your job, Major. We'll handle the rest."

The call ended abruptly, leaving Major Adams staring at the phone in her hand. The brass didn't seem surprised by the news, but they didn't seem to have any more answers than she did. *What theories could they possibly have? And why did they seem so reluctant to share them?*

She shook her head and turned back to her team. They needed answers, and they needed them fast. The fate of the world's navigation systems depended on it.

Monica Adams dialed a number from memory, her fingers trembling slightly as she pressed the buttons. She needed someone who had been in her shoes, someone who might have a broader perspective. The line clicked, and a familiar voice answered.

"Colonel Barnes," the voice on the other end said, gruff but friendly.

"Tom, it's Monica."

"Monica! Long time no hear. What's going on?"

She took a deep breath. "Tom, we're losing GPS satellites at an alarming rate. PreDawn can't find any natural causes. I need your take on this."

There was a pause before he spoke again, his tone more serious now. "How bad is it?"

"We're projecting a ninety-seven percent loss within seventy-two hours."

"Jesus Christ." He let out a low whistle. "That's catastrophic."

"Exactly. I called because I need your insight. What could be causing this?"

He sighed deeply. "Look, Monica, assume that if they're taking out our birds like this, it's not just about inconvenience or simple disruption. They're intent on causing massive problems, casualties, and likely freezing much of our economy."

"You think this is an enemy attack?"

"In our role, we always need to assume that," Barnes said firmly. "Our paranoia keeps us sharp. If someone takes out GPS, what might they go after next?"

Her mind raced through the possibilities: GOES weather satellites, communication satellites... She knew most of those were only a few hundred miles up compared to the GPS satellites' 12,000-mile altitude.

"Tom," she began cautiously, "the GPS satellites are much higher than those others."

He grunted in agreement. "An enemy would start with either the most vital or the closest targets first. You need to assume they hit the most vital first as I can't imagine who would have assets that high up."

The implication of his words sank in slowly. "So, we could be looking at attacks on our weather and communication satellites next? Do you think it could be cyber-attacks or something else?"

The man was silent several seconds before answering. Adams was unsure of her friends' current posting, but she got the feeling he was much more in the know than her or her current superiors.

"Something else," he said, his voice flat. "You need to contact those other agencies and privately share whatever intel you can."

Monica nodded, even though he couldn't see her through the phone. "Thanks, Tom. I appreciate it."

"Stay sharp, Monica," he said before ending the call.

She put down the phone and turned back to her team with renewed determination. There was no time to waste; she decided to follow her friend's advice over her superiors at least on this one point. She needed to coordinate with other agencies immediately if they were going to mitigate whatever was coming next. Still, Tom's comments about taking out what was vital or closest frightened her. What out there might be closer to objects 12,000 miles out in space?

"Alright everyone," she called out, drawing their attention back to her, "we've got new orders..."

Widespread GPS Outages Spark Concern — Officials Quietly Blame Chinese or Russian Cyberattack

"Though no formal attribution has been made, multiple senior intelligence officials speaking under condition of anonymity have confirmed that the GPS disruptions affecting aircraft, container shipping, and military units across the eastern U.S. are being treated as a 'hostile probe' — likely the work of either China's Unit 61398 or Russia's GRU.

"'We've seen packet spoofing before,' said one official. 'But not at this scale, and not across multiple defense-critical channels. This feels like a signal — not just interference.'

"Publicly, the Department of Transportation has attributed the issue to 'solar activity and algorithm drift,' though independent analysts note that similar anomalies have not been reported globally."

The Washington Sentinel* | *Byline: Jayson Keller, National Security Correspondent

CHAPTER TWENTY-FIVE

Abandoned Skate Park
Paris, Texas, USA

The sky was bleeding rust and gold as the sun slipped behind the horizon. The air smelled faintly of hot asphalt, sagebrush, and the remnants of a grass fire from earlier in the week. Everything felt brittle. Drought-hardened. Like the world was tired of holding together.

They gathered at the dead skate park out by the drainage canal—just like they always did when the news was too much. No boards anymore. Just phones, sarcasm, caffeine, and questions nobody really had answers to.

Ty sat cross-legged on the chipped concrete of a drained bowl, hoodie sleeves pushed up, earbud hanging from one side. "Alright, guys. Look. Don't roll your eyes. But I think something's happening."

Asha took a lazy sip from her half-melted iced matcha and shot him a side glance. "You say that every week."

"I know, but this time's different."

Zee sprawled on the bleachers above, tapping through an obscure chat thread on his tablet. "That's what people say right before they get shadow-banned or disappeared."

"No, seriously," Ty continued, holding up his phone. "Have you even looked at any of this stuff? A whole village out west or somewhere just went off-grid. Starlink blinked out for two days, and cell coverage is down over half the continent. The military is on high alert. And whatever the hell that was in New York. Lots of crazy theories on that. And all those random UFO reports."

Asha raised an eyebrow. "So, a fiber line went down. Or a data center glitched. Not exactly proof of what? Alien extermination squads?"

Ty shook his head. "Damn, girl, no. It's not just that. Look here—satellite telemetry from NOAA showed a weird radiation pulse over the Andes just before the blackout. That data's already been pulled from their site. But mirrored servers caught it."

Zee looked up. "What kind of pulse?"

"They say gamma. Brief but powerful. Something real. Not atmospheric noise."

The three friends were kids, and while dismissed by the adults that saw them lounging in the park, they were not stupid. In fact, what bound them together was their shared love of science, math, and the subjects most of their peers hated.

"That... should not happen without someone noticing," Asha said, a little quieter.

Ty nodded. "Exactly. But no media coverage. No scientific statements. Nothing. Which means it either wasn't natural—or someone's hiding it."

Zee leaned back against the steel rail and stared out toward the tree line. "This makes, what, seven disappearances this year? Not counting the refugee ships off the Indian coast or the Arctic research team that went dark?"

"And the Mars transmissions they buried," Ty added. "The ones from the European Rover that wasn't supposed to be transmitting anymore."

Asha frowned. "I thought they said that was solar interference?"

"They always say that."

For a few moments, the only sound was the low drone of cicadas and the distant whine of an overworked transformer.

"I don't know," Asha said. "Part of me wants to believe it's nothing.

Just random. But part of me... I don't know. Something's off. The world's not just breaking. It feels like it's being reset."

Zee nodded slowly. "Like we're on borrowed time, and no one wants to say it out loud."

"Think about it," Ty said. "You know how every generation talks about 'change'? How things were hard but they pushed through? Ours... we don't get that. We get collapse in real-time. Climate. Economics. Truth. All decaying faster than we can react."

"And the people who caused it," Asha muttered, "are the ones still holding the controls."

Zee raised his cup in a sarcastic toast. "To the Boomer Industrial Complex: thanks for the wars, the carbon, the surveillance state, and the debt."

Asha snorted. "They'll say we're just bitter and lazy. That we should work harder. Like we're not hustling three side gigs just to cover rent. Still, we can't judge. They did their part, worked with what they had... what they knew."

"They aren't that sympathetic toward us. They aren't inheriting a planet on fire," Ty said. "They didn't have to code-switch their resumes to get through an algorithm just to get ghosted after an interview. They got pensions. We get burnout. They had moon landings. We get deep-fake presidents and microplastic in our brains."

Zee tapped his screen. "They also got clean oceans. Rain that didn't kill coral reefs. Stable weather. Affordable homes. Student debt was a joke back then. They lived their lives at the expense of ours and called it progress."

Asha was silent for a moment, picking at the edge of her nail polish. "Maybe it's not just human neglect. Maybe someone else out there expected us to do better."

Ty blinked. "What?"

"I'm just saying," she shrugged. "I read a theory someone overseas had. Made you think, you know? What if there is some kind of, I don't know... cosmic oversight? I mean, all these stories about the lights in the sky, the unexplainable tech... Maybe Earth was part of a larger galactic system, and we were supposed to evolve past greed, pollution, and destruction. And now they're stepping in because we failed the assignment."

Zee smirked. "You're saying aliens gave us a pop quiz and we flunked?"

"I don't know... maybe. Like they watched for a while. Waited for us to get our shit together. And when we didn't, some big poobah started damage control."

Ty nodded slowly. "Like a cleanup crew."

"Or a reset button," Zee added.

Silence again. But it was heavier now.

Finally, Asha stood, brushing off her jeans. "Okay, even if you're right, even if it's all connected... What the hell are we supposed to do about it? We're just people. Burned out, broke-ass, and buried under a mountain of noise."

Ty stood, too, phone in hand. "We cut through the noise. We can mobilize; hell, that's our generation's superpower. Get pissed off and share what we know. We find the real signal underneath all the bullshit. And let the world know."

Zee looked up at them from his screen, then sighed and stood. "That's assuming we have time."

"Maybe we don't," Ty said. "But I'd rather go down knowing we tried than just keep doomscrolling till the lights go out."

They walked into the twilight together, their devices buzzing in their pockets—each one a window into chaos, silence, and maybe... a hint of truth.

Overhead, the stars were just starting to emerge. But not all of them were stars.

The three teens didn't say much as they walked back through the empty park. The lights in the parking lot were out—again—and the silence between them wasn't awkward. Just... unsettled.

They turned onto the old gravel trail that cut behind the retention pond and snaked through the scrubland behind the high school. This part of Denton was slowly being eaten by weeds and kudzu. Abandoned trailers, collapsed fences. Civilization fraying at the edges.

Asha was the first to stop.

"What's that?"

Ty turned. "What?"

"Up there."

She pointed skyward.

Zee followed her gaze, squinting. "Probably a drone."

Ty shielded his eyes. "That's no drone."

There—hovering against the stars—was a shape. Not a star. Not a plane. It moved too slowly. Too deliberate. A single, sharp point of blue-white light pulsed at its center like a heartbeat. Then, as if acknowledging them, the shape tilted, revealing its underside: a lattice of amber light in geometries that made no human sense.

It wasn't flying.

It was stationary, utterly silent, not blinking, not moving—until it did. In a fraction of a second, it zipped left, stopped dead, zipped again, paused midair, and then... vanished.

No contrail. No sound. Just gone.

Ty's mouth went dry. "Did you—did you see that?"

"I saw it," Asha whispered. "Holy shit, I saw it."

Zee stared blankly into the sky, blinking fast. "That... wasn't a satellite. Or a drone. Or anything that makes sense."

Silence again. Except now the world felt louder—crickets, wind, breath.

"You saw how fast it moved?" Ty said. "No sonic boom. No light trail. That was real."

Asha's hands were trembling. "We need to get off this trail."

"Why?" Zee asked. "You think it saw us?"

"I think," she said, steadying her voice, "we're not supposed to know what we just saw."

They started walking faster. A nervous pace. Not running—yet.

Ty checked his phone. No signal. "Seriously?" he muttered. "No bars?"

"Mine's dead," Asha said. "It was 60% ten minutes ago."

"Same here," Zee said. "Battery just nuked."

They walked in silence again. This time not from apathy—but alertness.

After a few minutes, Ty spoke up. "Okay... let's say that was a ship. Or drone. Or whatever. Why now? Why show up here, where we'd see it?"

"Maybe we weren't supposed to," Zee said. "Maybe we're just in the wrong place."

"Or the right one," Asha muttered. "For once."

They reached the road. The occasional car passed in the distance, oblivious. The world still mostly asleep.

Zee looked back toward the sky. "People won't believe us."

"No," Ty agreed. "Because they don't want to believe. It's easier to pretend it's fake. CGI. A glitch in the matrix. Weather balloon. God forbid we accept that something bigger is happening."

"That's how it happens," Asha said. "That's how civilizations fall. Not with fire and brimstone. But by looking away. Denial. Normalcy bias."

Zee's face was pale. "I used to think all the conspiracy people were just bored or lonely."

"They are," Ty said. "But that doesn't mean they're wrong."

They reached their cars. Asha's hands hovered over the door handle. "What do we do now?" she asked.

Ty looked up once more at the empty, silent sky. "We stop pretending this world still works the way we thought it did."

CHAPTER TWENTY-SIX

38°44′N, 104°50′W
Cheyenne Mountain Space Force Station

General Taylor stood in the bustling NORAD command center, his eyes fixed on the large radar screen displaying a mysterious object hurtling toward American airspace. The room buzzed with activity as analysts and technicians scrambled to assess the potential threat.

"What's the trajectory?" General Taylor barked, his voice cutting through the chatter.

A young lieutenant, her face illuminated by the glow of her computer screen, responded promptly. "Sir, the object appears to be on an impact course. Current estimates show it entering the atmosphere over the Gulf of Mexico in approximately 20 minutes."

General Taylor furrowed his brow, perplexed by the lack of urgency from the commanding officers. He turned to one of the Air Force command liaison officers, Colonel Johnson, who stood nearby, equally puzzled. NORAD was nominally an Air Force base, operated by both Americans and Canadians. The highest-ranking officer the general had met so far was a Canadian lieutenant general named Cabot. His American counterpart, Air Force General Walter McAdams, hadn't shown for the meetings earlier in the week nor the reception for the visiting general last night.

General Taylor was an observer here at best; he had no real authority, but his reputation and the ear of the president normally carried some weight.

"Colonel, why aren't we seeing any response from the alert units? Shouldn't they be scrambling jets and coordinating with local authorities by now?"

Colonel Johnson shook his head, his eyes darting between the radar screen and the various communication panels. "I can't say for certain, sir. My assumption is that it doesn't meet alert criteria."

General Taylor felt a growing unease in the pit of his stomach. Something wasn't right. He strode over to the communications officer, a seasoned sergeant with a headset pressed against his ear.

"Sergeant, get me on the line with the base commanders. I want to know why they're not reacting to this potential threat."

The sergeant nodded, his fingers punching the keyboard as he attempted to establish contact. Moments later, he looked up at General Taylor, a hint of confusion in his eyes.

"Sir, neither of the base commanders are available. It's like their communication systems are down. I've left word with both of their aides."

General Taylor's unease turned to alarm. He turned back to the radar screen, watching as the unidentified object continued its rapid descent toward American soil. The room fell silent, the only sound being the steady beep of the radar as it tracked the object's progress.

"Colonel Johnson, this base is supposed to be an early-warning center and a deterrent against enemy hostilities. Neither of those mandates seems to be a priority at the moment. I am about to have this sergeant get me an outside connection to the White House. If you don't want all hell coming down on you and every officer here, you will get your bosses' asses in motion and help me understand why this isn't an Alert Condition One."

As Colonel Johnson rushed to carry out the order, General Taylor couldn't shake the feeling that they were dealing with something far beyond their usual protocols. But the object's trajectory and the unresponsive base commanders all pointed to a situation that could quickly spiral out of their control.

"Sir." A young female airman was seated at her station, looking up at the general.

"Yes?"

"The intrusions happen too often. No one even reports them anymore. We know they aren't Russian or any of our known enemies. We can see the vectors."

This young woman was giving him more information than any of the brass in this place had, and yet, not even she seemed concerned.

"How do you know we aren't being attacked? Or that one of our enemies has developed something new—a hypersonic missile or something?"

She looked somewhat chagrined but shook her head. "They would've had to lift off somewhere on the surface, and we track all of that as well as all the orbital debris. Things like this fast-mover happen way too often, and our orders are to ignore them unless it is an immediate threat, or we see a corresponding launch from another terrestrial location."

The colonel reappeared with a questioning look on his face. He glanced at the airman before addressing General Taylor. "Lieutenant General Cabot is on his way. He will meet you in the analysis room. If you will follow me."

Great, the fucking Canadian, Taylor thought. He damn sure couldn't pressure him the way he wanted. "Where is McAdams?"

"I'm afraid the commander is...umm, regrettably detained," the liaison officer replied uneasily.

"Right." General Taylor growled before following the younger man out of the command center.

Taylor lit into the Canadian officer like a bloodhound pursuing a fugitive. "You don't even take incident reports on things like this? Does your command structure know about this?"

The man's smile did not reach his eyes. "General Taylor, I understand your concerns," Lieutenant General Cabot began, his voice calm and measured. "But as you're aware, this is a unique joint command structure. Our protocols and reporting requirements differ from those of a typical U.S. military base."

General Taylor's eyes narrowed, his anger simmering just beneath the surface. "I don't give a good goddamn about your unique command structure, Cabot. When there's a potential threat to both our nation's security, I expect a fucking response!"

Cabot's forced smile remained fixed, but his eyes hardened. "With all due respect, General, you are here as an observer. While we value your input, the day-to-day operations of this facility fall under our purview."

"Purview? Is that what you call ignoring a goddamned unidentified object hurtling towards our country?" Taylor slammed his fist on the table, causing a water tumbler to tip over.

Cabot leaned forward, his voice low and deliberate. "General, I assure you that we take every potential threat seriously. However, not every anomaly warrants a full-scale response.

"Do you realize the hardware we have at our disposal? Upgraded Early Warning Radar, AN/FPS-117 and AN/FPS-124, SBIRS, Space-Based Infrared System, Ground-Based Electro-Optical Deep Space Surveillance, Space Fence LEO detection Radar, Cobra Dane, and a half-dozen more systems even you aren't cleared to know about. We have our reasons for handling these situations with a certain level of discretion."

"Discretion? Is that a new code word for a cover-up?" Taylor's face reddened, his anger boiling over. "I swear to God, Cabot, if you and McAdams are hiding something..."

"General," Cabot began. "Approximately 25 million meteors enter Earth's atmosphere every day. Most of these are very small, about the size of a grain of sand, and they typically burn up upon entry. The larger ones result in meteors that we often see as 'shooting stars.' This amounts to an estimated 50-100 tons of meteoric material entering the Earth's atmosphere daily.

"Also, on average, around 100-200 pieces of space debris reenter Earth's atmosphere each day. This includes defunct satellites, spent rocket stages, and other fragments from space operations. Most of this debris also burns up upon reentry, with only larger pieces potentially reaching the Earth's surface.

“Add to that 100,000 commercial flights and several thousand military ones every single day. What I am saying is we know what we are doing here. Every object has to be course tracked on multiple systems, analyzed, and determined if it is even real or simply an electronic ghost, of which we have many. We don't fully understand everything that is out there, but we are on the job, sir."

"So, are you implying what we saw on radar back there wasn't real? It damned sure wasn't a 747 or a weather balloon coming in from Saturn."

"I am saying we deal with a tremendous amount of knowns and a small number of unknowns; our task is the same as yours is. We must keep our respective countries safe."

The general was winding up for another blow.

Cabot raised his hand, cutting off Taylor's tirade. "I understand your frustration, General. But I must remind you again that you are a guest here. We have our protocols, and we will handle this situation as we see fit."

Taylor stood abruptly, his chair scraping against the floor. "This isn't over, Cabot. I'll be taking this up with the joint chiefs and the president himself. If there's a threat to our nation, you'll be damned lucky if they let you continue tracking Santa Claus come December.”

Unconfirmed Reports of 'Skyquake' Off Gulf Coast Stir Online Panic

"At approximately 10:22 a.m., residents from Destin to Apalachicola reported hearing what one fisherman called 'a sonic boom that shook the soul.' Officials' initial claim is that it was a likely undersea tremor. NOAA has yet to confirm any seismic activity."

NPR Morning Report | By: Rachel Everhart, National Security Correspondent

CHAPTER TWENTY-SEVEN

0903 EST May 11
White House Oval Office
Washington, D.C., USA

"Emily, what I am telling you is that either one of our more sensitive military installations is full of incompetents, or there is a larger conspiracy to hide the truth from everyone."

The deputy chief of staff looked at General Taylor, then over to her friend, General Briggs, with some skepticism. "You're talking about NORAD, General. No one will believe me if I go after them."

"I'm just stating what I found. You asked me to go out there and kick over some rocks, and that is what I did. Look..."

Briggs cleared his throat. "That base has always run on its own set of rules. Never made sense to me to have the Canadians helping to run the thing."

Taylor nodded as he reached up and scratched his neck. Emily could see the man's discomfort with this topic. She knew he wasn't a believer, but that was why she was relying on him so much.

"You know I don't give a good goddamn about little green men. I do care a great deal about this country, though, and I see a threat to our national defense that no one but you seems to be taking seriously. When those lights falling from the sky turn into bombs or invaders, it's going to be too late."

"Any indications that any of those objects hit the surface?" Emily asked.

Briggs answered, "Nothing showing up so far, but that doesn't mean much. If it hit way out to sea, it might have gone unnoticed. Also, depending on the size, it likely wouldn't do much damage. They are right that tons of space rock fall on the planet every day."

They finished debriefing General Taylor, who stood and left, still clearly frustrated. "They are covering something up," Briggs said. "No other reason the base commander would have refused to even meet with him. He was a presidential liaison. That action is not just rude, it is insubordination."

Emily paused, her brow furrowed with concern. "There's something else, General. I think someone went through my office in the West Wing last night."

The general's eyes widened. "Oh? What do you mean?"

"I came in this morning, and things were missing. Files were scattered around, and my computer had been tampered with." Emily's voice trembled slightly as she recounted the unsettling discovery.

"Did you report it to security?"

"Not yet. I wanted to talk to you first. I'm not sure who I can trust right now. I don't think anything was taken, and anyone allowed in that area, even the cleaning crew, has been seriously vetted."

The retired general leaned forward, his expression grave. "Listen, Emily, this could be serious. If someone is targeting you, it means they're afraid of what you might uncover. You need to be cautious and increase your security detail. Truthfully, though, if you saw the signs, it's because they wanted you to. They want you rattled."

Emily frowned, her mind mulling over the implications. "So, what do you suggest?"

"First, have your office swept for bugs. They might have planted listening devices to monitor your activities. And have Trent check your personal vehicles for tracking devices, too. You can't be too careful."

As Briggs spoke, Emily couldn't help but wonder if his paranoia was crossing into delusion. The idea of being spied on and tracked seemed like something out of a conspiracy thriller. Yet, given the strange events unfolding around her, she couldn't dismiss his concerns outright.

"I'll arrange for a sweep as soon as possible," Emily said, trying to keep her voice steady. "But General, do you really think this is necessary? I mean, bugs and trackers? It sounds a bit extreme."

He fixed her with a piercing gaze. "Emily, if you are right about any of this, you're dealing with people who will stop at nothing to keep their secrets hidden. Who knows what else they're capable of?"

"I also have another question," Emily said. "Someone is trying to force an intelligence agent onto my group. Are you familiar with Daniel Groves?"

The general shook his head. "If he doesn't pass the sniff test, don't let him within a hundred yards of your committee."

"He mentioned Paul's disappearance and one other thing." She handed him the envelope Agent Groves had given her. The general quickly scanned the images and the information about Warehouse D.

"Not familiar with either, but my assumption is that it is something to take your eyes off the goal. In this town, you have to be more wary of your friends than your enemies. Beware of anyone offering gifts."

Emily swallowed hard, the awful weight of everything sinking in. She knew the general was right. If she was going to pursue this investigation, she needed to be prepared for the worst.

Her phone buzzed, and she studied the alert from Ohio. Calling Trent, she asked him for more details on the UFO report, then made one more call.

POLITICO Brief | Internal Memo Leak

Senate Intelligence Committee: "No Evidence of Alien Contact" Despite Military Briefings

"The closed-door report refers to 'unidentified high-speed phenomena' tracked over continental airspace. While multiple radar systems confirmed non-ballistic maneuvering, the official recommendation is to classify under weather anomalies."

CHAPTER TWENTY-EIGHT

38°53'N, 82°47'W
Lawrence County, Ohio, USA

The late-night call from Emily Carter had roused him from a fitful sleep, but Kaden Trembley was on the red-eye flight just after two AM. He hadn't planned on being out in the field with this committee, but Emily had said it was important.

Hours later, as he approached the scorched ground in the cordoned-off area, Kaden was surprised to see a young woman already examining something, her red hair pulled back in a ponytail and a determined look on her face. She turned to greet him, her green eyes sparkling with intelligence.

"Dr. Trembley," she said, extending a hand, "Natalie Reeves, MUFON lead investigator."

Kaden shook her hand, taken aback by her confident demeanor. He knew the unofficial UFO network of amateurs was highly motivated but sometimes questionable in their quest for evidence of extraterrestrial life. "I wasn't expecting MUFON to be involved."

Natalie grinned. "We've been tracking this type of anomaly for a while. It's really not like anything we've seen before."

As he crossed under the yellow tape and they approached the supposed ground zero of the alien touchdown, Kaden couldn't help but marvel at the precise demarcation between blackened dirt and weeds and the pristine meadow beyond.

"Radiation?" he asked one of the technicians nearby holding one of the new multi-band detectors.

The man in the white coveralls shook his head and kept sweeping the wand over the blackened earth.

"You say 'this type,'" Kaden began, "in what ways do you categorize this...event?"

The young woman smiled, obviously pleased to be taken seriously for a change.

"First, let me ask, have you seen anything like this before?" Natalie asked, her brow furrowed in concentration.

Kaden scanned the area a bit closer, then shook his head. "Not precisely, no. And I've studied nearly every major reported UFO sighting in history."

Both of them were making a slow circuit of the zone where others were taking measurements and photographs.

"This area is a known 'hot spot' for UAP sightings, so we keep a close watch on it. Some in my group believe it is a magnetic or gravimetric locus that the aliens center in on like a homing beacon."

"But you disagree?" Kaden asked.

She nodded. "It might be true, but honestly, I think it is over-speculation about a random data point. One that ultimately takes us nowhere."

Trembley was beginning to like this young woman. Her mind was sharp, her process very analytical, and she seemed to be trying very hard not to get in the way of the facts but to accept only what the scene was offering.

"There were witnesses," she said, pointing to a group of rattled locals being interviewed by someone in uniform.

"You spoke to them?" he asked.

"No," she said with a laugh. "I'm not so good at that part, so I usually let others handle it. I want facts; I want to know the why and the how. People's memories are easily manipulated or just plain wrong. I know we can't believe what we see with our own eyes."

Kaden marveled at the girl's words and smiled as he reached a gloved hand to pick up a twig that was charred black right to the outer edge of the circle, then looked at fresh and unmarred twigs just beyond. Natalie was indeed correct. Few people know how unreliable the mind—or more accurately, memories—are. Even vision is suspect. You literally cannot always believe what you see, much less what you remember.

"With AI-generated images and videos, no one can trust photographs anymore, no matter how convincing they look," she continued. "And don't get me started on drones. The rising level of sophistication and silent power systems are making them the most prominent false positives we see these days. I can't even tell the difference with some of them until we hit them with an IR camera. That usually reveals the truth."

"Natalie, you strike me as..."

"Not what you were expecting?" she asked with a grin. "I am a contract researcher for the group. One of many they have. Don't get me wrong. I want to believe, but I also follow the evidence. Evidence that I am tired of seeing swept away and buried."

"By people like me?" Kaden asked. He'd heard all the conspiracy theories many times before. 'Men in Black' showing up or the military. Always someone attached to a super-secret government program. Now he was with the government.

She shook her head and gave a rueful smile. "No, not you, Dr. Trembley. I know your background. I know you believe as well, and I feel like you want the truth to come out."

"So you don't reckon this was a drone... or some lads mucking about?"

"I didn't say that," the investigator responded cryptically as she squatted and lowered her head to the ground to look across at ground level. "In fact, I do think it was a drone. Just not one made by humans."

"Alien drones?" Now that was a new idea.

The woman pulled a few wayward strands of hair back and tucked them into her ponytail. "In my opinion, yes. Drones or maybe probes.

You've seen the footage of the so-called fast-movers. The Tic-Tac-shaped craft."

Kaden nodded.

"The flight characteristics of those vehicles were off the charts. The physics alone rule out any life form we are aware of being able to survive the extreme acceleration and G-force on those tight turns. We would be jelly."

"Ahhh," Kaden said, lapsing back into his role as a teacher. "Your only error is inferring or attributing anything human to your analysis. 'We would be jelly,' but the other life form may be jelly to start with or aquatic or anything else entirely. The math gives you the facts but not necessarily the truths."

She nodded and looked a bit sheepish but unapologetic.

"It's human nature to compare with what we know, but when it comes to truly alien life forms, that bias might be our undoing. Tell me, Natalie, what did you do before this?"

She smiled sadly. "Naval aviator."

That made sense to Trembley; her analysis had a pilot's viewpoint. "I imagine you have some stories of your own. Maybe some that drove you into this role."

She nodded, then added, "Yes...but they're off-limits for general discussion. Your assumption is correct, though. That is indeed why I do this, Doctor. I know we aren't alone. I also know there are human organizations that prefer we not know the truth. That alone is reason to search for the truth."

"Clever girl," he said, then realizing how patronizing that sounded, tried to backtrack.

She laughed and leaned in. "I'm Navy. I've heard much worse. Besides, coming from you, I appreciate the compliment."

As they worked, Kaden's mind tried to connect the dots. If the craft that made this was indeed extraterrestrial, then how might it fit in with everything else that was happening? He thought of Emily and her mission to uncover the truth. He'd promised her he would find the truth and was beginning to realize he was going to need more help.

Natalie seemed to sense his unease. "You okay, Doc? You look like you figured something out."

Kaden took a deep breath. "What is the real question for you, Natalie? I can tell it isn't 'Are we alone?'"

"No, I know that one. My question is, Why are they here?" She made more notes on her tablet as she talked.

The older man nodded. "I just can't shake the feeling that there's something much bigger going on here. This is just incidental."

Natalie nodded, her expression serious. "I've had that feeling for a long time. That's why I took on this role—to find the truth, no matter where it leads."

“Tell me, Natalie, fancy a bite to eat with me back in that little village down the road?"

She eyed him suspiciously; the man was probably old enough to be her father. His quaint British accent, however, seemed to hold nothing but respect for her.

Kaden continued, oblivious to her silent interpretations. "I have something I would like to run by you. Maybe interest you in working this problem from a different angle."

Her lips pursed into a face that was way too cute for a woman as serious as she obviously was. Natalie nodded in agreement, then went back to work. She was glad the man had taken her seriously. She would definitely listen to whatever else he had to say.

CHAPTER TWENTY-NINE

The diner was clean, neat, and exactly what one would expect in a small town in middle America. Natalie studied the chalkboard menu above the counter before ordering a club sandwich and potato salad. She'd traveled the country enough to know what was typically safe to eat. She checked her watch before filling a coffee cup and heading to a corner booth.

She sipped her coffee and studied the professor as he selected a salad and unsweetened tea before joining her. He was precise and somewhat handsome for his age, but he seemed to burn with an intense curiosity that she found appealing. Having encountered more government investigators in her career than she cared to remember, Kaden Trembley was a breath of fresh air.

She motioned to a man sitting alone near the door. "Friend of yours?"

The professor nodded. "His name is Trent. They make me take an escort into the field. I have no idea why." He'd seen him earlier as he deplaned but had forgotten about him afterward.

Natalie nodded approvingly; the man was very fit, and she liked that his eyes were everywhere except on her and Kaden. Apparently, this professor did warrant a certain level of respect. Still, she'd had uncomfortable visits from government officials in the past, and it hadn't gone so well for her either.

Kaden picked at his salad, his eyes occasionally darting around the diner. "So, you've been with MUFON for how long now?"

Natalie took a bite of her sandwich, chewing thoughtfully. "About three years. Around six months with CUFOS in between missions."

Kaden's eyebrows raised. CUFOS was the group originally started by Allen Hynek, a controversial figure from back in the Blue Book days of UFO hunting. CUFOS did have a reputation for applying a more scientific rigor to its investigations, but he could see the move. MUFON investigated a much broader range of incidents. "And before that, Navy aviator? That's quite the career shift."

She smiled. "Yeah, you could say that."

They sat in silence for a moment, the low hum of conversation around them filling the gap. Kaden finally spoke again. "You alluded earlier that you've had your own experiences."

Natalie's expression grew serious. Kaden watched as her eyes seemed to light with intensity.

She leaned in, lowering her voice. "Let's just say I have a deeper appreciation for cases like these. I had some missions... they weren't exactly routine flights."

Kaden leaned forward, curiosity piqued. "Would you tell me some of what happened?"

She sighed, taking another sip of her coffee before speaking. "It started as anomalous radar contacts. Our incident was similar to the 2004 Nimitz incident, but honestly, I am not allowed to discuss it."

Trembley fumbled in several pockets and eventually produced the government credentials Emily Carter had provided. "You see my clearance level, don't you? It supersedes even your military's Top Secret."

"Not the way it was explained to me," Natalie said. "Even if President Martin were sitting where you are, I would not be able to talk about it without fear of severe consequences."

Kaden was more than a bit shocked. "Your superiors said that?"

She shook her head. "No... not military. The agency." She glanced at the chair where Trent Rogers was sipping coffee and pretending to read something on his phone.

"They filed the incident reports," she said, her voice flat. "But they went nowhere. I was advised in no uncertain terms to 'forget' what I saw and not to mention it to anyone."

"Advised?" Kaden pressed.

Natalie nodded slowly, a bitter smile on her lips. "Pressured would be more accurate. Strong pressure from people in my chain of command and outside the Navy. The kind of pressure that makes you rethink your career choices if you don't comply."

Kaden frowned, setting his fork down. "That must have been quite frustrating."

"You have no idea," she replied quietly. "The more I pushed for answers, the harder they pushed back."

"So you left," Kaden said.

"I had to," Natalie admitted. "I couldn't stay and just pretend nothing happened when I knew something did."

Kaden studied her face, seeing a reflection of his own struggles with skepticism and disbelief from peers and superiors alike.

"And now you're with MUFON," he said.

Natalie nodded again, finishing her sandwich and wiping her hands on a napkin. "I needed to find the truth without someone constantly breathing down my neck. With MUFON, I have the opposite problem. To most of them, everything seems like aliens."

"Change of topic," Kaden said. "What is your take on the Fermi paradox?"

Natalie leaned back, a thoughtful look crossing her face. "The Fermi paradox. If aliens exist, where are all of them?" She took a deep breath before diving into her well-considered answer. "I've given it a lot of thought."

Kaden nodded, leaning in closer.

"First," she began, "if we can't trust the officials, maybe we've heard from them many times already. Who's to say the signals haven't been intercepted and classified?"

Kaden nodded; her answer matched one of his own.

"And second," she continued, "have we really looked or listened? Space is vast. No matter how much we search, we're only listening to our own little corner of the universe. And that's assuming they would use something as primitive as radio waves to communicate."

"That's a good point," Kaden mused, rubbing his chin thoughtfully.

"Lastly," Natalie added, "maybe they've transcended physical bodies and are all energy or pure data now. Imagine an advanced civilization evolving past their biological limitations. They could be living in a digital realm, far beyond our current understanding or perception."

Kaden's mind echoed back to similar conversations with students over the years. How many he'd asked this same question of. "So you're saying that our search methods are outdated?"

"More like naive," Natalie affirmed. "We're like ants trying to understand humans by listening for footsteps."

"And there's also the question of their intentions," she added after a pause. "Maybe they're avoiding us on purpose. We might not be ready for contact or pose some unknown threat to them."

Kaden nodded again, impressed by her insight. "You've certainly given this a lot of thought."

She smiled wryly. "Comes with the territory."

"Do you think there's a way to improve our search methods?" he asked.

"We need to think outside the box," Natalie replied confidently. "Look for signs of their technology or energy signatures rather than waiting for them to broadcast 'Hello World!' And we should consider all possibilities—biological, digital, and beyond."

Kaden took a deep breath, feeling a renewed sense of why he was here. "Your perspective is refreshing."

"I'm glad you think so," she said, finishing her coffee. "Why do I feel like this is a job interview?"

Kaden leaned back in his seat, absorbing everything she had said. "Well," he began slowly, "if we're going to uncover what's really happening up there, I believe we're going to need every bit of genius-level talent and genuine experience we can get."

Natalie's eyes met his, filled with determination and something else—maybe hope.

Kaden smiled for the first time since they'd sat down. This might just be the ally the team needed.

Natalie leaned back. "So, what's your take on all this, Dr. Trembley? You've been studying UFOs for years. What do you hope to find?"

Kaden's eyes lit up with that familiar spark of curiosity. "Honestly, Natalie, I want to prove once and for all that we are not alone. I want to understand their technology, their intentions, and why they're here."

She nodded slowly, absorbing his words. "But you must know how dangerous this is. The government doesn't want this information getting out."

Kaden shrugged and took a deep breath, choosing his words carefully. "You're right. But I don't think the entire government is in on it."

Natalie raised an eyebrow. "What do you mean?"

"For one, I firmly believe the White House is largely in the dark," Kaden said. "The president might get briefed on certain high-level issues, but when it comes to the nitty-gritty details of UFO sightings and encounters? I'm quite certain he's not fully informed. In fact, I think they—and I mean the senior staff included—are being deliberately misinformed."

Natalie frowned. "That's a bold statement, especially from someone who is essentially from the government."

Kaden leaned forward, lowering his voice. "Think about it. The sheer number of sightings, the reports that get buried or dismissed—these aren't isolated incidents handled by one central authority. It's fragmented."

"Fragmented?" she echoed.

"Yes," Kaden said firmly. "Different agencies handle different aspects of it—some in the military, some in intelligence agencies, and others in private sectors contracted by the government. They all have pieces of the puzzle, but no single entity seems to have the whole picture."

Natalie stared at him, processing what he was saying. "So, you're saying it's compartmentalized to the point where even the president might not be included in the 'need to know' category?"

"Exactly," Kaden replied. "It's easier to control information that way, to prevent leaks and manage public perception."

She rubbed her temples, feeling a headache coming on. "Someone must be coordinating it, though. I mean, this could be way bigger than I ever thought."

Kaden nodded solemnly. "And that's why we need to work together —combine our resources and knowledge if we're going to get anywhere."

Natalie looked him straight in the eye. "I'm intrigued, Kaden, but don't take this the wrong way. You're the enemy."

Kaden's expression softened. "Touché. But I did buy you lunch, and even you shouldn't let distrust stop you from finding the truth."

Natalie slowly uncrossed her arms and extended her right hand across the table. Kaden grasped it firmly.

Natalie powered on a large-screen iPad and began scrolling with her finger. Obviously, she had something specific she wanted him to see.

Natalie's fingers danced across the iPad screen, pulling up a series of case files. Kaden leaned in, his eyes widening as he took in the information.

"These are some of my top cases I've personally investigated," Natalie explained, her voice low. "None of them made it to the press."

Kaden's brow furrowed as he studied the first file. "Why not? This looks significant."

Natalie swiped to the next case. "They all share striking similarities. Look at the patterns in the sightings, the descriptions of the craft, even the reported behaviors of the objects."

Kaden nodded slowly, his analytical mind already picking up on the connections. "You've applied some sort of analytic filtering process to these, haven't you?"

"Absolutely," Natalie confirmed. "I've ruled out the marginal cases, the clearly delusional witnesses, the publicity seekers, and the outright fakes. What you're seeing here are only the cases that withstood my level of rigorous scientific scrutiny."

She swiped through a few more files, each one causing Kaden's eyebrows to rise higher. "This is... remarkable," he muttered.

"It gets better," Natalie said, a hint of excitement creeping into her voice. "These cases? They've all passed my personal bullshit test. And believe me, after years in the Navy and MUFON, my bullshit detector is finely tuned."

Kaden's eyes darted back and forth, absorbing the details. "The consistency in the reports is undeniable. The same triangular craft design appearing in multiple locations, the similar light patterns, the reported gravitational effects..."

Natalie nodded emphatically. "Exactly. When you apply scientific rigor and filter out the noise, you're left with a small fraction of cases that can't be easily explained away."

She pulled up another file, this one featuring detailed sketches and measurements. "This case in Mississippi in particular stands out. Multiple witnesses, physical trace evidence, and corroborating radar data from a nearby airport."

Kaden's mind took in all the implications. "Natalie, this is groundbreaking. Why haven't you or MUFON gone public with your findings?"

Her expression darkened. "Remember what I said about pressure? It's not just the military. There are forces at work that don't want this information getting out. Even our group feels the pressure, but mainly, my investigation isn't done. Lots of data points but little in the way of correlation."

"I maintain," Kaden began, "that since the pressure is from humans, some of the craft are likely human-made as well. What is your general stance on how much of this is simply experimental aircraft? Human-made top-secret aircraft?"

"Same, up to a point. We've had experimental aircraft testing since the Wright brothers. It's how we learn what works and what doesn't. I personally assume Area 51 and whatever took its place is a joint DARPA, military, and military contractor proving ground for new and possibly exotic technologies.

"Some of what we're seeing is undoubtedly our own craft, and I personally think some of what I encountered were unmanned drones, simply due to the flight characteristics. Like I said, there is a limit to the amount of inertia and G-forces a human body can withstand."

"So, you don't jump automatically to the little green men mindset?"

She refilled her glass from a nearby pitcher and shook her head. "I didn't say whose drones."

"Again? Aliens using drones?" Kaden said questioningly.

She shrugged. "Wouldn't that make sense? That's what we do."

Indeed, it did make sense, and he was liking Natalie's approach even more. He felt he understood why Emily wanted him out here today. He made a decision and unclasped his leather briefcase, sliding a folder across the table to Natalie.

"Are you ready to go down the rabbit hole?" he asked.

She studied the White House seal on the cover. "Don't you mean, do you want to take the red pill?"

Kaden smiled. "I am going to read you in on everything I know. To be fair, I should probably have an NDA from you and a mountain of other paperwork, but I don't think you want that, and I want your opinions." He proceeded to tell her about the Mars stones and everything else he'd learned over the recent months. She then read through all of the investigations one by one.

"What's your take on all this?" he asked as she closed the file.

Natalie stared out the window, her eyes fixed on a point somewhere in the cloudless sky. "We are facing two distinct threats."

"Tell me more," Kaden said.

"The government, agency, Men in Black, or whatever are desperate to keep both the alien connection and whatever secret technologies the country has under very tight control. Personally, I believe they will stop at nothing to control the narrative, and they've been doing a damn good job since at least 1947. Intimidation, coordinated disinformation, and the use of more forceful means when necessary."

"And the second?"

"Aliens," she said. "They are real, and they are stepping up the frequency and scope of their terrestrial encounters."

"Why now? What is the purpose, and what connection do they have to the government cover-up you describe?" Kaden could see the machinery in the girl's mind whirring, attempting to put the desperate pieces into place.

"We're sharks," she said before sipping her coffee again and turning to face him once more.

"Pardon?" he asked in confusion.

"I think they are experimenting on us. The aliens have been tagging us for years, like we do predators such as sharks or bears. They've been doing their own threat assessment. As to the connection to the Men in Black—no idea. As to the why now, I can only think of one reason."

CHAPTER THIRTY

1323 CDT June 1
Northeast Florida, USA

Nancy scrubbed the last plate, the warm, soapy water soothing her tired hands. The kids were glued to the TV, some animated show blaring through the small house. She glanced at the clock, 1:23 PM. Plenty of time before she had to start dinner.

A faint siren in the distance caught her attention. She paused, dish towel in hand, and strained to listen. The sound grew louder, closer, mingling with an odd, high-pitched whistling.

"Is there a fire?" she muttered, turning towards the window. The sky looked normal, blue, and calm.

Before she could ponder further, the ground beneath her heaved violently. Nancy screamed, grabbing the counter for support as dishes rattled and crashed to the floor. Earthquake? Her mind raced. *This is Northern Florida, not an earthquake zone!*

The thought evaporated as the house shook with an intensity that seemed to come from everywhere at once. She stumbled forward, driven by a primal need to reach her children.

"Kids!" she yelled, but her voice was swallowed by a deafening roar.

In an instant, the roof tore away with a sickening crack, like a giant ripping paper. The walls followed, disintegrating in an explosive blast. Nancy was thrown to the floor, shielding her head as debris rained down. Dust and smoke filled the air, choking her lungs.

Coughing violently, she forced herself up, heart pounding. Everything sounded like she was underwater. Her vision dimmed and blurred, but she made out the shapes of her children huddled together by the remains of the upended sofa. She scrambled towards them, every muscle screaming in pain.

"Mommy!" her daughter cried, tears streaming down the child's face.

Nancy pulled them close, covering their heads with her arms. The world around them was chaos, a cacophony of destruction.

"It's okay, it's okay," she whispered, though she didn't believe it herself.

The next blast wave hit them like a freight train, flattening what little remained of their home. The force sent them sprawling, but Nancy held on to her children with every ounce of strength she had left.

And then, as suddenly as it began, the chaos ebbed. The noise receded, leaving an eerie silence in its wake. Nancy cautiously lifted her head, dazed and groggy; she surveyed the wreckage around them.

Nancy Ramesh made the instant decision to flee. She looked up from her living room floor to see ominous dark clouds roiling and folding in on themselves. She ripped a shirt into rags and quickly tied one around each child's nose and mouth, then did the same to her own. She grabbed a few things that she could quickly locate, then pulled both her children up from where they were still hiding.

They heard an explosion, and one of her neighbor's screaming sounded close. Nancy's hands were shaking uncontrollably as she threw random items into a sack. She looked for the refrigerator in hopes of finding bottled water but couldn't even be sure that what she was crawling through was even the kitchen. There was just so much destruction.

Nancy left what remained of her home, her heart racing, with her two young children in tow. Smoke filled the air, and she could smell the burning metal. She couldn't believe it. The airbase where her husband was stationed was destroyed. Massive clouds of dirt and ash still blocked out the sky in that direction.

Whatever had hit the base had been strong enough to wipe out most of Willowcrest, too. The off-base subdivision where many of the officers lived had once been a refuge; now it was rapidly becoming a raging inferno that Nancy and her children had to quickly escape.

She moved through the neighborhood in a daze, her feet crunching on broken glass and debris. Around her, houses lay in shambles, their walls crumbled and roofs caved in. The once quiet streets were now a hellscape of twisted vehicles, burning debris, and shattered concrete.

TJ, her oldest, was saying something, but all Nancy could hear was a roar like a jet engine. "I can't hear you!" she yelled, only hearing the words inside her own head. She reached up and felt a liquid draining from her ear.

Oh, God! I'm deaf.

As they turned a corner, Nancy let out a choked sob. There, lying in the middle of the road, was the body of her neighbor, Mrs. Johnson. The elderly woman's face was frozen in a mask of terror, her body partially crushed beneath a fallen telephone pole. Nancy quickly shielded her children's eyes, but she knew it was too late. They had already seen too much.

Further down the street, Nancy spotted Junior Thompson, the president of the HOA, sprawled across his front lawn. Most of his head was gone, blown clean off by some unseen force. His arms and legs were bent at unnatural angles, and blood pooled beneath his shattered body.

Nancy's mind reeled as she tried to make sense of the devastation around her. What could have caused this? Who would do such a thing? She thought of her husband, stationed at the airbase, and felt a sickening sense of dread wash over her.

As she hurried her children along, Nancy couldn't shake the feeling that this was just the beginning. Whatever had attacked the airbase, whatever had laid waste to her neighborhood, was still out there. And she had no idea how to protect her family from it. She pulled TJ and Lynn close; both were shaking and crying as badly as she was. Who had attacked them? Was it over, or would they come back? She had never been so scared. "Please let it be over," she begged, looking up toward an uncaring sky.

An hour later, TJ asked again, "Are we going to find Dad now?"

His mother was still not sure what he was saying, and even if she had been, she had no idea how to answer the young boy, so she stayed silent. She rubbed the tears and the snot from her face with the ash-covered kitchen towel. They needed water, they needed a place to rest, they needed clean air to breathe, but everywhere around them was simply more destruction.

Hours later, Nancy and the children trudged forward; each step was exhausting in the debris-laden terrain. As the streets of the nearby town of Valparaiso came into view, they were unrecognizable, transformed into a nightmarish wasteland. Asphalt buckled and cracked, resembling the jagged teeth of some monstrous beast. Charred vehicles lay scattered like discarded toys, their metal skeletons twisted and blackened.

Buildings that once stood proud were now reduced to heaps of smoldering rubble. The air was thick with the acrid stench of burning materials and the faint, metallic tang of blood. Nancy's eyes stung, and her throat burned with each breath. She held TJ and Lynn close, their small hands clammy and trembling in her grasp. "My God! How far does all this go?" she asked aloud.

They passed what used to be the grocery store, now a mangled mess of steel beams and shattered glass. A flickering neon 'Open' sign, half-buried in debris, cast an eerie, sputtering glow over the scene. Nancy had to force herself to look away from the scattered remains of shoppers who had been caught in the blast.

Near the intersection where the local diner once stood, she saw a family huddled together, their clothes singed and faces streaked with soot and tears. The father cradled a limp, motionless child in his arms, his eyes hollow and vacant. The mother rocked back and forth, whispering a mantra of disbelief, her voice a haunting echo in the devastation.

Nancy stepped over a fallen lamppost, her foot sinking into a patch of scorched earth. She glanced down and saw a child's bicycle, its frame bent and wheels melted. A sob caught in her throat as she imagined the joy it once brought. Now it was just another piece of wreckage in this landscape of horror.

Ahead, a man stumbled out of the ruins of what used to be the town hall. His clothes were in tatters, and his skin bore the telltale signs of severe burns. He looked at Nancy with wild, desperate eyes, reaching out as if seeking solace. She could offer him none; she was barely holding herself together. She rushed past hurriedly.

Nancy led her children past the shattered remains of a school bus, its bright yellow paint charred and peeling. Inside, the seats were empty, but she could see the faint outlines of where children had apparently been sitting, etched into the dust and grime. She squeezed her eyes shut, trying to block out the horrific images that threatened to overwhelm her.

She kept moving, navigating through the wreckage, her mind numb and body on autopilot. The once-familiar streets were now an alien landscape, devoid of life and hope. As she walked, the only sounds were the distant crackle of flames and the occasional groan of a collapsing structure.

Nancy's heart ached with every step, but she knew she couldn't stop. For TJ, for Lynn, and for herself, she had to keep going. The world had become a nightmare, and all she could do was survive it.

CHAPTER THIRTY-ONE

1313 CDT June 1
30 Miles South of
Campti, Louisiana, USA

Daniel Groves stepped off the helicopter, his boots sinking into the wet Louisiana soil. The sun had just risen, casting long shadows across the small town. He surveyed the scene with a steely gaze, taking in the haphazard arrangement of vehicles and scattered debris. The black-clad tactical team fanned out behind him, moving with practiced precision.

"Alright, let's secure the perimeter," Groves barked. His men nodded, dispersing to their assigned positions.

Groves approached a group of locals standing together near a battered pickup truck. Their faces were pale, eyes wide with fear and confusion. A man in his forties stepped forward, nervously twisting a dingy baseball cap in his hands.

"You must be Mr. Beauchamp," Groves said, glancing at his notes.

"Y-yes, sir," the man stammered. "You the government guys?"

Groves shook his head at the way the man said government. "Yes, you were smart to contact us." He showed the man a badge and ID. The badge was real; nothing else on the identification was, though.

"We didn't know what to do. Sheriff Clanton just said we were nuts and we needed to lay off the hooch. But hell, man, one minute everything was normal, and then... lights, noise... our trucks just died."

Groves nodded curtly. "You're safe now. We need to ask you a few questions about what you saw."

Beauchamp swallowed hard, glancing nervously around the lumber yard. "We were just finishing up for the day," he began, his voice shaky. "It was getting dark, and we were heading back to camp when we heard this humming sound, like nothing I ever heard before. We looked up, and there it was—a big, shiny craft, just floating there in the sky."

Beauchamp paused, his eyes distant as he relived the moment. "It had these lights, all different colors, and it was moving so smooth, like it was gliding on air. Then this... well, this really bright light hit our truck, and the thing quit."

"Tell him about the aliens," a short, Hispanic man said.

Beauchamp turned and glared at the smaller man. "Yeah, then these creatures came out. They didn't walk; they just sorta glided towards us. They had these big, demonic eyes. Solid black. We couldn't move, couldn't do nothing. Next thing I know, there's a bright light, and we're all just standing there, back at camp, like nothing happened, but we all felt it. We knew it was real."

Groves wiped the sweat from his brow and made his notes. "You guys are loggers?"

"Yes, sir, under contract for Trammel and Sons out of Campti."

"How long have you been out here?" Groves wasn't even sure where 'here' was. All these places began to have a certain sameness after a while.

"Little under three months. Got some old-growth timber we're thinning. Hard to get to for the locals. Can't get their skidders in there, so we brought in our floating bog-haulers."

Groves eyed some equipment nearby that looked like a cross between a drag racer and a seriously lifted four-wheel drive truck. The tires were massive with deep horizontal ridges instead of tractor tread.

"You normally stay here or somewhere back in town?"

"Why don't you want to know about them aliens?" one of the other men asked. "They fucked up our trucks. Only one of our phones is working. And Larry swears he was probed...you know...back there in the behind."

Groves ignored the question. While he questioned the witnesses, military transports arrived and began loading up the damaged vehicles. Engineers in hazmat suits scanned the area with Geiger counters, murmuring into their radios.

Over the next several hours, Beauchamp and his men were asked to describe again and again the strange lights in the sky, a sudden surge of heat, and then complete power failure. As they spoke, Groves kept an eye on his team's progress. He made notes occasionally. This part was mostly for show, but occasionally, he learned something interesting.

"We're almost done here," one of his men reported quietly.

Groves pulled out his phone and dialed a secure number. "This is Groves. The scene is contained. We've got fewer than a dozen witnesses."

"Good," a voice on the other end replied. "Make it all disappear."

"Understood," Groves said before ending the call.

He turned back to Beauchamp and the others. "Thank you for your cooperation. We'll need you to come with us for further debriefing."

Beauchamp's eyes widened in alarm. "Where are you taking us?"

"Just standard procedure," Groves said with an almost reassuring tone that did little to mask the underlying command.

The tactical team moved in swiftly, guiding the locals toward waiting transports. No one resisted; fear had already done its job.

As the last of the vehicles were loaded up and began to roll out, Groves took one final look around. The town would wake up soon to find nothing out of place—no signs of any strange events from the night before. The logging camp would be empty, and people would assume the workers had moved on.

As incidents went, this one was easier than most. Being a larger group, that was always cause for concern. That was why he'd brought in the tactical team. Thankfully, this one could be swept away quietly.

Sure, families would ask questions. Accusations might be made, but nothing much would matter. They might have to pay a visit to the local sheriff. Groves checked his notes. Clanton. If the loggers had made an official report, it would need to be erased. The county might get a new patrol car out of this if they played nice. That wasn't his job, though. His talent was containment.

He checked his field report once more before filing it up to D.C.

The men's description of the visitors didn't fit. It was a rough edge in an otherwise smooth case file. Gibson would have questions. Hell, the man always had questions, but this one was a wrap.

Then the Trident team's personal alarms started blaring. "What in the fu..."

"Cover!" Groves yelled. "Everyone take cover."

He had no idea what they were about to face, but the number of alert tones indicated it was imminent. He crouched behind one of the very solid transports. Somewhere high overhead, he heard a sound unlike anything he'd heard before. Not in the military and not in the years working with NovaCore.

It was a sound like a zipper opening onto a giant furnace from hell. It ended in a distant explosion that they felt more than saw.

"Jesus Christ!" one of his men said. "That was fucking close."

Groves stood and tried to peer through the thick pine forest to the southeast, where he could just see the top of a dirty, ugly cloud rising high into the sky. *Someone just got the shit knocked out of them,* he thought.

"Time to get the fuck out of here! Corral them damn Cajuns and head out!" he yelled to his second, who was still staring eastward. Groves waved his hand in the air, signaling the pilot to restart the engines. He was damn sure not sticking around.

Controlled Detonation Flattens 6-Mile Radius in Central Florida — Air Force Denies Involvement

"Eyewitnesses claim a bright flash lit up the sky 'like a second sun' before a blast shattered windows as far north as Tallahassee. The Pentagon says the explosion was part of 'a mishap with routine weapons testing.' Initial reports of civilian casualties are still unconfirmed."

Associated Press Bulletin | Reporter: Malik Chen

CHAPTER THIRTY-TWO

1203 EST June 3
NovaCore Offices
McLean, Virginia, USA

"We are facing more incidents than we have teams to handle right now."

Gibson shook his head. "Daniel, you're a good operator. I would say talented even, but you think small. Use the resources better. Your guys don't need to handle every report of a strange light yourselves. We have assets up and down the line from military to local law enforcement. Prioritize the mission. Our job is mainly to control the narrative, not get bogged down in the logistics."

The operative pursed his lips and was obviously unhappy with that but gave a nod. "Do we have any ideas on why things are..."

"Above your pay grade, Daniel. Off the record, no. It is somewhat unprecedented in the history of the Ground Observers."

"Reports I'm getting from the field," Groves began, "well, sir, they don't fit with our data. The bodies in Chile, for example."

Gibson looked away from the man to study the lights twinkling on the shoreline far away. "Yes, our containment crew was very thorough. The reports have caused some ripples inside the group as well."

"All of them we could identify were missing persons. None were from Chile. Only a few were even South American. Many had been missing for years," Groves said. His words held an edge of tension he was forcing himself to keep muted.

Gibson placed a hand on Groves' arm and turned to face him. "Do you have any idea how many people go missing each year? It's quite astonishing."

"No... no, sir, I don't."

"Six hundred thousand in the U.S. alone. Worldwide, the number is estimated to be over eight million. The oldest individual we identified from Chile was a young woman from China who disappeared nine years ago. In nine years, approximately seventy-two million others disappeared without a trace. Do you really feel like a handful of bodies on a remote mountainside in South America is going to amount to anything?"

"They erased an entire town, though," Groves said. "Even you have to admit that is..." the agent struggled to find the right words, "extreme, sir."

"We can't control what our benefactors do, Groves. Only our species' reactions to it. That is our only real mandate. We don't have to understand, much less agree. They are aliens with very alien agendas. Who the fuck knows what they're doing with these people?

“Now, I want to know about your current assignment. That is my only reason for coming all the way out here tonight. You said you had an update."

Daniel Groves tapped the screen to activate his tablet and handed it to his boss. "Emily Carter's team is in place. She's got some real talent on it, and unfortunately, POTUS's position seems to be shifting from casual interest to genuine curiosity."

"You're getting this from our embedded assets at the White House?"

"We have every meeting space closely monitored, sir. We can listen and watch most conversations during mealtime, but yes, the assets are confirming most of the intel as well."

Gibson scrolled through the tablet, his eyes narrowing as he absorbed the information. He handed it back to Groves with a nod.

"Good work. Now, let's discuss how we're going to handle this situation."

Gibson paced, hands clasped behind his back. "First, we need to discredit Carter's committee. A slow burn should work well. Start with subtle leaks to the press about their very existence, then complete lack of qualifications. Emphasize any past failures or controversies. Make it seem like this is just another government waste of taxpayer money."

Groves nodded, taking mental notes.

"As for the president," Gibson continued, "we'll use our donor network. Have them express concerns about the economic and political impact of entertaining 'alien conspiracy theories.' Remind him how this could affect his legacy and re-election chances."

He stopped pacing and turned to face Groves. "I want detailed dossiers on every committee member. And I mean detailed. Family, friends, finances, skeletons in the closet—everything. We need leverage on all of them."

"Understood, sir," Groves replied. "What about Emily Carter herself?"

Gibson's lips curled into a cold smile. "She's the linchpin. She knows nothing else about her brother's disappearance. And she damn well better not. Do find something... anything we can use to rattle her. I take it she didn't take the bait on Project Sentinel?"

"No, sir, nothing yet," Groves reported.

He paused, considering. "And get me everything on the rest of her family, too. Parents, cousins, old flames—anyone we can potentially use as pressure points."

"So, standard protocols, sir?"

Gibson knew what he was asking... or not asking. "Nothing about this is standard, Groves. This is the White House, and we must never let anyone there learn the truth. They serve the people. But we... we protect the people. Only we know the real threat that has been hanging above our heads for the last seven decades. Your teams must be discreet until you can't be."

"We may have a problem then, sir." Groves flipped the tablet back and showed him two of the committee members again. An older man, distinguished-looking with a neatly trimmed beard, and a somewhat younger woman with red hair, striking features and a determined expression. "These two are believers, zealots. On their own, they mean nothing, but together... well, that's another matter. Also, they seem to be eluding our surveillance. We have yet to get a clear recording of their discussions."

"Paranoid?" Gibson asked.

"You could say that. Both have been burned before, and they are cautious and meticulous. They seem to have an agency escort most of the time as well."

Gibson scrolled through the brief file for each. Taking them out was an option, but since they now had a direct connection to the president, that likely would raise questions. He pointed to one. "Let's go full brushfire on this one. If that doesn't stop the other one, then you know what to do. They are both too smart to be let off the leash."

Groves winced but nodded in agreement. Brushfire would ruin anyone's life. When the Observers wanted to discredit someone completely, Brushfire was how they did it.

"Now tell me what we are doing about that mess down in Florida."

CHAPTER THIRTY-THREE

0903 EST June 3
White House West Wing
Washington, D.C., USA

Emily stood at the head of the conference table, scanning the faces around her. Despite the importance of this meeting, a cloud of frustration hung over her. This was her team—albeit the best she could gather under the circumstances.

Natalie Reeves sat with her arms crossed, eyes sharp and calculating. Next to her, Kaden Trembley leaned forward; as usual, he was already engrossed in some images on his tablet.

Emily cleared her throat to draw their attention. "First off, thank you all for being here. I know how difficult it was to clear your schedules and be here today, as well as meet the commitment I am asking for."

Trent Rogers nodded. "It's disappointing that NASA refused to send anyone," he remarked. "Their stance on UFOs has been frustratingly rigid, especially when some of their own astronauts have been very vocal about their own experiences."

Elena shook her head. "It is telling, though, isn't it? The organization most equipped to handle these phenomena is refusing to engage publicly."

General Taylor folded his hands on the table. "We don't need NASA to move forward. We've got enough talent right here."

"Agreed," Emily said, but she couldn't help feeling a pang of frustration. They had reached out to several other experts and agencies only to be met with refusals or demands that made collaboration impossible. They had even blocked Kaden's recommendation of Nathan Carlson, who was retired from there, although he still frequently consulted with them.

Natalie broke the short silence that followed. "I'm not sure I should even be here. I'm no longer military, and I have no scientific background per se. Also, we—those of us in the UFO hunting community—usually look at the government as the enemy. No offense, Ma'am."

Emily quickly looked around the table again before responding. "You may be our most important addition, Natalie. I trust Dr. Trembley's recommendation, but you also represent the American public. That 65% of the U.S. population who believe that UFOs are real or that extraterrestrial life could exist. I also want you to hold on to that distrust of the government, as I share it as well. We will be trying to get to the bottom of that mess, too."

Emily gave a brief intro of Natalie and Kaden, then continued with other introductions. "We are also delighted to have Alana, who is skilled in environmental science and survival tactics. She has navigated extreme environments including a long duration stay in Antarctica and conducted biological field studies. Her specialty is extremophiles.

“I think we can assume any life form that is not native to this planet could be classified as such an organism. As I understand it, Alana, these organisms thrive in extreme environments that would be inhospitable to most forms of life. These environments can include extreme temperatures, pressures, salinity, acidity, or alkalinity, where conditions are so harsh that life, as we know it, would generally struggle to survive. So how does your knowledge help this group understand the potential threat?"

Alana had a detached way of speaking that was a bit off-putting.

Her looks were more rugged or handsome than pretty, but her voice belied her small stature.

"Extremophiles have adapted to live in very challenging conditions and can be found in a wide range of extreme habitats," she began. "To an alien species, oxygen could be poisonous. Our air pressure at sea level could be too thin. We need to understand what a truly non-human species might be dealing with if they are visiting us. I'm sorry, but I find the likelihood of a typical alien exiting a flying saucer and having a mental session with a human contactee rather absurd. Just them being able to breathe our atmosphere would be incredibly unlikely.

“There is also the possibility that if they are malevolent, they use other extremophiles to help with their invasion—spreading parasites or virus-like microorganisms to kill and decimate the planet before they ever come in person. They could even be those organisms. Perhaps they just hitched a ride on a chunk of asteroids and made it to Earth with no technology at all. One theory is that just such an organism is what kickstarted life on this planet billions of years ago. Others could be deep in the sea or frozen in the Antarctic, waiting for the day they can reanimate and begin reproducing.”

Beside her, Dr. Samuel Greene leaned back in his chair. "Damn, that's some scary stuff."

Kaden had heard Dr. Greene speak several times at conferences but had never met the man. Emily introduced the noted astrophysicist. He was more of a big-picture man, a theorist. He hobnobbed with celebrity cosmologists and theoretical physicists when he wasn't giving lectures.

"I'm not sure what I am doing here, either," he said with a laugh. "I'll bring coffee and taste-test all the pastries."

An older man, Rigel Thomas, looked thoughtful before chiming in. "My best asset is that I solve puzzles. That may not be of any immediate need, but if you find something, bring it to me, and I will give you an answer."

"I do want to be transparent with you all," Emily added, her voice steady but tinged with a hint of frustration. "Our group is smaller than initially planned."

She paused, choosing her words carefully. "We had targeted a larger roster, but circumstances... intervened. Many potential members couldn't commit at this time due to various reasons."

Kaden raised an eyebrow, sensing there was more to the story. Emily caught his look and continued, "I won't sugarcoat it. Some candidates didn't pass the White House vetting process. Others..." She trailed off, then squared her shoulders. "Let's just say their demands were incompatible with our mission."

Colonel Walker leaned forward, his military bearing evident even in the casual setting. "You made the right call, Ms. Carter. We need a cohesive team, not a collection of egos."

Emily nodded appreciatively. "Exactly, Colonel. This committee has no room for prima donnas. We're here to work, to uncover the truth, and to protect our nation—perhaps even our world."

Dr. Elena Schmidt spoke up, her voice quiet but firm. "Quality over quantity. I'd rather work with a small, dedicated team than a large, fractious one."

Kaden was deeply touched to see his friend and former student as part of the team. He knew Elena was still struggling with what happened with her Elysium project and couldn't imagine the strings Emily pulled with ESA to get her here, but she looked good, especially for all she had been through.

"Okay. I had some of our support staff put together a short video. I think it frames up nicely what we are up against." Emily clicked the remote, and the large flat screen came to life.

The black screen offered up a single word: Disclosure. A solid beat of dramatic music introduced a series of fast-cut scenes from interviews, congressional hearings, and what appeared to be found footage. 'A secret program... A hidden truth... Who or what is in our skies, and what does our government really know?'

The following scene cut to video footage from the Phoenix Lights incident—a mass sighting of strange lights in the night sky over Arizona in 1997. Thousands of witnesses, including former Governor Fife Symington, described the event as otherworldly.

The former Arizona Governor appeared in an inset window in the bottom right: "It was enormous, it was silent, and it was hovering right over the city. I am convinced it was from beyond this world."

The Phoenix Lights, witnessed by thousands, was one of the most compelling mass UFO sightings in history. But it was just the beginning.

David Grusch (former U.S. Air Force officer and intelligence official testifying at a congressional hearing): "Absolutely, the U.S. government is in possession of UAPs. We have sources confirming craft of non-human origin."

The next scene cut to a noted senator from Florida: "These objects defy our current understanding of flight, and they're here in our skies."

"From the Tic Tac UFO sighting by Navy pilots in 2004 to the USS Nimitz encounter, where unknown craft outmaneuvered our most advanced jets, the evidence is piling up. Pilots, military officials, and intelligence officers are speaking out."

Commander David Fravor, Navy pilot, USS Nimitz Incident: "It wasn't behaving by the normal laws of physics. This was something not from this world."

The narrator continued: "In a hearing held on July 26, 2023, former U.S. intelligence officer David Grusch dropped bombshells about crash retrieval programs, alien craft, and non-human biologics—statements that shocked Congress and the public alike."

David Grusch: "Biologics came with some of these recoveries."

Congresswoman Nancy Mace from South Carolina asked during the hearing: "Were they human or non-human?"

Grusch very seriously answered: "Non-human."

The screen cut to eerie music and flashing images of UAPs: from the mysterious Phoenix Lights to the Rendlesham Forest Incident in the UK, where military personnel encountered UFOs on the ground—the text said, 'These are not isolated events.'

An unnamed former Pentagon official appeared in silhouette: "Powerful people don't seem to want this information out there. But the public deserves to know.

"As the pressure mounts, Congress and the Pentagon are being forced to address these disturbing revelations. Is the government hiding proof of extraterrestrial technology? Have alien craft really crashed on Earth? And what about the non-human intelligence that might be operating them?" Every voiceover was accompanied by equally dramatic video.

A former senior defense official that everyone in the room recognized said: "This is no longer a question of if these objects are real, but what they are and where they come from."

"But not everyone agrees," the narrator continued. "Despite the seemingly overwhelming evidence, some of the most well-known officials and agencies continue to routinely debunk the UFO narrative."

NASA Administrator: "As of today, NASA has found no credible evidence that suggests we have been visited by extraterrestrial life. We have teams studying UAPs, but most of these events can be explained by natural phenomena or human-made objects."

The video cut to officials from the Department of Defense and Intelligence Agencies. A Senior Defense Intelligence Official: "We remain open to new findings, but at this time, the vast majority of these sightings can be attributed to foreign adversaries, technology testing, or airborne clutter."

Cut to footage of the 2019 Navy 'Pyramid' UFO video: Narrator: "The infamous footage showing pyramid-shaped objects hovering above the USS Russell was cited by UFO enthusiasts as definitive proof. But the Pentagon later declared these were likely drones or unmanned aerial systems."

Cut to a news clip of the infamous Roswell Incident in 1947: "Even the Roswell Incident, one of the most debated cases in UFO lore, was officially explained as a downed weather balloon, part of the top-secret Project Mogul."

Noted UFO Skeptic and Investigator: "Many of these sightings can indeed be explained by atmospheric conditions, camera distortions, or simple misidentifications. People want to believe, but science demands proof, and most of these claims don't hold up under scrutiny."

"The debunkers hold firm—UFOs are just misidentified earthly objects, with natural or human-made origins. But with increasing whistleblower testimonies and mounting pressure for transparency, are they telling the whole truth? What are we not being told?"

Former senior defense official appears on camera: "If these sightings are just atmospheric or man-made objects, why are they appearing in restricted military airspace? Why do we still lack an official explanation for the UAPs documented by our own military and commercial pilots?"

Former Pentagon official: "There's an active effort to dismiss and downplay. But the American people deserve to know if we're dealing with advanced technology beyond our understanding.

"This is our mission—a showdown between those seeking to expose the truth and those insisting there's nothing to reveal."

Final cut to a clip of various members of Congress all saying essentially the same statement: "The American people are being lied to... It's time for the truth." The screen faded to black with a dark gray question mark.

"Whoa!" Natalie said. "Color me impressed." The others nodded in agreement.

Emily smiled and nodded. "I thought this would work better than a PowerPoint." Everyone laughed. "Look, I think this sums up what we are after and what we might be up against. In 2022, Ronald Moultrie, the Under Secretary of Defense for Intelligence and Security, testified before Congress in a historic public hearing on Unidentified Aerial Phenomena. That UAPs pose a potential national security threat, emphasizing the importance of thorough investigation and the collection of reliable data on these phenomena.

"We are committed to a focused effort to determine their origins. UAPs pose potential national security risks and must be investigated, and any threats they pose should be mitigated."

"I respect that man," Emily continued. "Sadly, neither I nor the president feel that this has been done in a more meaningful or comprehensive manner. You, and yes, I am looking at every one of you, I am charging you to do your part to make sure we have looked at this threat seriously. Are we all in agreement on that point?"

Every head nodded in unison.

CHAPTER THIRTY-FOUR

1404 CDT June 4
Beta Site Prepper Enclave
Ozark Mountains, Arkansas, USA

Marcus stared at the phone before putting it away. Leaving yet another voicemail for his old girlfriend hadn't been easy for him. The relationship had been wonderful... right up until it wasn't. Now he'd asked her for help in confirming how bad things were getting, and so far, she hadn't responded.

He also was out on a limb offering her a spot here at Beta Camp. He was unsure on many levels how wise that was. She fit many of the criteria, and he knew she could hold her own in a crisis, but she hadn't been vetted by anyone but him. That went against the bylaws.

He snorted an internal laugh. Who was he kidding? Assuming they weren't all being a little nuts—it didn't look like most of the others were taking the call-out seriously. So far, only about a dozen vehicles were stored under the cliff-side parking area. The last hundred feet of the mountain had been undercut over the eons and now provided perfect shelter for the cars and trucks from anyone looking down. Camo netting helped conceal the vehicles even more.

The parking area itself was almost two miles from the main enclave, but they had side-by-sides and other smaller vehicles to run people back to their cars if needed. Honestly, the setup had been purposefully designed to be inconvenient. Cars were too easy to spot and track to be allowed closer, and none of them intended to stay reliant on their cars to survive. The entire purpose of the enclave was to be self-sustaining.

Marcus nodded to Jack as they surveyed the fortified enclave taking shape before them. Years of meticulous planning and preparation had led to this moment.

"Perimeter defenses look good," Jack reported, checking the monitors. "Motion sensors are all green."

Inside what they jokingly called the war room, a flurry of activity surrounded them as survivalists scurried about, setting up living quarters and checking the compound's outer perimeter. The remote Ozark location provided natural cover, but they had enhanced it with man-made barriers and hidden defensive positions.

In the center of the enclave stood a large underground bunker designed to withstand virtually any attack. It housed the operations center, emergency living spaces, and ample food and water reserves. Solar panels and wind turbines supplied sustainable power. Farther out, most of the members had their own cabins. They didn't look like much from the outside, but all were modern and well-equipped on the inside.

"Any word from Alpha Camp?" Marcus asked, his brow furrowed with concern.

Jack shook his head grimly. "Yeah, sort of. Another group heading down said they heard from a friend down there." The man scrunched up his face like he'd tasted something sour. "Isaac might have... well..." He looked off before continuing. "He might have his hands full. Seems like a lot of the roads are blocked off... something about a huge wildfire. Also, they're encountering a lot of religious groups all claiming God's wrath and shit."

Marcus cursed under his breath. He knew Alpha was more exposed than this camp, but this was just too soon to be having problems.

"Isaac has Luther, and the others should be okay, but..." Jack's voice trailed off, the implications clear.

If it came down to survival, it would inevitably become a bloody affair in these uncertain times. Marcus wished there was another way, but they had to protect what they'd built at all costs.

"Let's double our own outer patrols for the next few nights and keep me updated," Marcus ordered. "If any of those lunatics come sniffing around here, we'll give them an unforgettable lesson in humility. Tell me something, Jack. Do you think we are all nuts?"

"A little bit... probably, Marcus, but being cautious. Being prepared is about survival, not what others may think of us."

"But UFOs? Aliens?"

"Does it make a difference?" Jack said, squatting down and looking up at him. "A threat is a threat, and I choose survival over death or slavery or whatever crap is coming downstream toward us. Hell, you know damn well I love it out here. It's peaceful, beautiful country, clean water, and great resources. Most of you are probably hoping it's a three-month pause on your normal life. Maybe six months. Over time, whether the threat is real or not, we are going to have problems. We could really use someone who has specific knowledge of the threat."

Jack stood and walked off toward the water cisterns. Marcus checked his phone again. "Come on, Natalie," he whispered. He was needing some answers, and she was the only one he knew to call on something like this.

CHAPTER THIRTY-FIVE

2243 EDT June 4
Edisto Beach, South Carolina, USA

The clear night sky was devoid of moonlight. The ocean waves made a gentle sound as the couple lay back on the blanket after yet another round of enthusiastic lovemaking. Sophie's head rested on Matt's chest, both of them breathing deeply, basking in the afterglow.

"That was incredible," Matt said, running his fingers through Sophie's hair.

She smiled, her eyes half-closed. "You always know how to make it special."

They lay there for a while, enjoying the serenity. The night was peaceful, the kind of peace that makes you feel like you're the only two people in the world. The rhythmic sound of the waves lulled them into a comfortable silence.

"Fancy a swim?" Sophie asked suddenly, lifting her head to look at Matt.

Matt chuckled. "Isn't that how that Jaws movie started?"

Sophie laughed, the sound blending with the whispering waves. "Yeah, but I promise not to get eaten by a shark."

He shook his head, still smiling. "Alright, but if I see even one fin, I'm out of there."

They both turned to look toward the ocean horizon. Off to one side, something caught Matt's eye.

"What do you think that is?"

Sophie followed his outstretched hand. "Shrimpers maybe," she said unconvincingly.

Even now it was closer. An unmistakable glow was quickly coming into view, traveling parallel to the South Carolina coastline a mile or two offshore. The eerie bluish light seemed to be moving fast just beneath the surface.

"Man... that is bizarre," Sophie whispered, her eyes wide with awe.

"Yeah," Matt replied, sitting up. "What the hell is it?"

They watched as the light grew closer, revealing its massive size—way bigger than even the largest of cargo ships. It seemed to stretch on forever.

"That thing must be a mile long," Matt said, his voice filled with amazement.

They continued to watch in stunned silence, the reality of the moment sinking in. The glow was mesmerizing, casting an otherworldly hue over the ocean.

"I think we need to go," Matt said, turning away from the ocean to get his things.

Sophie continued to watch transfixed for a moment more, then turned to follow, only... Matt was gone. She looked up and down the beach but saw nothing but shadows in the dim light.

Sophie's heart raced as she scanned the empty beach. "Matt? This isn't funny!" Her voice cracked with fear. "Come on, cut it out!"

Trembling, she rushed to the blanket, fumbling to pull on her shorts and t-shirt. As she straightened up, a chill ran down her spine. She instantly knew she wasn't alone.

Slowly, Sophie turned. A tall, thin figure loomed between her and the glowing craft now just offshore. Her breath caught in her throat.

The air grew thick, heavy with an otherworldly presence. Sophie's limbs felt leaden, her movements sluggish as if time itself had slowed. A high-pitched whine filled her ears, drowning out the rhythmic sound of the waves.

Suddenly, a brilliant, white light engulfed her. Sophie tried to scream, but no sound came out. Her body lifted off the ground, suspended in midair. Panic gripped her as she realized she had no control over her movements.

The world around her blurred and distorted. Sophie's vision tunneled, and she felt herself being pulled towards the towering shadow. The last thing she saw was the endless expanse of the night sky before everything went black.

When Sophie regained consciousness, she found herself in a sterile, white room. Strange symbols adorned the walls, pulsing with an eerie light. She tried to move, but her body wouldn't respond. Terror seized her as she realized she was paralyzed, lying on a cold, metallic surface.

More of the tall, thin figures with large, almond-shaped eyes surrounded her. Their skin was a pale color with strange black markings, and they moved with an unnatural fluidity. Sophie's mind reeled, unable to process what she was seeing.

One of the beings approached, holding a long, needle-like instrument. Sophie's heart pounded in her chest as it drew closer. She wanted to scream, to run, to do anything, but she remained frozen, helpless as the creature loomed over her.

The needle-like instrument pierced Sophie's skin, sending a searing pain through her body. She wanted to scream, to thrash, to fight back, but her muscles remained locked in place, unresponsive to her desperate commands.

In her mind, Sophie cried out for Matt, then her mom... for anyone to save her from this nightmare. But deep down, she knew no one could hear her silent pleas. She was utterly alone, at the mercy of these otherworldly beings.

The creatures moved around her, their long, spindly fingers probing and prodding her flesh. Sophie felt the cold touch of metal against her skin as they attached strange devices to her temples, chest, and abdomen. The devices hummed to life, sending pulsing jolts of energy coursing through her body.

Images flashed before Sophie's eyes, memories she had long

forgotten mixed with visions of worlds she had never seen. She saw towering cities of glass and metal, vast landscapes of red sand and twin suns, and the endless expanse of space dotted with countless stars.

The pain intensified as the beings continued their experiments. Sophie felt like her body was being torn apart, piece by piece, only to be put back together again in ways that defied nature. Her mind reeled, struggling to make sense of the alien sensations assaulting her senses.

Time lost all meaning in this sterile, white prison. Sophie had no way of knowing how long she had been there, subjected to the relentless probing and prodding of her captors. Minutes, hours, days—it all blurred together in an endless cycle of agony and terror.

Through the haze of pain, Sophie's imprisoned thoughts drifted to Matt. Was he somewhere in this place? Was this the underwater ship they'd been watching? Was he enduring the same horrors? Or had he escaped, left to wonder what had become of her? The uncertainty was almost as unbearable as the physical torment.

As the experiments continued, Sophie felt herself slipping away, her mind retreating to the deepest recesses of her consciousness in a desperate attempt to escape the unimaginable reality of her situation. She clung to the memories of her life before, to the love she shared with Matt, as the last vestiges of her humanity were stripped away by the relentless alien probing.

In the absolute depths of her despair, Sophie prayed for an end to the nightmare, for the sweet release of oblivion. But even that small mercy seemed beyond reach in this hellish realm of cold, clinical cruelty.

CHAPTER THIRTY-SIX

1328 EDT June 5
Crestview, Florida, USA

'Breaking News!' The red graphic blazed across the screen, and a pretty female reporter began her broadcast.

"Behind me, you can see a massive fire raging, and military officials are telling us an incident has occurred on the southern side of Eglin Air Force Base in Okaloosa County. All roads in the area are closed to thru traffic, including the very popular Highway 285. Residents we have managed to speak with said they heard a loud explosion right before followed by a small earthquake. We know they store a large number of combat ordnances for the 33rd Fighter Wing as well as the 919th Special Operations Wing and others. We have unconfirmed statements of casualties, but so far, no indication that this might have been a terrorist attack."

The voice-over from the male reporter on the anchor desk chimed in with a note of well-crafted concern. "Allison, any truth to some of the rumors we are hearing that the U.S. Navy has put a blockade offshore to prevent visitors anywhere near the area?"

"Yes, Bill, we've heard some of the same suggestions, and a Naval spokesperson said there were some unrelated fleet maneuvers in the area as part of a readiness drill, but no blockade. It seems unlikely, as Eglin is over eight miles from the ocean. Still, it could be a precautionary step."

Back in the news studio, they showed archived footage of past forest fires as well as video images of large C-130s landing at one of Eglin's airfields.

Bill nodded gravely, his practiced anchorman demeanor on full display. "Thank you, Allison. For our viewers who may not be familiar with Eglin Air Force Base, it's one of the largest military installations in the world, covering over 460,000 acres in the Florida Panhandle. It's been a crucial testing ground for the Air Force since World War II."

He paused, allowing the gravity of the situation to sink in. "Eglin is known for its extensive bombing and gunnery ranges. In fact, it was the site where the GBU-43B Massive Ordnance Air Blast, or MOAB, was tested back in 2003. That's the largest non-nuclear bomb in the U.S. arsenal."

Bill's expression softened slightly. "However, despite the alarming visuals, we've received unofficial word from military personnel that this incident appears to be the result of a controlled detonation gone awry. The unnamed source suggested they were apparently conducting routine disposal of outdated munitions when an unexpected chain reaction occurred."

He turned to face a different camera. "While the fire looks dramatic, authorities assure us that it's largely contained to an unpopulated area of the base. No civilian casualties have been reported, and only minor injuries to personnel have been confirmed so far.

"The base commander, Colonel Diana Hawkins, issued a statement moments ago, saying, 'We understand the public's concern, but I want to assure everyone that this situation is under control. Our emergency response teams are working tirelessly to extinguish the fire, and we expect to have it fully contained within the next twenty-four hours.'"

Bill's mechanical tone became reassuring. "Officials say the EPA has been notified and will be monitoring air quality in the surrounding areas, but initial reports suggest no immediate danger to nearby communities. Local residents are advised to stay indoors if they have respiratory issues, but no evacuations have been ordered at this time.

"In other news, a powerful rogue wave struck near Cancun, Mexico, inundating the neighboring town of Merida. 'Waves like this are uncommon but not unheard of,' the local mayor said. There were no indications of injuries or casualties, and it looks like it is back to calm seas and sunshine at the neighboring resorts. With that, let's turn it over to our storm-center desk to check out our own weather for this coming weekend. Carmen, how are we looking?"

Within hours, the news had spread to the national press with the headline 'Massive Wildfire Threatens Military Base.' The normal cast of villains, including climate change, drought, and land management mistakes, was trotted out for the masses to digest. To the tens of thousands fighting to make their way out of the impact zone, this was of little comfort. In fact, the amount of news getting into the disaster area was only slightly better than the meager amount of aid that was coming in, primarily from Navy ships fifteen miles offshore.

CHAPTER THIRTY-SEVEN

1455 CDT June 5
Northeast Florida, USA

The road they were on seemed to go on forever. The Florida scrub pines offered little in the way of shade, but at least they were seeing signs of life again. TJ and Lynn were taking turns riding in the old wagon Nancy had found near a destroyed mobile home. Occasionally, others would silently join their sad pilgrimage for a while, then they would drift away, leaving them alone again.

Nancy trudged along the desolate road, her feet aching with every step. TJ and Lynn followed close behind, their faces etched with exhaustion and fear. The sun beat down mercilessly, making their thirst even more unbearable. They had been walking for hours, searching for any sign of help, water, or food, but the landscape remained barren and unforgiving.

TJ, being the older of the two, tried to be brave for his little sister. He held Lynn's hand tightly, offering what little comfort he could. Nancy's heart broke as she watched her children suffer, knowing that she had to stay strong for them. She fought back the tears that threatened to spill, focusing instead on the task at hand.

As they walked, Nancy's mind raced with questions. What had

happened to their home? Who had attacked the airbase? Was it a nuclear strike? The thought made her shudder. She knew that if it was, their chances of survival were slim. But she couldn't dwell on that now. Her priority was finding help for her family.

Hours passed, and the sun began to set. Nancy knew they couldn't keep going much longer. TJ and Lynn were on the verge of collapse, their small bodies pushed to the limit. Just as she was about to give up hope, Nancy spotted a small stream in the distance. Her heart leaped with relief.

"Look, kids! Water!" she exclaimed, pointing toward the stream.

TJ and Lynn's faces lit up, and they quickened their pace. As they approached the stream, Nancy couldn't help but think of her husband. He had always been their protector, their rock. But now, deep down, she knew he was gone. The realization hit her like a ton of bricks, and she struggled to keep her composure.

The water might be bad; it certainly didn't smell good, but they were out of options. They'd passed a few convenience stores—or the ruins of them, at least. Most had already been picked clean by other survivors. Of the few people they saw, no one was rioting or shouting or even crying.

Nancy knelt down by the stream, cupping her hands to bring the cool water to her lips. TJ and Lynn did the same, drinking greedily. For a moment, they forgot about their troubles and savored the momentary relief that the water brought.

But as the sun dipped below the horizon, Nancy knew they couldn't stay there. They needed to find shelter for the night. It seemed inconceivable that they were in essentially no-man's land, a section of the Florida panhandle with virtually no people, few stores... really nothing other than some logging companies' temporary camps. Her babies were exhausted, and so was she. Behind them, smoke still rose from where the airbase had been. She wasn't good at gauging distance but knew they had walked all day.

As night fell, Nancy stumbled upon a small metal shack near the train tracks, its rusted exterior offering a glimmer of hope in the desolate landscape. The oppressive heat and humidity clung to her skin, making every breath a struggle. Sweat poured down her face, stinging her eyes and mixing with the tears she fought to hold back.

TJ and Lynn followed close behind, their small bodies struggled to keep up. Their skin, once fair and smooth, was now angry and red, blistered from the unrelenting sun. They whimpered softly, their hunger and pain evident in every step.

As they approached the shack, Nancy's heart sank. It was barely big enough for the three of them, and the interior was just as unforgiving as the world outside. The metal walls radiated heat, making the air inside stifling and unbearable.

Still, she ushered her children inside, trying to create a makeshift bed out of the few rags and pieces of cardboard she could find. Her children curled up together, their eyes heavy with exhaustion and despair.

Nancy sat down beside them, her mind racing with doubts. She had thought leaving Willowcrest was their only chance at survival, but now she wasn't so sure. They hadn't seen a single working car all day, and the only other humans they'd encountered had long since abandoned the road for God knows where.

The weight of her decisions pressed down on her, suffocating her with guilt and fear. What if she had made the wrong choice? What if staying in Willowcrest would have been safer? Maybe she should have gone to look for her husband. She had no way of knowing, and the uncertainty was tearing her apart.

As the night wore on, Nancy held her children close, trying to provide what little comfort she could. But even as she whispered reassurances and stroked their hair, she couldn't shake the feeling that she had failed them. She'd never felt so utterly alone or this afraid. Still, she wanted to appear strong for her babies... not that it mattered. How long would she be able to protect them from the truth?

CHAPTER THIRTY-EIGHT

1508 EDT June 7
White House
Washington, D.C., USA

Emily rubbed her eyes in frustration. Files and documents were scattered across her desk. Most had nothing to do with the UFO committee, but that was what was occupying her thoughts right now. She was spending countless hours digging into the SCET's investigations, and the deeper she went, the more the pattern of misdirection became apparent.

First Kaden, and then Dr. Greene had both privately voiced very similar concerns that the government would suppress or contaminate any findings the task force came up with.

She needed a second opinion. Picking up her phone, she dialed Trent's number. The intelligence agent was turning into a good sounding board for her theories.

"Hey, Emily," Trent answered after a few rings. "What's up?"

"Trent, are you in the building? I need to talk to you about a few things," she said.

Trent sounded upbeat. "Sure, I'll be over in a few minutes."

"So what's up?" he said, coming in the door with two cups of coffee.

"Oh, thank you," Emily said, taking the cup. "I just want to run a few incidents by you."

"For the committee?"

"Oh... um, yes," she said, taking a sip. She sometimes forgot they both had other duties in this grand palace. "I need your general opinion as far as your working knowledge within the intel community." She saw his left eyebrow arch. "Nothing specific. Not going to ask you about protocols or the phone in your shoe. No secret squirrel stuff.

"But look at Project Blue Book. It appeared serious, but that group was assembled really just to debunk credible sightings. Or the O'Hare incident—November 7, 2006, when multiple United Airlines employees, including pilots and ground staff, reported seeing a metallic, disc-shaped object hovering over Gate C17 at Chicago O'Hare International Airport.

“Listen to this. ‘Witnesses described the object as silent, stationary for several minutes, before it suddenly shot upwards at an incredible speed, punching a hole through the cloud cover. The Federal Aviation Administration totally dismissed the sighting, attributing it to a weather phenomenon, but the witnesses were adamant that what they saw was not an airplane or a natural occurrence. Despite its significance, no official investigation was conducted, adding to the speculation and mystery surrounding the event.’

“Here's another and another." Emily flipped reports out until she had a small stack. "These are just the public ones; if we get into the classified encounters, that stack would fill my office."

"Look here," she said, pulling out a photocopy of a newspaper article. "Stephenville, Texas. 2008. Ever heard of that one?"

Trent raised his eyebrow. “This is just the public stuff? Looks like the syllabus for a college course in ‘Things That Shouldn’t Exist.’” He shook his head.

"True," she said derisively. "Read here. Dozens of residents, including a local pilot, observed large, silent lights moving at high speeds in the sky. Witnesses described the object as enormous, sometimes over a mile wide, and displaying unusual light patterns. Initially, the U.S. Air Force denied any military activity but later did admit that F-16 jets were conducting training exercises in the area. Radar data obtained later supported the presence of unidentified objects. It briefly did get a good amount of media coverage, but no one sent in any type of officials to investigate. Our airspace, Middle America, Air Force jets in pursuit, and yet it's just ignored?"

"I get it, a lot of misdirection," Trent said, "but what are you asking of me?"

"Not just misdirection. A complete and systematic program of misinformation, coercion, and outright lies. Just like in 2017 when the Pentagon acknowledged the existence of the Advanced Aerospace Threat Identification Program, more often called AATIP, it was seen as a step toward transparency. However, since then, despite loads of additional evidence and videos being released, there has been a pattern of conflicting information, such as the Pentagon initially acknowledging UAPs but then downplaying their significance while offering no clear conclusions.

"I'm sorry, but this back-and-forth mixture of confirmation and ambiguity has led me to believe that the government or military or someone in charge is indeed deliberately creating confusion to prevent any coherent understanding of UFOs while acknowledging them enough to seem transparent. The optics are that the government is on the case, but the reality is the exact opposite."

Emily set her coffee cup down and tapped a slender finger on the stack of reports. "I want to know, before we go any further, are we the bad guys?" Lowering her voice, she continued, "I'm starting to think there's a deliberate effort to misdirect us in our investigations. Could the government, military, or our intel community do that to us, a presidential task force, and could they have continued to do it successfully for, oh... say, the past seven decades?"

Trent paused for a moment before responding. "I've seen my fair share of cover-ups, but this would require a level of coordination that's nearly impossible. Just think about it: coordinating between military and civilian authorities on this scale? It's not just improbable; it's practically impossible without someone slipping up. None of the cases you mention even involve the same government or military departments."

"That's what makes it so baffling," Emily replied. "The more I dig, the more I find conflicting narratives and disinformation. It's like they're playing a game of smoke and mirrors."

"You've got a point," Trent conceded. "But who... or why would they go through all this trouble? What's the endgame?"

Emily leaned forward, tapping a file on her desk. "Misdirection. They steer public attention away from the truth by creating false narratives, confusion, and doubt."

"So, like you say, they're acknowledging just enough to seem credible while they're keeping us all in the dark?" Trent asked.

"Exactly," Emily said. "It's like they're giving us breadcrumbs but leading us away from the real story."

"There is one entity that could manipulate a lie this big," Trent said. "Someone with considerable influence over all these agencies and military commands."

They both looked up in the general direction of the president's executive residence. Emily shook her head.

"It crossed my mind too, but no. For one thing, he isn't that smart, and I don't mean that the way it sounds. The fact is, I don't think anyone who has ever held that office would have been smart enough to come up with this level of obfuscation. Secondly, politicians simply can't keep anything that secret. Someone would know. I would know."

"I know you're close, so I would accept that, but it leaves really no one on the suspect list for exactly the points I mentioned," Trent said.

"Hypothetically, if you were that person or persons, how would you wield that influence? How would you keep the lid on the biggest secret the world has ever known?" Emily asked.

Trent exhaled sharply. "That's a damn good question to ask." He sipped his coffee while formulating a response.

"First, I imagine the people would actively monitor all key channels —air traffic control, intelligence feeds, and civilian reports—to detect an anomaly before it becomes public knowledge. Once alerted to a potential UFO sighting, their priority would be dispatching field agents to the location under the guise of federal or military personnel, arriving faster than any local authorities or media. Their immediate task would be to assess the credibility of the sighting, verifying whether the event involved extraterrestrial activity, an experimental aircraft, or a false alarm.

"Next, I'd guess that if the event is confirmed, the team would secure the area by establishing a perimeter, either by restricting civilian access under the pretense of a government or military investigation or by issuing vague safety concerns like hazardous materials. They would have to work fast to remove or maybe just tamper with any physical evidence, including UFO debris or biological material. High-priority items would be transported to a secure facility for further study or destruction, while more common items, like scorch marks or landing sites, would be erased or altered to appear as natural phenomena.

"Nowadays, they would also need to confiscate or erase any recorded data, seizing video footage, photos, or sensor readings from witnesses or surveillance equipment. They might use legal cover, citing national security concerns, or, in extreme cases, erase digital evidence remotely through hacking or electromagnetic pulses. And yes, I do know we have the technical ability to do that.

"To handle witnesses, they would need to deploy teams to interrogate and debrief anyone who encountered the event, gauging the reliability of their accounts. Witnesses might be coerced into silence using non-disclosure agreements, legal threats, or financial incentives. If necessary, witnesses would be discredited publicly by planting stories that undermine their credibility, associating them with conspiracy theorists or fringe groups. I also have to assume in the most critical cases, witnesses would be detained or possibly even killed to keep the secret.

"Finally, I think the so-called Men in Black would occasionally have to implement a media disinformation campaign, flooding the news with alternate explanations—like drones, weather phenomena, or aircraft malfunctions—to dilute the UFO sighting's significance. They might also leak false stories that lead the public down confusing or conflicting paths, ensuring that any lingering belief in the sighting becomes mired in doubt, skepticism, or outright disbelief.

"In the end, the encounter would be buried under layers of doubt, legal obfuscation, and misdirection, leaving the public with only vague rumors while the truth remains carefully locked away."

Emily nodded. "Very thorough case study, Agent Rogers. Shame you've never given this topic any real thought," she said with a note of sarcasm. "Seriously, though, much of that rings suspiciously close to what all these reports say."

"I have given it a lot of thought, and the agency trains us to think along these lines. It's not the answer that matters, but why the answer is given. The truth is often layers deep, and if you are simply looking superficially, like many of our politicians, media, and even law enforcement do, it is simply lazy. There are ways of taking advantage of that tendency in order to promote the perception you prefer."

Emily considered his words and found that indeed, the pattern was there as plain as day. What she didn't have was a smoking gun. Nothing that pointed at anyone in a position to have that type of power.

"We're looking for a Dr. No or Ernst Blofeld," Emily muttered, unsure if the young agent would get the old James Bond reference.

"Spectre," he said, surprising her. "It would take a group. Not just an individual. Probably a fairly large group."

"Agreed," Emily said. "This is what I want you focusing on—the how and the who might have the means to do this. Also, it seems our Ms. Reeves might be the most helpful and the most at risk since she already feels that we, the government, are the enemy. Keep a close watch on her."

"Alright," Trent said with a note of resolve in his voice. "But you also be careful, Emily. If there is a cover-up this extensive, there are powerful people who won't take kindly to us poking around."

Emily nodded. "I know. But we can't let SCET become just another footnote in a long history of government disclosures that turn out to be just another vehicle for covering up the facts."

CHAPTER THIRTY-NINE

1133 EDT June 7
Reston, Virginia, USA

Laura Bennett pulled into the corporate office park, her eyes scanning the gleaming glass and steel buildings. It wasn't the typical location for a lead on a UFO story, but she'd learned to follow every thread, no matter how unlikely.

She parked her car and strode toward the entrance, her heels clicking against the pavement. As she approached, a sleek, black sedan caught her eye. There, in the back window, was an emblem she'd seen before—a gold trident on a charcoal gray rectangle.

Laura discreetly snapped a picture with her phone. She'd already encountered that symbol in her research, but the connection remained elusive. For appearances' sake, she stopped and scrolled the screen of her iPhone, then backed up to look at the address on the sign. Pocketing her phone, she entered the building, appearing unsure if she was in the right place.

At the reception desk, a polished woman greeted her with a practiced smile. "Welcome to Alcon Industries. How may I assist you?"

Laura returned the smile, masking her suspicion. "I'm Laura Bennett, a journalist. I was told your company does business with the federal government." That line usually got a reaction one way or the other. "My column is a bit of a watchdog for the taxpayers. I was hoping to learn more about what your company does."

The receptionist's expression flickered, her eyes hardening. "I'm sorry, Ms. Bennett, but we don't often discuss details of our business with the media. If you'd like, I can provide you with our standard press release or give you the contact email for our media representatives."

Laura leaned forward, her gaze intense. "I'm not interested in a press release. I'm investigating a story, and I believe your company might be involved."

The receptionist's smile turned brittle. "As I said, we don't discuss our business. I'm sorry, but I'm going to have to ask you to leave." The woman never stopped smiling, although her words were icy cold.

Laura hesitated, weighing her options. She could push harder, but risking getting thrown out would only draw unwanted attention. She needed to be smart about this.

With a curt nod, Laura turned and walked out, her eyes taking in every detail. The receptionist's defensive attitude only fueled her suspicions. Alcon Industries was not the name her source had given her, nor did it appear on any of the signage.

As she climbed into her car, Laura pulled out her phone and studied the picture of the gold trident emblem. It was a small clue, but it was a start. She put the car in drive and cruised the parking lot, looking to see if any other cars had the same badging.

Three did, and she snapped pictures of each. Toward the rear of the main complex, she saw a secured area with additional vehicles—black suburbans, vans, and even a few tractor trailers. The yard was guarded by a security fence and numerous solid-looking guards who definitely appeared up for the job. She was not the type of journalist to break the law or go sneaking in after hours. She could pay people to do that or simply find another way.

"You understand what I want—right?"

"Yeah, yeah," the teen boy said a few hours later. Amazing what fifty bucks and a little time searching the internet could do.

He pulled the small drone from its padded case and flipped out the four rotors. He snapped the tiny GoPro camera into place like he had done it a million times.

"They won't be able to hear you?" Laura asked.

"Does it matter? Geez, lady, the sky's are free. This is America." They were positioned a mile from the industrial park, far enough that the kid felt confident no one could track the small drone. The footage would be routed directly to her iCloud account, so she wasn't even going to wait for the boy to retrieve his drone.

"The other fifty," he said before launching. She handed him the cash.

They watched the monitor as the kid expertly flew the drone low to the ground, weaving around numerous buildings until it reached the secure yard behind Alcon. There, he hovered over the top of a semi-truck as it wound its way into the parking area. The drone footage was crystal clear, capturing every detail in high resolution.

At first, no one seemed to notice the small device buzzing overhead. A passing train nearby offered enough noise cover that they risked moving closer. Laura leaned in, her eyes glued to the screen.

"Holy shit," she muttered.

The teen's eyes widened. "What is it?"

Laura pointed to a group of men in black-clad tactical gear racing toward two of the SUVs. They moved with military precision, their automatic weapons at the ready.

"Whoa," the teen exclaimed. "That looks like something out of 'Call of Duty' or something."

Laura considered the possibilities. What were heavily armed men doing at a supposed tech company office? She watched as the SUVs peeled out of the lot, tires squealing.

Suddenly, the image on the screen jerked wildly. The teen swore under his breath.

"What's happening?" Laura demanded.

"They spotted us," he said, his fingers dancing over the controls. "I'm trying to—"

The screen went black.

"Uh-oh."

Laura and the teen bolted for her car, hearts pounding. As they scrambled inside, the boy's face was a mask of anger.

"My drone! That thing cost me a fortune," he whined, slamming the passenger door.

Laura gunned the engine, tires squealing as she peeled out of their hiding spot. "Relax, we're far enough away," she said, eyes flicking to the rear-view mirror. "Can they track that back to you?" She knew little of the FAA registration process.

The teen shook his head, some of the tension leaving his shoulders. "Oh, hell no, bought it off the gray market. No regs."

Laura nodded, her mind already racing to analyze the footage they'd captured. She needed to get somewhere safe to review it properly.

"Look, I need that footage," she said, glancing at the sullen teen. "How much for the drone?"

His eyes lit up, sensing an opportunity. "It was a custom job. At least a grand."

Laura snorted. "Dream on, kid. I'll give you another two hundred."

"Four hundred," he countered quickly. "And that's a steal."

Laura weighed her options. The footage could be crucial to her investigation, and she didn't need an angry teenager causing problems.

"Fine," she sighed, reaching for her wallet. "Four hundred, but that's it."

The teen grinned, practically bouncing in his seat as Laura counted out the bills. She handed them over, shaking her head at his eagerness.

"We good?" she asked.

He nodded, stuffing the cash into his pocket. "Yeah, we're good. You got some crazy footage there, lady. Hope it was worth it."

Laura's expression hardened. "Oh, it was. Now, get home before anyone starts asking questions."

CHAPTER FORTY

0851 PDT June 9
Mt. Wilson Observatory
Pasadena, California, U.S.

"Doctor Cho?" The young woman's voice grated on his nerves like fingernails on a chalkboard, and Cho struggled to contain his aggravation.

"What is it?" he snapped.

The younger astronomer ignored the man's harsh tone. "The alignment seems off again. This time by fifty arcseconds."

"That's ridiculous," Cho shouted angrily. "No collimation error would be that large unless we've had an earthquake or someone fed the target coordinates incorrectly."

The young woman looked around at the other workstations for support, but none of her colleagues seemed willing to face the irascible older man with her. "No, sir, I double-checked Aaron's entries myself, and Coleen and Yoshi verified the target RA and Dec for the night's observations."

"Shit," Cho moaned. His time on the CHARA Array was very

limited, and now he was losing a second night to the damned misalignment.

"Yoshi, see if you can confirm with Flagstaff. Maybe we have an atmospheric anomaly. If they pretend not to hear us, bribe them with scotch. Worked last time."

The man nodded but looked doubtful. The Navy Precision Optical Interferometer near Flagstaff, Arizona, NPOI, also used an array of telescopes to perform optical interferometry, but they didn't often share information. The whole situation was ridiculous, as both sites were part of a global team working on spotting asteroids potentially heading toward Earth. Once they got closer, they were reclassified as Near-Earth Objects.

NEOs, or more often NEAs (Near-Earth Asteroids), are asteroids whose paths bring them close to Earth's orbit. They are classified into different groups, such as Atira asteroids when their tracks are entirely within Earth's orbit and Amor asteroids for objects between Earth and Mars. A few others, like Apollo and Aten asteroids, cross Earth's orbit only rarely.

The CHARA Array on Mount Wilson Observatory in California consists of six telescopes working together to perform observations. This array provides extremely high-resolution images by combining the light from multiple telescopes.

Cho studied the night's imaging. When searching for NEOs, his team employed a systematic approach using multiple images of the same sky region taken at different times.

First, they captured a series of images over several hours or nights, ensuring they had a consistent view of the area. By aligning these images so that the background stars and galaxies remained fixed, any movement they could detect could be attributed to the objects themselves.

Then they compared those aligned images using sophisticated software and manual inspection by Aaron and Tracey to identify objects that shifted positions. These moving objects were tracked, and their motion was measured to calculate their orbits.

If an object's orbit brings it within 1.3 astronomical units of the Sun, it is classified as a Near-Earth Object. This meticulous process of identifying and tracking moving objects against a relatively stationary background is crucial for monitoring potential threats and gaining a better understanding of our cosmic neighborhood.

Cho knew he was demanding; in fact, he knew he was an asshole, but no one argued with his results. They didn't have to like him to see his brilliance. He studied the images on the large display screens, rapidly switching between baseline images from previous nights and then back to tonight. The aberration had shown up three days ago and was back again tonight—distinct clusters of stars and stellar objects that were clear and sharp in one view and blurry a short time later.

It seemed likely that Tracey was correct: at least one of the optical telescopes was misaligned, but if so, why was it not consistent? This array didn't use cryogenic cooling like some of the infrared scopes did; in those, temperature variations could potentially cause a similar problem, one that would occur infrequently and then correct itself.

"You see something?" Aaron asked.

Cho had his finger on the display near one of the tiny dots of light and, with his other hand, began flipping the images on the screens rapidly. Focusing on a single object at a time, he could see it move out of focus and then back into clarity.

"Yes, there is an issue, but it is not with the array."

His entire team looked back at him in confusion.

They had been observing a small patch of sky in the general vicinity of the Taurus constellation. In fact, CHARA could achieve resolutions as fine as 0.2 milliseconds. Cho knew the detail he was observing was like looking at a single hair strand held at arm's length.

He stayed focused on the live feed, which showed the same blurring. "Recalibrate and focus the array on backup targets Echo and then Delta."

The collective groan was unsurprising, as this would entail a great deal of work. "We must determine whether this aberration is localized or a widespread issue. To verify this, we must refocus our observations on different areas of space. This will help us know with certainty whether the blurring phenomenon is unique to the initial patch or indicative of a broader problem."

Cho's team of young astronomers got busy while he went back to looking at the blurred images from Taurus. External factors could cause blurring, including gravitational lensing and interstellar medium variations, which is the matter that exists in the space between stars within a galaxy. The ISM consists mostly of hydrogen and helium, dust, cosmic rays, and magnetic fields. These variations can affect the propagation of light and other electromagnetic radiation traveling through space. He knew that shouldn't be a significant factor with observations within our own solar system, though.

What really bothered him was why only some of the objects blurred while others did not.

CHAPTER FORTY-ONE

0645 EDT June 11
Northeast Florida, USA

Nancy crouched in the dim light of the metal shack, trying to make herself comfortable on the hard dirt floor. TJ and Lynn lay beside her, their small bodies exhausted from another day's ordeal. She needed to relieve herself but didn't want to wake the children. Gathering her courage, she slipped out of the shack, the smoky fog swirling around her like ghostly tendrils.

The early morning air felt cool against her skin, a stark contrast to the oppressive heat of the day. She moved a few paces from the shack, scanning the desolate landscape for any signs of danger. As she began to unbutton her jeans, she sensed something—a presence.

She turned slowly, her heart pounding. There, standing motionless in the fog, was a vague shadow. A shadow that was slowly resolving into a man. He was tall and broad-shouldered, his silhouette towering over the sparse landscape. The fog parted enough for her to see his face: a large and intimidating Black man with eyes that seemed to pierce through the haze.

Panic gripped her. She froze, her mind fearing the worst. Friend or foe? He stood still, almost statuesque, not making any move toward her.

"What do you want?" she managed to whisper, her voice trembling. The man remained silent, his expression unreadable in the dim pre-dawn light.

Nancy's breath quickened. She took a cautious step back, keeping her eyes locked on him. He didn't move, didn't speak. She felt the urge to scream but knew it might wake the kids, drawing attention she didn't want.

"Who are you?" she asked, louder this time, hoping for a response. Again, nothing. The man's presence alone was enough to send shivers down her spine.

She backed up further, nearly tripping over a rock. The tin shack seemed miles away now, the safety of its flimsy walls too distant to reach. Her heart pounded louder, a drumbeat of fear echoing in her chest. She considered running, but her legs felt like lead.

In a moment of desperate resolve, she clenched her fists and steadied her voice. "I have kids in there," she said louder, trying to sound braver than she felt. "If you mean us harm, I won't let you."

The man did move, just a slight tilt of his head. It was enough to send a fresh wave of terror through Nancy. She turned on her heel and bolted back to the shack, her mind screaming at her to get inside and lock the door.

Nancy was frozen with fear. Her body shook uncontrollably, and she was covered in an icy cold sweat. At any moment, she expected the big man to burst through the flimsy door, but that didn't happen. Her kids kept sleeping, the shafts of light cutting through the shack's walls brightened, and slowly she realized she had relieved herself after all. The smell was the last thing she needed.

Then the odor of wood smoke overwhelmed even her own stink. It was apparent the attack had triggered numerous fires in the dry Florida heat, but this seemed closer... different.

Nancy's heart pounded in her chest as she looked around the edge of the door. The big man was still there, now sitting by a fire. She could also now smell coffee and bacon.

She watched, transfixed, as he poured steaming coffee into a metal cup and set it on the ground. Then, to her surprise, he looked up directly at her and motioned with his hand, indicating that the cup was for her.

Nancy's mind tried to make sense of it all. What was his intention? Was this a trap? Her instincts screamed at her to grab the kids and run, but something held her back. Despite his intimidating appearance, the man's demeanor seemed non-threatening, almost friendly.

She glanced back at TJ and Lynn, still sleeping peacefully. The thought of waking them and fleeing into the unknown was daunting. But could she trust this stranger?

Slowly, cautiously, she opened the door a bit wider. The man remained where he was, not making any sudden moves. He gestured again to the cup, a silent invitation.

Nancy hesitated, her hand on the door. She knew she had to make a decision. The smell of the coffee was enticing, a reminder of the comforts of home they'd been forced to leave behind. And the man, despite everything, seemed to be offering a small kindness.

She took a deep breath and stepped out of the shack, keeping her eyes on the big man. He nodded, acknowledging her presence. Nancy nervously walked toward the campfire, each step measured and cautious.

As she approached, the man stood up, towering over her. Nancy's heart skipped a beat, but he simply took a step back, giving her space. He motioned to the cup again, then to a spot on the ground covered by an old towel where she could sit. She sat cautiously, thankful not to be sitting on the dew-covered ground.

Nancy reached for the cup, her hand trembling slightly. The warmth of the metal was comforting against her skin. She raised it to her lips and took a small sip. The coffee was strong and bitter, but it was the best thing she'd tasted since the explosion.

She looked up at the man, who was now sitting across from her, his own cup in hand. He met her gaze, his eyes deep and inscrutable. Nancy knew she was taking a risk, but something told her that this man, whoever he was, meant her no harm.

For a moment, they sat in silence, the crackle of the fire the only sound. Then, the man spoke, his voice deep and rumbling. "Name's

Luther Haines," he said. "Big Luther Haines to most people. Looks like you could use some help."

Nancy winced at the man's deep, resonant voice, then slowly nodded. She couldn't help but feel gratitude toward this imposing stranger who had appeared out of nowhere.

"I'm Nancy," she said, her voice barely above a whisper. "Those are my kids, TJ and Lynn, in the shack. And... thank you."

Luther nodded, his expression softening. "You folks look like you've been through hell," he said, taking a sip of his own coffee. "Were you close to the base?"

Nancy hesitated, unsure of how much to reveal. But something about Luther's steady gaze compelled her to speak. "Our home, our whole neighborhood backed up to the base... it's gone. Destroyed in the attack, or whatever it was."

She swallowed hard, fighting back tears. "We've been walking for days, trying to find safety. Food, water, shelter... it's been hard to come by."

"I understand, Miss, and I know you have no reason to trust me, but I mean you no harm. I caught a glimpse of you and the little ones yesterday. What I saw worried me, so I circled back to check on you."

Nancy looked at him, puzzled.

He shook his head. "You were drinking from standing water. That ain't safe, neither is about a dozen other things I noticed."

She nodded, "I don't know what I'm doing, Luther. My husband was on the base. I just knew we had to get away... so many people..."

Luther nodded; he got it. The kids were lucky their mom wasn't in shock. At least she was doing something.

"Yeah, lots of folks gone. That's just the way it is."

"You know about the attack? About the base?"

He sipped his coffee and leaned over to crack some eggs into the pan with the bacon. "Nothing reliable. Just heard a few people talking, you know. Mostly on the radio. No cell service nowhere.

“They say the base is totally gone. Not the whole thing, you know. Hell, that's one of the biggest bases in the U.S. But the airfields, hangars, officer quarters—all the main stuff is now the newest bay on the Gulf Coast. One man said it had to be nine miles across. Sorry,

Miss Nancy, but ain't no one has seen anyone alive that was at the airbase."

Her face contorted into an unattractive grimace. "I... I think I knew that as soon as it happened. Are we at war?"

"Now that is a really good question and one I can't answer. I've heard nothing that makes me think we are other than that tremor last night. You may not have noticed, but it sounded and felt similar to when Eglin got hit, but a little farther away."

Nancy had heard it and felt the ground shake again. "It woke me up. I thought it was a thunderstorm."

"Yeah, off to the west a bit. I saw the... what do you call it? The impact eruption. Lit up the sky like a volcano. I'm guessing it was from over toward Pensacola. If they hit our airbase, they may have taken out the naval air station over there as well."

He dished her up some eggs and bacon on a metal plate.

"Eat up; I'll cook some more eggs when your kids wake up. That's all I have on the bacon, though."

She took a bite, trying hard not to shove the contents of the whole plate in her mouth. "So," she said between bites, "what else was I doing wrong?"

He smiled as he almost delicately ate his own food. "Water was the main thing. Have to drink from fast-moving water supplies or treat it. You know, boil it, add some chlorine or even bleach, or simply check some of these houses for wells. No one out this far is on city water. You find the well, push the cement cap off, and lower a bucket or water bottle or whatever you have."

He took another bite. "You passed how many houses with chicken coops? Eggs and chickens. Eggs you could eat raw; calories matter when you're in survival mode."

"I don't want to steal."

"How many live people you seen? It ain't stealing if it's what is keeping your little ones alive. Hell, even cans of dog food would do. You won't like it, but calories matter. You'd be surprised what else you can eat right around here. Also, your boy—what's his name again?"

"TJ," Nancy said.

"Yeah, TJ has blisters on his feet. Probably bad. I saw him limping yesterday and can tell from his tracks he's favoring one foot. The boy ain't wearing no socks and got some crappy shoes. Probably need to treat them and let him rest today, get him in some socks."

"He doesn't like wearing them, and he loves those sneakers. They're from a line by his favorite NBA players."

"Yeah, I know where they're from. They're junk. Might have to do until you can find something better, but check his feet. Check all of your feet. Nothing running out here, so we're all gonna be walking for the time being."

"So how do we get..." She didn't even know how to ask. Nancy still had no clue where they were going. "How do we get somewhere safe?"

Luther leaned forward, his elbows resting on his knees. "Ain't nowhere that's truly safe right now," he said. "But I think you're safe to stay here a while, catch your breath. I've got some supplies I can share."

Nancy's eyes widened in surprise. "You'd do that? For strangers?"

Luther shrugged, a hint of a smile playing at the corners of his mouth. "The way I see it, ma'am, we're all in this together now. Gotta look out for each other."

He stood up, his large frame unfolding. "I'll rustle up some breakfast for your little ones. Then we can talk about where you're headed, see if I can point you in the right direction."

Nancy watched as Luther moved toward a battered old backpack, pulling out a few eggs and other containers. She felt a wave of relief wash over her, still mixed with a tinge of suspicion. In this new and dangerous world, could she really trust anyone?

CHAPTER
FORTY-TWO

1345 CDT June 12
Beta Site Prepper Enclave
Ozark Mountains, Arkansas, USA

Marcus's heart raced as he took the satphone from Jerome, his knuckles turning white. After more than a week of silence from the Florida enclave, the sudden call filled him with a sense of dread.

"Marcus, it's Isaac," the voice on the other end crackled, faintly audible amidst the static. "We've been hit... it's bad."

That was not at all what Marcus expected to hear. He was just worried about the members at the enclave.

"What do you mean 'hit'? What happened?" Marcus demanded, his voice tight with concern.

Isaac's words came in short, painful bursts. "Lee says it was a kinetic energy weapon, Marcus. I've got scouts out now checking the damage. Looks like they targeted Eglin, the airbase, directly. The destruction... man, it's unimaginable. In fact, we have a new bay on the coast that runs up past the main base terminals."

Marcus felt his stomach drop, a cold sweat breaking out on his forehead. "Jesus...how many casualties?"

There was a long pause, and for a moment, Marcus thought the connection had been lost. Then Isaac spoke again, his voice heavy with grief. "No way of knowing. Intercepted part of a National Guard call indicating upwards of 60,000. Many, many more are injured, some critically. The call got cut off before they said more. Also, the aid camps they're trying to set up are a joke, and supplies are already running out. Alpha camp is okay, but we are nearly ground zero...this whole area is a disaster."

The revelation hit Marcus like a punch to the gut. He had assumed the enclave's predicament mirrored the official reports of a training accident and massive wildfire. But this... this was something far more sinister.

"What about federal help? Surely the authorities must be sending some kind of coordinated aid?" Marcus asked, though he already suspected the answer.

Isaac let out a bitter laugh. “Federal help? Sure. Just as soon as they finish arguing about where to land the press helicopter. Check in with Swannanoa on how that went. No one's coming, Marcus. They're covering it up. We've heard some of the national reports. They're not even close to the truth. We're on our own, and we're barely hanging on. You were right to put out the call. The nation is under attack. We just happened to be first."

Marcus closed his eyes, his mind reeling from the shock. The severity of the situation was far worse than he had imagined. His people, his friends, were suffering, and the world was turning a blind eye.

"Isaac, listen to me," Marcus said, his voice steady despite the turmoil within. "I'll do everything in my power to get you additional help. I still have some contacts from my Navy days. I'll see what I can do."

But even as he said the words, Marcus knew it was a long shot. If the true extent of the devastation was being concealed, his old channels might be of little use.

"I appreciate it, Marcus," Isaac said, his voice tinged with exhaustion. "But don't put yourself at risk. We should be okay. We didn't get all the supplies in and are way behind schedule on projects and new builds. But we didn't plan on thousands of desperate survivors wandering through the forest. Just... just, hell, you guys be ready. If they can do this down here, to a military base no less, then no one is safe."

The call ended abruptly, leaving Marcus standing in the middle of the compound, the satphone still clutched in his hand. The weight of his friend's words settled heavily on his shoulders.

He had to do something. The people in the Florida enclave would likely be okay; sadly, this is what they'd planned for. Still, he couldn't bear the thought of all those others suffering while the world ignored their plight. But where could he turn? Whom could he trust?

Marcus paced outside his cabin, the satphone clutched tightly in his hand. He couldn't shake the desperation in Isaac's voice. He was pissed off, and the anger was beginning to take over with every call he made. With a deep breath, he dialed the next number.

"Central Command, this is Lieutenant Commander Carmichael speaking."

"This is Marcus Smith, SEAL Team-4 retired. I need to speak to someone in domestic ops to report a critical situation along the Gulf Coast—"

"I'm sorry, sir, but this isn't a help line. If you have an emergency situation, please contact your local authorities."

"I'm not in the disaster area," Marcus said, trying very hard to keep his voice and temper in check. "A friend just informed me that the Gulf Coast of northern Florida is one big disa..."

The line went dead. Marcus cursed under his breath and dialed again, this time reaching out to his old SEAL instructor.

"Chief Walters, it's Marcus Smith."

"Marcus? Damn, son, it's been years. How you been, and what can I do for you?"

"Chief, I'm good, but I've got reliable intel about a massive attack on Eglin AFB. Maybe tens of thousands dead, more injured. Someone seems intent on covering it up."

There was a long pause. "Mark, look son, that's a serious accusation. Are you sure about this?"

"Positive, sir. We need to get the word out. Try and get some real help to the area."

"Look, son, I can't act on unverified information. If there was an attack of that magnitude, we'd know about it. They had a training accident—just a fire that's proving a real challenge—but that's all. I'm sorry, Commander, but my hands are tied."

Marcus felt his frustration mounting as he dialed his last hope—Congressman Jim Harper, an old Navy buddy now representing Mississippi's central district.

"Jim, it's Marcus. I think I need your help."

"Hey, man, what's going on?" he asked.

"Something odd. I have reliable word there's been an attack on Eglin. It's bad, Jim. Really bad. They're covering it up, but thousands are dead or injured."

"Whoa, slow down. An attack? Marcus, that's impossible. I was just briefed this morning about the training accident. Just some large ordnance and wildfire in that area. Nothing about an attack."

"Jim, I'm telling you, it's not what they're saying. I have people on the ground—"

"Marcus, stop. Do you realize what you're implying? That our government is lying about a massive attack on a military installation on our own soil? That's insane."

"But Jim—"

"No, Marcus. I'd be laughed out of my own office. Who would even do that? Terrorists? Man, I don't know what game you're playing or if you're pulling my leg, but I want no part of it. Please don't call me again with this kind of shit."

The line went dead, leaving Marcus standing in stunned silence. He had exhausted his best contacts, and each attempt had left him feeling more isolated and desperate than before. The truth was out there, but no one seemed willing to listen or help. All of it was reinforcing his position that everyone had to depend on themselves in a real crisis.

He made a few more calls, but if they even bothered to answer, no one was listening. He wanted to throw the expensive phone into the side of the nearby rock face. That frustration did spark one more person, though. Someone else who tried their best to raise an alarm that no one cared to acknowledge.

Marcus hesitated for a moment, his thumb hovering over Natalie's number displayed on the phone screen. They hadn't spoken in years, not since their falling out over their near mutual decision to leave the Navy. But the nature of recent events and genuine concern for his friend had compelled him to reach out. Still, she had not returned his recent calls.

He hit the call button and held his breath as it rang.

"Marcus?" Natalie's voice came through, surprised but not unwelcoming.

"Hey, Nat," he said, his own voice rough with emotion. "Look, I know I'm probably not your favorite person, but how are you, and do you have a minute to talk?"

There was a pause, and then Natalie sighed. "I'm good. How is Retro?"

Marcus closed his eyes, the weight of his own situation bearing down on him. He reached down and scratched behind the dog's ears and smiled. "He's good, he misses you. Listen, Nat, I called because... because I wanted to check in on you and also ask a favor. I need your help."

He could almost hear her eyebrows raise through the phone. "You need my help? That's a first." Marcus laughed, a sound that made all the memories come flooding back to her. Sunday mornings lounging on the bed with him. Walking the dogs in the water near their cabin. The smell of his body after he showered.

"Please, just hear me out," Marcus pleaded, his voice cracking. "I've got people down in Florida, good people, who are in trouble. There's been an attack, a bad one, but it seems like it's being covered up. Thousands are dead or injured, and no one seems to be acknowledging it or coming to help."

Natalie was silent for a long moment. "An attack? Marcus, are you sure?"

"I'm positive," he said, his frustration bleeding through. "I've tried everything, Nat. Called in every favor, talked to everyone I know. But no one will listen. It's like they're all in on it, like they're all part of some big conspiracy. Either that, or the cover-up is so complete that no one is questioning it. My friend, Isaac, has spotters over near Eglin AFB. They indicate an entire chunk of the coastline is just gone."

"I... I don't know what to say," Natalie murmured, her own voice heavy with emotion. "That coastal area is highly populated. This is a lot, Marcus. I mean, I've been investigating some strange things myself, but this... no way they could keep something like that secret. Think of the outside organizations that would immediately know something was up: the airlines, delivery drivers, trains. Any corporation with locations or offices in the area."

"I know it sounds crazy," Marcus said, his heart aching. "But I swear to you, it's the truth. And I'm out at the Beta camp, and I know I can't do this alone. I need someone I can trust, someone who will believe me."

There was another long pause, and then Natalie spoke, her voice soft but determined. "I always believe you, Marcus. And I want to help. I'm actually in a place right now where I might be able to do some good. Let me see what I can do."

Relief washed over Marcus, so strong it nearly brought him to his knees. "Thank you, Nat. Really. I don't know what I would have done..."

"Don't thank me yet," she said, a hint of their old banter creeping into her voice. "We've got a lot of work to do. But Marcus... it's good to hear your voice again. Despite everything."

Marcus felt a lump form in his throat, a rush of old feelings threatening to overwhelm him. "Yeah. You, too, Nat. You, too."

CHAPTER FORTY-THREE

1301 EDT June 14
White House West Wing
Washington, D.C., USA

Natalie stormed into the SCET conference room, her face flushed with anger. She slammed a stack of papers onto the table, causing Emily and Kaden to flinch. Trent Rogers stepped close to intercede, but Natalie's expression caused him to take a step back.

"You think you can keep this under wraps?" Natalie's voice dripped with venom. "People are dying in Florida, and you're sitting here twiddling your goddamn thumbs!"

Emily stood, her posture rigid. "What are you talking about, Natalie?"

"Please don't play dumb with me, Director." Natalie jabbed a finger at the papers. "Eglin Air Force Base. That 'controlled detonation' bullshit? It's a massacre."

Kaden's brow furrowed. "How do you know this?"

Natalie laughed bitterly. "I have eyes and ears everywhere, Trembley. Unlike you government lackeys, I don't wait for official reports. My organization has a network of watchers. I also have friends in the affected zone."

Emily's eyes narrowed. "Natalie, if you have information about an ongoing casualty event, you need to share it. Now."

"Oh, now you want to know?" Natalie's voice rose. "This is the fucking White House. If you people aren't up to speed on this, how the hell could you ever catch up on UFOs?"

"Not the same thing," Emily insisted. "If people are in danger—"

"They've been in danger!" Natalie exploded. "Wake up! Your precious government is lying to you, to everyone! Again!"

Kaden stepped between them. "Natalie, please. Just tell us what you know."

Natalie took a deep breath, her hands shaking as she spread out satellite images and eyewitness reports. She'd been busy since getting off the call with Marcus. "My friend has contacts near Eglin AFB. They saw... something. Not a fire. Not a craft. More like a meteor; they called it a kinetic energy weapon. And the casualties? They are in the thousands, maybe tens of thousands. I contacted MUFON, and one of our main assets got a drone up and said the entire base was gone. It's a crater backfilling with ocean now."

Emily's face paled as she examined the evidence. "If this is true..."

"If your boss is also in the dark, then someone very high up is keeping a lid on this," Natalie finished Emily's thought, her eyes blazing with intensity.

Emily turned to her military advisors, Colonel James Walker and a newcomer, Major Lisa Chen, who shifted uneasily in their seats. Their nervousness was palpable, and Emily's suspicion grew.

"Why would they?" Emily asked, her voice sharp. "It's obvious we would know as soon as the smoke clears. This is an attack not just on American soil but on an American military base. That is a literal black eye no one in uniform will want to own."

Colonel Walker cleared his throat. "Director Carter, we need to proceed with caution. Jumping to conclusions..."

"Conclusions?" Natalie scoffed. "I'm not jumping to anything. I'm showing you hard evidence of a catastrophe that's being officially covered up."

Colonel Walker spoke up, his voice measured. "We understand your concerns, Ms. Reeves. But we have protocols, chains of command. We can't just—"

"To hell with your fucking protocols!" Natalie slammed her hand on the table. "People are dead, and more will die if we don't act now. Your fucking cover-ups are why we are here in this room."

Trent, who never joined in on the discussions, voiced his concerns. "Rumors are Ms. Reeves is correct." While the others had access to scientific or military information, Trent was tied into the nation's intelligence community.

Kaden, who had been quietly studying the satellite images, looked up. "She's right. This isn't just some random UFO sighting or a mysterious disappearance. This is a direct attack on a military installation apparently from space. We need answers, firsthand evidence."

Emily nodded, stacking up the various data points. If her own advisors were in the dark, then the cover-up ran deeper than she had ever imagined.

"Colonel," Emily said, her tone leaving no room for argument. "I want a full report on everything related to Eglin Air Force Base: personnel, operations, research projects—everything. And I want it yesterday. Also, speak with General Taylor. See if this could tie into what he saw at NORAD."

The officer glanced around the room but nodded his assent.

"Natalie," Emily turned to the investigator. "You and Agent Rogers keep digging. If there's more evidence out there, we need it. The rest of our agenda is suspended until we know the facts about this event."

Natalie gave a curt nod, her anger still simmering beneath the surface.

Kaden caught up with Trent and Natalie just outside the conference room, his footsteps echoing against the sterile corridor.

"Hell of an entrance, Natalie," he said, a half-smile breaking through his concern.

Natalie glared at him, her arms crossed tightly over her chest. "You think that's funny? Did you see how quick they were to feed bullshit to the media? Brushfire, ordnance accident. Ugh! The press is like lapdogs to whatever lies the government wants to tell."

Kaden nodded, the weight of her frustration hitting him. "I get that, but we have no idea this was UFO-related, do we?"

She rolled her eyes, her voice dripping with sarcasm. "Of course not. But it's the same M.O. Looks like a page right out of the UFO cover-up handbook: create chaos, deflect attention, and sweep the real story under the rug."

Kaden leaned against the wall, watching her pace like a caged animal. "The scale of this, though... it's unprecedented. You think they'd go that far?"

"It's not unprecedented, Kaden. That's the thing." Natalie's eyes were sharp, and her voice held a tight edge as she glanced between Trent and Trembley. "You remember the Northeast Blackout back in 2003, right? They tried to pass it off as human error—just a glitch in Ohio. But I don't buy it, and neither should you."

Trent frowned. "That's the one that knocked out New York and parts of Canada, right? They said it was some kind of electrical fault."

"Yeah, that's the official story," she snapped, her hands gripping the edge of a door. "August 14, 2003. Fifty million people left in the dark. New York City, Toronto, Detroit, Ottawa—all went down like dominoes. And they expect us to believe it was just a 'cascading failure' from one malfunction in Ohio? Please." She practically spat the words.

Trembley raised an eyebrow, leaning back cautiously. "So you think it was something else?"

"I know it was," Natalie insisted, her voice rising. "They claimed it was some software bug at a FirstEnergy Corporation facility, that operators missed the warning because the alarm system failed. But think about it—how does a bug in Ohio take down the grid for fifty million people? It doesn't add up. The government wants us to think it was a technical glitch, but that's just a convenient cover."

Trent was watching her closely. "So, what's your theory?"

She leaned in, her eyes intense. "UFOs," she said bluntly. "There were multiple reports of strange lights in the sky before the blackout. And not just any lights—fast-moving, erratic, beyond anything we know how to control. Same kind of stories you hear in every major blackout, going all the way back to 1965 and 1977. This isn't a coincidence; it's a pattern."

Trent leaned back, absorbing her words. "So you think they're covering this up, now?"

"Absolutely," Natalie hissed. "They've been covering it up for decades. And I'm tired of it. It's the same story, over and over. The truth is out there, but they think they can keep us in the dark. Just like they did to millions in 2003. The only difference between then and now is the number of casualties."

Natalie stopped, her blue eyes fierce. "If they think they can hide something big, you bet they would. It's all about control. They want to shape the narrative and keep us all in the dark."

Kaden felt physically ill. "So you really believe this is connected? That we're looking at something extraterrestrial?"

Natalie threw her hands up in exasperation. "Yes! What else could it be? The patterns, the cover-ups, the military's immediate response? It screams UFOs. Or something worse. We can't ignore it just because the brass doesn't want us poking around."

Kaden considered her words, his mind racing. "Look around. Natalie, we are part of the government, and I don't think anyone in this building knew what you just said back there."

"Then this country has an even bigger problem than a missing airbase. Satellite images will show what has happened there soon enough, but someone is buying time or looking to protect whomever did this," Natalie said.

Trent motioned for them to keep their voices down. "You guys, I mean, we are a minor committee studying a fringe issue that may not be relevant to any of this. No one will listen to us. I am not even sure Director Carter can act on the information you just dropped in her lap."

"She can go to the president," Natalie said. "If he's not part of the cover-up, then he can get answers."

"But if you are wrong, her credibility will be zero. Yours, too, I'm afraid," Trent said.

"Look, Natalie, I agree with you, but the scale is mind-boggling. I'd love to stay, but I have to catch a flight to the West Coast. Agent Rogers, please keep her out of trouble," Kaden said, patting her on the shoulder.

Natalie watched her colleague go. She knew the reputation of MUFON and the fact that they tended to side with the more dramatic side of events, but she prided herself on being the outlier. She had always demanded proof, and she had enough this time to feel confident she was right about the attack. She was less sure of the extraterrestrial origin, but one thing at a time...

"So where do we begin?" Trent said after the professor was gone.

Natalie eyed the handsome man closely before answering. "I have an idea, but I may need some help." She rushed to catch up to Colonel Walker, who was leaving with Emily. Natalie was going to need a favor.

CHAPTER FORTY-FOUR

1217 EDT June 16
38°48'N, 76°52'W
Joint Base Andrews, Maryland, USA

"You're a UFO investigator, right?"

"Yes, Agent Rogers," Natalie said as the car moved deftly through D.C. traffic.

"Look, it's just Trent, okay? I mean, outside of the zoo."

She knew he meant the White House and was beginning to appreciate the analogy.

"Sorry, I was just curious why you are running point on this?"

"Investigating the cover-up?"

He nodded.

"That's what I've always done. Much of what we do on incident investigations is to see who has gotten there before us and what they did to throw us all off the trail."

That echoed many of his own suspicions, but he wanted to hear it from her perspective. "You mean others screw with your investigations? How often does that happen?"

She eyed the man driving with a look of hopelessness. "Trent, you have been in nearly every one of the task force meetings. You must know it happens every single time. If the site hasn't been corrupted, the individuals coerced, or the media tipped off to some reason that the entire scene is a hoax, then we know it was likely a non-event."

"Who are these people, Men in Black, CIA?" Trent asked.

"Who do you work for?" Natalie asked.

"I... I work for the American people," he said, grinning. "Just like you."

"I get your point, but it just seems... you know, impossible."

The car pulled into Joint Base Andrews an hour later.

"This is your idea?"

"Yeah," she said. "Do you get airsick?"

Trent shook his head as he donned the flight suit.

"No," she said, coming around the lockers. "Put these on first."

"They look like my grandmother's compression socks. And not even the sexy ones—these scream varicose veins."

"Serve the same purpose, too. Put on all the base layers and then the jumpsuit. We won't be pulling any major G-forces, but better safe than sorry."

Natalie still couldn't believe Emily had actually arranged what she wanted. They had tasked a semi-retired F-14 two-seater trainer. She wasn't checked out on the newer generation fighters, but she knew this baby.

Natalie strapped into the cockpit and glanced back at Trent. "Ready to see the damage firsthand?" she asked, a hint of a smirk playing on her lips.

"Ready as I'll ever be," Trent replied, trying to mask his unease. The jet roared to life, and Natalie wasted little time on pre-checks. Minutes later, they screamed down the runway, the G-forces pressing them into their seats. Just as they lifted off, Natalie sent the jet into a near-vertical climb.

"Jesus, Natalie!" Trent's knuckles whitened as he gripped the sides of his seat. "You trying to give me a heart attack?" Emily had told him to stay close to her, but this seemed more than reasonable.

"Just making sure you're awake," she said, laughing. The jet leveled out, and they were soaring above the clouds, heading towards the Gulf

Coast. Seconds later, she hit the afterburners, and the reliable bird climbed up past Mach 2.

"You're enjoying this way too much, Ms. Reeves," Trent said, trying to keep his breakfast down as Natalie banked the F-14 hard to the right. The G-forces pressed him into his seat, and he let out a soft groan.

"It's Natalie, and sorry, just anxious to get us there, Agent Rogers," Natalie replied over the comms, a hint of a smile on her face. "Besides, didn't you want a close-up look?"

Trent took a deep breath, his eyes fixed on the horizon. "I did, yes. I've been known to be an idiot at times."

As they leveled out, Natalie grinned and glanced at the slight reflection in the canopy that she knew was the agent. "So, Trent, what's your story? How'd you end up on this task force?"

Trent's gaze drifted off for a moment before he focused on Natalie again. "I used to work in counter-terrorism, but after 9/11, I got pulled into a special projects unit. We dealt with... unusual threats."

"Unusual?" Natalie raised an eyebrow. "You mean like UFOs?"

Trent nodded. "Among other things. Let's just say I've seen things that I'd rather never see again."

Natalie chuckled. "I think I can handle it, Agent Rogers."

Trent's expression turned serious. "I'm not sure you can, Ms. Reeves. This stuff... it gets under your skin. It changes you."

Natalie's eyes narrowed. "I've seen things, too, Agent Rogers. Things that'd make your blood run cold."

The aircraft flew on in silence for a moment before Trent spoke up again. "I guess we all have our demons, don't we?"

Natalie's gaze returned to the horizon. "Yeah, we do."

The F-14 continued its steady course toward the Gulf Coast, the only sound the roar of its General Electric F110 turbofan engines and the softer hum of the instruments. As they flew, Trent and Natalie sat in comfortable silence, each lost in their own thoughts but both aware of the other's presence.

Trent broke the silence first. "You know, Natalie, I never thought I'd be having this conversation with a UFO investigator."

Natalie smiled, her eyes crinkling at the corners. "Life's full of surprises, Trent."

The aircraft hit a patch of turbulence, and Trent's stomach dropped. "Oh, joy."

Natalie laughed. "Just a little bump, Trent. We're almost there."

As the F-14 leveled out again, Trent let out a sigh. "I hope so, Ms. Reeves. I really do."

The northern Florida coastline came into view, a scarred landscape where the massive weapon had impacted. Fires still burned in some areas, smoke plumes rising high into the sky.

"Take some pictures, Trent. Use the controls like I showed you. I need to line up for refueling."

Trent saw the shadow of a giant plane descending from the heavens toward them.

Natalie was silent for a moment, taking it all in. Her eyes glazed over, and suddenly, she wasn't in the cockpit anymore. She was back in the Navy, on a routine flight over the Atlantic. The radar had picked up an anomaly, and before she knew it, she was face-to-face with a glowing, pulsating craft. It moved with impossible speed, darting around her plane like a predator toying with its prey. Then, a blinding light enveloped her cockpit, and everything went black.

"Natalie! Snap out of it!" Trent's voice pierced through the fog of her memory. She blinked rapidly, realizing they were approaching the refueling tanker a bit too fast.

"Sorry, but I'm fine," she said, shaking off the flashback. But her hands trembled as she maneuvered the jet into position.

Trent noticed. "Are you sure? This isn't exactly the time to zone out."

"I'm fine," she repeated, more firmly this time. The refueling probe connected, and the jet's fuel gauge began to climb. "See? No problem."

Trent didn't look convinced but kept his mouth shut. He hated flying, especially in situations like this. The idea of being thousands of feet in the air, relying on a narrow tube for fuel, made his stomach churn. He focused on his breathing, trying to stay calm.

Natalie, aware of his discomfort, couldn't resist one more jab. "Relax, Trent. It's just like filling up your car, only, you know, in the sky. With the fuel tanks hanging in the sky above you."

"Yeah, real comforting at Mach 2," he muttered, eyes fixed on the massive fuel tanker that seemed way too close.

"Nah, we slow down to about 300 for this." The refueling complete, Natalie radioed her thanks, then pulled away and banked back toward the Gulf Coast. "Hang on," she said. "We're going to get a closer look."

Trent clenched his jaw, determined not to let her see just how much he hated this.

"Damn!" was all either of them could say as she banked left and descended through the clouds. The air force base was indeed a smoking ruin. Much of the southern end of the base was now part of a new bay filled with blue gulf waters and the occasional splinters of ruined buildings poking through.

"All those people," Rogers said in disbelief.

"Tell me something, Trent. Does this look like a brushfire or an ordnance accident to you?"

"God, no," the agent said truthfully. "Looks like an atom bomb went off. Maybe several."

Natalie had been running sensor scans since arriving on-station. No radiation detected. No, this was something more conventional.

Natalie glanced at the radar and saw two blips climbing rapidly toward them. She frowned and keyed the radio. "Unmarked jets at my six o'clock, this is Lieutenant Natalie Reeves, requesting identification and mission intent. I have clearance from the White House."

No response. The jets continued to close the distance.

"Trent, we have company," she said, her voice tight. "And they don't look friendly."

Trent craned his neck to see the approaching aircraft. "What do you mean?"

"I mean they're not answering, and they're moving in fast."

"Should we—"

"Hang on," Natalie interrupted, flipping a series of switches. She pulled the jet into a sharp turn, trying to get a better angle on the newcomers. They were the more modern F-35s. She saw they were dark and unmarked but skillfully mirrored her maneuvers, staying right on her tail.

"Unmarked jets, this is Lieutenant Natalie Reeves. Identify yourselves immediately. We are on special tasking from the White House." She waited, but the radio remained silent.

"Okay, Trent, this is getting serious. If they're not responding, they might be hostile."

"What do we do?" he asked, gripping the sides of his seat.

"We might need to cut this trip short. Hold on tight." Natalie banked hard, accelerating away from the former air base. The unmarked jets followed, their intentions clear.

"Why aren't they answering?" Trent's voice was tinged with panic.

"Could be a lot of reasons, none of them good," Natalie replied. She pushed the jet to its limits, weaving through the sky in an attempt to shake their pursuers. The unmarked jets stayed on her, matching her every move.

"Unmarked jets, this is your final warning. Identify yourselves or we will take defensive action." Natalie didn't wait for a response. She executed a high-G turn, hoping to throw them off. The jets followed seamlessly, closing the gap and lining up into firing position.

Natalie heard the intermittent beep; they were painting her craft with radar.

"Trent, this might get rough," she said, her voice steady but tense. "I'm going to try and lose them in the clouds." Not that that would do anything to blind the other jets' radar.

She dove into a thick bank of cumulus, the F-14 shuddering as it cut through the dense vapor. The unmarked jets followed, their dark silhouettes barely visible in the swirling mist.

The missile lock tone sounded throughout the F-14.

Natalie checked her instruments, noting the unmarked jets' positions. "They're still on us," she muttered.

"Can't we call for backup?" Trent asked, his voice strained.

"Already did," Natalie replied. "But we might have to rely on ourselves for now."

She leveled out, skimming just above the cloud tops. The unmarked jets maintained their relentless pursuit. Natalie took a deep breath, her mind racing through options. "Get ready, Trent. We're going to need every bit of luck we can get."

The radio crackled, but it wasn't the unmarked jets. "Reeves, this is Command. Do you read?"

"Command, this is Lieutenant Reeves. We have two unmarked jets on our tail, F-35s but not responding to hails. Requesting immediate assistance."

"Copy that, Lieutenant. Hold tight for five mics; help is on the way."

Natalie's hands danced over the controls, her eyes flicking between the instruments and the unmarked jets in her mirrors. "Okay, Trent, time to show these guys what we're made of."

The F-14 shuddered as she pushed it to the limit, banking sharply and diving through the clouds. The tone of the radar lock fell silent. Still, the unmarked jets followed, their engines roaring, their presence a constant threat.

"They're still on us!" Trent's voice was filled with fear.

"I know," Natalie said through gritted teeth. "But we're not done yet."

She yanked the stick, sending the jet into a series of tight, unpredictable maneuvers. The G-forces pressed them into their seats, making it hard to breathe. Trent clung to his seat, his knuckles white.

"I think I just pissed myself."

"Aren't you glad I made you put on your grandmother's underwear now?" she asked.

Natalie leveled out for a split second, then abruptly cut the throttle, allowing the jets to overshoot her position. She slammed the throttle back, the F-14 rocketing up behind them.

"Nice move," Trent gasped.

"Thanks, but they're not done," Natalie replied, her eyes narrowing. The F-35s looped around, closing in once more.

A warning beep filled the cockpit. "They're locking on to us again," Trent guessed, his voice just above a whisper.

Natalie's mind raced. "Hold on," she muttered, diving again, skimming just above the treetops. The unmarked jets mirrored her move, their presence a constant shadow.

"They're just trying to scare us away," Natalie said, more to herself than to Trent. "But I don't doubt they'll shoot us down if we don't leave."

She pulled the jet into a steep climb, the more maneuverable F-35s following closely. As they reached the peak, she rolled the aircraft, diving back down in a tight spiral. The jets fired, rounds streaking past her wings, tracers lighting up the sky.

Trent's breath came in ragged gasps. "They're shooting at us!"

"Stay calm," Natalie said, her voice steady. "We can do this."

She leveled out again, pushing the jet to its maximum speed. The other jets were newer, relentless, and their weapons systems primed. Another warning beep filled the cockpit. The other pilots were good, and she was a bit rusty. Still, it was coming back to her fast.

"Natalie," Trent's voice was strained. "Do we have any weapons?"

Natalie's eyes flicked to the empty missile racks. "No," she admitted, her voice tight. "This is a trainer. We're flying unarmed."

Trent swallowed hard. "So, what's the plan?"

"Out-fly them," she said simply, determination etched in every line of her face. "We've got skill, and we've got brains. That has to be enough."

The F-14 roared through the sky, a sleek predator with no claws, but Natalie's skill and determination were more than a match for any foe. The F-35s continued their pursuit, but Natalie's maneuvers kept them at bay, each move more daring than the last.

Another line of tracer rounds streaked past, missing by inches. "That was too close," Trent said, his voice shaking.

"Just hang on," Natalie replied, her eyes focused, her mind racing. "We're not done yet."

One of the craft lined up again just behind the F-14, perfectly positioned for a firing attack. The other hovered off to the side, ready to support. Natalie's eyes flicked to the radar, seeing the blip that meant they were in serious trouble. Her hands gripped the controls, ready to perform a dramatic and very dangerous maneuver. She grasped the throttles, ready to hit full power and dive to the deck.

Just as she was about to execute the move, two F/A-18E/F Super Hornets appeared on the radar, zooming in from above. Their presence was a welcome sight.

"Two bandits at six o'clock," came the calm, authoritative voice over the radio. "This is Viper-One and Viper-Two. We have you covered, Lieutenant Reeves."

Natalie felt a wave of relief. "Copy that, Viper-One. We could use the assist."

The Super Hornets wasted no time. They locked their radar onto the two unmarked jets, painting them with an unmistakable threat. The bad guys didn't hesitate. Realizing they were outmatched, they bugged out, breaking formation and peeling away at high speed.

"Looks like they're retreating," Trent said, his voice filled with relief.

Natalie exhaled deeply, the tension easing from her shoulders. "Thanks for the save, Viper-One. We owe you one."

"Anytime, Reeves. Just doing our job," the voice replied, cool and collected.

The skies cleared, and the immediate danger passed. Natalie leveled the F-14, her mind still racing from the close call. Trent's knuckles gradually regained color as he loosened his grip on the seat.

"Let's head back," Natalie said, her voice steadier now. "We've got a lot to report and we're bingo fuel."

Trent nodded, still processing the intensity of the chase. "Yeah, let's get out of here."

Natalie set a course for their D.C. base, the Super Hornets escorting them for the first hundred miles. The adrenaline still coursed through her veins, but she felt a renewed sense of purpose. They had survived, and now they had to figure out who was behind the unmarked jets. And what the real story was about the destruction they had seen and filmed. Marcus had been right, she thought.

The horizon stretched out ahead, clear and calm, a stark contrast to the chaos they had just endured. Natalie used the odd canopy to mirror a glance back at her passenger, who was finally starting to relax.

"Guess this job isn't so boring after all," he said, a hint of a smile tugging at his lips.

Natalie laughed. "No, Trent, it definitely isn't."

CHAPTER FORTY-FIVE

0903 EST June 08
White House Oval Office
Washington, D.C., USA

Emily stepped into the Oval Office, her eyes locked on President Martin. Her mouth was dry, and her chin jutted forward as she approached his desk. She didn't bother with small talk, her gaze piercing as she spoke.

"Mr. President, I need to ask you something uncomfortable." Her voice was firm but respectful, a tone that brooked no evasion.

Martin's expression remained calm, a practiced politician's mask. "Of course, Emily. You are my acting chief of staff. What's on your mind?"

She didn't hesitate, her words coming in a rapid, controlled flow. "The 'incident' at Eglin Air Force Base. The one they're calling a 'controlled detonation gone awry.' I've seen the footage, sir. I've talked to people. And I know this was no accident. Nor is it contained. This is a mass casualty event, isn't it?"

Martin's eyebrows rose, a calculated gesture of surprise. "I'm not aware of any evidence pointing to—"

Emily cut him off, her voice rising. "Please... please don't play dumb with me, Mr. President. I've worked with you long enough to know when you're stalling. I've seen the reports, the satellite imagery, and now one of my own people has seen it first-hand. This was no accident. It was a deliberate attack. And I want to know why you are helping cover it up. We should be flooding the area with aid and broadcasting for civilian assistance. Instead, we are, what? Hosting a state dinner for the vice-premier of Who Gives a Fuckstan?"

Martin's smile was a faint, condescending curve of his lips. "Emily, you're getting ahead of yourself. We're still investigating—"

"I'm really not getting ahead of myself, sir," Emily interrupted, her eyes flashing. "I'm trying to catch up and uncover the truth. People have died... are still dying. More military airmen just like my brother and their families. No, sir, when it comes to the safety of this country, I won't be silent."

The president's expression didn't waver, but Emily saw the faintest flicker of annoyance in his eyes. He knew she wasn't afraid of him, that she would push until she got the truth.

"Emily," he began, his voice smooth as silk, "I understand your concerns, but you need to trust that we're doing everything in our power to—"

"No, Mr. President," Emily said, her voice low and deadly. "You asked me to get to the bottom of what was going on."

"That was about UFOs," he said, standing up suddenly, his face reddening. "What is going on in the Gulf is a military situation."

"Oh?" she said. "A situation that involves a big chunk of coastline being vaporized?"

He lowered his eyes and sat back on the edge of the wooden desk, knowing she knew pretty much what he knew. He nodded once.

Emily had talked to Natalie as soon as she had landed and could not believe the footage she and Trent had delivered. She was not going to bring up the opposing jets just yet, but that was potentially an even bigger worry. Martin's administration was not as secure or powerful as she'd thought. Now she wondered whom she could trust. Perhaps the cover-ups did begin in the Oval Office.

"It's bad. It is really bad, Emily. Someone hit us, and we have no idea who. The joint chiefs and the national security advisor want to keep it quiet for now."

"Keep it quiet?" she said in an accusing tone. "Because it was an attack on American soil?" she guessed.

The president nodded again. "And it was a military base, two actually. Pensacola Naval Air Station was hit, too, the very next day. Someone took out two of our front-line strategic bases with no warning, using weapons we can't even begin to understand."

Emily digested the news and began to calm herself by pacing back and forth in the historic office.

Emily stopped and faced President Martin again. Her voice was measured but urgent. "Sir, scientists have theorized for years that if an alien race were to initiate a first strike, they would likely use orbital bombardment with kinetic energy weapons. These KEWs could be aimed off the coast to generate massive tidal waves and also target key infrastructure."

She watched the president's face intently for small micro-expressions. She knew at once this information wasn't a surprise to the man.

The president sighed, rubbing his temples. "Why tidal waves?"

"Efficiency," she stated flatly. "Fifty percent of our population lives within fifty miles of the coastline. Along with that, many of our industrial, technical, and financial centers, plus... well, us, the government. If you extend that out to 250 miles, the numbers go up to around seventy percent. Large enough waves could decimate us and most other major countries on Earth without using any conventional weaponry or risking any assets in battle."

"Emily, I think you're getting a little too wrapped up in your committee's theories. We have no concrete evidence that this was anything close to, what...an alien attack."

Emily stepped closer, her eyes unwavering. "Mr. President, the precision of these strikes, the type of destruction—they align perfectly with what my experts have predicted. These weren't conventional attacks.

They're beyond anything any nation on Earth is capable of. You can't just dismiss this."

Martin crossed his arms, skepticism etched on his face. "So, you're saying these attacks were orchestrated by aliens? Based on what? Some vague theories?"

"Not just theories, sir," Emily pressed on. "It's not a lot yet, but I just got you to admit that there even was an attack. If this were a terrestrial power, there's going to be some trace, some chatter. Radiation, for God's sake, but there's nothing. Just silence. I get my version of the daily security brief, too, you know."

He shook his head, clearly unconvinced. "Emily, I appreciate your dedication, but jumping to conclusions about extraterrestrial involvement—"

"It's not jumping to conclusions," she interrupted. "It's following the evidence. We have to consider every possibility, especially when our usual explanations don't fit. If we ignore this and it's true, the consequences could be catastrophic."

The president stared at her, his expression hard to read. She felt like she was getting through to him...maybe. Finally, he spoke, his voice softer. "Alright, Emily. Let's say, for argument's sake, that you're right. What do we do then? How do we even begin to defend against something like this?"

Emily took a deep breath, knowing she had to be clear and concise. "We start by taking these threats seriously. Mobilize our resources, strengthen our defenses. And most importantly, we need to be transparent with the public. They deserve to know what's happening. Keeping them in the dark will only lead to more panic and chaos. If people learn you're part of covering this disaster up, your presidency is over."

"I can't do that," the president said sadly. "I'm sorry, Emily, but I just can't."

"You can't tell the American people the truth, sir?"

He licked his lips and looked out the window. Emily saw his right hand had a slight tremor. "You asked me if I am part of a cover-up. I am not. Pete is heading up the effort to contain it. Honestly, I am staying as far away from it as possible."

He patted the Resolute desk and gave a slight chuckle. "My predecessor left me a letter... you know, tradition. He said, 'Have fun chatting with Valiant Thor.'"

Emily had heard that name before but couldn't place it.

President Martin's gaze remained fixed on the window, his voice barely above a whisper. "Valiant Thor. That's what they called him. An alien who supposedly walked among us, right here in Washington, D.C."

Emily's brow furrowed. "Sir, I don't understand. Are you saying—"

"I'm saying that according to highly classified documents, in 1957, an extraterrestrial being calling himself Valiant Thor allegedly made contact with President Eisenhower." Martin turned back to face Emily, his expression grave. "The story goes that this human-looking alien lived here for three years, offering advanced technology and solutions to numerous global problems."

Emily's mind raced, trying to process this information. "But why haven't we heard about this before? Why keep it secret?"

Martin shook his head. "Because it sounds insane, Emily. A humanoid alien walking into the Pentagon, offering to solve all our problems? It reads like bad science fiction. But the records... they're extensive. Detailed. And they're corroborated by multiple high-level officials from that era."

"What happened to him?" Emily asked, her voice full of questions.

"According to the files, he left in 1960, promising to return when humanity was ready." Martin's lips twisted into a bitter smile. "Whatever that means."

Emily took a moment to absorb this revelation. "And you believe this, Mr. President?"

Martin's eyes met hers, filled with uncertainty. "I don't know what to believe anymore, Emily. But I do know that if there's even a fraction of truth to that or what you just suggested, we're dealing with forces far beyond our comprehension."

Martin leaned forward, his elbows resting on the desk, his hands clasped tightly. "Emily, I need you to understand something. Admitting that UFOs and aliens are real, much less the fact that they just attacked us, would have devastating consequences for the American people... hell, for the entire world."

Emily frowned, her mind grappling with the implications. "But sir, doesn't the public have a right to know? Especially if we're already under attack?"

The president shook his head, a weary sigh escaping his lips. "It's not that simple. Every religion would revolt. People's entire belief systems would be shattered. Civil unrest would be rampant. Riots, looting, mass hysteria. Society as we know it could very well collapse." Martin's arms gestured wildly as if he was talking to a crowd.

He stood up, pacing behind his desk, his voice growing more intense. "Every person who has sat in this office has realized the same thing. Humanity just isn't ready for a truth like that. The consequences would be too severe. Too damned unpredictable."

Emily bit her lip, torn between her duty to the truth and her understanding of the potential fallout. "But how can we defend ourselves, rally the nation, if we're keeping them in the dark?"

Martin stopped pacing, his gaze fixed on the portrait of Washington hanging on the wall. "We do what we've always done. We fight in the shadows. We protect the people without them ever knowing the true nature of the threat."

President Martin stood and leaned on the back of his chair, the weight of the world clearly visible on his shoulders. "Emily, there's something you likely do not know. Something none of us like to admit, but our military is not prepared for a full-scale battle, much less one involving highly advanced extraterrestrial technology," he admitted, his voice tinged with frustration and a hint of defeat.

"All of those magnificent weapons our defense contractors keep selling the Pentagon—well, if we had to use them in a sustained battle, every smart bomb and most of our other advanced weapon systems we have... they'd last us maybe a week, possibly two."

Emily's eyes widened, the truth of his words sinking in. "Sir, are you saying that all the billions we've spent on defense might be for nothing against this kind of threat?"

Martin nodded, rubbing his temples as if to stave off a headache. "We spend millions—hell, billions—on these weapons. Billions of taxpayer dollars, and they look great when we take out a truck full of extremists who declare war on that peaceful village on the other side of the hill."

He paused, looking her directly in the eye. "But when you break it down, the adjusted cost of killing a single enemy combatant during World War II was under $10,000 in 1940s dollars. Today, that number is over $2 million. Two million dollars per person in that ratty-ass technical truck we just took out with a predator strike."

Emily's mind mulled that over. What the man was revealing was ridiculous. "So you're saying our current strategy and arsenal are not just expensive but fundamentally flawed for what we're likely to be facing?"

"Exactly," Martin said. His expression grim. "We've been focusing on low-intensity conflicts and counterinsurgency operations for so long that we've lost sight of what it means to fight an existential threat. Our advanced systems are incredible for what we've been using them for—expensive as hell, but incredible. Against an enemy with superior technology, though... we might as well be throwing rocks."

Emily's thoughts flashed to the SCET committee and their daunting task ahead. "So, what do we do? How do we even begin to prepare for something like this?"

Martin sighed deeply, leaning forward again and then staring out the window toward the gardens. "I simply don't know. I need to talk with Pete."

Emily frowned but nodded slowly, understanding the enormity of their situation. "I still firmly believe the people need to know what's at stake."

He turned back to Emily, his expression resolute. "Your committee, your investigations—they're more important now than ever. But the circle of knowledge must remain small. I can't afford for this to leak."

"I can't be part of a cover-up, sir. We've seen enough of that already. The vast majority of people already believe in alien life. Give them some credit. I think the people of this country will surprise you."

Emily took a deep breath, steadying herself. "Mr. President, do you remember learning how Copernicus's heliocentric model changed everything back in the 16th century?"

Martin frowned, then looked up at the ceiling, clearly trying to understand where she was going with this. "Yes, I'm aware. It suggested for the first time that the Earth wasn't the center of the universe."

"Exactly," Emily continued, her voice gaining strength. "Before Copernicus, the prevailing view was that Earth and humanity occupied a special, central position in the cosmos. His heliocentric model suggested otherwise. It radically diminished our cosmic importance and upended deeply ingrained beliefs. People were terrified. They felt lost and insignificant."

Martin's expression softened slightly, as if he began to see her point. "But eventually, humanity adapted. We learned to accept our place in a much larger universe," he said.

Emily nodded, pressing her advantage. "Precisely. It was disruptive, but it was the truth. And isn't it better to live with the truth, no matter how uncomfortable, than to live in ignorance? Especially if something out there poses a tangible threat to our way of life?"

The president sighed, rubbing his temples again. "Hell, Emily, ten percent of the people out there still think the Earth is flat. Look, you're asking me to consider something that could destabilize everything—governments, global economies, not to mention the religious implications for every faith on Earth—"

"And what if ignoring it leads to our destruction?" she asked.

Emily's voice was fervent now, almost pleading. "We can't afford to stick our heads in the sand. We have to confront this head-on. Humanity needs to know so we can prepare, so we can fight if necessary."

Martin looked at her, admiration and a bit of frustration showing in his eyes. "You're asking me to make a monumental decision. One that could change the course of history."

"Yes, I am," Emily said, her voice steady. "But it's a decision that needs to be made. We can't keep living in the dark, pretending everything is fine. The world deserves to know the truth. We deserve to be prepared. Those people in Florida deserve our support."

The president's gaze dropped to his famous desk, his fingers tracing the grain of the wood. "You're not the only one to suggest that aliens might be behind this attack. The clues are there, just as you say, but I just can't do it...not yet, Emily. We need conclusive evidence, and assuming we get it, I need a plan. We can't just throw a bombshell out there without a strategy to contain or control the spin."

Emily felt a glimmer of hope. "Then let's make a plan, sir. Together. Let's figure out how to reveal the truth in a way that minimizes panic and maximizes our chances of survival. That's part of my job here."

Martin nodded slowly, the weight of the decision settling on his shoulders. "Okay, Emily. I'll take what you've said under advisement. But we need solid proof, and like I said, I need to see a reasonable plan for disclosure. One that doesn't have us on our knees. Trust me, we need to be careful. Very careful."

CHAPTER FORTY-SIX

0607 MST
37°06′N, 111°52′W
Private Desert Estate
Central Arizona, USA

"Incoming call for you, Mr. King."

He studied the rugged landscape, watching the rising sun paint the Arizona bluffs in brilliant pinks and oranges. He tapped the screen on the unusual-looking phone, and he heard the telltale sound of his encrypted line accepting the caller.

The report was concise and unsurprising. Gibson was excellent at handling the tactical issues when dealing with a potential risk at the very high level that they were currently facing. Owen King wanted to be kept fully informed. Gibson's report was brief and informative.

Since its inception, the Observers' mandate had been clear: keep the secret—no matter what. Only once had a sitting president ever gotten close, and that had been before Owen was even born. That man paid the ultimate price, and the situation hadn't changed at all in the decades since. The president was fine asking questions. Hell, they all did. What went on at Area 51? Do we have a flying saucer from Roswell? Are there any breakthroughs in technology that have been derived from UFO-related research? Or the new classic, what really went on with the Navy and the USS Nimitz encounter off the California coast in 2004?

The idiots didn't even know the real questions they should be asking. Most assumed they were all powerful and that no one would deliberately mislead them. The truth was the president was just part of a system. A system that had more layers and more secrets than anyone would ever think possible.

The intelligence community, the military, and even the defense contractors like NovaCore all had sensitive and secret files that no sitting president would ever be given access to. It was on a compartmentalized need-to-know basis, and like all the others, President Martin didn't need to know.

The real trick was keeping their focus elsewhere. As Bill Clinton once alluded to, a considerable portion of presidential responsibilities involves maintaining and managing national security, foreign policy, and defense-related matters, with domestic policy playing a somewhat secondary role in terms of urgency and resources.

The irony of that is that the national press now focuses almost all its attention on domestic policy issues and makes mountains out of the most mundane items on the POTUS's desk, then eviscerates the people in charge when something goes wrong. It's a bad system, but it works to keep attention off of activities that Owen King strongly preferred to stay in the dark. Through key placements, healthy campaign donations, and an internal structure that was bound to the very framework of the U.S. power structure, nothing was off-limits to the Earth-based Observers.

To his predecessors, that had been a comfortable thought. They could exist in total anonymity. Even he had to admit the architect of the system had been a mastermind. Owen picked up the small device encased in Lucite from his bookshelf. It didn't look like much but had really been the start of it all. The object was gold, about the size of a postage stamp and only as thick as a credit card. None of them knew what it was back in the 1940s, but some of his predecessors eventually figured it out.

Within years, they had deduced the integrated circuit's functionality and produced their own, as well as a side project of creating transistors. From that, the floodgates opened up with technological breakthroughs from pacemakers to computers. All from this one tiny fragment from an extraterrestrial craft.

King's people estimated that reverse engineering that one device advanced human technical capabilities forward by a hundred years. Since then, they had found more crash sites and made even more astounding discoveries. The biggest, of course, was direct contact back in the fifties. Man, he would have loved to have been around for that one.

As the keeper of the secrets, he felt he held a noble position. One that both protected humanity and pushed us into a much brighter future. The downside was the overriding requirement to keep the aliens' influence and activities a secret at all costs. It was inhumanly cruel but necessary.

The warning had been clear since July 20th, 1952. The human race was not alone in the universe. Nor were we all that special, but we could benefit from allowing interstellar observers to study our planet as long as the truth was never revealed.

Over the years, his group had taken to calling themselves by the same name as the aliens. The aliens had only made official contact on two other occasions, and neither had been welcomed. Now, though, Owen felt a sea change in the tenuous relationship. The frequency of the alien incursions, as well as the level of negative outcomes, pointed to something more sinister.

As Owen made his one call, the phone chirped pleasantly before being answered. The voice was male, confident, and well-educated. "Stellar Ops."

"Bryce, it's the chairman," King said. No one at this level would even recognize the name of Owen King. Such was the compartmentalized nature of the Observer's organization. Still, the man's tone took on an even greater level of respect.

"Yes, sir. What can we do for you?"

"I need an update on the tracking project. Do we have a location on our friend's current operations hub?"

"Nothing definite, but we are picking up increased activity out near Enceladus. Just some increased subspace transmissions and visuals on what look like their smaller probe craft, you know, the modified suborbital pods."

Increased activity on a moon of Saturn? How does that fit in with what we know? Owen wondered.

"Nothing on our own moon?" They were nearly certain the aliens were using either Earth's own moon or possibly Mars as a forward observation base but had never been able to get any real proof. The assumption was that the base was deep underground and camouflaged completely. Bryce Thompson was also one of the proponents of at least one deep-sea base in the Atlantic as well.

"Zero lunar contacts so far, sir."

King was troubled; increasing activity on Earth had to be coming from somewhere. The challenge was that the aliens didn't want to be discovered and were damn good at minimizing any useful intel. Blurry pictures and evasive radar tracks weren't just a problem for amateur UFO hunters. The Observers also struggled to track their benefactors just as much.

"How many satellites do you have tasked to this currently?"

"Two dozen if we count the military and Russian ones."

Owen knew what he meant. They could use most of the other countries' hardware at times, but the Russians and Chinese, just like the U.S. spy satellites, primarily looked down at the planet's surface. The whole world was so preoccupied with what was going on down here that they were blind to what might be happening out there.

"I'll make some phone calls to our ESA office and get you access to those as well. We need to keep a full sweep going, and Bryce..."

"Yes, sir?"

"Increase the range. Use the James Webb. If you get a target, just make sure none of those get released into the JPL data feed."

"Yes, sir, we know the play. Thank you, sir."

Owen watched out the massive windows as the shadows on the

bluffs receded deeper into the valley. Something was definitely up, and he didn't like not having all the facts. One way or another, he was going to find out what was going on up there.

CHAPTER FORTY-SEVEN

1728 EST June 21
White House Situation Room
Washington, D.C., USA

Emily rushed to the White House situation room, her heart pounding with a sense of impending dread. As she entered, the tension in the air was palpable. President Martin stood at the head of the table, his face etched with concern as he stared at the grainy video feed projected on the screen.

General Taylor, who had managed to gain entry after a tense standoff with the secretary of defense, stood off to the side, his arms crossed and his expression grim. Emily caught his eye, and he gave her a subtle nod, acknowledging the gravity of the situation.

The video feed showed a massive object hurtling through space, its trajectory unmistakably aimed towards Earth. As the image zoomed in, the object's scale became apparent, dwarfing any man-made satellite or spacecraft.

"What are we looking at here?" President Martin demanded, his voice strained.

One of the advisors, a balding man with thick glasses, stepped forward. "Mr. President, our initial analysis suggests that this object is of deep-space origin. Its size and velocity are unlike anything we've ever encountered."

"Like a meteor?" the president asked.

"Similar, sir, but no, it's not coming from the direction of the asteroid belt. It is coming in out of our system's ecliptic."

"What the hell does that mean?" the president yelled. "Never mind. Does it show any sign of intelligent control? Could it slow down?"

"It means gravity's still undefeated, sir," General Taylor said in a tone lacking all respect.

"Slight control changes," the bald advisor said. "Yes, although they are within the margin that could just be sensor errors," the nervousness in his voice more pronounced now, "slowing down is a possibility, but the physics..."

"It's going to hit," General Taylor said, speaking up. "Nothing traveling that fast can stop in the distance between it and the ground."

A murmur rippled through the room as the implications sank in. Emily glanced at General Taylor, who remained stoic, his earlier warnings now vindicated.

"Where is it headed?" the president asked, his gaze fixed on the screen.

"Based on its current trajectory, we believe it's on a direct course for Alaska," another advisor replied, pointing to a map on the table. "If it maintains its speed, impact is estimated within the next 14 hours."

The advisor took a call, his face going white as a sheet. "Correction, sir. We seriously underestimated the object's speed. Impact is imminent within the next thirty minutes."

The room fell silent, the weight of the revelation hanging heavily in the air. Emily had difficulty considering the potential consequences of another such event. The devastation, the panic, the global ramifications—it was almost too much to comprehend. Deep down, she knew this was what had happened in Florida. Still, no one in the room seemed to want to bring that up. Would they try to silence this one, too?

President Martin turned to his advisors, his jaw set with determination. "We need to mobilize our forces immediately. I want every branch of the military on high alert. We must be prepared for any fallout from this. Is there any way we can intercept?"

The military men looked at one another, then shook their heads. "Nothing we have can intercept something traveling that fast," the SecDef said, shaking his head.

"Mobilize everyone you need. Notify the governor and ask him to mobilize guard units. Call up everyone you need," the president ordered. "If we can't stop it, we have to respond. First to help our people, then to attack whoever did this. I want a war plan by this afternoon, gentlemen. This is America, and we don't turn the other cheek."

"Mister President, I suggest we raise the defense condition to Fast Pace. DEFCON 2," the admiral, who was the ranking member of the joint chiefs, said.

"October 1962," the president said with a sigh. "That was the last time we were at that level during the Cuban Missile Crisis. But yes. Make it so, gentlemen. DEFCON 2."

As the advisors sprang into action, Emily caught General Taylor's gaze once more. In that moment, a silent understanding passed between them. They had been right all along, but now the stakes were higher than ever.

6.8 Earthquake Shakes Remote Interior Alaska — No Casualties Reported

"At 3:41 a.m. local time, the U.S. Geological Survey recorded a 6.8 magnitude earthquake centered in a remote region of Alaska's Koyukuk River basin. The tremor, while intense, occurred far from population centers and resulted in no reported injuries or structural damage.

"Officials noted the quake's shallow depth—just 18 miles—and categorized it as 'a rare but natural release of tectonic stress.' When asked about rumors of a visible flash or crater formation, USGS spokesperson Dana Kepler replied, 'Likely visual misperceptions caused by atmospheric conditions or northern lights activity.'

"Military aircraft were observed in the area shortly after the quake, reportedly conducting routine flyovers as part of NORAD readiness drills."

USGS Update via Associated Press | Byline: Lydia Marks, Environmental Science Desk

CHAPTER FORTY-EIGHT

1040 PDT June 23
Oregon Coast, USA

"You've seen today's paper?"

He nodded, unable to speak without letting his emotions take over.

Sarah sighed and joined him, staring out the large windows to the sea. She slipped her hand into his. "They're doing it again."

Kaden nodded. "I know," his voice broke as the words tumbled out.

He glanced down at the column in the Post, his stomach twisting into knots as he read the headline: 'Disgraced Professor Under Investigation for Sexual Misconduct.'

The words blurred before his eyes, but certain phrases stood out with horrible clarity: 'unnamed sources'... 'disgraced British professor Kaden Trembley'... 'sexual harassment'... 'government task force'... 'witnesses from Colgate University'... 'intent on filing charges.'

His hand trembled as he reached the paragraph implying this wasn't his first offense. The reporter had even included a line about one alleged victim being under eighteen at the time.

"This is... this is absurd," he whispered, his voice cracking. "I've never —I would never—"

"I know," Sarah squeezed his hand. "It's character assassination, plain and simple."

Kaden folded the newspaper with shaking hands. "They're trying to discredit me before I can speak out."

"The timing isn't coincidental." Sarah took the paper from him and tossed it onto the coffee table. "Right when your committee starts making real progress."

"These allegations..." Kaden ran a hand through his disheveled hair. "They're completely fabricated. The university has already called. My sabbatical looks to be permanent."

Sarah's eyes narrowed. "That's what makes it so insidious. They're banking on the public not fact-checking. The damage is done the moment people read the headline."

"My reputation..." Kaden's voice trailed off. He'd spent decades rebuilding his credibility, fighting against ridicule from peers, pushing against institutional resistance. Now, with a single newspaper column, they were trying to destroy everything.

"This is what they do," Sarah said, her voice hardening. "When they can't silence you with ridicule, they try to destroy you personally."

"But why? I'm just an old man looking for answers," he said, his voice cracking.

Sarah squeezed his hand. "No, Kaden. You're a scientist looking for the truth. That scares the hell out of them." She picked up the paper and shook it. "This just means you are closer than you think."

"It won't end," he muttered. "It'll get worse."

She nodded.

"You need to distance yourself from me... from this. Don't let it ruin your reputation, too."

"Honey, you know I know how these games are played. I can handle it. It's you I'm worried about. I always worry about you."

Kaden sank into the armchair, suddenly feeling every one of his years. Sarah had endured so much because of him. The whispers in faculty lounges, the canceled dinner invitations, the way colleagues would subtly steer their graduate students away from his seminars.

"You've already sacrificed too much," he said, looking up at her. "Your position at Princeton—"

"Was stifling me anyway," she interrupted, the corner of her mouth turning up. "I want to spend more time here anyway."

"Sarah." His voice was gentle but firm. "We both know that's not true. You were on track for department chair before you publicly defended my research."

She turned away, staring out at the churning ocean beyond the window. The silence between them spoke volumes.

"I remember the night Dean Harrington called you into his office," Kaden continued. "You came home and wouldn't tell me what he said, but I heard you crying in the bathroom."

Sarah's shoulders stiffened. "Ancient history."

"Then there was the move from England. Leaving everything behind. Your mother—"

"My mother never approved of anything I did anyway," she said with forced lightness.

Kaden leaned close to her, placing his hands on her shoulders. "And now they'll come after you again. The same people who planted this story will dig into your past, your family. They'll try to discredit your research, too."

She turned to face him, eyes flashing. "Let them try."

"I can't ask you to go through it all again." Kaden's voice cracked. "Not the isolation, not the ridicule, not watching your career opportunities vanish one by one."

Sarah cupped his face in her hands. "You never asked. I chose this—chose you—because I believe in the work. In the truth."

"The truth," he echoed hollowly. "What good is the truth if it destroys everyone who touches it?"

She pressed her forehead against his. "The truth is worth fighting for. Always has been. Besides... most of my career is behind me. I'm ready for some quiet."

Kaden closed his eyes, overwhelmed by her loyalty. All these years, through the academic exile, through the mockery, through the loss of everything they'd worked for, she had remained steadfast. His champion when no one else would stand with him.

"There will be more," he stated flatly.

"I know," she said, worry and weariness coloring her words. "You speak with Emily yet?"

"Mmm, yes," he said distractedly. "She says it is to be expected, and she agrees with you. It means we are making someone very nervous. We should be careful, but that I still have the full confidence of her and the president."

"That's good. Right?"

"It's good... until it isn't. If I become too much of a news story or embarrassment, that support will evaporate faster than nitrogen on hot pavement."

"You could walk away," she suggested, already knowing he wouldn't.

"Someone has to do this, Sarah. You were right. I am that person."

CHAPTER FORTY-NINE

1057 EST June
17Private Residence
Washington, D.C., USA

Natalie paced her hotel room, phone pressed tight to her ear. Three calls to Marcus, three times straight to the damned generic voicemail. She jabbed the end call button with her thumb.

"Dammit, Marcus." She tossed the phone onto the bed. "Pick up your damn phone."

The images from the Florida flyover haunted her—scorched Earth where buildings should have been, the bizarre behavior of the unmarked jets that intercepted her. Mostly, though, she thought of the countless lives lost on land and out at sea.

Her phone buzzed. She lunged for it, but her shoulders slumped when she saw Trent's name instead of Marcus's.

"Any luck reaching your friend?" Trent asked when she answered.

"No." Natalie ran a hand through her hair as she stared up at the ceiling. "His compound is off the grid and probably in communication blackout. I do need to warn him about what's happening in Florida."

"About that." Trent's voice dropped. "The Pentagon classified everything we saw yesterday. Top secret, compartmentalized. Even within SCET, it's restricted information."

"I briefed Emily. She has the footage and was headed to talk to the president. They can't just erase what happened to those people," Natalie hissed.

"Somebody thinks they can, and they are." Trent paused. "Look, I'm not saying it's right. But we both know there are consequences for sharing classified intel. You recall all those papers you signed when you got to the White House."

Natalie leaned against the window frame, watching rain streak down the glass. "So, we're supposed to pretend we didn't see what had to be the graves of hundreds, maybe thousands, of bodies? That the base wasn't obliterated by some 'controlled detonation?'"

"I'm just saying be careful." His tone softened. "Especially with outside contacts."

"Marcus isn't just some 'outside contact.' He's—" She stopped herself.

"He's what?" Trent asked, curiosity evident.

"Someone I trust," she finished. "Someone who deserves to know what's coming."

"Natalie." His voice took on an edge she hadn't heard before. "I like you. I respect you. But this isn't just about following rules. People who've leaked less have disappeared."

The implicit warning hung in the air between them.

"Are you threatening me, Trent?"

"The opposite." He sighed. "I'm trying to protect you. Whatever we saw in Florida, whatever you think it means—keep it to yourself. At least until we understand who and what we're dealing with."

Natalie stared at her reflection in the rain-streaked window. "Fine."

It wasn't fine, and despite her military background, she wasn't much of a rule follower. Agent Rogers did have a point, though. She needed to talk to Marcus in a less obvious way. At this point, everybody on SCET was beginning to feel watched. She had already been briefed on what was going on with Kaden. It pissed her off and made her want to go public more than ever.

After hanging up with Trent, Natalie drummed her fingers against the windowsill. The standard communication channels were compromised—that much seemed likely. Her brief exposure to naval intelligence had taught her that when powerful people wanted to listen in, they usually found a way.

She pulled out her phone and used a private messaging app to contact her old MUFON partner Larson.

"It's Nat," she said when he replied. "Need your advice on something sensitive. How paranoid are you feeling these days?"

Larson replied dryly, "On a scale of one to ten? About fifteen."

"Perfect. I need to contact someone off-grid without leaving digital breadcrumbs. What would you use?"

"Not over this app," he replied immediately. "But I know a guy who knows a guy. Give me an hour. If you're still in D.C., I'm not far."

She confirmed, and ninety minutes later, her phone buzzed with a text containing only an address for a coffee shop downtown.

The paranoia was contagious. Natalie took a rideshare car to reach the location. Inside the coffee shop, Larson sat in the corner, looking the same as every other time she'd seen him.

"These government types," he muttered as she slid into the seat across from him. "You look good, Nat. Being a public servant works for you."

"I'm not a Fed," she declared with a smile.

"Good," he said. "They've got eyes and ears everywhere. Stuff is really getting crazy out in the field. What can you tell me?"

She considered offering him something but shook her head. "Not much. Seems like we were on the right track, though. So what do you have for me?"

"There's something new on the market." He slid a brochure for hiking equipment across the table. "German engineering. Triple encryption, bounces off private satellites. The NSA's still working on cracking it."

"Sounds expensive."

"Very." He sipped his coffee. "But we've got connections, though. Our people have been testing these for months."

"I don't have that kind of money, Larson. And I really only need to make one call."

"Don't need it." He lowered his voice further. "I've got one. Consider it borrowed. No digital trail if we do this right."

Natalie raised an eyebrow. "What's the catch?"

"No catch. Just promise you'll tell me what's really happening when this is all over." His eyes sparkled with curiosity. "Whatever you've seen... it's bad, isn't it?"

She nodded.

"Thought so." He finished his coffee. "I'll have it sent to you via overnight courier. The package will look like camera equipment. Instructions inside."

"Thank you."

"Don't thank me yet." Larson stood to leave. "Just be careful whom you trust, Reeves. Even the people you think you know."

She finished her coffee and considered what he'd said. Whom did she really trust? No one here in Washington, that was for sure. Kaden? Yes. Trent? Maybe; he seemed genuine, but he was a trained intelligence officer. Probably the one person in her inner circle she shouldn't trust. Truthfully, she didn't have many personal friends. Mostly, what she had were a few work acquaintances over the years who had grown into casual friendships—the kind you could call twice a year or send a birthday card to, and everything was fine.

At 8:30 the next morning, Natalie was holding the device. It was small, black, and felt solid. Typical German engineering, she thought. She dialed Marcus's phone, and he surprisingly picked up after one ring.

"Hello? Who is this?"

The sound of his voice was a comfort despite his cold greeting. "It's Nat. I have an update for you, but..."

"But you would be breaking the rules to let me know, right?"

"Yes."

"Are you home or in your car?" he asked.

"No, Marcus. I do recall all the stuff you taught me. No place that might have listening devices. I am in a public park by the river with a supposedly untraceable phone."

"What kind?"

She told him, and he whistled. "Get me a few of those, okay?"

"It's borrowed, but sure, as soon as I win the lottery. Look, I did a flyover of the North Florida Coast, and you were right." She proceeded to tell him everything she saw, as well as the unmarked jets trying to chase her away.

"Goddamn! I'd hoped my guy was wrong or just exaggerating. That's got to be some massive cover-up," he said worriedly. "How in the hell can they expect to keep that secret?"

"I don't know, but you're right, no one up here seems to be acknowledging it."

"Why would that be, Natalie?" he asked.

She liked the fact that he still asked for her opinion. They had been good together; she had forgotten that. "They're protecting an even bigger secret," she answered.

"Or a bigger threat," he said.

"So what are you going to do, Marcus?"

"I've got people down there—another enclave, in fact. They were well-positioned to be self-sustaining, but I need to verify they're okay."

"You're going down? You'll never make it through all the roadblocks. The military is running the show from what we saw."

"I'm not sure, Natalie. I can't do nothing at all. They're my people."

She knew who he meant by that remark—the preppers and survivalists that, in her mind, he had chosen over her. "Okay, just be careful, please?"

"Always. I have Retro to watch my back."

CHAPTER FIFTY

0645 EDT June 19
Northeast Florida, USA

TJ skipped along beside Big Luther, chattering excitedly about his favorite superheroes and the latest video game he wished he could play. The burly man listened patiently, a hint of a smile tugging at the corners of his mouth as he adjusted the straps of his heavy backpack.

"You know, Big Lou, you kinda remind me of the Hulk," TJ said, grinning up at him. "You're all big and strong and stuff."

Luther chuckled, a deep rumble in his chest. "I'll take that as a compliment, little man. But I don't think I'd look too good in green."

Nancy watched the exchange from a few paces behind, her brow furrowed with unanswered questions. She quickened her pace to catch up with Luther, Lynn dozing in her arms.

"Luther, I appreciate everything you've done for us," she began, her voice low. "But I need to know where we're going. You keep saying somewhere safe, but what does that mean?"

Luther glanced down at her, his expression unreadable. "It's a place I know, off the grid. We'll have shelter, supplies, and a chance to regroup."

Nancy bit her lip, her eyes searching his face. "And you're sure it's safe? With everything that's happened, I just... I need to be certain."

"I understand," Luther said, his tone softening. "I know you've been through hell, Nancy. But you have to trust me. I'm not going to let anything happen to you or your kids."

TJ tugged on Luther's sleeve, oblivious to the tension between the adults. "Hey, Big Lou, can you tell me another story about when you were in the Army? The one with the tank was so cool!"

Luther ruffled the boy's hair, his gaze lingering on Nancy for a moment before he launched into another tale of his military exploits. Nancy adjusted Lynn in her arms, trying to quell the unease that churned in her gut.

They had been traveling with Luther for the past two days, and he had been incredibly kind, as well as showing them all how to spot danger, forage for edibles, and, of course, take care of their feet. He hadn't managed to find TJ any better shoes yet, but he had some ideas on that, too.

"Can I ask what you were doing up near the base?" Nancy asked. "I mean, I know you said you lived somewhere south of here."

"I was..." He seemed unsure how much to say. "I was just looking around. We'd had some reports of stuff—unusual things going on. My friends sent several of us out to investigate."

"So, where are they now?"

A shadow crossed the big man's face. "Ain't heard from 'em, not since the impact. Most comms are down or limited to short range, though."

"Sorry," Nancy said, deciding to put her daughter back on the wagon. "You sure the blast wasn't a nuke?"

He nodded. "Pretty much, yeah. If it was, we'd all be getting sick by now. I'm not sure what it was. You probably don't remember it, but years ago they were testing something called the MOAB. Supposedly the biggest conventional bomb in the United States arsenal.

"Tested right there at the base. Way up past Duke Field, but we heard it when it cooked off. It shook the ground, too, but nothing like that one the other day. Nah... that was something else entirely. Whatever that was, it carved out a chunk of Earth like that asteroid that killed the dinosaurs did."

"You ever seen a dinosaur?" TJ asked, grinning.

"Geez, how old do you think I am, boy?" Luther growled like something prehistoric, then playfully grabbed the boy and swung him up to his shoulders.

Despite their situation, Nancy enjoyed seeing her kids coming alive again. They were more resilient than adults, and Luther seemed to know just how to bring the kid out in all of them.

By mid-afternoon, the heat was beginning to really wear them down. Luther suddenly crouched low, his hand raised in a silent command for Nancy and the children to stay put. He crept forward, his eyes narrowed as he surveyed the gathering of locals at the edge of the clearing. Many of them looked haggard and worn, their clothes tattered and their faces etched with fear and desperation. But what caught Luther's attention was the arsenal they carried—an assortment of rifles, shotguns, and handguns.

Nancy edged closer to Luther, her voice a whisper. "What's going on? Why do they have so many weapons?"

Luther shook his head, his expression grim. "Could be a lot of reasons. Desperation, fear, paranoia. When the world goes to hell, people start looking for someone to blame. And they'll do whatever it takes to feel safe... or eat."

He watched as a man in a tattered flannel shirt stepped forward, his hands raised in a gesture of prayer. The others followed suit, their heads bowed and their lips moving in silent supplication. Luther's brow furrowed as he tried to make out the words.

"They're praying," Nancy murmured, her eyes wide. "But for what?"

Luther's jaw clenched. He had seen this before, in the aftermath of disasters and conflicts—people turning to religion, to faith, in a desperate attempt to make sense of the chaos. But he knew all too well that faith could be a double-edged sword.

"Protection," he said, his voice low. "From whatever they think is happening or what is coming next."

Nancy looked at him, her face etched with worry. "And what do you think is coming, Luther?"

He didn't answer right away, his gaze still fixed on the gathering. He had his suspicions, based on what he had seen and heard in the days leading up to the impact—Marcus's warnings of strange sightings in the sky, of unexplained phenomena and government cover-ups. But he knew better than to voice those thoughts aloud, especially to a woman with two young children to protect.

"I don't know," he said, his tone measured. "But whatever it is, we need to be ready for it. And that means staying out of sight and keeping our heads down."

He motioned for Nancy and the children to follow him as he backed away from the clearing, his senses on high alert. They had to keep moving to find somewhere safe to hole up until they could figure out their next move.

Luther was a God-fearing man and had seen his share of things he rightly believed had been the work of the Almighty himself, but he also had seen and heard the other side of faith—acts of atrocities done in the name of religion. To be honest, that was what he feared most: scared people amassing under any particular ideology. All it took was one spark to turn them into a mob.

Luther's mind drifted back to Edna, her bright eyes full of hope and faith, the way she had thrown herself into the church's activities with an almost desperate fervor. They had married young, full of dreams and plans for the future, but it wasn't long before she seemed more drawn to the promises of a charismatic preacher who spoke of salvation and redemption in the face of worldly sins. As a vet, Edna began to see Luther as evil, too.

The preacher had a way of making people believe he had a direct line to God, his words a soothing balm to the weary souls of the congregation. He talked about the end times, about preparing for the coming of the Lord, and how only the faithful would be spared. Edna had been taken in by his charm and his certainty. She spent more and more time at the church, her devotion growing with each passing day.

Luther, on the other hand, had always been more skeptical. He respected faith, but he couldn't shake the feeling that the preacher was more interested in power and control than in any divine mission. He saw the way the preacher manipulated his flock, how he used fear and guilt to keep them in line, promising salvation in exchange for unwavering loyalty and generous donations.

It was when Edna started to talk about giving up everything they owned, about moving to a remote commune the preacher was setting up, that Luther put his foot down. He had argued with her, trying to make her see reason, but she was too far gone, her faith in the church unshakeable. One day, she just packed her bags and left, taking their two-year-old daughter with her. Luther came home to an empty house, never seeing either of them again, or the preacher.

That loss had scarred him deeply. He'd spent years searching for them, following every lead, every rumor, but they had vanished without a trace. The experience left him with a deep mistrust of anyone claiming to speak for God. He had seen how easily people could be led astray and how dangerous individuals could rise to power by exploiting the fears and hopes of the vulnerable.

As he led Nancy and the kids away from the clearing, Luther swore to himself that he would never let anyone else fall victim to such manipulation if he could help it. He had seen the dark side of faith, and he would never trust another preacher or man of God as long as he lived.

CHAPTER FIFTY-ONE

0903 EST June 19
White House West Wing
Washington, D.C., USA

Natalie sighed as she leaned against the wall outside the conference room. The morning's briefing had been intense, filled with discussions of recent sightings and unexplained phenomena. Trent approached, two steaming cups of coffee in hand.

"Thought you could use this," he said, offering her one.

"Thanks." Natalie took a sip, savoring the bitter warmth.

Trent hesitated, then asked, "So, I've been meaning to ask... is there someone special waiting for you back home?"

The question caught Natalie off guard. Her mind immediately flashed to Marcus, her ex-fiancé. The memories came flooding back—their slow-burn romance, the sudden proposal, and then the slow unraveling as her work and her regret over Paul consumed her.

"I... it's complicated," she finally said.

Trent nodded, understanding in his eyes. "Isn't it always?"

Natalie took another sip of coffee, buying time. "There was someone. We were engaged, actually. But the work... it just got in the way."

"What happened? I mean, if you don't mind me asking."

She did mind, but not as much as she expected. "He couldn't handle the long hours, the travel, and the fringe theories. Said he felt like he was competing with aliens and ghosts for my attention."

"Do you ever regret it? Choosing the work over..."

"Over a normal life?" Natalie finished. She paused, considering. "Sometimes. But then I think about what we're doing here, the truth we're trying to uncover. This is a massive leap forward over my work at MUFON, and I enjoyed that. How could I walk away from it?"

Trent nodded, his expression thoughtful. "It's not an easy path we've chosen. Most people think we're nuts."

"No," Natalie agreed, curious about how the agent increasingly felt like he was part of the team, not just its protector. "It's not."

"So what's their story?" Natalie asked, changing the subject.

Trent followed her gaze to Emily and General Briggs, who were speaking quietly. "Ahh, the general."

Natalie hadn't known the man was a general. It was obvious he was ex-military, but she'd rarely seen him interact with General Taylor or Walker. Briggs was an informal and irregular attendee at the meetings.

"That man is a legend around this city. A true power broker and a very old family friend of the director. Carter mentioned to me once that he was the one who encouraged her to start this task force. In my opinion, he is likely the reason she is one office away from the president as well."

"He has that kind of pull?" Natalie asked.

"Oh, yes, and more."

"Does he have a title? I mean, he just seems to come and go," Natalie said as she finished her coffee and dropped the cup into the waste bin.

"Officially, no," Trent said. "I'm sure he's called a special advisor or liaison or some other bullshit, but he is whatever he wants to be. He's not political and doesn't seem to be out for personal gain, which puts him at odds with ninety-nine percent of the people in this town and makes him invaluable to whomever is in charge. He's networked into everything and uses his access and friends to be in the know before anyone else."

"So he's in intelligence... like you."

Trent smiled and shook his head. "Nothing like me, no. I look for information people are trying to hide. General Briggs looks for the people doing the hiding and why they are doing it."

Trent tossed his empty cup as well and then smiled at Natalie. "Nice job on changing the subject there, too. You are smoothly effective."

Natalie blushed slightly but fought it off with a smirk.

"So, if you won't have dinner with me, do me one thing."

"I never said..."

Trent held up his hands. "I want you to be careful. I know you have a concealed carry card. I suggest you start carrying a weapon. If you don't have one, I'll get you one and check you out on it."

"What makes you think I'm not carrying already?"

He smiled. "I checked with the gate guard. No one gets into the White House with one, which means you would have to check it at the sentry station along with your smartphone. I asked... no gun."

"You are observant, Agent Rogers. I'll give you credit, but yes, I have one, and I am current on my range qualifications." She stepped toward the door, then paused. "You really feel like I'm in danger?" She smiled, recalling a very similar conversation with her old boyfriend.

He pointed toward the general and Emily, who were still talking discreetly. "That should let you know how damn serious this task force has become. Someone doesn't like what we are doing, and yes, I think everyone in SCET is in danger." He picked up his notebook and exited into the main corridor.

A few minutes later, Natalie exited via the guard station and followed Trent to the parking area. She jogged to catch up with him. "Hang on, Rogers. You can't just say something like that and leave."

His warning about danger had unsettled her, but there was something else nagging at her thoughts. As they walked side by side, she couldn't help but steal glances at him, noticing the confident set of his shoulders, the sharp line of his jaw.

Was her interest in him purely professional? She had to admit there was a certain chemistry between them, a spark that she couldn't quite ignore. But was it just the thrill of working together on something so momentous, so world-changing?

She shook her head, trying to clear her thoughts. This was hardly the time for such distractions. They might be on the verge of uncovering something real, a truth that could shake the very foundations of society. She needed to focus on the work, on the mission at hand.

And yet... there was something about Trent that drew her in. His dedication, his intensity, the way he seemed to understand the weight of what they were doing. It was refreshing to find someone who shared her passion, her drive.

But no, she couldn't let herself get carried away. Whatever this was, whatever she might be feeling, it had to take a backseat. The stakes were too high and the risks too great.

As they reached the parking lot, Natalie paused, turning to face Trent. "I appreciate the warning," she said, her tone professional. "And I'll take your advice about the gun. But let's keep things focused on the work, okay? We can't afford any... distractions."

Trent met her gaze, his eyes searching hers for a long moment. Then he nodded, a hint of a smile playing at the corner of his mouth. “Of course. Aliens first. Flirting later.”

Natalie nodded, satisfied. She turned to leave, but Trent's voice stopped her.

"But Natalie? When this is all over... maybe we can revisit that dinner invite."

She paused, her heart skipping a beat. Then, without turning around, she allowed herself a small smile. "Maybe. We'll see."

And with that, she walked away, her mind already turning back to the task at hand, even as a small part of her wondered what the future might hold with Agent Trent Rogers.

CHAPTER FIFTY-TWO

1057 EST June 22
Old Town Office Park
Alexandria, Virginia, USA

Kaden stepped into the lab, the air thick with the smell of old documents and the hum of excitement. Elena, his former student, greeted him with a familiar look in her eyes.

"Thanks for stopping by, Kaden."

Her new temporary lab was a testament to her dedication, every inch of space filled with reports, diagrams, and artifacts relating to the Mars stones discovery.

"You said it was important, Elena," Kaden said.

"How are you doing?" she asked.

He knew she had heard about the scandal and probably reached the same conclusion as others on the committee. "I'm okay. I guess at a certain point, you just have to accept these tactics as a cost of making progress."

She nodded, then touched his arm tenderly.

"Kaden, I've been through everything," Elena said, gesturing toward the chaos around them. "I think we've been looking at this the wrong way."

He nodded, intrigued. "Go on."

Elena took a deep breath, her voice just above a whisper. "I believe aliens may have always existed here on Earth. They've been living here, potentially even maintaining a hidden base."

"On Earth?" Kaden asked, confused.

"And maybe on the moon or, obviously, Mars," she said. "If down here, it would have to be concealed or so remote we would never find it. Antarctica, under the sea. But hundreds or thousands of years ago, they could have been nearly anywhere. The global population was so much smaller and so scattered; a base could have been..."

"In Africa, perhaps?" he offered, finishing her sentence.

Elena nodded. Kaden considered that and the implications. He wanted to believe, to let Elena's enthusiasm infect him. But the professional repercussions of pursuing such unproven claims loomed large in his mind.

"I've gone back over 10,000 years," she said. "Prior to the last Ice Age, the planet looked very different."

Kaden nodded. "Most of it was a snowball."

"Some of it," she corrected. "But not all. In truth, the Last Glacial Maximum only covered about eight percent of Earth's surface and around twenty-five percent of the land mass." Kaden knew that already but was failing to see where she was going. "You've seen these."

"The Nazca lines in Peru," he said, looking at the pictures on her screen.

Elena pointed at the screen displaying the intricate patterns of the Nazca lines. "This area and much of South America stayed ice-free during this time. These geoglyphs have always been a mystery," she began. "Conventional theories suggest they were created by the Nazca people for religious purposes, possibly to be seen by deities from the sky. But what if there's more to it?"

"Impressive, but the Nazca lines are only a few hundred years old, aren't they?"

Elena smiled, and it washed over Kaden as if he were a young man again. "You are, of course, right," she said. "But we now know that the Nazca were essentially copying symbols from a much older culture known as the Paracas.

"Think about it," Elena said, tapping on an aerial image of a massive hummingbird etched into the Earth. "The precision, the scale—these were made to be viewed from above, from an altitude impossible for the Nazca people without flight. Some believe they were a form of communication or even a landing guide for extraterrestrial visitors."

Kaden nodded slowly, eyeing the always intriguing figure of the Nazca spaceman. "So you think these lines might be markers or signals for alien ships?"

Elena's excitement grew. "Exactly! And it's not just about being seen from above. The symbols themselves might hold deeper meanings—patterns, codes that align with constellations or specific planetary systems. Look here," she pointed to another image showing overlapping and somewhat random geometric shapes. "These designs are too complex to be mere artistic expressions."

Kaden rubbed his chin thoughtfully. "That would imply that extraterrestrials had significant interaction with ancient civilizations."

"Or even guided them," Elena said softly, her voice filled with awe. "These civilizations could have received knowledge or technology from extraterrestrial beings, explaining sudden advancements in architecture and astronomy."

"But why would aliens help them? What would they gain?" Kaden asked.

Elena paused, her gaze distant as if peering into ancient history itself. "Maybe it was a form of symbiosis. Aliens could have required resources or certain conditions only Earth could provide at that time. In exchange, they helped upgrade the current farming techniques, irrigation, or weather prediction. They showed them how to use the stars to know when to plant crops. They offered them the next step in technology."

It was intriguing but not exactly new as far as theories went. Then Elena pulled up a new image. It showed a very different landmass, one filled with thick vegetation.

"Amazon jungle?" Kaden asked, questioningly.

"Yes," Elena said. "The Nazca, or more accurately, Paracas lines are intriguing because they are so well preserved. That is due to the desert conditions in that location. Several years ago, as the rainforest was being lost to logging and agriculture, they began to find shapes there as well."

She showed several images with rudimentary shapes spread out over large tracts of land.

Kaden thought he might have heard that before, but it was not his field of study, so those facts tended not to take root as well.

“Last year, ESA launched a new Landsat with LIDAR, you know, the photo sensors that can penetrate through trees to sense the actual ground beneath. The dark, green foliage of the Amazon basin disappeared, revealing the ground beneath as a literal patchwork of images, roads, and obvious settlements.

"My word. There must be hundreds of these..."

"Thousands," Elena said. "Maybe tens of thousands. Obviously, the rainforest was not as thick back then. During the Ice Age, it may have been more of a subtropical climate than tropical. These glyphs spread out to cover an area almost as large as the United States. These ancient people were all over down there, paying homage to something in the sky, something they revered almost as god-like. Beings who were just as real to them as their neighbors in Peru thousands of miles away."

"Or Africa, even farther away," Kaden said.

He flipped back through many of the images, his mind silently curating the more salient points.

"Elena, I am impressed. It's a bold theory. You’re beginning to sound like a younger me," he said cautiously. "But what makes you think we have enough evidence to support it?"

Elena's eyes locked onto his. "The symbols on the Mars stones, you know they're not just random markings. They're from here, and that suggests a far deeper connection between Earth, Mars, and the space beyond than we could have ever imagined."

Elena seemed to sense his uncertainty. "Kaden, I know this sounds crazy, but this is proof, as long as we get a chance to pursue it."

Kaden placed a hand on the younger woman's arm. Her white lab coat was wrinkled and stained—nothing like the prize student, assistant, and much more that she had been to him years earlier.

"What's going on, Elena? Where is this onrush of passion for fringe theories coming from? You were always the logical one of us. The standard candle that we loved to dash our romantic theories against."

She looked away briefly. "It's not just about the stones, Kaden. It's about what happened to Alex."

Kaden's brow furrowed. "Alex? What are you talking about?"

Elena's voice dropped to a whisper. "He was part of our team, one of the ones who discovered the stones."

"I remember the lad's name," Kaden offered. "What about him?"

"After they locked us out, he disappeared. Dropped off the radar—no one has heard from him in months. I think it's connected, Kaden. I think someone or something doesn't want us to know the truth."

Elena's words painted a picture more complex and sinister than he was ready to face. He looked at her, seeing the determination in her eyes, and knew he had to make a choice. Was he ready to confront his past mistakes and prioritize truth over fear of consequences? Or would he let caution and fear dictate his path once more?

"You're on a presidential commission now, Elena. Both of us are. We have a chance to find out the truth once and for all."

She nodded. "I do thank you for endorsing me for that. But..." Kaden could clearly see the woman was conflicted. "What if it is just all for show, like all the committee hearings and press conferences have been up to this point? What if they just want to contain us, control what we know, and if they need to—set us up for failure?"

Kaden considered the implications of Elena's words. The image of Alex, a brilliant mind lost potentially to the shadows, flickered in his thoughts. He couldn't shake the feeling of déjà vu. The name James Forrestal again bubbled up from his subconscious, a ghost from the annals of UFO history.

Forrestal was the first U.S. Secretary of Defense, had been a towering figure in his day, known for his relentless advocacy of UFO investigations. His death in 1949—falling from the 16th floor of Bethesda Naval Hospital—had been officially ruled a suicide.

Kaden's former colleagues had already labeled him as a fringe scientist, and another wild goose chase could cement his reputation as a pariah. He looked around at the chaotic room, every artifact and document calling out for someone to help reveal their truths.

"If we go down this path," Kaden began, his voice thick with uncertainty, "we will need concrete proof. If we don't have it, this could destroy us—destroy me. At the level we are now, nothing will escape scrutiny."

Elena stepped closer, her eyes locking onto his, bringing back old feelings he'd long abandoned. "Kaden, I know you're scared. I am, too. But think about what you've already accomplished. You've pushed boundaries no one else dared to touch."

"That's the problem," he sighed. "I've been on the edge for so long. One more wrong step and I'll fall off."

Elena placed a hand on his shoulder, her grip firm but comforting. "Your past doesn't have to define you. Remember when you first taught me about looking beyond the obvious? You always said that real breakthroughs only come from taking risks."

He felt a pang of nostalgia, remembering those days when curiosity and ambition burned bright within him.

"You can't let fear dictate your actions now," she continued. "If we let this slip through our fingers because we're too afraid of what might happen, we'll regret it forever."

Kaden's gaze softened as he absorbed Elena's words. She was right; fear had been a constant companion, whispering doubts into his ear and keeping him from reaching his full potential.

"I've already lost too much to this obsession," he murmured, almost to himself.

"Maybe," Elena replied. "But think of what we stand to gain if we're right."

He turned away from her, walking over to the lab window and staring out into the vast expanse of sky visible through the glass. The city lights below twinkled like stars against a dark canvas. He gazed up, watching the jets lining up for the nearby airport, thinking of all the other lights he'd seen that were much less simple to explain.

"We aren't alone," Kaden whispered.

"We've never been alone," she added, stepping up beside him.

"What we're seeing now isn't a beneficial alien interaction, Elena. In fact, it seems to be the exact opposite."

She nodded, "Something changed. We need to know what."

He would help Elena bring her findings before the task force, and for Kaden Trembley, that was just the next step. Finding the truth was what ultimately mattered.

CHAPTER FIFTY-THREE

0903 EST June 21
White House West Wing
Washington, D.C., USA

Elena watched her friend leave. She knew her emerging theory was way out there on the fringe, but she just couldn't let it go. She was an astrophysicist, but her first love and her minor were in geology. Now, that one was proving more useful than the other.

She was enjoying working with the other members of the task force. Each was brilliant, at least in their own field, and more importantly, open-minded to ideas like this. Other than Alana, whom she found a bit of a loner. Kaden had always been her rock; even when they weren't really talking, she always knew he would be there for her.

Elena carefully adjusted the microscope, focusing intently on a newly received sample from a Martian meteorite. As she examined the intricate details of the rock, her mind wandered to the seismic data they had also collected. Could it possibly support one of her more recent hunches?

She immersed herself in the volumes of data she now had access to, poring over every detail with a keen eye. As she delved deeper, other intriguing possibilities began to take shape. The pieces of the puzzle started to fit together, forming a picture that both excited and unnerved her.

She meticulously jotted down notes, ensuring that every observation was accurately recorded. Using state-of-the-art equipment, she captured high-resolution images of the sample, preserving the intricate details for further analysis.

Elena's fingers clicked absently on the keyboard, backing up her findings to her shared cloud drive. The data she'd collected from the Martian seismic activity correlated too well with the unusual seismic patterns here on Earth. It had to be more than a coincidence—but what? Maybe gravimetric devices, maybe even underground bases or transport systems. She felt a thrill whenever she was on the cusp of a breakthrough, and this felt like one.

Her old friend, Kaden, would be harder to convince, but to her, there was mounting evidence pointing to two conclusions. Aliens had been visiting and possibly staying on Earth undetected for a very long time. And the more surprising theory was that, judging by the data, there was likely more than one species involved in the visitations.

For Elena's findings to be true, the extraterrestrials must have mastered some method of controlling gravity at the quantum level. They could potentially stay hidden underground or under the sea inside a virtual bubble of null gravity.

She'd painstakingly spent much of the past forty-eight hours mapping out data points that she now guessed were potential entry or exit points for the UFOs. Her next step was to use some of Kaden's grad students' data to overlay UFO sightings to see how many matched up.

Outside, a fleeting shadow crossed the lab window, unnoticed by Elena, who was too engrossed in her work. The lab's overhead lights flickered ominously, casting brief, unsettling shadows around the room. She felt a sudden chill and glanced around nervously. Shaking off the eerie sensation, she refocused on her task, determined to present her findings to the SCET team in the next day's session.

The lab door whispered open, its well-oiled hinges barely audible in the hushed room. A shadow detached itself from the darkness beyond, materializing into a stocky figure cloaked entirely in black. The intruder's face was hidden behind a featureless black mask, dimly reflecting the glow of computer screens like a void with physical form.

Elena's fingers paused over her keyboard, another chill creeping up her spine. Something primal, buried deep in her lizard brain, sensed the predator's presence before her conscious mind could process it. The faintest rustle of fabric, a whisper of displaced air—it was enough.

She spun in her chair, eyes wildly searching for the threat. Time seemed to slow as her gaze locked onto the advancing danger. The assailant's arm was already in motion, a glint of metal catching the light as it arced toward her.

Elena's mind screamed a warning, fight-or-flight instincts kicking into overdrive. She saw the attacker's muscles tense beneath the black fabric, preparing to close the final distance. In that frozen moment, she cataloged details with scientific precision—the height and build of her assailant, the controlled grace of their movements, and the complete absence of hesitation in their approach.

Her body reacted on pure instinct. Elena's hand shot out, grasping for anything she could use as a weapon or shield. Her fingers closed around the first object they found—a heavy binder full of new research notes. She brought it up just as the masked figure lunged, closing the gap between them with terrifying speed.

She tried to scream, but a gloved hand clamped over her mouth. A brief, violent struggle ensued as she knocked over a tray of tools in a desperate attempt to break free. The crash echoed through the lab.

The operative silenced her swiftly, leaving her motionless on the floor. He hurriedly searched the room, zeroing in on Elena's laptop containing her critical data. In seconds, he'd secured it and vanished into the night, leaving chaos and uncertainty in his wake.

CHAPTER FIFTY-FOUR

2007 EST
NovaCore Offices
McLean, Virginia, USA

"Jesus Christ, King. Raymond is already fucked. If the truth about any of this gets out, we won't just be arrested—we will hang for treason."

Owen King offered one of his trademark smiles. He, too, was shaken by the recent events, but he knew better than to let this asshole see it. "Pete, you are the national security advisor. You can control what the president sees and does better than anyone. Now, yes, we have some exposure down on the coast."

"On the coast?" the older man said. "What about everywhere else? Are you blind to the fucking news, man?"

"Of course not, Director," Owen said smoothly. "After all, we help generate many of those headlines. Cloud the media with enough sensationalistic headlines that the truth never stands a chance."

"What about the airbase?" Pete asked, clearly fed up with Owen King's nonplussed demeanor.

"What about it?" King spread his steepled fingers in a questioning gesture. "We have a comms blackout covering a fifty-mile radius. No cell service, no internet. All news media is being kept away, and of course, the highways are all shut down to inbound or outbound traffic. The Navy and Coast Guard are busy keeping boat traffic away."

"News will get out. It's too big a story...too many casualties to just sweep under the rug."

"I don't disagree. The story will get out, but it will be 'our' story. One that we control the narrative on."

"Oh?" the national security advisor said questioningly. "I am eager to hear this one. How in the hell are you going to spin this to cover up all the fucking evidence? We lost a chunk of the state of Florida for God's sake! This isn't some farmer's field in New Mexico or a backwater village in South America. This is the Gulf Coast of America. It's a goddamn mecca for sun-worshipers and snowbirds. I've already heard estimates north of 45,000 casualties, so what 'narrative' do you have that will explain all this away?" Pete did air quotes sarcastically as he said it.

Owen King leaned back in his chair. "Here's the narrative," he began, voice steady and confident. "We attribute the explosion to a natural gas pipeline and storage facility rupture combined with a rare geological event—a sudden, unexpected collapse of a massive subterranean cavern. Florida is riddled with sinkholes. The site engineers for the pipeline failed to adequately assess the geologic strata."

Pete frowned but didn't interrupt.

"The impact site will be explained as the epicenter of this catastrophic combination. The gas explosion caused the initial blast, which led to the ignition of the wildfire. As for the coastline changes, we can say the cavern collapse resulted in unprecedented subsidence, shifting the ground and causing parts of the coastline to sink."

"And the cell outage?" Pete asked, crossing his arms.

"The electromagnetic interference from the explosion disrupted local cell towers. We'll release a statement that engineers are working around the clock to restore service. As for the blackout radius, we'll say the disaster led to a series of cascading failures, including taking down part of one of the major fiber-net gateways along the East Coast."

Pete's skepticism was palpable, but he seemed to be considering the idea. "What about the sheer scale of the casualties and the fact that Eglin was obviously destroyed?"

"We'll emphasize the unexpected nature of the geological event. The gas company will issue an apology, stating they were unaware of the cavern's instability. Sadly, later on, we will begin making suggestions that the Air Force was stockpiling unregistered and dangerous new types of bombs."

"What, like a neutron bomb or something?"

Owen smiled. "Or something. The point is, someone will need to take the heat for it, but it damn sure won't be either of us."

King leaned back in his chair and propped both hands behind his head in a well-practiced move to show how relaxed he was.

"We'll also highlight the heroic efforts of first responders, who, despite the odds, managed to save countless lives. Human interest stories will follow, showcasing the resilience and unity of the affected communities."

"And how do we explain away the military presence?"

"Routine disaster response. The National Guard and other military units were mobilized to assist with evacuation and emergency services. It's not uncommon for the military to be involved in large-scale natural disasters. We'll frame it as a coordinated effort to ensure the safety and security of the population."

Pete sat back, rubbing his temples. "It's risky. People are going to ask questions."

"Of course they will," Owen replied smoothly. "But questions are manageable. Answers are what matter, and we control the answers. We'll flood the media with expert analyses, interviews with geologists, and stories of survival. It'll create enough noise to drown out any dissenting voices."

A heavy silence settled between them. Finally, Pete nodded slowly. "Alright. Let's go with your narrative. But if this blows up in our faces..."

"It won't," Owen interrupted, his smile returning. "We've weathered worse storms. We'll get through this, too."

Pete sighed, the weight of the decision evident on his face. "How does this explain what happened up the road in Pensacola?"

"Easy, the pipeline went through there." King had already been advised that there were indeed massive natural gas lines throughout the area. "That section of the coast has overbuilt massively the last few decades; shortcuts were taken. Officials will be arrested for taking kickbacks. A transport ship in the bay was helping stress test the new gas lines, and when they failed, the pressure caused a secondary disaster in Pensacola. That one was much smaller anyway."

The national security advisor shook his head. "Does it not bother you at all? All these lies, all the deaths. Hell, man, the fact that your goddamn aliens just bombed us?"

"Of course it does," Owen said truthfully. "Still, we know this is minor compared to what they could have done. Somebody broke the accord—we are going to find out who, and that person will face the wrath of all the Observers."

Owen's eyes gleamed with calculated confidence. "Trust me, Director. We got this. This is what we do best."

"He's going to be a problem," Gibson said, entering from an adjacent room just after the director left.

Owen King nodded in agreement. "He is, but it's his ass on the line. We could all disappear tonight. He's too high profile."

"What about when he finds out it's closer to a hundred thousand deaths?"

"Let's hope math isn't one of his strong points," Owen said.

"You know what Stalin said about the death of millions," Gibson said, his face curving into an unnerving grin.

Owen nodded, but his mind was already elsewhere. Earth's visitors were increasingly taking direct action. In his mind, that could only get worse, and if so, he too might need to make some arrangements.

CHAPTER FIFTY-FIVE

1745 EST June 22
Georgetown
Washington, D.C., USA

Dr. Stephen Greene adjusted his tie as he stepped out of the cab in front of the Georgetown University auditorium. The evening air was crisp, and the street buzzed with the excitement of students and faculty heading to his lecture on extraterrestrial possibilities.

"Thank you, sir, for the ride," he called to the cabbie, fishing a few bills from his wallet.

As he turned towards the building, a group of students waved, recognizing him from his recent appearances on science podcasts. Stephen smiled, his spirits high. Tonight's talk could be big. He just wished he could do more than simply hint at his new gig working steps away from the president.

He glanced at his watch. Still fifteen minutes before he was due on stage. Plenty of time for a quick breath of fresh air to clear his mind and get his public persona tuned up.

Stephen strolled down the sidewalk, rehearsing key points in his head. The streetlights flickered on as dusk settled over the city.

A scuff of shoes behind him barely registered until a rough hand grabbed his shoulder, spinning him around.

"Wallet. Now," a gruff voice demanded. Stephen found himself face-to-face with two men, their features obscured by dark hoodies.

"Take it easy," Stephen said, raising his hands. "I don't want any trouble."

One of the men lunged forward, driving a fist into Stephen's stomach. He doubled over, gasping for air.

"We said, wallet," the other man growled, shoving Stephen against the brick wall of a nearby alley.

Stephen fumbled for his pocket, his quick mind analyzing even as his body spasmed in pain.

A swift kick to his knee sent Stephen crumpling back to the ground. One of the assailants grabbed his hair, slamming his head against the wall.

"Stop," Stephen wheezed. "Please, I'll give you whatever you want."

The men exchanged a look, their eyes cold and calculating. One of them pulled out a knife, the blade glinting in the dim light.

"This isn't about money, doc," he sneered. "It's about keeping your mouth shut."

Stephen's eyes widened with realization. His instincts were right; these weren't random thugs. That small mental acknowledgment was quickly followed by the resounding fact that it would be his last.

As the knife descended, Stephen's last thought was of his wife back home in Albany and his colleagues at SCET. He hoped they would be safe.

Alana Bishop's cross-trainers made no sound as she walked briskly down the dimly lit street. Her eyes darted from side to side, scanning her surroundings with practiced precision. Years of training and fieldwork had honed her instincts to a razor's edge. While her seat on the SCET committee had been more mundane, her habits were so ingrained as to be part of her DNA.

A flicker of movement in her peripheral vision caught her attention. She didn't turn her head, but her muscles tensed, ready for action. Two men in dark clothing were climbing out of an SUV. She could have been wrong, but it looked to her like they were trying hard to blend into the shadows.

As she approached the next intersection, she noticed a third figure emerge from an alley ahead; he appeared to be moving to cut off her path. Her suspicions confirmed, these guys were targeting her. Her instincts and threat assessments let her know this was a serious situation.

Alana kept her pace steady, not giving any indication she had noticed the mercenaries. She slipped her hand into her jacket pocket, fingers brushing against the compact multi-tool she always carried. As she approached a narrow alley, she ducked in swiftly, blending into the shadows as best she could.

She could hear the heavy footsteps of the men closing in behind her. Quickly, Alana pulled a thin wire that was wrapped tightly around the handle of a small tool and stretched it across the alley at ankle height, securing it tightly between a power conduit and a heavy wooden pallet. She backed away slowly, positioning herself for a better vantage point.

She moved silently to the far end, positioning herself behind a stack of crates. Her breath was calm and measured. The men entered the alley cautiously, their eyes struggling to adjust to the sudden darkness.

"Spread out," one of them whispered. "She can't have gone far."

One of the mercenaries moved forward, his foot catching on the wire. He stumbled and fell heavily to the ground, cursing under his breath. The sound echoed through the alley, drawing the attention of his companions.

"Damn, man. What happened?" another man asked, stepping closer to help his fallen comrade.

"Think that bitch set a tripwire," he growled. "Be careful."

Alana used their distraction to slip further down the alley, finding a rusted fire escape ladder. She climbed swiftly and silently to the second-floor landing, peering down at the scene below.

The men regrouped, scanning their surroundings with increased caution. Alana spotted a small metal pipe leaning against the wall nearby. She grabbed it and hurled it as far down the alley as she could. It clattered loudly against the concrete and bricks, causing all three men to whip around in alarm.

"She's down there!" one of them shouted, pointing towards where the pipe had fallen.

Alana used their momentary confusion to move along the fire escape toward another building's rooftop access. She used the multi-tool to force open a maintenance door and slipped inside, descending quickly through a stairwell that led her back to street level on another block.

As she emerged from the building, she blended seamlessly with a group of late-night pedestrians. Her heart pounded, but her mind remained sharp and focused.

The attackers would realize soon enough they had been outsmarted. But by then, Alana would be long gone. She called Emily Carter as she'd been instructed to do.

~

Natalie Reeves read the text twice before acknowledging it with a single-word reply. The director's warning at least explained why Trent was not hovering over her like a protective shadow tonight.

She had already made two full circuits around the block on the outskirts of D.C. The brick building was old, really old for this part of town. Natalie was curious by nature and meticulous as an investigator. She also carried a very healthy... or unhealthy lack of faith in what others told her.

Warehouse D, the address marker on her GPS said this was the right place. But was it the actual Warehouse D? That had been something Emily Carter had mentioned in one of the first meetings. The Army colonel had clamped the conversation down quickly, but Natalie had added it to her notes to check out all the same.

Coming up with an actual address had proven much more challenging. There were no fewer than forty-two buildings in the greater D.C. area using that same moniker. Thankfully, with Trent's help, she'd narrowed the field down to only three. The first on her list had turned out to be a burned-out husk. This monstrosity was number two.

Natalie parked her nondescript government sedan a few blocks away and walked back, blending into the evening shadows. She paused at the edge of the warehouse's lot, her eyes scanning for any signs of surveillance equipment. She didn't spot any obvious cameras, but that didn't mean they weren't there. Years of training had taught her to assume she was always being watched.

She approached cautiously, noting the closed loading bay doors. The building looked abandoned; no cars were parked in the adjacent lot, but appearances could be deceiving. Natalie moved closer to an ancient door that seemed ready to come off its rusty hinges. She pushed it gently, slipping inside.

The interior was a maze of dusty crates and long-forgotten machinery. She peered inside and identified the cast iron parts as most likely belonging to a farm implement production line of some sort. A few of the items looked vaguely familiar. She moved on through the shadows, her eyes adjusting to the dim light filtering through broken windows, her footsteps stirring tiny dusty swirls on the old wooden floor.

Natalie's instincts told her to look for hidden surveillance equipment again. She spotted a small, blinking light on one of the rafters ahead—a covert camera. "Typical," she muttered under her breath, making a mental note to stay out of its line of sight.

She continued deeper into the warehouse, passing rows of empty shelves and a derelict forklift sitting angled with only three wheels on it. An open shipping bay caught her eye. The bay was clean—too clean for an abandoned building. Fresh tire tracks marked the floor, leading to a large metal crate positioned conspicuously in the center.

Natalie approached the crate, noticing a small keypad lock on its side. She jotted down its serial number before moving on, her eyes sweeping the area for more clues.

A set of double doors at the far end of the warehouse beckoned her. They were slightly ajar, and she could see a faint glow emanating from within. Pushing one door gently open, Natalie found herself in a room filled with computer terminals and filing cabinets.

She rifled through some papers on a desk, finding documents

marked 'Project Sentinel.' Her pulse quickened as she skimmed through them—most were heavily redacted, but keywords like 'extraterrestrial,' 'containment,' and 'resource allocation' stood out.

Standing back, Natalie scanned the room once more. To someone like her, this smelled like a trap—a well-hidden, baited trap. One she had just walked right into. She turned and raced for the door as the smell of gasoline and the giant 'whoof' of flame sounded far behind. She had just reached the old door when the interior of the building erupted in flame.

Natalie doused her smoldering clothes with water from her tumbler before sliding back into her assigned car. She was uninjured but pissed at herself for not being even more cautious. Telling Trent she'd come out here on her own was going to be tough, but first, she had to let Emily know someone was definitely targeting all of them. Also, since Emily had this information first, it was probably meant for her if anyone.

CHAPTER FIFTY-SIX

1003 EDT June 24
White House Oval Office
Washington, D.C., USA

The president's fists slammed onto the polished oak table, the sound echoing through the Situation Room. "What the hell else got hit? And who did it?" His eyes scanned the room, demanding answers from his top advisors.

General Weston cleared his throat, stepping forward. "Sir, the strikes were surgical. They targeted very specific military logistics and transportation hubs."

"Go on," the president urged, his face a mask of controlled fury.

Weston pointed to the large screen displaying a map of the United States. Red dots marked the impact zones. "Major food distribution centers in Virginia and the Midwest, power generation facilities across the Northeast, hydroelectric sites in Missouri, Idaho, and Illinois, and key logistics hubs along the coasts were all struck. It's clear these strikes were designed to cripple our infrastructure."

The new Secretary of Homeland Security, Linda Reyes, interjected, her voice steady but concerned. "This wasn't a decapitation strike. There were no political targets. Most major cities are untouched. The intent seems to be disruption rather than mass casualties."

The president's jaw tightened. He felt this was his punishment for not raising the alarm when Florida was hit. Emily had been right; that was just a first strike, and the public damn sure should have been told. "So, what's the motive? And more importantly, who even has the capability for this level of precision?"

Director Harris of the CIA leaned forward, adjusting his glasses. "We're still gathering intel, but preliminary analysis indicates this isn't the work of any nation-state we're familiar with. The coordination and precision imply an advanced technological level well beyond current military weapon capabilities. No radiological fallout either, sir. These appear to be KEW weapons. Orbital bombardment."

The president's eyes narrowed, the implications weighing heavily on him. "Are you suggesting this could be extraterrestrial?"

Harris paused, weighing his words carefully. "It's a possibility we aren't dismissing, sir. The nature of the attacks and the absence of known terrestrial signatures point toward an unknown origin."

The room fell into a heavy silence, the gravity of the revelation settling like a thick fog over those advisors who were unaware of the Eglin attack.

General Weston was the first to speak again, trying to refocus the discussion. "Mr. President, our immediate concern should be stabilizing the affected regions. We've mobilized National Guard units and are coordinating with FEMA to ensure essential services are restored. Unfortunately, with so many of the nation's highways and rail lines impassable and the number of operational airports and bases dwindling, our options are limited."

Reyes nodded, her expression grave. "We've also increased security at other critical infrastructure points to prevent further attacks."

The president paced from side to side in front of the room, firing questions like arrows. "How? Tell me, Secretary Reyes. What measures can we employ to thwart another wave? If you had known this was coming, what could you have done?" Frustration oozed from him as he pivoted, looking for new targets. "And the public, Emily... David? What do we tell them?"

Press Secretary Daniel Harper spoke up first, "We need to address the nation, reassure them that we're in control and taking all necessary measures. But we must be careful not to incite panic."

The president nodded, his expression resolute. "Prepare a statement. I want to address the nation within the hour. And keep me updated on any developments. We need to figure out who did this and why."

As his advisors moved to execute his orders, the president stared at the map, the red dots searing into his memory. The country was under attack, and the enemy remained elusive and utterly unknown.

Once the room emptied, Emily Carter guided Colonel James Walker from the Situation Room to a nearby office. "A word, please, Colonel."

"Of course, Director Carter."

"Not Director, just Emily. Let's keep this off the record." Emily had known not to mention anything about the Eglin strike in the meeting. The president hadn't offered much detail, so she had followed his lead. Walker had been in the SCET meeting, though, and was probably read in on the prior strike.

"Of course, ma'am... I mean, Emily. What do you need?"

"This strike... I assume it came from space... deep space like the others?" she asked.

Colonel Walker met her gaze, understanding her implication. "It definitely came from space."

Emily's brow furrowed as she nodded, already fairly certain it had. "I feel sure I know the answer, but any chance it was just random chance?"

Colonel Walker folded his arms, his face thoughtful. "The odds of a KEW strike being naturally occurring are infinitesimal, Emily. Asteroids and meteors do impact Earth, but their paths are chaotic and unpredictable. They don't target specific locations with this kind of precision."

Emily's brow furrowed. "But let's entertain the possibility. What are the chances?"

Walker took a deep breath. "First, consider the atmosphere. Most asteroids burn up before reaching the surface. Those that do make it are random, not controlled. They ablate, burn off, and scatter debris across wide areas, not direct hits on specific targets."

"How precise are we talking on these?" Emily leaned in, her eyes intent.

Walker pointed to the map still showing on the display in the other room. "Take another look at the impact zones. Each strike hit a high-value target with pinpoint accuracy. A naturally occurring object would have a random spread, not this level of precision. The truth is, even our own KEWs could not reach even a fraction of that degree of accuracy."

Emily nodded, understanding dawning. "So, these strikes had to be guided, aimed."

"Exactly," Walker agreed. "Kinetic energy weapons, or KEWs, are designed to strike with incredible force and accuracy. They don't just fall from space; they're directed."

Emily's eyes narrowed. "And the trajectories?"

"We're running reverse tracking on them now," Walker said, pulling up a screen with data. "The initial analysis shows these projectiles were possibly launched months ago from somewhere outside the ecliptic plane. That means they were in deep space, directed here deliberately."

Emily considered the man's words. "So, something out there planned this attack well in advance. These KEWs weren't just random debris."

Walker nodded grimly. "Tailor-made for this strike, Emily. Whoever did this had the technology to plan and execute an attack with a long lead time."

Emily looked at the data screen on her tablet, the weight of the expanding destruction settling heavily on her. "Fair to say we're dealing with an enemy far more advanced than we are."

"Indeed," Walker agreed. "We need to find out who or what is behind this—and fast."

Emily straightened, determination in her eyes. "What is the Pentagon's war game scenario for an alien invasion, Colonel?"

The man looked decidedly uncomfortable. He mumbled something nearly unintelligible.

"I'm sorry, James. What was that?"

He met her gaze. "The United States does not have a defensive plan for such an attack."

Emily was beside herself, angry at the very system she was a part of. "We have, at a minimum, table-top scenarios for the most outlandish attacks possible. How is it we don't have one for this?"

Walker bobbed his head a few times, wondering the best way to answer. "The war game attack scenarios are developed based on the likelihood of occurrence as well as what we know about the potential enemy. No offense, ma'am, but little green men attacking didn't meet that standard. But it has at least been discussed. Any defense would need to be a joint coordinated effort, likely with the Air Force leading the assault, but they have routinely been unwilling to discuss it in any great detail."

The acting chief of staff studied the man. She liked Walker; he was a good military advisor and, as far as she knew, had never tried to bullshit POTUS. "You better start working on it, Colonel. We're starting to lose important chunks of our country. I have a feeling we're going to need solutions fast."

She was glad the president was at least going to brief the public, but her own enthusiasm was severely diminished by the task she had to do next—condolence letters for the families of two members of SCET.

No Coordinated Attacks Confirmed — White House Attributes Fires and Explosions to Infrastructure Failures, Civil Unrest, and 'Opportunistic Misinformation'

"The American people deserve clarity, and that's what we're here to provide," said White House Press Secretary Daniel Harper. "There is no credible evidence of a foreign attack or domestic terrorism campaign linked to recent events in the Midwest and Atlantic regions.

"The explosion outside Roanoke appears to have originated from a neglected propane storage facility operated by a defunct agribusiness cooperative.

"The St. Louis incident, previously speculated to be an airstrike, has been officially linked to an abandoned rail yard where amateur fireworks were stored illegally and detonated by local gang affiliates.

"Fires reported in Indianapolis and outside Pittsburgh have been traced to electrical grid overloads caused by outdated equipment and poor regional maintenance.

"It's unfortunate that a few online influencers have used these unrelated events to fuel fear, panic, and dangerous conspiracy theories. The Department of Homeland Security is actively working to curb the spread of misinformation and protect American minds as well as bodies."

Official White House Statement | Press Secretary Harper, National Address Summary

CHAPTER FIFTY-SEVEN

The mountain of material uncovered so far was compounded by the loss of two of the team's members and attacks on several others. Emily was no fool; she knew the score, and it was obvious she was getting too close to the truth.

"Obviously, what we do here matters. All we have to do is watch the news for the daily disasters to fully understand that extraterrestrials are real. President Martin is planning to address the nation. I've seen a recent draft of his speech, and it carefully alludes to but avoids admitting aliens might be behind the attacks.

"I think we have to face the possibility of SCET being made public, which may actually be a good thing since it is apparent from the recent attacks that we are being targeted. In that regard, a couple of our members have sadly resigned or will no longer be joining us for other reasons."

While Trent and a few others knew of the ongoing threats and attacks against members, she had decided not to reveal the deaths of Greene and Schmidt until later. Kaden, she knew, would be devastated by the news.

"Now, if or when this goes public, it is likely that each of us will be sought out for interviews. We will be touted as experts and also likely blamed for everything that is going on, including the cover-up. The timing is terrible, but I felt it best if each of us had a solid understanding of when the visitations started, and maybe we can come up with some explanations for why they are turning violent. We need to be concise as this will all likely be in a brief to President Martin as well. Kaden and Natalie, please walk us through what you have."

Doctor Trembley rose and walked to the front of the table and clicked on the large flat-screen display. He nodded to Natalie to start the slide deck.

"I know everyone wants to see another PowerPoint, but trust me, for this we are going to need it. You see, we are going to have to go back... way back. Doctor Green had been assembling much of this, and I'm not taking credit, but I will add my points where I can."

Natalie flipped through a series of images.

"This is The Tulli Papyrus, an alleged transcription of an Egyptian document that supposedly describes a sequence of mysterious fiery disks in the sky around 1480 BCE."

A painting appeared next, depicting an ancient city with what clearly looked like a UFO firing a beam of light into one of the buildings.

"The Annunciation with Saint Emidius from 1486," Kaden said.

"Next, a fresco in the Visoki Dečani Monastery in Kosovo from the mid-thirteenth century depicts the crucifixion of Jesus, flanked by two figures in what appear to be flying machines. The 'Madonna of the UFO' or 'Madonna of the Flying Saucer' is a painting located in Palazzo Vecchio in Florence in the Hall of Hercules. As you can see over in the background, there is a man and a dog looking up at a flying saucer in the sky. The man is even pointing at it." The shot zoomed in to show that section.

"Another seldom-mentioned report of strange aerial phenomena dates back to 1561, when residents of Nuremberg, Germany, described an aerial battle followed by the appearance of a large black triangular object, which was recorded in a broadsheet or type of newspaper of the time."

Kaden motioned for Natalie to speed through many of the others, including stone glyphs from Nepal, petroglyphs from Italy, and Australia. "The sarcophagus lid of the Mayan ruler Pakal the Great in

Palenque, Mexico, features intricate carvings that some interpret as depicting Pakal piloting a spaceship."

They continued to flip from screen to screen as Trembley picked up the narrative again. "Some of these are debatable, of course. I am not trying to convince anyone that any single image is an authentic representation of a UFO or an alien. Taken as a whole, though, they present a very compelling case that aliens have been visiting us for a long, long time. Possibly since the dawn of man." The final image was a rudimentary cave painting showing some horned animals running and a circular flying disc overhead.

"I wish Elena was here, as she has her own theories along these same lines that I find quite intriguing." He pulled up the geoglyphs and explained the possibility of ancient aliens in South America and Africa.

"Now, we want to skip ahead by many centuries. Post World War Two, to be exact. You may ask, 'Why then?' Well, something seems to have happened after we dropped the atom bomb. We have developed a theory, but it will be a bit controversial, so I'll save it for the end.

"Besides us cracking the atom down in New Mexico, we had mastered air travel. Airmen in the service often mentioned balls of bright light they called Foo Fighters trailing their craft." Kaden saw Natalie tense up at the mention of that.

"The first well-known sighting of what would be termed a 'flying saucer' occurred on June 24, 1947, when Kenneth Arnold, a private pilot, reported seeing a series of nine unidentified flying objects near Mount Rainier, Washington. Arnold described the objects as moving at incredibly high speeds, which he estimated to be around 1,200 miles per hour, and compared their motion to 'saucers skipping on water.' This description led to the widespread use of the term 'flying saucer' in the media.

"The next month, the so-called Roswell incident occurred. It is so well-documented that I don't think there is any need to spend more time on it. The thing is, this seems to set off a rash of incidents during the next few years. Incidents that seemed to set both the government and the military back on their heels."

Emily Carter seemed anxious. "Professor, I get the history lesson, but we have limited time."

Trembley smiled. "You want me to get to the ever-lovin' point, do you?" his British accent coming in strongly.

"The recurring theme," Kaden emphasized, "is control and containment. We've been given just enough information to keep us from blowing ourselves up, but likely not enough to understand or utilize their technology fully without supervision."

Kaden's eyes met each person in the room one by one.

"Our advancements in nuclear technology might have drawn their attention," he said, his tone soft but firm. "And since then, it seems our leaders have been operating under an unspoken rule: reveal too much about their existence or capabilities, and there might be dire consequences."

Natalie nodded in agreement beside him.

"That," Kaden concluded, "is why I believe we're being monitored—and why this cover-up is so meticulous, well-entrenched, and enduring.

"My..." he glanced at Natalie, "our, current belief is that a relatively small but powerful organization is likely behind this cover-up. Unsure if they would be military, government or what not. This mysterious organization, which we've taken to calling the Special Projects Group, would need to have far reaching capabilities and funding."

The meeting had been running long, and Emily felt exhausted but had two more questions. "Natalie and Kaden, thank you. Your work in this has been remarkable, as is your analysis. I have two concerns, and I hope you can clear them up quickly before we end. First one: What about the rest of the world? Does the influence of your Special Projects Group extend globally? We know many other countries have incidents as well and, like us, seem to also have cover-ups."

"That is a point that we simply don't know," Kaden answered. "Perhaps the SPG, as I'll call them, must have a worldwide presence. They certainly should have the resources. We are quite confident they are embedded in virtually every level of our own government, intelligence, and military. It may also be that the alien threat was shared with other major governments early on, but that seems unlikely as that secret would have been very hard to contain."

Emily seemed to accept that. "Number two: Why now?"

Kaden sat down, and Natalie gave the response—not one that she nor anyone else in that room was really prepared for.

"Invasion."

"Seriously?" the colonel said, standing up quickly.

"Occupation...cohabitation, call it what you want," Natalie said. "The aliens seem about ready for us to admit the truth. Disclosure is coming, and I think it's in the aliens' hands now. I don't know if this is the consequence they potentially threatened us with back in the fifties, but I would guarantee it is coming."

Emily's face was pale. "Professor, do you agree with this?"

Kaden nodded. "I'm afraid I do, Director Carter, one hundred percent."

"Jesus," Emily muttered uncharacteristically. "I've got to take this to the president." She looked at her notepad and scratched through a note. Then she seemed to reconsider. "Okay, I have a third question now. Obviously, the big threat is the aliens, but their motivation is unknown. Humans, we may be better able to figure out, so Kaden and Natalie, what do you think this SPG will do next?"

The two glanced at each other before Natalie took the lead. "We've been giving that considerable thought, and it is difficult to answer. If they are in close contact with the invaders, they may aid them in their assault. In discussing this with Agent Rogers and the professor, I don't feel that is likely. Personally, I think they have to be assuming they have failed. They're panicking. They are also likely about to have their flow of money cut off permanently. I think they are likely in chaos, desperate, and very likely making mistakes for the first time since 1945."

Emily sighed and sat back heavily. "Look, everyone. I need to let you know that we've lost two very talented members of this task force this week under questionable circumstances. Two more of you had very close encounters," she said, eyeing each of the remaining members in turn. Kaden's expression went to horrified, and he rushed briefly from the room. Emily had expected a strong reaction but continued on.

"If what Kaden and Natalie indicated is correct, and the mysterious Special Projects Group is out there controlling what we know and is as well-placed and well-funded as suggested, what is the likelihood that they know what we have just discussed?" She looked to Agent Rogers first.

Trent looked over at Natalie, who gave him a slight nod.

Agent Rogers cleared his throat, his eyes scanning the room before he spoke. "Director Carter, we've taken extensive precautions to ensure the security of our discussions here in the White House. We employ state-of-the-art electronic countermeasures, conduct regular sweeps for listening devices, and limit access to this wing to a select few individuals with the highest clearance levels."

He paused, his expression grave. "However, given what we've learned about the SPG's reach and resources, I have to be honest—we can't be certain our efforts are anything close to foolproof."

Rogers leaned forward, lowering his voice. "The truth is, we don't know the full extent of their infiltration or their technological capabilities. It's possible—even likely—that every word we've said here could be passed along to them in real time."

The room fell silent as the implications sank in. Rogers continued, his tone resolute. "I believe we represent a significant threat to their operations. If they have an exit strategy, they do not want us getting in the way. They've already shown they're willing to take drastic measures to protect their secrets."

He looked each person in the eye as he spoke. "We all need to take extreme precautions. Vary our routines, be cautious about whom we trust, and assume you are under constant surveillance. Our lives may depend on it."

Emily smiled and nodded for Natalie to take over.

"Our general agreement is that Roswell seems to mark the first time that the government, namely the U.S. Army, suppressed the truth about UFOs," Natalie began, picking up where Kaden had left off. "There were several government projects set up to investigate extraterrestrial incursions, including Majestic or MJ-12, Sign, Grudge, and Project Blue Book. Some of these were missions directed at national security, while others were clearly designed to discredit witnesses and bury the incidents from further scrutiny.

"In total, from 1948 to 2012, the U.S. alone has had nine different programs with the supposed central mission of uncovering the truth about UFOs. To date, none of these government-backed studies have provided credible results and only vague dismissals of the veracity of such craft, exotic technologies, or alien encounters.

"One important sub-note here is that James Vincent Forrestal, the first U.S. Secretary of Defense, died under mysterious circumstances in May of 1949 after falling from a 16th-floor window at the Bethesda Naval Hospital." An image of the man appeared on the large display. "Forrestal's death has been surrounded by numerous conspiracy theories and suspicions of foul play due to various irregularities in the official accounts and the context of his death.

"There are various claims and theories regarding his connection to UFOs. Some sources suggest that Forrestal intended to reveal the truth about UFOs and extraterrestrial phenomena, which may have contributed to his mental breakdown and subsequent death. These theories often link his declining mental health to his involvement in top-secret UFO-related projects and the pressure he faced from those who wanted to keep such information hidden."

CHAPTER FIFTY-EIGHT

Emily looked to the members of the military in the small room. "If I am understanding you, Ms. Reeves, your conjecture is that this is when a cover-up started—one that is still very actively running to this very day."

"Yes, ma'am—that is in fact our conclusion. This group started with suppression but quickly moved on to more overt tactics to keep the truth from the public, including redaction and even death." A visibly shaken Kaden had returned and began passing out binders with the full report and all of the incidents of note.

"Was this group the so-called Majestic 12?" Emily asked.

Natalie nodded, flipping to the next slide. "Ma'am, while the idea of Majestic 12 is widely circulated, there's substantial evidence suggesting it was a sham—a distraction, if you will, to divert attention from the real decision-makers."

She paused, letting her words sink in. "The documents that surfaced about MJ-12 were riddled with inconsistencies and inaccuracies—language usage, typeface errors, and anachronistic references. It appears someone went to great lengths to fabricate these papers."

Kaden added, "The true orchestrators behind the scenes were likely a much smaller, more clandestine group. This group had direct access to the highest levels of power and the ability to manipulate media narratives and suppress information effectively."

Natalie continued, "Our research indicates that these real decision-makers were embedded within various government agencies, military branches, and private defense contractors. They had no official name, no easily identifiable structure, and that's what made them so effective. They could operate with complete impunity."

Emily leaned forward, intrigued, her brow furrowing. "And you are saying this group still exists today?"

"Yes, ma'am," Natalie replied. "Their operations have evolved with technology, becoming even more sophisticated. They have access to surveillance, advanced counterintelligence techniques, and, in our opinion, considerable leverage over influential figures."

Kaden interjected, "The goal of Majestic 12 was to create a lightning rod for conspiracy theories, to distract and discredit genuine inquiries into UFO phenomena. By the time anyone realized MJ-12 was a ruse, the real operatives had already buried the truth under countless layers of misinformation."

Emily glanced at the binder, then back at Natalie. "If Majestic 12 was a fake, who are these real decision-makers? Do we have any names, any leads?"

Natalie sighed. "Sadly, that's the challenge. They're ghosts. Our best leads point to a few influential figures in the military-industrial sector, possibly some high-ranking military officials, and a handful of powerful political operatives. But nothing concrete. They're experts at erasing their footprints."

Emily tapped her pen on the table, her mind racing. "We need to find these people. Expose them. It seems that now, the need for a cover-up is mostly irrelevant."

"Agreed," Kaden said. "But we must proceed carefully. I feel sure, due to recent actions, that they won't hesitate to silence anyone who gets too close. We've already seen the lengths they'll go to."

Emily nodded, determination hardening her features. "Then we'll just have to be smarter. We need to dig deeper, find the connections, and expose the truth."

Natalie and Kaden exchanged a glance, their resolve matching Emily's.

"General Taylor, would you, Colonel Walker, and Agent Rogers mind stepping out for a moment? I have a sensitive question for Professor Trembley, and I'd prefer not to put either of you in a compromising position with your CoC."

After they left and the door closed again, Emily stood and went to the screen where the decades- old image of former Secretary of Defense James Forestal's body hung below a window of a brick building. She seemed to be forcefully moving the pieces into place, so she could know what the correct questions to ask might be.

"The President of the United States is somewhere in this building—the commander-in-chief of all the country's armed forces, arguably the most powerful military force in the world. In your opinion, is this cover-up that has been going on for over seventy-five years still a military operation? Because I can assure you, the president is in the dark on it."

Natalie had retaken her own seat and looked at Kaden before answering. "We don't believe so; however, they must have military cooperation at very high levels, particularly in the Air Force and Military Intelligence. Too many of the incidents—the more legitimate incidents—have involved members of our armed forces."

"So, someone who can direct military high command?"

Kaden leaned back. "No, Emily. They don't necessarily need to manipulate it from the top. The U.S. Military is a vast, oftentimes dysfunctional, organization. The Special Projects Group would only need to have leverage over a few mid-level commanders in each branch to achieve what they need.

“Our data suggest that all the presidents, other than possibly Bush Senior and Eisenhower, are in the dark by design. This is simply too big to have in the hands of a politician, ma'am."

"Why Bush Senior?"

"He was briefly the head of the CIA. There is a very real possibility that the SPG started on the intelligence side of the government Although now, we feel sure it must be independent."

"And Eisenhower?"

"I'll get to that in just a moment, Director," Kaden said.

The assistant chief of staff digested all this and was trying to come up with a reasonable narrative that she could share with POTUS. "Why? What is the point of all this obfuscation?"

Natalie clicked the remote, and the screen behind them changed. "That is the real question, but I suggest you bring our military guys back in for this."

Emily did so, and the meeting continued. "Why the cover-up, the fake disclosures, and all the other misdirection?" she asked.

"Only two real possibilities," Kaden began," and our strong feeling is that both are correct. Number one: the Special Projects Group likely has exotic alien tech in their possession and probably has since Roswell. They are likely making money by reverse engineering it, extracting new technologies over time, then licensing it or, more likely, setting up detached companies to take it to market." The screen began filling with the logos of many Fortune 100 companies.

"Each of these has brought out products with technical advancements without the prerequisite iterations or evolutionary foundations that would suggest a technical leap forward has been made. These all also have some tie-in to DARPA, the military, or a black-budget project at some point in the past."

"Professor, these companies are worth hundreds of billions of dollars. They are some of the best-known brands in the world," Emily said.

"Trillions," Natalie responded. "The top two are valued at over a trillion each. None of them existed prior to 1947. In fact, most didn't exist before the late 1980s." The companies were mostly high-tech and biotech firms, as well as a few weapon systems, aeronautical, and robotics.

"So money is reason one?" Emily asked.

"Yes, Ms. Carter, but not just money— a near-infinite amount of money and, with it, the technical advances to keep the U.S. in particular on the cutting edge of defense capabilities," Natalie offered.

Emily made a note on her pad—something she wanted to revisit later.

"Number two," Kaden continued, "well, this one is going to be a bit tougher to accept. The other reason the Special Projects Group has been so effective at marginalizing any real investigation or acceptance of extraterrestrial life could be, and in our mind 'is,' most likely the result of a threat by the aliens themselves."

"Wait, what?" the general voiced loudly.

"I know it seems difficult to accept, but hear me out and see if you can at least agree in principle."

Kaden stood up, adjusting his glasses as he walked to the center of the room. He paused for a moment, gathering his thoughts before speaking.

"Consider this—since the end of World War II, we have witnessed an unprecedented surge in UFO sightings and incidents. Now, why would that be? What changed so drastically in our world?" Kaden clicked the remote again, displaying a map marked with post-World War II nuclear test sites.

"Like I mentioned, we became a nuclear power," he continued. "The first atomic bomb was detonated in 1945, and suddenly, our tiny blue planet was capable of unimaginable destruction. Not just to our species, but potentially to our very environment and even beyond."

He pointed to a series of photos depicting high-ranking military officials and intelligence operatives. "In 1952, during the Washington D.C. UFO incident, unidentified objects were tracked on radar over restricted airspace near the Capitol Building and here at the White House. Jets were scrambled to intercept these objects, but they outmaneuvered our most advanced aircraft."

General Taylor's face tightened as Kaden spoke. "A top Air Force official later stated that the objects displayed capabilities far beyond any known aircraft at the time."

Kaden flipped to another image of a distinguished-looking man. "Consider Dr. J. Allen Hynek, initially a skeptic hired by the Air Force for Project Blue Book. His job with the project was to debunk UFO sightings. Over time, he became convinced that there was something truly extraordinary occurring—something that couldn't be explained away by conventional means."

The next slide showed President Dwight D. Eisenhower. "In 1954, there are unverified reports suggesting Eisenhower met with extraterrestrials at Edwards Air Force Base under a cloak of absolute secrecy," Kaden said. "What if these meetings were not just about exchanging technology but about setting boundaries?"

Emily leaned forward, her eyes narrowed in concentration.

"Let's look at it from the aliens' perspective," Kaden went on. "Suddenly, it's the 1950s—we are like children playing with matches next to a gas station. If extraterrestrial civilizations are monitoring us—and I believe they are—they'd have every reason to put us on 'galactic probation.'"

He flipped through more images: declassified CIA documents mentioning UFOs, scientists like Carl Sagan expressing cautious interest in extraterrestrial life, and more recent whistleblowers like Bob Lazar who claimed to have worked on reverse-engineering alien technology.

Emily polled the entire group. The discussion wavered on a few points, but the consensus was obvious—near one hundred percent. As the meeting ended and the group dispersed, Emily motioned for Kaden to stay behind.

"There is a lot of conjecture in your findings, Professor, as well as a considerable amount of well-deserved paranoia. That is not to say I think you are incorrect. Assuming even part of it is true, who can we trust and what can we do to stay the course? I have to assume that everything is being monitored, even here in one of the most secure rooms in the country."

"Not only that, Director," Kaden said cautiously. "You can't even trust your own team."

"I must trust someone," she said grimly.

She stood to leave before turning back and quietly slipping a note into his hand. "I'm so sorry, Kaden."

CHAPTER
FIFTY-NINE

1057 EST June 25
Private Residence
Washington, D.C., USA

Kaden sat in his dimly lit D.C. apartment, the tears coming more freely now. The scrap of paper lay on the desk beside him, the glow from his computer screen casting a pale light on his face. He hated Emily Carter for withholding that detail from him until the end of the meeting but understood her motivation.

Elena was dead. He'd assumed...no, he'd hoped she was just absorbed in her work at her lab. Several of the members had erratic attendance as their own work made it difficult to personally attend all the committee meetings. Doctor Green had been the other fatality. He, too, was a great loss, although not a personal one like Elena.

For the first time, the once clear-cut pursuit of truth felt murky; maybe the cost was too high.

He pushed back from his desk, running a hand through his thinning hair. Every revelation on this path seemed to pull him deeper into an abyss. Kaden had been searching for extraterrestrial life for almost forty years, and until the last few months, he'd made relatively no progress. Now it seemed the aliens were going to do it for him. Except they weren't coming with lavish technological gifts and plans to help usher mankind into a higher state of being. No, they were coming with weapons, malicious intent, and perhaps a total disdain for the human race.

His curiosity had overcome him, and he'd opened their shared cloud backup and begun searching more of her recent updates. He knew he'd been one of the last people to see her alive. Her theories had been well thought out but still unusual. Were they why she was killed or just that she was part of the White House committee? Even in her last moments, the science was the important thing.

Kaden stared at the printouts spread out before him—images of the Mars stones, geological maps, ancient artifacts, and classified documents. Yesterday, these would have fueled his determination. Now, they seemed to mock him, each one a reminder of the colossal weight of truth. The cost of truth had become staggering. Elena and Steven had paid with their lives, and now he wondered if he had anything left to offer. He'd made his pitch to the group, and now they could do with it what they wanted.

His phone buzzed, snapping him from his thoughts. It was Sarah Mitchell. She had always been his anchor, the one person who could cut through the noise in his head.

"Sarah," he said, his voice wavering more that he intended.

"How did it go?" she asked.

"I... I don't know if I can do this anymore," he said, ignoring the question. He dared not mention Elena's death. Sarah knew of his history with his former student and very much did not approve.

"Kaden, what's going on?" Her voice was calm, yet it carried an edge of concern.

"I... I don't know anymore. Sarah...just seems like everything is spinning out of control. People are dying. It's not even about proving UFOs are real; in a few more days that point will be moot."

"Listen to me," she said firmly. "You are one of the smartest people I know. If anyone can figure this out, it's you. Obviously, something real is going on here. Is it aliens, or is it humans?"

"It's both," he said with a sigh. "We've laid out a very convincing argument for an ongoing and malevolent alien presence and a human cover-up." He considered the warnings that someone could be listening in...then decided he just didn't care.

"But what if I'm wrong?" His voice cracked. "What if we're too late, or my obsession has clouded my judgment...again? What if I'm helping put the world on edge for nothing? The president is being briefed on our report. He is planning to address the nation. Do you know how much of a spotlight that could shine on all of us?"

Sarah sighed. "Kaden, sadly, self-doubt is part of your process. But remember why you started this. Remember the evidence you've gathered, all the data you and your team put together. This isn't just in your head."

Kaden's grip tightened on the phone. He knew she was right, but he was not feeling stable enough to accept her words. "I used to be so sure, so confident. Now... it feels like I'm losing my grip on reality."

"Kaden Trembley," she said forcefully. "You must stay focused," she urged. "This is bigger than you or me. The truth on this is finally screaming to be heard. Don't let the pressure break you."

He wanted to believe her, to feel the solid ground beneath his feet again. But the shadows in his mind were growing darker, more insistent. The cost of this mission was becoming too high, threatening to consume him entirely. He'd always been a bit morose. Melancholy, or maybe malaise, is what they would have diagnosed a century earlier. Now it went by other names.

"Thank you, Sarah," he managed to say, though his voice was almost a whisper.

"Stay strong, Kaden," she replied. "I do have some other distressing news for you, though."

"Go ahead."

It was obvious from her tone that she really preferred not to. "Jasper Maxwell passed away this morning. I know you two were close."

The news hit Kaden like another hammer blow. Even after the multiple revelations at their last meeting, he'd assumed his friend would always be there. Cancer didn't care for assumptions, it seemed.

Kaden thanked Sarah for everything and checked the time for the

West Coast before dialing Jasper's daughter, Laney, to offer his condolences.

Kaden sat there afterward, the silence of the room pressing in on him. His inner demons clawed at the edges of his sanity, but he knew he had to keep going. He had a glass of wine and then another.

The knock on his door startled him. He checked his watch—past 10:30. Opening it slightly, he was relieved and very surprised to see Natalie standing there.

"Have you eaten anything, Professor?" she asked.

"Oh...um, yes...no. I mean, I'm not sure," he said, drying the last remnants of tears from his face. He didn't much want company, but much like Sarah, Natalie seemed to bring out the best in him. He opened the door wider and waved his arm.

She grinned and slid in the door, holding two takeout plates of food. "Come on, join me. I have something I want to run by you."

Kaden poured the young woman a glass of wine before taking a tentative bite of the noodles and vegetables. "I don't often eat Thai food. Usually, it's too spicy for me, but this is delicious." He also hadn't appreciated how hungry he was. That was one of his problems—getting immersed in his work to the point he didn't take care of his basic needs.

"I hate to seem rude, Natalie, but why are you here? We've made what might be our final report to the committee."

"I just needed a sounding board—someone smart I could bounce some ideas off," she said before taking another bite of Pad Thai. "The aliens are really stepping up their activities and don't seem nearly as concerned about being discovered."

Kaden sat there processing what Natalie was saying. She was smart, too, but her brain seemed to work very differently from his own.

"We also know they have a human element that may be complicit in some or all of their activities," she continued. "Lastly, it seems like global unrest is at an all-time high. We are one flashpoint away from seeing society unravel."

Kaden nodded. "I don't disagree, but I'm just an astrophysicist. My grasp of what is going on down here is..."

"Don't bullshit me, Professor. You care very much about what goes on down here. Your reputation is the most precious thing in the world to you. Sorry to be so blunt, but I need to have a plan. I think all of humanity needs a plan. What do the stars tell you, Professor?"

Kaden was taken aback but recovered enough of his composure to calmly discuss what he'd observed in the skies. "No dramatic increase in aerial phenomena. Solar activity is at a minimum right now, and from a purely cosmic perspective, we have nothing to be concerned with.

"Honestly, Natalie, we have to be mindful that interstellar travel is, if not impossible, very nearly so, at least in any real practical sense. The distances any other civilization would need to travel are simply too great. The time it would take for even our closest neighbor would be from hundreds to hundreds of thousands of years."

"As we understand the physics involved," she said, finishing her meal and picking up her wine.

"Yes. As we understand it."

"I think we have to assume we are wrong on that point, Professor," she responded. "They are here. Now what do they want?"

He nodded in obvious defeat on that point.

She and the professor had discussed this a few times before, so she knew the man's standard answers: "colonization, natural resources, strategic advantage, slave labor, or perhaps just to stop humankind from advancing any further. Perhaps they know in time we will become a threat."

"That would actually also fall under strategic advantage," he added.

Natalie nodded but didn't seem to be listening to him. She was now pacing the floor, sipping wine as she thought through the information she had. "Once before, we agreed that much of the encounters seemed to indicate that the aliens fear us. They are tracking us, studying us, looking to learn about us, for what? So they can defeat us?"

"That is a possibility, but it indicates an enormous dedication over what is possibly a timespan of millennia. If conquering us was the goal, why didn't they do it in the fifteenth century when the global population was a fraction of what it is now? Also, now we seem to have a much better means of retaliating."

"All true, Kaden, if... and this is a big 'if.' If we are encountering the same species."

He walked over and joined her as she looked out at the capital skyline. "What do you mean, Natalie?" Her words reminded him of his last conversation with Elena.

Her face scrunched up in a way he'd learned was part of her processing. "I think there is a new and much more aggressive alien presence here now."

Kaden shrugged. "There has always been a great deal of diversity in the supposed sightings. But I've just been going over some of Elena's research. She seemed to feel as you do—multiple species, one of which could operate suboceanic or subterranean and seems to have a firm control of gravitics. She indicated a smallish gray species and a taller lighter one."

"Elena was one of them, wasn't she?"

Kaden knew what she meant. He nodded. "And Greene."

"Damn! I asked Rogers, but if he knew, he wasn't saying.

"Anyway, I'm less concerned about the physical descriptions. I'm basing this on tactics and behavior. We need to be studying what's changed. One thing I believe is they have limited force strength. Not enough to take out all of the population. So, they're hitting softer targets, disrupting our communications and leadership. Command and control is what the military would call it. The main weapon they're using right now is fear, and that's helping them tear the world apart without firing a shot. Well, without firing too many shots," she corrected.

Kaden considered her position and had to admit it made a lot of sense. "And the human counterparts? What is their role? Surely they aren't just going to help sell out the human race to an alien overlord."

She shook her head. "My belief is they were just opportunists, mostly out for themselves. They were a tool, possibly even an unwitting one, of the original aliens but not these newcomers. They're out of their league." She removed her phone from her pocket and tapped a few screens. "Look at this."

It was a grainy, still image of a lavish compound ringed by tree-covered hills. He used his fingers to pinch and zoom in on several things. One was very obviously a body missing its head, lying in a dark pool on the ground. The most striking item was the silhouette of a dark craft that seemed to be hovering several feet off the ground.

"North Korea," Natalie answered before he could ask. "Trent helped me get these. Mount Myohyang, we think, which is located in the northwest part of the country. That looks to be the Myohyangsan Residence, which is thought to be one of the premier's secluded mountain retreats.

"The image is part of a video that was smuggled out through China last week. No one seems to know who has the rest of it, but it passed all the verification tests as authentic."

"Who is that on the ground?" Kaden asked.

Natalie shrugged.

"I think we need to get eyes on the entire country, remote parts of Africa, and Australia as well. Anywhere this new species could be operating from unobserved needs to be monitored by satellite, drones, ground assets, ships, or overflight."

"You think they're operating from a base here on the planet?"

"From a practical standpoint, yes," she answered. "If there were a mothership up there, I think you would know it. That's why I'm here. Depending on their craft's speed and range, the moon or somewhere else could also be viable, but I'm leaning toward a terrestrial threat. If they're underwater or, as Elena said, underground, it will be even harder to detect, but I think that might also hinder some of their operations.

"They're testing our capabilities and probing our defenses, but there is only so much a small force should be able to accomplish. If we can find them and stop them now, we might have a chance."

"And if we don't?"

Natalie finished off her wine and turned to face him. "We're fucked."

Kaden nodded in agreement. "Natalie, I need to come clean with you on something—a bit of a burden I have been carrying since just before I met you, in fact." He proceeded to tell her everything Jasper had told him. She absorbed it all without speaking.

"The Observers," she mused. "Sounds better than SPG, and it fits with everything said in our meeting today. I do wish you had told me earlier, but I guess I don't blame you. Still, your friend could have been a little less cryptic. Now that he's dead, do you think we could go to his home and maybe find out more? It would really help if we knew who was running this group. We need intel—practical and actionable information—so we can be ready for this fight."

"Maybe," he said with a shrug. "But I rather doubt it would be that close to him. I got the distinct impression that very little he did was beyond the scrutiny of that organization."

"We need a name, Kaden. Your friend had 70 years of knowledge about the cover-up. Last year, or hell, even last month, that was just an annoyance. Now, not just knowing it could be apocalyptic."

CHAPTER SIXTY

1837 CDT June 27
Northeast Florida, USA

The heat was sweltering, but Nancy Ramesh and her two children followed their new friend. She had nowhere else to go, no one to turn to. She knew how dangerous this was, but the world had changed... for all she knew, it was like this everywhere. She looked up at the sound of an approaching plane. A military jet flew by very low. Someone was up there at least. Maybe there would be help soon.

Nancy's kids, TJ and Lynn, watched intently as their mother took the lead. TJ clung to his stuffed rabbit, his eyes darting between the adults, while Lynn's tiny fingers gripped the edge of Nancy's shirt.

As the hot afternoon began to dim, Luther stopped beneath a large cedar tree and slipped out of his pack. "Let's set up here for the night," he said. He pointed at Nancy. "Why?"

She thought about it. This had become a ritual between them. She realized the man was trying to teach her how to survive—lessons that she'd never had nor often needed in her normal life. She first eyed the area: a slight rise with a tree line fifty to a hundred yards away. "Good sight lines," she said confidently.

"Which is important, why?"

"So we can see anyone... or any animals trying to get close."

Big Lou nodded as he began to unpack his camp gear. "Go on."

She assumed there must be fresh water around; she thought she could smell it, but she had yet to see a source, so she didn't list that.

Nancy squinted, trying to think of more reasons. "The trees give us some cover from above," she said, her voice gaining strength. "We won't be as easy to spot from the air."

Luther grinned. "Good. Two more."

She scanned the area, noting some hills and downed logs. "The terrain over there could also provide some natural cover if we needed it. We could hide behind it if need be."

"Right, right," Luther agreed, laying out his sleeping bag. "One more."

Nancy chewed her lip, looking up at the sky, now painted with hues of orange and purple. "It's almost dark," she finally said. "Better to set up camp now while we can still see what we're doing."

"Exactly," Luther nodded approvingly. "You did good."

Luther took a sip from his canteen and handed it to Nancy. "Get some water in you. It's gonna be a long night."

She took a grateful gulp and passed it back. "Thanks, Luther. I don't know what we would have done without you."

"You'd have managed," he replied, though his tone softened. "But I'm glad to help."

Nancy began setting up her own sleeping area, pulling a blanket from her newly improvised pack and laying it on the ground. She noticed TJ's eyes drooping and pulled him close, kissing the top of his head. "You tired, buddy?"

He nodded, barely keeping his eyes open. "Will we be safe here, Mom?"

She glanced at Luther, who was already scanning the perimeter, ever watchful. "Yes, TJ, we'll be safe."

Luther pulled some piece of gear out of his bag. It was about half the size of a toaster.

"What's that?" TJ asked.

"Power block," Luther said. "Like a generator, but uses batteries instead of a gas engine."

TJ looked at his mom, confused, and she seemed to be as well. "You have power? You could charge a cell phone?"

"Sure," he pointed to the connector port and handed her a converter. "Won't do any good, though; no cell signal anywhere."

"I could listen to my playlist or scroll through pictures," she said with a grin.

"That's fine. I need to make a call on the Marine band." He plugged in what looked to be a thick portable radio and raised an antenna. He moved the dial to channel 16. Instantly, the sounds of other broadcasts echoed through the campsite. He turned the volume down. The chatter was obviously from other people in distress.

"Luther..."

"We need to listen." Luther's tone remained firm. "They might have some advice that helps us."

"Luther..." she started but was interrupted by another voice, rising above the din.

"Mayday! Mayday! This is the cargo ship Triton. We were struck days ago by massive waves and have major structural damage! We're taking on water fast—" The call faded into static, the urgency replaced by a chilling silence.

"Can you believe this?" Nancy shook her head, her stomach twisting. "What kind of world are we living in?"

Luther kept his eyes on the radio, focused and determined. "Nancy, information is the most important survival tool you have. Never get so caught up in the moment that you forget to look for an advantage."

A faint voice cut through again. "Coast Guard, please respond! We are losing power! There's too much debris! Repeat, we are in a—"

Then silence. The eerie stillness settled in, and Nancy clutched her children tighter.

"I'm sorry to say this is just the beginning," Luther murmured, shaking his head as he fiddled with the radio, searching for more signals. "We need to know what's happening out there."

Luther's deep voice cut through the stillness. "I'll take first watch. You all get some rest."

Nancy nodded, feeling a strange sense of relief. For the first time in what felt like ages, she trusted someone other than herself or her husband to keep her family safe. She settled down beside her kids, pulling the blanket over them.

As the last light of day slipped away, Nancy found herself whispering a silent prayer of thanks. Despite everything, despite the chaos and the fear, they had found a small measure of safety for now. And in this world turned upside down, that would have to do. She listened as Luther scanned the dial for several more minutes before putting it away.

The final broadcast she heard was the most heart-wrenching. A young-sounding air force pilot who had been forced to ditch his plane at sea said, "The whole fucking airbase was gone." He stated flatly there were no survivors and that the impact's blast wave flipped his prop plane into the ocean as he was lining up for approach. Somehow, the plane was still afloat two days later, and he was drifting farther from land. The boy was crying and asking anyone who heard him to contact his mother in Ohio and tell her he loved her.

"The world is filled with suffering," she whispered. Her own family's tragedy was just one dim outpost among a literal sea of victims.

CHAPTER SIXTY-ONE

Marcus cut the Land Rover's engine, the sudden silence amplifying the sounds of the forest around him. Dawn was just beginning to break, casting long shadows through the pines of Blackwater River State Forest. He'd driven through the night, avoiding main roads where possible after spotting the first military checkpoint a few miles farther south outside the little town of Springhill.

"Come on, boy," he whispered, opening the door for the German Shepherd. The dog hopped out, stretching his muscular body before sniffing the air cautiously.

Marcus pulled camouflage netting from the back of the vehicle, working methodically to cover the Land Rover. Years of training had prepared him for this moment, though he'd hoped it would never come. The southern Alpha Site was less than two hours away by car, but the roadblocks made that route impossible.

"We're hoofing it from here, buddy," he told Retro, who watched him with alert eyes.

Marcus checked his tactical backpack—water, rations, first aid, ammunition for his sidearm, and the handheld radio he knew would be useless. The jammers were powerful enough to block even the most basic signals. He'd tried every frequency during the night drive, hearing nothing but static.

He pulled out his handheld GPS unit, marking their current position with practiced precision. The small screen showed their location just inside the Florida state line. The forest would provide good cover, but the journey ahead would be challenging.

"Twenty miles straight-line travel," he muttered, studying the terrain. "Probably double that with the detours we'll need to take around the airbase or... whatever's left of it. Hope you're ready for a scenic detour through hell, buddy."

Retro's ears perked up, sensing his master's tension.

Marcus knelt beside the dog, checking the tactical vest he'd fitted him with. "You're carrying your share, too," he said with a half-smile, adjusting the small pouches containing additional supplies.

The distant rumble of vehicles on the highway reminded him why they couldn't stay put. Whatever was happening at the Alpha Site, he needed to get there to find out if the others had made it.

"Someone's gone to a lot of trouble to isolate this area," he said to Retro, who tilted his head in response. "Let's find out why."

Marcus moved with practiced efficiency; his footsteps were nearly silent on the forest floor. Years of SEAL training and risky missions had taught him how to become a ghost in environments like this. Retro, also highly trained, padded alongside him, ranging out several dozen yards occasionally to search ahead. The dog's instincts perfectly aligned with his master's intentions.

"Go low, boy," Marcus whispered, dropping to a crouch as they approached a small clearing. He scanned the area, looking for movement, listening for anything out of place.

By midday, the heat had become oppressive. Marcus stripped off his outer jacket, carefully rolling it and securing it to his pack. He'd rationed their water, taking small sips only when necessary. Retro seemed to understand the gravity of their situation, never whining for extra water or treats.

When they came across a small stream, Marcus tested it first, checking for discoloration or unusual odors before allowing Retro to drink. He filled their canteens and dropped in purification tablets.

"Lunch time," Marcus muttered, spotting a natural lake ahead. He set a simple fishing line from his pack and some flexible branches. They caught several fish that he quickly scaled and fried over a small camp stove.

They moved on, maintaining a steady pace through the dense undergrowth. When Marcus spotted a small family of hikers in the distance, he immediately signaled Retro to hold position. They remained motionless until the group passed, never knowing how close they'd come to the man and his dog.

In the late afternoon, he set out snares, then they began circling the area where he wanted to camp. The snare yielded results by dusk—a plump rabbit that Marcus cleaned with practiced efficiency. He built a small, nearly smokeless fire using a hole with a fire below ground level, with dry twigs, cooking the meat quickly before extinguishing every ember.

"Not exactly five-star dining," he said to Retro, sharing the lean protein. "But it'll keep us moving."

As darkness fell, Marcus found a defensive position—a small depression beneath a fallen oak that offered cover from three sides. He laid out a thin thermal blanket and checked their perimeter one final time before settling in for a few hours of rest.

"Four-hour rotations," he told Retro, though the dog already seemed to understand the drill. "You take first watch." Even Marcus knew the dog couldn't tell time, but Retro understood the intent. Stay on guard and make occasional recon patrols until Marcus took over.

Dawn broke as Marcus and Retro crested a small ridge. They'd traveled through the early morning, pushing hard to make up time. The forest had thinned, giving way to scattered pines and open patches of sandy soil. Marcus dropped to his stomach at the ridge's edge, pulling out his compact binoculars. The smell of smoke was much stronger here than it had been so far. He'd also been smelling something else—water... salt water.

"Jesus Christ," he whispered.

Where the main part of Eglin Air Force Base should have been, a massive lake, or perhaps this was the new bay, stretched for miles. The devastation was total—hangars, runways, administrative buildings—all gone. In their place, scorched earth pushed up into ridges followed by acres of twisted metal. Black smoke still billowed from several locations despite what must have been days of firefighting efforts.

The military presence was overwhelming. Humvees and troop transports formed a perimeter around the entire area. Soldiers in protective gear moved methodically through the wreckage, collecting samples and loading debris into sealed containers. Overhead was the constant buzz of helicopters and aircraft.

"That's no training exercise or gas explosion," Marcus muttered, adjusting the focus on his binoculars.

He counted at least six different agencies by their vehicle markings—Air Force Security Forces, Army, FEMA, CDC, and others he didn't recognize. The coordination was impressive, almost rehearsed, as if they'd prepared for exactly this scenario.

Retro growled softly beside him. Marcus placed a calming hand on the dog's back.

"Easy, boy."

A convoy of unmarked black SUVs rolled through a checkpoint. Men in black tactical suits emerged, conferring with military officers. They didn't wear insignias or name tags—another red flag. On the SUVs was a small insignia, one he thought he recognized.

"Government types," Marcus whispered. "But not the kind that show ID."

To the east, a section had been cordoned off with specialized equipment. Workers in sealed suits operated what looked like ground-penetrating radar. Others collected soil samples, sealing them in metal containers before loading them onto refrigerated trucks.

Most disturbing were the body bags—hundreds of them, maybe thousands, lined up in neat rows on the tarmac of what had once been a secondary runway. Military personnel were systematically documenting each one before loading them into refrigerated trailers.

"This isn't cleanup," Marcus realized. "It's evac...or containment."

He watched as soldiers turned away a civilian vehicle at a checkpoint nearly two miles from the impact site. The driver appeared to be arguing, pointing toward what might have been his home. The soldiers remained impassive, weapons visible but not raised. Eventually, the vehicle turned around.

Marcus shifted his position slightly, focusing on the far side of the devastation where a line of C-17 Globemaster transport aircraft waited on what remained of a secondary runway. Crews worked with practiced skill, loading equipment and personnel.

"They're bugging out," he whispered to Retro, who remained motionless beside him.

This wasn't just containment—it was evacuation. The realization was a shock. In all his years of military service, he'd never seen the Air Force abandon a major installation like this.

Through his binoculars, Marcus watched as technicians dismantled sensitive equipment from a partially collapsed building. They weren't just taking weapons and vehicles—they were salvaging servers, communications gear, and what looked like specialized research equipment.

"They're pulling everything that matters," he muttered. "Taking it somewhere else."

A colonel gestured urgently to a group of airmen, pointing to a priority list on a clipboard. The urgency in his movements told Marcus everything he needed to know. This wasn't a standard redeployment—it was a strategic withdrawal.

Marcus traced the direction of the loaded aircraft as they took off. Northwest. Away from the coast, toward the interior. Toward more defensible positions.

"Somewhere safer," he concluded. "Somewhere hidden."

He'd seen similar operations during his SEAL days—the rapid relocation of critical assets when a base became compromised or vulnerable. But never on American soil, and never with this level of coordination.

A truck passed by carrying what looked like prototype aircraft parts, carefully wrapped and secured. The insignia had been hastily painted over, but Marcus could almost guess the shape. In either case, he understood this was black projects. The kind of technology that officially didn't exist.

"They're not just relocating operations," Marcus realized. "They're going into hiding."

Marcus checked his position on the GPS. The Alpha Site camp was still fifteen miles southeast, but the extent of what he was seeing changed things. Whatever had happened here wasn't natural or an accident, and very definitely wasn't being reported accurately. Also, he wasn't going to be able to get across the base or that new stretch of the Gulf of Mexico unnoticed. He needed a new game plan.

CHAPTER SIXTY-TWO

Marcus and Retro kept to the shadows, moving only at dusk and dawn when the shifting light played tricks on sentries' eyes. For three days, they'd traced the perimeter of the exclusion zone, searching for gaps in the military cordon.

"Some operation they're running," Marcus muttered as he shared jerky with Retro. The dog's ears perked up, then flattened again as he chewed. "No press, no civilians, no questions."

The exclusion zone stretched for miles in every direction, swallowing what had once been suburbs, shopping centers, and parks. In the silence of this new no-man's-land, cut off from all communication, Marcus felt the weight of isolation pressing down.

"Wonder what's happening out there, boy." He scratched behind Retro's ears. "No news, no updates. What happened here might just have been the first strike. The world could be ending, and we wouldn't know."

At night, lying on his back watching aircraft lights crisscross the sky, Marcus found his thoughts drifting to Natalie. Her fierce intelligence, the way she'd challenge him on everything, and how she'd run her fingers through her coppery red hair when deep in thought.

"Dangerous thinking," he whispered to himself. But in the emptiness, memories were a comfort he couldn't deny.

He remembered their last real conversation before everything fell apart. Her determination to expose what she believed was true, and his insistence on preparing for the worst. Both protecting people, but in fundamentally different ways.

"Should've tried harder," he told Retro, who watched him with knowing eyes. "Should've found middle ground."

On the fourth morning, they reached the coastline—or what was now coastline. The Gulf had claimed miles of land, creating a jagged new shoreline of half-submerged buildings and twisted infrastructure. According to the GPS, he was near Navarre, but no sign of a town remained.

Marcus studied the water through his binoculars. No nearby boats patrolled this section—maybe too shallow, too many hazards. Maybe their way across.

"Might be our chance," he murmured, calculating distances and tides. If he could make it over to the barrier island half a mile offshore, he might be able to move south past the air base.

Retro suddenly stiffened, a low growl rumbling in his chest.

Marcus froze, slowly lowering himself to the ground. Fifty yards away, a military patrol suddenly emerged from the tree line—four soldiers in full tactical gear, weapons ready, methodically sweeping the area.

"Down," Marcus whispered, placing a hand on Retro's back.

The patrol moved closer, their boots crunching on the debris-strewn ground. Marcus pressed himself deeper into the underbrush, willing himself to disappear. Retro, sensing the danger, remained perfectly still.

One soldier paused, raising a hand to halt the others. He turned slowly, scanning the area, his gaze passing over their hiding spot once, then returning.

He'd seen something.

The soldier's gaze swept over Marcus's position as he raised his weapon to a firing position. The other men began selecting similar firing lanes.

Marcus's mind raced. These guys hadn't slogged through the swamps or navigated the dense underbrush. They were too clean, too unscathed by the harsh terrain of Eglin Air Force Base's vast expanse.

Bombing ranges, dense forests, swamps—it was a punishing landscape for anyone unprepared. And these men were pristine.

Slowly, Marcus signaled Retro to stay put, moving away from the dog's protective stance.

"Stand up! Hands where I can see them!" the soldier barked, his voice echoing through the dense forest.

Marcus cautiously straightened, raising his hands to shoulder height.

"Easy there," Marcus said calmly. "I'm just passing through."

Two of the soldiers advanced, weapons trained on him. Their gear was blackout—no insignias, no names. Not regular military.

Private contractors.

One of them stepped forward, helmet visor reflecting Marcus's face back at him. "You're in a restricted area," he stated flatly. "Identify yourself."

Marcus kept his voice steady, knowing any sudden move could turn deadly fast. "Name's Alton Smith. Just a hiker who got lost."

"Hiker?" The lead soldier scoffed. "In this fucking place? Give me a break."

Marcus shrugged. "Didn't see any signs. Figured I'd find my way out to the coast and signal for help."

The lead soldier wasn't buying it. "Drop the act." He nodded to another soldier who moved in closer, checking Marcus for weapons.

Marcus felt the tension crackle in the air like static electricity before a storm. These men had orders to follow, and they wouldn't hesitate to execute them if pushed.

"Listen," Marcus said carefully, watching as they patted him down. "I'm no threat to you guys. Just trying to get some help. My home is gone."

The soldier searching him pulled back, nodding to the leader that Marcus was clean—no weapons visible. Thankfully, they hadn't spotted his gear pack over near Retro.

"You're coming with us," the lead soldier said firmly.

Marcus's eyes darted around—trees thick enough for cover, but no clear escape routes without drawing fire. He needed a plan and fast.

"Alright," Marcus replied evenly, "but can you at least tell me who you are?"

"None of your concern," the leader replied sharply, gesturing for Marcus to move forward.

As they began walking, Marcus noticed how methodically they moved—silent hand signals, precise formations. These weren't just any contractors; they were elite.

Retro followed quietly at a distance, gaze locked on Marcus for any signal. The dog's silent loyalty was a small comfort in an otherwise tense situation.

They trekked deeper into the forest and closer to the water, each step amplifying Marcus's unease about what lay ahead and what these men were really after.

The lead soldier's grip tightened on Marcus's arm as they neared the water. Marcus could now see the faint outline of a boat in the distance. They were planning to transport him, which meant this was more than a simple patrol. He must have tripped a proximity sensor or maybe a drone using IR had spotted him.

"Move faster," the soldier ordered, shoving Marcus forward.

Marcus's mind raced, calculating his options. The dense foliage around them provided cover, and if he could create enough chaos, he might have a chance. His muscles tensed, ready to spring into action.

In one fluid motion, Marcus twisted his body and delivered a devastating kick to the knee of the nearest soldier. The sickening crunch of bone echoed through the trees as the man crumpled with a scream.

Without missing a beat, Marcus spun and drove his boot into another soldier's chin. The impact sent the man sprawling backward, hitting the ground with a heavy thud.

But the last soldier moved with deadly precision. Before Marcus could react, the butt of a strange-looking rifle slammed into his side. Pain exploded through his ribs as he staggered back, struggling to stay on his feet.

The soldier didn't relent. He swung again, this time connecting with Marcus's jaw. Stars danced in Marcus's vision as he fought to stay conscious.

Adrenaline surged through him. He ducked under another swing and threw a punch at the soldier's face. It landed with a satisfying crack, but the man hardly flinched. Both were now driven by sheer determination.

They grappled in the underbrush, trading blows in a brutal dance of survival. Marcus felt his strength waning as the soldier pressed his advantage. A powerful strike caught Marcus in the gut, knocking the wind from his lungs and sending him to his knees.

Breathing heavily, Marcus briefly considered raising his hands in reluctant surrender. Sensing victory, the soldier smirked triumphantly, adjusting his grip on the rifle.

Suddenly, Retro appeared, launching himself from the side with ferocious speed and precision. The dog's jaws clamped down on the soldier's arm, tearing through fabric and flesh. The soldier screamed in agony, dropping his weapon as Retro shook violently.

Marcus seized the moment of distraction. With every ounce of strength left in him, he lunged at the disarmed soldier, tackling him to the ground.

The forest erupted into chaos once more as man and dog fought together against their wounded captor's desperate attempts to break free. The man was good...and damned determined. Several times he squirmed out of Marcus's grip. But the man's blood loss was beginning to affect his reflexes.

Marcus felt the soldier's grip weaken. With one final, powerful blow to the side of the man's head, his opponent dropped, unconscious. The forest fell eerily silent, the only sound his ragged breathing and Retro's low growl as he kept a wary eye on the other incapacitated soldiers.

"Good boy," Marcus whispered, patting Retro's side. "We did it."

He quickly assessed the situation. Three men lay unconscious, scattered across the forest floor. Their weapons were advanced and unfamiliar, indicating they were part of something much bigger than a standard military operation. He quickly studied one of the rifles, then gathered all three. Using an unfamiliar enemy weapon went against his training, but he wanted to know what he was up against if he encountered more of the goons.

Marcus knelt beside the leader and rifled through his pockets, finding a radio, a small encrypted device, and a folded piece of paper with coordinates. He pocketed these items, knowing they might be useful later.

He stood and took a moment to think. He couldn't leave them here; they'd eventually wake up and report back. But killing them wasn't an option either. That just wasn't who he was.

"Restrain them," he muttered to himself.

He gathered zip ties from his pack and began securing their hands and feet. It was a temporary solution, but it would buy him some time.

Retro stood guard, ears perked for any sign of movement. Marcus worked quickly, binding their hands behind their backs and tying their feet together with duct tape he'd stashed in his pack. He also used the tape to cover their mouths. It was unlikely anyone out here would hear them, but it would also delay their escape or rescue.

Once finished, he dragged them into the thick underbrush to hide them from any passing patrols. He knew it wouldn't take long for their absence to be noticed, but every minute counted.

As he stood back to survey his work, Marcus wiped sweat from his brow and took a deep breath. The plan he was developing was still doubtful, but he'd bought himself some precious time and maybe something else.

"Let's move," he said to Retro, signaling for the dog to follow as they made their way toward the shoreline. In the weak moonlight, he could see the remnants of a hotel, or maybe it was apartments descending into the water. The lawn was still manicured and lush in a few places that hadn't been scorched.

The soldiers' radio crackled with static as they moved out of earshot, signaling that backup might already be on its way. Marcus knew he had to move fast before the situation escalated further.

With Retro at his side and renewed determination, they made it to the water's edge and into the small boat anchored a dozen feet offshore. He hoisted the dog in and then himself, pulled up the anchor, and hit the start button on the dash. He turned the boat east and headed for the far shore, praying he didn't hit anything along the way.

Markets Surge As Economic Growth Tops Expectations — Dow Up 1,400 Points

"In a stunning show of resilience, U.S. markets rallied sharply today after the Department of Economic Stability reported an unexpected 2.8% GDP growth for last month, handily beating Wall Street forecasts.

"Analysts attribute the surge to increased defense-sector output, emergency infrastructure contracts, and 'regional economic realignment initiatives' across depopulated metro zones.

"Secretary of Commerce Linna Meyers praised the report as 'evidence that American ingenuity thrives under pressure.' She added, 'What we're seeing is the beginning of a new, leaner economy — efficient, dynamic, and focused on rebuilding smart.'

"Investors shrugged off disruptions in air traffic, isolated unrest, and ongoing communication outages, instead doubling down on emerging markets in logistics, drone manufacturing, and biometrics.

"The White House called the rally a sign of 'market confidence in the nation's recovery trajectory.'"

CNBC Breaking | Market Minute With Jenna Thorne

CHAPTER SIXTY-THREE

0903 EST June 30
White House Oval Office
Washington, D.C., USA

Emily Carter shifted uncomfortably in her seat, trying to ignore the prickling sensation on the back of her neck. Across the table, Pete Cavanaugh's gaze bore into her, his expression unreadable. She had never cared much for the man, but when the president requested her presence at this meeting, she couldn't refuse. She already sensed the gains she'd made with Martin slipping away. There had been no speech, no information released to the nation. A press conference had been called and then abruptly canceled.

President Martin looked at them both. "Emily, I've asked Pete to sit in, as some of your findings obviously touch on national security. You offered me a pretty grim outlook when we spoke yesterday. Can you go through some of that again? Please give us a 30,000-foot overview of what conclusions your team has so far."

Emily took a deep breath, steeling herself for the task at hand. The SCET team had only scratched the surface of the myriad events they were investigating, and now she had to present a coherent overview.

"Mr. President," she began, "we've been looking into the incidents of

UFO sightings, orbital impacts, and related phenomena globally. Our findings are preliminary, but here are the key points we've identified so far."

She glanced at Pete, whose expression remained impassive, then back at President Martin. "First, we are seeing a greater number and longer duration of encounters with alien craft as well as a lot more recent cases of so-called abductions and disappearances. Many of these are deemed highly credible. One of these cases involves a group of bodies found last month in Chile that seems to be tied to this. They are still tracking DNA, but early indications suggest many of these individuals were from a community in Nevada that no one can now seem to locate.

"We feel it is clear that the recent KEW attacks on our country are a clear indication of both alien involvement and hostile intent. My team's conclusion is that the encounters with UFOs go back millennia. For the past seventy years or so we have been visited by a number of alien species, mostly benign.

"There is also evidence that a small group of humans may have been in contact and even collaborated with the aliens to keep their presence secret. We feel that this arrangement has recently changed. Something is triggering these more violent encounters. SCET is taking the position this is an invasion — the first strike of a global war with a non-human species."

President Martin leaned forward, his eyes narrowing. "Do you have any leads on who or what is behind this coordination?"

Emily hesitated before continuing. "We do have theories that strongly point toward a new unidentified but aggressive species with advanced extraterrestrial technology. We do not have any leads on the human collaborators, but my report suggests they are likely close to but not officially part of the government, military, or both."

She took a deep breath and continued, "Lastly, through our ESA connections, we've discovered symmetrical patterns on Mars rocks engraved with symbols. These markings resemble historical and possibly ancient Earth symbology and languages, strongly suggesting ancient alien contact and influence in our past."

Pete's eyes rolled with a look of exasperation. "Are you saying there's a historical connection between these extraterrestrials and Earth?"

Emily nodded slowly. "Pete, it's a very real possibility… one we can't ignore. It appears that someone transported ritualistic stones from Earth to Mars within the past 15,000 years. Since the scientist, a member of my committee, was banned from ESA after the discovery and recently murdered in her lab here in D.C., I am giving that information a great deal of credence."

President Martin interjected, "What about the military? They seem much less inclined to accept your alien theory."

Emily sighed inwardly; this was where it got tricky. "Sir, we have reason to believe many of our senior officers could be compromised into keeping the aliens' existence a secret."

"Even now?" Pete barked. "Hell, we are under attack. Who in our own military would even think of doing that if it were true? I'm sorry, but that is an outrageous statement, Emily."

"General Taylor's recent concerns about unidentified objects entering our airspace and NORAD's lack of alerts, even when some of these targeted critical infrastructure, further aligns with our findings," Emily added, ignoring the senior advisor's outburst.

Pete shifted in his seat. "And what about civilian sightings and abductions?"

"We tend to take those less seriously, although the event in New York City can't be easily dismissed out of hand due to the sheer number of initial videos and reports."

Emily paused to let her words sink in before concluding her overview. "In summary, while we're still piecing together the full picture, it's clear to me these events are interconnected through advanced alien technology that predates modern civilization and continues to affect us now.

"It is further our current assumption that there is likely a high-level cover-up by humans wanting to discourage any serious discussions of the threat such an alien species might pose."

President Martin nodded thoughtfully. "Thank you, Emily," he said softly.

"Pete, your thoughts?"

The other man leaned forward, like an attack dog guarding his food bowl. "Emily, your theories about alien conspiracies are, quite frankly, absurd," Pete began, his voice dripping with condescension. "I have evidence here that suggests you've been manufacturing false leads to convince the president of problems that simply don't exist."

He slid a folder across the table, and Emily's heart sank as she flipped through the pages. Photographs, documents, even some excerpts from the SCET meeting transcripts—all carefully crafted to paint her as a paranoid conspiracy theorist. One outright called Natalie Reeves a publicity-seeking alarmist who got drummed out of the Navy after getting her wingman killed. Another contained medical records for Kaden Trembley, where he was treated for depression with a possible bipolar disorder.

"This is ridiculous," she protested, but Pete cut her off with a wave of his hand.

"I know you are new to the CoS role, but the president needs to focus on real issues," he continued smoothly. "Israel, the growing threat of terrorist infiltration, the pending prisoner swap with Iran, the damn earthquake in Alaska. These are the real matters that require his attention, not your little wild goose chase."

Emily felt her cheeks burn with humiliation as the president and advisor exchanged glances. She knew how this looked, how Cavanaugh had masterfully undermined her credibility in just a few short minutes.

"The Alaska quake was the direct result of an object from space. Also, until yesterday, we hadn't involved the president for the very reasons you bring up. Our only mission is to give him an unbiased review of the data and any threats we uncover."

Cavanaugh laughed, a harsh, grating sound that echoed through the historic room. "Emily, everything that goes on in this building concerns the president, and me for that matter. When this gets out, and it will, that the president of the United States had an officially sanctioned task force trying to find ET, what do you think his opposition is going to do?"

He leaned back in his chair, a smug smile playing across his lips. "They'll tear him apart. They'll paint him as a crackpot, a lunatic who's more interested in chasing little green men than running the country. It'll be a political nightmare."

Emily felt her blood boil. On one level, she knew Cavanaugh was right, but she couldn't let him bully her into submission. "With all due respect, sir, I think it's more the president's campaign advisors who should worry about the political implications of our work. I was under the impression that the NSA's role is to protect national security, not to play politics."

Cavanaugh's eyes narrowed. "Don't lecture me about national security, Ms. Carter. I've been doing this job for two sitting presidents now. And I'm telling you, this little side project of yours is a disaster waiting to blow up."

He turned to the president. "Sir, I strongly advise you to shut this down before it goes any further. We can't afford to have the White House associated with this kind of fringe science and alien nonsense. The political fallout for the entire party would be catastrophic."

President Martin looked torn. Emily could see the wheels turning in his head, weighing the potential risks against the need for answers. "Emily, I understand your passion for this project, but Pete raises some valid concerns. We need to think carefully about how we proceed."

Emily took a deep breath, trying to keep her composure. "Mr. President, I know this is a sensitive issue, but we can't let fear of political backlash stop us from seeking the truth. If there really is an alien threat out there, we need to know about it. We must be prepared. We can move the committee out of the White House if that is better."

"No, I need you here at least until Dick is back at work." The president stood and thanked them both. "Let me review this and get us on more solid footing. Thanks, Pete." With that, the meeting was over, and Emily was quite sure she had lost this round.

As the meeting adjourned, Pete reached out and caught her elbow, his grip just a little too tight for comfort. "A word in private, Emily," he murmured, steering her into the corridor and turning into the next empty conference room. Just the fact that he was touching her was reason enough for her to file a complaint, but Emily knew she had to play the game, and accepting the load of crap from this stuffed shirt was part of it. Best to go ahead and find out what he really wanted.

The door clicked shut behind them, and Pete's cool facade dropped. "I want you gone," he said bluntly, his eyes cold. "Your little crusade ends now. You're a liability, and I won't have you jeopardizing our real work with your fantasies."

Emily wrenched her arm from his grasp, her heart pounding. "Yeah, you made that point pretty clear. Still, I know what we've learned, what we've uncovered," she hissed. "You can't just sweep this under the rug. This is a national security matter, maybe the biggest one ever."

"Watch me," Pete replied, a cruel smile playing at the corners of his mouth. "You have no idea the powers at play here, the strings I can pull. Walk away now, Emily, while you still can. You keep your career and your reputation. Because if you don't, I'll make sure you're not just discredited, but destroyed."

Emily walked away, forcing herself to remain calm. In truth, even her boss had occasional issues with the National Security Advisor. Cavanaugh's role and the chief of staff's often overlapped in duties. Frankly, since the advisor role was less 'official,' they often enjoyed better access and a more personal relationship with POTUS. Still, the man had crossed the line. He was winning brownie points protecting President Martin's legacy instead of the country. *Fucking politics as usual...*

She strode down the hallway, her heels clicking against the polished marble floor. The anger bubbled inside her, threatening to spill over. How dare he? How dare Cavanaugh try to intimidate her, to bully her into silence?

Emily knew the stakes were high. The evidence they'd uncovered, the patterns they'd pieced together—it all pointed to a truth that was too big to ignore. And yet, here was Pete Cavanaugh, more concerned with political optics than the safety of the American people. Growing parts of the country were disaster areas or completely uninhabitable, and that asshole was worrying about polling numbers.

She thought back to the dossier he'd presented, the carefully curated 'evidence' designed to undermine her credibility. It was a masterful piece of manipulation; she had to admit. But it was also a clear sign that Cavanaugh was desperate to shut her down. They had spent considerable time drumming up dirt on her team members. She felt sure some of it would soon find its way to the press.

As she turned the corner, Emily nearly collided with Trent Rogers, her trusted colleague on the SCET team. "Whoa, Emily, where's the fire?" he joked, but his smile faded as he took in her expression.

"Trent, we have a problem," she said, her voice low and urgent.

"Cavanaugh is trying to shut us down. He's more interested in protecting the president's image than actually investigating the truth."

Trent's brow furrowed. "That's not good. What's our next move?"

Emily sighed, running a hand through her hair. "I don't know. But we can't let him win. We cannot allow him to hide this. Too many people are relying on us."

Trent nodded, his jaw set with determination. "Agreed. But what would his angle be? It's obvious we're under attack, and even if we aren't on the right track with aliens, someone is definitely hitting us."

Emily knew he was right, but this was part of the game in D.C. Her friend was correct; she needed to choose the hill she would die on. Was it going to be this?

CHAPTER SIXTY-FOUR

0903 EST July 01
White House West Wing
Washington, D.C., USA

Emily was still fuming the next day at her committee's scheduled meeting. She looked around the table; the group was far smaller now than it had been a month earlier. Still, she was confident in this group and its ability to convince people to actually pay attention. She was unsure whether to go public if Martin and Cavanaugh tried to clamp a lid on it.

"I thought you all needed to see this," Emily said before clicking the remote. The White House seal on the large flat screen disappeared to reveal a shot of space, with Earth just visible at the bottom of the screen. "This video was taken by the Air Force X1B space plane in high orbit. The video showed nothing of interest until a long streak of light shot by from the upper right and straight down toward Earth. That was what took out the Florida panhandle...and Eglin AFB.

The room fell silent as the video played, the eerie stillness of space shattered by the sudden streak of destruction. Natalie leaned forward, her eyes narrowing as she studied the footage.

"That's not a meteor," she said, her voice low and tense. "The trajectory is all wrong. It's too controlled, too precise."

Emily nodded grimly. "Exactly. We knew from the targeting aspect it likely was not a meteor. This was a deliberate attack, not some freak celestial event."

The video looped, the streak of light slamming into the Earth's surface again and again. Each time, Natalie felt a knot tighten in her stomach. She considered the scale of devastation it had caused, the lives lost in an instant, and Marcus's desperate plea for help as well as his pleas for the people in the impact zone.

"Can you slow it down, freeze it on screen?" Kaden asked nervously.

Emily nodded. "The X1B is brimming with some of the best optics in space. We have a very clear shot of the impactor."

The next image was clearly what Emily had wanted them to see. It showed a streamlined, metallic-looking rod, bluntly pointed on one end, with a slight bulge in the middle and small nubs or maybe fins at the rear.

"It's a KEW," Natalie said in awe.

"Yes," Emily agreed. "Not as large as the ones we had on the drawing board for Project Thor. Those would have been the size of a telephone pole, but this one is estimated to be only about six meters."

"I recall the damage estimates from the original kinetic energy weapons assessment. They were nothing on the scale of what this did," Colonel Walker said.

"You're right. Those were expected to have a blast radius of only about 500 meters at most. It would have been a tactical weapon, but they were found to be nearly impossible to control as they had essentially no flight surfaces," Emily said.

"These weapons—and we are relatively sure the one that hit the nearby Naval Air Station seventy-three hours later was a smaller or slower version of the same thing—took out thirty miles in every direction of the Florida coastline. The difference was not mass. So what was it?"

"Speed," Kaden said.

"Right. The famed Rods from God were expected to reach Mach

35. These were apparently accelerated to much higher velocities. The scientists are suggesting possibly up to nine times as fast."

"The math doesn't work," Kaden offered, making notes on his pad. "The friction of the atmosphere at speeds that high would cause anything to burn up entirely. Yes, speed and mass are somewhat interchangeable, but at that speed, the mass would simply be too great."

"Unless they have something that protects it," Natalie suggested. "Like shielding, or perhaps they have developed super-dense alloys—metals that can rapidly dissipate heat."

Kaden nodded and chewed on his pen.

"But why target Eglin?" asked Walker, his brow furrowed. "Why not all the other bases, many of which have a lot more strategic weaponry?"

"We think it was to send a message," General Taylor said, speaking up for the first time. "They were letting us know they can take out what they want at any moment, and you can damn well bet where we are sitting is also high on their list. If the next step is a decapitation strike, God help us all."

"There is one other possibility, General," Natalie said. "They're scared of us...of what we are capable of."

Emily considered that point and nodded. She scanned the faces and settled on Dr. Kim. "Sam, do you have something to add?"

"Just thinking through the possibilities. It's obvious, to me at least, that whatever is behind the UFOs has been observing us for a very long time, yet officials have kept implying they needed proof. This is very clear proof, and yet we still see no outrage, no admission—in fact, no backing away from the persistent lie that UFOs are not real."

"You mean a conspiracy to conceal the truth?" Natalie asked.

"Yes, yes," Kim said. "They have proof, overwhelming proof, but still no action."

"They've had proof for years, Doctor," Natalie said with a snort. "Likely seventy years at least. My group worked on one case in Puerto Rico in 2013 at the airport in Aguadilla involving a U.S. Customs and Border Protection aircraft. The crew of a DHC-8 turboprop plane spotted and recorded a strange object using their thermal imaging system shortly after takeoff. The object, described as having a pinkish to reddish light, was observed flying over the ocean and the airport, moving at varying speeds between 40 to 120 mph. At one point, the object entered the water and continued to travel without losing speed—an ability not characteristic of known aircraft or natural objects.

"For whatever reason, the video wound up in the hands of Homeland Security, showing the object maneuvering at high speed over land before it seemingly split into two objects. My understanding is someone at Homeland contacted the Air Force to review the footage and advise them on what it was. The object demonstrated characteristics that did not match any known human technology, leading to speculation about advanced or possibly extraterrestrial origins. The Air Force literally told them they should contact MUFON.

"To me, this is a classic example of sweeping the truth out of the light. Give it to military intelligence or the NSA, CIA, or whatever alphabet agency you want to keep a lid on it. The conspiracy is real and needs to be at the heart of this group's mission."

General Taylor was nodding. "Jellyfish."

Emily looked at him. "Care to elaborate?"

General Taylor leaned forward and seemed to be trying to reach a decision on something. He exhaled, rubbing his temple. "The Puerto Rico thing? Yeah...that's just a taste." His voice was low, deliberate. "Any of you all heard of the Jellyfish encounter?"

Very few nodded; most didn't. Taylor smirked. "Of course you haven't." He keyed in his security code, his fingers moving swiftly across the secure tablet. The lights dimmed, and the main display came alive with a flickering video feed. "I'm not supposed to show you this. Frankly, I shouldn't even have it."

The screen lit up with grainy, night-vision footage, timestamped October 2018 and tagged to an Iranian military base. Guards patrolled the perimeter of what looked like an aircraft hangar. Routine, until the floodlights flickered. A pulse of light distorted the feed for a second.

"Right there," Taylor pointed, pausing the footage. Hovering just outside the perimeter lights was an object, shimmering and translucent —like a creepy flying jellyfish suspended in mid-air. Its edges pulsed with soft light, tendrils of energy drifting down, almost touching the concrete.

Kaden leaned forward. "That's not..."

"Nope," Taylor cut him off. "No UFO—this thing just...shows up."

He resumed the footage. The object hovered, silent and still, its tendrils moving like they were tasting the air. Guards scrambled, raised rifles, shouted orders. It didn't budge. Then, without warning, it began a long, slow transit over the secure wall and across the entire military compound.

“Watch this part," Taylor said, tapping the screen.

The object shifted, elongating, almost stretching itself, then it descended. Not just hovering anymore—it moved through the air and dropped seamlessly into a body of water just outside the installation, vanishing below the surface without so much as a ripple. "Transmedium," Taylor said flatly. "In and out of water like it's not even there."

"Wait, it's now underwater?" Emily asked, stunned.

Taylor nodded. "Seventeen minutes. Cameras catch the guards running around, vehicles scrambling. No one has any idea what they're dealing with. Then it comes back up, same way it went in. Angled out at forty-five degrees and gone. Drone lost tracking within seconds."

"What kind of propulsion could do that?" Kaden asked, his voice barely above a whisper.

"None that we understand," Taylor replied. "I'm going to be honest with you all, I'm not supposed to be talking about this. Hell, I'm not supposed to know about it. But I'm tired of the games. We have encounters like these every month—sometimes every week—and they don't add up. Is this a probe, a craft, a living creature?"

The room was silent. Taylor powered off the tablet and tucked it under his arm. "You want to understand what we're up against? Start with the truth. I've heard everything you guys have found. Let me assure you, as bizarre as this one is, get used to it. It's only gonna get weirder."

The meeting broke down, as it often did, into small groups discussing the video and aspects of their own specialties. They had the room for another twenty minutes. Emily noticed Kaden sitting quietly, staring at some papers. She moved her chair closer.

"Professor."

He looked up, the normally curious spark in his brown eyes now a faint ember. "I'm sorry about Dr. Schmidt...Elena."

He nodded his thanks. "It's my fault."

Emily wasn't good in this role but felt deeply for the man's grief. "It's not, Kaden." She pointed up to the video screen, still showing some of the destruction. "It's their fault. Whomever is out to stop us isn't going to go quietly."

She knew the professor had once again been under attack in the press and had been quietly let go by his university. Then the crap that the NSA advisor had complicated. Even the president had questioned letting the man stay on the team. "The optics will be bad if this gets out," he'd said.

It was already out. It seemed everything but the truth was out. That was part of their playbook. Whoever was behind this loved obfuscation, misdirection, and literally burying any shreds of fact under a mountain of hearsay.

"You going to the service?" Emily asked. She knew it was a small private affair. The White House had sent a sizable donation and a presidential letter praising Emily's service to her country and the world.

"If I can get a flight, yes," Kaden answered wearily. Most flights were being grounded now, and non-essential travel was discouraged.

Emily patted his hand. "I can help with that."

She'd chosen not to mention the last meeting with President Martin nor the somewhat uncertain status of the committee. Despite the cold reaction from the executive office, she still hoped she could persuade the man to a more deliberate and intelligent course.

She felt a presence and saw General Taylor move up behind her as they watched the professor leaving. "He's taking it hard," he said.

"He is," Emily admitted. She'd also heard that Dr. Greene's wife was under medical care after news of his death. Things were not going well for her team, and she felt personally responsible.

She turned to Taylor, "Next time you want to drop a bomb like the Jellyfish monster, give me some warning. That was the creepiest damn thing I've ever seen."

He laughed, "We thought it was, too. Everyone assumed it was a fake. When it checked out...well, let me just say I'm glad I wasn't on that base. I would have pissed my pants."

CHAPTER SIXTY-FIVE

1448 GMT July 02
St. Aelred's Church, Lower Marston
Gloucestershire, Cotswolds, England

Kaden stood solemnly at the edge of Elena's grave, a gentle breeze rustling through the cemetery just outside the quaint English village. The gray skies above mirrored the heaviness in his heart as he grappled with the weight of his failures and the loss of his brilliant colleague and friend.

He had flown to England to pay his respects, but the journey had been marred by more grim news. A text from Sarah Marshall informed him that she'd made it to Jasper Maxwell's memorial service and that his daughter had passed along a memento from Jasper. Yet another key figure in their alien investigation had passed away. Kaden felt a twinge of guilt at his muted reaction to Maxwell's death, especially in contrast to the profound grief that consumed him now, standing at Elena's final resting place.

The realization that he was more affected by the loss of one individual than the deaths of many gnawed at his conscience. Mitchell's quote on the subject rang in his ears. 'The death of one man is a tragedy...' Kaden hated himself for this disparity in his emotional response, viewing it as a fundamental flaw in his character. But even more than that, he loathed himself for failing Elena.

She had been a brilliant mind, a dedicated researcher, and a trusted ally in their quest to uncover the truth about extraterrestrial life. Now, she was gone, and Kaden couldn't shake the feeling that he had let her down. If only he had been more vigilant, more proactive in ensuring her safety, perhaps she would still be alive.

As he stared at the freshly turned earth of her grave, Kaden felt the weight of his shortcomings pressing down on his shoulders. The pursuit of truth and the obsessive drive to validate his theories had consumed him, blinding him to the dangers and the human cost of their endeavor.

He shook the hand of her brother and hugged a niece he thought he might have once met. Strangers going through the motions of saying goodbye. Elena didn't have a lot of friends. Like himself, her near-compulsive focus on her work tended to drive people away. Those here were mostly people who knew her through that work. That was where her life mattered. It was sad, but not in the way one might think. Kaden felt it was people like Elena who helped push the species forward. They gave their entire lives hoping for one breakthrough. She had made hers.

The unforgiving gray skies released their watery burden, and Kaden soon found himself at the village pub. The Feathered Dog was sparsely packed, so he put in his order for a pint and slid into a booth toward the back.

Kaden nursed his beer, the dark amber liquid reflecting the dim light of the pub. The weight of recent events pressed heavily on his shoulders, and he found himself questioning everything he had believed about his life's work.

For years, he had dreamed of the day humanity would make contact with extraterrestrials. He had imagined jubilant celebrations, a global sense of unity, and an unprecedented leap forward in scientific understanding. But reality had proven to be far more sinister and chaotic.

Instead of bringing people together, the alien presence had sown discord and fear. The world teetered on the brink of panic, with governments scrambling to maintain order and religious extremists decrying the aliens as harbingers of doom. The scientific community, which

Kaden had always believed would lead the charge in understanding and communicating with alien life, was now divided and under attack.

Kaden took a long swig of his beer, grimacing at the bitter taste that seemed to mirror his thoughts. The excitement and wonder he had always associated with the possibility of alien contact had been replaced by a gnawing sense of dread and hopelessness.

He reflected on the personal toll his pursuit had taken. Elena's death weighed heavily on his conscience, and he couldn't shake the feeling that his obsession had indirectly led to her demise. His strained relationships with other colleagues, the isolation from friends and family, the countless nights spent poring over data and chasing leads—all of it seemed futile now.

He had believed that uncovering the truth about extraterrestrial life would be his crowning achievement, a gift to humanity that would usher in a new era of enlightenment. Instead, it felt like he'd simply opened Pandora's box, unleashing chaos and destruction upon the world, and Kaden felt a deep sense of defeat.

His phone buzzed, and he checked the message. Natalie was checking in on him. She gave a quick update before asking again if he was okay.

Her concern brought a fresh tear to his eye. Like Elena, he'd dragged Natalie into this as well, but she seemed to be flourishing, if anything. He'd always been quite good at spotting talent; maybe that was where he should have focused more of his efforts. He took another pull from the pint and sent a bland but honest response.

It's time they know about the Observers. Should I have revealed that sooner? Would Elena still be alive if I had?

With hindsight, Kaden realized that a global cover-up was profoundly necessary. Not all of it, of course, but even now that the truth was getting out there, society was tearing itself apart. Humanity hadn't been ready. Not for the truth, nor for whatever technological gift aliens might have bestowed.

The football game over the bar was replaced by a special bulletin on riots near Westminster. The prime minister was enacting a curfew in all major cities, and Reserve Forces were being put on standby. Video showed a lorry burning in the street as people were in a pitched battle against the police. Kaden looked away, unable to bear much more.

He stared into the depths of his nearly empty pint glass, swirling the remnants of the liquid. The pub's ambient noise faded into the background as his thoughts consumed him. He reflected on humanity's long history of violence, intolerance, and self-destruction. From ancient wars to modern atrocities, humans had consistently proven their capacity for cruelty and shortsightedness.

The promise of alien contact, once a beacon of hope for unity and advancement, now seemed like a cruel joke. Humanity, with its petty squabbles and inability to overcome its baser instincts, was woefully unprepared for the cosmic stage.

His lips tightened as he considered the irony. For centuries, humans had gazed at the stars, dreaming of what lay beyond. Now that the beyond had come to them, they responded with fear, violence, and chaos. The very subject that had driven exploration and scientific advancement was now tearing society apart.

Kaden drained the last of his beer and stood up, fishing out his wallet. As he placed some crumpled notes on the table, he leaned close to the rain-soaked window, his voice only a whisper.

"Maybe we don't deserve the stars after all."

With those words hanging in the air, Kaden turned and walked out of the pub. The door swung shut behind him as he stepped into the pouring rain, the cold droplets mingling with the tears he could no longer hold back.

CHAPTER SIXTY-SIX

1257 EST July 03
Private Residence
Washington, D.C., USA

Natalie Reeves looked at the phone number on the screen in surprise.

"Hello...Laura."

"Hi, Lieutenant Reeves," the reporter said. "It's been a while."

"Just Natalie these days. What can I do for you?" Natalie was immersed in the data dump of UFO witness files Kaden had secured from God knows where. She really didn't have time for a side project right now, but she owed Laura Bennett. The reporter could have gone to press when they talked years earlier, but she hadn't. That had probably kept Natalie from being brought up on an Article 32 hearing for a possible violation of the Uniform Code of Military Justice. Her life would have been over.

"I need your help, Natalie," Laura began. "Truth is, I need someone's help, and you are the most competent and informed person on this that I can think of to ask."

"What's it about?" Natalie asked, her curiosity piqued.

"It's similar to what we discussed years ago." Natalie instantly knew the reporter's cryptic response meant she didn't trust that the call was secure. The nature of the call was obvious; UFOs were the only common ground the two women had ever discussed.

Natalie set down the folder she was holding. "You want to meet, grab lunch or something?"

Laura suggested an alternative. "Did you and your boyfriend ever marry?"

"Marcus?" Natalie laughed. "No, I'm afraid not. Turns out dating a guy who keeps bug-out bags and boxes of ammo under the bed is complicated. Why?"

Laura gave a slight sigh. "Nothing really, I just had some questions that I thought he might help with, too."

"We could probably get him on a call when we get together. We're still on good terms. Not sure exactly where he is, but I'm just outside the beltway working on a project."

Laura hesitated. Natalie was a little unnerved at the reporter's normally stoic demeanor. If she didn't know better, she would say the woman was scared...terrified even. "Laura, is this about a story... or something personal?"

"Can it be both?" Laura said, followed by a humorless laugh. "Let's meet at the same place we did last time, okay? Tomorrow at one?"

Natalie checked her watch. Norfolk was a drive, but she could make it if she left right after her weekly SCET committee call in the morning. Reluctantly she said, "I can do that."

It was a solid three-hour drive to the meeting. Natalie had plenty of time to consider why she was doing it, as well as to fight all the memories of the first time she and Laura talked—just after her second and third encounters with that damned unexplained aerial phenomena on a training flight off the coast of Georgia. She was scared, pissed off, and angry at the system that didn't seem to take her seriously.

All that hate had been a big part of what eventually drove her fiancé away. She'd strongly considered going to the press, and who better than the Post? Ultimately, it was the reporter, Laura, who talked her down. Natalie had a good story, but she had no real proof, and Laura knew it would tank the young officer's career. She had helped get her off the ledge, and even though she eventually left the service, Natalie managed to do it on her own terms.

She pulled into the parking lot of the small, nondescript lunch spot near Chesapeake Bay. The salty sea breeze filled her lungs as she stepped out of the car, bringing back memories of her time in the Navy. She spotted Laura already seated at a table outside near the water, her blonde hair dancing in the wind.

As Natalie approached, Laura stood up and greeted her with a warm hug. "It's good to see you, Natalie."

"You, too, Laura. It's been too long," Natalie replied, settling into the chair across from her.

The two women fell into easy conversation, catching up on their lives since they last met. Laura shared stories about her latest investigative pieces, while Natalie talked about her work with the SCET committee and her ongoing research into UFO sightings.

As they spoke, an aircraft carrier sailed into port, its massive silhouette cutting through the sparkling waters of the bay. Laura noticed Natalie's gaze lingering on the ship.

"CVN 77. The Avenger," Natalie said, watching it pass. "The George H.W. Bush," she said reverently.

"Do you miss it?" Laura asked.

Natalie sighed, a wistful smile on her face. "Every day. There's something about being out there on the open sea, the thrill of flying those jets, the camaraderie with your fellow officers. It's a feeling that's hard to replicate back here."

Laura nodded in understanding. "I can only imagine. But it seems like you've found a new purpose with your current work."

"I have," Natalie agreed. "But sometimes, I still feel that pull, you know? I managed to get some time recently in a trainer. It helped." She briefly wondered if she should tell Laura about that flight but decided to wait for now. She knew that would violate her agreement with the White House.

The two women sat in companionable silence for a moment, the sound of gulls and the distant hum of the ship filling the air. Finally, Laura leaned forward, her expression turning more serious.

"I need your help with something important," Laura said. She took a deep breath, her eyes fixed on Natalie. "You know that for years, I've been collecting stories like yours—testimonies and evidence about UFO sightings and encounters. At first, it was just a side project, something to pursue in my spare time. But the more I dug, the more I realized that there's a much bigger story here."

She pulled out a thick folder from her bag and placed it on the table. "I've got sources from all over the world, Natalie—pilots, military personnel, scientists, and ordinary people who've had extraordinary experiences. And then there's you, of course. Your story was one of the first that really made me sit up and take notice."

Natalie nodded, remembering their first conversation years before. "I remember. But what made you decide to pursue this now?"

Laura shrugged her shoulders. "It's the sheer volume of evidence, Natalie. The consistency of the stories, the patterns that emerge when you start to connect the dots. And then there's the government's response."

She flipped open the folder, revealing a stack of documents. "The congressional disclosure hearings, the denials, the cover-ups. It's all so obviously manufactured, designed to keep the public in the dark. And now, with this sudden rise in unexplained phenomena, it feels like something big is happening, and the powers that be are scrambling to keep a lid on it."

Laura didn't want to get into too much more but was intrigued that Reeves' work now seemed to be on a more official basis. "So, can I quote you as an official White House source now?"

Natalie laughed. "No, sorry. They've asked me to clear anything official through channels first. I am just here as a friend today." She leaned forward, her interest piqued. "So, what's your plan?"

"I need proof, Natalie. Same as always, really. Something concrete, something I can take to my editor and say, 'Look, this is real, and we need to tell this story.' I've got leads, but I need help following them up, verifying the information, and putting the pieces together."

Laura looked at Natalie, her eyes pleading. "That's where you come in. With your background, your experience, your connections, you're uniquely positioned to help me. I know it's a lot to ask, but I wouldn't be here if I didn't think it was important."

Natalie sat back in her chair, considering Laura's words. She knew the reporter was right. As part of MUFON, she always believed the truth needed to come out, and if she could help make that happen, she had a responsibility to do so. Now, she was slowly developing a more nuanced understanding of what disclosure involved. While her SCET involvement placed few limits on what she potentially could say to the press, her own good judgment did. Shit, people were dying over this already.

"What can I help with?" Natalie asked. "My own personal encounter was years ago."

"Well, I'm more focused on the human component. I have a lead on what I think is a major player in what I am beginning to think is an organized cover-up. Something you mentioned after your encounter."

"The government suits?" Natalie asked.

"Well, that was what I was hoping for, but not where the lead took me. You ever heard of Alcon Industries?"

Natalie looked confused, then shook her head.

"Industrial park about thirty miles from D.C. I tried bluffing my way in and got nowhere. The building I went to is large, though. Big enough to be a manufacturer of some kind, but what I saw around back looked more like a paramilitary group rolling out on a mission. A domestic mission."

"That sounds dangerous, Laura. You sure you weren't spotted?"

"Well, I walked in the front door and showed my credentials, yes, but they didn't know I stuck around to see the rest of the operation. But you're sure you've never heard of them?"

Natalie considered it and sipped her glass of wine. "No, but that doesn't mean much. I assume you've tracked the company, property tax records, and stuff."

"Shell company, none of the leads go anywhere tangible," Laura said. Her tone was weary with dejection. "I keep chasing this thing, and it's like grabbing at smoke. I found one small connection: a bill of lading from a now-defunct shipping company indicating someone with the initials O. King had authorized the secure access the driver needed for the delivery."

"Doesn't ring a bell," Natalie said, shaking her head. "You know what Alcon sounds like, don't you?"

"One of those government black-ops programs," Laura said.

"Yeah, my guess as well."

The women ordered some food and ate while continuing to discuss the case. Natalie didn't feel free to get into specifics the committee was investigating, but she did update Laura on some MUFON cases that might be helpful. Laura also let her browse through the folder she had. Most were previously known incidents to her group.

"You mentioned Marcus when you called? What do you need with him?" Natalie asked.

Laura gave a smile; she obviously wanted to ask more about the breakup but stuck to the business at hand. "I saw a window sticker in a few cars that I can't quite place, but I feel sure it had a military connection."

"One that Marcus might know?" Natalie guessed.

The other woman nodded. The two had become good enough friends over the years that Laura knew a lot about Natalie and her ruggedly handsome boyfriend back then. Marcus had been a Navy SEAL back in the day—not something he discussed anymore, but he seemed to know everything going on with the shadow warriors.

Laura showed Natalie the photo of the gold trident symbol. Something about it did look familiar to Natalie as well, but she couldn't place it. "Let's do a video call and see if he can help."

The call went to his voicemail. "Probably still off the grid or something."

Laura airdropped the file to Natalie's phone. "If you get him, you can ask him about it. I already checked online, and nothing came up. Very odd. Normally, you find too much stuff on any image you search for. Seems almost like someone was keeping it scrubbed from the web."

Natalie tried to gauge if Laura was on the right track or not. She, herself, had been much more centered on the alien craft than the cover-up, but since joining SCET, that paradigm was shifting.

"I think you're on the right track, Laura. In fact, I think the aliens are the ones causing all of the havoc around the world—the power outages, the GPS going down, food and fuel shortages. In fact, I would blame them for everything, including this rather forgettable bottle of wine." They both gave a nervous laugh.

"I'll check with Marcus when I can get through. In the meantime, you be careful."

They finished lunch, exchanged a few notes with current contact info, and headed to their cars. Both women hugged and promised to stay in touch this time, even though both knew they probably wouldn't. The trip had been friendly but generally unproductive. Neither woman noticed the pair of rental cars that pulled out and discreetly followed each of them as they turned back toward D.C.

CHAPTER SIXTY-SEVEN

Natalie merged into traffic, her mind still processing what Laura had shared. She was working with the government now, but she had always assumed someone in the government was behind the UFO cover-up. She had her own encounters with the infamous Men in Black.

A half-hour from Richmond, her mind seemed to shift into combat mode without her consciously knowing why. As she glanced in her rear-view mirror, a nondescript sedan caught her attention. It had been behind her for the last few turns, maintaining a consistent distance. Her instincts, honed by years of military training, whispered a warning.

Getting closer to the capital city, she made a series of random turns, her suspicions growing as the sedan matched her every move. Natalie's cold logic wasn't fazed by the realization that she was being followed. MUFON had worked for years on the outside, and every team had tales of intimidation by locals and officials alike. Being followed was just part of it. Still, she wasn't on a MUFON case, and in theory, no one knew she was here.

Natalie was driving a government sedan she'd checked out of the motor pool. They were all managed by the same national rental company and virtually indistinguishable. Tapping the nav screen, she brought up the closest rental lot and entered it into the navigation system. She made a number of random turns and even a three-point turnaround to change directions and backtrack. She no longer saw the tail car but decided it best to assume that they likely had a tracker on it as well.

Spotting the rental lot filled with similar cars, Natalie seized the opportunity. She deftly maneuvered her vehicle into the lot, weaving between the parked cars until she found a spot to hide her own. She cut the engine and ducked down. She watched as minutes later the sedan slowly cruised past the lot entrance.

As the car passed, Natalie caught a glimpse of the occupants—two serious-looking men. The car moved a hundred yards down the road, and then she saw brake lights. She left the key fob on the seat, eased open the passenger door, grabbed her bag, and crouch-walked out of the lot.

She picked a direction with the most pedestrians and did her best to blend in with the shoppers, office workers, and anyone else who happened to be on the streets in the Richmond suburb. She watched reflections in the mirrored buildings and thought she had made a clean break when she caught another glimpse of the white sedan. Using her phone, she hit record and videoed in the direction of the approaching car.

She made several more random direction changes and soon found herself passing a playground and then a school. "Shit!" She knew she was heading into a more residential area. With less cover, she would certainly stand out. She thought about who she could call; only one name came to mind, but he couldn't help her here, and she hadn't been able to get him on the phone anyway.

Natalie's mind went into overdrive calculating her next move. She couldn't risk leading them back to her home. Suddenly, an idea struck her. She pulled out her black phone, clicked to encrypt her number, and dialed the local police.

"911, what's your emergency?" the dispatcher asked.

"This is Trish Johnson. I'm an assistant at Jefferson Elementary School," Natalie reported as she eyed the sign she'd just passed. "There's a suspicious white sedan with two weird-looking dudes inside. I may be wrong, but they seem to be taking pictures of the students. They can't just do that—right?"

The dispatcher's tone shifted, urgency coloring her words. "We're sending officers to the scene immediately. Can you describe the vehicle?"

Natalie provided a detailed description of the sedan and its occupants.

"I went to that human trafficking seminar a few months back," she added. "They said to report anything suspicious. I hope that's okay." As she ended the call, she heard sirens in the distance, growing louder by the second.

Seizing the moment, Natalie tapped the app for a car service and marked a pickup location several blocks away. She watched as police cruisers sped past, heading towards the school. She caught sight of the sedan, now caught in the middle of the police response. She allowed herself a tiny smile. Those high-school acting classes had come in handy after all.

Natalie breathed a sigh of relief as the Lyft driver merged onto the highway, putting distance between herself and her pursuers. But the relief was short-lived, replaced by a growing sense of unease. She tried Laura Bennett's cell, and it went straight to voicemail.

Back in her condo, she went over the entire conversation with Laura. Coming to a decision, she called Emily and filled her in on everything. With some of the new security protocols, she should have notified the director immediately, but her original thinking was that today's meeting was a personal one...not SCET related. Now she was not so sure.

"Yes, Director Carter."

"It's just Emily, hon. Look, you did well. Kaden was smart bringing you onboard. When he gets back, I want the three of us to sit down and go over next steps."

Natalie noted the strain in the woman's voice. She wasn't sure if it was the pressure of the job or her task force that was causing the stress, but Emily Carter definitely sounded different. Still holding her phone, she pulled up the video of the two guys and pulled some still images of their faces. Scrolling back, she saw the photo Laura had sent her. She could try again to follow up on that lead.

CHAPTER SIXTY-EIGHT

0645 EDT July 03
Northeast Florida, USA

Luther, Nancy, and her two children trudged through the desolate landscape, the remnants of civilization scattered around them like broken toys. The silence was oppressive, punctuated only by the sound of their footsteps and the very distant hum of helicopters.

As they rounded a corner, a vehicle appeared in the distance, its lights flashing against the smoky backdrop. Luther's hand instinctively went to his hip, a gesture that didn't escape Nancy's notice. She tucked TJ and Lynn closer, her eyes fixed on the approaching vehicle.

It was a pickup truck. Through the windshield, the front seat appeared filled with boxes and supplies, and its doors were marked with the emblem of the Community Emergency Response Teams. The driver, a middle-aged man in a CERT shirt, stepped out and approached them.

"Need some help here?" the man asked, his voice firm but kind.

Luther eyed him warily. "We're looking for a safe place. Just somewhere we can get some food and shelter."

The man nodded. "I can help you with that. There's a shelter about ten miles from here. We've set up a temporary base with supplies and medical care. Red Cross is supposed to come in, but hell...who knows? It's not perfect, but it's better than being out here."

Nancy looked at Luther, a silent plea showing in her eyes. He nodded reluctantly. "Okay, we'll take it."

The CERT volunteer helped them load into the truck, his movements on automatic as if he'd done this countless times today. As they drove, Luther watched the landscape roll by, his thoughts a jumble of uncertainty. He had other destinations to get to, but he wouldn't be able to take Nancy and the kids there.

As they pulled in, they could see the shelter was essentially three large tents, their interiors bustling with people in various states of distress. The CERT volunteer led them to a registration desk, where a harried woman in a red vest greeted them with a weary smile.

"Welcome. We'll need to register you and your family. Please, let's get you settled."

Luther hesitated; all this was coming more suddenly than he expected. His eyes nervously scanned the crowded tent. He didn't like this one bit. But he knew it was temporary, and for now, it was better than being out in the open.

"I think these people can get you settled," he told Nancy, his voice low. "But I'm gonna need to go."

Nancy glanced at him. “Where will you go?”

Luther shook his head. "I just need to check in with my own people. But I'll be back."

Nancy nodded, her voice a whisper. "Be careful, Luther." She hugged the big man tightly. He had been a savior, and now he was leaving.

Luther's gaze lingered on her, then he turned and walked away, disappearing into the chaos of the shelter.

The volunteer's voice cut through the noise. "Sir, you can't just leave. You need to register—"

“It’s Big Lou. And no, I don’t do forms before coffee.”

Luther was already gone, lost in the sea of faces and the desperation that hung in the air like a thick fog.

TJ began to cry. "I want to go with Big Lou!"

Nancy felt the same, but having a cot to sleep on for a change would be welcome, too. She took the form and the stub of a pencil and began to write.

Nancy shuffled through the crowded tent, her children clinging to her sides. The sheer number of people crammed into the space was overwhelming. Desperate faces peered out from makeshift beds and cots, their eyes hollow and haunted. The air was thick with the stench of unwashed bodies and fear.

"Wait here," the harried woman said.

Another volunteer, her red vest stained and wrinkled, approached them again a few minutes later. "This way," she said, her voice flat with exhaustion. As they wove through the maze of cots, the woman leaned in close. "Word of advice—don't leave anything valuable out. Not even for a second."

Nancy clutched her backpack tighter, suddenly aware of the eyes following their every move.

"And keep those kids close," the volunteer continued, her gaze darting to TJ and Lynn. "Don't let them wander off, especially over that way near the fence. Just... just don't."

They reached an empty cot tucked in a corner. The volunteer gestured halfheartedly. "Here you go. Bathroom's outside, food line starts at six. Good luck."

As the woman walked away, Nancy felt a chill run down her spine. The camp hummed with an undercurrent of danger. Angry voices rose and fell in the distance. A child wailed, the sound raw and piercing.

Nancy's mind flashed back to Luther's face when the CERT volunteer had suggested this place. She understood now—the tightness around his eyes, the way his jaw had clenched. They weren't just refugees finding sanctuary; they were now prisoners, trapped in a cage of desperation. Luther knew what this place would be like even before he saw it.

She pulled TJ and Lynn close, her voice barely a whisper. "We stick together, okay? No matter what."

"I don't like this place," Lynn said, tears already streaming down her cheeks. "I want Daddy."

Nancy pulled her daughter tight. She feared she wasn't strong enough to survive this, despite the faith that Luther seemed to have in her. She pulled TJ's shoes and socks off and treated the blisters with some of the cream Luther had given her. "Keep your foot dry and out of the dirt while your shoes dry out."

As night fell, the sounds of the camp grew more ominous. Shouts and screams punctuated the darkness. Nancy lay awake, her children nestled against her, wondering if they'd made a terrible mistake.

After a sleepless night, Nancy eased off the cot, letting her children continue to sleep. Her back hurt even worse than the prior nights when she'd used the ground for a bed. As she stretched, a hoarse whisper caught her attention.

"Don't leave your kids here."

She turned to see an older woman on the neighboring cot. The woman's left arm ended in a blood-stained bandage, the stump where her hand should have been.

Nancy's stomach churned. "I... I was just going to use the bathroom and see about breakfast."

The woman shook her head, her eyes haunted. "Give it a half hour. Them volunteers don't get in any rush."

Nancy glanced at her sleeping children, then back at the woman. "What do you mean?"

"It's just surplus military rations or MREs most days. And your kids gotta be with you if you want them to get anything." The woman's voice dropped lower. "Not enough to go around most days."

Nancy's heart sank. She'd hoped for something more substantial, something to help her children regain their strength. "How long have you been here?"

The woman's eyes clouded. "Too long. Lost track of the days." She gestured with her stump. "Lost this to infection last week. They ran out of antibiotics last Monday."

Nancy felt a chill run down her spine. She looked around the tent, really seeing it for the first time. Desperation hung in the air like wood smoke. People huddled on their cots, their eyes hollow and wary.

"Thank you," Nancy whispered to the woman. "For the warning."

The woman nodded, then turned away, curling into herself on the cot.

Nancy sat back down, pulling TJ and Lynn close. She stroked their hair, her mind racing. This place wasn't safe. It wasn't sustainable. But where else could they go?

She thought of Luther, wondering if he would come back as he said. Wondering if they should have stayed with him instead. Where was he heading anyway? That had bothered her ever since she met the man. He was incredibly kind and helpful but also secretive. Never once did he let on that he had a specific destination in mind.

Nancy Ramesh sat on the edge of a worn mattress, the fabric threadbare as she fought to reclaim a sense of normality. The sounds of children laughing and families whispering filled the air around the refugee camp, yet there was a strong undercurrent of desperate tension. The blue pre-dawn light settled over the makeshift enclave as the sun struggled to rise above the horizon, and shadows retreated over the haphazardly constructed tents.

As she looked around, her heartbeat quickened. This place felt like a mirage, an insubstantial temporary refuge that might collapse at any moment—much like the life she once led. It was a swirling whirlwind of emotions, memories flooding in while she grappled with the harsh present reality. No matter how many smiles and words of comfort she offered, the gnawing fear of instability lingered within her.

Nancy's mind drifted back to Afghanistan, where her husband had worked as a translator for American forces. He had spoken of hope and freedom, of building a future together. But the whimsical dreams were shattered the day the Taliban returned, seizing control with violent intent. As they'd fled, they had watched their world unravel—friends, neighbors, a home evaporating into dust.

In the silence of her thoughts, she drew upon the strength that their past had nurtured. They hadn't just lost a house; they had left behind a life filled with possibilities—their cherished belongings, dreams of a small coffee shop where they could share Afghan culture, and their hopes for a future. All that now drifted alongside the final view of their destroyed home.

Now, within the confines of the camp, Nancy was reminded daily of her marginalized identity. People eyed her, whispering questions she could feel hanging in the air—did she practice Islam? Did her appearance align with their beliefs? Yet, Nancy found herself sidestepping such inquiries, unwilling to confront their implications or place herself within any predefined narrative. The pain of loss was tangled with her fear of judgment.

Trust had never come easily for her, especially after witnessing betrayal during her flight from Afghanistan. Many of those she called friends had become shadows when the power dynamics shifted. Those moments rang in her ears like chains clanking, tethering her heart to solitude. Suddenly needing to justify her beliefs felt like entering a battlefield all over again.

She considered her two children, still asleep despite the growing sounds of awakening from the rest of the camp. They were the only thing keeping her from despair. She had to be strong for them, not just to protect them but to find a way out of this mess. "You'll be fine," Nancy whispered, brushing a bit of hair from her son's face, wishing he could stay this way forever. "We'll be fine." She just needed to make sure that was true.

CHAPTER SIXTY-NINE

The enclave lay nestled in the dense Floridian wilderness, hidden from the untrained eye by thick underbrush and camouflaged fencing. Disguised defenses dotted the perimeter—pits masked by leaves, trip-wires, and silent alarms. Inside, a small community bustled with purpose. Members hauled pipes to draw water from a nearby stream, checked weapons, and inventoried supplies.

Big Lou stepped through the main gate, his large frame casting a shadow over the entrance. The guards recognized him immediately, nodding their acknowledgment as he passed. He had always been a key outside scout for the enclave from the moment it went active, someone they trusted implicitly.

"Luther," one of the guards called out. "Good to see you back safe, brother."

He managed a tight smile but didn't slow his pace. His thoughts were miles away, tangled up in memories of his missing wife and the immediate danger threatening Nancy and her kids back at the aid camp.

He found Isaac near the central tent, poring over supply lists and terrain maps with several other members. Isaac looked up as Lou approached, his eyes narrowing slightly.

"Big Lou," Isaac greeted him curtly. "What's brought you back so soon?"

"We need to talk," Luther replied, his voice steady but urgent. "Any word from the other camp?"

"Marcus is supposedly on his way but no updates. Also, the feds are still not admitting to what happened here."

"That figures," Luther said. "Look, I saw a lot of groups out there. They're going to be getting desperate any day now. I think we need to raise the alert level."

Isaac nodded. "Already in process, my friend. We've had a number of stragglers cross the perimeter alarms already."

"What are you doing with them?" Luther asked, fearing the worst.

The other man shrugged. "Limiting what they see and scaring them away. Not sure how long that will last, but we don't want to start shooting. It's obvious our camp is more exposed than we thought."

Luther considered that. They had put a lot of work into where they chose to set up. Buying the land alone had taken nearly a year. Isaac was right, though, the local population was just too large. Someone was bound to stumble across it, especially in the current situation.

"I want to bring someone in. A single mom and her two kids."

Isaac's brow furrowed. "You know our policies, Lou. We can't just let anyone in. We're all members who have paid our annual dues for years, along with considerable blood and sweat to have this place. We discussed at length that no outsiders could be allowed in... ever!"

"I know," Lou said, exhaling deeply. "But this is different. They're in real danger out there."

Isaac folded his arms across his chest, glancing at the others before nodding for them to give some space.

"Where are they now?"

"I left them at a makeshift aid camp over near Messer's Creek. The place smelled like raw sewage and death."

Isaac shook his head. "Then they're better off than most out there. They don't know anything about us, do they?"

"Of course not," Luther said. "I know the rules. I just think this woman could be an asset."

"Look, big man, we've been preparing for years," Isaac began once the others drifted out of the tent. "Every decision we make is about survival—about protecting what we've built here."

Lou nodded, understanding the gravity of what he was asking. "I wouldn't be here if it wasn't serious, Isaac. I've seen what it's like out there—the desperation—the chaos. Nancy and her kids won't survive without help."

Isaac sighed heavily but remained silent for a moment, contemplating. "Lots of people won't survive, my friend. That is the awful truth of all this. Choosing to do what is needed beforehand also comes with the realization you will likely hate yourself later for some of the choices you must make to keep it quiet and defend it."

"Look, Isaac...I get it, but keep in mind I paid dues for a family, and it's just me. I think I should be able to bring these three in as part of my family. Adopted family," he said, grinning.

Before their conversation could continue further, a shout rang out from the east perimeter guard. Both men turned toward the noise as armed guards hurried past them.

"What's going on?" Isaac demanded as they reached the gate.

"Not sure," one of the men said. "We've been spotting some larger groups of stragglers getting way too close the last few days. Looks like they were scouting us out."

A group of about a dozen heavily armed strangers stood just outside the enclave's boundaries. Their leader stepped forward, hands raised in what seemed like a gesture of peace. He held a Bible in one of his upraised hands.

"God led us here!" he announced loudly, his voice carrying over to everyone present. "We only seek refuge."

Tension spiked instantly among the enclave members; weapons were raised cautiously but firmly.

Isaac moved forward to negotiate, but Big Lou sensed trouble brewing in the look of this group—a volatile mix of desperation and fanaticism that could ignite at any moment.

"God, huh?" Luther said with a snarl, walking up to the gate.

"You need to just turn around and start walking," Luther said, his voice edging higher as he did so. "Forget you ever came across this place."

"Look, friend," the spokesperson said. "We just want a place to rest for the night. Maybe a bite to eat if you could spare it."

Isaac turned to Luther. "See what I mean? Nothing is safe, even out here."

"Look," Isaac moved past the gate and attempted to deescalate the situation. "We are just barely getting by ourselves. You can go to the aid camp not ten miles from here."

The stranger put down the Bible and turned back to his men. "No, I don't think we want to do that, brother."

The situation spiraled when one of the stranger's enforcers made a sudden move toward Isaac. In a flash, Luther's protective instincts kicked in; he lunged forward and struck down the attacker with an elbow strike to the face and then went after their leader, who was already drawing a sidearm.

"I am not your brother," Luther growled as his massive frame barreled toward the so-called religious leader, his eyes blazing with fury. "God didn't lead you here," he growled, his voice a low rumble of thunder. "It was the angel of death."

His fist connected with the man's jaw, a sickening crack echoing through the air. The Bible tumbled from the leader's grasp as he staggered backward. Luther didn't relent, following up with a vicious punch to the man's solar plexus that left him gasping for air.

"You ain't no man of God," Luther snarled, unleashing the hatred and anger that had been building for years on the man. Grabbing the leader by his shirt collar, he headbutted him, blood spraying from the man's now-broken nose. "You're just another vulture."

The man's followers reacted, drawing weapons. The air erupted with gunfire, bullets whizzing past Luther's head. He ducked, using the leader's body as a shield. A round caught the man in the shoulder, and he screamed in agony.

Luther spun, hurling the leader into his own men. As they stumbled, he charged forward, his massive hands finding purchase on another attacker's throat. With a roar, he lifted the man off his feet and slammed him into the ground. The impact was brutal, leaving the attacker motionless.

A bullet grazed Luther's arm, but he barely felt it. Adrenaline surged through his veins as he grabbed the fallen attacker's weapon. He turned, firing with deadly accuracy. Two more of the group fell, their chests blooming red.

The enclave's defenders had rallied, beginning to return fire from behind cover. Luther dove behind a stack of crates, his breath coming in ragged gasps. He peeked out, spotting the religious leader crawling away from the firefight.

With a snarl, Luther lunged out from cover. He closed the distance in seconds, his boot coming down hard on the man's wounded shoulder. The leader howled in pain, trying to roll away. Luther kicked out at the man's head, nearly separating it from his now-broken neck.

The gunfire soon faded, leaving an eerie silence punctuated only by the groans of the wounded and dying. Luther stood amidst the carnage, his chest heaving, blood spattered across his face and clothes. The enclave's defenders emerged from their positions, weapons still at the ready. They cautiously approached the downed men. Several more shots rang out as they finished off the wounded.

Luther's eyes scanned the battlefield, taking in the bodies strewn across the ground. His gaze fell on Isaac, crumpled near the gate, a dark stain spreading across his chest. Luther's stomach twisted as he realized the cost of this small victory.

"Check the woods for runners," he barked, his voice hoarse. "Make sure none of them got away." *So this is what it's come to already.*

As the enclave's guards moved to secure the area, Luther turned and saw what he feared the most—his friend and mentor lying on the ground. He knelt beside Isaac's body, a small wound high on his chest, blood still bubbling out. He closed his friend's eyes, a wave of guilt washing over him. This wasn't what he had intended when he came seeking help for Nancy and her children.

The other members of the group gathered around, their faces bearing witness to the seriousness like never before. They looked to Luther, their eyes seeking guidance in the wake of Isaac's sudden death.

"What do we do now?" someone asked, breaking the tense silence.

Luther stood, his imposing figure commanding attention. He surveyed the group, noting the fear in their eyes. These people needed leadership, and with Isaac gone, that responsibility likely now fell to him.

"We bury our dead," Luther said firmly. "Then we fortify our defenses. This won't be the last attack we face. How did these people find us so quickly?" He tried to prioritize the next steps. "We must do better at staying hidden. No cook fires, cold camp only for the next few days."

As the group dispersed to carry out his orders, Luther found himself alone with his thoughts. The newly added weight of leadership settled heavily on his shoulders. He had come here seeking refuge for Nancy and her kids, but now he was responsible for an entire community. Could they allow anyone who found the camp to leave alive?

He considered the implications of what had just transpired. The strict rules that had governed the enclave—the very rules he had hoped to bend for Nancy—now seemed both necessary and insufficient. How could they maintain their security without losing their humanity?

As he helped strip meager supplies and gear from the strangers and helped dig graves for the fallen, Luther grappled with the moral ambiguity of their situation. His actions had saved the enclave, but at what cost? The brutality he had unleashed disturbed him, yet he knew it would be necessary again in the future.

Several hours later, another commotion at the perimeter set him on full alert. This time he heard a dog as well. He didn't like dogs, and they seemed to feel the same toward him. Reluctantly, he dragged his weary body back toward the action.

CHAPTER SEVENTY

Luther limped toward the gate, muscles tensed for another fight. His hand gripped the rifle tightly, finger hovering near the trigger. The shouting had died down, replaced by excited murmurs from the lookouts.

When he reached the perimeter, Luther's exhausted eyes widened in disbelief. There, illuminated in the fading light, stood Marcus Smith—the leader of all the camps, the visionary who'd brought them together. A German Shepherd stood alert at his side, ears perked forward.

"Marcus?" Luther called out, his voice cracking with emotion. "Is that really you?"

Marcus nodded, his face weathered and drawn but unmistakable. "Permission to approach, Luther. We've come a long way."

Without hesitation, Luther threw the heavy wooden barricade aside and rushed forward. He embraced Marcus fiercely, clapping him on the back with enough force to make the smaller man wince.

"Easy there, big guy," Marcus chuckled, returning the embrace.

The German Shepherd growled, hackles rising at the sudden movement toward his master. Luther stiffened, eyeing the dog warily. He'd never been comfortable around canines—something about their unpredictability made his skin crawl.

Marcus noticed the tension. "Retro, stand down. He's family."

The dog's posture relaxed somewhat, though his eyes remained fixed on Luther.

"He's saved my life at least once already on this trip," Marcus told Luther. "Best partner I could ask for out there."

Luther took a deep breath and knelt down, extending his hand palm up. "Hey there, boy. Sorry about the rough welcome."

To his surprise, Retro approached cautiously, sniffed his hand, then allowed Luther to scratch behind his ears. Luther found himself pulling the animal into a friendly embrace, his fear dissolving as the dog's warm body pressed against him.

"Man, I am glad to see you guys," Luther said, rising to his feet. His voice broke as the events of the day caught up with him. "Isaac's dead. We just fought off some religious nuts. It's been... it's been a hell of a day."

Luther led Marcus through the compound, their boots crunching on gravel as they moved between cabins and storage sheds. He detailed the confrontation with the religious group while Marcus shared his harrowing journey through the military cordon.

"We lost three good people today," Luther said, his voice heavy. "Isaac went down fighting."

Marcus nodded grimly. "Sounds like him. He was a good man; we will all miss him."

They reached the main supply building, a converted barn with reinforced walls and a metal roof. Inside, shelves lined with canned goods, medical supplies, and ammunition stretched from floor to ceiling. Marcus discreetly studied the inventory with a practiced eye, checking expiration dates and counting boxes.

Marcus told Luther of all that was happening out in the world and what he had seen around the impact site. They moved through other parts of the enclave, Marcus taking time to speak to the ones he knew personally and offering pleasantries to the rest. Retro, now free of his combat harness and gear, was off frolicking with a group of children. The killer canine was just a big fur ball when off duty.

"Water filtration's holding up," Luther reported. "But they've told me they're down to sixty percent capacity on diesel. I imagine the generator's been running often since the grid went down."

Marcus ran his hand along a shelf of ammunition, noting the depleted stock. "They've used quite a bit."

"Had no choice," Luther said. "They have to hunt, and well, things are pretty bad here."

Marcus stopped back at the supply hut and rummaged through his gear bag, handing Luther and then Alex, the group's quartermaster, each one of the new weapons he'd taken off the PMCs. "I haven't had time to check these out, but they look nothing like I've seen before. I'm assuming energy weapons, but so far, I can't even see the energy source or battery. You guys keep these two, and I'll hang on to the other. Use them cautiously, but this is what you're up against out there." He also left them the small comms radio so they could listen in to the military command channel, assuming they didn't change frequencies. He eyed the other device but decided to hang on to that himself.

After completing their inventory, they stepped outside. The evening air carried the scent of pine and distant smoke. Marcus gazed across the compound, taking in the defensive positions, the garden plots, and the worried faces of the survivors. Several of the group's other leaders had gathered closer.

"I have to agree with Isaac. I don't think this is a viable location anymore," Marcus said.

Luther's shoulders slumped, but he didn't argue.

"Alpha had never been set up as completely as Beta in the Ozarks, but it was still very nice," Marcus continued, gesturing toward the cabins they'd built together. "It was always risky putting this near both a military base and a tourist destination. Now the water's fouled, communications are nonexistent, and you have jack-booted mercenary thugs roaming the woods not fifteen miles from here."

Luther spat on the ground. "Yeah, those weren't regular military I saw afterward either. Private contractors, like you said. Didn't even bother identifying themselves properly."

"Exactly my point," Marcus said. "Whatever happened at Eglin is big enough that they're willing to shoot civilians asking questions. We're too close to the epicenter here."

Luther leaned against a nearby table, eyes fixed on Marcus. "So, what's the play?"

Marcus met his gaze steadily. "You're in charge, Luther. You make the decisions from here on out."

Luther's brow furrowed. "Me? But—"

"No buts," Marcus cut in. "I've seen what you can do. You're a natural leader. You are the right man for this."

Marcus pulled an iPad in a tough case from his pack and began scrolling through maps and files, his fingers moving with practiced ease. The device's glow cast a stark light on the man's bruised and dirty face.

"Look here," Marcus said, pointing with a stylus at the screen. A detailed map of the area came into view, marked with various notations and symbols. "Getting this group safely to the Beta site will be nearly impossible under current conditions. The roads are blocked, and the military's got checkpoints everywhere."

Luther peered over Marcus's shoulder, eyes narrowing as he took in the map. "What about resources? If we even make it there, won't we overtax their supplies?"

Marcus nodded grimly. "I'm afraid so. We could take a few, but we need another solution."

He used the stylus to draw a rough boundary around a section of the map. "This is the blackout zone and military exclusion area. All movement inside this line is heavily monitored. All normal comms traffic, including radio and cell, is blocked."

Luther studied the map, recognizing landmarks and roadways now marked as no-go zones.

"We can't move everyone at once," Marcus continued. "We'll need to break into smaller groups, travel at different times, and find temporary safe havens along the way."

Luther rubbed his chin thoughtfully. "That means coordinating multiple rendezvous points and ensuring everyone has what they need for the journey."

"Right," Marcus agreed. "And we'll need to secure more supplies—food, water, medical gear—before we even think about moving out. There's something else. Refugees are going to be streaming away from the coast by the tens of thousands. This exodus will look like the survivors flooding across Europe from Syria years ago."

Luther nodded, "Perfect. Let's set up some hot cocoa and hope

FEMA shows up before the mothership does." His mind refocused on the plan. It was risky, but leaving was their only option.

Marcus handed Luther the iPad. "You'll need this for coordination and communication between groups." He pulled out a second device from his pack—a satellite phone. "It works only occasionally here, but hopefully that will clear up. This is your lifeline," he said, pressing it into Luther's hand.

Taking a deep breath, Luther accepted the weight of responsibility now placed upon him.

"We'll make it work," he said firmly.

"We have to," Marcus replied.

"So, where should we go?" Luther asked, studying the map. "Remember, these people paid for years to have resources and dwellings ready for them in case of a situation just like this."

Marcus smiled. "I think you're going to like what I have in mind. But...you guys will have to hold out here for a bit longer."

Kraft Foods Launches 'Quiet Comfort Meals' Campaign to Support National Unity

"Each family-sized tray will include a QR code linking to a curated playlist of calming sounds and patriotic speeches. Kraft declined to comment on supply shortages at its Chicago plant."

CHAPTER SEVENTY-ONE

1403 EST July 09
K Street
Washington, D.C., USA

Laura Bennett strode down K Street, her heels clicking against the pavement with a sense of purpose. The sun hung low in the sky, casting long shadows across the bustling sidewalks of Washington D.C. She had just wrapped up one more off-the-record interview, and her mind was still sorting through some points of the information she'd learned.

The aide to the high-ranking senator had been forthcoming, but the depth of knowledge on the possible UAP cover-up still wasn't coming together. Laura knew she needed more if she was going to keep the story alive.

As she turned the corner, a familiar sight caught her eye: two men sitting in a nondescript sedan parked across the street. Natalie's earlier message had heightened her awareness. Now she had seen them multiple times over the past few days, always in different cars, but their faces were etched in her memory. They had been following her and not even trying hard to hide the fact.

Her curiosity piqued, Laura quickened her pace, her high heels clicking on the pavement. She approached the car, her eyes locked on the tinted windows. The men's silhouettes were unmistakable, even in the fading light.

Laura's journalistic instincts kicked into high gear. Who were these men? Who did they work for? What did they want with her? The questions swirled in her mind as she weighed her options. She could ignore them, pretending she hadn't noticed their presence. But that wasn't her style. She was a reporter, and she needed answers.

With a deep breath, Laura crossed the street, her strides purposeful and determined. She approached the car, her heart pounding in her chest. As she drew closer, the men's faces came into focus. They were young, probably in their early thirties, very fit, with nondescript features and dark glasses covering unreadable eyes.

Laura tapped on the driver's side window, her knuckles rapping against the glass with a sense of urgency. The men inside barely acknowledged her presence, their gazes fixed straight ahead. She knocked again, harder this time, her frustration mounting.

"Can I help you, gentlemen?" Laura asked, her voice firm and authoritative, as she tapped on the window again and called louder. "Hey!" she called out, her voice sharp and demanding. "I know you've been following me. Who are you? Who do you work for?"

Behind the dark tinted windows, the men remained silent, their expressions unreadable. She pulled out her phone, ready to take a video of the two. Then, to Laura's shock, she heard laughter, their mocking tones echoing within the confines of the car. They were making fun of her, treating her like some kind of nut.

Laura's cheeks flushed with anger and embarrassment. She opened her mouth to retort, but before she could utter a word, the sound of a siren whoop filled the air. A police car pulled up beside her, its lights flashing red and blue.

An officer stepped out, his eyes narrowing as he approached Laura. "Ma'am, what seems to be the problem here?" he asked, his tone stern and authoritative.

Laura tried to explain the situation. "These men have been following me for days," she said, pointing to the car. "I just wanted to know who they were and why they were tailing me. Look, my name is Laura

Bennett. I work for the Post. I'm a journalist. Like I said, these guys have followed me."

The officer glanced at the car, then back at Laura. "Ma'am, you're standing in a public street. I'm going to need you to step away from the vehicle," he said, his hand resting on his holster. "You're creating a disturbance."

Laura's heart sank as she realized the optics of the situation. She had no proof, no evidence to back up her claims. And now, she looked like the crazy one, harassing innocent bystanders on the street.

With a heavy sigh, Laura stepped back, her shoulders slumping in defeat. The officer spoke briefly to the men in the car, their laughter still ringing in her ears. She watched as they drove away, disappearing into the sea of traffic, leaving her with more questions than answers.

Pulling her car out of the parking garage minutes later and still fuming, Laura drove toward home. Her grip on the steering wheel tightened with each passing thought of the mocking laughter from the men in the sedan. She needed to clear her head and gather her thoughts.

The organic food store came into view, and she decided to stop for supplies. Maybe some comfort food would help take the edge off. Laura parked her car and stepped into the store, grabbing a basket and wandering down the aisles. Fresh produce, organic snacks, and a couple of bottles of her favorite wine all found their way into her basket. As a splurge, she opted for some double chocolate brownies at the bakery counter.

Exiting the store, Laura's instincts kicked back in. She scanned the parking lot, her eyes darting from car to car, looking for any sign of the sedan or its occupants. The lot seemed ordinary enough, but she still couldn't shake the feeling of being watched.

Laura loaded her groceries into the trunk, her mind mulling over thoughts of who could be behind her surveillance. She considered calling Chris but dismissed it. The last thing she wanted was to drag her on-again-off-again girlfriend into this mess. Christine had enough on her plate already without adding paranoia to the mix.

Sliding into the driver's seat, Laura let out a heavy sigh. The week's lack of progress had taken its toll on her, and all she wanted was to get home and pour herself a glass of wine. She started the engine and pulled out of the lot, heading toward her townhouse.

As she drove through the city streets, Laura's mind wandered back to the interview earlier that day. The aide had been evasive but still slightly informative, hinting at layers upon layers of secrets that needed uncovering. But every answer led to more questions, more dead ends. The UFO issue was one of simply too much evidence instead of not enough.

Even the Air Force's own investigation, Project Blue Book, had documented over twelve thousand reports and ultimately declared over seven hundred as unexplained. She had filed a FOIA to gain access to the actual files being stored down in Alabama, but so far, no response.

Reaching her house, Laura parked and carried her groceries inside. The familiar scent of home brought a slight sense of relief as she set the bags on the kitchen counter. She uncorked the Italian wine and poured herself a generous glass before sinking into her couch.

Laura slipped her heels off and savored a bite of brownie followed by a sip of wine, enjoying the combined taste as she tried to unwind. Her files were stacked on the table just waiting for her to dive back into them, but she nudged them farther away with a toe. Not tonight, maybe not all weekend. She just needed a break. A hot bath and PJs seemed in order. Heck with cooking dinner.

She leaned back on the overstuffed sofa, letting the tension of the day drain away.

Then a sudden sound, and the lights went out.

CHAPTER SEVENTY-TWO

Emily sipped her coffee, her eyes glued to the television as she watched the parade of White House officials on the Sunday morning news shows. The vice president, Pete Cavanaugh, and others were out in full force, their faces etched with feigned sincerity as they spun a web of lies to the American public.

She gripped her mug tighter, the ceramic warm against her skin. The president had promised to address the nation, to finally shed light on the truth behind the UFO sightings and the escalating global crisis. But instead, he had retreated to his beach house in Rhode Island, leaving his minions to perpetuate the deception.

"You are the national security advisor, Mister Cavanaugh," the host of the supposedly heavy-hitting news show on NBC began. "In the past few weeks, we have seen a rash of catastrophic incidents affecting our nation as never before."

The host, Melanie Clarke, glanced down at her notes briefly before meeting his gaze again. "First, there was the massive explosion in New York City that shattered windows across the boroughs and caused widespread electronic failures."

Cavanaugh nodded slightly, maintaining his composed demeanor.

The anchor paused for a moment to let that sink in before moving on. "Second, there is an ongoing catastrophic incident at Eglin Air Force

Base involving unexplained explosions and much more significant casualties than first reported. Initial reports suggest an external attack, yet details remain scarce."

The advisor's face remained impassive, but a flicker of unease crossed his eyes.

"Third," the host pressed on, "major airlines have most of their fleets grounded due to erratic GPS outages."

Cavanaugh shifted slightly in his seat but didn't break eye contact.

"And finally," she said, her voice lowering with intensity, "the recent collision course of an extraterrestrial object towards Alaska, which prompted the president to raise the defense condition to DEFCON 2. The public is still in the dark about the true nature of this threat."

The host leaned back, allowing her words to hang heavily in the air. "These incidents have caused widespread fear and speculation. Can you provide any clarity on these matters? Is there a coordinated effort to address these threats?"

Cavanaugh cleared his throat and leaned forward slightly, smiling at the camera. "Indeed, Melanie, we've hit a bit of a rough patch." He spread his arms as if it were no big deal. "Let me assure you," he began, choosing his words carefully, "the government is taking all necessary steps to ensure public safety and address these incidents thoroughly.

"While collectively it might seem like something sinister, the truth is, we are a large country with a very complex infrastructure; things do fail. Normally, it's spread out, and we don't pay much attention to it. The GPS satellites went down due to a faulty software upload. They are working to correct that as we speak. Airlines can operate without the NavSat systems and are reverting procedures back to do just that.

"The Gulf Coast incident has been a truly difficult situation," he said. "Our initial understanding appears to have only been partially correct as the blast was apparently started when a large natural gas pipeline in the area ruptured. This was not even on the airbase, but the airbase did see significant damage, and our troops are on the front lines down there now helping the injured and delivering aid to those who are cut off. Just a horrible situation, and I know our hearts and prayers are with all of those families."

"And Alaska?"

Pete smiled and said, "That one is far easier to explain. The object came from space, a natural occurrence. Our experts tell me the Earth passed through the remnants of an unmapped asteroid cloud, and several came down. One was apparently large enough to trigger our seismic sensors along the coast."

"And the rise in alert status," Melanie asked.

"Just an abundance of caution," Cavanaugh said. "Our Alaska bases are on the front line, some of the closest military assets we have to Russia. We take no chances up there."

"So, you thought the attack was from them?"

The security advisor laughed out loud. "No...no, of course not. However, we must assume our enemies watch us as closely as we watch them. Had our assets been knocked offline during the crisis, then it was possible Russia could have taken advantage of the situation. Raising the defense posture of the armed forces was just a precautionary step. Nothing to be alarmed over."

Emily changed to another station, catching Vice President Thompson squaring off against Senator Alex Reynolds. The senator was at least bringing UFOs and orbital weapons into the discussion, but Thompson, a former trial attorney, was dismantling the man with a withering arsenal of what appeared to be solid facts to the contrary.

Face the Nation, CBS Studios, Washington D.C.

Moderator Stacey Thomas's calm demeanor stood in stark contrast to the palpable tension between Vice President Thompson and Senator Alex Reynolds.

“Gentlemen, shifting to the recent attacks on our infrastructure, Senator Reynolds, you've been vocal about the administration's handling. Your thoughts?"

The senator slammed his hand on the table. “Thoughts? This administration is asleep at the wheel! The crippling of our cell and power networks is a catastrophic failure of national security. President Martin's inaction is appalling.”

An unfazed vice president smiled for the camera. “Senator, that's simply not accurate. We're working diligently with our agencies to—"

Reynolds interrupted the VP, his voice rising. “Diligently? We've had multiple major outages in the past month alone! The American people deserve truth, not spin. These aren't coincidences. They're coordinated attacks, possibly even—"

"Possibly even what, Senator? You're not going to resurrect the UFO conspiracy theories again, are you?"

The senator leaned forward, a hint of a smirk. "Ah, but that's where you're wrong, Mr. Vice President. I have it on good authority that President Martin himself has assembled a UFO committee." Reynolds turned to the camera. "Yes, folks, behind closed doors, they're acknowledging what they deny in public. Care to comment, Mister Vice President?"

A slight shadow crossed the VP's face but was gone in an instant." I'm not aware of any such committee, Senator," leaning forward, his voice taking on a slightly aggressive tone. "And even if there were, I doubt it's something serious enough to discuss on a Sunday morning talk show. Your sources, as usual, are likely misinformed."

"Oh, come now, Mister Vice President! You expect us to believe you're out of the loop on this one? That's rich, even for this administration."

Stacey enjoyed a rousing verbal joust but needed to keep the show on track and on time. She interrupted, attempting to steer the conversation back on track. "Gentlemen, let's focus on the infrastructure attacks. Vice President Thompson, can you assure the American people that these food and power outages are not a sign of a broader vulnerability?"

"Absolutely, Stacey. Our investigations indicate these are isolated but interconnected incidents. Fate seemed to have worked against us this time, cascading one problem into another. Rest assured we're working closely with our public and private partners to enhance our grid security and reassessing our food distribution systems. The president's infrastructure bill that is still stalled in Congress would have gone a long way in shoring up both these items."

Senator Reynolds jumped in like the attack dog he was, his voice dripping with skepticism. "Isolated incidents? That's what they said about the New York City explosion and the Eglin Air Force Base disaster. When will this administration stop downplaying the truth?"

As the cameras cut off, Senator Reynolds and Vice President Thompson were still engaged in a heated yet hushed exchange.

"You can't keep the truth hidden forever, Mister Vice President. The American people will see through your smokescreen."

"Alex, we've known each other a long time. Hell, I like you. I remember when our boys played baseball on the same team. Look, I'm not concerned about your conspiracy theories. Focus on legislating instead of speculating. Your constituents want leadership right now—not finger pointing."

The moderator stood and approached the two men; she was ready to leave, and her producer was urging her to close down the discussion. "Gentlemen, I believe we've reached the end of our allotted time."

As the studio staff began to disassemble the set, Senator Reynolds swiftly gathered his belongings. "Thank you, Stacey. Always a pleasure."

The vice president was already gone before the host turned around.

Emily gritted her teeth as she heard what they said. Each one of their responses was a complete distortion of the truth. They mentioned gas line explosions, misidentified meteors, and the government's dedication to full disclosure. But Emily had seen the proof and had been involved in the cover-ups herself.

She wanted to scream, to shatter the television screen and expose their lies for what they were. But she remained still, her anger simmering beneath the surface. She had dedicated her career to serving her country, to upholding the principles of truth and justice. And now, she found herself at odds with the very institution she had sworn to protect.

Emily set her mug down on the coffee table, the liquid sloshing against the sides. She reached for her phone, her fingers hovering over the keypad. She had contacts, sources who could help her expose the truth. But she hesitated, the weight of her loyalty holding her back.

She leaned back against the couch, her thoughts roiling with the implications of what SCET was uncovering. The world was on the brink of something monumental, something that could change the course of human history. And yet, the powers that be were determined to keep the public in the dark, to maintain their grip on power at any cost. Was it all just politics? Or...something even darker?

Emily knew she couldn't sit idly by, couldn't allow the lies to continue unchallenged. She had to find a way to bring the truth to light, to hold those in power accountable for their actions. But just like her recent run-in with that snake, Pete Cavanaugh, she also knew that the road ahead would be treacherous, that she would be going up against forces far greater than herself.

She closed her eyes, taking a deep breath to steady herself. She had never backed down from a fight, and she wasn't about to start now. This mission had originally been to discover what had happened to her brother, but now it was much bigger. She would find a way to expose the truth, to bring justice to those who had been wronged. And she would do it on her own terms, no matter the cost.

CHAPTER SEVENTY-THREE

2144 GMT July 14
Oregon Coast, USA

Kaden sat on the patio of Sarah's bungalow, the sound of the Pacific surf crashing against the shore providing a soothing backdrop. He sipped a glass of wine, savoring the rich flavor as he watched the sun dip below the horizon, painting the sky in vibrant hues of orange and pink.

Sarah emerged from the kitchen, carrying two plates of steaming pasta. The aroma of garlic and herbs wafted through the air, making Kaden's mouth water. She set the plates down on the table and took a seat across from him.

"This looks amazing, Sarah," Kaden said, picking up his fork. "I've missed your cooking."

Sarah smiled, but there was a hint of concern in her eyes. "Enjoy."

The food was delicious, and they ate mostly in silence as they watched the sun settle down over the ocean. Kaden could tell his friend was troubled. His own mind was a storm-tossed ocean crashing against rocks.

"So, how was it?" Sarah asked.

"The service? It was fine," he said. Sarah knew of his history with

Elena Schmidt and did not approve. Kaden knew that did not mean she ever wished ill on the woman. That was not who Sarah Mitchell was.

Sarah looked like she wanted to say more but suddenly got up from the table and went into an adjacent room, coming back seconds later with something wrapped in brown paper. She placed it on the table between them.

"Kaden, I think we need to talk."

Kaden paused, his fork hovering over the plate. "About what?"

Sarah took a deep breath. "About your obsession."

"With pasta?" he asked, stabbing a wandering tortellini. “Oh. The aliens. Right. That, too.”

She laughed. "Yes, with finding the truth about UFOs and extraterrestrial life."

Kaden set his fork down, his appetite suddenly gone. "It's not an obsession, Sarah. It's my life's work." He paused for a moment, then nodded. "Okay, it's also an obsession."

Sarah reached across the table and took his hand. "I know, Kaden. But I'm worried about you. Last time, you asked me to keep an eye on you, and well... to be honest, I know you’re doing important work. It's just... well, you seem so consumed by it this time. I'm worried you're losing sight of what's really important."

Kaden pulled his hand away, feeling defensive. "And what's that?"

"Your health, for one thing," Sarah said. "You're not sleeping—you're barely eating. And your relationships. When was the last time you called your sister?"

Kaden looked away, unable to meet her gaze. She was right, of course. He had been so focused on his research and now the final reports with SCET that he had neglected everything else in his life.

"I just... I feel like I'm so close, Sarah," he said, his voice barely above a whisper. "I can't give up now."

Sarah sighed. "I'm not asking you to give up, Kaden. I'm just asking you to take a step back and reevaluate what you're doing. Is it really worth sacrificing everything else in your life?"

Kaden didn't have an answer. He picked up his fork and took another bite of the pasta, savoring the rich flavors. Sarah was a great cook and an even better friend. They ate in silence for a few minutes, the only sound the crashing of the waves against the shore.

"The truth is, I'm worried, Sarah, but not about me."

"What about?"

He wanted to tell her all of the truth, but that might just ruin the most important friendship in his life.

"Is that it? The thing from Jasper?" he asked, changing the subject.

"Yes, you should call his daughter when you have time."

He nodded absently as he removed the thick brown paper. Several more layers of packaging were beneath it. The contents were about seven inches long and maybe as thick as his wrist. Feeling the weight and unusual shape, he'd guessed what it was before the final wrapping fell away.

"Is that a meteorite?" Sarah asked.

Kaden lifted the blackened object up for them both to see. 'The relic from an ancient alien battle,' Jasper had said. The object's weight still threw him off. Something about it simply screamed alien relic. He passed it to Sarah, who took it reverently and studied the charred remnant closely. "I know you always considered my ideas to be outrageous," he said. "I now am coming to believe they weren't outrageous enough."

Sarah was surprised at how serious her friend sounded. "What do you mean?"

Kaden filled her in on everything Jasper had told him as well as what Emily cleared him to discuss with colleagues. She was especially shocked at the devastation Natalie had seen in Florida.

"A KEW impactor? That correlates with what our colleagues always said might be a first strike from an alien force," Sarah said.

Kaden nodded. "It is one of the likely options, probably one of the better ones for humanity. It indicates they don't want to upset the ecosystem. They didn't use nukes or biological agents."

"So, they just want the people gone," Sarah stated.

"Or the military," Kaden said, appreciating again how quickly his friend picked up on salient facts. The woman had a mind like a computer but rarely published or even spoke on her primary research.

"So, do you believe me now?" he asked.

"No." She shook her head emphatically before pouring them both more wine.

"I don't disbelieve you, though," she added.

Sarah swirled her wine glass thoughtfully, her gaze fixed on the deep red liquid before lifting it to meet Kaden's eyes. She let out a soft sigh, her voice calm but carrying the weight of a quiet internal struggle.

"Kaden, I know the data points are compelling. I've seen many of the same figures, run the same simulations, and read the same reports. Mathematically, the probability of life beyond Earth makes sense. Statistically, it's almost inevitable that we're not alone in this universe. And yet..." She paused, setting her glass down with a gentle clink. "I just... can't accept it."

Kaden raised an eyebrow. "You're a cosmologist, Sarah. The vastness of the universe is literally your field of study. How can you deny the possibility?"

She gave him a small, rueful smile. "That's exactly the problem. I know how vast the universe is. I've spent my entire career unraveling the mysteries of the cosmos, trying to make sense of phenomena that are already almost incomprehensible. Black holes, dark energy, multiverses —it's all abstract yet rooted in physical laws I can trust. But aliens? Intelligent beings? I know it's irrational, but... my mind simply rejects it."

Sarah leaned back in her chair, arms crossing lightly. "It's not that I don't see the evidence. I do. It's just that, for my entire life, extraterrestrial life has been in the realm of science fiction, not science fact. There's a part of me, no matter how much I try to rationalize it, that simply refuses to let go of that ingrained disbelief. It's like a cognitive dissonance I can't shake. I should be able to accept it, but I just can't."

Kaden smiled gently. "You think you're wrong, don't you?"

"Oh, absolutely," she admitted, a touch of frustration creeping into her voice. "Logically, I know I'm most likely wrong. The odds of Earth being the only cradle of life in a universe this old and expansive are minuscule. But knowing that doesn't change how I feel. It's almost like... there's a barrier in my mind that refuses to let me cross into that new paradigm."

She shook her head softly. "I can study the laws of physics, I can measure cosmic background radiation and search for dark matter.

Those things fit into a framework I've spent years building. But sentient beings from other planets? It breaks something fundamental in my worldview, and I'm not sure how to reconcile that. I think I hide behind Enrico Fermi's damn paradox."

"He wanted to know: if they exist, where are they? They are here, Sarah."

She nodded, then took a slow sip of her wine, looking out into the distance. "It's strange, I know. Maybe it's just fear of the unknown, or maybe I'm clinging too tightly to the ordered way things 'should' be in my mind. Either way... it's not that I don't believe you. It's that I don't think I can."

They'd had the conversation many times over the years. Kaden knew her position. It wasn't radically different from many people, maybe even most people.

"You know," Kaden said, "what you're describing is exactly how entire groups of people—or even institutions—can manipulate that very same cognitive bias to dismiss the possibility of extraterrestrial life or UFOs. It's not just individuals like you who struggle to accept the idea. It's deeply ingrained in our human psyche, this need to maintain a sense of control and certainty in our understanding of the universe, or just uncertainty in general."

He paused, choosing his next words carefully. "Think about it—if the vast majority of people, including scientists, are wired to resist the concept of intelligent extraterrestrial life, despite the logic, then it becomes easy for skeptics or even governments to lean into that bias. They can frame anyone who brings up aliens or UFOs as delusional or irrational simply because they're playing into the default assumption most people already have—that it's just too far outside the realm of what can be called 'normal.'"

Kaden set his glass down and leaned forward slightly. "The thing is, it's not about the facts or the evidence in these cases. It's about the narrative. If the majority of people are instinctively uncomfortable with the idea of aliens, then it's incredibly simple to discredit anyone who challenges that worldview. They don't even need to engage with the science or the data. They just have to play into the existing skepticism and inherent fear of the unknown."

He glanced at Sarah, gauging her reaction before continuing. "It's why people like me, who push for serious consideration of these possibilities, are often labeled as crackpots or conspiracy theorists. It's not because the evidence doesn't exist—it's because society, on some level, isn't ready to accept it. And those in power know that. They know it's much easier to dismiss and ridicule some things than to deal with the upheaval it might cause if people actually started to trust the facts and believe."

"So you think you were persecuted for speaking the truth?" Sarah asked, smiling, obviously trying to get a rise out of him.

He sighed, running a hand through his hair. "Aye... I was, too. But you see, it's a form of psychological gatekeeping. By framing the idea of extraterrestrial life as something only 'crazy people' like me believe in, they maintain the status quo. People don't question what they're told if it fits neatly into their pre-existing beliefs. And if anyone steps outside of that, they're dismissed—not because they're wrong, but because society isn't ready to shift its paradigm."

Kaden looked at Sarah, his tone softening. "What you're feeling? That resistance? It's completely natural. But when it's amplified on a societal level, it becomes a tool. A destructive tool to suppress ideas that are uncomfortable, even if they are completely true."

He let his words hang in the air for a moment, watching as Sarah considered them. "The truth is, it's not that aliens don't exist. It's that people are conditioned to reject the possibility because accepting it would force them to confront a universe that's far more complex—and far more uncertain—than they'd like it to be."

"So we disagree," Sarah said. "I still think you're brilliant, but you will never change my mind, nor likely the billions of others out there. Still, I will gladly go to the next space movie with you."

She looked up at the darkening sky, then back to Kaden. "I worry about you like you worry about them." She pointed up. "Don't let them take over, okay?"

He knew what she meant. This was one of the reasons he'd come here. He needed to feel grounded. If he was being honest, he wanted to feel cared for. He was, in truth, devastated and guilt-ridden over Elena's death—something he would not bring up again tonight. "I'll try, Sarah.

You know I must find the truth. Learn what they're doing here, but yes... I'll try harder to find a balance."

Sarah smiled, reaching across the table to squeeze his hand. "That's all I'm asking." She reached down to pick up the pile of wrapping paper for the artifact. "Kaden?"

"Yes."

"I think this is also for you." She handed him a sheet of thin paper that had fallen out from some of the others. It had writing on it in small, precise lettering.

"That's Jasper's handwriting," Kaden said.

CHAPTER SEVENTY-FOUR

Kaden rubbed his tired eyes, looking away from the monitor. He turned to Sarah, his voice taking on a more strident tone.

"Looks like I'm going to need to go meet someone—Dr. Adrian Cho. Javier says he might have information we could use. I'm going to ask Emily to set it up."

Technically, Sarah was not part of SCET, and sharing any information violated the working agreement, but Emily had been open-minded when she formed the group. 'Use whomever you need to help get to the truth.'

Sarah nodded. "I've heard of him... a bit of an odd bird. You think he can help, or is this just another wild goose chase?"

Kaden knew that even with the validation his White House connection offered, that carried little weight with his counterparts in the scientific community. Sarah was always protective of him. She cared for his reputation far more than he did. Still, even he was familiar with government committees turning on one of their own in the past.

One noted example was when Project Blue Book hired a professor of their own to give their sad little group at least the appearance of scientific legitimacy. "Dr. J. Allen Hynek was an American astronomer and professor; Hynek played a significant role in three major Air Force projects: Project Sign, Project Grudge, and Project Blue Book, which investigated UFO reports from 1948 to 1969."

"Who?" Sarah asked.

Kaden caught himself; he hadn't realized he'd been contemplating out loud.

"Professor Hynek?" he responded.

Sarah raised an eyebrow. "Of course. Blue Book or Project Grudge. Hynek was involved with that, right? The Air Force commission?"

"Yeah," Kaden nodded. "He started out as a skeptic. The Air Force brought him in to provide scientific credibility. They wanted someone who could debunk the sightings, make it all go away."

Sarah folded her arms, listening intently.

"Project Blue Book was the third of three studies conducted by the Air Force," Kaden continued. "It began in 1952 and was the most publicized effort to investigate UFO reports. Hynek's role was to analyze these reports scientifically."

"Did he always try to debunk them?" Sarah asked.

Kaden shook his head. "Initially, yes. The Air Force was more interested in dismissing the reports than investigating them thoroughly. They were concerned about public hysteria and the potential for mass panic."

"Sounds familiar," Sarah muttered.

"But Hynek's perspective shifted over time," Kaden said, ignoring her comment. "He started seeing patterns and evidence that didn't fit conventional explanations. He began pushing back against the Air Force's dismissive approach."

Sarah leaned forward, intrigued. "What about that swamp gas incident?"

Kaden sighed. "That was a turning point, but not in a good way. In 1966, there were multiple sightings in Michigan. Hynek was sent to investigate and concluded that what people saw could be explained by swamp gas reflecting light."

"Swamp gas?" Sarah scoffed.

"I know," Kaden said, grimacing. "It sounded ridiculous, even to him. But he was under pressure from the Air Force to find a non-alien explanation. Congress got involved because the public wasn't buying it. They saw it as a cover-up."

"And Hynek defended that explanation?"

"He did," Kaden admitted. "But it hurt his credibility with both the scientific community and the public. However, it also marked a shift for him personally. He started advocating for more serious scientific inquiry into UFOs."

Sarah nodded thoughtfully. "So, Dr. Cho... you think he might have proof or what?"

Kaden shrugged. "I'm not sure what to think. If he is that valuable, he probably should also be on the team, not just someone we consult with. Either way, Javier seems to think he might have corroborating information I need."

"Great, so when do we go?"

"We?" Kaden asked, surprised.

"Yes, we. I said I wasn't a believer; I never said I wasn't interested."

Emily set up the meeting and admitted Cho was already on her radar. She'd been in contact with one of his bosses in the last few days.

After an unpleasant red-eye flight into LAX and several hours in an even more unpleasant-smelling rental, Kaden and Sarah arrived at the Mount Wilson Observatory. He read the handwritten sign that said, "Go Away!" rolled his eyes, and pressed the buzzer. A crackling voice responded, "State your business."

"Dr. Cho? I'm Dr. Kaden Trembley. Emily Carter set up a meeting."

Silence. Then, "Third floor. Don't touch anything." A loud buzzing unlocked the door.

"I've only heard rumors about this guy. Brilliant, but... eccentric," Sarah said in a soft whisper as they climbed the stairs.

"Wonderful," Kaden said without enthusiasm.

They found Cho hunched over a cluttered desk, surrounded by star charts and blinking monitors. He didn't look up as they entered.

"You're the UFO guy," Cho stated flatly.

Kaden bristled. "I prefer 'astrophysicist studying unexplained aerial phenomena,' but—"

Cho waved a dismissive hand. "Yeah, yeah. Same difference. What do you know about the Hyades cluster?"

Kaden blinked, caught off guard. "Uh, open cluster in Taurus. About 153 light-years away. Why?"

Cho's eyes lit up. He spun his monitor around, revealing a complex star map. "Because something's wrong with it."

Sarah leaned in, squinting. "What are we looking at?"

"Anomalies," Cho said, his fingers flying across the keyboard. "Fluctuations in stellar brightness, unexplained gravitational effects. At first, I thought it was instrument error, but..."

Kaden's pulse quickened. "But what? Problems with the optics?"

"Don't be ridiculous. Telescopes are perfect. We had cryosystems purged twice and ran recalibration each time. Then we went through our entire suite of control observations to make sure. We're not looking at Andromeda here—we study NEOs."

The man's tone was frantic, and his speech pattern difficult to follow, but both Sarah and Kaden got the gist. "You cross-checked with oth—"

"God, yes, man. Why do you think I went straight to the top?"

Sarah used her thumb and forefinger to zoom out on the display. Cho was correct; the star clusters appeared crystal clear, then blurry, then clear again in a later image. "Atmospheric distortion?" she said, not looking up.

"Yes, no," said Cho. "I mean, that's one of the first things we checked."

Dr. Cho pulled up another set of images. "The night before last, we got a little time on Hubble."

Kaden leaned closer, his eyes narrowing as he examined the screen. "Hubble's pretty reliable. What did you find?"

Cho zoomed in on the same section of the star cluster images. "Most of the clusters snapped back into sharp focus, but a half dozen were still blurry."

Sarah frowned, her gaze flicking between Cho and Kaden. "And you're sure it's not an issue with Hubble?"

Cho nodded emphatically. "We triple-checked everything—instrument calibration, atmospheric conditions, even gravitational lensing from nearby objects. None of it explains why only these specific clusters are affected. Also, even if it was an issue, all of the same stars should still be blurred, not just a few."

Kaden considered the possibilities. "Could it be some kind of external interference? A localized phenomenon affecting only those clusters?"

"That's what I thought," Cho said, his voice tinged with excitement and frustration. "But then I found this." He pulled up a new set of data points and overlaid them on the star map.

"Infrared and visible spectrum light analysis," Sarah said, recognizing the red shift in the images and reading the data on the sidebar. Chandra?"

Cho nodded. "Not current data, but we began tracking backward days, then weeks. The blur has shown up inconsistently for the last six months."

"The light levels have changed?" Kaden said, looking over at Sarah. "Stars don't typically do that. There are a few variable stars, but none in this grouping. In fact, some of these are actually galaxies, not stars or planets. They should only get brighter if the star is going supernova." Of course, Sarah was well-versed on this as well but knew talking about it was part of Kaden's process to understand new data.

"All of them going supernova at the same time," Cho said, laughing. "Yeah... I think not."

Kaden was still studying the star charts intently. Sarah, on the other hand, realized the strange man already had an idea of what they were seeing. "You know what it is, don't you?" she asked.

"Indeed," the man said, smiling.

He motioned for them to follow. They trailed behind until they wound up in a dingy conference room. The paneling was old, and the chairs were worn. He motioned for them to sit, then dimmed the lights and turned on an old-style overhead projector. He tilted it down until it was shining nearly in their eyes.

Cho then repeated the process with two other projectors that were sitting on rolling carts to either side.

"Stars?" he said. "Or galaxies?"

Then he left the room hurriedly. "Be right back."

"He's nuts," Kaden said.

"Doesn't mean he's wrong," Sarah said.

The little man came dashing back into the darkened room with even more noise than when he'd left. He moved back down front, and they heard chairs moving. After several minutes of him fumbling with something, he called excitedly, "What am I holding?"

"I have no idea," Kaden said. "The light's too bright."

"What about now?" Cho asked.

Kaden and Sarah could see slight differences in the brightness of the light. He assumed it was Cho holding something up. If he thought the bright light would help illuminate the object, he was mistaken.

"Professor Trembley, can you flip the light on by the door?"

Sarah patted his arm. She knew her friend was getting frustrated by the antics of the astronomer. "I got it."

The light came on, and Kaden dropped his notepad. A dozen or more people were beside Dr. Cho, all of them holding something like airplane models mounted on sticks. Cho brought one of them forward.

Kaden saw it wasn't a model airplane at all. It was some sort of spaceship. "Colony ship from my Star Wars collection," the man said excitedly. All the others held similar models.

Kaden began to speak, but Cho held up his hand. The demonstration had been effective, but he needed a minute to let his own brain catch up.

"A ship," Sarah asked as the gears clicked for her, too.

"A fleet of ships," Kaden corrected. "Hiding in the starlight."

"How is that possible?" Sarah asked. "They would have to constantly readjust to take into account the orbit of the Earth around the sun."

"The solar system moves as well," Cho added.

Kaden nodded, lost in thought. "The Earth moves at a speed of about 67,000 miles per hour around the sun," he said, more to himself than to anyone else. "That's roughly 18.5 miles per second."

Cho's eyes gleamed in agreement. "Exactly! And that's just our orbital speed."

Sarah tilted her head. "But the solar system itself moves through the galaxy, too."

"Yes," Kaden continued, warming to the topic. "Our entire solar system orbits the center of the Milky Way at an astonishing speed of approximately 514,000 miles per hour. That's about 143 miles per second."

Cho gestured towards the star charts on the wall. "And if you consider our galaxy's movement through space, it's even more complex."

Sarah looked at Cho, intrigued. "You're referring to the Milky Way's motion relative to other galaxies?"

"Exactly," Cho replied, nodding. "The Milky Way itself is moving through space at roughly 1.3 million miles per hour, or about 361 miles per second, relative to the cosmic microwave background radiation."

Sarah's eyes widened. "So this only works if they are heading toward Earth. That seems very deliberate."

"Yes... yes. Very planned," Cho said, shooing the last of his team to get back to work.

Kaden wanted to finish the topic. "You're saying these ships would have to adjust not only for our orbit around the sun but also for our solar system's orbit around the galaxy and the galaxy's movement through space?"

Cho grinned. "Precisely. It's an astronomical ballet, one that would require constant recalibration and adjustment. We think it is definitely a grouping of intelligently controlled craft, and most likely they need a forward observer to help keep mostly in the Earth's visible path to the stars they are using for cover."

"Still, that would be a near Herculean task. Even different observatories on the planet would have slightly different perspectives," Kaden said.

"Probably why the view to us here comes in and out of focus," Cho said. "They can only use an average adjustment. What position keeps them concealed from most of the Earth and our space-based telescopes?"

"Should we base anything specific on the direction they're coming from? Would that be their home planet?" Sarah asked.

"Great question," Cho said, "but we don't think so. The one common point of all these background stars and galaxies is they are very distant."

"Meaning they don't move around much from our point of view," Kaden said. He bent to the table and picked up the Star Wars model. "One thing I don't get. Assuming your assertion is correct," he moved the ship in front of one of the projectors that was still on, then held it off to the side. "In deep space, the ship would be invisible to us even if it was the size of a planet."

"Ah, yes, very perceptive, Professor. In the deep recesses of space, the albedo of an object might be so low that it would be nearly undetectable, as it reflects very little light and absorbs most of the ambient radiation. But as it gets closer to a star like our Sun, the sunlight starts to illuminate the object, increasing its albedo. This increase in reflectivity means that the object now reflects a higher proportion of the incident sunlight, making it brighter and more visible to our telescopes.

“For instance, a distant asteroid with a rocky, carbonaceous surface might initially have an albedo of just 0.03, indicating it reflects only a small percent of any light that hits it. As it moves into the inner solar system, sunlight illuminates its surface, potentially increasing its albedo to around 0.1 or higher, depending on its composition and surface features. This increase in reflectivity allows astronomers to detect it with greater ease using optical telescopes and other observational instruments.

“So, as these objects were in deep space, their albedo, or reflectivity, was minimal, likely meaning they were not using the stars for cover. Like a Top Gun fighter pilot, though. You know, Maverick? Attack from out of the sun. Blind your enemy to your attack. As they start to encounter more sunlight, that will dramatically change their visibility."

"So they are already encountering solar energy from our local star?" Sarah said. The nervousness in her voice was pronounced. “They are not as distant as those stars.”

Kaden ran a hand over his beard. "If they've been hiding in plain sight for this long... we need to figure out their intentions fast. Any idea on size or distance?"

Cho leaned forward, his voice a whisper now. "Not yet. Likely it will be several more weeks before we know exactly. That, Professor, is probably why the White House let you come here. To figure out what we're dealing with before it's too late. Soon, the fleet will be unable to stay undetected by more of our scopes. Then it's going to be chaos."

Kaden couldn't understand why the man was smiling. He, himself, was in full panic mode.

CHAPTER SEVENTY-FIVE

0612 UTC
38°04'N, 77°16'W
Observer's Detention Facility
Virginia, USA

Laura Bennett looked at the wall in front of her. It was gray metal, just like the floor and just like the ceiling. She hadn't been awake when they captured her. The lights went out, or maybe they knocked her out. Either way, this was where she woke up.

She'd had a friend once; he'd worked for a competing paper but handled field reports with the Russia desk. The KGB picked him up on trumped-up spy charges and held him indefinitely while they waited for America to come to the table with an offer of a prisoner swap.

This was not like that. There would be no reprieve for her. No national outrage when she failed to show up for work next week. Nor would her imprisonment be subject to any humane conventions. These Trident guys seemed to be calling all the shots. She'd overplayed her hand once too many times, and now it was coming back to bite her in the ass.

Laura heard a heavy door open and close somewhere nearby, then footsteps. She counted them, mainly just to occupy her mind. She wasn't getting out of here—she had no illusions about that.

The metal slide in the door pulled back. "Food," the man said, leaving the tray in the slot for her to take.

Say what you want, but the food here was actually really good. Metal trays and plastic spoons diminished the overall impression, but she would still give it a solid four stars on Yelp. Apparently, the black-budget covered more than just the essentials for Trident.

Laura had already lost track of time...and days. Had she just eaten lunch, or was that dinner? The lights in the cell never went off, and the guard routines rarely varied. They hadn't threatened or abused her since her capture. Nor had they even asked her many questions. She felt sure that would change. What she'd learned was likely the only thing keeping her alive.

Trident Tactical Services was an internal security contractor for NovaCore. Learning that from the congressional aide must have been the link that triggered her captors into action. She'd gotten too close and therefore had to be removed.

That meant that NovaCore was indeed the most likely group at the top of this very complicated pyramid of defense contractors, military hardware providers, politicians, and the U.S. intelligence community. While everyone, including her, had assumed there was a government cover-up, that apparently was not the case.

Owen King, the CEO of NovaCore, was practically a ghost as far as the public knew. He was rarely photographed; nothing was known of his personal life, nor even where he lived. They had several corporate offices inside the Beltway. Alcon Industries had turned out to be a shell company of NovaCore.

So, who did King report to... anyone? Laura thought.

She'd been tracking the origins of NovaCore and had uncovered a group of founders from much smaller companies in the fifties and sixties. This small group came together under several names and eventually bought the small aerospace firm NovaCore, adopting their name as the corporate moniker.

Many of the founders had come out of the military, and a few from major defense contractors like McDonnell Douglas, Grumman, and Raytheon.

They originally set up smaller companies with names like Northguard Defense and Lockwave Systems; those were the only ones she could recall without her notepad. Even though these companies were new and relatively small, they filed more patents in ten years than the next half-dozen of their much larger competitors.

Laura paced the room, wanting the story to come together before she met whatever fate they had in store. Like Natalie Reeves, she, too, was obsessed with finding the truth.

Why would the greatest secret in the world be in the hands of a private company? she silently asked herself. Over and over, she mulled that over. Then it hit her; it was so obvious she didn't know how she'd ignored it until now. *Holy shit!*

Government agencies, even at the highest security levels, were subject to congressional oversight, including being hauled before subcommittees. Worse for a secret like this was FOIA, or the Freedom of Information Act. Private entities are not subject to FOIA. This means they do not have to disclose their records or activities to the public, allowing them to operate with an even higher degree of secrecy and confidentiality.

They would also be able to protect discoveries and proprietary information from being disclosed. In addition, and most importantly, they could also earn a profit from it.

As she finished her meal, the cell door opened suddenly, and a man in a gray business suit stood there. His face was as unreadable as it was forgettable. Rarely had she seen someone so aptly described as nondescript.

"Hello, Ms. Bennett. Are you ready for a little talk?"

CHAPTER SEVENTY-SIX

Laura lay on the cold concrete floor, every inch of her body throbbing with pain. She winced as she tried to shift her weight, the bruises and cuts on her skin a stark reminder of Gibson's ruthless interrogation. Her mind drifted to thoughts of Natalie and many of the others she had interviewed over the years—people who had faced unimaginable threats and yet stood their ground.

"I can't keep this up," she whispered to herself, her voice barely audible over the incessant hum of the overhead lights.

She thought about her investigation, how every step closer to the truth seemed to push her further into this abyss. Had it all been worth it? Her eyes welled up with tears, not just from the physical pain but from the crushing weight of doubt that gnawed at her spirit. Maybe her efforts had only complicated things, making it easier for the conspirators to tighten their grip on the truth.

Sleep took her and offered her a small mercy of relief before the door creaked open, and Gibson stepped back in, his presence filling the small room with an oppressive air. He crouched down next to her, his eyes cold and calculating.

"Laura," he began softly, almost kindly. "You've shown incredible resilience. But let's face it—everyone has a breaking point."

"Go to hell!"

Laura's head snapped back from the force of Gibson's blow. The slap stung, but the boot to her chest that came next caused her to briefly pass out. A stream of water dumped on her woke her with a cry. She could taste blood on her lips. His goon, a hulking figure with dead eyes, stood silently behind him, a menacing shadow.

"Who have you talked to?" Gibson's voice was icy. "We want names."

Laura coughed, struggling to find her voice. "Go fuck yourself! I'm not telling you anything."

Gibson nodded to his goon, who grabbed Laura by the hair and yanked her head back, exposing her neck. The pressure was agonizing, but she gritted her teeth, refusing to give them the satisfaction of a scream.

"We can do this all night," Gibson said calmly. "Or you can make it easy on yourself. Start talking."

Laura thought of everyone she had contacted recently—the scientists, the former military officers, the whistleblowers. Giving up their names was not an option.

"Go to hell," she spat out.

The goon's fist collided with her stomach, knocking the wind out of her. She gasped for air, her vision blurring.

"Your iCloud and email passwords," Gibson demanded. "What are they?"

Laura closed her eyes, focusing on anything but the pain. "You're wasting your time," she managed to say.

Gibson leaned close. "Do you use any trip-switch protocols? Any data dumps if you don't check in?"

Laura's heart pounded in her chest. She had indeed set up a fail-safe, but she couldn't let them know that.

"You're delusional if you think I'd tell you anything," she said through clenched teeth.

The goon twisted her arm behind her back until she thought it would snap. "Answer him!"

Gibson continued, unfazed by her defiance. "How much does your editor know?"

Laura felt a cold wave of fear wash over her at the mention of Jack, her editor. She couldn't drag him into this nightmare.

"You're sick," she hissed. "I'm not telling you anything." She'd endured countless sessions by now. The only one that really terrified her was the waterboarding. They hadn't done that in her cell, so maybe that wasn't on the schedule for today's fun and games.

"1055 Rosewood Court. Isn't that right?" the man said with a sneer.

Laura knew that was Jack's address.

"And let's not forget about lovely Christine," he said, flipping through a screen on his tablet. "Oh, she's in Falls Church. I like it out there." The man looked at the guard holding her. "Maybe we should take a drive out there later today."

The goon laughed and nodded.

"You're not getting what you want," Laura hissed. "The press is the people, and the people won't be silenced."

"You journalists all like to think of yourselves as the guardians of truth, the champions of free press and all that bullshit, don't you?"

"That's right. We aim to report the facts and hold power accountable," Laura struggled to say the words her old journalism professor used as a mantra.

Gibson gave a humorless grin. "Let me remind you of a few things. Ever heard of Operation Mockingbird? During the Cold War, the CIA had journalists on their payroll, planting stories and shaping public opinion to suit their needs. Your so-called free press was nothing but a puppet."

"That was decades ago. Things are different now," she said weakly.

"Different?" Gibson snarled. "How about the lead-up to the Iraq War in 2003? The media parroted the government's line about weapons of mass destruction without questioning the evidence. Even your prestigious New York Times, among others, played a significant role in drumming up public support for that war. Thousands died because the press didn't do its job."

"Mistakes were made, but that doesn't mean the entire institution is corrupt," Laura said, the bite of the tired old arguments getting her blood going again.

"Mistakes? That's putting it lightly. Let's talk about the News of the World scandal in the UK. Hacking into phones, including those of murder victims, just to get a juicy story. The Murdoch empire showed the world just how low the press could go for a scoop," Gibson said.

"That was in the UK, not here."

“Face it, honey. Your industry is so unreliable, no one can believe anything you print. We should let you run your stories. No one can stop doomscrolling their social feeds long enough to pay attention to any rumors your free press might offer.”

"We strive to be better, to learn from these mistakes, and even at our worst, we report the facts, not the made-up echo chambers of TV or your feeds on social media."

"Strive all you want, but know this—the truth you think you're protecting is always at risk, always under attack. Question your beliefs, because sometimes you will discover that the watchdog you depend on was just another lapdog for someone else."

Gibson sighed and stood up, motioning for the goon to take her. The two men dragged her to a brightly lit room where she was strapped to a chair. A young Asian woman in a lab coat jabbed a hypodermic into her arm, which immediately felt like it was on fire. The sensation was so realistic Laura found she couldn't even look at it. The pain spread, and the agony increased. She smelled flesh burning and could hear the crackling of her charred skin even as she knew it was an illusion.

The next few hours were a blur of pain and questions that Laura barely registered through the haze of agony. Every fiber of her being wanted to give in, to make it stop, but she held onto the only thing she had left—her silence.

She would not betray those who trusted her, no matter what they did to her here in this godforsaken place.

Laura clenched her fists, summoning whatever strength she had left. "I won't... give you... anything," she managed to say through gritted teeth.

Gibson smirked. "You’re brave, I’ll give you that. But bravery won't keep you alive." He paused, letting his words sink in. "Join us. You’re smart and resourceful. You could be a valuable asset. We could use someone with your credentials pushing our version of disclosure to the masses."

For a moment, Laura almost considered it. The pain would stop; she could rest. She could even continue investigating from within, perhaps find another way to expose the truth later on.

But then a wave of self-loathing washed over her. Could she really betray everything she stood for just to escape this hell? Her mind flashed back to Natalie's unwavering resolve and the stories of courage she'd heard from countless others who had witnessed alien contact and fought against insurmountable odds to be believed, to stay employed, and even to keep living. She owed them more than her own safety.

"Don't... think so," Laura rasped, spitting blood onto the floor. "You can't own every journalist. You can't shut down every outlet that refuses to spread your lies."

Gibson's expression hardened. He stood up and walked toward the door without another word, leaving Laura alone with her thoughts and doubts once more. Another of the men took over as interrogator and nodded to the woman in the lab coat. More injections followed, and Laura soon knew she would have no secrets left after this night.

The guards took her back to her cell, where she slumped to the floor like a pile of discarded flesh. As she lay there, feeling every bit of brokenness within herself, Laura realized that bravery had its limits. She wasn't Natalie; she wasn't invincible. But maybe that was okay. Maybe acknowledging those limits was a form of strength, too.

In that brightly lit cell, Laura Bennett faced her own humanity—and decided she wasn't ready to give up just yet.

Somewhere in the dark, she heard a familiar sound. A tapping from somewhere close. It had been there for days... or nights. She still had no reference for time. No clue how long she had been there. The tapping had to be from another prisoner, but she was in a metal box half the size of a train car. Whoever it was might as well have been on the moon. Despite that, she found the corner closest to the sound and tapped back. Just a simple gesture, but even this crumb of human contact helped tremendously.

CHAPTER SEVENTY-SEVEN

2007 EST July 16
NovaCore Offices
McLean, Virginia, USA

"Where were you?" Owen snapped several hours later.

That had not been what Gibson expected. "Very sorry, sir, I was handling a small problem."

Gibson shifted uneasily under Owen's piercing gaze. "The Bennett woman. The reporter. She was getting too close."

Owen's eyes narrowed. "What did you find out?"

"Not much yet. She's tough, wouldn't give anything up easily. Claims her editor doesn't know anything, that she was working this story alone." Gibson rubbed his chin. "But I don't buy it. She had photos of one of our Trident sites. Drone footage. Someone's been helping her."

"And the files?" Owen pressed.

"She had them well hidden. Encrypted. My team's working on cracking them now." Gibson hesitated. "There's something else. Under our drug therapy, she mentioned several potential sources including a congressional aide and... Natalie Reeves."

Owen froze, his glass halfway to his lips. "Natalie Reeves? Are you sure? Reeves from SCET, the presidential commission? Natalie Reeves, the same lone investigator from that crazy UFO group who we can't seem to manipulate?"

Gibson nodded grimly. "Afraid so, yes, sir. Under duress, the reporter said Natalie might be able to link you to everything. To the disappearances, the cover-ups. Everything. She must have been the unknown subject the team tailed back from Norfolk last week."

Owen drained his glass and slammed it down, his mind racing. Natalie Reeves. If she was involved, if she knew even a fraction of what was really going on...

"Where is this reporter now?" he asked, his voice dangerously calm.

"Secure location. My men are... seeing what else they can get out of her." The implication hung heavy in the air.

Owen stood abruptly, his chair scraping harshly against the floor. He braced his hands on the table, head bowed.

"Finish it," he said quietly. "Get what you can from her, then get rid of her. Her and anyone else who knows anything. We can't afford any loose ends. Not now."

Gibson nodded curtly. "Understood, sir. And the files?"

"Destroy them, of course. All of it. Every last byte." Owen turned to face the window, his reflection haggard in the glass. "No one can know. We have to maintain control."

"What about the others? Trembley, Carter, the rest of them on that panel? They're not going to stop digging."

"Then we'll bury them." Owen's voice was cold, resolute. "I'll talk to Pete. He can help. Whatever it takes. We're the only thing standing between our world and God knows what. These secrets must stay buried. Make no mistake, we are in a shadow war. As usual, we do what must be done. No matter the cost."

CHAPTER SEVENTY-EIGHT

"It's them, sir."

"You cross-verified?" Owen knew even before the man answered in the affirmative. "Any word from Gibson yet?" The question was directed at his personal assistant, who just shook her head.

He was going to need to handle this himself. It was, after all, the main reason for him being here. The local Observer's lone responsibility was to answer the aliens when they made contact. It didn't matter that the last time had been his predecessor's predecessor way back in the seventies. He knew the protocols.

He keyed in his sixteen-digit passcode and entered the most secure space of any NovaCore facility. The entire room was isolated and disconnected from the outside world when active. It was, in essence, a giant SCIF. Totally secure, totally designed to prevent any unintended ears from listening in.

Owen King entered the secure room, heart pounding as he approached the ancient communication system. He hadn't felt this anxious since taking over the helm of the ground-based Observers.

The ancient piece of computer tech was against one wall, the tiny display in the midst of all those knobs and dials. Owen knew that top engineers from Palo Alto Research Park, Hewlett-Packard, and MIT had jointly worked on the behemoth back in the sixties. Of course, none of them knew the true purpose. In truth, it was less a computer and essentially just a receiver.

As the man had said, the amber light was flashing on and off. The listening station had been modernized multiple times over the years based on the original plans, but for some reason, they had never been able to get the incoming signal light to work on the new one like it did on the original. Therefore, the beast of a comms system sat to one side like a disapproving parent watching its offspring struggle with even the simplest of tasks.

The original version had been a text-based system. The notes indicated that the alien species did not use a language per se, and when they tried, the syntax and sentence structure were so odd as to be unintelligible, so a version of text messaging was used. It was likely the earliest version of email, and that it came from inhabitants of another world was a hidden irony.

The current system was much more high-tech and included voice or text options. All Owen had to do was speak his words, and the speech-to-text converter would translate his words to the aliens. Since they didn't use language in the same way, no one actually knew if the upgraded system would work at all.

"Observer station WDCAlpha-01," he said nervously. He was glad none of his people could listen in on this conversation. He did not like showing weakness, but in this case, that was exactly how he felt.

"Observer WDCAlpha-01 accepted," the system responded in a stilted, mechanical voice.

'Synchronizing' displayed on a screen and Owen suddenly 'felt' another presence in the room. Suddenly, he knew he was communicating with a purely alien presence. What all did they know? Could they read his thoughts? Did they know all he had done to help keep them secret? Moreover, did they know how much of their tech he had recovered and profited from?

He swallowed down a building urge to vomit and took a deep breath. "Purpose of increased incursions and hostility needs clarification." He knew to be succinct in his words to avoid confusion.

There was a pause before the reply came. "Monitoring exceeded safety limits. Termination of Human Experiment initiated."

Owen felt a chill run down his spine. "Termination? Clarify purpose of termination."

"Human species failed to meet essential criteria for sustainable cohabitation. Irreversible environmental degradation and repeated internal conflicts detected. Observer initiative cannot proceed within current parameters."

"We're making progress," Owen pleaded, his voice cracking. "Environmental policies, technological advancements—our efforts are helping ensure the peace!"

"Insufficient. Rate of increased social regression and potential for irreversible damage to planet-wide systems surpasses thresholds. Species deemed unfit for continued habitation and participation. Terrestrial observers such as WDC-Alpha have abused the privileges offered, withheld technology from your species, and profited off of our generosity. A044 interim monitoring required."

Oh, God! They know everything. His dad had been right about them. Owen's hands shook as he scribbled on his notepad. The rebuke toward him and this specific Observer station were bad enough, but the last part had him frozen in place. *A044? What the hell is that?* Something about the name struck an even deeper level of fear in the man.

Another pause. "Senior species A044 will assume monitoring duties. Full handoff in 14.8 lunar cycles."

"They will arrive in just over a year?" Owen asked.

"Advanced scouts currently establishing ground base facilities. The increase in incursions and violence detected is from A044 scout teams."

Owen's breath caught. "You mean the encounters we've been investigating—the hostility isn't from you?"

"Correct. A044 initiating preliminary occupation protocols. Human species exhibits intelligence comparable to other member societies but lacks social or ethical maturity. Humans are the spoilers of Eden. Overwatch protocol is deemed non-essential. Without protective intervention, self-destruction and planetary ruin is a certainty."

Owen felt his world crumbling. "Is there no option for intervention, assistance? We have maintained your secrecy, facilitated countless advancements—surely there is a way to co-exist peacefully?"

"Protection mechanisms are ineffective. Decision irrevocable. Terminate Planetary Experiment 2273 in 1.35 planetary cycles. Human self-destruction is imminent without more direct oversight. A044 will request additional information and acquired tech from WDC and others."

Owen's vision blurred with unshed tears. He knew this was more than they had ever communicated before, but this seemed final. "What will A044 want from us? What are their intentions? Will we have a role in the future of our planet?"

"A044 aims to stabilize and exploit planetary resources; colonization is an ancillary goal. Human cohabitation potential assessed as minimal. Previous protections nullified. Goodbye WDCAlpha-01."

The finality of the statement struck Owen like a hammer blow. He stumbled back from the console, the weight of the revelation crashing down on him—a horrifying realization that Earth had been a zoo, and the monitoring aliens had merely been the zookeepers. Now, a new, and apparently even less compassionate guardian was taking over, one who viewed humanity as little more than interesting but ultimately non-essential inhabitants of a world they would soon call their own.

He stumbled from the room, drenched in sweat, the words echoing endlessly in his mind. Humanity had failed. They had failed. He had no doubt that in time, his own group's efforts would all be exposed and subsequently condemned by the masses. Then, everything he valued was doomed to disappear, leaving Earth at the mercy of an uncaring galaxy, with Owen King held up as the man who gave it all away. He fumbled for the door controls and stepped out.

Gibson was there with a bottle of water.

"Looks like we need to talk."

"Yeah," Owen said sarcastically as he downed the water. He looked down at his pad, then shook his head. "We aren't prepared for this." Then collapsed to the floor.

Gibson and two security men carried their boss back to his office. Once he woke up, Owen poured himself a single malt and downed it, followed by another. He sat heavily at the conference table and looked out over the D.C. skyline.

Gibson watched his boss for any clarification about what the historic communication had involved. Owen King looked exhausted, older even. His clothes were wrinkled and sweat-stained. He'd read staff reports on the prior two sessions in the sixties and another in 1976. On both occasions, the report said the human directors left the listening station looking much the same as his boss did now.

"It's all over," King finally said.

"What do you mean?" Gibson asked, his eyes wide.

"I mean we failed the fucking test. Whatever the goddamn test was. We fucked up."

Gibson had his doubts about Owen King, but this was a side of the man he'd never seen.

"We've done our best to keep them hidden. Do they understand how hard that is now that everyone has a camera in their phones? Where one image can circle the world in seconds via social media. Do they understand the extent we have to go through just to keep the big stories from getting out, much less the stupid anal probes and cow mutilations?"

King shook his head, "I think they see that we brought much of that tech to market. We made money off technology we should have been keeping secret."

"So what do we do now?" Gison asked, genuinely worried.

"I need to think. Not sure it matters, but they indicated a change of management was coming."

Gibson leaned against his office door minutes later digesting what King had said. Maybe they still had time to salvage the arrangement. He was committed to doubling down on efforts to keep the truth about the alien Observers from ever getting out. He was less sure Owen King would be on board with that.

CHAPTER SEVENTY-NINE

2057 EST July 24
Private Residence
Washington, D.C., USA

Natalie paced the small motel room, her phone pressed tightly to her ear. Each ring felt like an eternity. She glanced at the clock on the nightstand, the minutes ticking by with agonizing slowness. Finally, the call connected.

"Rogers."

"Trent, it's Natalie. I need your help."

A pause. "Natalie? What's going on?"

She took a deep breath, her voice trembling slightly. "It's Laura Bennett. I think she's in danger."

"Laura Bennett?" Trent's tone shifted from casual to serious. "The journalist? What's happened?"

"I can't reach her, but I just got a compressed file supposedly from her. I think it was a timed send. There was only a single line with the file." Natalie said, her words coming out in a rush.

"What was the line?" Trent asked.

"If you're reading this, I've been silenced."

"Damn," Trent muttered. "That's not cryptic at all. Always nice when journalists go full Mission: Impossible. Can you access the contents?”

"Some of it. She's been digging into some heavy stuff—UFOs, government cover-ups, you name it. She mentioned a paramilitary group before she went silent. Lots of interview notes. It will take me a while to go through it. I’ve tried her phone several times, but now I’m getting nothing but radio silence from her."

"That doesn’t sound good," Trent replied, his voice steady but concerned. "Do you know where she lives?"

"Not exactly," Natalie admitted, frustration evident in her voice. "Emily was going to touch base with her editor, she may know. I think she has a small place downtown, somewhere close to her office."

"Alright," Trent said, his voice calm and reassuring. "Give me a minute."

Natalie could hear the sound of typing in the background as Trent worked on his computer. She bit her lip, anxiety gnawing at her insides.

"Got it," Trent said after a few moments.

"What is it?" Natalie asked anxiously.

"Wait," Trent said, his voice suddenly guarded. "I've got her address, but I'm not comfortable just giving it to you."

Natalie's grip tightened on her phone. "What? Why not?"

"Because you've already got people following you from Norfolk, remember? Those armed men tailing you weren't mall security, Natalie."

She paced faster, running her free hand through her hair. "I lost them."

"This time," Trent countered. "Look, I get it. You're worried about Bennett. So am I. But rushing in alone might be exactly what they want."

Natalie stopped at the window, peering through the blinds at the dimly lit parking lot. "I can handle myself."

"I know you can. You're ex-Navy, and you've got skills most people don't. But we may be dealing with something bigger than either of us anticipated." His voice softened. "Wait for me. I can be there in forty minutes, and we'll go together."

Silence stretched between them. Natalie closed her eyes, weighing her options. The memory of those men following her car flashed in her mind—they looked menacing, and somehow, she knew they were armed and wouldn't hesitate to eliminate her if challenged.

"Natalie?"

"Fine," she relented. "Forty minutes. Not a second longer."

"I'll be there," Trent promised. "And Natalie? Don't open the door for anyone but me."

"Roger that." She ended the call and tossed her phone onto the bed.

The walls of the motel room seemed to close in around her. Forty minutes. She glanced at her gun sitting on the nightstand, then back to the window. Somewhere out there, Laura Bennett was in trouble—possibly because of information Natalie had shared with her.

Waiting felt like betrayal, but Trent was right. Whatever they were up against had resources, training, and a clear willingness to eliminate problems. Going in alone would be playing right into their hands.

Forty-three minutes later, Trent's government-issue sedan pulled into the hotel parking lot. Natalie was already waiting outside, leaning against her rental car with her arms crossed.

"You're late," she said as he approached.

"Traffic." Trent's expression was grim. "Let's go. I'll drive."

The journey to Laura's apartment was tense and quiet. Natalie stared out the window at the passing streetlights, her mind roiled with possibilities, none of them good.

"I'd like to know more about what you and this reporter were discussing. What exactly did Laura tell you about her investigation?" Trent asked, breaking the awkward silence.

"Some paramilitary security group that she feels is connected to something big. Military contracts, black projects. She thought they might be part of a government cover-up." Natalie turned to face him. "She said it was connected to the UFOs—the same group that came after me...after my encounter."

"The Men in Black?" he asked.

She stared at him, wondering if he was making a joke, then nodded.

They pulled onto a quiet residential street lined with small cottages and older bungalows. Trent slowed the car, checking house numbers.

"That's it," he said, pointing to a cottage set back from the road. "Number forty-two."

The place was dark, no lights visible from the street. Laura's driveway sat empty.

"Car's not here," Trent observed as they parked across the street.

They approached cautiously, staying low and moving quietly. The cottage seemed unnaturally still against the backdrop of distant city noise.

Trent raised his hand, signaling for Natalie to stay back. "Let me check first," he whispered, his right hand moving to rest on his service weapon.

He crept along the side of the house, peering through windows. Natalie followed a few paces behind, ignoring his instruction. The living room was visible through the first window—furniture in place, nothing obviously disturbed, but completely dark.

“Heading around to the other side. If I get shot, avenge me by going after whoever designed these god-awful porch lights,” Trent said, disappearing into the dark.

Less than a minute later, he was back. "I don't see anything," Trent whispered. "No signs of forced entry. She's probably not home."

Natalie moved to another window, cupping her hands around her eyes to block the reflection. The kitchen was empty, dishes stacked neatly in a drying rack.

"We need to get inside," she said firmly.

"Natalie, we can't just break in. That's illegal, even for me."

Without hesitation, Natalie grabbed a small garden stone from the flowerbed. Before Trent could stop her, she smashed it against the door window. The glass cracked with a sharp snap, then shattered.

"What the hell?" Trent hissed, looking around frantically. “Do you always have that much confidence or just enjoy breaking and entering?”

Natalie reached through the broken window, careful to avoid the jagged edges, and unlocked the door from the inside.

"There's no one here," Natalie said, her voice echoing in the empty house.

Trent moved through the rooms, his pistol at the ready, checking corners and closets with purpose. The living room opened into a small dining area, everything in its place. Too much in place.

A collection of coffee table books sat perfectly aligned on the glass surface. The throw pillows on the couch looked freshly fluffed, arranged with geometric precision. Even the mail on the counter was stacked with unnatural tidiness.

"Something's not right," Trent muttered, scanning the shabby chic aesthetic of the space. Decorative baskets lined shelves in perfect symmetry. Artisanal candles stood untouched on pristine end tables.

His training screamed at him. This wasn't a lived-in space. It was a display home, a staged facade.

The kitchen gleamed under their flashlight beams—spotless countertops, unused appliances still sporting their energy efficiency stickers. Not a single dirty dish in sight.

"Look at this," Natalie called from the bedroom. She pointed to the closet where clothes hung with exact spacing between hangers, color-coordinated, pristine.

“No one lives like this,” Trent said, holstering his weapon. “Unless Pottery Barn is running a witness protection program.”

"But why?" Natalie asked, her mind racing through possibilities. "Why create this elaborate setup?"

"To make it look like Laura has a normal life?" Trent suggested. "A cover story?"

His instincts prickled. In his years of service, he'd seen similar setups—safe houses designed to project normalcy while hiding something else entirely. But this felt different. More deliberate. More controlled.

"Here, help me," he said as he pulled the cushions off the chairs, then moved to the sofa. Natalie joined in, understanding that the ruse may not be as thorough as it seemed.

Brown crumbs lined a spot between cushions. "What is that? Cookie? Brownie?"

"Not sure," Natalie answered. She took some between her fingers, then smelled it. "Chocolate."

They stripped the covers off the bed, checked the washer and dryer for clothes, then went through the trash cans inside and out.

"Checked her mailbox," Trent said, walking up holding a stack of mail. "Looks like she hasn't checked it in a week or more. No trash, no food in the fridge. No clothes that aren't clean. Shower is dry, and her toothbrush looks brand new."

"Also, her luggage all seems to be in her closet," Natalie added.

"I need to check with her employer, but..." Trent said tentatively.

"But what?"

He reached over, gently touching her arm. "My instincts say she was taken, and this place was thoroughly cleaned. Nearly all signs of her being here recently have been erased."

That was what Natalie was feeling as well. "Those men who followed me. They probably had a team on Laura, too."

"We'll find her, Nat. Just keep yourself safe. Sounds like you both were working on the same story. If you have pissed off the same people, then you could be next. Especially if they discover you received her emergency dump files."

CHAPTER EIGHTY

Natalie finally got through to Marcus on his satphone, her voice crackling with the interference of the failing satellite network. "Marcus, can you hear me?"

"Loud and clear, Natalie," Marcus replied, relief evident in his tone. "Thank God you called. You okay?"

"I am. What about your people on the coast?"

"It's as bad as you said it was. Maybe worse. Looks like they're abandoning the airbase. Or what's left of it."

He took a pause while static cut into the call. "I think all military bases are targets right now; hopefully, someone upstairs has enough sense to disperse our assets."

"I'm still trying to get someone to get aid down there, but now there are lots of other areas needing it. We'll keep trying, Marcus."

"Good to hear; I know they need it," Marcus said. "Look, Nat, I wish you would consider coming down here. It will be safer. I know civilian GPS is down, but I could get you close enough with Long-Lat coordinates."

Natalie's voice held steady despite the emotions swirling through her. "Listen, Marcus, I didn't mention it before, but I'm now part of a presidential task force investigating these UFO incursions. I can't leave right now. I'm not sure it would be a good idea even if I could."

Marcus's concern cut through the static. "I know what you fear even more than the aliens. Look, you don't need to be concerned about us—that's not it. I get it—you're committed to this task force, but think about your safety for a moment. Beta camp is secure. You could help the country from here."

Natalie shook her head, even though he couldn't see her. "Marcus, I appreciate the offer, but my place is here right now. We need to figure out what's going on and stop it at the source."

Marcus sighed heavily. "You're stubborn as ever, Natalie."

“And somehow that’s still not the worst thing anyone’s called me this week,” she replied.

“Just promise me you'll stay safe."

"I will," she assured him, though both knew it was a promise that might be hard to keep. Look, I'm working on something with a friend, and she would like your opinion. You okay if I send an image?"

Marcus took paranoia to new levels. He instead sent her a cloud account link. "Drop it there; it's more private."

She did so, then gave him time to access the file.

"Natalie... hon. What are you mixed up in? This isn't part of your alien hunting, is it?" The man's tone was more than just concerned. He seemed on edge.

"It... could be related, yes. I thought I recognized it but just couldn't place it. My friend saw several cars outside an office she was investigating with that in the window. Does it mean anything to you?"

"Yeah, I'm afraid it does. Is your end of this line secure?" he asked.

"Very. Like I said, I'm doing some high-level work right now. They got me a Blackphone."

"Damn, sounds like you really moved up from MUFON. About time you left those clowns."

"They aren't clowns, they’re just enthusiastic." It was true, they had a bit of a reputation. "I haven't left but am working on this commission, trying to get to the bottom of the recent rash of UFO incidents."

"Okay... well, then. I'd like you to do something for me if I answer your question."

She considered that a moment. Despite their past, he was an honorable man. She could commit to whatever to get to the truth. "Okay."

"I want you to go down to the range and run several boxes of ammo through your sidearm. I want you to do it several times a week until you are as good as you used to be."

The request was not what she had expected. "I can still shoot, Marcus." She smiled at how similar this conversation was to the recent one with Trent. *Guys... Why did they think guns were always the answer?* "What's this all about?"

"Just do it, okay? I can send a friend to go over it all again if you need. It's more than just muscle memory. You need to be proficient, automatic, prepared."

He was serious. Marcus wasn't just screwing with her. He meant it. "You've still got a CCP, right? Carry that piece with you everywhere."

"They won't let me in the White House with a concealed carry card."

"They can check it at the gate. Just let them know it's on you before they check."

How the hell would he know what White House security was like? she wondered.

"Okay, Marcus. Now what does that symbol mean?" His paranoia was also setting her nerves on edge as well.

"TPS, Trident Protective Services."

The name set off alarm bells, but she didn't know why. "Why does that sound familiar?"

"You remember Dozier and Mercer?"

The names came to her along with the faces of the two hulking brutes. They had been friends of Marcus back in his early service days, and they'd all hung out every few weeks.

"SEALs?"

"Trident was started by a former SEAL commander named Jennings. I think he's gone now, but at least early on, they only hired former SEALs."

"So, Trident was probably the paramilitary guys my friend saw." That made sense. "Why do you think I need protection, Marcus?"

He didn't answer immediately, and she heard someone calling to him. "Do you need to go?"

"Gimme a minute?" she heard him say.

She heard more talking in the background and a familiar dog barking.

"I'm sorry, Nat, but we have some stuff going on here, too. Remember if you need to run away, just let me know. I'll drop a pin for you."

"So, Beta camp is off the grid?" she said, already knowing it would be.

"Way off." He took a moment before answering her previous question. "Nat, look, I lost track of my buddies after they signed up."

"Sorry."

He cut her off. "No, it was my choice. They just changed. They were juicing bad. I think it was screwing with their heads. Steroids can do that, you know?"

She didn't know but let him talk.

"Trident is not well-known, but they have a very bad rep in the marketplace. We would call them enforcers. They are not hired to keep the peace or offer protection. The people that run into them usually go missing."

Natalie chewed on the inside of her cheek, considering his words.

"Would these people be government contractors?" She wanted to know the connection. How deep did this go?

"Look, Natalie, I know you dealt with the government assholes back then. You couldn't talk about it, but I'm sure they came after you for wanting to speak the truth. I don't know for a fact that Trident might be on someone's black budget, but I damn sure wouldn't rule it out. They are serious players. Look, why don't I get some guys I trust to keep an eye on you and your friend?"

She really felt like she was imposing now. "No, Marcus, thank you, but we'll be fine. I just wanted your opinion on this, and you've been very helpful." Even she knew that sounded shitty to say. "I mean, I really appreciate everything, but don't worry about me. I'm a big girl."

"I know you, Natalie. You never give up on anything. You will keep pushing until you have the truth or it kills you."

She didn't want to mention that her friend she was doing this for was already missing. Now confirming Trident was part of all this was scaring her more; even Marcus seemed afraid of the group. Her emotions were getting the best of her, and she ended the call before she lost it. As she disconnected, she realized Marcus was wrong on one point. She had given up on one thing...

CHAPTER EIGHTY-ONE

2007 EST July 29
Gulfstream G280
Virginia to Arizona

The corporate jet cut through the night sky, its Honeywell turbofan engines humming with mechanical precision that Owen King found oddly comforting amid his internal chaos. He stared out the window, seeing nothing but darkness punctuated by distant lights—much like humanity's place in the universe, he thought bitterly. The scotch in his hand, his third since takeoff, did little to calm the trembling that had begun hours ago.

"Dad, maybe you should slow down." Emma's voice pulled him back to the cabin. Her eyes, so much like her mother's, held concern he rarely saw directed at him.

Owen drained the glass anyway. "I'm fine."

"You haven't been fine since you left that meeting." Emma moved to sit opposite him, her gaze steady and searching. "I've never seen you like this."

"Define 'fine.'" *If you mean not curled in a fetal position, then yes. Totally fine.*

The ice clinked in his empty glass as Owen set it down harder than intended. He'd built an empire on control—of information, of technology, of people. Now that control had slipped through his fingers like desert sand.

"There are things happening that I can't fix, Em." His voice sounded foreign to his own ears—ragged, uncertain.

Soon the Arizona ranch appeared below them, a sprawling compound nestled against the red rock landscape. Owen had built it as a sanctuary, a place removed from the world's prying eyes. Now it felt like his last refuge. The rumors were that the area held a "High Strangeness" due to numerous inexplicable events. Owen had used that belief to his advantage a few times but now he felt like it karma was kicking him in the shins.

As they descended, Emma placed her hand over his. "Whatever it is, we'll figure it out together."

Owen almost laughed. How could he explain to his daughter that an ancient species had just declared humanity's experiment over? That beings with technology beyond comprehension had deemed them unworthy of continued existence?

The jet touched down on his private airstrip, jolting him from his thoughts. Within minutes, they were in the main house, its soaring ceilings and glass walls offering no comfort tonight.

Owen poured another drink at the bar while Emma watched, arms crossed.

"You're scaring me," she said plainly. "This isn't like you. You don't run, you don't hide, and you certainly don't drink yourself stupid when there's a problem."

"This isn't a problem, Emma." Owen's hand shook as he raised the glass. "It's worse than that."

Morning sunlight speared through the bedroom windows, assaulting Owen's eyes with merciless intensity. His head throbbed, punishment for last night's indulgence. He rolled over, checking his watch—nearly ten. He hadn't slept this late in decades.

After a shower and three aspirin, Owen found Emily in the stable, already saddling two horses. She wore riding boots and a wide-brimmed hat, looking more relaxed than she had in months.

"Thought you might need some fresh air," she said, not mentioning his hangover or last night's uncharacteristic behavior.

Owen nodded, grateful for her discretion. "Good call."

They rode mostly in silence through the scrubland, the horses' hooves kicking up dust that sparkled in the sunlight. The vastness of the landscape usually brought Owen peace—the uninterrupted horizon, the distant mountains, the sense of possibility. Today, it only reminded him how small and vulnerable humanity truly was.

"Remember when I taught you to ride?" Owen asked, watching Emma handle her palomino with practiced ease.

"I was terrified," she laughed. "But you told me fear was just the mind's way of saying something mattered."

Owen smiled despite himself. "Smart guy, your old man."

"Sometimes." Emma guided her horse alongside his. "So, when are you going to tell me what's really happening?"

The question hung between them. Owen studied his daughter's face —determined, intelligent, so full of life and potential. How could he tell her that all of it—her future, humanity's future—had been deemed unworthy by beings who viewed Earth as little more than a petri dish?

"It's complicated, Em."

“I figured. You only get locked to a table when it’s really complicated. I think I can handle complicated."

Owen opened his mouth, then closed it. What could he say? That for decades, the Observers had maintained a fragile agreement with extraterrestrial intelligences? That humanity had been given time to prove itself worthy of continued existence, and had failed spectacularly?

"Some things, once known, can't be unknown," he said finally. "I'm trying to protect you."

"I don't need protection. I need the truth."

The afternoon light began to soften, casting longer shadows across the desert floor. Owen was about to respond when something caught his eye—a brief, unmistakable flash of light on a distant hill. His blood ran cold. In his heart, he knew that signal.

They were calling him.

"We need to head back," Owen said, his voice suddenly tight. "It's getting late."

Emma followed his gaze to the hill. "What's out there?"

"Nothing." The lie felt leaden on his tongue. "Just the sun hitting a rock."

"Dad—"

"Emma." His tone brooked no argument. "Ride back to the house. I need to check something with the property line."

She stared at him, hurt and confusion crossing her face. "You're shutting me out again."

"I'm trying to keep you safe." Owen reached across the space between them, squeezing her hand. "Please. Go back to the house. I won't be long."

For a moment, he thought she might refuse. Then she nodded curtly, wheeling her horse around. "Don't treat me like a child. Whatever this is, I deserve to know."

Owen watched her ride away, his chest tight with emotion. When she was safely out of sight, he turned his horse toward the distant hill, spurring it forward. Each hoofbeat carried him closer to a reckoning he'd hoped would never come.

His heart ached for her and also quaked at whatever he was about to encounter. No Observer had ever had a face-to-face encounter with an alien. *Why in the hell does the first have to be me?*

He stepped into the shallow wash of the sunbaked hillside and stopped dead. Bathed in the slanting amber of late afternoon, the solitary figure stood motionless in the depression—its skin a ghostly alabaster, with dark patterns that curiously resembled tribal tattoos, their lines converging into a network of what seemed like dark veins. The vaguely reptilian head, hairless and full of menace, inclined as if curiously sizing him up; its lidless eyes glowed with a molten copper light, reflecting the dying sun. A narrow slit formed its mouth—an abyssal crack that parted just enough to reveal nothing but utter emptiness. The air carried a faint scent with an unsettling tang, like iron warmed by desert heat. With deliberate slowness, the creature raised a slender arm, its veined markings rippling in the light, beckoning him forward.

Owen stepped forward, his legs moving without conscious direction, as if pulled by some invisible force. The creature's copper eyes never left his face, tracking him with predatory intensity. A warm wetness spread down Owen's leg, and he knew without looking that he'd lost control of his bladder. Shame mingled with terror as he realized the truth he'd always hidden from himself—beneath the power, the wealth, the carefully constructed facade of control, he was a coward.

The alien's presence crushed against his consciousness like a physical weight. This was no subordinate species, no messenger or scout. This was A044—the senior species. The knowledge materialized in his mind with absolute certainty, though no words had been spoken.

Ten feet away, Owen stopped, unable to force himself closer. The creature's skin rippled with subtle movement, the dark veined patterns shifting like ink beneath water. Up close, the thing was even more terrifying. While thin and tall, he could see corded muscles rippling beneath the thin white skin. It wore a semi-translucent suit over part of its body. The shimmering material pulsed with faint turquoise light that somehow made the thing look even more menacing and alien.

"You know why you are here." The mouth moved, but Owen wasn't sure if the voice was spoken or perhaps inserted directly into his mind, bypassing his ears entirely. It carried no emotion, just cold, clinical certainty.

King wanted to say he came here to get away from all this, but he knew the aliens seemed to know everything he did. "The termination of the monitoring phase?"

The thing let out what might be called a laugh. "Oh, no, this is simply official notification that your services are no longer required. The Hi'Grash' have now finalized the formal portion of the handover process."

The mechanical way the alien said it made King's blood run cold. "So, now what? What can we do to make this right?"

The alien, which had turned away as if to leave, turned back with a truly evil expression on its face. The slash of a mouth twisted into a very human-looking sneer. It moved closer in a terrifyingly inhuman manner.

"You... will know," it said as it stretched out a bony six-fingered hand

and touched a long curved nail to Owen's forehead. The desert suddenly went silent, and blackness took over Owen King's mind.

Owen jerked awake, his body trembling as consciousness returned. The desert had cooled, shadows stretching long across the scrubland. His first instinct was to check if the creature was still there, but he already knew the answer. The alien presence had vanished, leaving only the distant call of a nighthawk and the whisper of wind through the brush. *Was it even real?* Yes, he had no doubt of that.

He sat up slowly, his muscles protesting. His pants were dry but carried the unmistakable acrid smell of urine, a humiliating reminder of his terror. More pressing than physical discomfort were the images cycling through his tortured mind—visions the alien had inserted there with that single touch to his forehead.

Tears welled in Owen's eyes, spilling down his weathered cheeks. He had failed. The Observers had failed. For generations, they had maintained the fragile agreement, keeping humanity ignorant while the aliens studied Earth mostly from a distance. They had convinced themselves they were protecting mankind, that ignorance was mercy. Now he understood the truth—they had merely been collaborators, facilitating humanity's eventual doom.

In the distance, the lights of his ranch house glowed warm against the darkening sky. Emma was there, probably wondering where he was, perhaps angry at being sent away. His daughter—brilliant, fierce, beautiful Emma—would face a world of horror because of him.

Owen staggered to his feet, his legs unsteady. His horse was gone, likely spooked by the alien presence. He would have to walk back, alone with his knowledge and his shame. Each step toward the ranch felt heavier than the last.

"I'm sorry," he whispered to the empty desert. "I'm so sorry, Emma."

But apologies were meaningless now. The clock was ticking down on humanity's final hours, and Owen King—powerful, connected, wealthy beyond measure—was utterly powerless to stop it.

CHAPTER EIGHTY-TWO

1007 EST July 31
NovaCore Offices
McLean, Virginia, USA

Gibson eyed his boss closely. The man hadn't been the same since he'd returned from his ranch. He knew the message from the Observer species had shaken him, but this seemed to be something more. Owen's gaze drifted toward the window, lost in thought as if the world outside held answers to questions he feared to voice. Gibson noticed the lines on Owen's face deepening, a man weighed down by burdens no one else could see.

The real trouble brewed beneath the surface. His daughter had been with him during that trip, and Gibson couldn't shake off the feeling that Emma was more than just a concerned child. She had been asking questions, probing into areas she had no business exploring. That kind of curiosity was dangerous; it could expose vulnerabilities they couldn't afford right now.

"Sir," Gibson ventured cautiously, "we can't afford distractions. The projects you're considering shutting down—"

"They're a waste of resources," Owen interrupted, snapping back to reality. "We need to focus on what matters."

"What's that? Hiding behind classified reports?" Gibson stepped closer, keeping his voice low yet firm. "We have assets we can leverage here—technology that could yield billions and secure our position."

Owen's jaw clenched at the suggestion. "And what good is all that if it attracts attention? The Observers, or more accurately the Senior Species, are watching us."

Gibson straightened, frustration bubbling just beneath his calm facade. "They'll always be watching! We need to push forward, not retreat into shadows."

"I'm not retreating," Owen said quietly, though doubt seeped through his words.

The silence stretched between them, heavy with unspoken fears and uncertainties. Gibson noticed how Owen rubbed his temples as if trying to ward off an impending headache or worse—an impending realization.

"It feels like you're giving up," Gibson pressed, refusing to let up. "You can't show weakness now."

"Sometimes weakness is the only path to survival," Owen shot back defensively, but even he sounded unconvinced.

"What about Emma?" Gibson countered sharply, sensing a crack in Owen's resolve. "She's not going to accept the company pulling back from what she thinks is its humanitarian mission."

Owen stiffened at the mention of his daughter's name but didn't reply.

"Look," Gibson continued, softening slightly but maintaining his intensity. "If we don't act decisively now, there won't be anything left for her—or for us."

The weight of those words hung in the air as both men understood in different ways that time was running out.

Gibson closed the door as King fell into his chair. The encounter with A044 had shaken him to the core. He needed to reach out to someone in charge, to let them know what was coming, but strangely, he was trapped by his own network of embedded traitors. He sat atop a precarious pyramid, and if one stone loosened, all the conspirators knew it would be game over for them as well. The people he thought he owned were too smart, too powerful, and too dirty to ever willingly let the light of truth shine on them.

Gibson's smile was unconvincing an hour later as he watched Emma King wandering the NovaCore offices, her inquisitive nature evident in every question she asked. He knew what she was doing here—snooping around, perhaps seeking a way to understand the complicated web of secrets her father had entangled himself in. Gibson had always been a man who took matters into his own hands, and he saw Emma as a potential threat, not because she was a formidable adversary, but because she represented a weakness in Owen King's armor.

He approached her with a slight limp, a recent reminder of his advancing age. "Emma, I see you're quite the investigator," he said, his voice smooth but underlaid with a sharp edge.

Emma turned, her eyes narrowing slightly as she took in Gibson's demeanor. "Just trying to understand a bit more about what Dad does," she replied, her tone casual yet guarded.

Gibson nodded. "Well, if you're interested, I'm heading out to one of our research facilities today. It might give you a better idea of our operations. Would you like to ride along?"

Emma hesitated, her gaze flicking over Gibson before she nodded hesitantly. "Sure, that sounds interesting."

Gibson's smile widened, a cold calculation in his eyes. "Excellent. I'll have them bring a car around to the front. We can discuss some of the projects we're working on. It's a bit of a drive, but I think you'll find it... enlightening."

Emma followed him, her steps echoing in the quiet hallways. She couldn't shake the feeling that something was off about this invitation, but her growing curiosity about her father's work overrode her unease.

Gibson maneuvered the sleek company car onto the highway, stealing glances at the very young and very attractive Emma sitting across from him. The young woman's eyes darted between the passing scenery and the stoic man beside her.

"So, Emma, how are your studies going?" Gibson asked, his tone deceptively casual.

Emma shrugged. "Fine, I guess. Lots of work, but interesting."

Gibson nodded, tapping his fingers on the steering wheel. "Your father speaks highly of your aptitude. I know he's proud."

"I suppose," Emma replied, her voice tinged with uncertainty.

They lapsed into silence for a while, the hum of the engine filling the car. Gibson occasionally pointed out landmarks or commented on the weather, but the conversation remained superficial.

"So, what is it NovaCore does? What do you do, Gibson?"

Gibson's fingers drummed against the steering wheel as he considered Emma's questions. "Well, NovaCore is involved in a lot of cutting-edge technology," he started, his eyes on the road ahead. "Defense systems, primarily. We work on projects that help keep our nation safe."

Emma leaned back, crossing her arms. "Seems like we haven't been very safe lately. Still, that's a pretty vague answer. Can you be more specific?"

Gibson chuckled softly, a smile creased his brittle face. He hated the brat and wished he could strangle her and dump the body before he reached their destination. "A lot of what we do is classified, dear. National security and all that. But I can tell you we're developing technologies that will revolutionize defense."

Emma raised an eyebrow, clearly unsatisfied with his answer. "Like what? My dad always talks about the importance of his work, but he never gets into the details."

Gibson tightened his grip on the wheel, choosing his words carefully. "Think about it this way: imagine a world where threats can be neutralized before they even materialize. That's the kind of future we're working towards."

Emma stared at him, unblinking. "That sounds like something out of a science fiction movie."

Gibson's lips twitched into a brief smile. "Sometimes reality surpasses fiction. Some of the technology we're developing could change the balance of power globally."

"Like how?" Emma pressed, her curiosity piqued.

"You heard about the Zero Point Energy system? A reactor that literally makes electricity from the vacuum of space."

"Free energy?" she asked. "Like NovaCore could just give it away?"

"No... that's naïve. We would not give it away. It will cost a fortune to finish the research and then get the machines built. Your father's company is a for-profit endeavor. We exist to make money."

"We have money," Emma said with a sigh. "What the world needs is clean, free energy."

"Well, when you are running NovaCore, you can make those calls."

Emma tilted her head, considering his words. "Maybe... but tell me this. What about all these rumors I've heard? About alien technology?"

Gibson's expression hardened for a split second before he forced another smile. "Rumors are just that—rumors. People love to speculate when they don't have all the facts."

"But is there any truth to them?" Emma insisted.

He glanced at her briefly before returning his focus to the road. "What we do at NovaCore involves highly advanced technology, some of which might seem... otherworldly to those not in the know."

Emma narrowed her eyes. "So, you're saying there might be some truth to it?"

Gibson exhaled slowly through his nose, irritation flickering across his features despite his best efforts to mask it. "I'm saying that our work is complicated and often misunderstood by outsiders."

Emma leaned forward slightly, sensing an opportunity to dig deeper. "And you're okay with all these secrets? With people not knowing what's really going on?"

Gibson's jaw clenched subtly before he forced himself to relax. "It's part of the job," he said evenly. "National security isn't about transparency. It's about keeping people safe, even if they don't know how it's done."

As they drove further from the city, Emma's unease grew. She studied Gibson's profile, noting the hard set of his jaw and the coldness in his eyes.

Finally, unable to contain herself any longer, Emma turned to face him fully. "You're not a good person, are you?"

Gibson's smile was as cold as the dark windows of the Trident facility they approached. "No, I'm not," he answered, his voice dripping with a condescending tone that made Emma's skin crawl.

She shivered reflexively as the gates of the facility opened, revealing a complex of sleek, black buildings surrounded by layers of security fencing. The air was heavy with the smell of diesel and the distant hum of generators. The place was in the middle of nowhere, and it was creeping her out.

"Please, surrender your phone and purse to security before proceeding," Gibson commanded, his hand pointing to the uniformed man just inside the doors.

"Surrender?" Emma hesitated, not liking his choice of words. Her eyes scanned the surroundings nervously. The black-clad guards moved with a precision that seemed almost military, their eyes fixed on her as if sizing her up. Relenting, she handed over her belongings, feeling a rising sense of unease as they were taken away.

As they walked through the security checkpoint, Emma couldn't help but notice the layers of security: metal detectors, biometric scanners, and numerous reinforced doors. It was like entering a fortress.

"What is this place?" Emma asked, her voice barely above a whisper as she followed Gibson through the labyrinthine corridors. "What do you do here?"

Gibson's smile remained fixed, but his eyes seemed to darken, as if something had shifted inside him. "This is a research facility," he said, his voice smooth but lacking warmth. "We work on advanced technologies here."

Emma's gaze darted to the guards, their faces impassive behind their visors. "Advanced technologies?" she repeated, her skepticism clear. "It looks like a prison."

Gibson chuckled, the sound hollow. "Appearances can be deceiving, Emma. Sometimes, the most secure places are those that appear the least threatening."

As they turned a corner, Emma caught sight of rows of doors, each labeled with cryptic codes and symbols.

"Where are we going?" Emma asked, her voice firmer now, a hint of defiance creeping into her tone.

Gibson's smile faded, his expression becoming stone-like. "You'll see soon enough," he said, leading her further into the heart of the facility.

CHAPTER EIGHTY-THREE

1042 EST August 02
White House West Wing
Washington, D.C., USA

Emily Carter stood in the doorway of Raymond Whittner's office, her stomach knotting as she took in his haggard appearance. The chief of staff's skin had a sickly pallor, and dark circles rimmed his bloodshot eyes. He motioned for her to enter with a trembling hand.

"Sit down, Carter," Whittner barked, his voice raspy.

Emily perched on the edge of the chair, her back ramrod straight. "Sir, it's good to see you back at work. How are you feeling?"

Whittner ignored her question. "Let's cut to the chase. Your little UFO committee? It's done. Finished. We're putting it on indefinite hiatus."

Emily's jaw clenched. "With all due respect, sir, we've made significant progress—"

"Progress?" Whittner scoffed, a coughing fit interrupting his tirade. When he recovered, he fixed Emily with a glare. "The country's falling apart, and you're spending official time chasing fairy tales."

"These aren't fairy tales, sir. We have concrete evidence—"

Whittner slammed his fist on the desk. "Evidence? The only

evidence I care about is the president's tanking poll numbers. We need all hands on deck to address real crises, not waste resources on your pet project."

Emily leaned forward, struggling to keep her voice level. "Mr. Whittner, with respect, I believe someone's been manipulating us for years. This investigation is crucial to—"

"Manipulating who? The White House? Me?" Whittner's face flushed an alarming shade of red. "The only manipulation here is you trying to further your own agenda. It stops now."

"Sir, please. If you'd just look at the data—"

"Enough!" Whittner shouted, then doubled over in another coughing fit.

Emily rose, concern overriding her frustration. "Sir, are you alright? Let me call the doctor?"

Whittner waved her off, his breathing labored. "Get out. And don't even think about pursuing this further. Am I clear?"

Emily hesitated, torn between her duty and her convictions. "Crystal clear, sir," she finally said, her voice tight.

As she turned to leave, Emily couldn't fathom the change in the man's demeanor. The chief of staff could be a tyrant, but never to his staff. If anything, he was a giant teddy bear. Someone got to him—that much was obvious. What else would have dragged him in off what may have been his deathbed to deal with this one issue?

SCET was barely on the radar as far as White House committees went. It used very few resources and was ongoing at the president's own request. While she couldn't just tuck tail and run to the president, she still had a few tricks up her sleeve.

One upside to the chief of staff being back at work was Emily no longer had a protective detail who watched her every move. A young man named Ted had let her know earlier in the day that security assignments were being moved. Leaving the building shortly after eleven, she had a car service waiting at the northwest gate.

Her paranoia was not at full throttle yet, but the nature of her work made her wary even in the best of times. This was clearly not the best of times. The service let her off near Georgetown, where she kept her personal car in an underground parking garage.

It felt good to be driving herself once again. The sunroof was open on the Audi, and she had a desperate desire to just keep driving and put the nation's capital in her rearview mirror. Instead, she took an indirect route to a private yacht club well outside the city.

General Briggs met her at the iron gate and keyed her in. He was in a sweater and slacks, but Emily always felt like he was still in uniform. The man never actually relaxed despite being retired from the service for years.

"I got your message. Very clever."

Emily smiled; she had some covert tricks of her own. She worked in a house of secrets, yet everyone's assumption was that there were no secrets there. None you could count on being kept, at least. She held up her phone and waggled it side to side.

"I had a good teacher." The BlackPhone S with the new security chip made for supposedly unbreakable encryption. Even the NSA was having trouble cracking it. While she couldn't risk making phone calls inside the White House with it, the SMS messages did seem secure.

"So, Dick Whittner is back at work, eh?" Briggs asked.

"How did you..." Emily began. "Never mind, General, you were always two steps ahead of everyone else in this town."

"Word is the CoS is battling stage-four cancer. Colon or stomach or something. Being treated over in Baltimore at some private-care facility," Briggs offered as they sat on the deck overlooking the small marina.

Emily ordered a Diet Coke from the server, and the general tapped the side of his nearly empty tumbler. They waited until they were alone again before speaking.

"He's shutting SCET down. I think that's all he came in for."

"Means you are ruffling some feathers, maybe finally getting close to the truth. They're scared, Emily. Now might be the time to push even harder."

General Briggs hadn't asked her much in the way of details about her task force, but Emily felt sure he was well-informed. The man knew secrets she couldn't even begin to fathom. In D.C., secrets were currency, and Briggs knew exactly when and where to spend that currency. While officially retired, the scuttlebutt was he was running a counter-terrorism unit out of Baltimore, probably out of Fort Meade.

"Do you have a plan?"

Emily relaxed a little as she contemplated her next move. "I can keep most of my people active; I just won't be able to meet with them like we were. Most likely, Whittner will keep me buried in busywork until he figures out how to get rid of me or discredit me... or both."

"You do know how the game is played, don't you?"

They took their drinks. "Sandy," he said to the young server, "please have Chef Taylor make us a couple of those wonderful club sandwiches and add some of those house pickles."

Emily hadn't realized it, but she was starving. Briggs knew her better than she wanted to admit.

"I'm glad I didn't hear you say anything about following your boss's orders."

"I'm not here to play politics, General. POTUS is being kept in the dark, and the nation—possibly the entire world—is under threat, very possibly from extraterrestrials. Top that with a rogue element possibly embedded within the government and military whose sole mandate seems to be keeping all of it secret. I've lost two key scientists already, and no one seems to give a good goddamn."

The general gave a little laugh. His whole body shook as he took a quick sip of his bourbon. "Damn, you remind me so much of your dad when you talk like that."

He wiped at the corners of his mouth. Emily knew the man well enough to see that he was trying to reach a decision about something.

"In your opinion, Emily, what is the actual level of this threat?"

"Very high, potentially catastrophic," Emily answered immediately. She was not an alarmist and rarely took the worst-case scenarios as being the most likely, but the circumstances they had uncovered all pointed to this scenario.

"I think you are right, Emily, and I think it's time disclosure actually meant something real up on the hill. Stay the course, and let me see if I can get you anything helpful. But first, let's enjoy the rest of our lunch."

Markets Rally on 'National Resilience' — Dow Jumps 1,200 Points

"In an astonishing display of investor confidence, the Dow closed up 1,200 points today, despite three unexplained power outages in New York City and reports of orbital debris impacting military installations off both coasts.

"Economists say the rally is driven by record defense contracts and technology stocks—particularly firms tied to 'critical infrastructure rebuild' grants. No announcement has been made on whether this includes underwater city-protection walls.

"The Treasury called it 'proof that American ingenuity shines brightest under pressure,' while critics note that half the data servers feeding the market are currently offline. Global markets have mixed reactions—Tokyo is closed for emergency drills, and Frankfurt reports a mysterious 2-hour internet blackout."

Economic Policy Podcast August 03

CHAPTER EIGHTY-FOUR

1602 UTC
38°04′N, 77°16′W
Observers Detention Facility
Virginia, USA

Emma's pulse quickened as she followed Gibson through the sterile corridors of the NovaCore research facility. The heightened security measures—armed guards, biometric scanners, and reinforced doors—only amplified her growing unease. Gibson's demeanor had shifted from guarded to downright cold, his responses clipped and evasive.

As they walked deeper into the facility, Emma couldn't shake the feeling that something sinister lurked beneath the polished surface. The curious glances from staff and the hushed conversations that stopped abruptly as they passed only fueled her suspicions.

Gibson led her into a dimly lit observation room with displays showing a series of small rooms. This didn't look like anything else she had seen at any NovaCore facility. For that matter, the NovaCore logo wasn't on anything. The black-clad men wore a simple pitchfork-looking symbol.

"Wait with them until I send for you, Emma." Gibson pointed to the two imposing men before walking out.

Emma scanned the room. It was a typical-looking security office, although it had a lot more screens. She sat in one of the swivel chairs and began to spin in circles. The two guards watched her with leering expressions before eventually losing interest.

Her eyes widened as she took in the sight of people in orange jumpsuits on the screens, their faces etched with fear and despair. The realization hit her like a punch to the gut—these weren't just research subjects; they looked more like prisoners.

She picked up snippets of conversation from two guards speaking in hushed tones. "What do you think he's here to do?"

The other one shrugged. "Question D77 again, probably. He seems to have a hard-on for that one."

Emma's heart pounded in her chest as the implications sank in. NovaCore wasn't just conducting research; they were actively detaining people against their will. The thought made her stomach churn, and she knew she couldn't ignore what she was learning. She moved the cursor and began pulling up camera views on the screen she was sitting at. Searching the controls menu, she found the option she wanted.

Several levels below where Emma sat, Laura's eyes opened reluctantly. She groaned as she regained consciousness, the cold, hard floor pressing against her cheek. She eventually opened both eyes, blinking away the disorientation in the unrelenting brightness of the overhead lights.

What had awakened her was a sound. Something metallic. A sound that she had heard many times now and one that filled her with dread: the lock of her cell door releasing. She looked fearfully toward the opening. The door stood slightly ajar, but no tormentor was standing there this time.

She slowly rose to her feet, every muscle aching from the previous night's interrogation. Her fingers brushed the edge of the door cautiously. It creaked open further, revealing a dimly lit corridor beyond.

Laura's confusion and fear were fast turning into curiosity. This had to be a test; they were toying with her, but maybe this was her chance to find answers and perhaps a way out. She cautiously stepped farther into the hallway, her senses heightened, listening for any sign of approaching footsteps.

She moved quickly but quietly down the corridor until she spotted another open cell door. Inside, a man sat on a cot, his head in his hands. She was shocked that despite his frail appearance, she recognized him—his picture was in her notes on the UFO encounters.

"Paul," she whispered urgently, stepping into his cell.

He looked up, eyes widening in surprise and relief. "Hello," the man said weakly. They were both in the orange jumpsuits. "How did you get out?"

Laura explained to him the last few minutes before asking him if he could walk.

"Maybe," he said, getting up gingerly.

Together they looked in the adjacent cells, finding a small man who only spoke French or something close. He was very fit but seemed delirious. In two other cells, they found an older woman and a large black man, both of whom appeared to be drugged.

"Let's see if we can get out of here," Laura suggested.

Laura and Paul tried the steel door blocking their path, but it remained solidly locked, unyielding to their desperate attempts to force it open. Laura turned to Paul, her brow furrowed with concern. "Do you have any idea where we are?" she asked, hoping for some clue or insight.

Paul shook his head, his expression mirroring her own frustration and confusion. "I'm sorry, I don't," he admitted, his voice strained. "They've kept me drugged most of the time, and when I was conscious, they had me blindfolded during transport. I don't even know what year it is."

Laura sighed, running a hand through her disheveled hair. She glanced back at the other prisoners they had discovered, their conditions a testament to the cruelty of their captors. The French-speaking man continued to mutter incoherently, while the older woman and the large black man remained in their drug-induced stupors.

"We need to find another way out," Laura said, determination seeping into her voice. She refused to let this setback defeat her, not when she had already given up. "There has to be an alternative route or some weakness in their security."

Paul nodded and looked around, scanning the corridor for any potential leads or clues they might have missed.

As they stood there, the weight of their predicament bearing down on them, a faint sound caught Laura's attention. It was the distant hum of machinery, barely audible over the oppressive silence of the facility. She tilted her head, straining to pinpoint its source.

"Do you hear that?" she asked Paul, her eyes narrowing in concentration.

Paul listened intently, his brow furrowed. After a moment, he nodded. "Yeah, I hear it, too. It sounds like some kind of generator or maybe the ventilation system."

They followed the sounds, communicating with the small European man mainly through gestures. He was very fit and, coming to his senses somewhat, scrambled up a wall to glance out a high window. He turned back and shook his head.

"Probably just a mechanical room, no exit," Paul said. He then turned and looked at Laura. "How did you know my name?"

She gave a grim smile. "It's a long story," she answered. "But it looks like we have time for it." They were out of their cells, but they weren't getting any closer to freedom today. Still, just having someone else to talk to felt like a sort of freedom.

Emma's heart raced as she watched the silent exchange between Laura and Paul on the monitor, their desperation palpable even through the grainy footage. A mix of emotions filled her, the weight of their predicament pressing heavily on her conscience. These weren't terrorists. That much was obvious.

Driven by an obsessive need to uncover the truth, Emma's fingers flew across the keyboard, searching for any way to unlock additional cells and aid in their escape. The urgency of the situation fueled her determination, knowing that every second counted. Gibson could come back at any moment. The display screen was quickly flashing from one section to the next.

Just as she managed to unlock another door, the sound of the monitoring room's entrance sliding open shattered her concentration.

Emma's head snapped up, her eyes locking with Gibson's as he stepped inside, his face rigid with furious anger.

Gibson approached her, his footsteps echoing in the tense silence. "What do you think you're doing, Emma?" he asked, his voice low and menacing. "You're meddling in matters far beyond your understanding."

Emma's heart pounded in her chest, adrenaline spiking as she realized the gravity of being caught. Gibson's thinly veiled threats hung in the air, the consequences of her actions suddenly all too real.

"I... I was just..." Emma stammered, her voice trembling as she tried to find an explanation. "Who are they?"

Gibson's attention shifted to the monitor. Emma followed his gaze, momentarily caught up in the fear and shock of the revelation. She hadn't noticed the other screens until now. On one, an image of an apparently dead alien lingered there ominously.

As the weight of her discovery settled upon her, Emma knew that the danger she faced was now more immediate than ever. "Does my dad know about any of this?"

Gibson laughed, coming to a decision. "Who do you think sent me here?" He motioned to the two guards. "Holding cell. Now, you morons."

The men who'd been mostly trying to ignore her before Gibson came in now roughly pulled Emma to her feet and manhandled her out the door. Now NovaCore's second in command had two problems to get rid of—three if he included Owen King.

CHAPTER EIGHTY-FIVE

2057 EST August 05
Private Residence
Washington, D.C., USA

Trent Rogers leaned in close to Natalie, his heart pounding as he gazed into her captivating eyes. The growing sexual energy between them was obvious, a delicate dance of unspoken desires and hesitation. Natalie felt herself drawn to him, the magnetic pull of their connection growing stronger with each passing second.

As Trent's hand gently brushed against hers, a shiver ran down Natalie's spine. The air crackled with electricity, the promise of a passionate encounter hanging in the balance. She tilted her head, her lips parting slightly, inviting him to close the distance between them.

But just as Trent leaned in, his breath hot against her skin, he suddenly pulled back. Natalie blinked, her confusion evident as she searched his eyes for an explanation. The moment had been perfect, the chemistry undeniable, yet something fundamental had shifted in Trent's demeanor.

"Natalie, I..." Trent stammered, his voice tinged with an unfamiliar nervousness. He ran a hand through his hair, his gaze darting around the room as if searching for the right words. "I...I can't...there's something I need you to know."

“If you say ‘it’s not you, it’s me,’ I swear I’ll shoot you in the balls. Let me guess...you’re married? How many kids?”

“It’s D.C., no one is married here and no...no children.”

Natalie furrowed her brow, sensing that Trent's unease wasn't solely due to their near-romantic encounter. She reached out, placing a comforting hand on his arm. "What is it, Trent? You can talk to me." It wasn't like she had been giving mixed signals. She wanted this man... now!

Trent took a deep breath, his shoulders sagging under the weight of his words. "Natalie, you're in danger. I've lost two members of the task force already. Your friend, the reporter, is missing, and you have been followed."

"I know all that already, Trent. What has that got to do with this... with us?"

He flushed red and quickly glanced around. "I can't get distracted, and getting any closer to you emotionally..."

He trailed off, and she actually did get it. "Could put your mission in jeopardy," she finished for him.

"Would...not could," he said. "I’m doing all I can to stay professional and objective around you, but honestly, I can't. I want more, and that is dangerous. Also, I once cried during a grocery store commercial, so I may not be the steely-eyed operator you think I am."

"Okay," she said, disappointed. "Tell me more about what you said —I'm in danger?" Natalie asked, her voice barely above a whisper. "What's going on, Trent?"

He leaned in close, his voice low and urgent. "It's about your investigation, Natalie. The people you're looking into, the secrets you guys are uncovering... they're not going to let you continue without consequences."

Natalie's mind raced, piecing together the implications of Trent's words. She had always known that her pursuit of the truth came with risks, but hearing it from Trent made it all too real. Just like Laura, she was beginning to understand what they were up against.

"How do you know this?" Natalie asked, her voice trembling slightly. "What aren't you telling me, Trent?"

His gaze locked with hers. "I'd rather not say."

"Not an option, Agent!"

He seemed to want to look anywhere other than at Natalie right now. "Because someone in my chain of command has... well, I've been tasked with stopping you, Natalie." He paused to lock eyes with her.

"But I can't do it. I won't. I care about you too much to let them hurt you."

Natalie drew back in disbelief. She knew Trent was agency, but hell, that could still be nearly anyone. "What truth is it that's making everyone so nervous?" Her tone was neither angry nor sad, which surprised even her.

Trent shook his head. "I wish I knew. I think it has something to do with someone within the White House. Someone who very much does not want the task force to succeed."

"Whittner? The chief of staff? Emily indicated he'd been trying to shut down the task force. And when he failed, someone needed to take more direct action," Natalie said, mainly talking to herself. "Did your people take out Elena or Thomas? Do you know where Laura is or who has her?"

Natalie's wrath was coming on strong, and Trent put up his hand, feigning innocence. "No, I swear, I had nothing to do with it and had no idea my group might be part of the problem until yesterday."

His eyes dropped down to see Natalie's hand was no longer on his, and she had shifted several inches away. "Something about Whittner seemed to set it all in motion, though."

Trent's nervous energy made him get up from the sofa and refill his wine glass. "This will cost me my career if you repeat it, but I was part of a team that did a security sweep of his home. He's not doing well... you know. Well, we also put a surveillance package in his house. Before we left, I left a device to clone his phone the next time he recharged it. It looks just like his normal charger—standard agency stuff."

"You did what?" she asked incredulously. "You bugged the chief of staff's house and phone?"

Trent shrugged. "It's our job, Natalie." He took a few steps toward the window. "Not exactly a legal part. Anyway, there were a number of messages there to a local number, all very cryptic but obviously focused on your group. I mean, our group."

"Who was it?"

"That's just it. No one ever said. When I saw the transcripts of calls and texts later, that number wasn't even listed, nor were the messages."

"But you ran it anyway?" Natalie said with a hint of a smile.

"Not me, not through the agency, but I have a friend... an off-the-books friend."

She refilled her own glass, now more interested in where this conversation was going than the possibility of sex or rage.

"And?"

"Comes up as a local businessman. Name is Owen King."

"Owen King," Natalie repeated. "Why does that sound familiar?"

"He's the CEO of a company called NovaCore Technologies. Not a terribly large organization, but a key supplier in defense contracts. Also, he's a very eligible Washington bachelor—widower, actually—and occasionally shows up in the society pages."

Natalie shook her head. "I don't read that garbage. That's not it, but I came across it recently. Hang on." She slipped her laptop out of her bag and opened it up. Trent watched as her fingers danced across the keys. "Running a search," she said distractedly.

"Ah... okay, yeah. Trident Tactical Services, which is a subsidiary of Alcon Industries."

"Not following," Trent said. "Although I have been briefed on Trident before."

Natalie kept searching. "I used an AI program to help backtrack corporate timelines. My friend, Laura, was investigating Trident, and I had the AI search all property records, investors, tax filings—everything to try and nail down specific locations. In one of these, a lease appeared on some office space that indicated the owner was an Owen King."

"And you remembered that obscure bit of intel?" Trent said, impressed.

"Details matter, Rogers. And hey, I'm an investigator, too—not just another pretty face."

"Oh, but it is an incredibly pretty face," he said, leaning down and kissing her, surprising them both.

"What else does Laura know?" Trent asked.

Natalie shook her head. "That's the thing. I don't know. Since she is now missing, her file dump might be all we ever have."

"So NovaCore is...?" he asked.

"I think NovaCore is likely our mythical Special Projects Group. These are some of the conspirators we've been hunting, Trent. And if they've been controlling Whittner and whomever is in your agency's command structure, they could have assets everywhere. We need to pick King up."

Trent shook his head. "If you're right—and I'm beginning to believe you are—they'll never let us anywhere close."

"There is another problem," Natalie said, sighing. "I'm not sure there's anyone we could ask for help."

"I think I may know someone," Trent offered before leaning close and kissing Natalie again. *Distractions be damned*, he thought.

CHAPTER EIGHTY-SIX

38°52′N, 77°03′W
Strategic Military Command Center
Alexandria, Virginia, USA

Trent paced the length of General Briggs' private office while Natalie spread documents across his desk. The afternoon sun cast long shadows through the Venetian blinds, striping the room with bars of light and dark.

Briggs turned on a small device before turning his chair back to the two. "So, you're telling me this defense contractor—NovaCore—is orchestrating a massive conspiracy to conceal extraterrestrial contact while simultaneously profiting from reverse-engineered alien technology?" Briggs leaned back in his chair, his weathered face betraying neither belief nor dismissal.

"Yes, sir. A defense contractor with more secrets than a CIA company picnic. That is exactly what we're saying," Trent replied, stopping his pacing to face the general.

"The connections are pretty obvious. Natalie's reporter friend from the post traced financial transactions linking Trident Tactical Services and Alcon back to NovaCore. They've been quietly acquiring small tech firms that suddenly produce revolutionary advancements without explainable R&D processes. Most of these subsidiaries operate independently, so while it looks like NovaCore is still a minor player in the U.S. Defense Industrial Base, in truth, collectively they are one of the largest defense contractors in the world."

Briggs thumbed through the documents, his expression hardening. "This is compelling, but not convincing. You've got circumstantial connections and suspicions. I need hard evidence before I can take action against a company with these kinds of military and political connections."

"We understand that, sir," Natalie said. "That's why we need your help. With your clearance and resources, we could access the information needed to build a solid case."

Briggs set the documents down and fixed them with a penetrating stare. "Why aren't you taking this to Emily Carter? This is precisely what SCET was established to investigate."

Trent and Natalie exchanged uneasy glances.

"Sir, we're concerned about operational security," Trent said. "If NovaCore has infiltrated government agencies as deeply as we suspect, Emily could be under surveillance or even in danger if she authorized us to go after Owen King."

Natalie pointed to Laura's interview with the congressional aide. "You likely know of Congressman Paul Switzer from Indiana. Did you read any of the aide's answers to Laura's questions?"

Briggs nodded. "Yes, I know the asshole. Always front and center on the House side echoing Senator Reynolds' conspiracy theories. Yet your reporter says he is part of it?"

"Laura's feeling is that this runs deep through the entire government, military, and possibly the media. We needed someone we could trust implicitly," Natalie added. "Someone whose loyalty to Emily is unquestionable, but who operates with enough independence to move without drawing attention."

Briggs stood up, walking to the window. "Emily Carter is like a daughter to me. If what you're suggesting is true, she's in danger, and so is this country." He turned back to face them. "I'll help you, but we do this my way. And at the first opportunity where it's safe, we bring Emily in. Are we clear?"

"Crystal clear, sir," Trent nodded.

Briggs drummed his fingers on the desk, his brow furrowed in concentration. "What about hard evidence? If we're going to move against an organization this powerful, we need something concrete."

Trent leaned against the wall, arms crossed. "We could try to gather intelligence covertly, but it would be time-consuming. And there's no way to do it without involving others in the agency." His expression darkened. "Others that I have very good reason not to trust." He glanced at Natalie defensively.

"What about legal channels?" Briggs asked.

Natalie shook her head. "We could attempt to get a warrant, but that's assuming they don't own the judges, too." She pulled out a folder and opened it on the desk. "Look at these dismissals of numerous FOIA requests related to contracts with NovaCore subsidiaries. Different judges, different jurisdictions, but virtually identical language in the rulings. That's not coincidence—that's coordination."

"So we're looking at a presidential order," Briggs concluded. "Emily might be the only one able to secure that."

"Might being the operative word," Trent said.

Briggs swore, the expletive sharp in the quiet room. "Emily's star in the White House seems to be dimming at the moment. She's undoubtedly being undermined from within."

Natalie tapped an image of Owen King. "If we're right about this man and his connections, he wouldn't just sit back and let Emily investigate. He'd work to neutralize her."

"So we're stuck between impossible options," Briggs muttered.

"Not necessarily," Trent said, straightening. "What if we create a situation where Owen King reveals himself? If we can provoke him into action—"

"You want to use yourselves as bait?" Briggs interrupted, his voice sharp with concern.

"Not exactly," Natalie replied, a determined glint in her eyes. "But we need to change the playing field. They're expecting us to follow procedure, to work within a system they've already compromised. What if we don't?"

Briggs studied them both for a long moment. "You're talking about going outside official channels completely."

"I'm talking about a military solution, sir. About doing whatever it takes to protect this country," Trent said. "Isn't that what we all signed up for?"

The general mulled this over for several seconds. "The Posse Comitatus Act prevents me from legally doing anything resembling law enforcement on U.S. soil," he stood and walked to the window, looking out toward the Capitol, "that is without the president's specific authorization and only then, it is limited to wartime or a national emergency."

"You're retired, General, at least officially," Natalie suggested.

General Briggs stared out the window, watching the bustle of Washington, D.C. unfold beneath him. The chatter of political machinations and national concerns filtered into his mind, but his focus remained fixed on the potential implications of Trent and Natalie's proposal. His covert elite task force, a blend of active-duty soldiers and former special operators, operated in a gray area that allowed them wide flexibility beyond standard military constraints. Yet even for him, taking action against a U.S. defense contractor—especially one as powerful as NovaCore—felt perilously close to crossing an uncharted line.

He shook his head slightly, dismissing the thought. "We can't operate outside the law," he muttered under his breath. "This is dangerous territory. We risk actions that would likely have me judged even harsher than anyone at NovaCore."

Natalie and Trent stood silent behind him, their anticipation palpable. They could sense the weight of his decision hanging in the air, a tension thick enough to cut with a knife.

"I understand your concern," Natalie finally said, her voice steady. "But if Owen King is orchestrating a cover-up of this magnitude, we can't afford to wait for bureaucratic wheels to turn."

Briggs turned back to face them. "You both know how sensitive this situation is. We are dealing with national security here." He let the words linger before continuing. "A direct assault on NovaCore would not only raise alarms but could jeopardize everything we've worked for."

Trent stepped forward, determination shining in his eyes. "General, with all due respect, if the rumors are true, and you have an elite team at your disposal, then you can navigate these waters better than anyone else in this city. We need to be proactive if we want any chance at exposing this conspiracy."

"Let me ask you," Briggs said. "How do you know I'm not complicit? Maybe I'm a NovaCore plant."

The two looked at each other and shook their heads. "We don't," Natalie said honestly. "Emily trusts you, and we trust her. If we're wrong, we will probably both be dead within hours."

The general felt a pang of admiration for their resolve; it mirrored what he once felt in combat—the drive to confront danger head-on rather than wait for it to strike first. But confronting a company like NovaCore posed a different kind of battlefield—one fraught with legal repercussions and political fallout.

Briggs leaned back against the desk, steepling his fingers as he considered their argument. The capabilities of his task force gave him unique leverage; they were well-trained professionals accustomed to operating in environments where traditional rules did not apply. They could gather intelligence without raising suspicion or perform actions that regular military units would never be cleared to undertake.

Still, even within those operational parameters, there existed moral lines he had never crossed before.

"Let's poke the sleeping bear," he suggested cautiously, testing their reaction as he spoke aloud a half-formed thought that had begun taking shape in his mind.

As they formulated plans around tables strewn with papers detailing past UFO encounters and evidence against NovaCore's clandestine activities—a light bulb flickered dimly over General Briggs' head; maybe there was a way forward after all that didn't require sacrificing principle or protocol entirely...

His resolve strengthened quietly within himself while allowing them space to discuss strategies ahead—the nature of calculated risks bound tightly together by unspoken alliances forged through urgency over survival—all centered around protecting truths still waiting desperately beneath layers built up over decades...

CHAPTER EIGHTY-SEVEN

0903 EST August 06
White House West Wing
Washington, D.C., USA

"There is something else," Emily said softly after another long session. "Officially, this committee is shutting down."

"Shutting down?" Kaden's voice cracked with disbelief. "That can't be right. We've barely started. Well, I guess the apocalypse is now on a budget."

Natalie's jaw clenched, her eyes narrowing. "Who's behind this?"

The room erupted with overlapping questions; the tension palpable as committee members rose from their seats. Colonel Walker slammed his palm against the table, silencing everyone.

"Enough! Let Emily speak."

Emily raised her hands, waiting for the commotion to settle. "The directive came from higher up, but I understand it's not from the president." Her voice remained steady despite the storm brewing in her eyes. "I spoke with President Martin directly this morning. He was... surprised to hear about the shutdown order."

"Then who?" Trent asked, his expression darkening.

"I am not at liberty to say, but it's no secret we've had our share of detractors—from the national security advisor, Pentagon, and even the vice president." Emily's gaze swept across the room. "They're claiming resource allocation issues and a need to focus on 'verifiable threats' rather than, and I quote, 'chasing phantoms and conspiracy theories.'"

Dr. Kim shook his head. "After the KEW attack we just saw? That's absurd."

"So, is the reason that there was no presidential address?" someone else asked.

"It's deliberate obstruction," Natalie said, her voice cold with certainty. "Someone doesn't want us connecting these dots." She looked at Trent. He could volunteer who on his side was pulling the strings, but she knew he wouldn't.

"The president didn't overrule them?" Kaden asked. He'd wanted to let everyone know what he'd learned in California, but now that seemed unnecessary.

Emily's expression hardened. "I think he's being politically outmaneuvered. They're framing this as the president indulging in fringe theories while ignoring immediate national security concerns."

"So, that's it? We just... stop?" Alana's voice trembled with barely contained fury.

"No," Emily said firmly. "That's not what I said. I said officially this committee is shutting down. Officially."

Understanding dawned across the faces around the table.

"We're going dark," Colonel Walker stated—not a question, but a confirmation.

Emily nodded once. "The president can't openly support us right now, but he made it clear that our work must continue. Just not through official channels and not within these walls. I'll get word to you as soon as we have a new space."

"I can probably provide that," Walker said. "Some of our admin installations have secure space."

"Thank you, but no," Emily said. "No offense, Colonel, but I want to have separation between SCET and any possible enemies that might interfere with our work. We value your input, and you are a vital part of this group. That appreciation does not extend to your full branch of the service. Nor yours, Trent. Nor even my own."

She continued, "I understand the pressure we are all under—the attacks both personal and professional. They have hurt us; they have taken away some of our friends and colleagues. But we are not standing down. This is a battle worth fighting."

CHAPTER EIGHTY-EIGHT

1712 UTC August 08
National Harbor Yacht Club
Maryland, USA

The sun dipped low in the sky, casting a golden hue over the Potomac River as Emily Carter settled into the familiar confines of General Briggs' yacht. The sleek craft glided smoothly through the water, its hull cutting a clean line against the gentle waves.

"Remember when we first took this out?" Briggs asked, a smile tugging at his lips as he adjusted the sails. The wind caught the fabric, filling it like a great white wing.

"Of course," Emily replied, her voice warm with nostalgia. "You made me hoist the sails while you shouted directions like a drill sergeant."

Briggs chuckled, eyes sparkling with mischief. "You needed to learn! And as I recall, you hoisted a sail backward. I stand by my yelling. Seriously, Em, you never know when you'll need to commandeer a boat in an emergency."

She laughed. "Let's hope not. That was years ago."

As they passed Fort Washington Marina on their right, Emily let her gaze drift to the shore. The fort loomed like a sentinel over the river, its historical significance weighing heavily in her mind. She turned back to Briggs, whose expression remained focused yet distant.

"Okay, Bill, why'd you invite me out here?" she asked, trying to sound casual but unable to hide her curiosity.

Briggs tightened his grip on the wheel, navigating around a bend. "I wanted to give you some space away from everything at the White House," he said carefully. "You've been under a lot of pressure lately."

Emily sighed. "Pressure doesn't begin to cover it." The memories of tense meetings and hushed conversations flooded back—her investigation into UFO sightings and the continued lack of answers on her brother's mysterious disappearance only adding fuel to her anxiety.

They continued downriver toward Occoquan Bay, with the water reflecting shades of orange and pink as twilight descended.

"Something feels off about all of this," she confessed, glancing at him sideways. "I don't understand why things seem to be escalating so quickly."

"Things have changed." He paused for a moment, seemingly searching for words that wouldn't send them spiraling deeper into uncertainty. "There are forces at play that we're not entirely aware of."

Emily studied him closely as they motored past lush, green banks flanking both sides of the river. His demeanor suggested he carried burdens she couldn't fathom.

"What do you mean?" she pressed gently.

Briggs looked ahead, squinting against the fading light as if searching for answers on the horizon. "There's more happening than what's been publicly reported—especially regarding those UFO sightings and government actions surrounding them."

She furrowed her brow, trying to connect dots that felt scattered and vague. "You can't just drop hints like that without elaborating."

"Just... trust me on this one," he said softly but firmly.

The silence that followed buzzed with tension as they glided toward Occoquan Bay—a calm spot tucked away from the prying eyes and relentless surveillance of D.C.

Once anchored near a small inlet where they could drop lines securely to keep from drifting away in the current, Briggs relaxed his posture against the stern railings and gestured for Emily to join him at his side.

"Take a look," he said.

She stepped closer to him, leaning against the rail as he pointed toward land where fireflies flickered among dense foliage lining the riverbank.

"It's beautiful here," Emily admitted quietly. The tranquility washed over her like balm for wounds still raw from constant vigilance in D.C.

"You needed this break." His voice softened again as he added more seriously: "And soon enough, we will need our wits about us."

Her heart raced slightly at his words—the weight behind them resonated too deeply given recent events. She considered their shared history; there had always been an underlying bond forged through trust and shared experiences that sometimes felt thicker than blood.

"What are you saying?" she asked finally.

Briggs turned toward her fully now, gaze steady but grave beneath half-furrowed brows. "Whatever's coming next is bigger than any one person or organization," he warned solemnly before glancing away toward open waters that stretched infinitely beyond their small haven.

The evening air shifted slightly between them—a subtle acknowledgment that whatever lay ahead would require not just individual strength but unity among all of them.

Quietly, he took a device from a bag Emily recognized as an eavesdropping scanner. The general ran it over every inch of the boat before rejoining her, where he added a second device that emitted a slight hum.

"Signal blocker," she guessed.

He nodded.

Briggs pulled a weathered manila folder from his jacket and laid it flat on the polished wooden table between them. The papers inside were meticulously arranged, some with official stamps and others with handwritten notes in the margins.

"NovaCore Technologies," he said, tapping the top document. "They've been operating since the late 90s, but their real influence began after 2001. Military contracts, advanced weapons systems, and specialized communications infrastructure."

Emily leaned forward, examining the documents. Financial records showed massive government payments, organizational charts revealed connections to countless subsidiaries and deep links to intelligence agencies and every branch of the military, and satellite images displayed heavily guarded facilities in remote locations.

"They're everywhere," Briggs continued. "Virginia, Nevada, Alaska, and overseas operations we can't even track. But the pattern is clear—wherever there's been a UFO incident with physical evidence, NovaCore or Trident or Diamond or some other subsidiary personnel arrive before official investigators."

Emily's brow furrowed as she studied a photograph of Owen King, NovaCore's enigmatic CEO. "I've seen this man before. At the White House Christmas party last year. He was with Pete Cavanaugh."

"Of course he was," Briggs said. "Cavanaugh may have been their executive-level government shield for years."

Emily shook her head, processing the implications. "It makes sense. The cover-ups, the disinformation, the attacks on our committee members... but it's hard to believe a private corporation could wield this much power."

"Not just a corporation," Briggs corrected. "Think of them as a cult with government contracts, trillions in profits, and alien technology. They may have been assembling this group since Roswell. This is your Special Projects Group."

She pushed the papers back toward him, her mind already calculating next steps. "We'll need presidential authorization for direct action. Search warrants, asset freezes, detention orders for King and his leadership team. With Martin's signature—"

Briggs poured amber bourbon into two small glasses, handed one to Emily, and took a long sip from his own. His gaze drifted to the dancing fireflies along the shoreline, their intermittent lights reflecting in the dark water like distant stars.

After a moment of contemplation, he slowly shook his head. "No," he said quietly. "Martin can't know about this yet."

"Why not?" Emily demanded, setting her untouched drink down. "He's the president. We need his authority."

Briggs turned to face her, his expression grave. "Because we don't know how deep this goes or who else is compromised. NovaCore has had decades to embed themselves in our government. If we move officially, they'll see us coming."

Emily stared out at the water, watching the last light of day fade across the Potomac. The weight of Briggs' words settled between them like an anchor. After nearly three decades of friendship, she recognized the resolve in his eyes—the same determination she'd seen when he'd mentored her through her early career, when he'd supported her after Paul's disappearance.

She reached across the polished deck table and placed her hand gently on his forearm. "Bill, this isn't your fight," she said softly. The irony wasn't lost on her—how many times had he said similar words to her? "This doesn't need to be your hill."

Briggs looked down at her hand, then back up at her face. The lines around his eyes deepened.

"They'll destroy you," Emily continued. "Even if we manage to bring King in, nothing you find would stand up in court. Not without proper warrants, chain of custody, all the procedures we've spent our careers supporting."

The bourbon in Briggs' glass caught the fading light as he swirled it absently. "You think I don't know that?"

"I know you do. That's what worries me." Emily withdrew her hand and leaned back. "Best case scenario, it's a career ender. More likely, it's a military trial and lengthy prison time—for you and any of your top officers that go along with your orders. For what? To expose a truth no one wants to hear?"

Briggs set his glass down with deliberate care. "I'm at the age where my pension outlives my ambition. Besides, some truths need to be heard, Emily. Regardless of the cost."

"And who pays that cost?" Emily challenged. "Your family? The men and women who serve under you? The institutions we've both sworn to protect?"

A night bird called from somewhere along the shoreline. The sound hung in the air between them. Briggs glanced down at the signal blocker that still had a green LED glowing steadily.

"I've been in this game too long," Briggs said. "I've watched good people die because of secrets that should never have been kept. Your brother—"

"Don't," Emily cut him off sharply. "Don't use Paul to justify this."

Briggs' expression softened. "I'm not justifying anything. I'm just saying there comes a point when following the rules becomes its own kind of betrayal. Careers be damned, Emily. I'm an old man, and this is important. If we hit fast, we can shut this down. With King in custody and talking, the president will back the play. He'll retroactively sign the orders."

Emily looked away, unable to meet Briggs' gaze. She understood his position all too well—the same restlessness burned inside her. But unlike Briggs, she still believed in working within the system, even a flawed one.

"There has to be another way," she whispered, trying to convince herself more than him.

"Emily, I ran out of 'other ways' two wars ago."

CHAPTER EIGHTY-NINE

2007 EST August 10
Private Estate
McLean, Virginia, USA

Owen King pulled into the circular driveway of his McLean estate, the tires of his Bentley crunching over imported Italian gravel. The Georgian-style mansion loomed before him, its limestone façade glowing amber in the setting sun. Three acres of meticulously landscaped grounds surrounded the property, ensuring privacy from even his closest neighbors—tech billionaires, foreign diplomats, and fellow defense contractors.

"Emma?" he called as he entered through the grand foyer, his voice echoing off the twenty-foot coffered ceilings. The chandelier above—Swarovski crystal, custom-designed—cast prismatic patterns across marble floors imported from a quarry in Carrara.

His footsteps resonated through the silent house as he moved past the formal living room with its hand-knotted Persian rugs and antique Steinway grand piano. The built-in bookshelves housed first editions behind bulletproof glass—not that Emma had ever shown interest in them.

"Emma?" he called again, his voice taking on an edge.

The kitchen—all Sub-Zero appliances and Calacatta gold countertops—stood empty. No signs of afternoon snacks or homework spread across the island. Owen checked his watch and frowned. She should have been home hours ago.

A cold wave of panic crashed through him. Had A044 taken her? The aliens had made their position clear during their encounter—humanity was deemed non-essential, a failed experiment to be terminated. Had they started with his daughter?

Owen rushed up the curved staircase, taking the steps two at a time. "Emma!" he shouted, his composure cracking. He burst into her bedroom—finding it exactly as it always was. Her laptop was missing, but her bed remained neatly made, her collection of vintage vinyl records untouched on their custom shelves.

He pulled out his phone with trembling fingers and called her number. It went straight to voicemail. He tried again. Same result.

Owen braced himself against the doorframe, forcing himself to breathe. No, he reasoned, if A044 wanted Emma, they could have taken her in the desert or really, at any point. The senior species had demonstrated capabilities far beyond his comprehension. They wouldn't need to be secretive about it.

He remembered she'd stopped by NovaCore that afternoon—a routine visit. She often hung out at the company after school, using the state-of-the-art facilities or chatting with employees, many of whom she'd known since childhood. But she always texted when she had plans to be late.

"Teenagers," he muttered, trying to calm himself. Probably just being rebellious, asserting her independence. That had to be it. But as he wandered back downstairs to his study, doubt crept in. He poured himself three fingers of 30-year-old Macallan and sank into his leather chair.

The whiskey burned his throat but did nothing to erase the images A044 had planted in his mind during their last meeting. Cities reduced to ash. Oceans being restocked with... with something. The systematic dismantling of human civilization—not with Hollywood explosions and drama, but with cold, clinical efficiency. And those mechanical sentries; God, he hoped and prayed that vision of those abominations was false.

And he had helped them. For decades, the Observers had maintained the secret, allowing the aliens to study humanity while profiting from scraps of their technology. Owen had convinced himself they were shepherding mankind toward a glorious future among the stars.

What a fool he'd been.

He stared at the family photo on his desk—Emma at twelve, before her mother passed, leaving them nothing but each other. Before that, he'd kept his job at arm's length, never acknowledging the true reasons NovaCore existed. Then he'd shaken up the leadership, brought in Gibson, who quickly pushed them to diversify and to set up their own security force.

Owen drained his glass and set it down with a heavy thud. If A044 hadn't taken Emma, then where was she? And more importantly, would there even be a world left for her to grow up in?

Owen poured his fourth glass of whiskey, the amber liquid sloshing over the rim as his hand trembled. The crystal decanter clinked against the tumbler, a sharp sound cutting through the oppressive silence of the empty house. His eyes burned from staring at his phone, willing it to ring.

He dialed Emma's number again. The same familiar voice greeted him.

"This is Emma. Leave a message if it's important. If it's Dad, I'm fine, just busy."

"Emma, please." His voice cracked. "Just call me back. Whatever's going on, just let me know you're safe. Okay?" The whiskey had loosened his tongue, stripped away the calculated control he maintained in boardrooms and government briefings. "Just tell me you're safe, honey."

He ended the call and checked the security system for the hundredth time. No alarms triggered. The cameras showed nothing unusual—just darkness and the occasional fox prowling the perimeter. He'd called her friends, her school, even her favorite coffee shop. Nothing.

Gibson hadn't answered either. That was unusual, but not unprecedented, especially after hours. The man often went dark when handling sensitive operations. But tonight, the silence felt ominous. He briefly thought of calling Groves, their director of security, but he wasn't ready to turn that wolf loose on it yet.

"Damn it," Owen muttered, stumbling to the window. The lights of other mansions dotted the landscape, their occupants oblivious to what was coming. He pressed his forehead against the cool glass. How many of those homes would still be standing in a year? A month? Hell, a week?

He shuffled back to the sofa, his expensive Italian loafers dragging across the hardwood. The leather cushions received him with a soft hiss as he collapsed. The room spun slightly, the bookshelves and artwork blurring together.

Owen lifted his phone again, squinting at the bright screen. 2:17 AM. No messages. No calls. He dialed Emma's number once more, listening to the rings with diminishing hope.

"Emma," he slurred into the voicemail. "I've made mistakes. So many mistakes. But you were never one of them. You need to know that."

The phone slipped from his fingers, landing on his chest. His eyelids grew heavy, the whiskey finally overpowering his anxiety. As consciousness faded, images flickered behind his closed eyes—A044's inhuman presence, the clinical way it had dismissed humanity's worth, Emma's face when she was five and he'd missed her ballet recital, the way Gibson had looked at him when they'd discussed 'neutralizing' threats.

In his dreams, Owen stood in a vast desert, the sand beneath his feet not yellow but gray like ash. The sky above burned red, and massive structures—not buildings, but something else, something alien—rose from the horizon. A mechanical sentinel approached, its movements precise and inhuman. It extended an appendage toward him, and Owen tried to run but found himself paralyzed.

"You facilitated this," it said in A044's voice. "You prepared the way."

"Where's Emma?" he screamed, but no sound emerged.

The sentinel gestured, and Emma appeared, suspended in the air, her eyes open but unseeing.

"Non-essential," the sentinel pronounced.

Owen jolted awake, gasping, sweat soaking through his expensive dress shirt. The phone slid from his chest onto the floor with a clatter.

Sunlight streamed through the windows, harsh and unforgiving. His mouth tasted foul, his head pounded, and for a moment, he couldn't remember why he'd been drinking.

Then it all came rushing back. Emma. A044. The end of everything.

The sight of sunlight cutting through a skylight above finally registered in his fog-riddled mind. He grabbed his phone from the floor. 7:43 AM. No messages. No calls.

Emma hadn't come home.

Owen King slammed his office door behind him, the weight of dread pressing down like an iron shroud. He paced the polished floor, hands trembling as he ran through his options. The pit in his stomach churned with every passing moment.

"Call the police," he muttered, glancing at his phone again, desperate for a sign. No calls, no messages—nothing but silence echoed back. He shook his head; involving law enforcement could bring unwanted scrutiny to NovaCore.

Then it hit him like a lightning bolt—he didn't need the cops. He had resources. One of the departments within NovaCore specialized in tracking cell phone activity for security purposes. In fact, they even sold the tech to various security agencies. They could trace Emma's last location, maybe even her recent interactions.

He rushed down the four levels to the section of the underground facility, each step fueled by panic and determination. The sterile hallways buzzed with the low hum of technology, but all he could focus on was Emma's absence.

Eventually reaching the right department, he burst through the door, breathless and frantic.

"Get me everything you have on my daughter's phone," he barked at the startled technician. "Last known location, any activity—now!"

The technician blinked, never having met the boss in person but quickly nodded and checked the number on King's phone, fingers flying over keys as Owen's heart raced. Time was slipping away, and he needed answers before it was too late.

Minutes later, Owen King stared at the screen. Then he said quietly, "Track this other number as well."

Back in his office, King asked his secretary to summon Groves immediately.

Nearly twenty minutes later, Daniel Groves strode into Owen King's office with the silent confidence of a predator. His black tactical pants and fitted shirt seemed to absorb the light around him, making his broad shoulders and muscular frame appear even more imposing. A thin scar traced his jawline, barely visible unless you knew to look for it.

Owen hated how small the man made him feel in his own office. He'd hired Groves specifically for his intimidation factor, but being on the receiving end of that cold, calculating gaze never got easier.

Groves didn't wait for an invitation. He settled onto the leather sofa, legs spread wide, claiming the space as if it were his own. His eyes—pale blue and utterly devoid of warmth—scanned Owen's unshaven face, taking in the disheveled appearance, the obvious signs of a hangover.

"Gibson took my daughter Emma yesterday," Owen said, struggling to keep his voice steady. "Do you know where they went?"

Groves didn't immediately respond. He leaned back, resting one arm along the back of the sofa, studying Owen with the detached curiosity of someone examining an insect under glass.

"Interesting," he said, the word hanging in the air between them.

"Interesting?" Owen's voice rose. "My daughter is missing, and that's your response?"

Groves tilted his head slightly. "Gibson doesn't make unauthorized moves. You know that."

"This wasn't authorized," Owen snapped, slamming his palm on the desk. "I would never—"

"Wouldn't you?" Groves interrupted, his voice calm but edged with steel. "If Emma discovered something she shouldn't have? If she became a liability?"

The blood drained from Owen's face. "She's my daughter."

"And this is your company." Groves gestured around them. "Built on secrets that would destroy you both if exposed."

Owen felt sick. "I want her found. Now."

Groves stood, fluid and graceful despite his size. "I'll look into it. But King—" he paused at the door, "—if Gibson did take her to the detention facility, there might be a reason. A reason you gave him, perhaps due to your recent encounter?"

"The detention center? What encounter and what are you implying?"

"None of the rest of us have talked directly to them." Groves shrugged, gesturing skyward. "And you've been under considerable stress lately."

"What? Do you think I am under alien control or something? This is my daughter, for God's sake. Just get out! I'll deal with Gibson myself."

As the door closed behind Groves, Owen collapsed into his chair. Had he possibly caused this? Had he shown weakness or compliance where Gibson expected to see defiance? His second in command was driven, that was damn sure, and yes, Owen admitted he indulged his daughter, but she was all the family he had.

Gibson would have taken her if he thought King was about to throw it all away. He knew the bastard knew how to use leverage. Hell, that was most of his job. He also knew Gibson had no problem eliminating problems.

The thought was unbearable, but not impossible. And that terrified him more than anything A044 had shown him. He picked up his phone. "Nancy, have my car brought around—I'm heading out for the day." First, he had to find the location of his own detention center; he'd flown there twice but couldn't even recall what state it was in.

Owen King moved across the polished marble lobby, his footsteps echoing in the cavernous space. Floor-to-ceiling windows revealed his gleaming black Bentley waiting under the covered entrance, morning sunlight glinting off its perfect finish.

A prickling sensation crawled up his spine. He glanced back and paused mid-step—Daniel Groves stood motionless in a darkened hallway, watching him with those pale, predatory eyes. The man didn't even attempt to hide his surveillance, his muscular frame half-concealed in shadow like some nightmare creature not quite willing to step into the light.

King's pulse quickened. He diverted toward the reception desk, maintaining his practiced executive composure despite the sweat beading at his hairline.

"Good morning, Mr. King," the receptionist said, her professional smile faltering slightly at his disheveled appearance.

"Morning, Jessica." He leaned casually against the counter. "Could you touch base with Nancy? I need my schedule cleared for the day. Family emergency."

"Of course, sir. Right away."

While she reached for her phone, Owen slipped his hand into his pocket and found his key fob. Without looking down, he pressed the remote start button, feeling the slight resistance give way under his thumb.

The Bentley's headlights flashed once, twice. The engine purred to life, a distant, expensive hum. Nothing bad happened, and King let out a breath he hadn't known he'd been holding.

Jessica was speaking again. "Nancy says she'll reschedule your ten o'clock with Senator Brooks and—"

Owen glanced back toward the hallway. Groves was gone.

His stomach tightened. Where had he—

The world exploded.

The Bentley erupted in a blinding flash, a fireball expanding outward with terrifying speed. The blast wave hit the lobby windows like a giant's fist, shattering the reinforced glass into a million deadly shards that flew inward with hurricane force.

Owen dove behind the reception desk, dragging Jessica down with him as glass, metal, and concrete debris tore through the space where they'd been standing seconds before. The sound came a microsecond later—not just a boom but a physical force that compressed his lungs and set his ears ringing.

Alarms wailed. Sprinklers hissed to life, raining down water that mixed with the dust and smoke now filling the lobby. Through the gaping hole where the entrance had been, Owen could see the twisted, burning chassis of what had been his half-million-dollar car. The covered entrance had partially collapsed, concrete chunks scattered across the circular driveway like discarded toys.

"Oh, my God," Jessica sobbed beside him, blood trickling from a cut on her forehead. "Oh, my God."

Owen pulled himself up, his designer suit torn and soaked. Three security guards rushed into the lobby, weapons drawn, shouting orders that he couldn't hear through the high-pitched whine in his ears.

He'd been meant to be in that car. The bomb must have been set on a time delay after ignition. His eyes darted around the chaos, searching for Groves. The man was nowhere to be seen.

Had Groves planted the bomb? Or had he been warning Owen by watching him, keeping him from leaving? Either way, the message was clear—someone at NovaCore wanted him dead.

Emma. If they were coming for him, his daughter was in even greater danger. Owen stumbled toward one of the security guards, grabbing the man's arm. "Lock down the building," he shouted, barely able to hear his own voice. "No one in or out."

The guard nodded, speaking into his radio.

Owen glanced once more at the burning wreckage outside. A044 had promised humanity's end, but it seemed someone wanted to finish Owen King first.

As he made it to the stairs, he saw his security force assembling and realized the truth. Groves and Gibson were taking over. He raced up the stairs to his office.

CHAPTER NINETY

2007 EST August 11
Axxor Technology Park
McLean, Virginia, USA

Around the large table covered in maps and blueprints of the NovaCore complex, Natalie, Agent Rogers, General Briggs, and his tactical team leaders gathered. The table was cluttered with markers, schematics, and hastily scribbled notes. They'd been over the plan countless times during the night.

General Briggs leaned over the table, his stern face illuminated by the harsh overhead lights. "Listen up," he began, tapping a pointer against a detailed blueprint of the NovaCore headquarters. "This must be a precision operation. Our objective is to extract Owen King. We have little reliable intel, but satellite coverage indicates he should still be there."

He paused, scanning the faces around the table. "Team Alpha will secure the main entrance and provide cover. Bravo will take the southern approach through the maintenance tunnels. Delta, you'll infiltrate through the roof access points." His eyes locked onto each team leader as he spoke.

Natalie exchanged a glance with Trent. She saw her own determination reflected in his eyes. They had been preparing for this moment for only a few days, and she was still nervous. This wasn't her skill, but she wanted to be in on it. It felt like she had to be.

"Remember," Natalie added, "King is our primary target. We extract him alive. Any data on NovaCore's alien technology and operations is secondary but could be crucial. This mission is a bust if he winds up KIA."

Ninety minutes later, the tactical teams moved in with eerie silence, their footsteps muffled by the lush greenery surrounding NovaCore's imposing structure. Natalie, alongside Trent, supervised as the units split into their designated positions. Team Alpha took point at the main entrance, while Bravo slipped towards the maintenance tunnels. Delta vanished into the rooftops, their ascent aided by grappling hooks.

"Teams in position," a low, steady voice crackled over the comms device in Natalie's ear.

As Trent moved up with a female lieutenant named Garcia and approached the building, the acrid smell of burnt metal and gasoline hit them. A car, now a charred, smoldering husk, occupied a charred space near the front entrance. The once-polished finish had melted, resembling molten lava.

"What happened here?" Trent murmured, eyeing the destruction.

The lieutenant's gaze swept the area, her hand resting on the grip of her pistol. "Looks like our welcoming committee has got trust issues. Keep sharp."

Natalie was held back at the rear command station, a decision that didn't sit well with her. She paced, frustration growing with each passing second, until her blackphone buzzed. The caller ID read 'Owen King.' Her eyebrows shot up in surprise.

"Hello," she answered, voice low.

"Ms. Reeves, I... I need your help. I know you are looking for me; this is Owen King. I'm being held captive inside my own offices."

"Who is holding you, King?" she asked as she signaled all assault teams to hold position.

"Trident Security... they've turned on me."

"You're now a prisoner of your own security force, and you want us to come save you?" Her tone was incredulous, bordering on outright humor.

"I can explain later, but yes. My second in command took my daughter captive. I tried to leave, to come turn myself in, and my head of security blew up my car and driver.

"He... Groves is in charge here now. He's... ruthless. You must get me out, but be warned, it won't be easy. Ms. Reeves, I say this with complete honesty. The fate of the world depends on this. You must win; you must know what I know." Owen's voice was laced with desperation.

Natalie's grip on the phone tightened. "Mr. King, I—"

The line went dead.

"Trent, we have a situation," Natalie called out, already moving towards the executive entrance. "Owen King just reached out. He's being held captive inside by Trident Security, led by a man named Groves, in the executive offices."

Trent nodded curtly, his team awaiting his signal near the main entrance. "Roger that. My team will secure the lower floors, clear a path for you. You focus on extracting King."

With a sharp nod, Natalie followed them as they moved towards the executive entrance, her own smaller team following closely. She knew it was not going to be easy.

The simultaneous flash of muzzle fire and the high-pitched whine of the plasma rifles illuminated the dim corridor. It looked like a sci-fi movie, but it was all too real and deadly.

"Get down!" Natalie dove for cover, dragging one of her men with her as a volley of plasma rounds fired from the Trident forces ricocheted off the walls.

Lieutenant Garcia, eyes wide, pulled the pin on a flashbang. With a sharp toss, it landed amidst the approaching Trident troops. A concussive blast and disorienting flash momentarily stunned them.

"Now!" Natalie sprang up, firing her pistol in controlled bursts.

The elite tactical team followed suit, their suppressed weapons barking, adding to the cacophony of gunfire. Smoke filled the air as the team advanced, firing as they moved.

The Trident troops, momentarily disoriented, fell back, seeking cover from the onslaught.

The major running this operation's voice crackled over the comms. "We're taking heavy fire! Those damn energy weapons are cutting through our armor like butter. Casualties are mounting!"

Trent, his face grim, fired around a corner, covering Natalie's advance. "Don't stop! We have to push through!"

The wall next to Natalie exploded in a shower of sparks as a plasma bolt ricocheted off the metal frame. She ducked, feeling the heat wash over her.

"Frag out!" Garcia shouted, lobbing a grenade down the hall.

The blast sent a Trident soldier flying backwards, his armor charred and smoking.

"Keep moving!" Natalie shouted. "We have to reach King!"

A Trident soldier, wielding a plasma rifle, stepped into view. With a sharp hiss, he fired, the energy bolt searing past Natalie's face. She fired back, her bullets punching holes in his chest.

The team pushed forward through the smoke and chaos. Another Trident soldier loomed ahead, his rifle trained on them. Garcia fired first, her bullets ripping into his armor.

They cleared the hallway, bodies littering the floor, the acrid smell of gunfire and burning flesh filling the air.

"We're getting there!" Trent shouted, checking the schematic on his phone. "King's office is on the top floor!"

Trent charged forward, his gun firing in short, controlled bursts, taking down Trident soldiers with improving accuracy. Suddenly, a figure emerged from the smoke-filled corridor—Daniel Groves, his eyes locked onto Trent with an unnerving intensity.

"You picked the wrong day to play hero," Groves sneered, his voice low and menacing.

Without warning, Groves fired his sidearm, the plasma round gouging a deep furrow in Trent's side. Trent's eyes widened as he stumbled, his rifle dropping from his hand. Groves seized the opportunity, rushing forward and unleashing a devastating kick that connected with the side of Trent's knee. The sound of shattering bone filled the air as Trent crumpled to the ground, his face contorted in agony.

Natalie's vision blurred for a moment, her heart racing with horror. She whipped around, taking in the carnage around her. Most of her team lay motionless, either dead or severely injured. The weight of their sacrifice hit her like a sledgehammer.

All of this... just to get to one man? The thought echoed in her mind as she locked eyes with Groves. Her grip on her pistol tightened, finger hovering over the trigger.

"You're a monster," she spat, her voice trembling with rage and grief.

Groves chuckled, his expression unyielding. "I'm just a man who gets the job done, Ms. Reeves. And my job today is to ensure Owen King never leaves this building alive."

With a swift motion, Groves raised his sidearm, training it on Natalie. She stood momentarily frozen but dove as she caught a flicker of movement.

The frag grenade went off just behind Groves, who was literally launched over Trent's body into the middle of the corridor. He had his gun up and trained back on Natalie even as he rolled across the floor.

Natalie's ears were ringing, and she was having trouble locating her own rifle, but her eyes settled again on the black-clad man. Then she realized he was pulling the trigger. The only problem was nothing happened. His weapon was dead, obviously damaged in the blast.

She dove onto one of the plasma rifles nearby and came up, finger on the small nub she assumed was the trigger. Trent was moaning, and Groves was placing his gun on the floor with a smirk still pasted on his face. Her round bore a charred hole right through it.

CHAPTER NINETY-ONE

1227 EST August 12
NovaCore Offices
McLean, Virginia, USA

"We might have been able to get useful intel from him," Trent said as the team medic dressed his wounds.

"Groves was a dick," Natalie stated. "He was just like the people that came after me after my encounter in the Navy. Fuck him. We are about to go upstairs and take his boss down."

"Why did King call you, and how?"

"He said he wanted to come in. He thought I was the one person he could definitely trust to keep him alive. I guess having one of your own security chiefs try to murder you puts things in perspective," Natalie said.

Owen King stood defiantly in his luxurious office, the cityscape sprawled behind him through the massive windows. The calm he exuded seemed almost surreal given the chaos unfolding around him. As the door swung open, armed agents flanked by Natalie Reeves moved in efficiently, their faces set with determination.

King barely flinched, his expression one of mild annoyance. "You're Reeves?"

She nodded.

"Thank you for setting this up, but is this really necessary?" He adjusted his cufflinks as if preparing for a board meeting rather than an arrest.

Natalie stepped forward, her blue eyes blazing with anger. "Necessary? You have no idea what you've done, do you?"

King raised an eyebrow, a smirk playing on his lips. "Oh, Natalie, no need for the drama. Things got a bit out of hand, but I'm sure with your help we can clear it up."

She moved closer until she was mere inches from his face. "A misunderstanding? People are dying out there because of you and your cronies. This isn't some corporate merger gone wrong—this is the end of the world as we know it!"

King's smirk didn't waver. "And yet here I am, still standing. That should tell you something about who really holds the power in this town."

Natalie's fist clenched at her side. "You think you're untouchable? Your own people tried to kill you. Your little house of shadows is crumbling, and you're too delusional to see it."

He went to speak, but she cut him off. "What? Let me guess, you want your lawyer."

King gave a muted laugh. "God, no. I'm not totally sure who I can trust right now, but it damn sure isn't them. Look, I called you. I have something to offer...a lot of somethings, actually. But I also have an ask, two in fact, and they are big. You want my cooperation, you have it. One of my asks is time-sensitive, though, and it will be of great interest to you as well as me."

"King, I am not too concerned with your wants, and I am holding a rifle."

King's eyes narrowed slightly as he looked at her with something approaching genuine interest for the first time. "You're awfully sure of yourself for someone who's spent their career chasing shadows."

"And you've spent yours hiding behind them," she shot back.

He shrugged nonchalantly. "Call it what you will. At the end of the day, it's all about survival."

Natalie's voice dropped to a whisper, laden with venom. "Survival is all you'll have left after today."

Agent Rogers appeared in the doorway on crutches and holding one hand over a bloodied bandage. "You should listen to her, King. She just took out your boy wonder downstairs."

As they escorted Owen King out of his office in handcuffs, despite his plea for cooperation, he walked with an air of arrogance that suggested he still believed himself untouchable. For Natalie and her team, though, this was just one step closer to uncovering the full scope of his treachery and bringing a measure of justice to all those who had suffered because of him.

Natalie watched as several ambulances took Trent and several others to the hospital. As the APC pulled up to take King, one of Briggs' soldiers handed her a satphone. "The general."

Briggs wasted no time. "Go with King; keep him alive. As soon as this gets out, a lot of people are going to be gunning for him. Hell, half of Congress will likely be lining the streets to take a shot."

"Sorry about your men, General, but thank you," Natalie said somberly, climbing into the armored vehicle. "Where are we headed? Where will we be safe?"

"Probably best you don't know for now. Here's Emily—I read her in. This line is secure."

"Natalie, it seems like you've had a busy day. Owen King does look like our man. Very good work. We have a team headed over to his offices now, and I am going to get the president to authorize the operation and a full sweep on all NovaCore holdings."

A medic had checked Owen King out to make sure he had no weapons, transmitters, or anything he could use to do harm to himself. The woman nodded as she zip-tied his arms to the gurney he was lying in.

"That your boss? The infamous Emily Carter?" King asked, still with that smug undertone. Natalie nodded reluctantly.

"I have a message for her."

"He wants to speak to you, Director. Are you okay with that?"

"He's not yet under arrest, is he?" Emily asked.

"No ma'am, still off the books per the general's directions." Emily told her to put him on.

Natalie held the phone to the side of King's face. Almost at once, the smugness was gone. Now he was a totally different person. "Ms. Carter, I know you have a lot of questions for me, and I have the answers you seek; however, I am looking for a deal. Presidential immunity before I talk, and I want your help recovering my daughter, Emma. My second-in-command took her hostage earlier today."

"Why would he have done that, and why on Earth do you think I would go to the president asking for immunity for you?"

"He did that for leverage. Gibson knew I would talk, knew I would make a deal. He wants to make sure I know what it will cost me if I do. As for the immunity, we will get to that soon enough. For now, though, I just need to stay alive. Here is a gift, call it an act of good faith. Someone in the president's inner circle is one of mine. He's been working against you from day one. I can give you access to a file that the attorney general will accept as indisputable evidence."

King rattled off an address to a Google Drive folder. "I'll offer the passcode when I am in your secure facility. These are trying times for all of us, Director Carter. Believe me when I say that the worst is still ahead, and what happens to me doesn't really matter in the long run. I would like to know that my daughter has a chance, though. If you help free her, this will be the first of many wins you will earn."

The medic was holding a syringe designed to knock Owen King out for the ride. Natalie took the phone back and nodded for her to give him the shot. The man's eyes closed at once.

"Director," Natalie said. She could hear Emily and General Briggs discussing what King had just said.

"Yes, Natalie, stay with him and keep him safe. We will have to handle our White House rodent problem. I give you four stars on your investigative ability."

"Thank you, ma'am. We've put him to sleep until we get where we're going. You're not actually going to give him the deal, are you?" Natalie's mind was considering the possibilities; this was spinning into something much larger than she was prepared for.

"Not my call, but probably, yeah. I understand he called you and warned you about what was waiting for your assault force."

Natalie confirmed that, although doing so made her frown in anger. She rubbed a hand down the sleek rifle she'd not yet relinquished. "They still chewed us to bits. The captain was killed, and about half the others were either killed or wounded."

"Well, it does indicate King might have been attempting to turn himself in. It will add weight to his desire to cooperate. See if you can find out where his daughter is being held and who this Gibson is. Get with General Briggs and come up with a plan. I think we best keep this close for now, as I have no idea whom we can trust. Assuming he is right about the National Security Advisor, POTUS is going to be relying on us more than ever."

"Roger that, ma'am."

General Briggs got back on the line. "Reeves, you get that code from King, and I'll be getting authorization to send a team into the White House to take whomever it is into custody. That action will likely set off a firestorm, the ripples of which you may encounter where you are headed."

"You can arrest a cabinet member or presidential advisor?" Natalie asked, surprised.

"Military authority is my only option. It's unusual to say the least, but it is allowed, particularly in times of national emergency. We'll run it by the AG later, but I want to have the bastard under lock and key before then. All the other nasty little bastards are going to be trying to find your man, though."

"I got that, sir, and..."

"I know, you need some help, some additional trigger pullers. I'm working on that as well. Listen, I know you aren't an interrogator."

"No, sir." She laughed. "Pretty bad at it, in fact."

"We'll try and get you one. Hopefully, Agent Rogers can get patched up and join you. He's damn good at it. Get whatever you can from King. He seems to trust you, and we need to know what he has to offer before anyone will consider his immunity. Time is not our friend, Reeves. You understand what I am saying?"

"Roger that, sir."

"And Lieutenant, don't let him out of your sight. I am locking down his access to you alone. Hope you are comfortable with that."

"Understood, sir." She fully recognized the implication of him using her former rank. He'd given her an order, one with several implications.

She disconnected and looked down at the man who had caused her and God knew how many others so much harm. She felt the weight of the pulse rifle and really had to resist the urge to do exactly what the general had just warned her others would want to do. This bastard had to pay for everything he'd done at some point.

CHAPTER NINETY-TWO

1057 EST August 14
Old Town Office Park
Alexandria, Virginia, USA

Kaden Trembley disconnected the call. "She worries too much," he muttered. Again, he hunched over the computer, his eyes straining against the glow of the screen in the dimly lit lab. He pored over the satellite data, searching for any anomalies that might support Elena's theory of opposing alien species. The silence was broken only by the hum of the equipment and the occasional creak of his chair.

He'd gone through his former student's files previously. Elena was a very disciplined researcher and routinely saved backups to her cloud server, which Kaden had accessed not long after her murder. Some of the findings seemed rather far-fetched to him, but the concepts were intriguing. He was especially taken by the possibility of competing alien species visiting Earth.

Now that he also had more information from Jasper, he needed to check some of Elena's findings again.

The computer screen flickered, and the satellite feed he'd been checking disappeared. Kaden frowned, tapping the keyboard in frustration. "Come on, don't do this to me now," he muttered under his breath. The internet connection was dropping out now as well.

As he worked to restore the connection, a pang of guilt washed over him. Being back in Elena's lab, surrounded by her research and personal effects, was a stark reminder of her untimely death. Kaden couldn't shake the feeling that he had failed her somehow—that if he had been more supportive of her work, things might have turned out differently.

Lost in thought, Kaden almost didn't notice the lights in the lab flickering. He glanced up, his brow furrowed in confusion. It wasn't just the lab—through the window, he could see the city lights blinking on and off like a faulty string of Christmas lights.

Kaden rose from his chair and made his way outside. As he stepped into the cool, night air, he was struck by an eerie silence. The usual buzz of the city was absent, replaced by a stillness that sent a chill down his spine.

He looked up at the night sky, expecting it to be clear with the streetlights now off. Instead, he saw distant flashes in the few clouds, like silent lightning. Kaden's mind tripped over the possibilities—could this be part of the alien threat? He dismissed that thought as apophenia or confirmation bias—the tendency to perceive connections or patterns between unrelated things.

Around him, people went about their evening, complaining about the electricity but seemingly oblivious to the strange phenomena occurring above their heads. Kaden felt a sense of unease wash over him, knowing that he might be the only one who understood the gravity of the situation.

Whittner was out on medical leave again, and Emily Carter barely had time to settle into her post when the summons came. The urgent call dragged her into the situation room, where tension crackled like static electricity. Advisors crowded around a large table, their voices a cacophony of panic and speculation. She wanted to ask what was going on, but very quickly, she understood.

"We're seeing power outages in New York, London, Tokyo—and

other major cities across the globe, including here," one advisor shouted over the din. "Cyberattacks, maybe? Or some kind of coordinated natural disaster?"

President Martin stood at the head of the table, his face showing a strained calm. He glanced at Emily as she entered, his eyes reflecting concern, if not a trace of annoyance.

"Emily, thoughts?" His voice cut through the chaos, commanding attention.

Emily scanned the room quickly before speaking. "I'll need a minute to get up to speed, but this doesn't sound like cyberattacks to me. Maybe not natural disasters either," she began, choosing her words carefully. "The scope is too large and simultaneous."

"Solar storm?" suggested the NSA man, leaning back in his chair with a shrug. "We've had those disrupt things before."

Emily's instincts screamed otherwise. Her gaze drifted to the air traffic monitor on the wall. Planes blipped off radar one by one like dying fireflies. She stiffened.

"Is that a live view?" she asked the young man who was accessing the various data screens.

"The air traffic monitor," she said, pointing it out to the room.

"Yes, ma'am," the technician said. "All current flights in observable airspace."

Heads turned to follow her gesture. The implications sank in like lead weights; planes going off radar could spell catastrophic consequences.

"How can this be happening all at once?" another advisor demanded, sweat beading on his forehead.

The lights flickered above them, casting brief shadows that danced ominously across worried faces. Deep under the White House, Emily's eyes were drawn to a display that mirrored one of the views from the West Wing overlooking Washington D.C., now a patchwork of light and shadow as blackouts spread block by block. They could hear sirens wailing in the distance—a haunting soundtrack to their escalating crisis.

"This isn't just an outage," Emily murmured to herself but loud enough for those nearby to hear.

President Martin's knuckles whitened as he gripped the edge of the table. "I need answers now, people," he ordered. "Mobilize National Guard if we need to. All emergency protocols are on the table, and issue statements to calm public fears."

"Calm public fears?" someone echoed, somewhat incredulously.

Emily watched as advisors scrambled into action, some barking orders into phones while others furiously typed on department laptops, trying to piece together fragmented information.

"Solar storm or something benign," stubbornly repeated Cavanaugh, as if saying it enough times would make it true.

Emily's gut twisted in knots. She knew they were on the precipice of something far more sinister than anyone else in this room was willing to admit.

President Martin massaged his forehead, trying to understand the reports that were coming in. Military leaders stood around him, determined to maintain their composure.

"Mr. President," General Taylor began, his voice steady, "we believe these power outages and satellite failures could be isolated incidents. We suggest calm. We don't need the public in a panic."

"What about all those flights?" Martin asked.

"No confirmation on flights, could be lost transponder signals," the general suggested, nodding to the secretary of transportation, who was flipping through papers.

"We are showing numerous GPS satellites dropping out. That could be due to a solar storm, as Mr. Cavanaugh suggested," the middle-aged woman said, although you could see she was unconvinced.

Linda Reyes, the no-nonsense Secretary of Homeland Security, spoke up for the first time. While her role and Cavanaugh's seemed to overlap, their focus was very different, and the resentment toward the advisor was evident. "DHS is more focused on response than causes, Mr. President." The dig was a barely disguised criticism of Cavanaugh's solar flare claim. "To that end, we are mobilizing relief supplies already, but it is obvious that's not going to be enough. Coordination is going to be impossible if we don't get the cellular and GPS networks working reliably, especially in the more remote areas."

As the conversations raged, Emily's official phone buzzed in her pocket. She was one of the few allowed to have a phone anywhere in the

White House, but especially here. She glanced at the screen: a text from Kaden Trembley. She read it quickly, her eyes narrowing.

"This isn't just a comms or power glitch," Kaden's message read. "Lights in the sky and too many other anomalies. Not sure we can ignore the obvious anymore, Emily. This may be the first wave of the next attack."

Emily's jaw tightened as she looked up at Pete Cavanaugh, the National Security Advisor. He caught her gaze and raised an eyebrow. Someone in this room was a traitor, and she was betting it was him.

"You've got something to add, Emily?" he asked, his tone dripping with condescension.

She took a deep breath. "Professor Trembley just contacted me. He's observing significant atmospheric anomalies that suggest this is far more than a simple glitch."

Pete scoffed, crossing his arms over his chest. "Who? That British crackpot that said all that crap years ago? He always thinks the sky is falling."

The tension in the room thickened as air traffic controllers reported entire fleets of planes now missing from radar. Gasps and murmurs rippled through the assembled advisors.

"We've lost contact with multiple military flights as well," one of the data control officers reported over the speakerphone, her voice tinged with barely contained panic.

Outside the situation room, chaos reigned in Washington D.C. Traffic lights were out, and cars honked angrily as drivers navigated intersections without guidance. The normally bustling streets were now a scene of confusion and mounting frustration.

"General Taylor," Emily stood and addressed the man. She'd made a decision, a potentially career-ending decision. "In modern warfare, what is the initial plan of attack?"

Everyone but the general's face went blank. He understood what the woman was getting at. "First, we know the enemy. We study their strengths, weaknesses, tactics, and positions. We gather as much information as possible before making any moves. Second, we disrupt communications; take out their comm networks—satellites, radios, and any means they have to coordinate their forces. If they can't talk, they can't fight effectively."

Emily nodded and pointed to the various monitors around the room. "Then what, General?"

"We would go after their leadership. We'd aim to eliminate or disrupt their command centers where decisions are made. Without leaders, enemy forces will be confused and less organized."

President Martin's face grew pale as he listened to the reports. He turned to General Taylor. "How do you explain entire fleets of planes disappearing from radar? Is that part of an attack plan, too?"

Taylor shifted uncomfortably but continued.

"Absolutely, sir. Establish air superiority, sir. Whomever holds the high ground controls the battle. That hasn't changed in thousands of years."

"So, you are also saying we are under attack? From whom?" the president demanded.

Emily seized the moment. "We need to acknowledge the worst-case possibilities of what is happening here," she said firmly, her eyes locked on Pete Cavanaugh's. "If we downplay this any further, and we are wrong, we risk losing control entirely."

Pete's expression hardened. "And what would you have us do? Announce to the world that we're under some sort of mysterious attack? From whom? The little green men your committee keeps trying to find?"

Emily stepped forward, her voice unwavering. "Mr. President, we need transparency and decisive action—"

Pete cut her off, his voice rising in frustration. "Decisive action based on what? A hunch from one of your washed-up lackeys?"

The room fell silent, all eyes on Emily and Pete as they squared off in their disagreement.

And there it was. Emily realized she had been set up to fail from the very beginning. Cavanaugh was right to some degree. Almost everyone she'd managed to get on the SCET team had come with baggage of some kind. Baggage that made them easy targets and easily discredited. It was more of the same from a system of denial she'd been adamant in taking down.

The tension was palpable as President Martin weighed their words, the fate of millions hanging in the balance while outside D.C., disarray grew by the minute with no one officially admitting a problem existed at all.

"Emily, would you mind giving us the room?" the president asked, and just like, that she was no longer a player in whatever this game was. She had indeed finally chosen her mountain, it seemed.

CHAPTER NINETY-THREE

1845 EDT August 16
Northeast Florida, USA

Nancy crept through the rows of tents, her heart pounding as she took in the grim reality of the rescue camp. It hadn't been in great shape, but now just a few days later, the once somewhat orderly rows had devolved into a haphazard maze of makeshift shelters, their inhabitants huddled together in fear and desperation. The stench of unwashed bodies mingled with the acrid tang of smoke from the few remaining fires.

As she turned a corner, Nancy froze. A group of men were gathered around a still form on the ground, hastily covering it with a tattered blanket. She caught a glimpse of a pale, lifeless hand before it disappeared beneath the fabric. Death had become a constant companion in the camp, and sadly, the sight of it no longer shocked her.

Somewhere up ahead, a scuffle broke out as two women grappled over a meager supply of food one of them had obviously hidden away for later. Their shouts and curses pierced the air, drawing the attention of the other survivors. Nancy watched as the fight escalated, the women trading blows and tearing at each other's hair. No one intervened; everyone was just too focused on their own survival.

Nancy's gaze drifted to the far end of the camp, where the aid workers' tents once stood. Now, mostly empty spaces remained, the tents long since abandoned. The disappearance of the majority of aid workers had been the final blow to the camp's morale. Without their assurances that more help was coming, the survivors had been left to fend for themselves in an increasingly hostile environment.

She knew that they couldn't stay here much longer. They needed to find a way out before the camp consumed them all.

As the afternoon sun dipped lower, Nancy clutched TJ and Lynn close as she surveyed the chaos unfolding around them. The once mostly safe haven of the aid camp had devolved into a powder keg of desperation and fear. She could feel the change in herself, a steely resolve replacing the helplessness that had plagued her since the disaster struck.

"We're getting out of here," she whispered to her children, her voice low but firm. "Tonight."

As she began gathering what meager supplies they had left, Luther's words echoed in her mind. "Trust your instincts," he had told her. "They'll keep you alive when everything else fails."

Nancy's instincts were screaming at her now, warning her that the camp was no longer even a temporary sanctuary but a death trap waiting to be sprung. The entire place felt like a pressure cooker waiting to explode. She watched as a group of men huddled together. One of them, everyone knew him as a troublemaker, seemed to be taking the lead. While their voices hushed, their intentions were clear in their furtive glances and clenched fists.

"Mommy, I'm scared," Lynn whimpered, clinging to Nancy's leg.

"It's okay, baby," Nancy soothed, running a hand through her daughter's tangled hair. "We're going to be fine. Just stay close to me."

As the sun began to set, casting long shadows across the camp, Nancy overheard another heated argument near the haphazard food line.

"There's not enough!" a woman shouted, her face contorted with anger and fear. "We can't keep sharing with everyone!"

"Who died and left you in charge?" a man snarled back, his hand inching toward something hidden beneath his jacket.

Nancy pulled her children behind a nearby tent, her heart rate spiking as she considered her plan. She knew it was only a matter of time before the situation here exploded into total violence. They had to leave now, while they still had a chance.

"Listen to me," she whispered to TJ and Lynn, kneeling down to meet their eyes. "We're going to play a little game. We need to be very, very quiet and follow Mommy, okay? Like we're sneaking past a sleeping bear."

The children nodded, their eyes wide with a mix of fear and excitement. Nancy took a deep breath, steeling herself for what lay ahead. She knew the risks, but staying put was simply no longer an option. With one last look at the camp that had been their temporary home, Nancy led her children toward the perimeter, praying that Luther's lessons would be enough to see them through the dangers that awaited.

As Nancy navigated the chaotic landscape of the camp, her heart pounded with every step. She couldn't shake the feeling that she was being watched. Through the thick underbrush, she knew the perimeter fence was just ahead, its barbed wire strung between pine trees—a stark reminder of the desperation that had brought them to this point.

Suddenly, a figure emerged from the shadows. It was the man she had spotted earlier, his eyes fixed on her with a predatory intensity. His face was a map of stubble and scars, and his lips twisted into a sneer that made Nancy's skin crawl. He was a tall, imposing figure, his commanding presence seeming to draw her in, making her feel small and vulnerable.

"Looks like you're trying to make a run for it," he drawled, his voice low and menacing. "I've been watching you. You're not too hard to look at, and I know exactly what you need."

His eyes seemed to bore into her soul, their leering stare making her feel like an animal caught in a trap. His gaze roved over her body, lingering on her children before returning to her face. "You're a feisty one, aren't you?" he sneered. "I like that."

Nancy tried to stand taller, to meet his gaze with defiance, but her heart was pulsing in her ears, and her legs felt like jelly. She knew she had to get away from him, to protect herself and her children from this monstrous figure.

The man took a step closer, his eyes never leaving hers. "You're coming with me," he said, his voice firm and commanding. "And you're going to do exactly as I say."

With her body going numb with fear, Nancy reached down and gripped her children's hands tightly, preparing for a desperate fight for their freedom.

The man's laugh echoed through the dimly lit woods—a harsh and grating sound that sent a shiver down Nancy's spine. His hands moved to his belt, unfastening it with a slow deliberation that made her stomach churn. He didn't care that TJ and Lynn were there, their small faces pale with fear and confusion. To him, they were just obstacles, inconsequential details in his twisted game.

"You're not going anywhere, sweetheart," he sneered, taking another step closer. The belt slipped from his pants, the metal buckle clinking ominously to the ground. "Not until we've had a little fun."

Nancy's heart pounded in her chest, her breath coming in short, desperate gasps. She looked around wildly, searching for any escape, any chance to save her children from this monster. The trees blocked an easy escape; the fence ahead towered and seemed unscalable. The only way out was past the man she suddenly remembered was called Hudson, and he wasn't about to let them go without a fight.

"Please," she begged, her voice barely a whisper. "Don't do this. Not in front of my kids."

Hudson chuckled, a cold and cruel sound. "Kids are resilient," he said, picking his belt up. "They'll get over it. Besides, it's not like they haven't seen worse already, right?"

He took another step forward, the belt now wrapped around his fist, a makeshift weapon ready to strike. He didn't care if she was conscious or not. Nancy could see the lust in his eyes, the sickening desire that had nothing to do with her and everything to do with his need for power and control.

"Oh, yeah...you're a fighter. I like that," he said, his voice low and menacing. "But you're outmatched here, sweetheart. You might as well give in and enjoy it. Just make it easier on yourself, and maybe I'll leave your kids alone."

She couldn't fight him, not with her kids here. She couldn't risk them getting hurt. But she couldn't give in either; she couldn't let this monster win. She had to find a way out, had to save her children from this nightmare.

He was close now, too close. She could smell the stale sweat on him, could see the stubble on his chin and the cruel gleam in his eyes. She had to do something, had to act fast. But what? What could she do against a man like this?

Her eyes darted around, searching for anything she could use as a weapon. But there was nothing—just trees, pine straw, and piles of trash. She was out of options, out of time. Hudson was right in front of her now, his breath hot on her face, his hand reaching out to grab her.

She had to act, had to do something. She couldn't let him win, couldn't let him hurt her children. She had to fight, had to find a way out of this nightmare. But how? How could she possibly hope to defeat a man like Hudson?

Her mind made up, Nancy took a deep breath, steeling herself for what was to come. She had to be strong, had to be brave. For her children, for herself. She had to fight.

Nancy swung, and Hudson caught her arm, twisted it, then slapped her to the ground. Both her children screamed. She lay there in one of the hundreds of the camp's trash heaps, desperate for a way out of this mess. Luther's words came to her again: *Anything can be a tool...or a weapon.*

Nancy's eyes locked onto Hudson, her mind filling with hate as she wiped blood from her mouth. Her other hand probed the pile of trash until it closed around one of the thousands of discarded cans inside the heap. The can was bent, but she felt the lid still partially attached—jagged and sharp. Her attacker was leaning down to haul her up. Without hesitation, she swung it up and toward him with all her might.

The impact was brutal. The can's jagged lid worked like a blade, slicing deep into Hudson's throat and causing him to stumble back in agony. Nancy didn't hesitate; she used the momentary lull to grab TJ and Lynn, pulling them close as she darted toward the fence.

Hudson, clutching his throat in a desperate attempt to stem the flow of blood, stumbled through the underbrush toward her. His eyes were wide with pain and rage, and he yelled a muted scream of gurgled fury, but he was no less determined to catch them. Nancy knew she had to act fast to get them away from the crazed man.

She was in full survival mode now, and as they raced the twenty or so yards to the barricade, her gaze fell on a fallen limb. She leaned down, grasped it firmly, and turned back at Hudson, who now staggered toward her, still holding his neck, blood gushing between his fingers in rhythmic spurts. She turned, jamming the limb under the bottom strands of the wire fence and pushing up as hard as she could.

For an instant, it seemed like nothing was happening—the wire twanging ominously with the added pressure but refusing to give way under her strength. Hudson's footsteps were getting closer now; he was almost upon them.

But then, in a burst of strength that surprised even herself, Nancy managed to make some headway against the thick wire of their prison. The limb groaned under pressure as she forced it higher against the wire's reluctance to bend or break.

As she pushed with all her might against this makeshift lever, the wire finally yielded as vines and debris released it. Nancy felt herself gain a tiny measure of hope as the wire rose five, then seven inches above the ground.

She urged TJ forward, using a foot to push him under. Then he reached back for his sister, Lynn, and pulled her through. Now Nancy had a problem, though—if she let go of the tree limb, the barbed wire would flatten again to the earth, blocking her exit. She was straining with all her might but couldn't see a solution. The gurgle of the man stumbling toward her quickly spurred her into action.

Nancy strained against the limb, managing to wedge it against a nearby tree. The wire held, for the moment, creating just enough space for her to scramble underneath. She could hear Hudson's labored breaths behind her, the sound of his stumbling footsteps crunching on fallen leaves. Panic surged through her as she wriggled her upper body through the tiny gap.

Just as she was halfway through to the other side, Hudson reached her. His boot lashed out, connecting with her makeshift lever. The limb snapped away, and the barbed wire came crashing down. The sharp metal barbs punctured deep into Nancy's skin, pinning her lower half inside the camp. She cried out in pain and desperation, feeling the sting of metal digging into flesh.

Hudson's face twisted into a blood-filled smile. He seemed almost to enjoy her agony as he grabbed onto the wire, starting to drag her back toward him. "Thought you could get away?" he gurgled, his voice raspy from the injury she had inflicted.

Nancy's eyes widened in terror as she clawed at the ground, trying to pull herself free. The barbs were carving deep grooves into her tortured flesh. Her hands scrabbled for purchase on anything that might help her escape, but there was nothing but loose dirt and pine needles.

The man said something incomprehensible, then sneered through his bloodied mouth.

The barbs tore even deeper into her legs as Hudson yanked on her body with brutal strength. She could feel her skin ripping and knew she was losing blood quickly. But she couldn't let him win; she couldn't let him take her children.

"Mommy!" TJ's voice broke through the chaos, filled with fear and helplessness.

Nancy's heart clenched at the sound of her son's voice. She couldn't give up now. With renewed determination, she pulled against the man's weakening grip again, ignoring the pain that shot through her body. She had to get to her children; she had to protect them.

Somehow Hudson recovered and lunged forward again, but Nancy was ready this time. She grabbed a rock from the ground and swung it at him with all her strength. The rock connected with his temple, causing him to stagger back once more.

"Run!" Nancy screamed at TJ and Lynn, hoping they would listen even as she fought for her own life.

Her children hesitated only for a moment before turning and running into the forest. Nancy observed them leave, feeling both glad and afraid. She had bought them some time, but now she had to find a way to free herself before Hudson recovered completely.

Her blood-soaked legs were still mostly inside the camp, but she, too, was losing strength quickly. She managed to free one leg and a foot only to feel Hudson's hands wrapping around her other ankle. "Why won't you die?" she screamed.

Then she heard something that scared her more than her own situation: the voices of her children coming back. She felt herself blacking out, giving up, then lying back she saw boots and a man's legs between the kids. All this had been for nothing.

She looked back through the fence at Hudson, expecting to see the man gloating over his prize. Instead, he had a look of shock as he dropped to his knees, his hands suddenly releasing her foot as his bloody hand clutched at the shaft of a spear protruding from his chest.

Nancy's eyes closed as Luther bent down and gently removed her injured legs from beneath the wire, then easily pulled her up into his arms. "It will be okay, Nancy Ramesh." TJ and Lynn followed him as he disappeared back into the woods.

CHAPTER
NINETY-FOUR

2018 EST August 24
Private Residence
Washington, D.C., USA

Trent was busy on the computer while Natalie got them both a beer. She wasn't sure where this thing with the handsome man was heading, but so far, she liked it.

His fingers flew across his laptop keyboard, his brow furrowed in concentration. Suddenly, he froze, tapping the refresh button repeatedly.

"Damn it," he muttered.

Natalie set the beer down beside him. "What's wrong?"

"I've lost connection to the agency VPN systems. Can't get back in."

She frowned, swiping at her own phone screen. "That's weird. My Internet's acting up, too."

Trent pulled out his phone, dialing quickly. "I need to call my boss." The line remained dead. He tried Emily Carter next, with the same result.

Natalie picked up a remote and clicked on the TV. A harried news anchor appeared mid-sentence: "...widespread reports of cyberattacks and power failures across..."

The screen went black.

"Trent," Natalie said slowly, "I don't think this is a coincidence. There have been too many strange incidents and sightings lately. UFOs all over the place."

He shook his head. "Let's not jump to conclusions, Natalie. It could be something simple or—"

"Or what?" she challenged. "Come on, let's get a better look."

They hurried to Natalie's balcony. The sprawling cityscape of D.C. stretched before them, lights twinkling in the dusk. Suddenly, an entire sector to their left plunged into darkness. The blackout spread rapidly, block by block. Then her own apartment went dark behind them.

"My God," Trent breathed.

People began pouring onto the streets below, their voices a confused murmur rising into the dark night. Faces turned skyward, searching for answers.

An eerie silence settled over the city. No sirens, no distant traffic hum. Just the whisper of wind and muffled conversations.

Natalie pointed. "Look. Over there, the Capitol and White House still have power."

Trent nodded grimly. "Emergency generators. Great. Targets with backup generators. Like a glow stick in a haunted house."

They stood in tense silence, watching as Washington D.C. was swallowed by shadows, leaving only two islands of light in a sea of darkness.

Miles away, Emily rushed through the darkened corridors beneath the White House, her heart pounding. The power flickered erratically, casting eerie shadows on the walls. Sirens that had been blaring outside suddenly fell silent, leaving an unsettling void. Here she had considered to be one of the safest places on Earth, but it was also one of the biggest targets.

Secret Service agents urged her to return to the secure lower levels, but Emily pushed past them, determined to reach the main floor. She needed answers, and she wouldn't find them hiding underground.

As she emerged into the grand foyer, Emily froze. Through the tall windows, she saw a city plunged into darkness. The usual glow of streetlights and illuminated monuments was conspicuously absent, replaced by an inky blackness that seemed to swallow everything.

The only movement came from a mass exodus of vehicles attempting to flee the city center. Headlights snaked slowly through the streets as panicked citizens tried to escape the growing chaos, finding the darkened streets little more than vehicle prisons.

Emily's gaze shifted to the White House perimeter, where Capitol Police and Park Police had positioned their cruisers and an armored personnel carrier to block the entrances and exits. Red and blue lights strobed across the grounds. The sight sent a chill down her spine, reminding her of the haunting stories from 9/11 when the nation's capital last faced a devastating attack.

Remembering Kaden's message, she scanned the sky, her breath caught in her throat. Strange lights danced on the horizon to the south, their movements too erratic and purposeful to be dismissed as mere aircraft. Deep down, she knew her suspicions had been right all along. The alien threat was real, and it was happening right before her eyes.

But convincing the skeptical officials within these walls would require more than gut instinct. Emily still needed hard evidence, something tangible to prove that this wasn't just another unexplained phenomenon. She had to find a way to gather that proof, even as the world around her descended into darkness and confusion. The idiots!

SCET had been attempting to do that for months but so far had little in the way of tangible facts if she was being honest. Pulling the lid off the cover-up seemed minor right now. If the country was under attack, did it matter who knew about it beforehand?

Behind her, the elevator doors swung open, and she was surprised to see General Taylor striding out.

"You get kicked out, too?"

He shook his head. "No. Those damn politicians can't get their collective dicks out of the mud long enough to think any of this through."

He placed a gentle hand on her folded arms. "I appreciate what you tried to do, Emily. Just like you said, the threat is real, no matter where it's coming from. We must be on a war footing now."

"You heading to the Pentagon?" she guessed.

He peered out the window at the gridlock and shrugged. "That was my intent, but it looks doubtful. I should be able to reach high command from the SCIF," he suggested, looking toward the secure conference room reserved for the most sensitive discussions, "assuming the hard-line connection is still up."

"What are they doing down there?" Emily asked.

Taylor gave a sad chuckle. "If you can believe it, they're getting ready to address the nation. Martin has his speechwriters trying to come up with something calming and placating."

"But we don't know anything yet."

Turning to walk away, the man said, "When has that ever stopped them?"

"Get in front of the story," Emily mumbled to herself. Political communications lesson number one. "Look presidential, look in charge of the situation." Totally fucking ridiculous.

CHAPTER NINETY-FIVE

0612 UTC August 24
20°00'N, 170°00'W
Pacific Ocean

USS Jefferson City (SSN-759) Operating 200 nautical miles forward of Carrier Strike Group

"Sonar, Conn. What's the contact classification on bearing 240?" Commander Jack Reynolds asked, leaning over the sonar operator's shoulder in the submarine's control room.

Petty Officer Martinez adjusted his headphones, frowning at the waterfall display. "Sir, it's not acoustic. I'm picking up magnetic anomalies through the towed array, but nothing that makes sense. No cavitation, no machinery noise... just this weird magnetic signature moving way too fast."

Reynolds studied the display. As the forward picket for the Roosevelt's strike group, Jefferson City was tasked with providing early warning and reconnaissance beyond the carrier's immediate defense envelope. With satellite coverage becoming patchy possibly due to ongoing solar storm activity, the submarine had become the group's primary long-range sensor.

"Chief of the Watch, bring us to periscope depth," Reynolds ordered. "Prepare to launch ALTAIR. Radio, prepare to transmit contact report to Roosevelt."

"Aye, sir. Coming to periscope depth."

The submarine rose quietly through the Pacific waters. At 60 feet, Reeves watched as his crew prepared the specialized Autonomous Tactical Low-Profile Air Intelligence Reconnaissance drone. The ALTAIR was designed specifically for situations like this—when submarines needed eyes above the surface without compromising their position.

"ALTAIR prepped for launch," reported the UAS operator. "Drone configured for electronic intelligence gathering and aerial reconnaissance."

"Launch ALTAIR. Get us above this jamming layer."

The small UAV ejected from the submarine's sail, its rotors immediately spinning to life as it climbed rapidly through the ocean air. Within minutes, it had ascended above the electronic interference, its sensors clearing.

"Contact!" the UAS operator called out, his voice tight with disbelief. "ALTAIR has multiple unidentified airborne contacts bearing 240 true, range 380 nautical miles."

Reynolds felt his gut tighten. In twelve years of submarine operations, nothing in his training had prepared him for this. The jamming itself was considered a hostile act. Inbound aircraft approaching the carrier strike group raised that threat even more.

"Classification?"

"Unknown, sir. ALTAIR's showing what looks like... well, anomalous behavior. Sir, they're not following any aerodynamic principles that I understand. They're changing direction without banking, accelerating without visible propulsion."

ALTAIR was incredibly advanced, but there was only so much equipment you could place in a unit that size. The control room fell silent except for the hum of electronics. Through ALTAIR's sensor feed, they watched the path's objects moving across the sky in ways that seemed to defy physics.

"How many contacts?"

"Initial count shows seven... no, make that twelve distinct objects. They're not in a typical formation but seem coordinated. Range now 320 nautical miles and closing fast."

Reynolds grabbed the communications handset. "Comms, do you have the TR yet?"

"Still trying sir!"

"Try harder, Mister Jones. Get me the Roosevelt CIC now. Priority Flash traffic."

"Aye, sir. Roosevelt CIC, this is Jefferson City. Priority Flash message follows."

Reynolds took the microphone, knowing his next words would change everything. "Roosevelt, this is Jefferson City. We have launched ALTAIR UAV and confirmed multiple unidentified airborne contacts bearing 240 true, range 320 nautical miles and closing at possible hypersonic speeds. Contacts exhibit flight characteristics beyond known aircraft capabilities. We are observing coordinated broad-spectrum electronic warfare. Recommend immediate alert status. Jefferson City out."

As ALTAIR continued its surveillance mission above, Reynolds watched the impossible objects streak across his airborne drone's sensor feed, each movement confirming that they were facing something entirely outside human experience.

USS Theodore Roosevelt - Combat Information Center

Captain Ed Warren received the submarine's report in the Combat Information Center of the USS Theodore Roosevelt, the blue-lit tactical displays casting shadows across the faces of his watch team. The CIC hummed with controlled activity—a stark contrast to the chaos that would soon follow. Warren knew the PriFly, or Primary Flight Control, would also be buzzing with similar activity as LaBlat's crew members spun up planes, communicated with pilots, and monitored the tactical situation.

"Admiral Mitchell to CIC," came the voice through the sound-powered phone system.

Warren picked up the handset. "Warren here, Ma'am."

"Captain, I just saw the reports from Jefferson City of unknown contacts in our operational area. What's your assessment?"

Rear Admiral Diane Mitchell, the Carrier Strike Group commander, had been monitoring the situation from her flag bridge. Warren knew she'd want to ensure his air package readiness status before making any tactical decisions.

"Yes, Ma'am. Something's also jamming our long-range communications. No comms with Naval command. Recommending we go to Condition II and get our CAP expanded. I want more eyes out there."

"Agreed. Make it happen."

Warren turned to his tactical action officer. "Commander Hayes, sound Modified General Quarters. Get the Hawkeye airborne and double our Combat Air Patrol.

The 1MC crackled to life: "Set Condition II throughout the ship. Modified General Quarters, Modified General Quarters. All hands man your battle stations."

"Sir, we've lost all comms to Washington," his watch commander reported to the CO, his fingers racing across the tactical display. "All secure channels are down."

"Damn it!" Warren muttered, watching the electronic warfare displays flicker with interference patterns he'd never seen before. Deep in the CIC, the atmosphere was thick with the weight of impending action. Warren called his executive officer who presumably was on the bridge, Commander Kelly McAllister. "Status on Carrier Strike Group Readiness?" This would normally be the CSG's role but the captain knew she already had her hands full. The XO would handle the specific logistical moves the strike group might need to make. If it came down to it, every other ship out there would be used to protect the carrier.

"Negative, Captain. All command channels are down, but we are able to use shortwave to stay in touch—for now."

Warren swore again under his breath, eyes narrowing. This level of electronic disruption wasn't accidental—it was a deliberate attack. He had witnessed electronic warfare in his day, but this was beyond anything he'd seen.

Up in PriFly above, Air Boss Lieutenant Commander Lablat was already coordinating the launch sequence. "Get me two more Super Hornets airborne," he barked into his headset. "And prep the Hawkeye for immediate launch."

The flight deck erupted into its familiar ballet of organized chaos. Yellow-shirted aircraft directors guided the F/A-18E/F Super Hornets into position while the massive E-2D Hawkeye, with its distinctive radar dome, was moved toward the catapults.

Back in CIC, Warren ordered contact with his Aegis Missile Cruiser which supplied primary air and missile defense. Despite its massive size, the USS Teddy Roosevelt was essentially just a floating airport. The USS Gettysburg, on the other hand, was equipped with the Aegis Combat System, which integrated powerful SPY-1 radar, fire control, and missile launch systems.

"Roosevelt, this is Alpha Whiskey on Gettysburg," came the voice of Commander Lisa Torres. "We're also tracking those intermittent radar contacts, but they're unlike anything in our databases. Fast-movers, bearing 165 true, approximately 262 nautical miles and closing fast."

"Speed?" Warren asked.

"That's the problem, sir. We're clocking Mach 16."

Warren's blood chilled. Nothing in their arsenal could effectively engage targets moving at hypersonic speeds—not reliably.

"Torres, this is Warren. We've lost contact with D.C. and most of the CSG command comms. What's your intel on these threats?"

"Negative on solid intel, sir. Before they were cut off, PacFleet was speculating some kind of systemwide cyberattack or even an EMP strike. But, sir...also some wild rumor from JSOC that this could be non-terrestrial."

Warren exchanged a grim look with Hayes, who was silently mouthing the words 'non-terrestrial' before responding. "Understood, Gettysburg. Maintain your defensive posture. We'll attempt to re-establish command and maintain air cover. Roosevelt out."

"Admiral Mitchell, recommend we need to go to General Quarters," Warren said through the sound-powered phone. "These contacts are moving too fast to be conventional aircraft."

"Concur. Do it. Captain, do you think this is China?"

The General Quarters alarm pierced the air: "General quarters, general quarters, all hands man your battle stations! This is not a drill."

“Unkown, ma’am. TAO Hayes indicates no but is unable to further classify. The flight characteristics are off the chart. The AW just relayed an unconfirmed report from JSOC.”

The admiral cut him off before he could say more. “Yes, I am aware of what is being whispered. All I want to know is how to bring the bastards down; whoever they are. Remember Warren, this is sovereign American territory out here. We either dominate this space, or we don’t control anywhere.

Warren watched his CIC transform as sailors moved with practiced precision to their combat stations. The Condition I posture put every system on the ship at maximum readiness.

"Air Boss to CIC," Lablat's voice crackled through the comm. "Hawkeye-1 is airborne and establishing radar picture. CAP reports visual contact bearing 180 true, range 200 miles.”

As Warren approached, Lablat reported, “We’ve got two CAPs airborne, sir—each equipped with F/A-18E/F Super Hornets. We’re prepping another group for launch. The E-2D Hawkeye is about to go up as well to give us better radar coverage.”

“Good. Let's also have the Growlers on Alert-5 standby,” Warren replied. “We’ll need them for electronic warfare. Whatever we’re dealing with, they’ve already compromised our systems.”

The EA-18G Growlers were equipped with advanced electronic warfare technology designed to disrupt, deceive, and degrade any enemy electronic systems. They carried AN/ALQ-218 receiver systems that could detect and locate electronic threats.

Moreover, the Growlers could carry the ALQ-99 jamming pods. These pods emitted a powerful signal that could interfere with enemy radar and communications, effectively blinding them and preventing an enemy from knowing anything other than what they could see directly.

"Get those birds up as soon as possible," Warren said firmly.

“Patching in our lead hornet, Donaldson is Rimfire-1. You need to hear what he is saying,” Lablat said just as the sound on the phone took on a faraway muted quality.

"Roosevelt actual, this is RimFire-1. We've got visual on the bogeys

—non-conventional propulsion system and designs, no visible markings. Looks basically like a dart with stubby wings, reflective upper surface, and some kind of blue light pulsing... like it's alive."

Warren exchanged a grim look with his tactical action officer. "Maintain visual contact. Do not engage unless fired upon," LaBlat ordered. "AW, take over flight command."

"Copy that, but sir..." the pilot said, "... these things are moving faster than anything we've ever clocked. We can't keep up. The damn thing just blinks off my scope and seems to reappear miles away in seconds."

On the Gettysburg, Commander Torres coordinated with the Hawkeye crew, her voice steady despite the unprecedented situation. "Roosevelt CIC, Alpha Whiskey. Recommend we prepare SM-6 missiles for engagement. Whatever these are, they're demonstrating hostile intent through their electronic warfare."

"Concur," Admiral Mitchell replied.

Warren eyed the flight deck monitors and was tempted to go to PriFly himself, but this is where he belonged. The crew on deck moved with organized chaos, a dance of precision and frantic activity as they readied the Growlers for launch. Technicians checked and double-checked the jamming pods and receiver systems, ensuring everything was operational. Pilots donned their gear and received last-minute briefings, aware that they were about to enter an unpredictable combat environment.

Warren watched as the first EA-18G Growler taxied down the flight deck, its engines roaring to life. The aircraft lifted off, climbing swiftly into the sky where it would begin its mission to reassert control over the electronic environment.

"Growler-59 is airborne," Lablat confirmed through his headset.

As more Growlers launched from the deck of the Roosevelt, Captain Warren felt a sliver of hope amidst the chaos. With their advanced capabilities, these aircraft would give them a fighting chance against whatever was out there—whether terrestrial or not.

"Good," Warren replied, his eyes still on the sky. "Keep me updated on their progress."

Admiral Mitchell relayed her own instructions to the fleet of ships accompanying the TR, "All escorts, prepare for engagement. Rules of engagement are weapons free on my command."

The U.S. Navy historically maintained a cautious posture when it came to engaging in direct action, especially during the Cold War. That caution was rooted in strategic restraint, rules of engagement, (ROE), and the desire to avoid escalation with peer adversaries like the Soviet Union. But this posture began to shift in the late 1980s and transformed significantly after 9/11.

Thankfully, that caution began to erode in response to shifting global threats and regional provocations. The mining of the USS *Samuel B. Roberts* by Iran in 1988 marked a turning point. This and other incidents including the bombing of the USS Cole in 2000 shifted the posture to one of Proactive Engagement. What was the point of having the world's mightiest naval force if you were unwilling to use it?

Warren glanced back at the deck cameras where the next wave of Super Hornets was being prepped. The F/A-18 was a multi-role fighter-bomber, equipped with AIM-120 AMRAAMs and AIM-9X Sidewinders, giving it a formidable punch in air-to-air combat. It looked like they were going to be too late to the party, though.

"Alright, people! We're scrambling two more groups of Super Hornets," Lablat barked into his headset. "Nighthawk Group, you're up next. I want twenty birds in the air looking for those intruders. Let's move!"

The captain and CSG both knew that the F/A-18E/F Super Hornets were the most dangerous weapon they had. Lablat was holding at least two air groups in reserve. Probably smart to do so.

The deck crew seamlessly shifted into launch action, guiding the sleek jets into position over the catapult launch. Engines roared to life, and Warren felt the familiar vibration through his boots as the next group of Super Hornets catapulted off the deck, slicing through the twilight sky.

"We've got them on radar," a petty officer said tersely to Hayes. "Bearing southeast. Intermittent contacts. Looks like they're closing in fast. Holy shit... really damn fast."

"Understood," Warren replied, his gaze fixed on the horizon where their jets had disappeared moments before. "Eyes open and our defenses tight."

It seemed less than a minute before the radar man yelled, "Overflight in five... four... damn... one," and then in a somewhat relieved tone, "past us now."

Unbelievably, Captain Warren felt the Roosevelt shudder as something passed low overhead at near hypersonic velocity.

The carrier group maintained a 300-mile watch zone around the fleet. In fact, it was a no-fly zone for anyone other than approved craft. Now that zone had just been pierced by a group of potentially hostile craft going Mach 16. Sixteen times the speed of sound.

"Intruders are going hypersonic and turning back for another pass," the petty officer on radar yelled out.

"Contact! RimFire-1 has missile lock," came the excited voice seconds later from one of the FA 18's.

"Fire!" Mitchell commanded.

The AIM-120 AMRAAM streaked through the sky, its active radar seeker tracking the alien craft. For a moment, the CIC held its collective breath.

"Splash one! Target down!"

A cheer went up from the watch team, but Warren's relief was short-lived. Now the battle was absolutely on.

"More contacts incoming!" the radar operator called out. "Multiple bogeys, bearing 240 true, 85 miles out and closing fast!"

"Deploy ESSM and ready CIWS," Warren ordered.

CSG Commander Mitchell followed that with her own orders "All ships, weapons free! Get a firing solution on those damn things. I want all ships targeting as soon as they're in range. Support vessels move to cover primary."

The minutes dragged on as they waited for updates from the airborne units. The tension on deck was thick, each crew member focused intently on their tasks.

"Nighthawks reporting visual contact," came a voice over a speaker near the air boss's command chair.

"Copy that," Lablat responded swiftly. "Group One, maintain shadowing distance as possible and report any changes in behavior or heading."

Warren felt a flicker of unease as he listened in. His birds were flying blind against an unknown threat, each pilot relying on their training and instincts to guide them through this unprecedented situation.

Lablat spoke to Warren over the handset, a determined tremor in his voice. "We're doing everything we can up here, Captain," he said firmly.

Warren nodded appreciatively. "I know you are," he replied quietly. "And we're going to see this through. Let our boys know we are going to be firing on the intruders this time—stay clear."

As before, the alien craft stayed on course for the carrier, but unlike last time, began emitting brilliant flashes of blue-white beams at the escort ships at they approached. The Teddy Roosevelt came under fire.

The RIM-162 Evolved Sea Sparrow Missiles launched from the vertical launch systems throughout the strike group, while multiple Phalanx Close-In Weapons Systems spun to life, their 20mm Vulcan guns tracking the incoming threats.

But then the unthinkable happened.

"RimFire one and two have both gone dark," Lablat reported from PriFly, his voice tight with concern. "All systems failed simultaneously. They're going down."

Warren watched the tactical display as both F/A-18s fell from the sky, their pilots' desperate mayday calls cut short by what appeared to be a directed energy weapon.

"Launch SAR immediately," the Air Wing commander ordered.

The captain snatched up the sound-powered phone as it rang. "Admiral, we're taking casualties. Request permission to engage with all available assets."

"Permission granted, Commander. Defend this strike group with everything we have."

The alien craft pressed their attack, moving in impossible patterns that defied physics. The USS Gettysburg's Aegis system fired salvo after salvo of SM-6 missiles, managing to splash two more targets, but more kept coming.

Then came the devastating blow. A series of pulsed energy blasts struck the Roosevelt's flight deck. They seemed to be specifically targeting the bow catapults. Warren felt the massive carrier shudder under the impact.

"Damage report!" he called out.

"Forward catapults one and two are inoperative," came the reply from Damage Control Central. "Flight deck damage is significant, but waist catapults appear functional. Repair crews are already on it. Maybe thirty minutes until we can recover aircraft."

Warren realized the tactical implications immediately. They could bring their remaining birds home, but launching new sorties would be severely limited. He just hoped they had thirty minutes, otherwise more aircraft would be dropping into the sea.

The attack continued with surgical precision. Through the CIC's cameras, Warren watched in horror as the USS Chancellorsville took multiple hits, her superstructure erupting in flames. The destroyer was already listing heavily to starboard.

Lablat was getting desperate. “Next pass, fire on lock,” the air boss said to his pilots.

"Aye, sir. Fire on lock, roger," came the reply, though it was clear the pilot was already mesmerized by the craft.

The Super Hornets circled back, trying to reacquire their targets. Seconds ticked by with agonizing slowness before the lead pilot called out again.

The static on the line grew more intense as the pilot’s voice broke through once again. "It’s maneuvering now! Impossible angles! Jesus, it just made a 90-degree turn at hypersonic speed without losing momentum!"

"Can you get a lock?" the air boss asked with an eerie sense of calm.

"Negative, no lock," the pilot's voice crackled through the comms, frustration evident.

Commander Lablat was monitoring the radar screens intently. The bogeys danced across the displays, their erratic movements making them nearly impossible to track.

"Copy that," Lablat replied, keeping his tone steady. "Stay on him, keep trying."

The seconds ticked by agonizingly slowly as the pilot maneuvered, attempting to gain a weapons lock on the elusive craft.

"Bogey One still maneuvering wildly—no lock," the pilot reported again, tension creeping into his voice. "They're moving out of range fast."

“Lock acquired! Firing!”

A streak of light shot out from the Super Hornet as it launched its AIM-120 AMRAAMs toward the target. The radar lit up as the missiles homed in on their prey, cutting through the air at Mach 4. They couldn't catch the much faster alien-looking craft, but the Navy pilots had maneuvered into a near-perfect firing angle to cut off the alien craft.

“Missiles away,” the pilot confirmed, his voice tight with anticipation.

The bridge and PriFly held their collective breath as the missiles closed the gap. Then, a sudden burst of energy lit up the sky.

“Splash one! Target down!” Lablat gave a grim smile and issued new orders.

"Gettysburg reports heavy damage but still operational," TAO Hayes reported. "We've lost contact with three of our escort vessels. Enemy craft are going cold. Hostile is exiting the threat envelope, heading 270, angles 15." An incoming message from the AW echoed Commander Hayes’ observation.

Then, something heavy hit the bow of the carrier. To Warren, it seemed like the 100,000-ton ship had just hit a wall.

“XO?” Warren said, picking up the phone. “Bow support damage, sir. Also crack near waterline. One of those damaged craft just exploded about a half mile ahead. The blast wave from it was enormous.”

“Keep me posted,” Warren said, struggling not to let the absolute terror he was feeling get into his response. The U.S. had not had a carrier sunk since 1942, and he didn’t want the next one to be his.

He felt the ship tilting slightly. He surveyed the tactical display, now showing multiple friendly fleet contacts either sinking or dead in the water. The alien craft had struck with overwhelming force and precision, crippling his strike group in minutes.

“CO to CSG,” Warren called.” He updated the admiral on the condition of the ship as she relayed similar status of the support fleet.

“This was a goddamn massacre,” she said. The vitriol obvious in her words. “Can you recover all your birds?”

Hayes was shaking his head no, obviously hearing the question, too. “Doubtful, especially not with helos launching for Search and Rescue operations.”

“Do the best you can, Captain. We need to get our OPREP out as soon as we have a sat link.”

“Yes, ma’am. We need to stay on station for recovery and survivor pickup. Also to enact repairs on the bow.”

“Make it fast, Commander, the intel is likely more important than birds or lives right now.”

"Secure from General Quarters," Warren ordered grimly. "Set Condition II and focus on search and rescue operations and deck repairs. Limit all radio traffic to SAR coordination only."

As he picked up the sound-powered phone to notify his executive officer, Warren couldn't shake the feeling that they had just witnessed—and barely survived—the opening shots of something far beyond conventional warfare.

The surviving alien craft disappeared into the Pacific sky as quickly as they had arrived, leaving behind a battered carrier strike group and more questions than answers. In the span of minutes, the most powerful naval force on Earth had been humbled by technology that seemed to operate outside the laws of physics.

Warren looked around his CIC at the faces of his crew—professional, determined, but shaken by what they had encountered. Whatever these craft were, wherever they came from, one thing was certain: the rules of naval warfare had just been rewritten.

Back on the bridge, Warren could feel the enormity of the situation settling in. “Status report,” he demanded.

Commander McAllister's fingers gripped the back of a chair while watching over the shoulder of the comms station. "Captain, we're getting distress signals from multiple ships—the Pinckney and Paul Hamilton are both capsized; Shiloh is heavily damaged and taking on water. We’ve lost all contact with the Gettysburg."

"Damn it," Warren growled, gripping the edge of a console until his knuckles turned white. "Any sign of those enemy craft?"

"Negative, sir," another officer replied. "They've disappeared off scope."

Captain Warren ordered the hatch closed and all radio traffic to be limited to interfleet SAR. He couldn't afford for any other enemies to know how damaged his Pacific fleet was.

The destruction was mind-boggling. He needed to keep a level head if they were going to survive this onslaught. "Get damage control teams on those fires," he ordered. "And someone find out if our radar systems can be recalibrated to pick up those damn craft." He needed to know who... or what they were up against.

CHAPTER NINETY-SIX

0222 EST August 24
Multiple Locations, USA

In San Francisco, the power flickered out just after dusk. People spilled onto the streets, confused and fearful, murmuring. An eerie silence settled over the city, punctuated by distant sirens and occasional shouts. Without streetlights, the usually bustling city felt like a ghost town. Some folks dug out candles and flashlights, huddling together for warmth and reassurance.

In Miami, the heat was oppressive without air conditioning. Families sat on their porches, fanning themselves with newspapers and trying to make sense of the sudden blackout. Those who had old-style radios listened as they crackled with static, only occasionally delivering garbled news about widespread outages. Grocery stores were swamped with frantic shoppers grabbing canned goods and bottled water. Shelves emptied within hours, leaving behind barren aisles and a sense of growing desperation. The last tweet posted said: *First the humidity and mosquitoes, now the apocalypse—Florida really is extra.*

Over New York City, the skyline dimmed one building at a time until the entire metropolis was cloaked in darkness. Subways ground to a halt in their tunnels, trapping commuters in sweltering conditions.

The few working cell phone towers were overwhelmed as people tried to call loved ones, only to hear busy signals or nothing at all. In Times Square, the iconic billboards went dark, casting an unfamiliar shadow over the heart of the city.

Seattle wasn't spared either. The overcast sky seemed to press down even more heavily as lights flickered out across neighborhoods. People began lining up at the few gas stations that had solar or generator power, filling every container they could find with fuel, fearing it might be their last chance. Internet service was patchy at best; rumors spread like wildfire through text messages and old reliable word of mouth.

Down in New Orleans, the humid air felt even thicker as residents grappled with the sudden loss of power. Bars and restaurants closed early as their refrigerators warmed up and ice melted away. The French Quarter's usual liveliness was replaced by a tense quiet as people stayed indoors, unsure of what might come next.

Boston faced its own chaos as well; hospitals switched to emergency generators while traffic lights blinked out of existence. The grocery stores filled quickly with anxious customers stocking up on essentials—milk, bread, eggs—anything that could sustain them for an uncertain period. Store managers moved quickly to a cash-only basis and soon began increasing prices and limiting purchase quantities on essentials. Someone hung a handwritten sign. “Don’t bother to ask about toilet paper. We’ve seen this movie.”

As each area grappled with its unique challenges, one thing became clear: this was no ordinary outage or isolated incident. This slow-moving apocalypse touched every corner of life—leaving people grasping for answers in an increasingly dark world.

In Virginia, the Jackson family huddled around the kitchen table, their faces lit only by the flickering flame of a candle. Mark, the father, rubbed his temples as he stared at the meager supplies they had left. Canned beans, a half-empty jar of peanut butter, some stale crackers—hardly enough to sustain them for more than a couple of days. The hard-working commuter family lived on takeout and meal deliveries.

"We can't stay here," Mark said, his voice barely above a whisper. "We need to get to the cabin." Calling the old family getaway a cabin was being generous, but it had to be better than here.

Catherine, his wife, nodded, her eyes filled with worry. "But how? The car's almost out of gas, and the stations are all closed. We don't even have enough cash to buy more if they were open."

Their teenage son, Ben, fidgeted in his seat. "The power is out—they can't pump fuel without electricity. What about the bikes? We could ride them as far as we can and then walk the rest of the way."

Mark sighed, looking at Ben with a touch of hopeful sadness. "It's not that simple, son. The cabin is way up in the mountains. It's a long journey. It would be risky, especially with how little we have."

Lilly, their youngest at eight years old, clutched her stuffed rabbit and looked up at her parents with wide eyes. "Will we be safe there?"

Catherine forced a smile and stroked Lilly's hair. "Yes, sweetie. We'll be safer there than here."

They began gathering what they could use. Mark rummaged through drawers for batteries and flashlights while Catherine packed a small backpack with clothes and whatever non-perishable food they had left. Ben found an old map and spread it out on the table.

"Here's the route," he pointed out. "If we leave early in the morning, we might avoid any trouble on the roads."

Mark glanced at the map and nodded. "Good thinking, kid." He folded it carefully and slipped it into his jacket pocket.

As they gathered their supplies, reality began to set in—how little they actually had and how unprepared they were for such an undertaking. The car's gas gauge indeed hovered just above empty; their cash reserves were nearly nonexistent since banks had closed yesterday, and credit cards were useless.

They lived in an affluent section of Richmond. Few of the places accepted cash, and they had long ago moved to digital currency and cards for everything they needed. Mark tried to remember the last time he had even seen an actual paycheck. It simply showed up in his account. An account that he could no longer access.

Mark looked around at his family, feeling the weight of responsibility and poor choices pressing down on him. They had no choice but to leave; staying meant risking starvation, or worse, as full-on panic eventually would grip the city.

"Alright," he said. "We leave at first light."

The Jackson family loaded up their Toyota SUV in the pre-dawn darkness. Mark carefully arranged their meager supplies in the trunk while Catherine helped Lilly buckle into her seat. Ben took one last look at their house before climbing into the back seat.

As they wound their way through the neighborhood, the streets were eerily quiet. Houses stood dark and lifeless, giving the impression of a ghost town. The only sound was the low rumble of their engine as they crept along, trying to conserve what little gas they had left.

About fifteen minutes into their journey, Ben suddenly shouted, "Dad, stop the car!"

Surprised, Mark hit the brakes, the SUV lurching to a halt. "What is it?" he asked, alarmed.

Ben pointed excitedly at a house on their right. "That's Chase's place. Look, their garage door is up, and both their cars are gone."

Mark furrowed his brow, not understanding the significance. "Yeah, the power's out. No one shuts their garages manually. They probably did what we're doing. Why is that important?"

"They keep cans of gas in their utility shed," Ben explained quickly. "I helped Chase cut his grass a few months ago. I know where they keep them. And their cars are electric. They wouldn't have needed it."

Catherine's face tightened with concern. "But that would be stealing," she protested.

Mark and Ben exchanged a look, weighing the moral dilemma against their desperate situation. Without a word, they both unbuckled their seatbelts and jumped out of the car.

"Be careful!" Catherine called after them as they sprinted through the pre-dawn darkness towards Chase's house.

Mark and Ben returned from the shed, each carrying a gas can. The full one weighed heavily in Mark's hands. Ben struggled a bit with the half-full can, but determination fueled both their steps.

Mark unscrewed the gas cap on the SUV and carefully began to pour the contents of the full can into the tank. The smell of gasoline filled the air, sharp and acrid, as he tilted the can to ensure every last drop made it into their vehicle. He then handed the empty can to Ben and took the half-full one, repeating the process.

Catherine watched anxiously from inside the car, glancing back at

Lilly, who was humming softly to herself, oblivious to the gravity of their situation. "Hurry up," she whispered to herself, wringing her hands.

Mark finished pouring the gas and screwed the cap back on tightly. He turned to Ben, who was already closing up the utility shed behind them. "Good job, son," he said quietly, giving Ben's shoulder a reassuring squeeze.

They climbed back into the SUV. Mark started the engine, and they drove cautiously out of Chase's driveway, merging back onto their route towards safety. As they continued down suburban streets still cloaked in shadows, Mark's thoughts wandered. How many other houses were empty already? How many families had decided to flee? Some of them likely had resources they could use. He dismissed these thoughts quickly; he had to believe that most people were sheltering in place.

As they neared the main road that would lead them out of town, Mark's heart sank. Ahead of them was a long line of red taillights. Cars stretched out as far as he could see, all trying to do exactly what they were doing—escape.

Catherine let out a sigh of frustration. "We're not getting anywhere like this," she said, her voice tinged with desperation.

Ben leaned forward from the back seat. "Dad, is there another way?"

Mark rubbed his forehead, trying to think. "We could try some side streets," he suggested reluctantly. "But it might take us longer."

Catherine nodded slowly. "It's better than sitting here wasting gas."

With that decision made, Mark turned off onto a narrower road running parallel to their intended route. They weaved through residential areas and smaller thoroughfares, hoping each turn would bring them closer to their destination without encountering another blockade of vehicles.

As they navigated through quiet streets lined with darkened homes and unlit streetlamps, Mark couldn't help but feel a pang of guilt for leaving others behind—but his family's safety had to come first. It took almost two hours to come to the realization they weren't going anywhere.

With traffic lights out and other families apparently lower on fuel than they were, wrecks and stalled cars were blocking every path they tried. None of the GPS systems had worked in the last week, and he wasn't even sure there was an alternative route they hadn't tried. They had burned through a quarter tank of fuel and were still within ten miles of their house.

Mark carefully extracted the Toyota from the latest traffic jam to the sound of yells and honking horns. He pulled into an empty shopping center and parked in front of a Panera Bread as the sun came up. He looked around at his family in defeat. Sighing, he turned the car off and placed his head on the steering wheel.

CHAPTER NINETY-SEVEN

0644 UTC September 02
White House Security Area
Washington, D.C., USA

General Taylor sat in the dimly lit White House SCIF, monitoring the CIC control room aboard the USS Theodore Roosevelt thousands of miles away, eyes glued to the multiple screens before him. His fingers drummed against the metal table as he remotely monitored the activity on deck and the broader naval theater. A seasoned veteran, Taylor had seen his fair share of crises, but nothing compared to this.

"Status on satellite control?" Taylor asked, his voice carrying a steely calm.

"Still compromised, sir," a young officer back at the Pentagon replied, frustration evident in his tone. "We've got teams working round the clock, but every time we regain control, we lose it within minutes. We can see what they see, but they can't reach us."

Suddenly, one of the radar operators spoke up, alarm obvious in his voice. "Sir, we're picking up strange anomalies over the Pacific."

Taylor's eyes narrowed. "Define 'strange.'"

"Multiple unidentified objects moving at hypersonic speeds. They're not following any known flight paths."

Taylor considered Emily's warning as he, too, now saw the feed from the radar console.

"We have a bird in the area," another voice said as the view on one of the screens shifted.

The feed from a high-altitude military drone showed several lights traveling roughly in formation until each of the lights converged and became one. The feed glitched out and then went dark. Taylor's jaw tightened as he glanced at another monitor showing the Pentagon's situation room in D.C., where Admiral Alvarez and other joint chief military leaders were watching, as frustrated as he was. None of them had any direct contact with the carrier group.

At the Pentagon, anxiety hung thick in the air. High-ranking officials and analysts filled the room, their faces illuminated by flickering screens showing chaotic data streams.

"We're also dealing with a sophisticated cyberattack," one analyst said, pushing his glasses up nervously. "We can't even pinpoint the source."

An officer at the Pentagon interrupted with an urgent call: "We've lost contact with over half the planes in the air!"

A brief gasp filled the room as everyone turned their attention to the central monitors displaying blips disappearing off of radars one by one.

General Taylor's voice cut through the cacophony of disbelief and speculation. "What do we have on those anomalies?"

"Sir, they're defying our usual tracking methods. It's like they're... phasing in and out," a radar technician explained, clearly baffled.

Taylor took a deep breath and surveyed the room full of joint chiefs and senior advisors through his video link. Uncertainty clouded their faces as they scrambled for answers.

"We need to know who we are fighting," someone suggested hesitantly.

"We can't do that without confirmation or evidence," another retorted. A buzz of similar conversations filled the space.

Taylor had had enough of their dithering. "Shut up, all of you," he commanded sharply, drawing immediate silence. His gaze was icy and determined. "We don't have time for analysis paralysis. Our priority is regaining control over our airspace and satellites. Right now, we aren't fighting anyone; we are getting our collective asses kicked without ever seeing the enemy up close."

He focused on one of his top communications officers. "Activate all contingency protocols. Contact NORAD and CENCOM. I want backup systems online immediately."

"But, sir—"

"No buts," Taylor snapped. "Do it now."

The operations room burst into action, spurred by Taylor's decisiveness. Yet, amid the flurry of activity, an unspoken dread lingered—an awareness that they were up against something beyond human understanding or control.

General Taylor's gaze remained locked on the screen before him as the first signs of the assault unfolded. The grainy, real-time footage came from a high-altitude drone orbiting that section of the Pacific Ocean. The craft were blurry dots moving in and out of range like a dance, then making near ninety-degree turns without any decrease in speed.

"Damn!" he said reflexively.

"Commercial airspace in zone one closing in five minutes," came a voice from somewhere. "Predators in the air."

"Show it, monitor three," Alvarez ordered.

Taylor had to do a mental jump to recall where zone one was. South Florida. From the new drone view, he could see the power grid below, a sprawling web of streetlights and hovering icons indicating power transformers and lines critical to the region's electrical infrastructure.

"Zoom in," Taylor ordered.

The image magnified, showing intricate details of the power grid. Suddenly, a strange hum filled the speakers, growing louder until it was almost deafening. The radar screen showed a fleet of craft hovering above the site.

The drone picked up views of the sleek craft with stubby wings as they circled at just over 5,000 feet.

"What are they doing?" someone whispered behind Taylor.

In a heartbeat, one of the ships emitted a brilliant beam of energy—plasma-like and otherworldly—directly at the interchange. The light was so intense that it overwhelmed the camera sensors for a moment, turning everything white.

When the image cleared, chaos reigned. The once orderly grid had become an inferno of sparks and molten metal. Transformers exploded like fireworks, sending showers of debris into the air. Entire sections of the interchange collapsed under their own weight, succumbing to gravity and fire.

Taylor's jaw clenched as he witnessed the destruction unfold in horrifying clarity. "Get us visuals from surrounding areas," he barked.

New feeds popped up on additional monitors, showing entire neighborhoods going dark as the power grid failed. Streetlights flickered off one by one like dominoes falling into an abyss. Homes were plunged into darkness, leaving residents confused and scared.

"Sir, we're getting reports of massive blackouts across the bottom tier of states," an aide announced breathlessly.

Taylor nodded grimly, eyes never leaving the screens. "Inform FEMA and Homeland Security. We need immediate disaster response teams on standby."

He watched as more plasma strikes targeted other sites. His people informed him one by one. It was key internet hubs along the coast. Data centers erupted into flames, servers melting into unrecognizable lumps of slag. Communications towers toppled like felled trees.

A cold sweat formed on Taylor's brow. He knew these strikes weren't just about physical destruction—they were dismantling America's ability to coordinate a response. His fingers dug into the armrests of his chair as he realized how calculated and devastating these attacks were. He sent for the president but doubted the man would come up to see any of this.

General Taylor's attention snapped back to the Pacific theater as new drone footage appeared. The USS Theodore Roosevelt's deck erupted in flames, its proud silhouette marred by smoke and destruction. F/A-18s littered the deck, some still burning from direct hits.

"Dear God," someone whispered in the control room.

Through the grainy feed, they watched helplessly as support vessels around the carrier faced similar fates. The USS Gettysburg listed heavily to port, water rushing over its deck. Rescue helicopters dotted the sky like frantic insects, searching for survivors in the debris-filled waters.

"Can anyone raise the Roosevelt?" Taylor demanded.

"Negative, sir. All communications remain down."

The drone's camera caught glimpses of pilots ejecting from their aircraft, their parachutes tiny white specks against the vast ocean. Some jets simply dropped from the sky, their systems completely failed, while others spun out of control before crashing into the waves.

"Track those bogies," Taylor ordered, his voice tight with controlled fury.

"Sir, they're... they're gone. Just vanished off scope."

The high-altitude video feed showed the aftermath in stark detail—burning wreckage scattered across miles of ocean, rescue boats weaving between floating debris, and the mighty carrier Theodore Roosevelt transformed into a floating inferno. The pride of the U.S. Navy, reduced to a wounded giant in minutes.

Taylor's hands clenched into fists as he watched American sailors on smaller ships jumping into the Pacific, choosing the ocean over the inferno their ship had become. The drone's infrared picked up dozens of heat signatures in the water—survivors waiting for rescue.

"How many ships down?" he asked quietly.

"Three Arleigh Burke destroyers confirmed sunk, sir. USS Gettysburg going under. The Teddy Roosevelt still afloat but..." The officer's voice trailed off as another explosion rocked the carrier's deck. "Unable to determine its seaworthiness."

"Those striker craft are going to be unstoppable," the Air Force general stated flatly.

Admiral Alvarez broke in, "One new bit of intel coming in, gentlemen. Just receiving a preliminary Navy Blue communication. The CSG is also unable to raise the USN Jefferson City. So what took out the submarine? This was an airborne attack."

The room fell silent as they continued watching the rescue efforts through the drone's unblinking eye, everyone present knowing they had just witnessed something unprecedented in naval warfare—the complete devastation of a carrier strike group by an unknown force.

"They're crippling us," someone murmured.

Taylor's voice was steel as he responded, "They're testing us. Looking for vulnerabilities. This was the first strike, a sucker punch, but we drew blood, too... we will adapt."

But even as he spoke, he knew they were facing an enemy unlike any they had ever encountered. In one strike, the bulk of the Pacific Fleet was gone. Emily Carter had been right all along, but would anyone actually believe a non-terrestrial enemy?

~

Sarah Mitchell leaned against the railing of her balcony, a glass of Pinot Noir in hand as she gazed out at the vast expanse of the Pacific Ocean. The salty breeze whipped through her graying hair, and she closed her eyes for a moment, savoring the tranquility of the evening.

She had just ended a call an hour earlier with Kaden. Despite his brilliance, Sarah worried about his obsessive tendencies and the dangers they posed. "Be careful out there, Kaden," she had warned him, her voice laced with concern. "Don't let your pursuit of the truth consume you."

As Sarah took a sip of her wine, a bright light streaked across the darkening sky, catching her attention. She squinted, trying to make out the source of the anomaly. It looked like a meteor, but something about its trajectory seemed off.

The object grew larger as it approached, its fiery tail illuminating the clouds. Sarah's heart raced as she realized it was heading straight for the ocean. She gripped the balcony railing tighter, her knuckles turning white.

The impact was deafening. A blinding flash lit up the horizon, followed by a thunderous boom that shook the very foundation of Sarah's house. She stumbled backward, her wine glass shattering on the wooden deck.

The ground beneath her feet trembled violently, and Sarah struggled to maintain her balance. Bookcases toppled over inside her living room, spilling their contents across the floor. Pictures fell from the walls, their frames cracking upon impact.

As the shaking finally subsided, Sarah cautiously made her way back to the railing. Her eyes widened in horror as she saw a massive wall of angry water rising from the sea, towering over the coastline. The tidal wave, born from the impact of the mysterious object, raced toward the shore with terrifying speed.

Sarah stood frozen, her mind struggling to comprehend the scale of the impending disaster. She thought of Kaden and the warnings she had given him, realizing that they paled in comparison to the catastrophe unfolding before her eyes. Kaden had been right, and now she realized why he was so obsessed with making the world open their eyes.

The roar of the approaching wave filled her ears, drowning out the frantic beating of her own heart. As the wall of water neared, Sarah closed her eyes, a strange sense of acceptance washing over her. She had dedicated her life to unraveling the mysteries of the universe, but in this moment, she realized that some forces were beyond human understanding or control.

In the final seconds before the nearly thousand-foot wave crashed over her balcony, Sarah whispered a silent prayer for Kaden and all those who would be left to face the aftermath of this cataclysmic event. Then, the world around her disappeared in a swirling maelstrom of water and debris.

CHAPTER NINETY-EIGHT

2218 EST September 02
White House Oval Office
Washington, D.C., USA

"We need to calm the public but do so without revealing too much," insisted Communications Director Courtney Rollins. "Frame it as a series of unfortunate coincidences—cyberattacks, power grid failures, maybe even throw in some solar flare activity."

National Transportation Director Tom Wurthing shook his head. "Courtney, that just won't fly this time. People are seeing things in the sky. We can't just ignore that."

"Then we pivot to domestic terrorism," Rollins countered. "Suggest it's all part of a coordinated attack by extremist groups."

President Martin raised a hand, silencing the room. "Whatever we say, it needs to be believable. We can't risk losing what little credibility we have left."

As the team crafted their message, Emily Carter stood in the back of the room, her jaw clenched tight. She watched as they spun lies and half-truths, her frustration mounting with each passing moment. She'd been adamant about uncovering the truth and identifying the real threat, but the machinations of politics still pretended otherwise.

Finally, she couldn't contain herself any longer. "This is insane," she burst out, drawing all eyes to her. "We're facing an unprecedented threat, and you're worried about political spin?"

NSA Advisor Pete Cavanaugh fixed her with a cold stare. "Ms. Carter, this discussion is above your pay grade. I suggest you—"

"No," Emily cut him off, stepping forward. "We've seen the evidence. I know what's really happening out there. And I won't stand by while you feed the American people lies."

Cavanaugh's face reddened. "You're out of line, Carter. Your temporary authority nor your little committee don't give you the right to—"

"Fuck you, Pete! My committee has uncovered more important truths in the past few weeks than you have since you've been here," Emily shot back. "Or maybe you've just been hiding it all along?"

The room fell silent, the tension palpable. President Martin looked between Emily and his security advisor, his expression unreadable.

"Both of you, enough," he said firmly. "Emily, I understand your concerns, but we need to approach this carefully. Pete, I want a full briefing on everything your agency knows about these attacks. No more secrets."

Emily opened her mouth to argue further, but the president held up a hand. "That's all for now. We'll reconvene in an hour."

As the room emptied, Emily locked eyes with Cavanaugh. The presidential advisor's gaze was cold, promising retribution for her outburst. But Emily stood her ground, knowing that the truth was more important than any personal consequences she might face.

Despite the horrendous attacks, much of the country remained unscathed, and the hostilities had gone quiet. Scattered reports were still coming in, but this much seemed true. Emily felt sure the press secretary's plan would be approved. That was just how things worked here. Downplay the truth, obfuscate the facts, and keep the American people in the dark...literally and figuratively. It was hard to fathom they could still be trying to hold that line in the face of all this, but people wanted to choose what facts they believed, and too often a comfortable lie was the preferred truth.

The enemy's first wave of attacks had been devastating. The USS Theodore Roosevelt's carrier group had been hit hard. One of the stanchions of America's military might had been nearly taken out in a matter of minutes. Communications from much of the Pacific fleet had gone silent after a chaotic transmission detailing hypersonic and very erratic craft. Fleet destroyers opened fire in desperation, but the alien craft apparently decimated support ships with precision strikes. Search and rescue operations were underway amidst the wreckage.

Major military and logistics hubs across the globe had also taken severe hits. Globally, power outages and cyberattacks wreaked havoc on civilian life. Reports indicated widespread blackouts targeting key internet hubs and power grids, systematically crippling communication and essential services.

The Northwest Coast had experienced perhaps the worst, as a series of tsunamis overwashed the coast for miles inland. No one had any real guess as to the casualties, but it was going to be extremely high.

Despite the mounting internal disagreements, Emily had been brought back to the president's inner circle. He was a politician, but he also wasn't stupid. He needed someone close who could stand up to the other strong personalities around him. Someone he could trust. They needed to understand the full scope of this devastation if they were to mount any effective response against such an unprecedented threat, no matter what he said to the American people.

"General," Emily said as Taylor walked in and sat heavily in the chair across from her desk. Neither of them looked like they had gotten any sleep. "Any updates?"

Taylor shook his head. "Not..." He paused, considering what were likely countless reports of destruction and casualties. "Not so much. They hit us hard, but it could have been worse."

"Why wasn't it?" Emily asked, genuinely curious. She had been wondering the same thing.

He rubbed a hand across his unshaven face. "In our opinion—purely theoretical, mind you—they have insufficient numbers to wage a full-scale war. Their technology and weapon systems more than make up for it, but most likely, all this was just a distraction. Well...maybe more of a softening up of the target."

"You mentioned something like that in the situation room the other day. I was asking you about how we would execute a war. I don't think they let you finish."

He smiled. "Seems a bit prophetic now, doesn't it? They don't want to hear it, Director Carter. This is D.C. They all have their own truths to maintain. The last thing they need is contradicting facts."

"I want to hear. I think you said to learn all you can about the enemy, then once you start an attack, you disrupt all communications. What would happen after that?"

The general pursed his lips, considering it. "After that—it gets worse. Much worse. We would hit their leadership. We'd aim to eliminate or disrupt their command structure where decisions are made. Without leaders, their forces will be confused and less organized."

"Military or government leadership?"

"Both. However, our plans would typically prioritize military. Decapitating political leaders requires precision and is often just not worth the effort."

Emily was making notes now. "Then what?"

"Expand the assault," the general said. "Increase air and missile strikes. We would hit hard from the air, broadening the scope of our target lists. Before ever thinking of sending in ground troops, we use air power to take out high-value targets like military bases, missile sites, and airfields."

"Which they've already done?"

The general's face screwed into a frown. "They did some of that, not as much as you might think. Yes, they took out some key military and civilian targets. They made life tough on us, but they may have made a mistake. Much of our ability to wage war is still very much intact.

"If it were us, we would want to control the skies. Make damn sure our aircraft can fly safely, and the enemy's planes are grounded or destroyed. This gives us near-total control over the battlefield."

"What then?" Emily asked, making some notes and almost not wanting to know the answer.

"Once we've weakened their forces considerably, we would send in ground troops to take control of key areas, neutralize remaining enemy forces, and secure the region. Then it just becomes a job of holding onto the territory and preventing any counterattacks."

"So, if the aliens, or 'enemy forces,' follow anything similar to this, we are just in the opening rounds. The worst is yet to come," Emily said.

"Indeed," Taylor said. "Which is why Director Reyes of DHS and I have been urging POTUS to evacuate to a safer location."

Emily knew the frustration in the West Wing between the key decision-makers. It wasn't just her and Cavanaugh. Everyone seemed to have a different idea of what was a priority and what was the best move. As Churchill famously said, "Democracy is the worst form of government, except for all the others that have been tried."

Taylor gave a grim smile. "Emily, this is your aliens. You were not wrong. But...there is also something else to consider."

"What's that?"

"What I laid out is how humans would prosecute the war. That is not necessarily how an alien species would. Even now, some of their strategy is very obviously different from ours."

"Their behavior will be alien to us, we understand that, but some battle tactics will likely be nearly universal. Right?" she asked.

"Probably," the general acknowledged. "However, they likely have weapons that we can't even dream of, or worse, tactics that we would simply find...well, inhuman. Chemical, biological, or maybe something like autonomous attack bots or drones that could wipe out significant populations in minutes. We know they have been studying us; we know their craft can infiltrate our airspace, even penetrate the ultra-secure airspace around our facilities undetected.

“Even with all the information that SCET gathered, we barely scratched the surface of what the aliens might be capable of. We can't make the mistake of treating them like a human enemy. That will doom us. Unfortunately, that is the only way our military machine can function."

Emily recalled the Jellyfish infiltration the general had shown them. As creepy as that was, it might be nothing compared to whatever came next.

CHAPTER NINETY-NINE

2227 UTC September 03
25°07'01"N, 51°18'32"W
Al Udeid Air Base
Doha, Qatar

Even as the collaborators' mission was unraveling, the savage attacks continued unabated, with the air filled with the deafening wails of sirens and the gut-wrenching screams of the dying and desperate. The command center at the heart of the sprawling Al Udeid Air Base southwest of Doha, Qatar, descended into chaotic havoc. Soldiers rushed about, their faces twisted in horror as they surveyed the devastation wrought upon their once fortified stronghold.

Communication lines flickered and faltered, unable to carry the weight of the desperate pleas for help and instructions that bounced off the ether. Radios hissed and whined, offering only static in response. Every attempt to connect with command or other bases around the world proved futile as the sinister alien force struck with the precision of a master assassin.

The once-powerful command center lay in ruins, its once-proud structures now little more than debris strewn about the barren landscape. Powerful energy blasts had obliterated command and control, communications towers, and transport hubs in a flash, leaving only silence and devastation in their wake.

The stealthy A044 attack craft had shown no mercy, delivering their surgical decapitation attacks with cold, calculating efficiency. Their cloaking technology left defending forces completely unaware of their incoming fate until it was too late.

The commands that had once flowed through this center now lay quiet, the once-busy war rooms now echoing with the chilling reminder of the enemy's ruthless determination.

"This is fucked," muttered a soldier, anger and complete frustration in his voice. "Does anyone know how we can get in touch with command?"

The man beside him replied, "Shit, they're the reason we are all out here with our thumbs up our butts."

Without orders from their leaders, soldiers scrambled to maintain some semblance of order. However, the lack of centralized leadership left them struggling to coordinate any meaningful response. In some places, pockets of resistance attempted to organize, but they were quickly overrun by more alien attacks, leaving nothing but carnage in their wake.

With communication lines severed and their base left in shambles, the surviving soldiers could only watch helplessly as the alien force continued to press forward, their sinister intent clear for all to see. The alien craft's hit-and-run tactics were devastatingly effective. Nothing the soldiers had was capable of even matching the speed of the damn things, much less the destructive power.

Across the smoldering ruins of the sprawling Al Udeid base, Major Derek Collins stumbled through the wreckage, blood trickling from a gash above his eye. The acrid smell of burning fuel and melted electronics filled his lungs as he navigated the twisted metal and concrete that had once been the command center.

"Anderson! Rodriguez!" he called out, his voice hoarse from the smoke. "Anyone with a working radio, sound off!"

A figure emerged from behind a collapsed wall—Lieutenant Margaret Ruiz , her uniform torn and face smudged with soot. "Sir, I've got nothing. Every frequency is dead or jammed."

Collins wiped the blood from his brow. "What about the backup systems in Bunker Three?"

"Direct hit, sir. Seemed like they knew exactly where to hit us."

The implications were obvious. The enemy—the aliens—had targeted their communication infrastructure with surgical precision, isolating them completely. They had insider information or their intel was much better than humans'.

"Sir!" A young airman sprinted toward them, clutching a satellite phone. "I found this in one of the vehicles. It's still working."

Collins grabbed the device, hope flickering briefly before reality crushed it. "Who the hell do we call? Washington? London? For all we know, they're in the same shape we are."

The distant whine of the alien craft cut through the air again. Everyone tensed, eyes scanning the sky.

"Get down!" Collins shouted, pulling Ruiz and the airman behind a concrete barrier.

The alien vessel—sleek, almost translucent, with pulsing blue energy at its core—glided overhead. Unlike human aircraft, it moved with an eerie silence, the only sound a low electromagnetic hum that made teeth ache and electronics fail.

"They're not even trying to hide anymore," Ruiz whispered. "This isn't just a raid—it's an invasion."

As the craft passed, Collins watched it head toward the horizon where the city of Doha lay. His stomach twisted as he imagined what was happening there—the panic, the chaos, the slaughter. The trillion-dollar skyline would be rubble by day's end.

"We need to gather whoever's left," he decided. "Weapons, vehicles, supplies. If we can't communicate with command, we become our own command."

Ruiz nodded grimly. "And then what, sir?"

Collins stared in the direction the craft had disappeared. "Then we fight back. Because I'll be damned if I let those things take over without one hell of a goddamn fight."

CHAPTER
ONE HUNDRED

0957 EST September 04
11th Street NW
Washington, D.C., USA

"I am profoundly sorry, Professor," Natalie said.

The man's eyes cast down and seemed fixed only on the patch of asphalt just ahead.

Kaden and Natalie trudged through the clogged streets of Washington, D.C., dodging debris and panicked citizens. The power outages had turned the city into a labyrinth of traffic jams and confusion. They'd abandoned their car miles from the White House to continue on foot.

Natalie's hand found Kaden's shoulder in the darkness, her touch gentle but firm. Her voice softened, cutting through the distant sounds of chaos.

"She lived near the water, didn't she?"

His shoulders tensed beneath her palm. The silence between them stretched as he stared into the middle distance, his face half-illuminated by the occasional emergency light. Kaden had been out of sight since the news of the Oregon attack.

Natalie already knew the man couldn't hide his emotions, nor his depression, of which he'd had plenty lately. Still, she was trying to bring him back. She needed him; the country needed him now more than ever.

"She called me," he finally said, his voice hollow. "Right before. Said she was watching the ocean. She loved it there. It was serenely beautiful. Just like her."

Natalie swallowed hard. "The Cascadia fault. I heard they're saying it was a nine-point-two. The entire coastline..."

"Two million people." Kaden's words fell like stones. "At least. That's what they're estimating."

A military convoy rumbled past them, headlights cutting through the darkness. Neither of them acknowledged it.

"I'm so sorry, Kaden. I truly am."

He nodded mechanically, his eyes glistening in the dim light. "She was a fine woman and a better friend than I ever was." His voice cracked slightly. "She warned me about all this. Told me I was losing myself in theories while missing what was right in front of me."

Natalie squeezed his shoulder. "You couldn't have known."

"Couldn't I?" His laugh was bitter, empty. "Isn't that what we've been chasing all along? The signs were there."

They stood in silence for a moment, the weight of loss and realization pressing down on them both.

"She deserved better," Kaden whispered. "From me... from the world."

Natalie was unsure how to respond. "She was your champion, Professor, and what she would say right now is the world needs you now more than ever."

"I heard about your heroics taking that group down. Very impressive, young lady."

"I was mostly along for the ride, and we didn't take them all down, but we did get the key man, we think."

Kaden started to say something then abruptly stopped.

"We're almost there," he said, glancing at his smartwatch, which had surprisingly flickered to life.

"Good," Natalie replied, realizing he wanted to change the subject. "I don't like being out here this late without backup."

"Without Mister Trent, you mean," Kaden said with a small chuckle.

Kaden stopped walking suddenly, turning to face Natalie directly. In the dim emergency lighting, his features looked more pronounced, the shadows deepening the lines of his face.

"Don't let him get away."

Natalie blinked, caught off guard. "What?"

"I've seen how he looks at you. And how you look at him when you think no one's watching." Kaden's expression softened. "If you have feelings for him, make sure the lad knows it."

Natalie's mouth opened slightly, but no words came out.

"Don't make my mistake," Kaden continued, his eyes distant for a moment. "Don't let your obsessions blind you to the passions or the needs of others. I was so fixated on proving I was right about the extraterrestrial presence that I missed what was right in front of me." He swallowed hard. "Sarah deserved better."

"Kaden, I—"

"Life is too short, Natalie. We're seeing that now more than ever." He gestured vaguely at the chaos around them. "Whatever happens next, don't leave things unsaid. Human connection... people. They are what matter most. Keep them close."

Natalie's blue eyes met his, a complexity of emotions playing across her face. "I didn't realize you were such a romantic, Professor."

"Not romantic. Just a foolish realist." He turned to continue walking. "I'm just a tired, old fool, but listen to me on this. Just something to think about while we're trying to save the world. Remember—remember who you are saving it for."

They finally reached the White House, greeted by a virtual wall of security. After even more enthusiastic rounds of very rigorous safety checks, they were escorted inside, where Emily waited for them in her small office.

"It seems the committee isn't shutting down after all," Natalie said. The irony of what was going on wasn't lost on these three.

Emily looked at her as she motioned for them to sit. "SCET seems pretty irrelevant now," she said curtly. "We're in the middle of an alien invasion. The threat we were pursuing is obviously real."

Kaden didn’t waste time with small talk. With everything that had been going on, he hadn't been focused on his job. The one time in his life his obsessions were being proven, and he'd been mired in grief and guilt. Pulling himself together, he apologized for his absence. "Emily, you need to hear my update from Dr. Cho."

Emily’s eyes narrowed; she vaguely remembered who Cho was, but she gestured for Kaden to continue.

"Dr. Cho discovered anomalies in the Hyades star cluster," Kaden began, opening his bag and laying out a series of charts and data printouts on the table. "He suspects intelligently controlled spacecraft are using stars for cover as they approach Earth."

"We know about the craft; hell, they took out a dozen cities and our Pacific Fleet.”

Trembley shook his head. “No, no, no. This is a different group of craft. A full fleet of much larger ships. What we have now is just scouts or skirmishes. Just a warm-up for what is likely going to come next."

Emily’s blood ran cold. She leaned in, studying the data and quickly getting the more salient points. "So they’ve been hiding in plain sight?"

"Exactly," Kaden confirmed. "Initially, these objects were nearly invisible due to their low albedo. But as they approach our Sun, they are becoming detectable."

Natalie added, “Good to know we’ve officially crossed into ‘hold my beer’ territory. So, the random attacks are what? Just the prelude. It’s all coordinated and obvious that they’ve been planning this for a long time."

Emily’s face grew grim as she absorbed the information. "General Taylor feared a full ground force invasion... now I see that's not just paranoia."

"Correct," Natalie said. "What we are seeing is likely the precursor to a larger assault—ground troops included."

Emily exhaled sharply and stood up straight, her mind running through scenarios and contingencies. She had been constantly benched by her boss, at least as far as the truth was concerned, but this new intel was critical.

"We need to update General Taylor immediately," she said decisively. "If they will even let me in."

Emily strode purposefully toward the secure briefing room, Natalie and Kaden following close behind. The corridor was filled with frantic staffers rushing between offices; the sense of panic was growing.

As they approached the heavy, metal, reinforced door, a young guard stepped forward, his hand raised. "I'm sorry, Director Carter. I can't let you in."

Emily's eyes narrowed. "Excuse me?"

"Direct orders from the national security advisor." The guard shifted uncomfortably but held his ground. "You are not to enter without his express permission."

"This is absurd." Emily's voice dropped dangerously. "I'm the acting chief of staff. Cavanaugh doesn't outrank me here. Also, we have critical intelligence about the attacks."

"I understand, ma'am, but my orders are clear."

Emily's face flushed with anger, her fists clenching at her sides. She stepped forward, nearly nose-to-nose with the guard. "Listen to me very carefully. While you're playing doorman, people are dying. The president needs this information."

The guard swallowed hard but didn't move. "I am really sorry, ma'am."

Emily's arm twitched, her restraint visibly slipping. Natalie reached for her, but Kaden moved faster.

"Excuse me, son." Kaden gently placed himself between Emily and the guard, his tone calm and grandfatherly. "What's your name?"

"Corporal Davis, sir."

"Corporal Davis, I understand you're just following orders. That's commendable." Kaden smiled warmly. "But would you be willing to pass along a message to General Taylor? It's of vital importance regarding the nature of these attacks and the future of this nation."

The guard hesitated, glancing between them.

"The information we have could save countless lives," Kaden continued. "All we're asking is that you relay it to the general. He can decide what to do with it."

Davis's posture relaxed slightly, and he nodded. "I can do that, sir."

"Thank you." Kaden nodded appreciatively. "Please tell him Dr. Trembley has confirmed the attacks are coordinated and are likely preliminary to a much larger assault. He'll understand what that means."

The guard seemed shaken by the message. He nodded and motioned for another guard to take his place while he quickly slipped through the door.

Emily took a deep breath, her anger still simmering but under control. She gave Kaden a grateful look.

"Sometimes you catch more flies with honey, my dear," Kaden whispered.

“I was about two seconds from swatting the fly,” Emily muttered. "If we don't stop this advance force, what chance do we have against what's coming?"

The door opened, and Corporal Davis motioned them in. General Taylor was in conference with the secretary of defense and another member of the joint chiefs. Emily watched as the threat screen on the far wall flashed orange and then red. She wasn't sure what it meant but doubted it was anything good. What the military men were about to learn would elevate the threat to levels never even considered.

CHAPTER
ONE HUNDRED ONE

Undisclosed Location
Outskirts of Baltimore,
Maryland, USA

Owen King sat nervously at one end of a large stainless-steel table. Natalie Reeves strode into the room, flanked by two secret service agents and four uniformed soldiers who were so large they could have played pro football. The tension thickened as she surveyed the scene, her blue eyes narrowing with determination.

Owen's face twisted into a feeble smile. "Hello again, Ms. Reeves," he said, standing nervously. Somehow, he still couldn't keep the condescension out of his voice. "What a pleasure."

"Save the charm. You've got enough slime on you to fill a Senate hearing," Natalie spat the words. She walked up to him, her steps echoing in the hushed room. In one swift motion, she pushed him backward so hard that the heavy chair tipped over, sending Owen crashing to the floor with a thud. His head bounced off the polished concrete, a dazed look crossing his features.

The two agents looked ready to intervene. "So... should I write that up as 'light coercion' or 'accidental gravity-assisted diplomacy?'"

Natalie ignored the unusual bit of dark humor from the senior agent. "Just want us to be clear on who is in charge," she commanded, her old naval officer demeanor stepping front and center. The Secret Service agents moved to pick King up, but Natalie motioned them back. They exited back out to the corridor.

Once the door slammed shut, leaving only Owen and Natalie in the room, she leaned down, eyes burning with cold fury. "You are one massive fuck! A collaborator with an alien overlord who has been making the rules, kidnapping people, and experimenting on the human race for decades," she spat.

"I...I didn't have a choice," he pleaded. Despite his earlier demands, he seemed ready to talk. He knew if he didn't make a deal, he was a dead man.

"First, the code to the file and the name of the conspirator in the White House," Natalie demanded.

"Has news of my arrest been made public?"

Natalie looked confused. "No. Why does it matter?"

King looked nervous. "He could do some considerable damage if he knew I was about to start naming names."

"Just give us what we want. I hold an executive order and accompanying national security directive that revokes your right to habeas corpus, due process, legal counsel, or even the right to a defense."

Owen blinked up at her, fear in his eyes.

"Your violations are deemed so atrocious," Natalie continued, "you'll be lucky to avoid a public hanging on the White House lawn."

Owen struggled to sit up, blood trickling from a cut on his head. "You can't do this," he muttered. "I have rights."

"Not anymore," Natalie shot back. She stepped closer, her boots inches from his face. "You will tell me everything you know about this cover-up, your role, and every other collaborator that we need to be collecting. Not just here in the U.S., either. We know it's a worldwide cancer."

Owen's eyes darted around the room as if seeking an escape that wasn't there.

"Do you understand me?" Natalie demanded.

He nodded nervously. Natalie yelled for one of the agents to come back and set up the secure video link direct to Joint Base Andrews, where Emily and the president were waiting. The meeting had been set up quickly when they realized their pursuit of the truth was finally paying off.

"What about helping me recover Emma?"

"We'll get to that."

Natalie had given Owen King a paper with only six questions to start with. He had only minutes to frame his responses, and the homeland agent had attached electrodes to his head and arms. Not overly effective as a lie detector, but she wanted the man to worry about even the hint of lying.

From the flat-screen display, Emily Carter stared at King like she was shooting daggers from the screen. "We're ready, Ms. Reeves."

“First, the passcode to the file and the name of the senior White House officials.”

“Did you keep my arrest secret?” King asked again. “Look, these people will stop at nothing...”

“Clock's ticking, King. Write the answer.”

He wrote; Natalie saw the name and gasped.

“If he knows I am in custody, he will be on the run and both could do some serious damage to the country and your presidency. And come after me before I offer you what you need to know.” King eyed the video monitor as he answered. “Pete Cavanaugh.”

“Holy shit!” the president said.

"When and how did it start?" Natalie asked.

"My immunity deal?" King asked meekly.

"Not on the table at the moment," the president said in a voice that was equally menacing. "Give us the broad strokes now. If it seems compelling, I'll consider it. Otherwise, you will be redacted to a non-U.S. location for enhanced interrogation. If it is any consolation, nothing in the debrief will be permissible in court, assuming you ever see the inside of a courtroom."

Owen King swallowed hard, his hands trembling as he began to speak. "It started in 1947, after Roswell. The government realized we weren't alone and formed a secret group to manage the situation. We mostly called ourselves the Observers, or originally, the Ground

Observers. That was based on the aliens using the same term for what they were doing."

He paused, glancing nervously at Natalie before continuing. "Our mandate was simple: keep the secret at all costs and harness alien technology for the benefit of humanity. Our founders felt we were protecting people from a truth they just couldn't handle."

"Did the aliens require you to keep this secret?" Emily asked.

"Yes... I mean, no. Honestly, I don't know; it was before my time. It was implied that they did, but by the time I was fully read into the group, the protocols for total silence were firmly baked into the system."

King's voice cracked as he delved into the darker aspects of their mission. "I know, I know we... we've done terrible things. Armed response teams were deployed to silence witnesses. We drugged abductees, erased their memories. When that didn't work, we discredited them, drove them to the brink of madness."

Tears welled in his eyes as he recalled the most painful memories. "Some couldn't take it. They took their own lives, unable to reconcile what they'd experienced with the manufactured reality we forced on them. God help me, we let it happen. We always convinced ourselves it was for the greater good."

King's shoulders slumped, the weight of his accumulated actions finally seeming to crush him visibly. "I know it sounds monstrous, but you have to understand. We truly believed we were keeping the peace, preventing global panic. And...the technology we gained... it's revolutionized medicine, energy, transportation. We always told ourselves that the ends justified the means."

He looked up at Natalie, his face a mask of anguish. "I was only trying to do what I thought was right. To keep the peace. But now... now I see the cost was too high. We were just wrong. So terribly wrong. In the end, it didn't even matter."

Natalie eyed the screen but moved on to the next question. They would have time for a more in-depth debriefing later.

"Who in public office, the military, the scientific community, or the media is in alliance with you? Write the names on this paper as well as whether they know the full extent or are simply being paid to do what you ask."

King swallowed hard. He'd seen this question on the list moments earlier and dreaded it immediately.

"There are too many to name."

"No, there aren't," the president nearly yelled. "Your secret is too big. Hell, I was kept in the dark, as were most of my predecessors, I believe. Three people can keep a secret if two of them are dead."

Natalie picked up from POTUS, "Give us the top names, countries, and positions for now. We will get into the weeds later."

King scribbled rapidly, his hand shaking as he filled the paper with names. His face contorted with a mix of relief and dread, as if unburdening himself of a terrible weight while simultaneously sealing his fate. When he finished, he pushed the list across the table to Natalie.

She scanned the names, her eyebrows rising as she took in the implications. "Only fourteen?" she asked, skepticism evident in her voice.

King nodded, his voice hoarse. "The full truth... it's highly compartmentalized. Only eight actually know everything. The others... they're pawns, really. Paid well to follow orders without asking too many questions."

Natalie's eyes widened as she reached the ninth name on the list. "Raymond Whittner? The chief of staff?"

King nodded grimly. "He's not fully read in, but like Cavanaugh, he's been instrumental in keeping certain investigations from gaining traction."

The president's voice crackled over the video link, a mix of anger and disbelief. "I trusted that man. He's been by my side for years."

Natalie continued down the list, her face growing more serious with each name. "You've got a Nobel Prize-winning cosmologist here. And... Christ, the general in charge of our strategic nuclear arsenal?"

King slumped in his chair. "We needed people in key positions. People who could influence policy, control information, and... if necessary... have access to our most powerful weapons."

Natalie held the list to the camera so the others could read it. She then handed the paper to the agent who scanned it for the official case files.

Emily leaned closer to the camera, her voice tight with barely contained fury. "You have two of the richest men in the world on here.

The assistant director of the CIA. Former heads of major defense industries. This goes beyond just covering up alien encounters, doesn't it? What exactly were you preparing for?"

King's eyes darted nervously between Natalie and the screen. "We... we had to be ready. For anything. We were keeping a global secret."

Natalie heard President Martin giving orders to someone off-screen to pick up Whittner, the general, and everyone else on American soil. They needed to move quickly to get all the collaborators before any of them realized the head of NovaCore had been taken down.

Natalie was reluctant to move on, as there were undoubtedly many more names to extract from this piece of shit, but she pointed to her list of questions. "Number three. Where is your own exotic tech located? We want locations and descriptions, King. What have you built, and what is actually from the aliens?"

Owen shifted uncomfortably in his seat, his eyes darting nervously around the room. "We've... we've developed some remarkable technologies," he began, his voice barely above a whisper.

"Such as?" Natalie pressed, her patience wearing thin.

King swallowed hard. "There are anti-gravity pods, shaped like elongated eggs. They're fully autonomous, capable of complex flight operations without human intervention."

"Yes, I am fully aware of that one," Natalie snarled. "Cost my wingman his life."

Emily leaned forward, her interest sharpened to laser focus. "I want to come back to that, Natalie. What else?"

"We have craft that can travel underwater at speeds exceeding Mach 1.5," Owen continued, his words coming faster now. "In the atmosphere, they can hit ten times that speed with no visible flight control surfaces."

Natalie's eyebrows shot up. "I'm a pilot, and that sounds completely impossible."

King shook his head. "Not with the gravitics technology we've... acquired. There's also a large boomerang-shaped cargo hauler. Completely silent, invisible to radar. We use it for covert transport operations."

As Owen described more exotic achievements—quantum communication devices, energy weapons that could disable electronics without harming organic matter—Natalie noticed his growing discomfort.

"The other part of the question, Mister King. Where are these marvels built and stored?" she asked pointedly.

Owen's eyes darted away. "I... I'm not entirely sure. The facilities are spread out, you see. For security reasons. Everything with our group is compartmentalized."

Natalie slammed her hand on the table, making King jump. "Don't play games with us. Where are they?"

King's facade crumbled. "I truly don't know all the locations. Gibson... he handles the facilities and logistics. I was kept intentionally ignorant of many details."

The truth dawned on Natalie. King, for all his power, was just another layer in this onion of secrecy. The real answers might lie with Gibson or some other person who knew. But she'd seen that name on his list as well as the personnel directory for NovaCore.

"Where is this Gibson?"

"Umm... he... he's most likely at our detention facility?"

"Your what?" President Martin all but yelled.

"Your private jail?" Natalie prompted, urging him for an answer. He was turning into the equivalent of human jelly.

"Sometimes it was required. I... I am sorry, but we had to contain the truth through any means necessary. Also, the alien Observers sometimes bring subjects back. We collect them for processing."

"Processing?" Emily asked.

"See what they remember, decide if they should be sent back home or detained," King answered.

"How many alien species are we dealing with?" Natalie asked.

King shook his head. "Our best guess is only two currently. The original Observers, or as some call them, Grays. We know others have visited, but we have few details on them. We have very little actual contact with any of them. For the most part, the monitoring species, the Observers, were curious but left us alone."

"What changed?"

King relayed the basis of the communication with the aliens terminating the human monitoring. When Natalie pushed him for more details, the man turned deathly pale.

"The aliens that are starting to attack. They are species A044, and they are bad news."

"That's why you are cooperating, isn't it? You're even more scared of them than us," Natalie said.

King told them everything about A044, the scant bit of information the original aliens had shared, and the encounter in the desert.

"So, they are coming to occupy the planet?" President Martin asked.

Owen ran a hand through his sweaty hair, then shook his head. "They are going to colonize Earth. The days of passive observation are over. Their advanced scouts are already here. Most... maybe all of the recent incidents are because of them."

Natalie saw the president and Emily mute the video link and turn from the camera. Something was going on. Part of the president's protective detail leaned in and whispered in his ear, then the camera feed went black. She looked down at Owen King and again wanted to slap the man.

"Where are your detainees?"

He told her he wasn't sure. Then Emily unmuted the video link. "Is Laura Bennett at that facility?"

King looked worried. "That name..."

"Don't fucking play ignorant with me."

"Yes... yes, she is there... or was there. Gibson was going to... to eliminate her when he apparently decided to take my daughter. Please, Ms. Reeves. You have to help her. Emma knows nothing of any of this. She lost her mom when she was young and..." King broke down into sobs.

She had the agents take him back to lock up. King was probably heading to a military prison, one he would likely never leave.

She watched as they led him away, possibly to redirect him to an unknown location where he would be interrogated night and day for as long as he was there.

"Natalie?"

Emily Carter sounded rushed. "Yes, is everything okay?" Natalie asked.

"I am the new chief of staff. Whittner shot himself as agents stormed his house."

"Good Lord," Natalie groaned. "Congratulations?" she said questioningly, ending in a nervous laugh.

"Right, just what I wanted right now." Emily said. "More bad news, though."

All Natalie wanted to do was get to the location of the detainees King had told her about. What Emily said next changed that priority.

"Another incoming orbital weapon will be striking off the California coast within the next few minutes. This one will be a swarm of impactors, not just one."

"And you waited until now to tell me this?"

The human race was going to war.

"Alien Attack" or Climate Hoax? Why the Left is Using Orbital Strikes to Push Green New Deal

— **By Tucker Hartwell, Senior Political Correspondent**

While mainstream media pushes the "alien invasion" narrative, Tucker Tonight has obtained exclusive documents suggesting yesterday's California coastal strikes may be an elaborate false flag operation designed to advance radical climate legislation. Sources within the Pentagon confirm that the so-called "orbital bombardment" created destruction patterns remarkably similar to proposed climate disaster scenarios used by environmental groups to justify trillion-dollar spending packages. The timing couldn't be more convenient for Democrats facing midterm pressure.

"They've been telling us for years that climate change would cause massive coastal flooding and devastation," said former NOAA whistleblower Dr. James Mitchell. "Now suddenly we have massive coastal flooding and devastation, but it's supposedly from 'space aliens'? The American people aren't stupid." Multiple defense contractors with ties to green energy lobbying groups were reportedly conducting "atmospheric testing" in the Pacific region just hours before the strikes occurred.

As Congress prepares for emergency spending bills that could funnel billions toward renewable energy projects and coastal "reconstruction," one has to ask: who really benefits from this convenient disaster? While rescue teams work the rubble, Washington elites are already drafting legislation that looks suspiciously like the same climate agenda they've been pushing for years. Sometimes the simplest explanation is the right one - follow the money.

CHAPTER
ONE HUNDRED TWO

1246 UTC September 11
White House Oval Office
Washington, D.C., USA

The room buzzed with palpable tension as the briefing screens flickered to life. A news anchor's frantic voice filled the air: "Breaking news! An immense impactor has struck 200 miles off the coast of Los Angeles. The impact has triggered a massive tsunami heading toward the coastline. Evacuation orders are in place, but time is running out!"

Footage flashed across the screens, showing towering waves racing toward the shore. People ran through the streets, some clutching children, others with their arms filled with hastily gathered belongings. Cars clogged the highways, honking horns and blaring sirens creating a chaotic symphony of desperation.

The Situation Room hummed with tense energy as President Martin studied the tactical displays. Red markers dotted the California coast and now Colorado and Nevada, each representing newly confirmed alien sightings or orbital incidents.

"As you know, that was six hours ago. Casualty estimates are unknown but likely much higher than the Cascadia strike," the president said. This wasn't how he envisioned this particular session starting, but he wasn't the one dictating timelines and priorities at the moment.

"The pattern suggests coordinated reconnaissance," General Taylor explained, pointing to a cluster near Denver. "They're testing our response capabilities. After the Doha attack, we haven't seen any other hits on military installations."

President Martin nodded, his face drawn with exhaustion. "And our options?"

Pete Cavanaugh cleared his throat, drawing all eyes to him. His demeanor remained unruffled despite the crisis—tailored suit crisp, posture relaxed, as if discussing quarterly budget projections rather than an existential threat.

"Mr. President, I've prepared a comprehensive security response that I suggest we implement today." Cavanaugh's voice carried the practiced confidence of a man accustomed to being heard. "First, we order a national communications lockdown. All independent news outlets and social media platforms temporarily suspended."

The president's eyebrows rose. "Communications suspended, Pete?"

"To control the narrative, sir, prevent panic," Cavanaugh continued smoothly. "Second, we declare martial law in key metropolitan areas—New York, Los Angeles, Washington, Chicago. Full military control, enforced curfews, security checkpoints."

General Briggs shifted uncomfortably in his chair. "That's extreme. And Pete, is 'The Narrative' truly our biggest problem right now?"

Cavanaugh ignored him. "Finally, we need to activate the Continuity of Government Plan. We move senior leadership to secure locations—undisclosed, of course. The chain of command must be preserved at all costs."

The room fell silent. President Martin studied his national security advisor with newfound scrutiny.

"You're proposing we abandon the public and hide in bunkers?" General Briggs couldn't contain himself. "You want to turn American cities into war zones and black out communication? That's not defense—that's tyranny."

"Survival sometimes requires sacrifice, General." Cavanaugh's smile seemed fake. "If you're too weak to make it, maybe you're not the right man for the job."

The president raised his hand, silencing them both. "Pete, to me these measures also seem... excessive. We need to protect our citizens, not control them. Tell me what else you would have us do?"

"With respect, sir, we're facing an unprecedented threat." Cavanaugh leaned forward. "Conventional approaches won't suffice. The public will thank us when this is over."

President Martin exchanged a brief glance with General Briggs—almost imperceptible, but loaded with meaning.

The door opened, and Emily Carter came in with Linda Reyes, the head of Homeland Security. Both apologized for being late. Pete Cavanaugh immediately was staring daggers into both of the newcomers.

"I need time to consider all options," the president said carefully. "General Briggs, raise the alert level and prepare defensive measures for the affected regions. Standard protocols for now."

Cavanaugh's jaw tightened slightly—the only crack in his composed facade. "Standard? Mr. President, delaying decisive action could be catastrophic."

Cavanaugh circled the table, a predator stalking his prey. He tapped a button on his tablet, projecting an organizational chart onto the main screen—a pyramid with his title at the apex.

"What we need is Joint Defense Command—a unified structure with clear, singular leadership." His voice carried the false humility of a man pretending not to nominate himself for absolute power. "All military branches would report directly to this office for streamlined decision-making. No bureaucratic tangles, no conflicting orders."

Emily watched silently, her pen poised over her legal pad. Something in Cavanaugh's demeanor had shifted—the mask of the reasonable advisor slipping to reveal something far more dangerous. That was the hope in this bit of stagecraft, see what else they could wring out of the man before taking him down.

"Furthermore," Cavanaugh continued, "we should consider temporarily suspending state governments in high-risk zones. Governors, mayors—they'll only slow our response with their demands for explanation and resources."

President Martin's face darkened. "Suspend elected officials?"

"We can't afford democratic debate when the enemy is knocking on the door." Cavanaugh's tone turned icy. "The Constitution wasn't written with alien invasion in mind."

General Taylor, who had been listening with increasing horror, slammed his fist on the table. "Are you out of your goddamn mind, Pete? This isn't defense strategy. It's a coup!"

The room fell silent. Cavanaugh's lips curled into a smirk.

"I'm sorry if this makes you uncomfortable, General, but we require real leadership during this time of crisis." He emphasized the word 'real' with barely disguised contempt. "Not everyone has the stomach for what must be done."

Emily's pen moved across her yellow legal pad: *See if we can get him to name more names?* She angled the note toward the president, who gave an almost imperceptible nod.

"Pete," President Martin said, "who else supports this approach? I'd like to know which of my advisors share your... vision."

"I've discussed this framework with several key figures who understand the gravity of our current situation." Cavanaugh's eyes flickered momentarily. "Director Harmon at CIA is on board. Senator Blackwood and his committee would back an emergency powers act. And there are others who prefer to remain... discreet for now."

Emily added these names to her growing list, her face betraying nothing while her mind raced. Cavanaugh wasn't just proposing a coup—he was beginning to reveal his network.

"Discreet? Names, Pete. Who else do you have in mind for the key roles in your plan?" the president asked.

Cavanaugh hesitated, his calculated composure slipping for just a moment before he recovered. "I've had productive conversations with General Whitfield at Strategic Command and Director Coleman at NSA." His eyes darted briefly to Emily, then away.

"Interesting group of people," Martin said. "Certainly a capable group, but would those people follow this plan of yours? Let's face it, Pete, some of this is clearly unconstitutional."

"All of it!" Emily stated loudly.

"Can I ask why she is in this meeting?" Pete asked, glaring at Emily again.

The president ignored the man's question. "I'm waiting on your response, Pete."

"Yes, these people have very loyal teams who will operate under whatever guidelines I instruct."

"That you instruct?" General Taylor snorted.

Pete looked around nervously, sensing that he had perhaps overplayed his hand.

"I am simply the voice of the president, executing his orders as, hopefully, he will be going somewhere much safer than here."

"Mr. President," Emily interjected carefully, "perhaps we should consider multiple response scenarios before committing to any single approach. I'd like to present some alternative strategies that don't require suspending constitutional rights."

Cavanaugh's eyes narrowed at Emily. "Ms. Carter, with all due respect, this isn't the time for academic exercises. We need decisive action, not committee debates."

"Pete, are you still foolishly backing your statement that aliens aren't our problem?" Emily asked.

Cavanaugh stammered, clearly not expecting the direct accusation on his past opinions. "I don't have time for this," he said with growing exasperation. "Why don't you just let the grown-ups talk?"

"That's enough, Pete." President Martin's voice cut through the tension, steel beneath his measured tone. "I've heard your proposals, and frankly, I'm also concerned about their direction and your intentions. These aren't defensive measures—they're power grabs."

Cavanaugh's face hardened. "With respect, Mr. President, you're not seeing the big picture. The threat we face requires extraordinary measures."

"No, what I see is you suggesting we abandon the very principles we're sworn to defend." Martin gestured to General Briggs. "The General's approach maintains our values while protecting our people."

"Briggs?" Cavanaugh scoffed. "He's clinging to an archaic system and broken ideals. His tired, outdated methods will get us all killed."

"Enough, Pete," Emily stepped forward, her presence suddenly commanding the room.

Cavanaugh sneered. "Didn't know the president's secretary was allowed an opinion here."

Emily didn't flinch. "You're not suggesting defense. You're consolidating power. Martial law? Total media blackout? You want control, not protection for anyone other than yourself. Moving the president somewhere secure in a comms blackout means whoever is here calls the shots."

He stepped closer, voice lowering to a whisper. "You don't know what you're meddling with, Carter. You don't have the clearance or the balls. You never did."

Emily met his gaze, unyielding. "Yes, I do. And I also know treason when I see it."

Cavanaugh laughed, hollow and sharp. "Treason? You have no idea what's really happening here."

Emily called out loudly, "Now!"

The doors burst open, and a team of FBI and Secret Service agents flooded the room, weapons drawn. Cavanaugh's eyes darted around, calculating, his smirk cracking.

Emily stepped forward, papers in hand. "That's where you are wrong. Apparently, you were unaware that NovaCore was raided yesterday. We know all about who you've been taking orders from. You're a goddamn traitor, Pete. Not only did you sell out the president, you sold out the entire human race."

Cavanaugh's jaw tightened. "You're bluffing."

Emily's eyes went hard as steel as she removed a folded letter from her pad. "This is a warrant for your arrest, Pete Cavanaugh. Espionage. High treason. And about two dozen other federal offenses."

Three Secret Service agents roughly pinned him to the table, cuffing him as he thrashed. His perfectly tailored suit wrinkled under their grip, his carefully constructed facade crumbling away into tears.

He shouted, voice cracking. "You're making a mistake! You think this is over? This is just the beginning!"

Emily stepped closer, leaning in as he was dragged from the room. "Oh, I know it's just the beginning. But you won't be around to see it."

Silence hung heavily in the aftermath. Papers scattered across the polished table. Someone coughed. The president looked at Emily, stunned. "So, how much damage did he do?"

Emily pointed at Reyes.

"He may have doomed us all," the woman said, her face ashen. "The security protocols he implemented—they weren't designed to keep aliens out. They were designed to let them in...let them see and access everything. NovaCore and its subsidiaries are in every government office with back doors in software to security systems to plain old human turncoats."

She nodded to Emily. "That guy really missed his calling as a Bond villain. Thanks to the heads-up by the chief of staff yesterday, we were able to move quickly to isolate the more critical systems and monitor all outgoing feeds. On my word, the FBI is poised to arrest an additional 1,100 department heads, government officials, and related individuals. Thanks to this meeting, we now have several more names and departments to add."

"Good work, everyone," the president said. “Emily, Bill...I know that had to feel good. Sorry it took me so long to see things clearly."

CHAPTER ONE HUNDRED THREE

The room was barely a third full. Kaden had never noticed how bland it was. The people, the members of SCET, had been what gave it life. Brilliant minds, each of them. The loss of Sarah and Elena still weighed on him terribly. Now, he feared for the others as well. Especially Natalie Reeves, if he was being honest.

"Bill told me before I started this to choose wisely which hill I wanted to die on."

Kaden knew Emily was referring to the retired general, her close confidant. He smiled and nodded. "Military philosophy often emphasizes the wisdom of prioritizing the conflicts that truly matter."

"And does this one, Professor? Does it truly matter, or am I just chasing ghosts?" Emily asked.

"One does not necessarily preclude the other, Director Carter. We are all here for different reasons, but we have one goal."

"But people have died on my watch. A week ago, I only worried that the president was losing faith in me and that the committee was going to be shut down." She played with a pen on the table, spinning it in circles only to stop it suddenly. "How little we knew and how much I worried about how things looked."

"This is a town in which appearances matter more than the facts,"

Kaden said. "I, myself, have fallen victim to the self-doubt such things can foster. Ultimately, Director Carter, all that counts is the truth."

She wanted to share the information that Cavanaugh had been taken into custody, but that was not being released publicly for now. There was also the somewhat disturbing fact that they did not have solid confirmation from the federal holding facility that the weasel had ever arrived. Hopefully, that was one of the millions of comms failures, but one never knew.

The door to the conference room swung open, and in strode Trent Rogers. Kaden looked up, surprise evident in his eyes, while Emily straightened her posture, sensing a shift in the atmosphere.

"Director Carter," Trent began, his voice steady but filled with an undercurrent of excitement. "There are problems, growing unrest. And this time I'm not just talking about my digestive system."

Emily tilted her head, curiosity piqued. "Go ahead and share it?"

"Don't worry, it's only slightly more terrifying than usual. But personally, I think the president should have addressed the nation like he's promised." Trent moved closer, lowering his voice as if sharing a secret of monumental importance. "There now seems to be a growing resistance movement...within the government and the military."

"That sounds a lot like treason," Emily said. "Or a coup." She considered that chopping off the head of the snake had only made the rest of the Observers even more motivated.

"Agreed, but maybe not the worst thing that could happen. We've known we have been up against well-placed operatives from the ones now known as the Observers, but now, it seems they are all beginning to flee for the lifeboats. Some are still trying to hide in the shadows, but that won't last. Owen King's arrest seems to have initiated a massive plan of denial and counter-moves by his associates.

"High-ranking officials, military personnel, even some within intelligence agencies—they're all choosing sides, and thankfully, most of the influential ones are rallying against the conspirators. And now that we know who has been behind all of it—the cover-up, the attacks on this group and more—the fallout is beginning in earnest."

Kaden leaned forward, skepticism mingling with a flicker of hope. "Perhaps, Emily, we need to come up with our own plan."

Trent's eyes gleamed with conviction. "I think you should develop a plan to expose the conspirators on a global scale. To bring the truth to light and hold those responsible accountable."

"King's group is powerful, Agent Rogers. They have been at it for over a generation," Emily said. "What makes you think we can take them all down now, and does it even matter anymore?"

A soft knock on the door, which opened just enough for the president's aide to lean in. "Director Carter. The president would like you to join him in the Cabinet Room in five minutes, please."

Emily nodded and stood, gesturing apologies to the others.

"No...ma'am. I'm sorry, but please bring your entire team," the young man said. "President Martin wants to include each of you."

Ten minutes later, the discussion was already in full swing. Top military advisors and several cabinet members were included. No formalities, no posturing. This was a 'Get Shit Done' session, to use one of General Briggs' colorful catchphrases. "Okay, chemical weapons, biological weapons, pandemics, poisoning, or whatever it takes. By God, we are really up against it," Martin said.

"Professor, you told us the other day about the fleet of ships headed toward Earth."

"Yes, Mister President. That is still our biggest threat."

"So what can we do to fight back? There are potentially thousands of them coming, right?" Martin asked.

"Well, it's a lot, but as Kaden and Natalie have pointed out, there are a finite number of these creatures," Emily said. "Even if there are 100 ships, there are only so many weapons, germs, and aliens that you can stuff into that number of interstellar starships. We have nine billion people on Earth. We need to weaponize every single one of them."

"How?" the president asked.

"Well, sir, we know there's likely to be more attacks, likely more direct attacks. They have been probing us, doing experiments, tagging us for who knows how long."

"So," the president looked down at his hands, "you're saying they know everything about us?"

"No, sir, Mr. President," Natalie said, speaking up for the first time. "What that means is they're scared. They're scared of something we possess. We're dangerous to them; we just don't know how. Just like when we go out in the ocean and tag a shark. We want to learn more about it. We want to track its behavior. We want to seek to understand. To some degree, we do this so we can exert some other level of control over it in the future. That control may be just to not be eaten by them, but it's control. We want to modify that shark's behavior. We want to understand where the threat really is. That is what the aliens have been doing. They want to know what kind of danger we might be."

"That makes sense. Please tell me more."

Kaden eyed the military officers before adding his points. He knew they still disagreed, but it needed to be said. "Okay, sir, but you won't like it. As we've seen from this past week, we can't do very much to stop their initial attacks. We simply need to understand that. What we can do is isolate parts of our power grid so they're unaffected. There need to be areas or assets that are not going to be taken out by whatever devices—EMP, or whatever else they use."

Emily added, "We can start distributing food to more remote locations immediately. Our food distribution system is heavily dependent on just a few companies and a handful of distribution centers. Those are easy targets, and we need to widen that footprint today," she offered, backing up the professor's line of thought. "Staple goods, fuel, food, and essential supplies. Things that will keep people alive."

"Okay, I can understand that," President Martin said.

"Respectfully, sir, no, I don't think you do. Assuming this goes the way we think, this will need to be a global operation, every major power in the world. We'll need to adopt the same kind of war footing if we're to survive as a species. I think we have to assume this force is not just hostile but ruthless, and we need to take steps for the survival of mankind."

"I'm not sure what you mean. We are the greatest military power in the world. I see us taking heavy losses, but there will be survivors. The country will survive," the president said.

"Sir, in our opinion," an Army colonel said, obviously speaking for the others, "the United States of America will be finished."

The president's face went ashen. He was losing the country on his watch. No politician wanted to even consider that as a possibility.

"But, sir, so will China, the United Kingdom, Russia, South America, Australia, India. Every power on Earth will go down the same way. It will be the one great equalizer. Military strength will not matter. If they take out our electronics, our ability to command, and they hold the high ground, we will lose."

Emily knew this was impossibly hard for the president's military advisors to admit. They'd undoubtedly gone over it numerous times in preparing for this meeting. They also knew the president would likely want more options.

"Financial dominance will not matter. Overnight, we could find ourselves on a very level playing field with every other human civilization on Earth," Emily said. "We will be on our way to being just another third-world country."

"So, what will change things? Can we use our nuclear arsenal against the incoming fleet?"

Kaden glanced at the Army general before giving a slight nod. "We probably should, yes, although their effectiveness in space will be far less than on ground targets. Down here, the atmosphere magnifies the damage via the shock wave. You won't have that in space. Also, we have to assume the alien ships have shielding to counteract radiation, as that is something they would have to overcome to even travel interstellar distances. One other thing is using nukes could make it worse for ourselves. It could flood the upper atmosphere with radiation and cause global EMPs that finish off our electronics as well as any remaining power."

"Jesus, Mary, and Joseph."

"We feel like the aliens believe that if they take out our command and control, they take out our food supplies, take out our electricity, and take out our communications, then they will be able to walk all over us," Emily said.

"What will matter is our resistance and our survival—those people who are prepared to mount a guerrilla war against the aliens."

"Not our armed forces?"

"No, sir. They will almost certainly be subject to a withering barrage in the initial attacks."

The president could see this group had been putting in a tremendous amount of research and planning into all of this.

"Emily, I really enjoyed my briefings with Raymond much better." The president gave a little laugh and rubbed his eyes. "So, if I'm hearing you guys correctly, you do have a plan. You're saying we need to arm all of our citizens."

The chief of staff laughed. "This is America, sir. We're already armed. We just need to deploy them and give them the ammo, tools, training, and resources they need to succeed."

"How would this work, General? You've previously suggested that we prop up these camps of survivors, militias, preppers, and anyone else that might make a difference?"

"Yes, sir. As uncomfortable as it is for me to admit, if they attack, the alien fleet will win the war. We just have to make it so uncomfortable for the aliens to win the occupation that they eventually give up. As you said, it's a finite number. The math is in our favor. Theoretically, no matter what they bring to the table, we should be able to outlast them. We should be able to keep biting at their heels until they just give up and leave or... all die."

The general continued. "Since we are not sure how long it will take this fleet to arrive, we suggest every major power quietly begin widely dispersing their forces. Hide the troops, heavy artillery, and everything that would be useful in guerrilla warfare. All of the heavy maintenance armaments, those that require large crews or constant downtime, should be abandoned or scheduled for use in the first engagements."

Emily added, "That does mean, sir, that we need to keep some level of research ongoing. Our scientific and weapon development community must stay connected, viable, and obviously well-hidden. We need to protect them, so they can make use of the incoming scientific breakthroughs, reverse-engineered alien weaponry, understand their biology, and hopefully, even develop shielding and protocols that we can use to go back on the attack."

"That sounds like a tall order, Director Carter. That sounds like an Area 51 project. And who do you suggest putting something like that together?" President Martin had an interesting look on his face as he asked the question.

Emily gave a nervous glance to Natalie. The displeasure in what she was about to say was obvious. "Unfortunately, sir, there really is only one person, one group of people that I am aware of. Owen King is the obvious choice, along with his senior NovaCore teams."

CHAPTER
ONE HUNDRED FOUR

1801 UTC September 14
33°28′N, 94°02′E
Northeast Texas

High over Texas, the ovoid-shaped craft zigzagged through the sky with an erratic grace, like a dragonfly evading a predator. The other alien A044 strike craft, a sleek and menacing shadow, clung close behind. The F-18 fighter jets roared in pursuit, their pilots straining to keep up.

"That thing's barely on radar," Lieutenant Carson muttered, squinting through the cockpit's canopy. "Blinking in and out like a ghost."

"Eyes on the prize, Carson," Captain Harris barked through the comms. "Focus on the ovoid craft. It seems damaged." They had been briefed previously on other sightings of the Tic Tac-shaped craft.

The alien craft flickered, its image shimmering as it veered left, then right, dodging the pursuing craft's every move. Carson could almost see the strain in its maneuvers, like a wounded animal fighting for survival. The pale oval seemed more like a cube at times. Something about it was way beyond anything humans had built.

"Strike craft is stealthed," Harris said, his voice tense. "But I can see it. Keep your distance; don't engage directly. If the aliens want to fight each other, let 'em."

Carson's heart pounded as he nudged his jet into a tighter formation with the others. "Roger that. Just keeping an eye on it. Why would they be attacking each other?"

The sky lit up with brief flashes of light as the A044 Strikers fired energy bursts at the fleeing Tic Tac. The ovoid craft darted through the barrage, evading with a precision that defied human comprehension. Carson watched in awe; the technology at play was far beyond anything he'd seen. Command had taken to calling it an OvoCraft instead of the more common Tic Tac the media preferred.

"This thing's dancing circles around us," another pilot, Lieutenant Baker, chimed in. "Never seen anything like it."

"Stay sharp, Baker," Harris replied. "We need to box it in. Force it to ground if we can."

Carson adjusted his grip on the controls, his mind flipping through anything in his training that might help. The A044's cloaking made it a phantom, its movements only discernible by the OvoCraft's reactions. It was a deadly ballet in the skies, each maneuver a life-or-death gamble.

"Weapons hot," Harris ordered. "But hold fire until my command. We don't want to hit the wrong target."

"Understood," Carson responded, his thumb hovering over the trigger. "Which one would be the wrong one?" The OvoCraft's flickering image filled his sight, its desperation palpable. He felt a strange empathy for the alien craft, wondering what or who piloted it.

"The one being pursued," Harris said uncertainly.

The OvoCraft veered sharply downward, diving toward the north Texan plains. The A044 followed, relentless in its pursuit. Carson and the other pilots tightened their formation, ready to follow wherever the chase led.

"Hold steady," Harris commanded. "We've got it on the run."

Carson's jet shuddered as he descended, the ground rushing up to meet them. The OvoCraft's erratic flight pattern suggested damage, its movements growing more frantic.

"We're losing altitude fast," Baker warned. "This could get rough."

"Stay with it," Harris insisted. "This is our chance."

The OvoCraft flickered again, its form almost vanishing before Carson's eyes. He gritted his teeth, focusing on the craft as it dipped lower and lower.

A sudden flash erupted from the striker ship, an eerie, silent pulse radiating outward. Carson's cockpit instruments flickered, then died. The jet engine sputtered roughly and fell silent. Panic surged through him.

"Mayday! Mayday!" he yelled into the dead radio. "Systems are down! Ejecting!"

His fingers scrambled over the ejection handles. He pulled with all his strength. The canopy blew away, and he felt the violent thrust as the seat rockets ignited, propelling him skyward. The force pressed him back into the seat, and the jet shrank beneath him, spiraling downwards, now a lifeless hunk of metal.

A second explosion echoed through the air as Baker's jet followed suit. The striker's weapon had left them defenseless, mere passengers in their own dying aircraft.

Carson's parachute deployed with a jerk, slowing his descent. He glanced around, catching sight of Baker's chute blossoming open nearby. Relief mingled with fear as he took in the scene below.

The ovoid alien craft, no longer under pursuit, spun wildly out of control. Its sleek, white surface glinted erratically as it tumbled through the air, heading for a dense forest below. Carson's heart pounded in his chest, knowing the terrain well—a heavily wooded area near a large lake, the perfect place for the craft to disappear.

The alien ship plunged into the treetops, branches snapping and leaves scattering in its wake. Carson winced at the sound, the sheer force of its impact echoing through the forest. The craft vanished among the trees, a final, violent spin sending it crashing near the water's edge.

Carson's feet hit the ground hard, knees buckling slightly from the impact. He quickly unbuckled the harness, shrugging off the parachute. He scanned the forest, the smell of burnt electronics and pine filling his nostrils. Baker landed a few yards away, struggling to free himself from his chute.

"You okay?" Carson shouted, jogging over.

"Yeah, I'm good," Baker replied, breathless. "That was insane. Did you see where it went down?"

Carson nodded, pointing toward the lake. "Over there. Near the water. We need to find it."

"What about Harris?"

Baker shook his head, determination in his eyes. "Let's move. Before something else gets there."

Together, they dashed into the forest, branches slapping against their flight suits. The thick underbrush slowed their progress, but the sight of smoke rising in the distance spurred them on. They had to reach the crash site, and fast.

It took over an hour for Carson and Baker to navigate the dense forest, their boots sinking into the mud as they pressed forward. The sun dipped below the horizon, casting long shadows that made the terrain even more treacherous. They finally broke through the tree line and stood at the edge of the lake, panting and soaked in sweat. A line of downed trees and disturbed ground led into the lake.

"There," Carson said, pointing to the water. Just below the surface thirty yards offshore, the Tic Tac-shaped craft glimmered faintly in the twilight, like a ghostly apparition. It rested at a slight angle, one end buried deep in the lakebed. It looked less like an ovoid now; they could see the surface was made up of polyhedrons that caught the fading light with a multitude of shifting angles.

Baker knelt down, scooping up water with his hand. "How deep do you think it is?"

Carson squinted, assessing the distance. "Not too deep. Maybe twenty feet at most. We can manage it, but we need to be smart about this."

Baker nodded, stripping off his flight suit to reveal a standard-issue undershirt and pants. "We dive down, find the access hatch, and get it open. Simple, right?"

"Yeah, simple," Carson echoed, though his thoughts were filled with uncertainty. "We may need some tools or something."

"We have the knife and flashlight from our SEER kit. Not much else."

Carson nodded, slipping the light into his tactical belt and taking a deep breath. "Ready?"

"As I'll ever be," Baker replied, adjusting his own flashlight around his neck with the supplied lanyard.

They waded into the water, the cold shocking their systems and tightening their muscles. With synchronized nods, they took deep breaths and dove beneath the surface. The world above faded into muffled silence, replaced by the eerie tranquility of the lake.

Visibility was poor, but the faint glow from the craft's underside provided a guiding beacon. They swam toward it, the weighted belts helping them stay submerged. Carson reached the craft first, running his hands over its mostly smooth, seamless surface. No obvious entry points were visible.

The ship was about fifty feet long and probably half that wide. It had no wings, no flight surfaces of any kind. The surface felt oddly warm and unlike metal or plastic. Carson couldn't even describe it. He was touching something truly alien.

Baker joined him, their eyes meeting in silent communication. They spread out, feeling along the craft's hull. Carson's fingers finally brushed against a slight indentation on a lower edge, a panel almost imperceptible against the alien metal. He motioned to Baker, who swam over. Carson pointed up, and Baker joined him to get a breath of air.

"May have found a way in on the underside. It's nearly invisible but definitely feels like a seam or panel."

Baker eyed the darkening sky above nervously. Flashes of lightning showed the silhouette of the opposing craft still orbiting high above. "We need to be quick, man."

Together, they worked to pry the panel open. It resisted at first, but Carson's determination won out. The hatch gave way with a soft click, revealing an entryway just big enough for them to squeeze through. They exchanged another nod, the weight of their discovery beginning to sink in.

CHAPTER
ONE HUNDRED FIVE

0806 UTC September 12
Vatican City
Italy, Europe

The Vatican's grand Sistine Chapel, usually a place of hushed reverence, now echoed with frantic whispers and muffled sobs. Cardinal Alessandri stood before a group of trembling priests, his own hands shaking as he clutched a rosary.

"Brothers, we must remain steadfast in our faith," he said, his voice cracking. "The Holy Father calls for unity in these unprecedented times."

But even as he spoke, a young priest collapsed to his knees, wailing, "How can this be? Are we truly so insignificant in God's plan?"

Across the world in Mecca, the Grand Mosque was in chaos. Pilgrims who had come for spiritual enlightenment now found themselves grappling with an existential crisis. Sheikh Abdullah al-Turki addressed the crowd, his words broadcast to millions.

"Allah's creation is vast and beyond our comprehension," he declared. "We must approach this revelation with humility and seek to understand its place within our faith."

But murmurs of dissent rippled through the crowd. Some saw the aliens as a test from Allah, while others whispered of 'Jinn' and other dark forces at work.

In India, the ancient Kashi Vishwanath Temple became a focal point for Hindu reflection on the cosmic revelation. Swami Avimukteshwaranand addressed a gathering of devotees, many of whom sat in stunned silence.

"Our scriptures speak of multiple worlds and dimensions," he said calmly. "Perhaps these beings are simply another manifestation of the divine cosmic dance."

Yet even as he spoke, a group of saffron-clad extremists pushed through the crowd, shouting about the need to 'purify' the Earth of alien influence.

In a small town in America's Bible Belt, Pastor Jim Rawlings stood before his congregation, his face contorted with rage.

"These so-called aliens are nothing but demons sent to test our faith!" he thundered, slamming his fist down on the wooden pulpit. "We must stand ready to wage holy war against these abominations!"

His words were met with a mix of fervent "Amens" and horrified gasps. In the back pew, a family quietly slipped out, unable to reconcile this hateful rhetoric with their own religious beliefs.

Meanwhile, in a converted warehouse on the outskirts of Tokyo, a new cult calling themselves 'The Celestial Awakened' gathered in growing numbers. Their leader, a charismatic woman named Akira, preached with messianic fervor.

"The star beings have come to elevate us!" she cried, her eyes shining. "We must prepare ourselves to join them in ascension!"

Her followers swayed in ecstatic devotion, even as elsewhere in the city concerned family members pleaded with authorities to intervene.

The towering spires of St. Patrick's Cathedral loomed over the bustling streets of Manhattan, a stark contrast to the chaos unfolding beyond its hallowed walls. Inside, the air hung heavy with incense and uncertainty as parishioners packed the pews for yet another emergency service.

Eight-year-old Tommy fidgeted in his seat, his small hand tugging insistently at his mother's sleeve. "Mom," he whispered, his voice barely audible above the pastor's impassioned sermon. "If God made everything, did He make the aliens, too?"

Sonia glanced down at her son, her brow furrowed with a concern mixed with exhaustion. This was their third service this week, each one leaving Tommy with more questions than answers.

"Shh, honey," she murmured, smoothing his unruly hair. "Let's listen to Father Michael."

But Tommy persisted, his young mind grappling with concepts far beyond his years. "But if the aliens are real, does that mean the Bible got it wrong? Are we still special to God?"

Sonia bit her lip, unsure how to respond. The pastor's words washed over them, a torrent of reassurances and calls for faith in these trying times.

"Mom," Tommy pressed on, his eyes wide with confusion. "If God loves everyone, does He love the aliens, too? Even if they're... different?"

A few nearby parishioners shot disapproving glances their way, but Sonia couldn't bring herself to silence her son's genuine curiosity. She leaned down, whispering, "God's love is infinite, Tommy. I'm sure it extends to all of creation, even parts we don't understand yet."

Tommy nodded slowly, but his furrowed brow betrayed his lingering doubts. "Then why are people so scared? If God's in control, shouldn't we be okay?"

Sonia's heart ached at the innocence in her son's simple yet profound questions. She wrapped an arm around his small shoulders, pulling him close. "Sometimes, honey, even grown-ups get scared when things change. But that's why we come here—to remember that we're not alone."

As the sermon reached its crescendo, Tommy's questions continued to tumble out in a whispered stream of consciousness. "What if the aliens have their own God? Or what if they are like angels? Can we still go to heaven if there are other worlds out there?"

The beautiful church's peaceful atmosphere shattered as a brick smashed through a stained glass window, showering the congregation with shards of colored glass. Screams erupted as more windows exploded inward, followed by the sickening thud of Molotov cocktails hitting the floor.

"Idiots! Wake up!" a gruff voice on a microphone bellowed from outside. "Your God can't save you now!"

Flames licked up the ancient wooden pews as panicked parishioners scrambled for the exits. Sonia clutched Tommy to her chest, shielding him from the chaos erupting around them.

Father Michael's voice cut through the pandemonium. "Please, remain calm! This way to the—" His words ended in a wet gurgle as a group of looters burst up the steps to the altar, fists and clubs swinging, meeting the man's body in what was a horrific and relentless attack.

Sonia watched in horror as the pastor crumpled under the onslaught, his white collar stained crimson. Acrid smoke quickly filled the air, stinging her eyes as she stumbled towards a side exit, Tommy's face buried in her shoulder.

"Mom, I'm scared," Tommy whimpered, his small body trembling against hers.

"It's okay, baby," Sonia choked out, fighting back tears. "Just hold on tight." Flames were racing around the historic building with alarming speed. Already they were climbing the walls and licking the century-old timber beams high overhead.

As she joined the crowd rushing toward the door, Sonia's gaze fell on the crucifix above the altar, now wreathed in flames. A crushing wave of doubt washed over her. Maybe none of it was true. Maybe they'd all been fools, clinging to comforting lies in the face of a harsh, uncaring universe.

She pushed the thoughts aside, focusing on the terrified child in her arms. Whatever the truth, she needed to get Tommy out of here. Then, in a maddening scramble, she was pushed to the floor, and Tommy was dragged from her grasp by the crowd of arms and legs.

Sonia hit the ground hard, the impact knocking the wind from her lungs. Through the chaos of screams and crackling flames, she heard Tommy's desperate cries.

"Mom! Mommy!" His voice was raw with terror, growing fainter as the frantic crowd swept him away.

She tried to push herself up, but her limbs wouldn't cooperate. Panic clawed at her throat as she realized she couldn't move. The smoke burned her eyes and filled her lungs, making it impossible to call out to her son.

Suddenly, a tremendous weight crashed down on her back. Sonia heard the sickening crack of bones and felt a burst of white-hot agony. The pain was all-consuming, obliterating every other thought and sensation.

As the flames crept closer, licking at her clothes and hair, Sonia's world narrowed to a pinpoint of suffering. The grand questions that had consumed humanity since the apparent alien revelation—the nature of God, humanity's place in the universe, the future of faith—they all fell away.

In those final moments, Sonia no longer cared about extraterrestrial visitors or cosmic truths. The philosophical debates and religious upheavals that regularly seemed to shake the world to its core meant nothing now. Even her own beliefs, once a cornerstone of her life, crumbled to ash.

All that remained was the primal, animal instinct to survive and the crushing anguish of separation from her child. But as the fire began to consume more of her broken body, even those faded into a dull, distant ache.

Sonia's consciousness dimmed, the roar of the inferno fading to a muffled hum. Her last thoughts were not of aliens or gods or the fate of humanity. In the end, there was only darkness and the fading echo of her son's cries.

God's Wrath or Government Lies? Either Way, We're Selling Out of Our End Times Survival Kits

"I've said it for years, brothers and sisters—America has turned its back on the Lord, and now He's parting the skies. Whether it's angels or aliens, pestilence or propaganda, it's all been prophesied.

"But don't panic—prepare. With every donation of $300 or more, we'll send you our exclusive Revelation-Ready Resource Box, complete with freeze-dried manna, Genesis water tablets, and my new PPV series: Why God Hates Coastal Cities.

"Let the sinners scream. Let Washington fall. We serve a higher kingdom."

TBN America Live | 'Faith in the Fire' Broadcast with Pastor Royce Chandler

CHAPTER
ONE HUNDRED SIX

1057 EST September 14
Private Residence
Washington, D.C., USA

The world had always been a tinderbox, but now it burned openly. Despite the desperate insistence of global officials—clinging to narratives of terrorist plots, rogue nations, or freak natural disasters—the evidence was too stark, too overwhelming to deny. The skies had split with fire, and entire cities had been reduced to smoldering craters by weapons no human hand had ever built. These were not flying saucers from some B-movie fantasy; they were sleek warships, slicing through the atmosphere like blades, their energy cannons capable of turning buildings to ash with a single blast.

Faith in authority crumbled beneath the weight of undeniable truth. Governments scrambled for control, their denials drowned out by the roar of riots and insurrections. In Paris, the banners of revolution flew above smoldering streets; in Beijing, crowds flooded the plazas, tearing down monuments of power; in London, Downing Street burned. Several governments had already fallen, toppled by their own citizens or crushed beneath alien firepower, while the rest held on by a thread, whispering lies to a populace that was no longer listening.

As mainstream news confirming an alien presence spread, cities across the globe erupted in chaos. In Rome, thousands of protesters flooded St. Peter's Square, their angry chants echoing off ancient stone walls. "La Chiesa ha mentito!" or "The Church has lied!" they screamed, hurling stones at the Vatican's windows. Swiss Guards struggled to maintain order as the crowd surged forward, demanding answers from a Pope who remained conspicuously silent.

Meanwhile, in Mecca, pilgrims clashed violently with Saudi security forces. What began as peaceful demonstrations quickly spiraled into riots as frustrations boiled over. The air filled with tear gas and the crackle of gunfire as authorities fought to regain control of Islam's holiest site.

In the United States, a group of Christian fundamentalists stormed the gates of NASA's Johnson Space Center in Houston. Led by a firebrand televangelist, they accused the agency of colluding with 'demonic alien forces' and demanded the release of classified information. Armed security personnel were overwhelmed as the mob breached the facility, setting fire to laboratories and destroying years of research.

Local officials there were also overwhelmed as members of their own ranks joined in on the riots. Every remaining government scrambled to respond to the rapidly escalating crisis. In Washington D.C., President Martin authorized the deployment of National Guard troops to protect key infrastructure and religious landmarks. Similar measures were enacted in capitals around the world as leaders sought to prevent further violence and property damage.

The United Nations convened an emergency session, calling for calm and unity in the face of unprecedented challenges. But their pleas fell on deaf ears as conspiracy theories and extremist ideologies spread like wildfire across social media. Over half the member representatives failed to even show.

In an effort to combat disinformation, social media and tech giants implemented strict content moderation policies. But for every account they suspended, a dozen more sprang up in its place, each peddling its own version of 'the truth' about humanity's place in the cosmos.

Then there were the videos, many of which were obvious fakes, but a significant number seemed equally credible and horrifying.

Natalie Reeves scanned through the curated videos list MUFON had sent over. She clicked the play icon. Shaky smartphone footage captured from a high-rise apartment in Tokyo showed a massive, dark shape hovering silently over the city skyline. The object, easily the size of several city blocks, blacked out the stars as it drifted ominously overhead. Suddenly, dozens of smaller pods detached from the larger vessel, their lights pulsing as they descended toward the streets below. The video abruptly cut off as the entire city grid went dark.

"Jesus."

In the next clip, a live news broadcast from Rio de Janeiro was interrupted by panicked screams off-camera. The reporter, visibly shaken, turned to reveal a scene of chaos on Copacabana Beach. Evening beachgoers fled in terror as a series of strange, leopard-like creatures emerged from the forest. They moved in a stilted mechanical gait that was unsettling but still graceful. The camera struggled to focus on the entities, their forms seeming to shimmer and distort in the moonlight. Military helicopters roared overhead, searchlights sweeping the sand, but the creatures had already vanished into the city. The sounds of screams and scenes of explosions filled the areas the creatures had entered.

Another clip showed dashcam footage from a police cruiser in rural Montana capturing a high-speed pursuit of an unconventional nature. The officers were in hot pursuit of what appeared to be a semi-metallic cube skimming just above the highway. As the vehicle rounded a bend, the disc suddenly halted mid-air. A beam of intense blue light engulfed the police car, lifting the front end off the ground. The last frame showed the cruiser as it crashed back to the pavement hood first before the feed cut to static.

These videos were spreading like wildfire across social media platforms, each garnering millions of views within hours. Despite attempts by authorities to dismiss them as elaborate hoaxes, the sheer volume and consistency of the footage from around the globe made such explanations increasingly difficult to accept.

The last one on the list struck a nerve with the former naval aviator. The view was familiar to Natalie as it was a cockpit view from an F-16 jet, likely from a National Guard unit judging by the configuration. The pilots must have mounted a camera to the canopy to get a view like this. Or it was faked; she still wasn't sure which.

The roar of twin F-16 engines sliced through the sky, a pair of streaking missiles in pursuit of an unearthly adversary. Natalie squinted at the screen, her pulse quickening as she tried to categorize the sleek, angular lines of the UFO ahead of them. It somewhat resembled a hyperjet prototype she'd once glimpsed during a classified Navy briefing—an aircraft designed to operate seamlessly between atmosphere and space. Yet this craft was beyond anything human-made.

"Bravo One, visual on the bogey," came the crackling voice of the lead pilot over the radio. "This thing's playing hide and seek with our radar. Lock's impossible."

"Bravo Two, roger that," his wingman replied. "Visual contact confirmed. Switching to manual targeting."

The UFO darted left and right, almost playfully, evading the F-16s' every maneuver. The pilots, obviously skilled seasoned veterans, were struggling to keep pace, their aircraft straining under the extreme G-forces. Natalie could hear the tension in their voices, full of frustration and more than a trace of fear.

"Bravo One, it's like this thing knows our moves before we do. What the hell is it?"

"Bravo Two, stay focused. We need to get a clean shot. Wait—it's disappeared from radar again."

For a few tense moments, the radar screens in front of the pilot went blank. The pilots scanned the skies frantically, eyes peeled for any sign of the elusive craft. Then, as suddenly as it had vanished, the UFO reappeared, hovering ominously above the clouds.

"There it is! Bravo One, lining up for a shot," the lead pilot called out, determination evident in his tone.

"Bravo Two, covering your six. Make it count."

Just as the lead F-16 pilot was about to engage, the cockpit lights flickered and died. The roar of the engine sputtered into silence. Instruments went dark, leaving him hurtling through the sky in a powerless hulk of metal.

"Bravo One, you're dead stick!" the wingman shouted, panic creeping into his voice. "Eject, eject, eject!"

The wingman's jet banked sharply, disengaging from the pursuit to follow his stricken comrade. He watched with anticipation as the ejection seat finally shot free, a white parachute blossoming against the blue expanse. Relief washed over him—until he noticed the limp form slumped in the harness.

"Bravo One, respond!" he called out, his voice strained with urgency. "Bravo One, do you copy?"

There was no answer.

"Shit!" Natalie said. That was real. The authorities or Men in Black could deny it all they wanted, but she knew genuine when she saw it. That craft, though, its profile was nothing MUFON had ever cataloged. That bothered her greatly. This was the craft the military had been battling, and to think it was just a scout ship, a reconnaissance platform. As much as she wanted to be back in the game, the thought of flying against those things made her blood run cold.

CHAPTER
ONE HUNDRED SEVEN

0903 EST September 17
White House West Wing
Washington, D.C., USA

Natalie strode through the West Wing, her footsteps echoing in the hallowed halls. She found Emily in her new office, surrounded by stacks of files and a bustling team of aides.

"Congratulations again, Madam Chief of Staff," Natalie said, a hint of a smile on her lips.

Emily looked up, her eyes weary but determined. "Thanks, Natalie. Let's talk in the conference room. More secure. The SecDef is with the president in the situation room. California isn't the only place getting hit."

"Here?" Natalie asked worriedly.

"Nothing so far, but we are all on a ten-minute evac order, so we best talk fast."

Once inside, Emily's demeanor shifted. "What have you got?"

Natalie laid out her plan. "Somehow, the general has assembled a new team. We're going after the detainees."

Emily's brow furrowed. "You got the intel from that asshole King? Where?"

"He's still not positive, but from the description, we think Fort A.P. Hill in Virginia, and apparently they have at least one other detainee center at Fort Bliss, Texas. We are retasking satellite coverage over both."

Emily shook her head. "Inside Army bases? That's bold. Hiding in plain sight. Like putting a shark tank in a petting zoo. King and Nova-Core were into everything."

"We're taking down the facility at Fort Hill first. We have to use another team in Texas. Briggs thinks we can trust them, but it's obvious he has concerns."

"We all do. I assume Gibson and the asshole's daughter are supposed to be at Fort Hill."

"Yes, ma'am. And hopefully my friend, Laura Bennett."

"Oh, yes, the reporter. I like her, too. Spoke with her years ago."

Emily leaned back, processing. "You've done amazing work, Natalie. Way more than what you signed on for. No one will blame you if you sit this one out."

Natalie nodded, her jaw set. "No. I'm going on the raid. This is personal now, and we have to know more about the alien species King mentioned. Without us getting his daughter back, I'm not sure that asshole will offer anything more concrete. I wouldn't mind more military assets, though. Anyone else you can call on?"

"Hell, who knows? The general we brought in earlier is naming others left and right. We're looking at two dozen congressmen and five senators likely forced to resign, as well as hundreds of top brass all over the military. Hell, I don't know who we can trust; things are getting desperate. There's more," Emily said, her voice dropping. "I haven't said any of this until now for several reasons." She looked away as if trying to collect her thoughts.

Natalie thought it was a rare show of humanity from the newly minted chief of staff.

"Could you quickly tell me what happened that day? Your encounter, I mean. I've read the official report, but I knew that was bullshit long before today."

It seemed like an odd thing to bring up now. Natalie felt like she'd earned her spot on the team and shouldn't have anything else left to prove.

"This is a personal request, Lieutenant," Emily offered. "Please indulge me."

Natalie put a hand on her brow and stared at a spot on the wall as if it held the memories she was about to recount.

"It was a routine training flight off the coast of Georgia. Paul and I were fifty miles east of the carrier group. Clear skies, calm seas. We were at twenty thousand feet, just finishing a combat air patrol sweep."

Emily watched intently, her fingers steepled.

"Paul noticed it first. 'Natalie, you seeing this?' he called over the comms. I looked to my left, and there it was—an object hovering off his port side. It was white, shaped like a damned Tic Tac, maybe forty feet long. No wings, no rotors, no flight control surfaces. Just like the thing mentioned in the Nimitz encounter."

She paused, her eyes darkening with the memory.

"Paul tried to get a radar lock but couldn't. It was like nothing I'd ever seen up close—no heat signature, no radar return, just... there."

Natalie's voice grew tense as she continued. "Then it moved. Fast. One second it was hovering, the next it darted forward, maybe one or two kilometers. We tracked it down to the deck—the ocean surface where it went in. We could follow its course there as well—it left a hell of a cavitation trail.

"About ten minutes later, it shot straight out and up toward us. I jerked the controls up and to the right, but the thing was coming on a collision course. Then I saw Paul angling underneath me. It clipped his wingtip. His jet went into a spin. The UFO never slowed down; it was heading for space.

"The Air Boss was yelling in my ear to maintain visual contact," Natalie said, her tone bitter. "But what could I do? I watched Paul's F/A-18 spiral down towards the ocean. I was in shock but kept looking for him to eject. I watched until the jet splashed. It stayed mostly intact, but then I got another warning on my radar. The same craft, or maybe another one, was back and angling for me now. I had to take evasive action.

"The radar track showed the object moving erratically—up, down, side to side—impossible speeds and angles. Every call from the Air Boss became more frantic: 'Rammer-4, do you have visual? Rammer-4, what's your fuel state?' I only got glimpses of the other craft before it zoomed off. Honestly, all I could see was empty ocean where Paul should have been. His Hornet was gone; it must have sunk fast. I circled above his last known position until I was nearly out of fuel," Natalie continued.

She swallowed hard, her voice growing quieter. "I finally had to head back to the carrier or risk ditching. The search and rescue teams never found him or his jet."

Natalie leaned forward, resting her elbows on her knees and clasping her hands together tightly.

"They told me it must've been pilot error or mechanical failure," she said with a bitter laugh that held no humor. "But we both knew what we saw that day wasn't anything normal. Nor would either of us have done anything that would jeopardize the mission or our lives. Paul was one of the best pilots, best wingmen, I ever flew with."

Emily sat silently for a moment before finally speaking.

"I appreciate you sharing that with me," she said softly. "It helps me understand why you're so driven."

"There is something else I want you to know before you go with the assault team," Emily said. "Paul Klaussen was...is my younger brother."

Natalie felt like she'd been punched in the gut. Her eyes widened, and she stared at Emily in disbelief. The room seemed to spin around her as the implications of Emily's words sank in.

"Paul... your brother?" Natalie's voice cracked, and she felt hot tears welling up in her eyes. She blinked rapidly, trying to hold them back, but it was no use. The floodgates opened, and she began to sob uncontrollably.

Emily moved closer, her own eyes glistening. "I'm sorry, Natalie. I should have told you sooner." Emily's arms embraced her.

Natalie struggled to regain her composure, wiping her eyes with the back of her hand. "But... how? I don't understand."

Emily took a deep breath. "We had different fathers. That's why our last names are different. I'm sorry, I didn't make the connection at first. It wasn't until Kaden brought you in that I realized who you were."

The pieces started falling into place in Natalie's mind. She remembered Paul mentioning a half-sister once or twice, but she'd never met her. Never imagined she'd be sitting across from her now, in the White House of all places.

"I... I'm so sorry, Emily," Natalie choked out. "I tried to save him. I really did."

Emily reached over and squeezed Natalie's hand. "I know you did. And now you understand why this mission is so personal for both of us. The Observers have obviously taken countless lives and more prisoners than we know of over the decades. This is going to be a very bad day for a lot of people. Let's go make at least one thing right today. Do it for Laura. Do it for Paul."

CHAPTER ONE HUNDRED EIGHT

1403 UTC September 19
38°17'N, 77°00'W
King George County, Virginia, USA

Natalie, General Briggs, and a recovering Trent Rogers stood side by side with an expanded team of elite Army assaulters. The stoic determination on their faces reflected the gravity of the situation.

Natalie's knuckles whitened as she gripped the edge of the table. "We knew some of this was coming, but seeing it unfold... it's another thing entirely. Does this change our plans?"

General Briggs nodded grimly. "This is only the beginning. If we don't stop them now, we will never get ahead of it. We need the locations of all the NovaCore assets and facilities. King's second in charge, Gibson, is the objective."

Trent, still nursing his injuries but driven by sheer willpower, added, "I leave you guys alone for a few hours, and all hell breaks loose."

Natalie told him to shut up; it was no time for jokes, but still smiled.

She turned back to General Briggs, her voice steady despite the chaos on the screen. "We potentially have a lot of civilians in there. What's the play?"

Briggs's eyes glanced to a TV showing footage of waves crashing into coastal buildings, swallowing them whole. "We stick to the plan but accelerate our timeline. We can't afford any delays. Leave it to our enemy to put a facility smack dab in the middle of a goddamn Army base."

Natalie exhaled slowly, her resolve hardening. "One good thing: some of the personnel at Fort Hill are being reassigned to some of the disaster areas." The group knew they had no idea who on that base would be loyal to the Observers, and who would follow orders. That was one reason Briggs still wanted to keep the assaulting force small, limited to people he could trust.

They had discussed all options, and in the end, Briggs made the call not to alert the base commander. Not until they were inside the wire. It was a gamble, but it seemed like everything today was going to be.

As they prepared to head out, the screen showed a final clip from LA: first responders pulling people from wreckage and debris floating through city streets like abandoned toys in a child's bathwater. It reminded Natalie of scenes from Thailand or Japan in the aftermath of the mega-tsunamis.

The sense of urgency hit home for everyone in that room as they braced themselves for what lay ahead.

The dimly lit warehouse near the rural Fort A.P. Hill buzzed with controlled chaos. Rows of military gear and clean, mended Trident uniforms hung on metal racks, their dark hues blending with the shadows. Team members moved purposefully, donning the enemy's gear and not looking too happy about it.

Natalie tugged on the collar of her borrowed uniform, adjusting the fit. "This thing smells like three failed missions and a bad breakup."

"Don't worry. You wear it better than whoever bled in it last," Trent said dismissively.

She checked her gear one last time: a sidearm snug in its holster, a combat knife strapped to her thigh, and the pulse rifle clipped to her back. Across from her, Trent fastened his Kevlar vest, wincing slightly as he secured the straps over his barely healing injuries.

"You good?"

"Just hope I don't have to sneeze," he said.

General Briggs stood near a folding table covered with maps and blueprints of both Fort A.P. Hill and Fort Bliss. He looked up as each team member finished gearing up, his sharp eyes assessing their readiness. "Everyone gather round," he commanded, his voice cutting through the ambient noise.

The team formed a tight circle around the table. Natalie glanced at the faces around her—hardened veterans, skilled operatives, each one committed to the mission ahead.

Briggs pointed to the map. "We'll enter through Gate B-17, posing as Trident personnel transporting detainees from the NovaCore offices skirmish. Our IDs are legitimate and should pass inspection."

He looked around the group, ensuring he had everyone's attention. "Natalie, you'll be leading the detainee transport unit. Trent, you'll handle communications once we're inside."

Natalie nodded. "Understood."

Briggs continued, "The rest of you will form the escort detail. Remember your covers—we're transferring high-value targets who may have vital intel on recent attacks."

Trent spoke up, "And if we get questioned?"

"Stick to your story," Briggs replied firmly. "We've got backup plans in place, but we need to avoid raising any suspicion."

He paused, looking each team member in the eye. "This is it. We don't get a second chance at this."

Taking a deep breath, General Briggs stepped back from the table and addressed the team with renewed intensity. "Listen up! The fate of God knows what depends on what we do tonight. We've trained for this —every single one of you is here because you're the best at what you do. This operation isn't just about preventing an immediate threat. It's about ensuring mankind has a future."

He clenched his fist for emphasis. "Failure is not an option. Let's show them what we're made of!"

A ripple of determination spread through the group as they absorbed his words.

"Move out!" Briggs ordered. He would not be going with them as he was already working the problem from another angle.

The team filed into a convoy of military vehicles parked outside the warehouse. Engines roared to life as they began their journey toward Fort Hill, ready to face whatever challenges awaited them inside those fortified gates.

KTLA 5 Los Angeles | Local News Segment | Anchor: Jenna Westbrook

Disneyland to Close Early Today, All Day Wednesday for 'Planned Infrastructure Upgrades'

"In an announcement made just moments ago, Disneyland officials confirmed the park will be closing early today and remain closed all day Wednesday due to what's being described as 'routine maintenance and upgrades to guest experience systems.'

"While some social media users posted videos of unusually high surf near the coast and unusual atmospheric flashes earlier today, park representatives insist the closure was scheduled weeks ago.

"Anaheim police say the sudden increase in traffic along I-5 is unrelated to any emergency evacuation orders and urge residents not to spread rumors. No tsunami warnings have been issued.

"In the meantime, guests with Wednesday reservations can reschedule or receive a complimentary future park pass. Back to you, Mark."

CHAPTER
ONE HUNDRED NINE

1512 UTC September 19
38°04'N, 77°16'W
Fort A.P. Hill, Virginia, USA

The bus rattled as it moved down a desolate stretch of road. The trees pressed in on either side, and the soldiers, dressed for combat, sat quietly, weapons in hand, waiting for the final assault briefing. Major Hairston stepped to the front, his voice clear and authoritative.

"Alright, listen up. We're getting close to Fort Walker—what used to be called Fort A.P. Hill. I know some of you have heard the official briefing from General Briggs, but let me set expectations straight for those who haven't had the pleasure of visiting this place before.

"Fort Walker is big—76,000 acres of Virginia wilderness. And when I say wilderness, I mean it. This place is a whole lot of nothing. Thick forests, open fields, a few winding roads, and enough mosquitoes to carry you off if you're not paying attention. But that 'nothing' is exactly why it's the perfect place for what we're dealing with.

"See, Fort Walker isn't your standard base with permanent barracks and chow halls. It's a training ground, a place built for the kind of warfare that doesn't show up on the evening news. It's where the Army sends people to train for the harshest conditions—because out here, it's just you and the wild. No distractions. No comforts. Just the mission.

"So, what should you expect when we get there? Well, a lot of empty space. Long stretches of dirt roads and remote terrain, almost like stepping into the Stone Age. If you're looking for landmarks, good luck. Half the time you can't see ten feet into the tree line. You'll find some old mock villages used for urban combat drills, and maybe a few battered buildings tucked away that haven't seen a coat of paint since World War II.

"But don't let the 'nothing' fool you. It's what you can't see at Fort Hill that's important. The rumor is that they've turned this place into something special. Hidden secure compounds, underground facilities, places built to keep things off the radar. It's our job to find out what they've been hiding out here and to make sure whatever's buried deep doesn't stay that way.

"Now, a word on who we are up against. They are going to look and sound like you and me. They may be regular Army, as we can't be sure who is in league with the fucking aliens and who is on the side of humanity. Yes, I did say aliens. That is who is causing all the damn problems right now. The people we are rescuing ran into trouble with what we always referred to as the 'Men in Black.'"

Several of the troops looked down at their black Trident Security uniforms.

"Yes, we have the look and the gear. We'll hit the ground as if we own the place. We belong there as much as anybody. This is a transitional base, no regular garrisons. Soldiers cycle in and out all the time for training. That's likely one reason NovaCore chose this place: few permanent people around to ask questions. We may run into civilians from the FBI or NSA. Both use this base, as well as others for training purposes as well. If it comes to shooting, use your discretion, but remember who we are after.

"And remember—once we're inside, everything you see is need-to-know. We're not tourists on a field trip, and you're not telling anyone about what goes down here. We get in, we get out safe, and we move on. Our HVT is this guy." He held up a picture of a very nondescript Caucasian man. "Capture only, do not kill."

"So take a look around while you can, because once we hit Fort Walker, it's a whole lot of nothing—until it's not."

The major paused, looking each soldier in the eye, his tone lowering.

"And one last thing—stay sharp. This isn't just another training op. Fort Walker's been off the comms grid for days; they shouldn't know much of what is going on out here, so we can use that to our advantage."

The three unmarked buses pulled up to the guard gate, the hum of their diesel engines blending with the quiet tension in the air. The drivers, seasoned veterans all, maneuvered with practiced ease, stopping precisely at the designated checkpoint. Each bus had weapons secured in arm lockers as per protocol, except for the designated Trident guard for each group of fake detainees.

Emily and Trent exchanged nervous glances, their tension obvious. In contrast, the other passengers appeared relaxed, almost casual—a testament to their training and experience.

The lead bus driver rolled down his window as a guard approached. "Ranking officer?" the guard barked, his eyes scanning the bus interior.

Major Hairston stepped out of the lead bus, his uniform crisp and adorned with rank insignia. He presented his credentials—military ID, Common Access Card (CAC), and official orders—to the guard. "Major Hairston, reporting as ordered," he said, his voice steady.

The guard nodded, taking the documents. "Wait here," he instructed before heading into the guard station to verify the orders.

As this happened, other guards began a visual inspection of the buses. They walked around each vehicle, checking for anything out of the ordinary. One guard peered inside each bus through the windows, noting the calm demeanor of those aboard and their proper uniforms.

Back at the guard station, communication was underway with base command. Orders were being cross-checked against scheduled activities, and personnel clearances were verified.

Minutes felt like hours as Emily and Trent waited. Finally, the lead guard returned with Major Hairston's documents. "Orders verified," he said curtly, handing them back to Hairston. He motioned to his colleagues to raise the barriers blocking their path.

"Cleared for entry," he continued. "Proceed straight down this road until you reach checkpoint Bravo. Military Police will escort you from there to the detention facility."

Major Hairston nodded in acknowledgment before returning to his bus. He climbed aboard and relayed the instructions to the drivers.

The barriers lifted, and one by one, the buses moved forward into Fort Walker's vast expanse of wilderness. The convoy drove slowly but purposefully along winding roads flanked by dense forests. They followed directions provided by the guards until they reached checkpoint Bravo, where an MP unit awaited them in a desert tan Humvee.

With a nod from Major Hairston, they proceeded deeper into the base under military police escort toward their designated area—a staging ground for their mission ahead.

"Get those arm lockers opened. We are going hot in five mikes."

CHAPTER ONE HUNDRED TEN

The trio of buses hissed to a halt in front of the detention facility, the doors swinging open. The fake detainees shuffled off, their fake restraints clinking softly. Hidden beneath their loose-fitting clothes, weapons awaited their moment. The MP escort pulled away, leaving them alone at the entrance.

Major Hairston took the lead, his gaze sharp as he surveyed the surroundings. Detention center security personnel stood by, watching with practiced indifference. An observant Trident officer, however, wasn't as easily fooled. He zeroed in on Trent Rogers, scrutinizing his ID card with a frown.

"Hold on a second," the officer said, stepping closer to Trent. "Your ID looks off."

Trent stiffened but kept his expression neutral. “Really? That’s the same face I’ve used for three years. Maybe your scanner’s having a midlife crisis.”

The officer didn't respond immediately. Instead, he tapped into a handheld device, checking Trent's ID against the database. Seconds ticked by with agonizing slowness.

"Where are you guys from? Haven't seen you here before, and it looks like your ID isn't matching up," the officer finally said, suspicion clear in his voice.

"Hey, shut the fuck up," Trent said coldly. "Been with this clown corps for years. Your system is shit."

The man rechecked but shook his head again.

"Maybe it's you," Trent said, revising the plan on the fly.

Before the other man could respond, Trent hit him in the mouth with the butt of his rifle. The guard went down hard.

"See? You should've swiped right."

Immediately, alarms began to blare throughout the facility. Red lights flashed urgently, casting an eerie glow on the scene.

"We're blown!" Major Hairston shouted over the noise. "Move!"

Chaos erupted as guards and security personnel scrambled to react. Shouts echoed through the corridors as Natalie signaled her teams to split.

"Team One, head to the control room! Get those alarms off! Team Two, with me to the holding cells!" Flex cuffs and restraints were left behind as every assaulter quickly had their weapons out, looking for targets.

Natalie led her group down a narrow hallway while Major Hairston and his team headed in the opposite direction. The sound of boots pounding against concrete filled the air.

They rounded a corner and encountered their first set of facility guards. A quick skirmish ensued—Natalie's team moved with precision, disarming and incapacitating the guards before they could raise an effective alarm.

Natalie kicked open a door leading to another corridor and gestured for her team to follow. "Keep moving! We need those cells secured!"

As they pressed forward, more guards appeared from side passages and doorways. Natalie's team engaged them swiftly, their training evident in every calculated move. This contingent of Trident was not the seasoned warriors they'd faced at NovaCore.

Major Hairston's voice crackled through their earpieces: "Team Two! What's your status?"

Despite his years since leaving the military, Trent Rogers followed his team into the control room with the precision of a seasoned infiltrator. Moving silently, they slipped past a pair of guards engrossed in their monitors. Rogers signaled to his men, and within moments, the guards were taken down with swift, silent strikes. They collapsed without a sound. The team was not here to negotiate. This was an assault with violent, deadly intent.

Inside the control room, Rogers watched as one of the team's tech wizards positioned himself at the central console while the rest of the team fanned out to secure the perimeter. Fingers flying over the keyboard, the young woman initiated a hack into the facility's security system. Lines of code scrolled across the screen as she bypassed encryption protocols.

"Almost there," she muttered, concentrating. With a final keystroke, the alarms fell silent, and security cameras began cycling through the facility's monitoring zones.

"Alarms disabled," Rogers reported into his earpiece. "We're unlocking the cells now."

Across the facility, Major Hairston and his team fought their way through the cell block area. The guards put up fierce resistance, but Hairston's men advanced with relentless efficiency. They exchanged gunfire in the dimly lit corridors, the air thick with tension and the smell of gunpowder.

"Rogers, do you have a location on either of our detainee HVTs?" Natalie asked. Briggs had given mission priority for Gibson. She and Trent were equally committed to rescuing Laura Bennett and Emma King.

Trent was scanning the list, but none had names—simply ID numbers and a code that might have indicated the time and place of pickup. "Working on it," he called back.

"Shit! Unlock them all," he told the technician.

"Sir?" the young woman said nervously. "Are you sure you want to do that?"

Trent followed her gaze to one of the other displays and felt his knees going weak as he saw what she saw. Multiple cells contained what was undoubtedly aliens lying on beds or tables. They looked dead but could just as easily be asleep. "Yes, do it," he ordered, feeling far less sure than he sounded.

"Major Hairston, we've got something going on out here, sir. Something I think you are going to need to see."

Hairston knew the voice was that of Specialist Fisher on rear guard. She and five others were positioned back near the buses. He had no time to respond at that moment, though, as his team inside the prison had their hands full.

"Cover me!" Hairston barked as he reached for a keypad beside one of the cell doors. With Trent's team hacking support, it blinked green and swung open.

A young man stumbled out, speaking incoherently in some foreign language. The major tackled the man to the floor as energy rounds punched into the steel cell door they were using for cover.

Suddenly, a massive explosion rocked the building. Dust and debris fell from the ceiling as emergency lighting flickered on. "No grenades in the holding areas!" Hairston yelled into his comms. They knew the concussion could easily kill the very people they were here to save.

"Wasn't us," yelled one of his men from farther ahead.

"Sir?" Fisher radioed again. "We need you out front, like, now."

Trent Rogers stood in the control room, the tension mounting with each passing second. His earpiece buzzed incessantly with urgent calls from the base commander.

"What in the hell is going on over there at your facility? Identify yourself!" the commander's voice crackled, laced with fury.

Trent stalled, hoping to buy time for Natalie's team. "This is Captain Wilson. We're conducting a surprise inspection authorized by General Briggs."

There was a brief silence before the commander's voice returned, more menacing than before. "We don't show any such orders, and my men heard alarms and explosions. I'm sending a security detail to your location now."

The technician's eyes widened as she monitored incoming data streams. "Sir, something is going on. We're starting to lose control of the system. Someone is overriding our access."

Before Trent could respond, another explosion rocked the facility. The force of the blast sent him sprawling to the floor, debris raining down from above. He scrambled to his feet, his heart pounding.

"Natalie, do you copy?" he shouted into his earpiece, receiving only static in response.

Natalie staggered as the explosion reverberated through the building. She felt a sudden weight pressing down on her back and shoulders. Looking up, she saw that part of the ceiling had caved in, effectively cutting her off from the rest of her team. A massive shadow moved over part of the exposed sky.

"Laura! Emma!" she called out, desperation creeping into her voice. But there was no answer—only an eerie silence punctuated by distant gunfire and alarms.

She struggled to her feet, dusting off bits of concrete and metal from her gear. Her eyes scanned the rubble for any sign of movement but found none. A sinking feeling gnawed at her gut.

Suddenly, she spotted a figure emerging from the haze of dust and debris. The man's imposing stature and cold gaze were unmistakable—it had to be Gibson.

"Natalie Reeves," he said with a sinister smile, stepping closer. "I must admit, your persistence is almost admirable."

Natalie gritted her teeth, every muscle tensing as she faced him. "And you would be the asshole named Gibson," she spat his name like poison.

Gibson chuckled softly. "You're meddling in things you don't understand," he said, reaching into his coat pocket.

Natalie's hand hovered over her sidearm, ready to draw at a moment's notice. "Where are Laura and Emma?" she demanded.

Gibson's smile widened as he produced a sleek, black device from his pocket. "You're too late," he said cryptically, pressing a button on the device.

The walls around them began to hum with an unsettling frequency, and Natalie felt a sharp pain in her head as if something was trying to pierce through her skull.

"Surely you didn't think we just used locked doors to keep people quiet, did you?"

In the control room, Trent Rogers clutched his earpiece tighter as he tried once more to reach Natalie.

He struggled to focus as the technician beside him worked frantically to regain control over the system but shook her head in frustration. "It's frozen. We're totally locked out!"

Just then, another alarm blared through the control room—this one signaling an impending breach at their location.

The facility plunged into darkness as the power failed, silencing the alarms and the unsettling sonic frequency. Natalie didn't hesitate. She raised her pulse rifle and fired, the bright muzzle flash illuminating the grime and agony on her face. The shot hit Gibson in the shoulder, spinning him around with a grunt of pain before he disappeared into the encroaching shadows.

Natalie advanced cautiously, her rifle trained on the last spot she saw him. "Gibson! Show yourself!" she demanded, her voice echoing eerily in the sudden silence. The only response was the distant sound of metal clanging against metal as he retreated deeper into the facility.

She moved forward, her eyes adjusting to the dim emergency lights that flickered sporadically. She breathed in measured puffs, each step exact and intentional.

In the faint glow of an emergency light, she saw a trail of blood leading down a narrow corridor. "Got you," she muttered under her breath, following the trail with renewed urgency. As she rounded a corner, a sudden noise made her stop—footsteps echoing faintly from behind a set of double doors.

Natalie pushed through the doors and found herself in a vast chamber filled with rows of holding cells. Her eyes scanned each cell quickly but thoroughly, searching for any sign of Laura or Emma. The room was eerily silent except for the occasional drip of water from somewhere above.

A soft whimper caught her attention, and she swung her rifle towards its source. In one of the barred cells, huddled in a corner, was Emma King. Her eyes widened when she saw Natalie.

"Emma!" Natalie rushed to the cell door and began working on the lock. "Hang tight; I'm getting you out of here."

Emma nodded weakly, her eyes filled with both relief and fear.

"Can you walk?" Natalie asked, supporting Emma as they moved.

Emma nodded but winced in pain; a bandage was wrapped around her lower leg. "Yeah... but I think we need to hurry."

They made their way down another corridor lined with cells until they found a blocked door. Someone was banging on it from the far side. "Laura, is that you?" If there was a response, Natalie couldn't hear.

"I have one of the HVTs," she radioed.

"Nat, the major is giving an evacuation order. Something is going on outside," Trent said.

"Trent, I have Emma. I wounded Gibson, but he got away, and I think Laura may be behind this blocked door. I can't just leave. I need a few minutes."

Natalie gritted her teeth as she tugged on the jammed door, sweat trickling down her forehead. The metal groaned but held fast, refusing to budge. Her frustration mounted, each second feeling like an eternity.

Taking a deep breath, she tried to calm herself. Shouting echoed from further down the corridor, followed by a blinding beam of light that seemed to fill the space, illuminating every corner with an eerie glow. She shielded her eyes for a moment before focusing back on the task at hand. She heard Emma sobbing behind her.

"Here," Natalie said softly, handing Emma a bottle of water and a gel pack. "Drink this. It'll help."

Emma took them with shaking hands, nodding gratefully. "Thank you," she murmured before taking a long sip and tearing into the gel pack.

Natalie turned back to the door, determination steeling her resolve. She knew brute force wouldn't work here—she needed precision. With a swift motion, she drew her energy rifle and adjusted its settings, hoping to convert it into a makeshift laser cutter.

"Stay back," she warned Emma, who quickly retreated to a safer distance. "I have no idea if this will work."

Natalie aimed the weapon at the jammed edge of the steel door and activated the beam. A focused ray of energy shot out, slicing through the metal with ease. Sparks flew as she methodically cut along the edge, the sharp smell of burning metal filling the air.

The door began to give way under the intense heat of the laser. Natalie continued her work with meticulous care, ensuring she didn't miss any sections. The sound of metal being cut was almost deafening in the confined space, but she pushed through, her concentration unwavering.

Finally, with one last cut, the door groaned and shifted. Natalie stepped back and kicked it hard with her boot, but it still wouldn't budge. She tried again, then heard a male voice from inside telling her to stand back.

Something slammed into the door from the far side, again and again. In agonizing slowness, it began to separate from the twisted metal frame and concrete wall. With one final heave, the massive doors swung out toward Natalie and fell almost completely off, save for the bottom hinge.

A figure emerged from the shadows of the room, stepping over the mangled remains of the steel door. Natalie's eyes widened in disbelief as she took in the sight before her, her grip on the energy rifle loosening slightly.

The man standing in front of her was the last one she expected to see in this hellish place. Questions raced through her mind, each one more confounding than the last. How did he end up here? Had he been here the whole time?

Natalie opened her mouth to speak, but the words seemed to catch in her throat. She shook her head, trying to make sense of the situation. The man looked at her with evident relief, his eyes darting between Natalie and Emma.

"What... how...?" Natalie managed to stammer out, her usually composed demeanor cracking under the weight of this revelation.

He held up a hand, silencing her questions. "There's no time to explain," Paul Klaussen said urgently, his voice hoarse from disuse. His body looked emaciated and scarred. "Help me now, Natalie."

CHAPTER ONE HUNDRED ELEVEN

Paul led Natalie into the cell, his expression grim. As they entered, Natalie's eyes fell upon the battered and bruised body of Laura Bennett lying on the cold concrete floor. Her heart sank, and a wave of nausea washed over her at the sight of her friend's condition.

Laura's face was swollen and covered in cuts and bruises, her clothes torn and stained with blood. It was clear that she had endured unimaginable torture at the hands of her captors. Natalie knelt beside her, gently brushing a strand of matted hair from Laura's face.

"Laura," Natalie whispered, her voice trembling with emotion.

"I'm so sorry," Paul said. "The guards threw me in here with her when the building started coming down."

He placed a hand on Natalie's shoulder, his eyes filled with sorrow. "She never gave up hope," he said softly. "She told me that you and Emily never stopped fighting for me."

Natalie nodded, tears streaming down her face. She couldn't find the words to express the pain and guilt she felt for not being able to save Laura sooner.

"We have to get her out of here," Paul said urgently, snapping Natalie back to the present. "I don't think we have much time."

Together, they carefully lifted Laura's body, supporting her weight between them. Natalie's heart ached with each step, the reality of the situation sinking in. She had lost a trusted friend, and the weight of that loss threatened to crush her.

As they made their way out of the cell, Emma joined them, her eyes widening at the sight of Laura's lifeless form. She opened her mouth to speak but thought better of it, instead focusing on helping them navigate the chaotic corridors.

The sounds of gunfire and explosions grew louder as they moved, a stark reminder of the danger they were in. Natalie tried to formulate a plan to get them all out of the facility alive, but her mind was stuck on Laura's cold body.

"We need to find the others," she said finally, her voice strained with emotion. "I don't want to leave anyone behind."

Paul nodded in agreement, his weakened body not diminishing his determination. They quickened their pace, Laura's body weighing heavily between them as they pushed forward, desperate to escape the nightmare they had found themselves in.

In an adjoining corridor, Natalie and part of her assault team regrouped. The adrenaline from the rescue mission was starting to wear off, replaced by a growing sense of dread. Natalie felt it, too, but she accepted it was the loss of Laura; she also felt buoyed by the fact they had recovered Paul.

"All the other cells on this side are empty," one of her team members reported, his voice echoing in the now eerily quiet corridor. "Well... not empty, but no one is still alive."

Natalie nodded, her mind considering the full implications of the secrets this place held.

Emma spoke up, "I saw most of the holding cells. I don't think they kept a lot of people here. It seemed like maybe they used this place for other stuff."

"We need to get out of here then," Natalie said, her voice steady despite the fear that gnawed at her. "We don't know what else might be lurking in this place."

The team moved swiftly, their footsteps echoing off the concrete walls as they made their way toward the exit. Another on her team joined them helped take Laura. Natalie led the way, her weapon at the ready, scanning the shadows for any sign of movement.

Suddenly, a brilliant blue light flooded the corridor, blinding them momentarily. Natalie shielded her eyes, squinting against the intense glare. As her vision adjusted, she caught a glimpse of something that made her blood run cold.

There, in the center of the light, stood a tall, thin, alien creature, its form unlike anything she had seen even in her worst nightmares. Its skin was a pale white with dark patterns, its limbs long and spindly, and its large eyes glowed with an otherworldly malevolence.

But it was what the creature held in its arms that made Natalie's heart stop. There, dangling limply from the alien's grasp, was the limp form of Gibson, his face frozen in a grotesque mask of terror.

Before Natalie could react, the light vanished as quickly as it had appeared, plunging the corridor back into darkness. She blinked, her eyes struggling to adjust to the sudden change in illumination. Gibson and the creature were both gone.

"What the hell was that?" Paul whispered, his voice trembling with fear.

Natalie shook her head, unable to find the words to describe what she had just witnessed. She knew one thing for certain, though. Whatever that creature was, it was not of this world. And it had just taken Gibson with it.

She and her team burst through the facility doors, emerging into the harsh afternoon sun. They skidded to a halt, confronted by a tense standoff. Armed soldiers from Trent's team faced off against military police and base personnel. Major Hairston stood in the middle, hands raised in a placating gesture, his voice carrying over the tense silence.

"Everyone, lower your weapons! We can talk this out!" the major shouted, trying desperately to keep both sides from pulling the trigger.

But most eyes seemed drawn upwards. Hovering ominously above the building was a massive alien craft, its sleek surface shimmering in the sunlight. The sight of it left everyone momentarily stunned, frozen in place by the sheer impossibility of what they were witnessing.

The hum was so loud it set teeth on edge. It was round, maybe fifty meters across and a dull aluminum gray with what appeared to be a small hexagon pattern on the underside in a slightly darker gray.

"They came for the bodies," Emma whispered. "They are going to level this place."

The spaceship suddenly darted hundreds of meters up and came to a sudden stop.

"She's right. We have to get away from the building," Natalie yelled.

Despite the standoff, everyone recognized the danger from above and raced away from the building, diving behind the buses and Hummers used by the base security detail.

"Move, move!" Natalie shouted, her voice rising above the chaotic clamor. Soldiers and personnel alike sprinted for cover, their eyes flicking back up to the alien craft looming ominously overhead.

The ground seemed to vibrate with an unearthly hum as the spaceship hovered even closer. Just as Natalie threw herself behind a Humvee, a blinding flash of green light erupted from the craft. She shielded her eyes with her arm, her heart pounding in her chest.

The building didn't so much explode as simply disappear. Everything within fifty feet—walls, floors, equipment—turned to dust. It was as if reality itself had been erased in an instant. One moment it was there; the next, it was gone.

The air was filled with a fine gray powder that settled slowly to the ground. Natalie blinked through the haze, trying to process what she had just witnessed. The man who'd been carrying Laura's body now lay dead beside her. Paul struggled to heave the reporter's body over his bone thin shoulder.

"Everyone okay?" Natalie called out, coughing on the dust that now filled her lungs.

There were groans and coughs from around her as people began to emerge from their hiding spots, brushing off the fine layer of dust that had settled on them. Paul appeared beside her, his face a mask of shock.

"What kind of weapon does that, Nat?" he asked, his voice shaking.

"I don't know," Natalie replied grimly, her eyes still locked on the spot where the building had stood moments before. "But whatever it is, it's not something we can fight with conventional means."

Emma clutched Natalie's arm, her eyes wide with fear. "My dad must know what those things are. He could help us fight them. We need to get to him."

Natalie nodded, not wanting to tell her about her father right now. A change in the hum caused them to look up as the alien craft sped up and away with an almost supernatural speed, leaving a vacuum of tension in its wake.

Hairston turned sharply to the base commander who was lying not far away, the major's face red with fury.

"Commander, explain yourself! Why are you ignoring orders from your superiors? Why were you allowing a non-military group to detain American citizens on your base?" His voice echoed with righteous indignation.

Some of the base personnel began to shift uneasily, exchanging uncertain glances. The moral weight of their actions seemed to be sinking in, and Natalie could see several soldiers lowering their weapons ever so slightly.

The commander's face twisted into a sneer. Without warning, he drew his sidearm and aimed at the major. Time seemed to slow as Natalie's heart leapt into her throat. She wasn't qualified to be part of this. She knew that now.

A shot rang out—but it wasn't from the commander's gun. One of Natalie's team members had acted faster, putting a bullet through the commander's chest. He crumpled to the ground, eyes wide in shock.

Chaos erupted instantly. Guns fired from all directions as Natalie and her team fought their way through a hailstorm of bullets. They moved with balanced precision, using every bit of cover available as they angled diagonally into the growing battle.

"Follow me," Trent yelled as he took Laura's body from Paul's arms.

Natalie didn't want to leave her team, but she had her orders. Get the detainees out of there.

"We're almost there!" Trent shouted over the rising din of chaos minutes later, leading Emma and Paul toward safety. Natalie stayed close behind, ensuring no one got left behind in the chaos. "Apparently the smaller ships weren't all they had."

"Apparently not!" Natalie agreed enthusiastically.

As they neared the extraction point, helicopters appeared on the horizon, growing louder by the second. She could tell by the comms chatter that the final stand behind them was brutal—hand-to-hand combat ensued as they grappled with determined adversaries. A lone soldier charged them from behind. Natalie ducked a wild punch and delivered a swift kick to her assailant's knee before dispatching him with a well-placed elbow strike.

Finally, they reached the waiting transport helicopters. With hearts pounding and bodies aching, they boarded the detainees one by one. Natalie counted twenty-seven detainees and one Laura Bennett. Some were in nearly as bad a shape as Laura.

As they lifted off, leaving the chaos below them, there was a brief but profound moment of relief among them all. Natalie couldn't stop staring at Paul. A large gash across his forehead was bleeding freely and looked like he had taken some shrapnel to his right leg. He wasn't in great shape, but he was alive. The medic was already working on him, and he had a weak smile as he stared back.

"We made it," Emma whispered, tears streaming down her face as she clung to Natalie. "Thank you!"

"Yeah," Natalie replied softly, her own eyes wet with unspoken emotion. "We made it."

Below, more choppers were landing, and this time they were disgorging support troops for Major Hairston's remaining assaulters. General Briggs had indeed done his part.

CHAPTER ONE HUNDRED TWELVE

38°52′N, 77°03′W
Strategic Military Command Center
Alexandria, Virginia, USA

At the front of the secure command room, a 3D map of Fort Bliss flickered on the screen, the markers for the Texas assault team flashing red to indicate casualties. Leaders from various agencies and branches of the military gathered around, all seeming to be in utter disbelief at what was happening.

General Briggs slammed a fist onto the table, causing a ripple in the hologram. "This was a massacre!" he barked, his voice strained. "We've lost nearly everyone. Only a handful even managed to evacuate."

Emily Carter's eyes were red-rimmed; this day had taken its toll on her in more ways than one. "And the detainees?" she asked, though she already knew the answer.

"All were executed," General Taylor said flatly, his jaw clenched. "No one left for interrogation."

A heavy silence settled over the room, punctuated only by the soft hum of the electronics around them. The brutal reality of their failure sank in, and with it came an overwhelming sense of defeat.

An Air Force colonel shook his head in disbelief. "How could this happen? We had the element of surprise. We should have had the upper hand."

"It's not just about Fort Bliss," General Taylor interjected, his voice low but filled with an edge of steel. "This goes deeper. The conspirators have entrenched themselves throughout our ranks. Loyalty to the Observers runs deeper than we even feared.

"It's not just an ideology. Hell, who would sell out humans to the aliens? We think it is more about them just trying to save their own skin. They feel the president has lost control already. They know they are screwed if they surrender. To them, it's about survival."

Heads nodded around the table as the weight of his words hit home. The U.S. military was fractured, its loyalty split between those who served their country and those who served a hidden agenda.

"But where were the aliens?" Emily wondered aloud, breaking the heavy silence that had descended over the room. "They've been so active everywhere else, even at Fort Hill—why didn't they intervene at Fort Bliss?"

Natalie Reeves leaned back in her chair, her mind racing through possible explanations. "Maybe it wasn't part of their plan," she suggested quietly. "Or maybe... they wanted this to happen."

"That doesn't make sense," Emily argued, shaking her head slowly as if trying to clear away foggy thoughts. "Why would they let us tear ourselves apart when they've shown they can easily take direct action?"

The room fell into another bout of silence as each leader pondered this mystery, their minds grappling with questions that had no immediate answers. "Why get involved?" General Taylor said. "Why bother taking action if we are going to try and destroy ourselves?"

"We need to reassess our strategy," General Briggs finally said, breaking through their collective reverie. "Find out who we can trust, who's left, and where our true allies are."

Emily and Natalie eyed each other. There was an even bigger issue to deal with—one that no one was mentioning yet. There was more of this so-called ‘Species A044’ on the way. What was going to happen when even more of them showed up?

“I guess you heard?” Emily said.

Natalie shook her head; this sounded like more bad news.

“Cavanaugh is in the wind. Part of the detail that took him into custody was compromised. Two dead agents were found in a swamp thirty miles from the capital. Slimy bastard did have friends all over.”

“Damn,” Natalie said. “That on top of letting Gibson get snatched just makes my day.”

Emily nodded. “We knew we were in for some tough fights, Natalie. I’m just glad you are with us.”

Natalie smiled and turned back to the general. "Sir, we need to talk about Owen King and his daughter."

Briggs looked up from the maps and data strewn across his desk, his brow furrowed. "What about them?"

"Emma deserves to know the truth, to see her father again. Also, it's key to getting what we need from him," Natalie argued, her voice filled with conviction.

The general leaned back in his chair, his expression hardening. "Not until we have everything we need from the man. King's a damn fortress of information, and we're not risking it—not for sentimentality."

Natalie's eyes narrowed. "But, sir, think about what Emma's going through. She's been through hell, and she needs answers. Keeping her in the dark, keeping her from her father... it's not right."

Briggs's face reddened, but he nodded. "Right? You think any of this is right? We're at war, Reeves. War with an enemy we do not understand, and Owen King might be our only hope of figuring out their endgame."

"I understand that, but—"

"Do you? Because from where I'm sitting, it looks like you're letting your emotions cloud your judgment."

Natalie bristled at the accusation. "With all due respect, sir, I think you're underestimating the power of human connection. If we show Owen that we have Emma's best interests at heart, it might be the leverage we need to get him to tell us the rest."

Briggs shook his head, a mirthless chuckle escaping his lips. "I'm not sure that man knows enough to help us at this point. He was coming to us for protection, remember?"

The room fell silent as the two stared each other down, the tension growing noticeably. Natalie knew Briggs had a point, but the thought of keeping Emma in the dark, of denying her the chance to see her father, felt wrong on a fundamental level.

"Sir, I—"

"We can let him know she is alive... nothing more. By the way, his request for immunity is a non-starter at this point."

Natalie knew she was overstepping an invisible line, and Briggs had been a tremendous asset, but she still needed some sort of closure. Notifying Laura Bennett's family of their loss had been one of the hardest things she'd ever done. Yes, there were literally millions dead this week, but it was the one that mattered, right now.

Emily's shoulders sagged. This had been a day of epic ups and downs. "I'm going to go see Paul," Emily said finally. She leaned in and hugged Natalie once more and whispered, "You do what you need. I will always have your back."

Natalie nodded. Bringing back her brother Paul had unlocked a side of the woman she'd never seen before.

~

Emily approached the heavily guarded hospital room. Armed soldiers flanked every entrance, their faces stern and watchful. She took a deep breath, steeling herself for what lay beyond the door.

As she entered, her eyes immediately locked onto the figure in the bed. Time seemed to stand still.

"Paul?" she whispered, her voice barely audible.

Her brother turned his head, a weak smile spreading across his gaunt face. "Em..."

Tears welled up in her eyes as she rushed to his side, all composure forgotten. She grasped his hand, squeezing it tightly as if afraid he might disappear again. Bending her head over his chest, she began to cry.

"I thought I lost you forever," Emily choked out, her voice trembling with emotion.

Paul's grip tightened on hers. "I'm here. They couldn't take me."

Emily leaned up and studied her brother's face, noting the dark circles under his eyes and the hollowness in his cheeks. Bandages masked more recent wounds, but his injuries didn't appear life-threatening. Some weight loss, certainly, and a haunted look in his eyes that spoke of trauma endured. But he was alive, and that was what mattered most.

"The doctors say you'll make a full recovery," she said, trying to keep her voice steady. "You're safe now."

As she spoke those words, Emily couldn't help but glance at the armed guards positioned around the room. Their presence was a stark reminder that while this moment brought immense relief, the danger hadn't fully passed.

Paul followed her gaze, his expression darkening slightly. "Are we really safe, Em? What's happening out there? More of those aliens?"

Emily hesitated, torn between shielding her brother from the harsh realities and being honest about the ongoing crisis. Before she could respond, a nurse entered to check Paul's vitals, providing a momentary reprieve from the weight of unanswered questions.

Emily sat beside her brother as she tried to condense the chaos into something digestible. She took a deep breath, meeting his questioning gaze. She had already been told by Natalie that Paul had seen no news since he was taken, but Laura had filled him in with what she knew while she was able.

"Paul, there's a lot you need to know," she began, her voice calm yet firm. "We've been dealing with alien attacks on a global scale. It started with isolated incidents but quickly escalated into full-blown assaults on major cities and military installations."

Paul's eyes widened, anger etched on his face. "Aliens? Yeah, we saw them in the prison. It just seems so unreal. I always knew what hit my jet wasn't one of ours. Still, none of it seems real."

"I know," she said, squeezing his hand reassuringly. "But it's real. We've had confirmed sightings and encounters."

"Natalie said Los Angeles was mostly gone...and Moscow."

Emily gave a sad nod. "It's bad, Paul. I won't lie to you. We are in a war."

Paul's brow furrowed as he tried to process this information. "And the military? What's their role in all this? Some at the base seemed to be on the side of my captors."

Emily hesitated, choosing her words carefully. "The military is split, so is the government. There are factions within our ranks loyal to the Observers—the covert group that held you. They've been collaborating with the aliens for decades. They've been working in the shadows, covering up the truth to control alien technology and influence."

Paul's face hardened. "So, this conspiracy goes back years?"

"Decades," Emily confirmed, her tone somber. "They've kept the public in the dark while manipulating events from behind the scenes. But not everyone is complicit. We have people within the government and military finally fighting back, trying to expose the truth."

She paused, searching for something positive amidst the turmoil. "Despite everything, there's hope. We've formed alliances with those willing to stand against the Observers and fight for transparency and justice. We are making progress."

Paul studied her for a moment before shaking his head again. "It sounds like you're trying to put a positive spin on something that's fundamentally terrifying."

Emily's shoulders slumped slightly as she exhaled deeply. "I was hoping for cautiously grim, but I'll take fundamentally terrifying if it sounds more honest. Actually, I'm just trying to find some light in all this darkness, Paul. We need hope now more than ever."

"It sounds to me like the worst is yet to come. But, hey, at least being held, I missed the COVID pandemics."

Emily smiled despite herself and took her brother's hand. "No, it's serious Paul. Apparently, all we have encountered so far is an advance scout force. A full armada is on the way."

Paul gave a sad laugh. "I think I was safer back in my cell. But hey, you're the president's chief of staff. So... congratulations on that. Never would have seen that coming. No offense, but I figured you'd end up running some egghead think tank or a vineyard. Or maybe both."

"Thanks. He is a good man but a somewhat misguided one. He trusted people he never should have, Washington's national pastime," she muttered. "Right after plausible deniability." The sadness in her voice diminished the upbeat tone she'd hoped to maintain.

Paul looked at the IV tube in the hand Emily was holding, then outside at the darkening sky. "Use some of that influence to get me reinstated to active duty as soon as you can. Put me somewhere I can make a difference. Natalie, too. Sounds like you're going to need us."

Emily followed her brother's gaze outside, knowing he wasn't wrong.

CHAPTER
ONE HUNDRED THIRTEEN

Undisclosed Location
Outskirts of Baltimore,
Maryland, USA

Trent gripped the steering wheel tighter as he navigated the back roads toward the secure facility. His shoulder throbbed where the bullet had grazed him during one of the previous firefights, and the stitches along his ribcage pulled with each breath. The doctor had been crystal clear: two weeks of bed rest, minimum. But here he was, three days later, playing chauffeur for a reunion that technically wasn't supposed to happen.

"How much longer?" Emma asked from the passenger seat, her voice small but steady.

Trent glanced at her. The girl had been through hell at the detention center yet somehow maintained a composure that people twice her age couldn't manage.

"Twenty minutes, give or take." He shifted in his seat, wincing as pain shot through his side. "You okay?"

Emma nodded, staring out the window at the passing trees. "I still don't understand why they don't want me to see him."

"Politics. Security concerns. Take your pick. It's like Hogwarts rules around here—except instead of magic flowing everywhere, it's just endless bureaucracy." Trent sighed. "Your father knows things that make him valuable and dangerous at the same time."

"Natalie said he helped you."

"He did." Trent navigated a sharp curve, grimacing as the movement pulled at his wounds. "That's partly why she arranged this. She believes everyone deserves a chance to see their family, especially now."

The unspoken truth hung between them—with alien attacks escalating worldwide, tomorrow wasn't guaranteed for anyone.

"She follows her gut," Trent added. "It's what makes her good at what she does."

"And you? What are you following by helping her go against orders?"

Trent almost smiled. The kid was perceptive. "Let's just say I've spent enough time following orders without questioning them. Sometimes the right thing isn't in the official playbook, kid. Besides, she scares the crap out of me—and she's usually right."

They fell silent as Trent turned onto an unmarked gravel road. The security checkpoint appeared ahead, a simple barrier with two armed guards who looked decidedly unofficial—Briggs' people, not regular military.

"When we get there," Trent said, slowing the car, "you'll have thirty minutes. That's all Natalie could arrange."

Emma nodded, straightening her posture. "I understand."

Trent pulled up to the checkpoint, his side screaming in protest as he leaned out the window to present his credentials. He shouldn't be here. He should be in a hospital bed, following doctor's orders. But Natalie had asked, and somehow that had been enough.

Natalie stood in the doorway of the nondescript block building, arms crossed against the autumn chill. Her hair caught the late afternoon sun, giving it an almost copper glow. She nodded at Trent as he pulled up, her expression softening briefly before returning to the professional mask she'd been wearing since Fort Hill.

"Right on time," she said as Emma climbed out of the car. "He's waiting inside."

Emma hesitated for just a moment before squaring her shoulders. Natalie placed a gentle hand on the girl's back.

"Thirty minutes, like we discussed. Agent Pearson will stay with you."

Emma nodded and followed the stone-faced agent through the door. Once they were inside, Natalie turned to Trent, her green eyes assessing his condition.

"You look like hell."

"Thanks. Feel worse." Trent leaned against the car, trying to hide his discomfort. "Doc said I should still be horizontal. Still, I do love emotionally fraught reunions. They pair so well with bullet wounds."

"Yet, here you are." A ghost of a smile crossed her face. "I appreciate it."

"Don't thank me. The real hero here is a little guy named Tramadol. I'd name my firstborn after him if I didn't think it'd raise eyebrows." He nodded toward the facility entrance. "How's King?"

"Cooperative. Too cooperative, which makes me suspicious." Natalie moved closer, lowering her voice. "We've confirmed most of his intel about the collaborators. Lots of legislators, including four more high-ranking senators, numerous congressmen, and at least a dozen more high-ranking military officers are being quietly detained."

"And the NSA?"

"Pete's been arrested... rearrested. He appeared to be preparing to leave the country."

Trent whistled low. "Running scared."

"Or running to something." Natalie rubbed her temples. "The attack on LA and San Diego was worse than they're saying on the news. Preliminary casualty estimates are in the millions. I hate to even see the global deaths already."

A heavy silence fell between them. The weight of what they weren't discussing—their all too brief romantic encounters before everything went to hell, the charged moments during the rescue operation—hung in the air.

"When this is over..." Trent started.

Natalie shook her head. "If this is ever over."

"When," he insisted. "We should talk about... you know."

"Not now." Her voice was gentle but firm. "We need clear heads."

Trent nodded, understanding. The world was falling apart around them. Personal entanglements would have to wait.

"Any word from Kaden?" he asked, changing the subject.

Her face darkened. "No, and I'm not sure we will. I think he feels he's done enough."

"And you?" Trent asked. "Where is Natalie Reeves focused next?"

Natalie looked to the side, then pulled Trent into an embrace and a kiss. "I don't know, Trent, but I think the fight is barely starting. This war is going to take all of us. I may see if I can get my flight status reinstated permanently."

He nodded. "You should... don't take this the wrong way, but your real value is down here."

She looked at him questioningly. "How's that?"

"I saw how you cut through the bullshit the last few months. You are a hell of an investigator but an even better leader. You have both a technical and tactical understanding of what we're up against."

"Thanks, but I assume SCET and my presidential commission are over now. Emily got what she wanted when we pulled Paul out of that hell."

"SCET was never Emily's," Trent said, the smile on his face expanding. "You and Professor Trembley took over as soon as you walked in the room. Even Colonel Walker knew you two were the ones who would find the answers. Now, depending on what that girl can get from her father, we may have better insights into A044 than we could have dreamed of."

"We've lost so many good people already, though, Trent."

"And we're going to lose more... probably a lot more, but you have to stay in the fight. Promise me you will."

"I will if you will," she said after a long pause. His expression let her know she'd struck a nerve. "What is it?"

He suddenly looked uncomfortable. Trent ran a hand through his hair, wincing as the movement pulled again at his stitches. "There's something else," he said, his voice dropping lower. "With all the shakeups in leadership at the agency, they're moving people around. I'm being promoted and reassigned."

Natalie's eyes widened. "What?"

"Yeah. Apparently, surviving two alien incursions qualifies you for middle management."

"When?"

"As soon as I'm cleared for duty." He looked away, focusing on the tree line beyond the facility. "Can't tell you where, but it's related to what we started with SCET. The A044 alien threat is becoming the priority across all agencies now."

"That's..." Natalie's voice caught. She blinked rapidly, her composure finally cracking after everything they'd been through. A tear slipped down her cheek, followed by another. "That's not fair."

Trent reached out, brushing a tear from her face with his thumb. "I know. I agree." His touch lingered on her cheek. "But it's what's necessary. We're both bound by duty, by a need to step in and do what others won't."

Natalie nodded, trying to regain control as more tears fell. After facing down alien threats and government conspiracies without flinching, it was this moment—this goodbye—that finally broke through her armor.

"This isn't goodbye, Natalie," Trent said softly. "Not unless you want it to be."

She looked up at him, her green eyes shimmering with tears. "What does that mean?"

"It means I'll find you. When I can. If you want me to." His voice was steady, but vulnerability showed in his eyes. "Whatever's happening out there, whatever's coming for us—you and I found something here. Something worth holding onto."

Natalie wiped her eyes with the back of her hand. "I thought we needed clear heads."

"We do. But clear heads don't have to mean empty hearts." Trent took her hand in his. "I've spent my whole career following orders, keeping my distance. For once, I don't want to walk away from something that matters. Someone who matters. Also, for the record, this is the first time I've ever made a woman cry without screwing something up."

Natalie shook her head and laughed as she squeezed Trent's hand, the warmth of his touch anchoring her in the chaos their lives had become. The facility's perimeter lights flickered on as dusk approached, casting long shadows across the gravel driveway.

"So, what happens now?" she asked.

"Now we wait for Emma to finish with her father. Then I take her to the safe house while you—"

The facility door swung open with a metallic creak. Agent Pearson emerged, his normally impassive face tight with urgency.

"Ms. Reeves," he called, motioning sharply. "King's asking for you. Says it's critical."

Natalie and Trent exchanged glances. She straightened, instantly shifting back to professional mode despite the tears still drying on her cheeks.

"What's happened?" she asked, already moving toward the door.

"Don't know the details, ma'am. He was talking to his daughter when he suddenly went pale. Started demanding to see you immediately."

Trent followed close behind, ignoring the stabbing pain in his side. "Is Emma okay?"

"She's fine. Shaken, but fine."

CHAPTER ONE HUNDRED FOURTEEN

Owen King sat again in the sterile interrogation room, his hands cuffed to the table. The door opened, and his daughter Emma entered, escorted by a guard. Owen's heart leaped at the sight of her, relief washing over him.

"Emma," he breathed, his voice cracking with emotion.

She looked at him, her eyes a mixture of emotions. "Dad." Her tone was flat, guarded.

As the guard left them alone, an awkward silence stretched between them. Owen struggled to find the right words. "I'm so sorry, Emma. I never meant for any of this to happen."

Emma's gaze hardened. "But it did happen, Dad. People died. Lives were ruined. And all for what? NovaCore's profit? Your goon kidnapped me!"

Owen flinched at her accusation. "It wasn't just about profit, Emma. I truly believed I was protecting humanity. I'm sure you saw them... the creatures. The aliens... they're not here for peaceful coexistence. They want to conquer us, or worse, destroy us."

"And you thought the best way to handle that was to conspire with them? To help them infiltrate our world?" Emma shook her head in disbelief.

"I... no, we thought we could control the situation, use their technology to strengthen our defenses. I realize that was naive, but our group's original intentions were good." Owen's shoulders sagged, the weight of his actions bearing down on him. "We didn't realize until it was too late that we weren't dealing with the ones in charge."

Emma studied her father, seeing the toll the recent events had taken on him. Despite her anger, a part of her still saw the man who had raised her, the man who had always tried to do what he thought was right. She missed her mother more than ever at that moment. She would have known what to say, what to do.

Owen looked at his daughter, tears welling in his eyes. "I never wanted to hurt you, Emma. You're the most important thing in my life. I'm so sorry for everything."

Emma reached across the table and, after seeming to consider it for a moment, placed her hand over his. "I know, Dad. But sorry isn't enough. You have to face the consequences of your actions. You have to make things right, as much as you can."

Owen met his daughter's gaze, seeing the strength and determination in her eyes. She had grown so much in such a short time, forced to confront the harsh realities of the world.

"You are asking for immunity before you tell them anything more. You can't do that."

Owen looked at his daughter, his expression pleading for understanding. "I have seventy years' worth of information... much of which advances our understanding and technology by thousands of years, Emma. I need to see this through; I need to be there for you, not rotting away in some prison."

"You won't be rotting away, Dad. You'll be dead. Just like me, just like everyone else you've ever known. Your damned aliens are wiping humanity out."

Owen knew his captors had likely briefed his daughter on some key points to get across, but these words were her own. She always knew what to say to get a reaction. In her own way, she was as much a manipulator as he was.

"They have the secrets to interstellar travel, to manipulating gravity, to virtually eliminating disease," he said. "We've been peeling back the layers on this for years. We just need more time."

"Could any of it have saved Mom?"

Damn, the kid knew how to sucker-punch, too. He shook his head. "No, but we've made progress since she passed. Some of the drugs we licensed to big pharma could have at least offered her more time."

Emma shook her head. "Always about the money, wasn't it?"

He wanted to say no, but she was mostly right. "It took a lot of money, Em. I'm sorry, but that is the truth. Keeping the secret alone cost billions each year. Doing the reverse engineering and working with exotic technologies required brilliant people... expensive people."

He was confident the conversation was being recorded, but he really no longer cared. Yes, they could use his own words to convict him, but he was sure they had plenty of evidence to do that already. More likely, he would face rendition to some foreign prison where he would never see the light of day.

"Grandad did this, too?"

"Yes, honey. They brought him in back in the seventies."

"And I suppose I was being groomed to join your little organization?"

Her snarky tone set his teeth on edge, but she deserved to know. "Maybe. I guess I hoped so, just so I could finally be honest with you, but that decision wouldn't have been only mine, and it was years off. I was almost twenty-three before I knew." He drew in a deep breath. "Also, it's not a little organization, hon. It's almost 80,000 people. Most have no idea they are part of it nor the alien connection, but it's big."

She huffed out, wanting him to know this wasn't the time for boastful words.

He lowered his head. "Sorry, that didn't come out right. What I mean is there are a lot of people worldwide who are working on this problem. Now that we don't have to work in the shadows or keep all the projects siloed, we could theoretically make much faster headway. The damn secrecy is what always held us back as well."

"You've met... talked with them... the aliens?" Emma asked, seeming to ignore his last point.

He nodded. "I've talked with the ones we call the Observers, but only once, and that was just a few weeks ago. It was a warning of sorts, and I think a goodbye. I have since met a representative of the attacking species. Species A044. That was what happened out at the ranch house. It was not a pleasant meeting."

"So, they were just using you?"

That was a question Owen King had been considering as well. "It's possible," he said finally. "I prefer to think they were protecting us as long as they could from this more hostile species. Our group has always maintained that extraterrestrials have a loose galactic hierarchy. Probably nothing as rigid as a government, but more likely trade arrangements and such. Earth was probably being watched and groomed so that one day we too might be asked to join. Assuming, of course, we survive our own self-destructive behavior."

"I don't understand," his daughter said, confused. "They're ruthlessly killing us, Dad. Did we fail their test or something?"

He shrugged. "I can't answer that. Perhaps this is just part of their plan to see how we deal with these invaders. My guess, though, is that yes, in some ways, we must have failed. Either we failed to keep the secrets they demanded or failed to become proper stewards of our planet. That, combined with the increasing expansion needs of this new, more hostile race of beings who seem to have a mandate to expand and colonize, prompted the Observers to simply give up on their little experiment called Earth."

"That sounds hopeless, Dad."

King wiped his eyes and leaned back. "It doesn't look good, Babygirl." He wanted so badly to reach up and brush the hair away from her face or simply give her the fatherly embrace she clearly needed, but his restraints stopped even the attempt.

"My father always believed the monitoring species, the Observers, were a remote outpost with aging equipment. That was why they occasionally crashed. I now tend to agree with him on that. I think they're tired of us and finally ready to go back home."

"Dad, I don't know if I can ever forgive you for what you've done," she said softly. "But I do accept that you thought you were doing the right thing, in your own misguided way. Still, that asshole Gibson was an evil prick!"

Owen totally agreed, but Gibson had been a prick who got things done. That had been all that mattered at NovaCore. All that mattered with the Observers. "Was he killed?"

"No, they snatched him," she said. "The aliens took him from the detention center."

That thought horrified Owen. If A044 had Gibson, *Oh, God!*

"What is it, Dad?"

"I need to see Natalie Reeves," he said to the agent standing in the corner. His tone was as flat as his expression.

Emma just looked at him, her eyes also glazing over with tears.

"Forget the immunity. Give them whatever the hell they need, Dad. Make this right."

He nodded, his eyes filling with tears. "I will, Emma. I promise. I'll do whatever it takes to make amends, to help fix what I've broken."

Emma hugged her father and left, and Natalie and Trent walked in. She had indeed followed her heart in letting King see his daughter. Now he needed to fill in all the blanks. She could see the man was sweating, and his eyes were welling with tears.

King's face was ashen, his eyes wide with something that looked like genuine fear.

"King," Natalie said, closing the door behind them. "What's going on?"

Owen looked up, his hands trembling slightly. "It's Gibson. He's going to give them everything."

"Give who what?" Trent demanded.

"A044. The locations of all the NovaCore facilities." King's voice cracked. "Emma just told me—Gibson survived Fort Hill. He was taken by their advance scouts."

"Yes." Natalie moved closer to the table. "What's at these facilities that's so important?"

"Everything," King whispered. "Weapons systems. Reverse-engineered tech. But more importantly, the defense grid we were building."

"Defense grid?" Trent's eyebrows shot up.

King nodded frantically. "It was our insurance policy. If the aliens ever turned on us, we wanted to have a way to fight back. Experimental weapons based on their own technology, mostly defensive." He looked between them, desperation in his eyes. "We called it the Exile Project. If

Gibson gives them the locations, they'll destroy our only chance at resistance before we can even deploy it."

Natalie leaned forward, placing her palms flat on the table. "Give me the locations. Now."

"I need guarantees first—"

"You don't get to make demands," Trent cut in sharply.

King's eyes darted to Emma, then back to Natalie. "I'm not asking for myself. For her. Safety. Protection."

"Done," Natalie said without hesitation. "Now talk."

"Ready?" she asked as she put her phone on the table, clicking the red record button. Owen began to talk. It was an unbelievable story seventy years in the making—intrigue, massive cover-ups, bribery, and corruption on a global scale, all designed to keep humans pacified and under control right up until the alien overlords decided they were tired of us.

Thirty minutes in, Trent left to take Emma and also get to Emily and Briggs with Owen King's warning. Hopefully, Natalie could get the exact location of the secret labs, but Trent knew he wouldn't be part of those operations.

"Fuck me!" Natalie said finally when Owen had relayed the last of his information.

She could almost understand the bizarre rationale the human Observers had for perpetrating such a hoax on the world. Still, it was stupid, greedy, and inexcusable. Natalie knew other interrogators would follow her. Owen would be wrung completely dry before they were done. Still, the man was on a short list of individuals who could possibly help humanity survive. She was damn glad she wouldn't be the one making that decision.

CHAPTER ONE HUNDRED FIFTEEN

0903 EST September 24
White House Oval Office
Washington, D.C., USA

The president turned from his security briefing to an agent whose eyes were fixed on the ceiling of the famous office, listening to something on his comms unit. "What the hell is going on?"

Almost at once, the phone on the desk began buzzing. More of the Secret Service protective detail rushed through two doors, and an alert signal broadcast throughout the White House.

"Please follow me, sir," one of the agents said. They ignored the presidential advisor as they whisked him from the office to a more secure section of the complex.

The room buzzed with tension, monitors flickering with live feeds from around the globe. President Martin, beads of sweat glistening on his forehead, slammed his fist on the table. "Who the hell can tell me what is going on?" His voice echoed through the underground bunker, bouncing off the concrete walls and reinforced steel doors.

A grim-faced aide rushed in, whispering into the ear of General Taylor, who nodded and turned to the president. "Sir, we're seeing other

KEW strikes around the world. One just took out another major pharmaceutical center in Kansas. The devastation is immense."

The president's eyes widened. "How many more of these can we expect? And why the hell are we still so blind to their source?"

"Colonel Walker, sir. He's the man you need," Taylor replied, signaling to an aide who promptly exited the room.

Minutes later, the door opened, and Colonel James Walker, a tall, imposing figure with a hardened expression, strode in. His presence seemed to bring a semblance of order amidst the unfolding chaos. He saluted sharply. "Mr. President."

"Walker, what the hell is going on out there?" President Martin demanded, leaning forward with a look of fearful determination.

Walker didn't flinch. "Mr. President, the strikes are precision attacks using kinetic energy weapons, likely deployed from high orbit or even trans-lunar. Our intel suggests these are not random acts but a coordinated assault targeting critical infrastructure globally."

"And we're sure this is the aliens?" Martin's voice wavered slightly, betraying his concern.

Walker glanced at General Taylor before responding. "Yes, sir, these are from the attacking aliens."

The room fell silent, the gravity of Walker's words sinking in. President Martin took a deep breath, his resolve hardening. "Gentlemen, what are our options?" Emily Carter had been sounding the warnings about aliens for months, so he was well aware the military officially didn't have a response plan in place.

General Taylor handed a phone he'd been using to an aide. "Mr. President, we are at war. You need to notify Congress."

President Martin's face contorted in shock, his eyes widening as the full weight of General Taylor's words hit him. He staggered back, gripping the edge of the situation room table for support.

"War?" he croaked, his voice barely above a whisper. Then, as if a switch had flipped, he exploded into action. "God damn it! How the hell did we get here?"

He whirled on Colonel Walker, jabbing a finger at his chest. "Your people knew about this, didn't you? All those reports, all those warnings—and yet we're still caught with our fucking pants down!"

The room erupted into chaos. Aides scrambled to help the senior staff gather more information, phones rang incessantly, and the cacophony of voices rose to a fever pitch.

"I want every available asset mobilized now!" President Martin roared, slamming his fist on the table. The impact sent coffee mugs clattering, spilling their contents across classified documents. "Get me the joint chiefs, the secretary of defense, and for God's sake, someone get Emily Carter in here!"

Colonel Walker stood his ground, unflinching in the face of the president's fury. "Sir, we've been advising preparation for this possibility, but the precision of the attack..."

"Advising?" Martin scoffed, cutting him off. "This doesn't look like preparation to me, Colonel. This looks like a goddamn disaster!"

Walker knew he was just an easy target, so he didn't take the man's anger personally. Still, Martin and all the other politicians that refused to look at the problem seriously deserved a large share of the blame.

The president turned to face the room, his face flushed with anger and fear. "Listen up! As of this moment, we are at DEFCON 1. I want every nuclear silo, every aircraft carrier, every damn peashooter we've got ready to fire. If these aliens want a war, we'll give them one they'll never forget!"

General Taylor stepped forward, his voice steady despite the tension. "Mr. President, we need to consider the global implications. We can't just start spinning up our nuclear arsenal without..."

"Without what, General?" Martin snapped. "Without considering the diplomatic ramifications? In case you haven't noticed, we're a little past diplomacy here!"

The room shook violently as another impactor fell. "Jesus, are they taking out the Capitol?"

Walker was using a laptop on the conference table now, the system linked together SOSUS and satellite feeds from all over the globe. "No, sir, that one was 125 miles off the New York coast."

President Martin took a deep breath, running a hand through his hair. When he spoke again, his voice was lower but no less intense.

"More coastal strikes? Jesus, Emily warned me about those, too.

Issue emergency evac notices for all major cities and bases along both coasts."

"Get me a secure line to our allies. And someone find out where the hell these attacks are coming from. We need to hit back, and we need to hit back hard."

Colonel Walker's face remained stoic as he surveyed the latest reports coming in. The digital map of the world before him was lit up with flashing red dots, each representing another devastating strike.

"Sir," Walker began, his voice tight, "we've just lost another major power plant in Pennsylvania. Rail lines in Europe are down, and communication hubs in Asia have been hit. The impact is going global."

President Martin's jaw tightened. "This is global? What about our allies? Have we heard from them?"

General Taylor, still on the phone, held up a hand. "Sir, the UK is reporting massive infrastructure failures. France is in chaos. Communications are spotty, but they're trying to coordinate with us."

An aide rushed into the room, eyes wide with panic. "Mr. President, sir..." The young man was ashen-faced. "News just in—Beijing's been taken out. Multiple KEWs."

The room fell silent, the weight of the news sinking in like a stone. President Martin's eyes flickered with a mixture of disbelief and horror. "China? My God, they're hitting capitals now."

General Taylor put down the phone, his expression grave. "Sir, this isn't just about disabling infrastructure anymore. This is about sowing fear and breaking the spirit of nations. They're targeting the heart of our allies."

President Martin's fist clenched at his side. "Then we need to strike back, and we need to do it now. I want every available option on the table. Walker, coordinate with NATO. General Taylor, prepare for a full-scale mobilization."

Walker nodded, already moving to relay the orders. "Yes, sir. I'll get on it."

Emily Carter entered the room, her face pale but determined. "Mr. President."

President Martin turned to her, a flicker of hope in his eyes. "Emily, are you up to speed?"

She nodded before glancing around the chaos in the secure situation room.

"Emily, I've asked everyone else. Do you have any indication of where these strikes are being launched from? Any way to predict the next target?"

Emily shook her head, frustration evident. "My science was running it down. They think they are originating out near the asteroid belt, but the precision and speed of these strikes make it incredibly difficult."

"What about King?" Martin yelled. "Does he have anything that will help with this?"

Emily shook her head. "I don't think so, but I have someone in with him now. Agent Rogers was just briefing me on another warning King did offer. He may be of no use, but we will need a military response soon."

President Martin took a deep breath, steadying himself. "Damn! Ok, keep me updated. Get with General Taylor. You have any asset you might need. Take a seat and get to work."

Emily nodded, her eyes steely with determination. "I'll do my best, Mr. President."

He wanted to tell Emily that he was sorry. He should have listened to her warnings. He should have taken the committee's recommendations more seriously, but it was too late for apologies or regret.

"Colonel Walker, a word."

The Colonel eyed Emily, then General Taylor before walking back to the corner where the president was standing. They spoke for several minutes before the Army colonel saluted, took an envelope from the commander in chief, then exited the room.

"I have the joint chiefs for you, sir," another military man said, pointing to the large flat screen.

CHAPTER
ONE HUNDRED SIXTEEN

1903 UTC September 27
Secure Bunker
TOC: Tactical Operations Center
Northern VA, USA

They'd evacuated the White House in the middle of the night. Now President Martin stood before the digital display showing Washington D.C.'s defenses, his mind momentarily drifting to another dark day in the capital's history.

"You know," he said quietly to Emily, "in August 1814, the British marched on Washington during the War of 1812. Admiral Cockburn and General Ross led their forces right into the heart of our young nation's capital."

Emily nodded, her eyes never leaving the satellite feed. "President Madison had to flee. The British burned the White House, the Capitol Building..."

"Yes," Martin continued, his voice heavy with the weight of history. "Just like we did, but there were those who stood their ground. Commodore Joshua Barney and his flotilla men at Bladensburg—outnumbered, outgunned, but they held their position while others retreated."

General Taylor approached, his tablet displaying new alerts. "Sir, we're getting reports of atmospheric anomalies above the city."

Martin looked up at the main screen, where thermal imaging showed dozens of objects descending through the cloud cover.

"Barney was wounded three times but refused to leave until ordered to by his superiors," Martin continued, almost to himself. "'They have given us the only fighting we have had today,' the British commander said of those brave men."

Emily felt for the president and the tremendous strain he was under. The nation was falling under his watch. Honestly, though, the entire planet was. To think that this was just the opening salvo in what promised to be a long and protracted battle for the future of mankind.

The room fell silent as the first impacts hit. The Washington Monument disappeared in a blinding flash, followed by the Capitol dome.

Suspected by many, the nation's capital is one of the most heavily defended pieces of real estate in the world. Most of the weapon systems are hidden, or so well disguised, few would ever guess.

General Taylor's voice cut through the tension. "Sir, we're deploying all available assets. Raven Rock Mountain Complex is fully operational and prepared to engage."

Martin's eyes flicked to the map of the region. "Raven Rock? What are our capabilities there?"

Taylor pointed to the display. "Raven Rock, also known as Site R, is one of our primary continuity-of-government facilities. It's equipped with anti-aircraft batteries, Patriot missile systems, and laser-based defense platforms."

Linda Reyes added, "The Mount Weather Emergency Operations Center. It has similar defensive capabilities, including THAAD missile systems and railgun emplacements."

Martin nodded. "What about Andrews Air Force Base?"

"Andrews," Taylor replied, tapping his tablet, "has a full complement of F-22 Raptors and F-35 Lightning II fighters on standby. The base also houses several squadrons of MQ-9 Reaper drones armed with AGM-114 Hellfire missiles. It's already taken several hits, but they are still operational."

Martin's gaze shifted to another part of the screen showing Fort Belvoir. "Fort Belvoir?"

"Fort Belvoir has Aegis Ashore missile defense systems and MIM-104 Patriot batteries," Taylor explained. "They're integrated into our NORAD network for real-time tracking and engagement of aerial threats."

Martin rubbed his temples. "What about naval support?"

"The Naval Surface Warfare Center in Dahlgren is operational," Taylor confirmed. "They've deployed their Zumwalt-class destroyers equipped with advanced radar and surface-to-air missiles. The USS Wisconsin is in Chesapeake Bay with SM-6 interceptors and RIM-162 Evolved Sea Sparrow Missiles. Most of our fleets in the harbors were protected from the recent tsunamis."

The president took a deep breath and nodded, absorbing the information. "Alright, General Taylor, do what you can against these bastards."

Taylor nodded briskly, issuing commands into his headset.

Emily leaned in closer toward the president. "We need to stay ahead of their strategy. They're targeting symbolic structures as well as our defenses."

Martin's jaw tightened as another explosion rocked the display, this time near the Pentagon.

"I know. Symbols can be replaced; people can't."

The Virginia bunker's command room buzzed with activity as screens updated with real-time data from various installations around Washington, D.C., each location armed and ready for what looked like an all-out war. A war on American soil.

"Got one of 'em," someone yelled. They watched as a video showed one of the sleek alien craft become fully visible as it ran through a virtual wall of rounds from a Patriot missile battery.

The image of the downed alien craft from the Patriot missile battery played on a loop, offering a brief moment of triumph.

"Got another one of 'em off the coast!" someone shouted.

General Taylor's eyes narrowed on the screens. "We need to maintain this momentum."

The hardened emergency bunker just over the border in Virginia was a fortified hole in the ground, nothing more. President Martin, standing slightly back from the command center, analyzed the broader picture. "General, their strategy seems chaotic and decentralized. They're hitting multiple targets to spread us thin."

Taylor nodded. "That's their plan, alright. But we've got layers of defense. They'll find it hard to penetrate all the way."

Just as more good news trickled in—reports of another successful interception near Fort Belvoir—the room fell silent as new data streamed onto the screens.

"Sir," an officer called out, "we're detecting multiple fast-moving objects changing course mid-air. They seem to be deploying something."

Martin's eyes locked onto the display showing thermal signatures veering sharply towards Raven Rock and Mount Weather. The lines on the screen moved like serpents, unpredictable and menacing.

"Bombs?" Martin asked.

"No, sir, zero detonations. Probes, drones, mines... no idea, but there are hundreds of them coming down all over."

"They're adapting," Emily murmured. "Some sort of ground force," she suggested.

General Taylor's face hardened. "Prepare for countermeasures. Deploy air-to-ground interceptors immediately!"

Commands echoed through the room as operators scrambled to adjust their defenses. The next impacts hit with a vengeance. Explosions rocked the foundations of Raven Rock, sending plumes of debris skyward. Mount Weather's defenses lit up in a desperate attempt to intercept the incoming barrage.

The tension in the room thickened as reports of damage and casualties streamed in. Raven Rock's radar array went dark, its primary systems offline.

"We're losing ground," one operator whispered, fear creeping into his voice.

President Martin clenched his fists, his gaze fixed on the carnage unfolding on the screens. They could now see close-up video of something mechanical moving behind the veil of smoke and debris.

"What in the hell is that?" someone asked.

"Emily, your experts said they would likely use kinetic weapons and tidal waves to soften up the coast. What comes next?" the president asked.

Emily tried to recall the conversation. "It will depend on their goals, but the elimination of command and control... our leadership, followed by some softening up of the local biosphere. A bio-weapon, chemical attack, or other mechanism to reduce natural threats. Then, once the planet is largely secured, an occupying ground force."

"I think they read the same playbook. In that regard, my days are likely numbered."

She wanted to disagree. She wanted to ease her boss's pain, but the president, like all of his predecessors, had brought this on himself to a large degree. Inaction or inability to act on reasonable threats should be a treasonous act.

For decades, the U.S. Government's main position on UFOs was one of absolute indifference. They focused on short-term, more immediate needs. Since no tangible threat was deemed to exist to the American people, the government shouldn't be spending time or money to study it, much less make preparations.

In truth, she had lost all faith in the industry in which she worked. Its collapse outside these walls mirrored what was going on in her own mind. Her priorities were now focused elsewhere. She wanted to get away, get Paul, and find somewhere safe to live out their last days.

A brilliant flash high in the sky was followed by a deafening thunderclap. "All defensive systems are offline," a technician called out, panic edging into his voice. "Missile batteries, rail guns, laser defense grid—nothing's responding!"

On-screen, they watched as swarms of smaller kinetic energy weapons rained down on the city, each impact precisely targeted. The Pentagon, Andrews Air Force Base, Fort McNair—all strategic military positions offline or obliterated in seconds.

"My God," Emily whispered. "They're systematically taking out every defensive position."

A brilliant blue beam cut through the clouds, slicing through the remaining government buildings as if they were made of paper.

"Just like 1814," Martin said grimly. "Except this time, there will be no Commodore Barney to make a stand."

The feed from the capital began to break up, static replacing the images of destruction as communication networks failed.

"Sir," General Taylor reported, his voice strained, "we've lost all contact with the Capitol. It's... it's gone."

"It's still there, General," Martin said. "Have some faith."

"The Pentagon is gone, too, sir," a young officer at a terminal said with a shaky voice. "All of it—a direct hit."

President Martin slammed his fist against the table, rattling coffee cups and tablets. "What about our orbital defenses? The Aegis system, anything!"

"All neutralized, sir," Colonel Yang replied, sliding a tablet across the table. "These last rounds of kinetic impacts were preceded by some kind of electromagnetic pulse that disabled our satellite and command network. We're effectively blind above the atmosphere as well as on the ground."

Emily studied the fragmented data streams still coming in from surviving military installations. "They're not just targeting command and control—they've hit power distribution, water treatment facilities, transportation hubs."

"It's a systematic dismantling of our infrastructure," General Taylor added. "The pattern suggests they want to cripple us without maximizing civilian casualties."

"Small comfort to those in D.C.," Martin muttered.

A communications officer approached with a secure satellite phone. "Mr. President, we have the Russian president on the line. Their strategic command center outside Moscow was also just hit. They're requesting immediate consultation under the Emergency Powers Protocol."

Martin took the phone, his expression grim. "This is President Martin." He listened intently, his face darkening. "Yes, we're experiencing the same. No, we don't believe this is an act by any terrestrial power." Another pause. “North Korea? No, we haven’t heard that. I agree. Full information sharing, effective immediately."

He handed the phone back to the officer. "Get leaders in Beijing, London, Paris, and New Delhi. Implement the same protocol."

"Sir," Taylor interjected, "the targeting algorithm they're using—it's precise to within centimeters. Nothing they do is random."

"They're surgically removing our ability to fight back as well as one hell of a decapitation strike," Walker said.

Martin studied the tactical display, where red impact zones continued to multiply across the country. "If they wanted to annihilate us, they could have. This is... containment."

"Or preparation," Taylor suggested quietly.

The bunker's lights flickered momentarily before emergency generators kicked in.

"They've found us," Yang said calmly, straightening his tie.

"General Taylor, what's our evacuation protocol?" President Martin asked.

"Air Force One is standing by at Site Romeo, sir. But given their ability to track and target with precision—"

"I understand." Martin cut him off. "Jack, the football?"

"The nuclear launch codes are secure, Mr. President."

Martin nodded, his face a mask of determination. "Then let's move. The United States Government may be on the run, but we're still in this fight."

Emily gripped the edge of the table, her knuckles white as they watched the satellite imagery of Washington, D.C. burning. The methodical destruction of the capital brought a chill that seemed to permeate the bunker despite its climate-controlled environment.

"What did President Madison say?" she asked, her voice barely above a whisper. "After the capital burned in 1814—what were his words?"

President Martin looked up from the tactical display, his face drawn with exhaustion and grief. For a moment, he seemed to age a decade before her eyes.

"Madison..." He cleared his throat. "After fleeing to Virginia, Madison wrote to his wife Dolley that the British invasion was 'the greatest humiliation which has befallen the government and the country since its independence.'"

He ran a hand through his silver hair, leaving it slightly disheveled.

"But what history doesn't emphasize is what he said to his cabinet when they reconvened in a tavern outside the city." Martin's eyes grew distant. "He told them, 'The republic stands not in its buildings but in its people and principles. We have lost structures of stone and wood, but not our resolve.'"

Emily nodded slowly, absorbing the historical parallel.

"Of course," Martin added with a bitter smile, "Madison had the advantage of facing human enemies who eventually withdrew. Our situation is..." He gestured helplessly at the screens showing destruction spreading across the country.

"Sir," General Taylor interrupted, "we need to move to the next secure location."

The president straightened his tie, a small, defiant gesture in the face of catastrophe.

"The question now," he said quietly to Emily, "is whether I'll be remembered as the president who lost Earth, not just the U.S. capital."

CHAPTER ONE HUNDRED SEVENTEEN

1500 EST Zerot Day
White House Grounds
Washington, D.C., USA

Several days after the annihilation of the U.S. capital, a sleek, obsidian vessel carved a shadow into the ruins of Washington D.C., touching down on what was once the White House lawn. Fire-scorched and littered with skeletal debris, the ground trembled slightly as the ship's gravitic pads hissed into silence.

From its underbelly emerged a single figure—tall, pale, and impossible to mistake for anything human.

Zyloth.

A junior tactician by Hi'Grash' standards, yet still carrying the authority to dismantle governments. He stood over eight feet tall, lithe and muscular beneath a seamless iridescent suit that pulsed faintly with threads of what could have been alien code. His skin, tight and textured like scorched marble, was veined with black fractals that curled across his elongated skull and down his neck like the roots of some ancient, diseased tree.

His eyes—deep crimson and orange, predatory—did not blink. They absorbed light. Reflected nothing.

Trailing behind him was a precision-locked honor guard of North Korean special forces, weapons slung casually, their loyalty earned through technology far beyond their understanding. They moved like dogs at heel—proud to serve, unaware of the leash.

Zyloth stopped before the fractured shell of the White House's north entrance, its columns now cracked and leaning like old men after a long war. President Martin stood among the remaining Secret Service agents, ash-covered, hollow-eyed.

The alien didn't bow. He didn't offer a hand. He didn't even look directly at Martin.

Instead, he inhaled—long and bored.

"The air smells of rot and plastic," he said. "Fitting."

Martin opened his mouth, but Zyloth raised a single clawed finger —not to silence him, but to dismiss the need for speech entirely.

"You are not here to debate. You are here to surrender."

General Briggs stepped between the alien and the president. Sporting numerous wounds from recent encounters, including an ugly flash burn to part of his neck, he drew himself up to his full height—still a foot shorter than the alien visitor.

"See here, we are not going to surrender. Not to you." His voice carried the weight of decades of command, though it cracked slightly from smoke inhalation.

Zyloth didn't even acknowledge the interruption. His crimson eyes remained fixed on some distant point beyond the president, as though Briggs were nothing more than atmospheric disturbance.

Several North Korean commandos rushed forward, their movements precise and unnaturally coordinated. They threw Briggs to the ground with brutal efficiency, weapons drawn and pressed against his temple and spine. The general grunted as his wounded body hit the rubble-strewn ground.

"General!" President Martin stepped forward instinctively but froze as Zyloth finally shifted his gaze—not to Briggs, but to him.

"Your species confuses defiance with dignity," Zyloth said, the words flowing with an unnatural cadence. "The difference is that dignity acknowledges reality."

Briggs struggled against his captors, blood seeping through his uniform where fresh wounds had reopened. "Mr. President, don't listen to this—"

A commando drove a rifle butt into his ribs, silencing him with a sharp crack.

Zyloth extended a hand toward Martin. From his palm unfurled a small metallic sphere that hovered in the air between them, pulsing with the same coded light as his suit.

"This contains the terms. Non-negotiable. Implementation begins immediately." The sphere projected a holographic document—pages of alien script interspersed with English translations. "Your military installations will be closed. Your population centers will be restricted and reorganized. Your resources will be cataloged."

Martin stared at the floating terms, his face ashen. Behind him, the remaining Secret Service agents exchanged desperate glances, hands hovering near weapons they knew would be useless.

"And if we refuse?" Martin asked, his voice hollow.

Zyloth's expression didn't change—it couldn't—but something like amusement rippled through the black veins across his face.

"You misunderstand. This is not a negotiation. It is an inventory process."

Martin stepped forward anyway. "We weren't told... who you are. Or what you represent."

Zyloth finally glanced at him. "I represent your total irrelevance. All that you presume is yours. Your cities. Your species."

He walked past Martin slowly into the building, inspecting the ruined pillars, the cracked bust of Lincoln now decapitated. "Your ancestors once conquered continents and enslaved entire civilizations without bothering to send kings or presidents. Why would you expect better treatment in your own undoing?

"I am not a diplomat," Zyloth said, his voice smooth but heavy with contempt. "I am a tactician. A mere functionary. I am here because no one of value in my clan wished to waste their cycles on this debris field of a planet. I volunteered to come here mainly at the request of our... new allies from what you call North Korea. Consider this a courtesy call."

He looked around the ruined grand foyer and gave something close to a smirk, though it twisted oddly across his sideways-moving mouth. "And you thought I was here to negotiate."

Martin stared, stunned, struggling for composure. "So what happens now? We report to Pyongyang?"

"You report to them, yes. They are obedient. Efficient. Capable of suppressing your species without unnecessary complication."

Martin's hands shook. "That's insane. You can't seriously believe we'll just submit."

Zyloth blinked slowly. "You already have."

He turned toward a crumbling wall where part of an oil painting still clung to the plaster—perhaps Jefferson or Adams, now smeared with soot. Zyloth touched it lightly.

"There was promise here. A spark. But your species, for all its noise and passion, confuses sensation for truth. You live in illusions. You weaponize fiction. And you crave authority... so we gave you one."

Martin tried again. "What are the Hi'Grash? What do you even want from us?"

Zyloth gave a low, rasping exhale—something between annoyance and pity.

"We want a clean acquisition. A biologically rich planet with adaptable labor units and orbital pathways. You're not special. You're not even particularly evolved. If your minds hadn't been so... entertainingly flawed, we would have scrubbed you entirely. But you have use. Some of you. Not eight billion. That would be... wasteful."

Zyloth turned to the North Korean commander at his flank, muttering something in a sibilant dialect that made the air shimmer briefly. The commander nodded and opened a metal case.

Inside: a bottle. Dust-covered. Deep amber.

Zyloth took it without ceremony. No toasts. No glass. Just uncorked it and inhaled.

"Bourbon," he said. "An accidental triumph of a doomed civilization."

Martin stared, furious. "Is this all a game to you?"

Zyloth drank deeply then pushed the bottle to Martin. Martin carefully took the bottle, careful of the alien's clawed hand.

"No, President. This is history. You are not the main character."

He stepped closer now, towering over the stunned leader. "I hope you resist. I hope your military tries to strike back. The cleanup would be faster. Simpler. But in the end, whether you kneel or burn is of no real concern."

He gestured toward the horizon, where the scorched skyline of Washington bled into a darkening sky.

"Enjoy your bourbon. It will be the last thing made by your species that isn't filtered through our approval."

With that, Zyloth turned away, already forgetting the man behind him. The honor guard fell into step, and together, they disappeared toward the ship.

The bourbon bottle had barely left his hand when President Martin surged forward, his voice cracking with something between desperation and rage.

"You can't just walk away from this!"

His words rang out across the rubble-strewn lawn.

His Secret Service detail flanked him instinctively, moving into protective formation. Weapons came halfway up. They didn't know what they could do—but training dies hard.

Zyloth didn't even stop walking.

But he did turn his head.

Just slightly.

That single gesture—slow, effortless—held more gravity than any shouted command. The alien's amber eyes locked onto Martin's, and what passed for a smile curled across his angular features.

Not cruelty.

Contempt.

"How profoundly human," he said, his voice low and venomous. "Still believing that noise equals relevance."

The president eyed the general still on the ground. Briggs was on his knees possibly trying to covertly reach a concealed weapon, maybe just praying for all this to end. The man's own suffering mirrored what had been done to the White House.

Zyloth extended two fingers—bent slightly, lazily—toward the North Korean commander walking at his side.

There was no discussion. No warning.

A sharp bark of orders in Korean cracked the air.

Suppressed gunfire followed like punctuation.

Three silenced bursts—then two more.

The Secret Service agents dropped in rapid succession. One gurgled, another twitched before going still. A final body hit the ground near Martin's feet, blood soaking into the gray dust. Every round a killing shot.

The president staggered backward, mouth open in horror.

"They were unarmed as we were instructed!"

Zyloth approached now, slowly, like a parent indulging the final tantrum of a child.

"You misunderstand, President," he said, voice like oil over glass. "Their purpose ended the moment I arrived. Protection implies value. You have none."

Martin stood frozen. Blood pooled near his shoes. One of the agents —a woman with a shattered radio still clutched in her hand—lay sprawled across a cracked tile that once bore the Presidential seal.

"What do you want from us?" Martin whispered.

Zyloth leaned forward, his smooth, pinched face mere inches from Martin's. The alien's skin shimmered faintly, as if catching signals from a distant star.

"Compliance. Silence. Labor. Fewer mouths.

"Our planet killers will soon control the remaining parts of your country. I was curious what the most powerful man in the world would be like; now I see he is nothing special, just like the rest of your species." He straightened and turned again without looking back.

General Briggs rushed at the alien, combat knife in hand. Despite the man's age, his movements were quick and unexpected to the men guarding him. Zyloth moved aside as if anticipating the man's strike. Briggs passed by Zyloth and directly into the path of rounds from commandos on the opposite side of the group. He slipped to the ground, blood leaking from a dozen new wounds. His eyes glanced at Martin before glazing over.

"Kill another president, clear another city—it's all the same to me," Zyloth said.

As the North Korean soldiers moved to fall in behind him, Zyloth paused once more and added, almost as an afterthought: "Keep resisting, though. It adds texture and nuance to the conquest."

And then he was gone, vanishing into the smoke and shadows, leaving Martin alone with the dead and the unbearable truth:

Earth no longer belonged to humans.

CHAPTER ONE HUNDRED EIGHTEEN

1645 EST Zero Day
DHS Temporary HQ
Washington, D.C., USA

Natalie hunched over her makeshift desk, the abandoned floor of the DHS building eerily quiet save for the rustling of papers and the frantic tapping of her fingers on the keyboard. Reports, maps, and data sheets were strewn about, a chaotic mosaic of the impending alien threat and the conspirators' machinations. The list of locations was known only to her and Trent.

Trent was working it from an intelligence angle, and indeed, they had already transferred him out of the area. She was monitoring the late general's unit, or what was left of them, as a military response to infiltrate and empty out each one. So far, they had been too late on the first three.

She reached for her phone, dialing Kaden's number for the umpteenth time. The line rang, each unanswered tone amplifying her frustration. "Come on, Kaden," she muttered through gritted teeth. "Where are you?"

Natalie ended the call when it went to voicemail again, slamming the phone down on the desk. She leaned back in her chair, running her hands through her hair. Kaden's expertise was needed now more than ever. His insights into the aliens' behavior and the fleet out there somewhere could be the key to surviving this crisis. She had also had no luck getting in touch with Dr. Cho. His proximity to Los Angeles might explain that, though.

The DHS system had tendrils into almost every person in the country. Emily had cleared the way for Natalie to have access to anything she needed. She turned to her computer as she scoured every database and communication channel available. Emails, encrypted messages, even old-fashioned radio frequencies—Natalie left no stone unturned.

But every path led to the same dead end. Kaden Trembley was a ghost, his last known location a credit card receipt from a gas station. She knew he took the news of the West Coast disasters quite hard. He was heading to Oregon. He had gone to help with rescue efforts after the catastrophic tidal wave and maybe find Sarah. But that was days ago, and since then, silence.

Natalie pushed back from the desk, the chair scraping harshly against the bare concrete floor. Time for humanity was running out. The alien fleet loomed on the horizon, and the conspirators' grip tightened with every passing moment. She needed answers; she needed Kaden's brilliant mind to help her navigate this labyrinth of alien threats and very human lies.

But all she had was silence and the gnawing fear that she might be too late. Natalie paused by the window, staring out at the city below. Somewhere out there, amidst the chaos and the rubble, was a path, a way to survive, maybe even triumph. And she would find it, with or without the professor.

A knock at the office door surprised her. She tucked the compact Glock into her waistband and opened the door. Amazingly, a man in a muddy delivery uniform stood there with an overnight envelope.

He held out a small device. "I know it seems crazy, but I need a signature," he said, passing over a small device. The young man's eyes kept darting toward the sky. In the distance they both heard a metallic crash followed seconds later by an unholy screech. The anxious driver hurried away.

Natalie shut the door as she saw it was from Professor Trembley and nervously pulled the tear strip and dumped out the contents. Two items tumbled from the envelope onto Natalie's desk. The first was a small note card, handwritten in Kaden's unmistakable scrawl. Her heart sank as she read his words:

'My Dear Natalie,

I'm so sorry for my sudden departure, but I simply can't take any more. I've done my part for better or for worse. Now that it is done...I wish I had been wrong.

The news about the destruction on the West Coast—about Sarah—has broken something in me. I've gone to find her remains or to join her. At this point, I don't care which.

My dear, you've become like a daughter to me these past months. Your determination, your brilliance, your unwavering courage in the face of impossible odds—they remind me of what humanity is worth fighting for.

The other item is from an old friend. You will understand why I didn't share it until now. He was in a position to know all but sadly failed to act until it was too late.

I will miss you every day until the end comes.

With love and regret,

Kaden'

Natalie's vision blurred with tears. She set the card down gently, as if it might crumble under the weight of her touch, and reached for the second item.

It was a single sheet of paper, neatly printed with a letterhead she didn't recognize. The text was formal, clinical—and utterly horrifying:

'A species designated in 1954 as A044 has a colonization fleet that will soon be entering the solar system. Long-range sensors detect 37 vessels of varying classifications. Conservative estimates place their arrival at Earth orbit late this calendar year.

As per Protocol Omega, all Observer assets are to be liquidated and evidence destroyed. The Human Experiment is officially terminated. Preliminary messages indicate A044 will keep a small portion of the population of the planet for breeding stock. The Observers are uncertain if that would be for slaves or food stock.'

There was more...too much more. Some of which was similar but different from what Owen King had finally offered up. Natalie's hands trembled as she read the document again, her mind refusing to accept its implications. The Human Experiment was over. Humans as slaves—or food?

The cold, detached tone of the memo made it all the more terrifying. This wasn't speculation or theory—this was an insider's confirmation of humanity's impending doom, written with the casual indifference of someone discussing a failed business venture. Someone with obviously more insight than even Owen King. She only had the initials of JM, but thanks to the computer terminal, she soon had the full dossier on Jasper Maxwell.

Interpreting what she had read, Natalie sent coded messages to her command group and a private one to Trent Rogers. The city was in ruins, and she had no idea how long the secure communications system would operate. It was time to move into the shadows.

She slid away from the desk and stood. Grabbing her pack from beside the desk, she checked the charge on the NovaCore plasma rifle and added the custom satellite phone before shouldering it and the backpack. She had a long journey ahead and might as well get going.

Almost 3,000 miles away, Kaden Trembley climbed through a mud-covered valley and over enormous downed trees. His mind wasn't focused on the stars, the alien threat, or even the devastation all around him. No, he was focused on his own stupidity—his incomprehensible blindness to what had always been right there in front of him.

He stopped, pulled the glasses from his eyes, and rubbed the tears away.

Kaden stumbled through the debris-strewn landscape, his heart heavy with the weight of realization. Sarah Mitchell, his mentor, his friend, and perhaps something more, was gone. The thought tore at his soul, a jagged wound that refused to heal.

He paused, leaning against a fallen tree, his chest heaving with emotion. How could he have been so blind? So consumed by his own pursuits that he failed to see what was right in front of him? Sarah had been there, a constant presence, a guiding light in the darkness of his obsession. And yet, he had pushed her away, relegated her to the periphery of his life, time and again.

Kaden's mind drifted back to their last conversation, the urgency in Sarah's voice as she warned him of the dangers of his path. He had dismissed her concerns, too focused on his own goals to heed her wisdom. Now, as he stood amidst the ruins of a world torn apart, he understood the depth of his folly.

Sarah had loved him, in her own quiet way. It was there in the gentle touch of her hand on his shoulder, in the way her eyes softened when she spoke to him. And he, in his stubborn pursuit of truth, had failed to reciprocate, to acknowledge the bond they shared.

Kaden's thoughts turned to the Observers, the shadowy group that had orchestrated so much of the chaos that now engulfed the world. They had believed they were helping humanity, guiding them toward a better future. But in their arrogance, they had sown the seeds of destruction.

Just as he had been blinded by his own obsessions, the Observers had been blinded by their own sense of purpose and superiority. They had played with forces beyond their understanding, manipulated the course of human history without regard for the consequences. And now, as the world burned, they were nowhere to be found.

Kaden pushed himself off the tree, his resolve hardening. He had to find Sarah, had to know for certain what had become of her. Even if it was a futile quest, he owed her that much. He owed her the acknowledgment of what she had meant to him, of the love he had been too foolish to ever admit to her.

CHAPTER
ONE HUNDRED NINETEEN

1714 EST Zero Day
National Harbor Yacht Club
Maryland, USA

Emily's fingers trembled as she gripped the steering wheel of the stolen military Humvee. The vehicle's engine roared through the deserted streets and broken roads of what remained of Washington D.C. Next to her, Paul sat slumped against the passenger door, his hospital gown replaced with ill-fitting clothes she'd grabbed from a staff locker room in the nearly abandoned hospital.

"You sure about this, Em?" Paul's voice was weak, barely audible above the loud rumble of the engine. His face was still gaunt, eyes hollow from months and years of captivity and whatever experiments they'd subjected him to. He did look better than he had days earlier.

"There's nothing left here for us," Emily said, her voice hard with conviction she hadn't felt until witnessing President Martin's meeting with the alien. "The president was attempting to negotiate with them. After everything they've done."

Paul turned his head slowly toward the window, his eyes widening as they drove past the Washington Monument—or what remained of it.

The once-proud obelisk now lay in massive chunks of white stone scattered across the scorched National Mall.

"My God," he whispered. "Is that...?"

"Yes."

They passed block after block of devastation. Buildings that had stood for centuries were now skeletal ruins. Fires still burned in some areas, sending plumes of black smoke into a sky that had taken on a perpetual reddish hue.

"The Capitol building is just...gone," Paul said, pressing his palm against the window. "And there's the Lincoln Memorial... Christ, Lincoln's head is just sitting there in the reflecting pool."

Emily kept her eyes on the road, swerving around abandoned vehicles and debris. "The first wave hit three days ago. Kinetic weapons from orbit. Then came some sort of mechanical guard dogs."

Paul stared at a group of civilians being herded by something—not quite like a dog in their movements. "Are those...?"

"I don't know. Maybe their ground force. I hear they have some more human collaborators, too." Emily's knuckles whitened on the steering wheel. "The joint chiefs are dead. Most of Congress, too."

They drove in silence past the Pentagon, now a smoking crater in the Earth.

"Where are we going?" Paul finally asked.

"General Briggs has a yacht at the marina. The Valiant. Forty-footer. He gave me the keys before..." Emily swallowed hard. "Before he and Martin went to face them at the White House. Said someone needed to survive to tell the truth."

Paul nodded weakly, his gaze fixed on the ruins of another monument as they sped past. "Everything I fought for... everything we believed in..."

"I know," Emily said, her voice breaking. "I know."

The Humvee skidded on loose gravel and came to a stop fifty feet from the thing squatting in the middle of the highway.

The pod looked like it had been punched into the asphalt from above—half-sunken, blackened, its outer shell still glowing faintly red. Steam hissed from vents along its flanks, and a deep, rhythmic thump emanated from inside, like a heartbeat trapped in metal.

Paul leaned forward. “Is that—”

The pod lurched.

Its surface shifted—segments unfolding with a grotesque mechanical grace, like steel petals blooming in reverse. Beneath, something moved. Sinew. Muscle. Wet, glistening tissue threaded with tubing and vein-like wiring. Limbs began to uncoil from within, too many at first to count. A jaw emerged—not hinged like a dog’s, but segmented, armored, folding inward with layers of cartilage and metal bone. The front claws dug into the asphalt as it dragged itself forward, still forming.

“Oh, God,” Paul whispered.

The creature’s spine flexed as its legs locked into place. The final pieces of the pod clamped over its back and chest like armor plating, snapping down with a wet, metallic crack.

Then it looked up.

Eyes—not lenses, but glossy, organic eyes—blinked to life beneath the armor. The wardog raised its head and let out a low, electronic growl. A single step forward sent spiderweb cracks through the pavement.

“Emily—go!” Paul shouted.

She slammed the accelerator, and the Humvee roared to life. Behind them, the thing dropped into a runner’s crouch—then exploded into motion, tearing after them down the ruined highway, faster than anything that big had any right to be.

The marina came into view, a scene of utter chaos. Half-sunken vessels littered the waterway, some still smoldering. Bodies floated face-down in the water. Emily pulled the Humvee to a screeching halt at the end of the dock.

"We need to move fast," she said, helping Paul out of the vehicle. His legs wobbled beneath him, and she shouldered some of his weight. "The Valiant should be at the end of Pier C."

A distant mechanical howl echoed through the devastated cityscape behind them.

"What the hell was that back there?" Paul asked, his head snapping around.

"The wardogs. I hear that they hunt in packs." Emily quickened their pace. "We don't want to be here when it...or they arrive."

They stumbled down the wooden planks of the pier, passing abandoned boats and upturned dinghies. The Valiant stood out—a sleek forty-foot yacht with a white hull, seemingly untouched by the destruction around it.

"That's it," Emily said, fumbling with the keys. Her hands shook as she unlocked the cabin door and helped Paul aboard. The general had kept it fully stocked this last month just in case. Paul helped her free the mooring lines, and she pushed them away from the dock.

Another howl, closer this time, followed by several more in response.

"Emily," Paul's voice was urgent. "They're coming."

She rushed to the controls, inserting the key and bringing the engines to life with a reassuring rumble. Through the windshield, she spotted them—five metallic quadrupeds with elongated heads racing along the shoreline, their movements unnaturally fluid. To her, they looked more feline than canine, but the approach was simply unnerving.

"Hold on," she called to Paul as she throttled forward, the yacht lurching away from the dock.

One of the mechanical beasts leaped onto the pier, its metal claws splintering the wood as it charged toward them. Emily pushed the throttle harder. The gap between the yacht and the pier widened to ten feet, then twenty.

The lead dog reached the end of the pier and launched itself toward the boat. It fell short, splashing into the water with a hiss of anger, then began swimming toward them at surprising speed.

Paul collapsed into the captain's chair, watching as the shoreline slowly receded. The mechanical creatures paced at the edge of the water, their faceless heads tracking the yacht's movement. The one in the water began losing distance and turned back to rejoin its packmates.

"Where are we heading?" Paul asked, his voice hollow.

Emily stared ahead at the open water, the ruins of Washington D.C. smoldering behind them. Her hands gripped the wheel, steadying herself.

"I have no idea," she admitted. "Just somewhere that is not here."

CHAPTER
ONE HUNDRED TWENTY

1917 CDT Day +3
Beta Site Prepper Enclave
Ozark Mountains, Arkansas, USA

"So President Martin finally came to his senses?"

Marcus snorted. "He's a politician. Not sure that's even possible. Hell, I voted for the guy; he seemed better than the rest, but he's just one man. Congress is like a pool full of sharks. Anything Martin wanted done, he had to do by presidential order."

"Executive order," David said.

"Oh? Right, executive order."

They had seen clips of the press conference in front of a ruined White House. The capital was essentially gone, as were so many other places. Little actual information was getting out, and what was filtering through seemed beyond comprehension.

"How long are we going to be out here, Marcus?"

In the light of the campfire, he wasn't sure which of the women had voiced the question. It was on everyone's mind, though. No matter what reasons motivated them to drop off the grid and move to a prepper compound, even these people craved normalcy and social interaction. They wanted to know what their grandkids were up to, how the Cubs did on their last road trip. Humans are wired to prefer the company of others.

"Everyone out there is trying to figure out how to get here or someplace just like here. I need all of you to listen, and this won't be easy to hear."

Marcus drew in a deep breath, the significance of what he was about to say not lost on him. "The world as we knew it is about to be gone. The aliens are real, and the government that seemed intent on covering it up, much less admitting they were a threat, is gone. We can't rely on anyone but ourselves now. This is home."

The group exchanged glances, a mix of emotions on each of their faces. They had prepared for this moment, but the reality of it was still hard to grasp.

"I know we've all made tremendous sacrifices just to be here," Marcus continued, his voice steady. "We've left behind our old lives, our families, our friends. But look around you. This is our family now. We've faced challenges together, and we've come out stronger for it."

Nods of agreement rippled through the group. They had faced some hardships of their own—damaged supplies, internal conflicts, a medical crisis, and the constant fear of discovery. But they had been mostly unscathed by the recent events.

"We were right all along," Lynn, the former paramedic, said. "All those years of preparing, of being called crazy. It was all worth it."

"And aliens are real."

"But what now?" Jake, the engineer, asked. "Do we stay here forever, cut off from the world?"

Marcus sighed. "That's a decision we'll all have to make together. The immediate threat may have passed, but we could be facing something worse. The world out there is still in chaos. We have to weigh the risks and benefits of reintegrating into society—if there is a society. We will send scouts to our coastal camp to see how they're doing and try to establish communication and trade. We know of other enclaves out there. We'll reach out and work to find common ground."

"What about Big Lou and Alpha Site?" Jake asked.

Marcus smiled. He'd been back a few weeks but had shared little of what went on there. "Alpha Site has been relocated to a much more secure location. They also had to take in some additional guests, so I'm expecting they'll need more of our assistance in the days ahead. Luther has things under control, but let's just say they are on more of a military footing now."

"Military?" Mike Johnson asked.

Marcus nodded. "Isolation is no longer an option for Alpha camp. They're going to be more exposed. Lou and some of the new recruits are preparing for the likelihood of direct action. We found a place that was tailor-made for that purpose."

The group fell silent, each lost in their own thoughts. The idea of returning to their old lives seemed almost foreign now. They had become a tight-knit community, relying on each other for survival.

"Whatever we decide," Marcus said, breaking the silence, "look, we can't forget who we are. The guidelines that have kept us safe. The importance of being prepared, of being self-sufficient. We have to pass that knowledge on to others."

Heads nodded in agreement. They knew their experience during the alien crisis would have a lasting impact, not just on their own lives but on society as a whole.

"For now, let's focus on the present," Marcus said. "We have each other, and we have our skills. We'll take things one day at a time and figure out our path forward together." He felt Retro stiffen under his hand.

"I just hope the worst is over." David said, echoing the thoughts of others.

"It's not over. It's just barely begun," a voice from the darkness said just as a perimeter alarm went off.

Marcus turned in the direction of the new voice, reaching for his sidearm. "Who are you, and what do you mean?"

Natalie Reeves walked closer to the fire, a teenage boy trailing behind her. She dropped her duffel. "It's just begun. The aliens have deployed what they are calling Planet Killers and...a large alien fleet is headed this way. Also, I'd like you to meet Chad. I found him a day ago.

He has an interesting story to share. Oh, and you may want to put spotters out to the Southwest. According to Chad here some downed pilots are heading this way with a new friend."

The young man stepped forward and smiled shyly.

EPILOGUE

James Walker stepped off the helicopter, his boots crunching on the gravelly soil of South Dakota. The whir of the rotors died away, leaving an eerie silence. The trip west had been one of the most convoluted he'd ever undertaken. He looked around, taking in the barren landscape. No buildings, no roads, just an endless expanse of scrubland stretching to the horizon.

"Colonel Walker," a voice called out, snapping him back to the present. A man in fatigues, insignia indicating a rank of captain, approached and saluted crisply. "Captain Harris, sir. Welcome to Blackrock."

Walker returned the salute, eyeing the captain critically. "Blackrock, huh? Seems like a whole lot of nothing out here, Captain."

"Yes, sir. That's the point," Harris replied, a hint of a smile tugging at his lips. "Follow me, sir. The briefing is about to start."

Walker fell into step beside Harris, his curiosity piqued. The orders in the president's letter had been brief and undeniable. This was where he was supposed to report. Wherever 'here' was. They walked a short distance to what looked like a natural rock formation. Harris pressed a hidden panel, and a section of the rock slid open to reveal an elevator. Walker raised an eyebrow but said nothing, stepping inside.

Harris placed his right hand on a translucent panel, and several images appeared behind his finger pads confirming his identity. The elevator descended smoothly, and moments later, the doors opened to a bustling underground facility. Uniformed soldiers and others in lab coats or coveralls moved about with purpose, the hum of machinery filling the air. Walker stepped out, taking in the sight. It was a stark contrast to the desolate surface above.

"Right this way, Colonel," Harris said, leading him through a series of corridors. They arrived at a conference room where a handful of high-ranking officers and officials were already gathered. Walker recognized a few faces, including General Weston.

"Colonel Walker," Weston greeted him, rising from his seat. "Glad you could make it. Welcome to Project Dark Forge."

"General," Walker nodded, taking a seat at the table. "Can I ask what all this is?"

Weston leaned forward, his expression grave. "You can, but first, we need you to forget your assumptions. Believe me, we require your expertise. Not everyone up there seems to be against us."

Walker felt a chill run down his spine. "The extraterrestrial, sir? That's not exactly what the reports indicate."

"That's true," Weston confirmed. "We've been tracking the UFOs for weeks, and it appears they're moving to a new phase with their ground strikes. Dark Forge is our country's covert asset to this threat. It was developed outside of normal channels with a history that goes back... well, too far to get into just now. We've known for some time that a lot of different species have been to Earth. We can tell from the configuration of types of craft and tech being used."

The general paused to let that sink in. "One thing seems constant, though. In the files we have in our possession, it seems many of them describe a species that sounds a lot like A044. Colonel, none of them care for the Hi'Grash. That said, most of these extraterrestrials are peaceful explorers...mostly. The point is, we need someone with your experience to take command and coordinate our efforts."

"You're not in command?" Walker asked uncertainly.

The general shook his head. "I stepped in on an interim basis. The people aware of this unit are very few. I retired from it a dozen years ago.

I haven't been on active duty for the past five. No, this is a younger man's game."

Walker nodded, already scanning the data. The president had been clear. Get out to this mysterious unit and take command. Now he was beginning to understand why.

General Weston turned to Captain Harris. "Captain, give Colonel Walker the tour. Show him what we're working with."

"Yes, sir," Harris replied, motioning for Walker to follow him.

They left the conference room, walking down a long corridor lined with reinforced glass windows. Walker caught glimpses of various laboratories, each filled with strange, otherworldly devices and buzzing with activity.

Harris stopped at a large, heavily secured door. He placed his hand on another scanner, and the door slid open with a hiss. "Welcome to the tech bay, Colonel."

Walker stepped inside and was immediately struck by the sheer scale of the operation. Engineers and scientists moved between massive pieces of machinery and aircraft, their surfaces gleaming under the harsh fluorescent lights. One aircraft caught his eye—it had sleek, almost organic lines and a surface that seemed to shimmer and change color as he watched.

"That's the X-97," Harris said, noticing Walker's gaze. "It's a prototype based on ART, or technology we've recovered from various crash sites over the years. Its surface can mimic the environment around it, making it nearly invisible to the naked eye and radar."

Walker walked closer, running his hand along the smooth, cool surface of the craft. "Incredible," he murmured. "And this was reverse-engineered from what, did you say?"

"Alien Recovered Technology," Harris pointed up toward the sky, or at least where the sky should have been. "But it's not just aircraft. We've got energy weapons, propulsion systems, even medical devices that are light-years ahead of anything we currently have in civilian use."

They moved to another section of the bay, where a group of scientists was working on a device that looked like a large, transparent cylinder filled with a shimmering blue liquid.

"And what's this?" Walker asked, fascinated.

"That's a stasis chamber," Harris explained. "We believe it can halt the aging process and put a person in suspended animation indefinitely. We're still testing it, but initial results are promising."

Walker nodded, taking it all in. "So, NovaCore and their Observer teams didn't get to every crash site?"

"That's right," Harris said. "The Air Force and regular Army beat them there many times. Just like the Observers, though, we've been disassembling and reverse-engineering this tech for decades."

They continued the tour, passing by various other projects—an anti-gravity platform that hovered silently above the ground, a set of exoskeletons designed to enhance human strength and endurance, and a room filled with alien artifacts that defied conventional understanding.

Walker paused in front of a large screen displaying a rotating 3D model of what looked like an alien city. "And this?" he asked.

Harris smiled. "That's our most ambitious project yet. It was recovered from an onboard system in one of the smaller ovoid-shaped drones. We believe it's a map of an alien settlement in our solar system, possibly on the moon or Mars. If we can decipher it, we might be able to find out more about who the original alien beings were and what they want."

Walker approached a cylindrical chamber that dominated one corner of the lab. Its surface shimmered like the surface of a bubble, refracting the fluorescent lights overhead. He couldn't help but stare in awe.

"What is this?" he asked, gesturing toward the device.

Dr. Amelia Chen, the lead scientist in the lab, stepped forward, a spark of enthusiasm lighting her eyes. "This, Colonel, is our prototype cloaking device. It operates on principles we've only begun to understand."

Walker leaned in closer, fascinated. "Cloaking? Like in the movies?"

"More sophisticated than that," she replied, adjusting her glasses. "We believe this technology is how their ships can disappear or appear at will, both in the sky and on the ground."

She waved her hand, activating the device. The shimmering surface shifted, displaying a mesmerizing array of colors that twisted and flowed like liquid. "The entire system is organic," she continued, her voice steady. “It’s based on a bioluminescent material that reacts to environmental stimuli.”

“Organic?” Walker echoed, intrigued. “How does that work?”

Dr. Chen pointed to a series of tubes snaking around the chamber, pulsating softly with a blue light. “These tubes are filled with a gel-like substance harvested from a specific type of algae found in the deep ocean. When stimulated by electrical impulses, it can bend light around it, effectively rendering the object invisible.”

Walker’s brow furrowed as he tried to comprehend the implications. “So, it’s not just a machine; it’s alive?”

“Exactly,” Dr. Chen said, a grin breaking across her face. “It adapts and evolves, responding to the environment much like a living organism. It’s still in the early stages, but we’ve had promising results. The potential applications are staggering.”

She turned back to the chamber, adjusting a few knobs. “We’ve managed to cloak small drones with this technology, and they’ve successfully evaded detection during test flights. It’s like playing hide-and-seek with radar.”

“Can it work on larger craft?” Walker asked, already envisioning military applications.

Dr. Chen hesitated, her expression growing serious. “That’s the next hurdle. Scaling it up poses some challenges, but if we can harness its biomechanical capabilities fully... then yes.”

The lab hummed with activity around them, but Walker’s focus remained fixed on the cloaking device, the reality of its existence shifting his understanding of what was possible.

Harris motioned him toward a large set of double doors marked "Propulsion." He handed the colonel a hard hat, ear protectors, and safety glasses before opening the secure door.

The doors to the propulsion workshop slid open, revealing a cavernous room filled with advanced machinery and the faint hum of energy. Walker's eyes widened as he took in the sight of engineers and scientists bustling around a series of sleek, elongated vehicles that looked like something out of a science fiction movie.

"Welcome to the heart of our operation," Harris said, guiding Walker further inside. The noise was loud as they passed through what had to be a foundry. "This is where we're developing the next generation of spacecraft propulsion systems."

Inside an adjacent section, the noise was less, but the scene was even less familiar. Walker noticed a central platform surrounded by consoles and holographic displays. In the middle of the platform stood a large, cylindrical device that seemed to pulse with an inner light. He approached it, intrigued by its otherworldly design.

"So no chemical rockets? No SpaceX or NASA?"

"No, Colonel. You've seen the flight characteristics of the alien ships. Rockets would never work for that. We can't compete with the enemy if we stick to only what we know."

"This, Colonel, is the Nyrris Drive prototype," Harris said, his voice tinged with pride. "It's based on the principles of something called the Nyrris Cosmic Transport system, or what we usually call the Voidstream."

Walker glanced at Harris, his curiosity piqued. "I've never heard of anything like that... Is it a warp drive? How does it work?"

Dr. Eliza Brennan, the chief propulsion engineer, stepped forward, adjusting her lab coat. "No, sir. The Nyrris Drive harnesses quantum fluctuations in the fabric of space-time to create corridors, or QTCs, that allow for near-instantaneous travel across vast distances. Essentially, it aligns the ship's quantum state with these corridors, enabling it to 'tunnel' through space."

"Like a warp drive creating a wormhole?"

She shook her head and said, "Call it what you want," then pointed to a series of intricate circuits and coils wrapped around the main drive. "These components generate highly localized gravitational fields, creating temporary gravity wells. This mimics the extreme conditions needed for quantum tunneling on a macroscopic scale."

Walker nodded, absorbing the information and wishing Trembley or one of the other scientists were here as well. "So, the ship doesn't travel through space in the conventional sense. It's more like it slips through a hidden pathway?"

"Exactly," Dr. Brennan confirmed. "Space—or more accurately, the galaxy—has an internal framework, or structure, resembling our body's own nervous system, or arteries and veins. We are just beginning to understand it all, thanks to discoveries made here and around the globe. Inside these spatial corridors, the usual rules of space and time don't seem to apply. The transition is seamless—no dramatic flashes or jumps. It's like merging with a highway that's always been there, but only accessible with the right technology. We believe this is why Earth has so many interstellar visitors."

"I don't understand," he admitted.

"Most people don't," the doctor replied. "While our planet is on a distant outer arm of our own galaxy, by studying some of the visitors' star maps, we've determined that it is just off a main corridor in the Voidstream. Think of it like Route 66 back in the old days. A relatively obscure distant town suddenly has a major highway running right beside it, even more so once the Interstate system was in place."

She led Walker to a nearby console, where a holographic display showed a ship navigating through a simulated quantum corridor. "Navigating within a QTC requires constant adjustment of the ship's quantum state. Even a minor misalignment could collapse the corridor and return the ship to normal space, leaving it stranded."

Walker studied the display, marveling at the precision involved. "And these ships... they're already being built?"

"A few, yes," Harris said, stepping back into the conversation. "We're in the final stages of constructing our first prototypes. Once perfected, these ships will redefine space travel and our ability to respond to extraterrestrial threats."

"So, what is the holdup? Why not have fleets of these things?"

Dr. Brennan looked a bit embarrassed. "It seems we solved the big problem but not the smaller one. You see, in this labyrinthine hidden network of the Voidstream, the on-ramps are irregularly spaced. This means we need more conventional means of propulsion to get us there. Based on some of the astrogation data files we have decrypted, it seems the closest one is still well outside our solar system."

"So you have a ship that theoretically can navigate to the stars via the, um... Voidstream, but it just can't get there to get started."

"Plainly put, Colonel, yes," Brennan responded. "It would also be so slow on the exit side as to be useless from any practical sense."

"What about the alien craft you are examining? They obviously have drive systems that can reach it."

She shook her head. "Unfortunately, most of them do not. We now know that much of what we have recovered were scout ships or drones probably from a mother ship or fixed base somewhere within the solar system. Our guess is that they are within the orbit of Jupiter. They can do fast, quick hops but not out past Pluto."

"So you can develop drive systems that do that? What is the technology?"

Harris jumped in before Dr. Brennan could respond, his voice steady and authoritative. "We're exploring several subspace propulsion technologies, Colonel. The primary focus is on integrating anti-gravity and zero-point energy systems."

He pointed to another section of the workshop where engineers were working on a large, disc-shaped object. "That's our latest anti-grav prototype. It utilizes a field generator to create a localized distortion in the gravitational field, effectively reducing the ship's mass to near zero. This allows for rapid acceleration and maneuverability without the limitations of conventional thrusters."

Walker nodded. "And zero-point energy?"

Dr. Brennan took over again, her enthusiasm evident. "Zero-point energy is derived from the quantum vacuum fluctuations present in all space. That one is proving much more challenging. We're developing a reactor that can tap into this inexhaustible energy source, providing a virtually limitless power supply for propulsion and other systems. The issue is that the substrate materials we have are inadequate for containment."

She guided Walker to another display showing a schematic of the zero-point reactor. "This beast can generate immense amounts of energy with minimal fuel, making long-duration space travel feasible. Combined with our anti-gravity systems, it will enable ships to reach the entry points for the quantum corridors."

Harris continued, "We're also looking into ion propulsion and plasma drives for intermediate-range travel. These technologies provide efficient, low- and high-thrust propulsion suitable for traveling within our solar system. They'll serve as the bridge to get our ships to the Nyrris corridor entry points."

Walker examined the various prototypes and schematics, appreciating the complexity and innovation behind each one. "It sounds like you've got all the bases covered."

"Not quite, but we're doing our best, sir," Harris replied. "But the challenge lies in integrating these systems into a single, functional spacecraft. Each technology has its own requirements and constraints, and balancing them is no small feat. The shielding for the Zero Point Drive alone will be immense; we're not sure it is even feasible."

Dr. Brennan nodded in agreement. "We're making progress, but there's still a lot of work to be done. Our goal is to develop a versatile fleet capable of responding to any extraterrestrial threat, whether it's within our solar system or beyond."

Walker took a deep breath, absorbing the enormity of their task. "Well, Captain and Doctor, it seems you have your hands full. I'll do everything in my power to support your efforts and ensure we're ready for whatever comes next."

"Thank you, Colonel," Harris said, his expression serious. "We'll need all the help we can get. We've heard that one of the other major players has one of the longer-range craft. If we could get one of those, it would make things much easier."

Walker smiled. "I'll see what I can do."

They continued the tour, discussing the various projects and their potential applications, each step bringing Walker deeper into the heart of Dark Forge's mission and the challenges they faced in protecting Earth from an unknown and ever-present extraterrestrial threat.

Captain Harris showed him the massive lift elevator for getting the prototype craft up to the surface. "We have a flattened mesa up top we can use for takeoffs, but they aren't appropriate for traditional landings, so only some of the vehicles can utilize it. Others have to be transported elsewhere for testing."

"So, some of the UFOs, lights in the skies—that's all you guys?"

"Yes, some," Harris answered. "We are so remote, and the tree cover is very solid that few people would see. But yes, our testing can be detected. That is one reason we take such precautions about not doing much locally. After Groom Lake shut down, we had to find other facilities, but Skunkworks sites are all over the place. These days, much of the testing we do is up in Alaska."

Walker felt a surge of excitement but also a great deal of apprehension. The technology was groundbreaking, but its implications were staggering. He walked back over to one of the exotic drive systems. "And you're confident all this is safe?"

Dr. Brennan laughed and exchanged a glance with Harris. "As safe as any pioneering technology can be, Colonel. We're constantly refining the process, learning more with each test. But the potential... it's limitless."

Walker nodded, feeling the weight of the future pressing down on him. This was more than just advanced propulsion—it was a leap into the unknown, a chance to explore and defend humanity on a scale never before imagined.

"So POTUS knew about all of this all along?"

Harris smiled and shook his head. "No politician has ever known of this site. The risks would be too great. General Bill Briggs drafted those orders. He just had to get the president to authorize them. Surely you noticed the lack of specifics in what was to be your duty station, including the detachment?"

"This is beyond anything I could have ever dreamed of," Walker stated honestly.

"And it's just the beginning," Harris said. "Welcome to The Forge, Colonel. This is where the future begins."

Walker gave a nod. As impressive as it was, he just hoped it wasn't all too late.

ABOUT THE AUTHOR

JK Franks is the popular author of numerous post-apocalyptic and near-future techno-thriller novels. He is an admitted tech geek, science nerd, cyclist, and storyteller. JK Franks' world was formed by a childhood growing up during the Space Age when he developed a love for books. He became an avid student of history and science and a regular reader of everything from reference books to dusty, old biographies. Once he discovered science fiction, he never looked back.

His work is mostly near-future thrillers, characterized by meticulous research, hard science, and a gritty, seldom-matched realism. "I hate stupid characters," states Franks. "Or even worse, smart characters, acting stupid." All of his work combines his passion for hard science fiction, well-crafted characters, and superb storytelling.

No matter where he is or what's going on, Franks tries his best to set aside time every day to answer emails and messages from readers. You can visit him on the web at www.jkfranks.com. Please subscribe to his newsletter for updates, promotions, and giveaways. You can also find the author on Facebook or email him directly at media@jkfranks.com.

OTHER BOOKS BY JK FRANKS

The Catalyst Series

Book 1: Downward Cycle

Life in a remote, oceanfront town spirals downward after a massive solar flare causes a global blackout. But the loss of electrical power is just the first of the problems facing the survivors in the chaos that follows. Is this how the world ends?

Book 2: Kingdoms of Sorrow

With civilization in ruins, individuals band together to survive and build a new society. The threats are both grave and numerous—surely too many for a small group to weather. This is a harrowing story of survival following the collapse of the planet's electrical grids.

Book 3: American Exodus

This companion story to the Catalyst series follows one man's struggle to get back home after the collapse. No supplies, no idea of the hardships to come; how can he possibly survive the journey? Even if he survives, can he adapt to this new reality?

Book 4: Ghost Country

Since the solar superstorm and CME almost two years before, the Gulf Coast town of Harris Springs, Mississippi, has suffered from gang attacks, famine, and hurricanes and has battled a crusading army of religious zealots. Now, they face their greatest challenge: outsmarting a tyrannical president and escaping an approaching pandemic.

Cade Rearden Thrillers

Book 1: State of Chaos

He's exhausted and brutally traumatized. Now, Spec-Ops Captain Cade Rearden must finally listen to the voices in his head...or everyone on Earth may die. If you like near-future technology, complex heroes, and high-octane action, then you'll love JK Franks' explosive new adventure.

Book 2: Midnight Zone

Nightmares are real in the cold, dark waters of the deep. National Security Agent Cade Rearden is used to secrets. Assigned to protect the ultra-dark-ops organization known as The Cove Project, he grapples with his role of defending a country still in crisis after a deadly super AI has devastated much of the U.S.

But when part of his team mysteriously disappears beneath the idyllic waters of the Caribbean, Cade finds himself thrust into a web of lies and mystery, at the heart of which lies an eons-old secret that somebody will kill to protect. Grappling with his inner demons and struggling to locate his friends, Cade stumbles upon a government cover-up...and terrifying creatures, hidden miles beneath the surface of the ocean.

The Fade Novels

The Night Gate

Since losing his daughter seven years ago, Pike Shepard has struggled to maintain a normal life for himself in the coastal community of Blackwater. It's a quiet life, until a beautiful scientist shows up on his doorstep with a desperate plea for help. Dr. Kate Cassidy has uncovered a new aspect to quantum entanglement: the ability to not just see the multiverse but a way to travel through it. Her device allows them to SideSlip between parallel dimensions that are at once familiar and quite bizarre, wondrous, and terrifying. Pike learns they aren't the only ones with this ability, and the others want them gone.

Savage Earth Series

Book 1: Nightmare Factory

In the not-too-distant future, a devastating global attack takes place and planet Earth is on the brink of extinction. In this sci-fi thriller, Master Sargent Joe Kovach has been through a personal hell as he struggles to adapt to his new enhancements. As battles escalates, so does his determination to uncover the group who triggered this brutal extinction event that has left the planet overrun by mechanical and genetic horrors.

Book 1.5: San Antonio

This isn't just the end of the world – it's a deeply personal story of Carla Garcia's fight to keep her family united and safe amidst chaos. After a devastating terrorist attack leaves society in shambles, Carla confronts dwindling supplies, haunting premonitions from her sister Meredith, and the slipping memory of her grandmother. In this close-knit struggle, where monsters lurk in the shadows and love is a rare treasure, every moment pulses with heart-pounding choices and the undying hope for a glimmer of light in the darkness.

Book 2: Eradication

In a world ravaged by a devastating attack, the remnants of humanity are barely clinging to existence. Months have passed since the enemy unleashed hordes of murderous creations that now engulf the planet. Amidst the chaos, One renegade group takes refuge on Earth's last remaining space vessels, orbiting above the desolate wastelands. They are Banshee Team, and they are alone beacon of hope in the face of annihilation. They are committed to uncover the truth behind the brutal attacks and lend their expertise to turn the tide of this merciless battle.

Book 3: Wastelands

In a world ravaged by a devastating attack, the remnants of humanity are barely clinging to existence. Months have passed since the enemy unleashed hordes of murderous creations that now engulf the planet. Amidst the chaos, One renegade group takes refuge on Earth's last remaining space vessels, orbiting above the desolate wastelands. They are Banshee Team, and they are alone beacon of hope in the face of annihilation. They are committed to uncover the truth behind the brutal attacks and lend their expertise to turn the tide of this merciless battle.

Connect with the Author Online:

** For a sneak peek at new novels, free stories, and more, join the email list at jkfranksbooks.com.

Facebook: facebook.com/groups/JKFranks/

Goodreads: goodreads.com/author/show/15395251.J_K_Franks

Websites: JKFranks.com or JKFranksbooks.coim

Twitter: @jkfranks

Instagram: @jkfranks1

www.ingramcontent.com/pod-product-compliance
Lightning Source LLC
Chambersburg PA
CBHW020602310726
48979CB00008B/1313/J
9781964509044